Power, Inc.

By the same authors:
America, Inc.: Who Owns and Operates the United States

By Morton Mintz:
The Therapeutic Nightmare
By Prescription Only
The Pill: An Alarming Report

Power, Inc.

Public and Private Rulers and How to Make Them Accountable

Morton Mintz & Jerry S. Cohen

The Viking Press

NEW YORK

Library of Congress Cataloging in Publication Data
Mintz, Morton.
  Power, inc.
  Includes index.
  1. Elite (Social sciences)—United States. 2. Power (Social sciences) 3. Conflict of inter-
ests (Public office)—United States. 4. Political ethics—United States. 5. Professional ethics.
I. Cohen, Jerry S., 1925—joint author. II. Title.
HN90.E4M56   301.5   76-23096
ISBN 0-670-57032-X

Printed in the United States of America
Set in Video Avanta

Acknowledgment is made to the following for the material indicated:

American Psychiatric Association: From "From Chaos to Responsibility" by Gerald Stern, American
Journal of Psychiatry, Vol. 133 (1976), p. 300. Copyright © 1976, The American Psychiatric Association. Reprinted by permission.

Buffalo Law Review: From "Secrecy and the Supreme Court" by Arthur Miller and D. S. Sastri.
Copyright © 1973 by Buffalo Law Review.

Columbia Journalism Review: From "The Fruits of Agnewism" by Ben Bagdikian, January/February
1973. From "Britain's Great Thalidomide Cover-Up" by Alfred Balk, May/June 1975.

Commonwealth of Pennsylvania (Insurance Department): From A Shopper's Guide to Dentistry by
Herbert Denenber.

Dr. George Crile: From The Surgeon's Dilemma.

Doubleday & Co. Inc.: From Job Power by David Jenkins. From Politics and the English Language
and England Your England by George Orwell. From Washington Cover Up by Clark Mollenhoff.

William J. Eaton: From "A.1: A Bill to Make . . .", The Guild Reporter, May 30, 1975.

Farrar, Straus & Giroux, Inc.: From Criminal Sentences: Law without Order by Marvin E. Frankel.
Copyright © 1972, 1973 by Marvin E. Frankel. Reprinted with the permission of Farrar, Straus &
Giroux, Inc.

Grossman Publishers: From Death in the Mines by A. Britton Hume. Copyright © 1971 by A.
Britton Hume. Reprinted by permission of Grossman Publishers.

Harper & Row, Publishers, Inc. From Dirty Business by Ovid Demaris (a Harper Magazine Press
Book). From The Case for Modern Man by Charles Frankel.

Harper & Row, Publishers, Inc., and Blond & Briggs, Publishers: From Small Is Beautiful by E. F.
Schumacher.

Harper's Magazine: From The Kennedy Vendetta by Taylor Branch and George Crile III. Copyright
© 1975 by Harper's Magazine.

Holt, Rinehart and Winston: From The Genteel Populists by Simon Lazarus. Copyright © 1974
by Simon Lazarus. Reprinted by permission of Holt, Rinehart and Winston, Publishers.

Houghton Mifflin Company: From Sin and Society by E. A. Ross. Copyright 1907 and 1935 by
Edward Alsworth Ross. Reprinted by permission of Houghton Mifflin Company.

Alfred A. Knopf, Inc.: From Supership by Noel Mostert. Copyright © 1974 by Noel Mostert. From
The CIA and the Cult of Intelligence by Victor Marchetti and John D. Marks. Copyright © 1974
by Victor L. Marchetti and John D. Marks. From Kind and Usual Punishment: The Prison Business
by Jessica Mitford. Copyright © 1973 by Jessica Mitford. All reprinted by permission of Alfred A.
Knopf, Inc.

The following page constitutes an extension of this copyright page.

For the Unborn

The idea of a rational democracy is, not that the people themselves govern, but that they have security for good government. This security they cannot have by any other means than by retaining in their own hands the ultimate control. If they renounce this, they give themselves up to tyranny. A governing class not accountable to the people are sure, in the main, to sacrifice the people to the pursuit of separate interests and inclinations of their own.

John Stuart Mill
Dissertations: Political, Philosophical, and Historical

During much of 1973, when numerous gross abuses of presidential power were being revealed in Congress, the courts, and the press, we became increasingly perplexed by a fundamental question: Was the Constitution in any way causally related to the abuses? This question was getting little or no attention amidst the torrents of words being written and spoken about Watergate. Eventually one of the authors of the present book wrote "Rethinking the Constitution," a "My Turn" column that *Newsweek* published in November 1973.

The column raised issues which have not gone away. "How many Americans are aware," the writer asked at the outset, "that a President on his own initiative can order a nuclear attack—but that not even the Soviet Union or China grants such ultimate discretionary authority to any one man? In those Communist countries a decision to begin a war that could end the world almost certainly would require the assent of the party leaders."

The article also pointed out that the Framers understandably had not anticipated the Industrial Revolution; they had no way to know that it would evolve "a crucial new power center: the giant—and now often multinational—corporations, interlocked with financial institutions which would come to rule us, just as surely as does the government." The writer suggested that the two-hundredth anniversary of our country would be an appropriate time to examine our present position. This book develops the questions raised in that article, and will expose the methods used by the powerful in both public and private sectors to avoid accountability. We offer a solution to the problem which would protect the fundamental rights our Founding Fathers intended reside with the people rather than with the powerful.

Acknowledgments

For indispensable guidance given with rare grace we will be everlastingly grateful to our editor, William Decker, to John J. Flynn, professor of law at the University of Utah, and to Arthur S. Miller, professor of law at the National Law Center of George Washington University.

We also have been the fortunate beneficiaries of valuable help of various kinds from Michael J. Faber, David Vienna, Rabbi Joshua O. Haberman, Herbert E. Milstein, John D. Hanrahan, George Lardner, Jr., Daniel Rapoport, John R. Pekkanen, Dan Morgan, Edward J. Walsh, William C. Lane, Jr., and Jonathan Rowe. For research on the origins of the concept of accountability our gratitude goes to Anita Mintz. Finally, we thank the *Washington Post* for granting a leave-of-absence to Morton Mintz without which this book would not have been possible.

Morton Mintz
Jerry S. Cohen

Washington, D.C.
May 1976

Contents

Unaccountability pervades American life—not merely the Presidency, not merely the rest of government, but all public and private institutions that exert substantial power over us and, inevitably, over future generations. The evidence lies all about us. But it is strewn helter-skelter in huge, chaotic scrap piles. So far as we know, ours is the first comprehensive attempt to pass a conceptual magnet over the fact heaps, to pull out information that illuminates, to organize it into some sensibly disciplined formations, and ultimately to draw from it valid—and fresh—conclusions. The magnet of course gets its charge from the particular experiences, judgments, and values of the authors.

What is accountability? The word more and more becomes common coin. In recent years it has been appearing regularly in newspaper stories. Yet there has been little exploration of its origins, of its multiple meanings and nuances, and of why it is centrally important. For a concise, rule-of-thumb definition, we will at once adopt this one, formulated by Arthur S. Miller, of the National Law Center of George Washington University: ". . . accountability, if it means anything, means that those who wield power have to answer in another place and give reasons for decisions that are taken; . . ."[1]*

Accountability—in elementary forms—is as old as civilization. Punishment is an example. The relation between servant and master is another. Consumer protection is yet another. India in 200 B.C. punished adulterators of grains and oils.[2] Greek and Roman laws prohibited the adulteration of wine with water.[3] Talmudic law, in an early rejection of *caveat emptor*, required the seller to inform the buyer of all defects.[4]

In nondemocratic or hierarchical forms of government accountability always runs upward. A monarch ruling by divine right holds his people accountable to himself, but holds himself accountable only to God. A fascist ruler also holds his people accountable to himself, but holds himself accountable only to himself.

In perfect accountability, John Stuart Mill said, "the interest of rulers approximates more and more to identify with that of the people in proportion as the people are more enlightened." Such accountability is of course beyond reach. Yet, Mill said, "identity of interest" is "an end incessantly to

*Numbered reference notes begin on page 591.

be aimed at, and approximated to as nearly as circumstances render possible, and is compatible with the regard due to other ends."[5]

In Periclean Athens (c. 490–429 B.C.) crude stirrings toward democratic accountability occurred. The Kleisthenean constitution provided that magistrates, who were empowered not only to administer and judge civil disputes, but also to decide and punish, had to come annually before the people— "judicially assembled"—to account for their general behavior. The scholar George Grote was not overly impressed by this form of accountability, having reason to suspect that the great powers of the magistrates, which were hemmed in by few laws and were subject to no appeal, "must have often led to corrupt, arbitrary, and oppressive dealing . . ."[6] Moreover, a later scholar, Thomas W. Africa, has said that the citizen "had no inalienable rights; his liberties were dependent solely on the state. . . . All of his freedoms were the result of a Greek's membership in a community; none were based on his status as a human being."[7] In Aristotle's time, Thomas Jefferson said, the Greeks "had just ideas of the value of personal liberty, but none at all of the structure of government best calculated to preserve it." As for Rome, it was, as seen by Jefferson, a nation "steeped in corruption, vice and venality . . ."[8]

Accountability in government coincides with that dimension of responsibility "in which the state imposes penalties on individual actions and in which officials and governments are held accountable for policy and action."[9] On the assumption that responsibility is an idea basic to morality as well as to ethical theory, the French philosopher L. Lévy-Bruhl, in 1884, sketched its history from antiquity—and found that the idea never had been studied or analyzed.[10] The American philosopher Richard McKeon, writing in the 1950s, said that "I was able to find no philosophic treatment of responsibility" until 1859 (in which year, in the interest of clarity, Alexander Bain had substituted the literal word "punishability" for the figurative term "responsibility").[11]

The *Oxford English Dictionary* cites a use of the adjective "responsible" in 1643, when the king was said to be "responsible" to Parliament. Jeremy Bentham used the noun "responsibility" in 1776. Alexander Hamilton, in no. 63 of *The Federalist,* used it in 1787, saying at one point, "Responsibility, in order to be reasonable, must be limited to objects within the power of the responsible party, . . ." Also in 1787, the noun *"responsibilité"* was used for the first time in French.[12] The English and French usages were first applied to the operation of political institutions in the context of the American and French revolutions.[13] In passing, it may be noted that neither the noun nor the adjective appears in classical Latin.[14] Not until after the fourteenth century did the adjective *responsabilis* appear in medieval Latin.[15]

. . .

The tradition that elected representative assemblies control the executive began with the English revolution of 1688. But it was a glory of the American Revolution that it launched true *public* accountability, i.e., accountability to the people, in the right belief that they are better judges of the common good than an elite or a king. "The full experiment of government democratical, but representative, was and still is reserved for us," Jefferson said. "The introduction of this new principle of representative democracy has rendered useless almost everything written before on the structure of government; . . ."[16]

Public accountability, E. Leslie Normanton has said, "calls for openly declared facts and open debate of them by laymen and their elected representatives," but

is capable of much more: it is, actually or potentially, a rich and open source of knowledge about how government services function in actual practice, and hence of ideas about how they ought to function. It casts a spotlight upon institutions which are shy of the public's gaze, but whose qualities and imperfections have a steady cumulative impact upon our daily lives.[17]

Public accountability is external, while ethical accountability—which depends on the moral judgment of an individual—is internal. Although public and ethical accountability interact in varied and volatile ways, "responsibility in the political sense if it is to have any real rationale must be based on responsibility in the ethical sense," according to the British philosopher A. C. Ewing. "I can be responsible for my actions without being specifically responsible to anybody other than myself. A theist no doubt will say that I am responsible to God, but I do not think that the notion of responsibility directly implies theism. What it does imply chiefly is blameworthiness if I do wrong, . . ."[18] The dilemma, which seems to us inescapable, is that one man's ethic is another man's vice. Shakespeare's Polonius, bidding farewell to his son Laertes, tells him:

> This above all: to thine own self be true,
> And it must follow, as the night the day,
> Thou canst not then be false to any man.

But was Polonius a self to which thou would care to be true? He was one of the things that was rotten in the state of Denmark. First he dumped a heavy ballast of homiletics onto Laertes, but then, as might a prototypical FBI or CIA director, dispatched Reynaldo, his servant, to Paris to snoop on his son:

> Inquire me first what Danskers are in Paris,
> And how, and who, what means, and where they keep,
> What company, at what expense; and finding

> By this encompassment and drift of question
> That they do know my son, come you more nearer. . . .

Becoming more specific, Polonius instructs Reynaldo even to hold out the "bait of falsehood," such as claiming to have seen Laertes entering a brothel. Thus would Polonius catch the "carp of truth" about whether his son's behavior accorded with the precepts he had sanctimoniously imparted. Finally, Hamlet kills Polonius in the act of eavesdropping. He was to his ownself being true.

Polonius had been wholly dedicated to his sovereign, holding "my duty as I hold my soul/Both to my God [and] to my gracious King." In Washington, many in the Executive branch have defined ethical accountability not to God, but to the President. Ethical accountability so defined can be unethical when it functions to deny the public knowledge of policies that may impel the country toward catastrophe, because it is the public as the ultimate source of legitimate power to which final accountability is owed. To be true to a misguided self, one might say, may mean being false to every man.

In *Resignation in Protest*, Edward Weisband and Thomas M. Franck point out some of the reasons for this situation, including the American reverence for team play, the awareness of most presidential appointees that they lack an independent political base, and the absence in the Constitution of a provision for internal accountability in the Executive.

The traditions and circumstances of parliamentary government are much different. In Britain, even in wartime, Cabinet ministers resign in protest against major government policies which they believe to be mistaken; promptly enlighten the public, sometimes with fiery speeches in Parliament, as to their reasons for resigning, are honored for their conduct, and reasonably may expect to return to power, even as Prime Minister. In the United States, high officials infrequently resign in protest, even in protest against policies as disastrous as those that took us into and kept us in the war in Southeast Asia. They cover up and lie about their differences with the President if they do resign, and thereby deprive the electorate of the information it must have if it is to give informed consent to its governance; are honored—or, at least, are not dishonored—for their dishonesty, and are comforted by the knowledge that to have been candid with the public rather than loyal to The Chief would have been politically suicidal. "If all the top State, White House and Pentagon officials whose recently published memoirs place them squarely in the camp of the doves had indeed been doves, Presidents Kennedy, Johnson and Nixon must have conceived, organized, administered and almost fought the war alone," Weisband and Franck said.[19]

Such doves might have fared poorly before the accountability tribunals once proposed by George Bernard Shaw. "Every person who owes his life to civilized society and who has enjoyed since his childhood its very costly protections and advantages," Shaw said,

should appear at reasonable intervals before a properly qualified jury to justify his existence, which should be summarily and painlessly terminated if he fails to justify it and it develops that he is a positive nuisance and more trouble than he is worth. Nothing less will really make people responsible citizens.[20]

The contemporary philosopher Charles Frankel formulated this sound general guideline for accountable decision making: "A decision is responsible when the man or group that makes it has to answer for it to those who are directly or indirectly affected by it."[21] It's worth a moment to illustrate this with a decision that assuredly would not have been made had the decision makers been directly affected by it.

In October 1974, the Occupational Safety and Health Administration (OSHA), a unit of the Department of Labor, proposed new federal standards for housing of migrant workers. Reporting in the *Washington Post,* Thomas W. Lippman pointed out that the proposed rules, among other things, would approve dwellings with neither windows nor electricity, and with ceilings less than seven feet high. An existing rule required that migrants be housed at least 500 feet from livestock; OSHA proposed to delete this, but to leave in existence a loophole through which employers could escape a requirement to meet any housing standards whatever.

As things stand, blueberry harvesters sometimes live in former chicken coops in Maine. Rats roam free in camps occupied by sugarcane workers in Louisiana. The rate of tuberculosis among migrant workers is seventeen times higher than in the general population, the rate of infestation by intestinal worms is thirty-five times higher, and the rate of respiratory and digestive diseases is two to five times higher. The proposed OSHA housing standards threatened to make the health of migrant workers even worse, an official of the American Public Health Association said. To make those who proposed the "atrocious" standards accountable, the AFL-CIO suggested "a fitting reward": "Send them and their families to live for a month in the kind of housing they have provided farm and other workers and work a full shift each day, preferably at stoop labor in the fields."[22]

Even in theory, however, it is sometimes difficult to apply the Frankel guideline. The success or failure, or wisdom or stupidity, of some decisions simply cannot be ascertained until months or even years after they are taken. Take long-term investments. Obviously, to judge them fairly soon after they are made is impossible. At the same time, D. C. Hague has written, "To wait until a decision can be fairly judged may mean that those who took the decision are no longer in the same department—or even in the same organization."[23]

Allowance also must be made for the need of decision makers to have independence of action, and for circumstances in which they must act quickly or even instantly, with opportunity for neither private nor public soul-searching. Oliver Wendell Holmes, the great justice of the Supreme Court, fought in the Civil War almost every day for four years. Most of his classmates were killed. The harrowing effects on him were profound and stayed with him all of his life. In commanding men under fire, he once told Thomas G. Corcoran, a Washington lawyer who had clerked for the justice, and who recalled the story to Carroll Kilpatrick of the *Washington Post,* "You never are sure you are right. But you have to act." Corcoran added, "The war made him understand that in the world of action you have to make decisions on insufficient information but you have to make them hard."[24]

In a technological age so advanced (or so extremist) that scientists are prepared to undertake genetic engineering, ethical accountability must transcend responsibility to kings, presidents, and defective selves. Even the familiar litany of values—truth, honor, justice, love, charity, compassion—will not suffice. We must be concerned, in contemplating accountability, with the legacy to be left for all subsequent generations. The Bible emphasizes that man does not own the earth, but is its custodian, or guardian. Fred L. Polak, of the Rotterdam College of Economics, saw the need, twenty years ago, to carry this concept much further, saying:

. . . I propose to lay down the thesis—new, seemingly one-sided and bold—that responsibility for the *future* (especially for the far-away, but also for the near future) forms the central core, is the crystallized essence of *all* responsibility of any kind, always and everywhere. Further, that this responsibility for the future is not only the all-encompassing responsibility, but is even prior to and a primary condition of man's responsibility in and for the present. Its function is considered to be fundamental for human *behavior* as *human* behavior, pertaining both to mankind as a whole and to man as an individual.[25]

Polak emphasized that the proposition was "sweeping" and "purposely strained here to its ultimate implications and farthest extensions . . ." His supporting arguments are much too complex and interwoven to be done justice here, but their texture perhaps can be suggested if the following passages are read in the light of recently perceived threats to the environment:

Responsibility without foresight is not only blind, it may even defy its own ends and result in its own distortion and destruction. The future is always there and we cannot simply forget all about it and lose ourselves completely in the present. . . . It is either we ourselves who consciously try to make the future, or others who are sure to make the future, both theirs and ours. . . .

If, finally, we only want an increasing mastery of the forces of nature, but not of time in the long view, nature and time in monstrous association will unite against man and his shortsighted civilization. If the pursuit of happiness is self-centeredly focused on today's problems, profits and pleasures (carpe diem), then, one day, the reckless evocation of "aprés nous le déluge" may become a bitter reality for the descendants we have repudiated by default. Then creative faith in the future may gradually, but completely be superseded by an impotent fear of the future, leaving man an easy prey for a coming onslaught of apocalyptic catastrophe.[26]

"It is a great consolation to me," Thomas Jefferson said in 1816, "that our government, as it cherishes most of its duties toward its own citizens, so is it the most exact in its moral conduct toward other nations. No voluntary wrong can be imputed to us."[27] This belief surely was ripped and torn by various American foreign adventures; but at Nuremburg, after World War II, as the historian Henry Steele Commager wrote, we still felt able to undertake "to outlaw as crimes against humanity such acts as indiscriminate bombing of nonmilitary objectives, mistreatment of prisoners, and reprisals against whole communities for the alleged misdeeds of individuals." Yet, he said:

We are now [1972] bombing rural hamlets and villages indiscriminately (that is the meaning of a "free fire" zone), dropping napalm and "daisy-cutter" bombs whose only use is the killing or maiming of civilians, using defoliates and herbicides to destroy the ecology, and destroying Vietnam with an over-kill prohibited by the laws of war which we ourselves prescribed! We had established the principle of accountability for "aggressive war" and for crimes against humanity at the German and Japanese war trials, convicted over 500,000 Nazis of crimes, hanged a score of them, and sentenced 720 Japanese officers to death. But so far the only war criminal to be brought to accountability in this war, for activities which cover the span of lawlessness from the destruction of villages to the massacre of civilians, is a lieutenant [William Calley] . . .[28]

Jefferson's pride in our role in the world—"No voluntary wrong can be imputed to us"—seems not to have rubbed off on modern Presidents, who, in a perversion of rational accountability, have undertaken to decide— usually stealthily—that other countries should not be trusted to work out their own destinies. The following exchange occurred at a press conference held by President Ford on September 16, 1974, after disclosures were made about the covert efforts of the Nixon Administration to topple the regime of the late Salvador Allende in Chile:

Q: Under what international law do we have a right to attempt to destabilize the constitutionally elected government of another country? Does the Soviet Union have a similar right to try to destabilize the government of Canada for example, or the United States?

A: I'm not going to pass judgment on whether it's permitted or authorized under international law. It's a recognized fact that historically, as well as presently, such actions are taken in the best interests of the countries involved.

Gerald Ford seemed not to grasp that he had no warrant to determine "the best interests" of Chile, just as a leader of that country has no warrant to decide what our best interests are.

Our charting of the vast domain of unaccountability would be incomplete unless we pass our conceptual magnet over Watergate, that mountainous Nixonian dump of burglaries, dirty tricks, lies, vile usages of secrecy and "national security," rapes of public agencies to reward friends and punish "enemies," blackmail to extract campaign funds, income-tax evasion at the highest level, and raids on the public treasury to support a lifestyle befitting not a President but a monarch.

First, no claim that "the system worked" could be made during the actual Watergate wrongdoings. *Nothing* had worked to block the various subversions at their inception, and *nothing* had worked to impede them once under way. There came a series of accidents—a stupid break-in at the offices of the Democratic National Committee in the Watergate Office Building, a guard vigilant enough to notice a door that, inexplicably, had been taped open; two reporters with the determination and freedom to pursue the story assiduously and alone; editors willing to back them, and a newspaper owner who resolutely backed the editors; a federal judge who refused to countenance an inadequate investigation and prosecution, but who in refusing abused his judicial powers; and the discovery, by the staff of the Senate Select Committee on Presidential Campaign Activities (Watergate committee), that the President had recorded conversations in the Oval Office and his suite in the Executive Office Building, and on several telephones. Only after such accidents did "the system" indeed begin to work and, ultimately, force Richard Nixon to flee the White House.

Second, Professor Arthur S. Miller has pointed out, Watergate was an aberration mainly as it resulted "from bringing into positions of immense governmental power individuals whose basic loyalty ran to the leader (the president) rather than to the people or to the law." At the same time, however, Watergate extended improper practices that had been followed for a long time, such as excessive secrecy (achieved, in part, by Executive privilege). "National security"—which no government body has yet defined—

was distended to justify a raid on a psychiatrist's office, to tap the phones of writers, lawyers, and others who were detached from defense and foreign-policy matters, or to do most anything else the White House wanted done.

Third, Watergate was, as former Senator Sam J. Ervin, Jr. (D–N.C.), the committee chairman, said, "unprecedented in the political annals of America in respect to the scope and intensity of its unethical and illegal actions." Yet not even that committee, let alone the Congress, addressed fundamental problems starkly posed by the scandal and its aftermath—problems that involve the basic distribution of power within the American government. Speaking bluntly about this, Professor Miller, who was senior consultant to the committee, said that it had been "the big bang of 1973," but expired in 1974, after seventeen months of labor, "with a whimper"—a final report that made thirty-four recommendations, none of which "squarely faces the critical question of a swollen presidency and a badly askew separation of constitutional powers."[29]

What was the lesson of Watergate? ". . . it is not that we had a President who was either blind or willful—but that there was nobody watching," Congressman Richard Bolling (D–Mo.) has observed. "We cannot have a system which depends on a benign executive—or a malign one. We've got to make the Congress work. There is no alternative. And if the Congress cannot be responsible, then the whole system of representative government and free-choice government is going down the drain."[30] Agreeing, Elizabeth Drew, a Washington commentator and author, emphasized that "Congress responds to great outside pressures. So, in the end, it comes down to us." She proposed that there be built "a web of accountability around the Presidency, around the Congress. The problem is not power; it is unaccountable power."[31] How the Constitution might build a "web of accountability" around *all* our powerful institutions is the challenge that ultimately we face.

I
The Obsolete Constitution

The Framers' Grand Design: Why It Failed

1

What did the Founding Fathers perceive to be government's principal purpose and justification? The answer advanced and argued by James Wilson, a leading colonial scholar and philosopher, was the happiness of society. Despite differences in approach, all of the Founding Fathers shared his view. Thomas Jefferson, author of the Declaration of Independence; James Madison, father of the Constitution and shepherd of the Bill of Rights; Samuel Adams, the testy revolutionary, and Alexander Hamilton, frustrated aristocrat and advocate of a strong Presidency—all of them agreed with Wilson.

To put this key point another way, no basic disagreement as to the sole legitimate end of government existed two hundred years ago, when the united colonies dissolved their political bonds with England. In forming a new government the Founders were, as the Declaration of Independence put it, "laying its foundation on such principles and organizing its powers in such form, as to them [the people] shall seem most likely to effect their safety and happiness."

After a decade under the Articles of Confederation, which proved to be highly unsatisfactory, the Framers in the hot summer of 1787 gathered in Philadelphia for the Constitutional Convention. They were preponderantly an extraordinary body of men: marvelously intelligent, high-minded, serious, knowledgeable about the various political systems the world had known and endured, and familiar with the thinkers and philosophers who had written on the nature and organization of government. All of this is evident in the record of the delegates' deliberations.[1] Moreover, the Framers, for the most part, also were experienced and practical politicians, many having served in colonial legislatures and in the Continental Congress. And, it is clear, they were aware that they were undertaking an act of historical significance—building a new government from the ground up.

To design a constitution that would achieve society's safety and happiness (concepts that incorporate liberty and justice), the Framers adopted two basic guidelines:

First, power must be allowed to concentrate neither in individuals nor in institutions. The delegates' experiences with King George III, with Parliament, and, in fact, with some of the colonial assemblies, had burnt into their consciousness the perception that concentrated power is unaccountable and a spawning ground of abuses.

Second, sovereignty—the ultimate power—must reside in the people.

3

This accorded with the philosophy of natural rights shared by the delegates, and with the view of James Wilson, which they also shared: "All men are by nature equal and free: no one has a right to any authority over another without his consent; all lawful government is founded on the consent of those who are subject to it."[2]

The delegates cherished no naive illusions as to the innate goodness of men or even as to their rationality. A fair reading is that they feared democracy almost as much as they feared despotism. Benjamin Franklin, the urbane, witty realist, did not hesitate to remind the convention of two passions that powerfully influence men: ambition—the love of power—and avarice—the love of money.[3] James Madison, delving into how a majority could be motivated to respect the rights of a minority, hardly could be accused of sentimentality:

A prudent regard to the maxim that honesty is the best policy is found by experience to be as little regarded by bodies of men as by individuals. Respect for character is always diminished in proportion to the number among whom the blame or praise is to be divided. Conscience, the only remaining tie, is known to be inadequate in individuals: in large numbers, little is to be expected from it.[4]

Alexander Hamilton captured the essence: "Give all power to the many, they will oppress the few. Give all power to the few, they will oppress the many."[5] Yet, the Framers recognized, they could best defend against tyranny by reposing ultimate political power in the people, not in any person or institution.

Some at the convention, fearing possible tyranny by the majority, wondered if the power proposed to be vested in the people was excessive. Madison allayed such fears:

The only remedy is to enlarge the sphere, and thereby divide the community into so great a number of interests & parties, that in the first place a majority will not be likely at the same moment to have a common interest separate from that of the whole or of the minority; and in the second place, that in case they should have such interest, they may not be apt to unite in the pursuit of it.[6]

He expressed a similar thought later when he argued, in *The Federalist,* for adoption of the Constitution:

Whilst all authority in it [the United States] will be derived from and dependent on the society, the society itself will be broken into so many parts, interests and classes of citizens, that the rights of individuals, or of the minority, will be in little danger from interested combinations of the majority.[7]

Here he foresaw that, as the country would grow and expand, shifting interests among the citizenry would restrain or nullify such tyranny as was possibly latent in the sovereignty resting with the people. To be sure, the people were not a perfect repository, but they surely were a safer one than any single element.

During debate on the duration of the term to be given the President, Benjamin Franklin wryly expressed the real meaning of sovereignty "in the people":

It seems to have been imagined by some that the returning to the mass of the people was degrading the magistrate. This [Franklin] thought was contrary to republican principles. In Free Governments the rulers are the servants, and the people their superiors & sovereigns. For the former therefore to return among the latter was not to *degrade* but to *promote* them. And it would be imposing an unreasonable burden on them, to keep them always in a State of servitude, and not allow them to become again one of the Masters.[8]

The dispersal of ultimate power among the people, then, was at once something more and something less than a natural right. It was simply the best of alternatives—the one least likely to evolve a despotic government and the one most likely to make government accountable to the citizens. The symmetry of the arrangement was distilled by Massachusetts into its Bill of Rights, passed in 1780:

All power residing originally in the people, and being derived from them, the several magistrates and officers of government, vested with authority whether legislative, executive, or judicial, are their substitutes and agents, and are at all times accountable to them.[9]

In constant awareness that the primary threat to the proper ends of society was arbitrary, unrestrained, and unaccountable power, whether political or economic, the Framers set out to bridle government so that while serving the people and securing their safety, it could not run away with their liberties and rights and thus convert their hallowed sovereignty into a sham.

At bottom, the tension was of course the ancient one between authority and liberty. But the Framers' grand design to resolve it was not merely new, but inspired. Their basic device was the separation of powers. Madison expressed the theory's underlying premise: "The accumulation of all powers, legislative, executive and judicial in the same hands, whether of one, a few, or many, and whether hereditary, self-appointed, or elective, may justly be pronounced the very definition of tyranny."[10]

Most delegates shared this view. Their dominant concern with power was not how it would be used, whether justly or unjustly, but that it not be allowed to concentrate. Consequently, the Framers decided that even those who would be elected—directly in the case of the House of Representatives, indirectly in the case of the Senate and the President—would be suspect in the particular sense that they would not be trusted to accumulate power.

In the intricate system of checks and balances, the Congress would check the Executive; the Executive, the Congress; the Judiciary, both; within the legislature the House would check the Senate, and the Senate the House; within the Judiciary, each judge would be independent of his brethren, yet subject to checks by them. The system thus would work to diffuse and compartmentalize power.

Furthermore, the Framers built accountability into the charter. Congress, explicitly as well as implicitly, would have the power that Parliament had grasped a century before in England: to hold the Executive accountable for the faithful execution of the laws. And the House of Representatives (but the Senate not until 1913) would be directly accountable to the electorate. In turn, the President, in the veto power, would have a device with which, to a deliberately limited extent, he could hold Congress accountable. In the case of the Judiciary, accountability would take the form of appointive power vested in the Senate, and the power of the purse and of limiting the scope of judicial review vested in Congress as a whole. At the same time, the Framers empowered the courts, through judicial review, to restrain the very branches empowered to restrain them.

The fifty-five Framers who gathered in Philadelphia did not invent the theory of separation of powers; neither did their alleged mentor, Charles Secondat, Baron de Montesquieu. The theory "bears some resemblance to, but is not the same as, the 'mixed constitution' well known to the ancient Greeks," Professor Arthur S. Miller has said.

Prominent in Plato's *Laws* and Aristotle's *Politics,* the theory of Aristotle's *Politics* was perhaps most clearly illustrated by Polybius, the Greek historian whose mixture of monarchy, aristocracy, and democracy had its greatest influence in Rome. Not until the late middle ages did separation of powers appear in the literature in anything like its modern form. But there is obvious overlap between the two theories. Both are concerned with achieving liberty under law; both are based on a conception that concentration of power means tyranny; and both appear to be predicated on a view of mankind as essentially irrational.[11]

The American Constitution established separate institutions to *share* power. This is fundamentally distinct from separating powers, Miller says, although "separation of powers" is the generally accepted shorthand.[12] What was new in 1787 was not only the quite rigidly compartmentalized arrangement of institutions, but an added and unique twist: the Framers divided the powers of the states (each of which also provided for its own separation of powers) from those of the federal government. The division was rooted in necessity. The original mandate of the Constitutional Convention had been to revise the Articles of Confederation, which, among other things, did not provide for a satisfactory Executive. Most of the delegates considered themselves to be citizens first of all of their particular states. As a practical matter, the states would cede power to a central government only insofar as they were satisfied that there would be no impairment of their ability to go on functioning as viable political entities. Happily, this practical concern of the states had in it the obvious potential to implement the foremost goal of the delegates: to prevent power from concentrating in any one place.

"If men were angels, no government would be necessary," Madison said. "If angels were to govern men, neither external nor internal controls on government would be necessary. In framing a government which is to be administered by men over men, the great difficulty lies in this: you must first engage the government to control the governed; and in the next place oblige it to control itself."[13] He was confident the Constitution would overcome the difficulty:

In the compound republic of America, the power surrendered by the people is first divided between two distinct governments, and then the portion allotted to each subdivided among distinct and separate departments. Hence, a double security arises to the rights of the people. The different governments will control each other, at the same time that each will be controlled by itself.[14]

At the same time, the Constitution satisfied those Founding Fathers who stressed efficiency as the primary reason why the Executive should be independent of the legislature.

During the four-month convention only relatively minor mention was paid to a bill of rights. This may seem odd, because the colonists, as English citizens, had asserted rights in petitions to the mother country, and because the states had believed it necessary to adopt bills of rights of their own. There was, of course, an explanation of the delegates' seeming indifference. They were confident that the Constitution they were drafting would be as potent an instrument as men could devise to prevent tyranny, and that a bill of rights also intended to prevent tyranny, but with a series of "Thou Shalt Nots," was essentially superfluous. This attitude carried over into the First Congress, in which legislators regarded other matters as more urgent. But because the states had won pledges during the debates on ratification that a bill of rights would be adopted—further to restrict the powers of the federal government—and because Madison was insistent, the First Congress finally did adopt the Bill of Rights, or the first ten amendments; it took effect in December 1791, three years after the Constitution itself had been adopted.

When the delegates had finished writing the Constitution, few were entirely happy with it, because they had compromised strongly felt views.

Yet, they knew, they had done their best, and by any reasonable standards that was extremely good, indeed. And when some balked at signing the document, Benjamin Franklin disarmingly reminded them that they as everyone were fallible:

Most men indeed as well as most sects in religion, think themselves in possession of all truth, and that wherever others differ from them it is so far error. Steele a Protestant in a Dedication tells the Pope, that the only difference between our Churches in their opinions of the certainty of their doctrines is, the Church of Rome is infallible and the Church of England is never in the wrong. But though many private persons think almost as highly of their own infallibility as of that of their sect, few express it so naturally as a certain French lady, who in a dispute with her sister, said "I don't know how it happens, Sister but I meet with no body but myself, that's always in the right—*Il n'y a que moi qui a toujours raison.*

As for himself, he was optimistic and would sign "because I expect no better and because I am not sure that it is not the best."[15]

The objection to the Constitution most often made in our day is that it is not, and cannot possibly be, "the best"; it is, the argument goes, a quaint anachronism that was appropriate to a mostly agricultural society with a population of four million (and an army of 719 officers and men) whose political needs were met mostly by local and state governments.

We disagree. We believe the Constitution can be made "the best." And we believe that the United States (and the world) would have been, and would be, much better off had the principles derided as out-of-date been faithfully observed rather than grossly violated.

"Would we be worse off," the historian Henry Steele Commager asked, "if Nixon had confined himself to the constitutional limitations of his office? Would we be worse off if he had been unable to wage war in Laos, invade and bomb Cambodia, mine Haiphong Harbor; . . . ?[16]

If the Constitution has not secured the safety and happiness of the people the proper course is to determine why, and then to seek to make in the Constitution such strengthening and healing changes as are necessary.

Samuel Adams, many years before the Constitution was adopted, said:

Is it not the uncontrollable essential right of all the people to amend, alter or annul the constitution and frame a new one whenever they think it will better promote their welfare and happiness to do so?[17]

Thomas Jefferson, forty years after the Constitution had been ratified, said he was not among those who "look at constitutions with sanctimonious reverence, and deem them like the ark of the covenant, too sacred to be touched." He went on to say:

But I also know, that laws and institutions must go hand in hand with the progress of the human mind. As that becomes more developed, more enlightened, as new discoveries are made, new truths are disclosed and manners and opinions change with the change of circumstances, institutions must advance also, and keep pace with the times . . . We might as well require a man to wear still the coat which fitted him when a boy, as civilized society to remain ever under the regimen of their barbarous ancestors.[18]

If the Founding Fathers miraculously could reassemble for the Bicentennial celebration, they would, we suspect, be reasonably satisfied that the form of government they devised two hundred years ago still performs its chores tolerably, and as well or better than most others. The federal establishment, they would find, does have a certain momentum that enables it to survive, to grow (too much), and even to deal with most of its day-to-day problems, no matter the competence or incompetence of those in charge.

But, we must also suspect, the Framers surely would find that the Constitution's most fundamental goal—securing the safety and happiness of the governed—has not been achieved. In the 1950s and 1960s, the eloquent Commager has recalled:

blow after blow rained down upon the American consciousness, dissolved American superiority, dissipated confidence and shattered complacency. In the sixties—it can almost be dated from the assassination of President Kennedy—Americans awoke with a sense of shock and incredulity to the discovery that the American dream was largely an illusion. Twenty million Negroes were second-class citizens—or worse. Thirty million poor made a mockery of the proud claim of an affluent society. For two hundred years Americans had laid waste the exceeding bounty of nature, cut down the forests, destroyed the soil, polluted the rivers and the lakes, killed off much of the wildlife and gravely upset the balance of nature; and now at last an outraged nature was revolting. Cities everywhere were rotting away; crime flourished not only on the streets but in high places; the supposed demands of security had qualified the institutions of democracy and of constitutionalism, and permanently shifted the balance in the relationship of the military to the civilian power. The nation which had invented revolution had become the most powerful bulwark against revolution; the nation which had fought colonialism and imperialism had become, in the eyes of much of the world, the greatest champion of both; the nation which Jefferson had dedicated to peace had become the most militaristic of great powers and was waging a pitiless war of aggression on a distant continent.[19]

By the fall of 1975, *New York Times* columnist William Shannon was experiencing "fleeting moments when the public scene recalls the Weimar Republic of 1932–33." He perceived "a new spirit of nihilism, a radical disbelief in any rational, objective basis for ethical norms or for orderly political change."[20]

For the failure of the Constitution to achieve the people's safety and happiness there are four chief explanations, none of which the Framers reasonably could have anticipated:

1. The great concept of separation and division of powers, designed to shield the people from that concentration of power perceived as the enemy of life, liberty, and the pursuit of happiness, has broken down.

2. The Framers did not design the Constitution to deal with, and it is not adequate to deal with, centers of private power that govern us, particularly but not exclusively the transnational corporations.

3. Particularly since the New Deal, there has been a proliferation of agencies and bureaus not recognized in the Constitution, which have become nonetheless a "fourth branch of government" which makes decisions affecting all aspects of our lives.

4. The sovereignty reposed in the people has disintegrated because the people do not have the means to make the wielders of power adequately and reliably accountable.

Separation and Division:
The Presidency

2

*Among the fundamental characteristics of monarchy is untouchability.
Contact with the king is forbidden except to an extremely few people or
as a rare privilege to be exercised on great occasions. The king's body is
sanctified and not subject to violation by lesser mortals unless he himself
so wishes. He is not to be jostled in crowds; he is not to be clapped on
the back; he is not to be placed in danger of life or limb or even put to
the annoyance of petty physical discomfort. Nor can he be compelled to
account for his actions on demand.*

*By the twentieth century, the presidency had taken on all the regalia of
monarchy except robes, a scepter and a crown. The president was not to
be jostled by a crowd—unless he elected to subject himself to do so
during those moments when he shed his role as chief of state and
mounted the hustings as a candidate for re-election. . . . The president
was not to be called to account by any other body (after the doctrine of
executive privilege was established). In time, another kingly habit began to
appear and presidents referred to themselves more and more as "we"—the
ultimate hallmark of imperial majesty.*

George E. Reedy
The Twilight of the Presidency

*With all its defects, delays and inconveniences, men have discovered no
technique for long preserving free government except that the Executive
be under the law, and that the law be made by parliamentary
deliberations.*

Justice Robert H. Jackson
Concurring Opinion in *Youngstown Sheet & Tube Co. v. Sawyer*

The apparently ineradicable impulse to exalt a President, in the absence of
a king—is but one of many interlocking factors that account for the decline
of the separation and division of powers as a barrier to concentration of
power in the White House. While fascinating, it is far from being the most
important factor, and in fact is more a symptom than a cause of the decline.

The preeminent factor was the growth of presidential power. "The last President to operate the White House as authorized by law was Franklin Roosevelt," two federal budget analysts, writing under the name "Ben Roberts," said in the *Washington Monthly.*

In 1933 he had six aides and a clerical staff of 40. This was sufficient to get him through the Depression. When Roosevelt proposed legislation in 1937 to increase the size and power of the White House, Congress voted it down. Eventually it agreed to give him six more personal assistants and to create the Executive Office of the President by moving the Bureau of the Budget from the Treasury Department. With this alteration, the White House prosecuted World War II.

The White House itself now [1975] includes more than 500 people. . . .

In addition to the White House itself, there are the Executive Offices of the President, comprised of more than a dozen separate "offices" or departments employing 1,600 people. By contrast to the congressional opposition to FDR's expansion plans, President Nixon's 1970 executive reorganization—which added almost 100 people to the presidential staff—faced almost no resistance.[1]

The Framers intended Congress to be the dominant branch of government. That is why they set up internal checks—the House on the Senate, the Senate on the House. But they did not think it necessary to provide internal checks within the Presidency, and in fact provided none.[2] Historically, some such checks have come from Cabinet members with, in the words of Arthur M. Schlesinger, Jr., "independent views, reputations and constitutiencies—men to whom even a strong President was compelled, often to his annoyance, to listen and with whom he had in some fashion to come to terms."[3] But these checks began virtually to disappear with President Nixon, who, during the 1968 campaign, ironically had promised to name to his Cabinet "the ablest men in America, leaders in their own right and not merely be virtue of appointment."[4] Once in office, Mr. Nixon deliberately humbled Cabinet members—many of them nonentities—while delegating power in the White House to such unaccountable inventions as a "Domestic Council" and to a swollen staff. As Watergate Special Prosecutor Archibald Cox said,

the hardest thing for me to understand was the final authority exercised by members of the White House staff over very senior officials elsewhere in the Government. No one in the White House of President John F. Kennedy—not even Theodore Sorensen—could have made the requests or issued the instructions of so youthful and minor but ubiquitous a figure as John Dean—not to mention [H. R.] Haldeman, [John D.] Ehrlichman or others of greater position than Dean. . . .

There are good reasons to fear such organizational arrangements . . . The power of Presidential aides is wholly autocratic. They are responsive and responsible to only one man. . . . Unlike every Cabinet officer, agency head and lesser official outside the White House, Presidential aides are subject to almost none of the checks of regularized procedure, of speaking for an organization and of having to respond to it.[5]

"Taken by and large," Professor Edward S. Corwin has said, "the history of the Presidency has been a history of aggrandizement." The evolution and growth of political parties—with each President heading his own—is one of the reasons for this. The Framers had neither contemplated nor intended such a development. Ironically, it was Thomas Jefferson, the great exponent of people's democracy, who developed the extra-constitutional role for the President and recognized in it a high potential to expand presidential power. Indeed, Professor Corwin said, "What we encounter in Jefferson for the first time is a President who is primarily a party leader, only secondarily a chief executive."[6] A century after the Jefferson Presidency, Woodrow Wilson would say that a President

cannot escape being the leader of his party except by incapacity and lack of personal force, because he is at once the choice of the party and of the nation.

He can dominate his party by being spokesman for the real sentiment and purpose of the country, by giving direction to opinion, by giving the country at once the information and the statements of policy which will enable it to form its judgments alike of parties and of men. . . .[7]

By 1975, the country had learned something more, most of all from Richard Nixon and Gerald Ford. Even if a President heads a minority party, his party leadership combined with his power to veto legislation makes him so formidable that he can dominate legislative programs. The Framers had not thought to create for the President a role similar to that of a British Prime Minister under the parliamentary system, but that is the role he has come to play without the internal checks and internal accountability which are prerequisites of sound parliamentary government.

Intended by the Framers to be the foremost branch, Congress was to balance and oversee the White House. For many reasons, prominently including the unexpected rise of Presidents as party leaders, Congress long has been floundering—and frequently in the wings rather than on-stage. The signs of disarray have been everywhere at hand. Consider:

1. The Framers proposed to make it impossible for "a ruler to take the nation into war. Henry Steele Commager has documented this to the hilt.

How revealing that even Hamilton, always ardent for power, provided in his famous draft constitution that the President was to be Commander in Chief and "to have the direction of the war *when authorized or begun.*" (Note in another version of this speech, "the direction of the war *when commenced*" (I Farrand 292 and III Farrand

624). This limited view of the powers of the Commander in Chief persisted almost down to our time . . .[8]

But, as Commager said, it was Madison, not Hamilton who justly could claim to be the father of the Constitution and its most authoritative interpreter. This is what Madison, writing as "Helvidius," said in 1793 about the power of the executive to make war:

Every just view that can be taken of this subject admonishes the public of the necessity to a rigid adherence to the simple, the received, and the fundamental doctrine of the Constitution, that the power to declare war including the power of judging the causes of war, is *fully and exclusively vested in the legislature,* that the executive has no right in any case, to decide the question whether there is or is not cause for declaring war, that the right of convening and informing Congress whenever such a question seems to call for a decision, is all the right which the Constitution has deemed requisite or proper.[9]

Madison added an observation that, Commager said in 1971, "we may take to heart today:" "In no part of the Constitution is more wisdom to be found than in the clause which confines the question of war or peace to the legislature and not to the executive department."[10]

But Congress long since has abandoned the question of war or peace to the Executive. In 1957 Congress authorized President Eisenhower to protect our "vital interests" in the Middle East, whereupon he dispatched 14,000 troops to Lebanon "to protect American lives and property." It was more vital to protect the Constitution—which would have meant doing no such thing. Congress having acquiesced, our "vital interests" later required our presence in Vietnam. What precisely were those interests? In 1967, Nicholas deB. Katzenbach, undersecretary of state, told the Senate Foreign Relations Committee that congressional declarations of war were outmoded—"thus neatly repealing a clause in the Constitution without the bother of congressional and state action," Commager said.

With the repeal uncontested by a Congress as hot as the White House for the worldwide anti-Communist crusade; and with Congress continuing to vote whatever funds were wanted by Presidents who meanwhile were emasculating the legislature, and with the men the press calls "conservative" leading the applause, President Nixon correctly concluded that he need have no compunction about starting a new war if he cared to. And so, in violation of the Constitution, and, as well, of international law, he started a secret war against Cambodia. Once a peaceful, lovely, self-sufficient nation, it quickly became a shattered hell, and, in the end, a brutal, closed Communist society.

When the time finally came, in 1974, to approve articles of impeachment, Congress had so often financed and consented to questionable and illegal activities that the House Judiciary Committee was able to approve articles of impeachment for unlawful wiretapping but not, Congressman Robert F. Drinan (D–Mass.) noted, "for unlawful war-making . . . for concealing a burglary but not for concealing a massive bombing."[11]

2. To meet peacetime crises starting in the 1930s, a President four times has declared a state of national emergency—Franklin Roosevelt in 1933 to deal with the Great Depression, Harry Truman in 1950 to prosecute the war in Korea, Richard Nixon in 1970 to deal with a postal strike, and Nixon again in 1971 to meet balance-of-payments and other international economic problems. Each time, the White House drafted and sent to Congress emergency statutes—470 in all—which gave the Executive fantastic discretionary powers. These included, the Senate Special Committee on National Emergencies and Delegated Emergency Powers reported in 1974, authority

to seize property and commodities, organize and control the means of production, call to active duty 2.5 million reservists, assign military forces abroad, seize and control all means of transportation and communication, restrict travel, and institute martial law, and, in many other ways, manage every aspect of the lives of all American citizens.

Thus, the Feed and Forage Act of 1861, intended to enable the United States Cavalry to requisition horse feed when Congress was out of session and unable to provide funds, was transformed by the Pentagon into a device to fund military activities in Southeast Asia that Congress had not authorized. Under another emergency statute, the President was empowered to "detail members of the Army, Navy, Air Force, and Marine Corps to assist in military matters in any foreign country," and under another to use whatever means may be necessary to abort any "subversive" acts by the government of Cuba. It is, the committee said, "distressingly clear that our Constitutional government has been weakened by 41 consecutive years of emergency rule," a "body of potentially authoritarian power" under which "[a] majority of the American people have lived all their lives . . ."

To be sure "[a]ggressive presidents" and "a long series of successive crises" contributed "to the erosion of the structure of divided powers, the bedrock of our constitutional system of government." Moreover, "in far too many instances, the Executive branch itself drafted the laws and cast them in such form as to give itself maximum advantage. It is understandable that the Executive branch, in drafting laws granting power to itself, did not provide for either oversight or for termination by Congress." In sum, at least in the case of the 470 emergency laws, "the Constitutionally prescribed roles of the Legislative and Executive branches have been reversed."

What role in this epochal reversal had Congress played? The committee, whose chairman was Senator Frank Church (D–Idaho), and whose co-chairman was Senator Charles McC. Mathias (R–Md.), was scathing. In addition to making provisions for neither oversight nor termination, successive Congresses had been "permissive." Conceding the urgent circumstances which had confronted Congress, it nonetheless had tilted the constitutional balance toward the Executive,

hastily without real scrutiny, without thorough hearings, and without the deliberation that such legislation should have demanded. For these reasons, Congress has not exercised its responsibilities prudently; it has not even reserved for itself the means to recoup its lost powers.[12]

Thanks principally to Church and Mathias, and with President Ford's cooperation, the Senate in 1974 passed a bill to terminate the four emergencies declared starting in 1933, to rationalize the handling of future national emergencies, to require a President to account for all significant invocations of emergency power, and to repeal obsolete emergency statutes. The bill died in the Ninety-third Congress because the House did not act. In 1975, however, the House passed a similar bill that was being considered by the Senate. The bill contained a provision under which the President could proclaim a national emergency when that would be "essential to the preservation, protection, and defense of the Constitution or to the common defense, safety, or well-being of the territory or people of the United States." In this vague language is a large potential for abuse: what in particular is the meaning of "essential to the preservation, protection, and defense of the Constitution"?

3. The "pattern of hurried and inadequate consideration"—the House and Senate together gave a total of eight hours of debate to the national-emergency bill of 1933, had no committee reports, and had only one copy of the bill on each floor—was repeated again and again, Senator Church noted, when laws with far-reaching implications were rushed through during World War II and the Korean War, and in the case of the Tonkin Gulf Resolution of 1964.[13]

4. Congress allowed a succession of Presidents to shift power from at least nominally accountable departments and agencies to unelected, unaccountable men in the Executive Office of the President, where government policy truly is made, without even requiring Senate confirmation of "the overlords of the executive branch," as Professor Philip B. Kurland called them.[14]

5. Without the ability to obtain information from the Executive, Congress cannot oversee it. Yet Congress allowed the White House to devise, refine, and enlarge various devices to withhold information and thus to frustrate the oversight function. Executive privilege is the classic example.

Dwight Eisenhower invoked it wholesale almost twenty years before Richard Nixon used it as the basis of his refusal to submit certain Watergate tapes requested by the Senate Select Watergate Committee. All this time, Congress had not so much as tried to define the privilege or to set general standards under which information must flow from the White House to Capitol Hill. Senator Sam J. Ervin, Jr. (D–N.C.) managed to get a bill through the Senate in 1973 to set such standards, but it died in the House Rules Committee.

6. For many years, Congress had appropriated funds, only to see the White House—required by the Constitution to faithfully execute the laws —impound them. The Nixon Administration developed impoundment to gigantic proportions, humiliating the Legislative branch by withholding more than $12 billion in each of three consecutive years (it took Senator Ervin two years merely to find out from the Office of Management and Budget, in 1971, how much was being impounded. In the budget year ending June 30, 1973, Professor Arthur S. Miller reported, the following were among the examples of funds deliberately appropriated by Congress, but withheld by presidential fiat: for the Model Cities Program, $105 million; for the Bureau of Indian Affairs, $53 million; for urban mass transport, $300 million; for the Veterans Administration, for grants to the states for extended-care facilities, $8 million; and for the nominally independent Federal Trade Commission, for seventy-two new positions intended to strengthen consumer protection, $620,000. "Possibly the basic trouble is that there is only one Sam Ervin," Miller said. It was Ervin (again) who introduced, fought for, and, in the Congressional Budget and Impoundment Control Act of 1974, finally got a law requiring that all impoundments be referred to Congress, which must give affirmative approval to each one if it is to be valid.[15]

7. Congress gives almost no review to the money that supports the White House. In addition to letting the President spend appropriations for the White House staff as he will; in addition to giving him a $1 million fund for emergencies (some of which, in 1974, went to entities as unemergent as the Federal Property Council), and in addition to a $1.5 million annual Special Projects fund (which the Nixon White House used to pay the travel expenses of E. Howard Hunt, Jr., and G. Gordon Liddy in preparing for the burglary of the office of Daniel Ellsberg's psychiatrist), Congress gives the President "blank check" funding. This makes it impossible even to figure out how much the President and his staff spend every year, "Ben Roberts" said in the *Washington Monthly*. "This form of . . . funding is more effective than the invocation of 'executive privilege' in keeping the courtiers of the imperial president beyond congressional supervision."[16]

Congress writes blank checks by allowing sundry federal agencies to bury White House expenses in their budget. The expenses involved "range from large—the $35 million that the Pentagon spends annually on the White House Communication system—to trivial—White House tourguides employed by the Treasury Department," Roberts said. The burial is often artful:

For example, what budget analyst attempting to review the White House's bankroll would think to examine the books of the National Park Service? Yet this division of the Department of the Interior spends millions annually on the presidency. The Park Service is responsible for the $1.2 million annually appropriated for operation of the Executive Residence. (Recently Park Service administrators found themselves defending the use of money from this fund to pay for Richard Nixon's personal valet and maid, detailed to his "Casa Pacifica" long after he had resigned as President) . . . The Park Service has spent over $3 million of its own funds since 1969 to repair the electrical and air conditioning systems in the White House.

The money spent by agencies such as the Park Service for the White House, "however necessary, frees official White House funds intended to cover such expenses for unreviewed and potentially undesirable activity," Roberts said. "More important, the other agencies' expenses for the White House cannot be reviewed because they cannot be found."[17]

"How odd to remember," Professor Commager has noted, "that when Thomas Jefferson walked back to his boardinghouse after giving his inaugural address, he could not find a seat available for him at the dinner table, or that a quarter century later President John Quincy Adams should have the same experience on a ship sailing from Baltimore to New York."[18]

Separation and Division: Congress

In the many years that I have been a member of Congress, the House has revealed itself to me as ineffective in its role as a coordinate branch of the Federal Government, negative in its approach to national tasks, generally unresponsive to any but parochial economic interests. Its procedures, time-consuming and unwieldy, mask anonymous centers of irresponsible powers. Its legislation is often a travesty of what the national welfare requires.

Congressman Richard Bolling
House Out of Order

The falling away of Congress from the grand role assigned to it in the separation of powers derives mainly from three basic factors: its faults, its nature, and its mission. The public hears a good deal about the faults, less about the nature and mission, and still less about the complicated, changing interrelationships between faults and nature and mission. The criticism of Congress of which the general public is usually most aware, incidentally, commonly comes from the White House. Such criticism is almost always self-serving, and often misleading, unfair, and intimidating, partly because there is no "Mr. Congress" to respond in kind to "Mr. President."

The faults of Congress that concern us in this chapter are those that, in the context of the intent of the Framers, may loosely be termed collective character defects. One classic example, cited in the previous chapter, was Congress' repeated grants of totalitarian emergency powers to the Executive with neither serious consideration of what it was doing nor provision for oversight or termination of those powers. Nothing in the constitutional design of the legislature required it to react mindlessly to presidential declarations of emergency, but it assuredly did so. Nothing in the design, similarly, compelled legislators to grovel before an Executive usurping the war-making power, to allow the White House to conceal its funding, or to allow Presidents to lie to Congress, to impose excessive secrecy, or to build up a bloated, unaccountable staff. Nothing in the Constitution told Congress that it had to deny itself a single computer for use in overseeing an Executive which, as of October 1975, had 7,830 computers programmed and operated by 114,286 employees.[1] Surely the Framers would be curious why in 1975, after all the brave talk about Congress reasserting itself, the House Appropriations Committee continues to borrow investigators from the FBI rather than hire its own.

Every member of Congress takes a solemn oath to uphold the Constitution. However, some senior members were told of the secret war in Laos, but did nothing about it, and this, as Ralph Nader has said, was "in violation of their oath to uphold the Constitution. They knew much about the lawlessness of the CIA and did nothing, again in violation of their oath to uphold the Constitution."[2] After the exposures of Executive lawlessness in the Watergate scandals, some legislators in 1974 drew up a list of reforms. The immediate point is not whether the recommendations were good or bad, adequate or inadequate—but simply that Congress was uninterested. Where was it written that Congress should lack, and it comes down to this, self-respect?

At Thurii in ancient Greece, Charondas, a member of the Pythagorean brotherhood, was purported to have devised an extreme and effective deterrent to the passage of unnecessary legislation: a politician proposing a new law had to do so with his neck in a noose, so that, in the event his motion failed, he could be hanged immediately. Reportedly, only three citizens had the nerve to propose legislation.[3] Nothing quite so drastic is in order on Capitol Hill. But there is a habit of passing laws and then failing to see to it that they are enforced, or are enforced properly—or to inquire if they are in fact enforceable. For several years until 1974, former Congressman Chet Holifield (D–Calif.) was chairman of the House Government Operations Committee. During his tenure, neither the committee nor any of its components ever held an oversight hearing on the Atomic Energy Commission or the National Aeronautics and Space Administration, two of the most important agencies in the committee's jurisdiction.

The Senate, in its power to "advise and consent" to presidential nominees to high government posts, has one of the most potent devices for conscientious oversight, but frequently simply throws it away. The inevitable result is not merely that bad appointments slip through, but that Presidents do not feel inhibited in making more of the same. No wonder that of the forty-five persons named in a five-year period ending in 1975 to nine regulatory agencies (the Consumer Product Safety, Federal Communications, Federal Power, Federal Trade, Interstate Commerce, and Securities and Exchange

SEPARATION AND DIVISION: CONGRESS

commissions, the Environmental Protection Agency, and the Food and Drug and Highway Traffic Safety administrations), twenty-four—more than half—came from industries they were supposed to regulate.[4] No wonder Presidents name unqualified large campaign contributors to ambassadorial posts. No wonder President Ford, in 1975, felt free to name political hacks to agencies as important as the Interior Department and the Tennessee Valley Authority.

Woodrow Wilson said that Congress was run by committee chairmen who "exercise an almost despotic sway in their own shires."[5] That is to say, while generally failing to hold the Executive accountable, Congress has made its own leaders accountable "only to their longevity."[6] Few men in the United States wield more power than Congressman George Mahon (D–Tex.), the seventy-six-year-old chairman of the House Appropriations Committee. To be reelected over the years, he has, typically, needed but to please the voters in a population of less than 500,000 in West Texas. The voters, also typically, hold Mahon accountable mainly for his performance in their behalf. But no reliable mechanisms exist to hold him accountable for his handling of something as awesomely important as the federal budget.

For nearly thirty years Mahon's heir apparent, Congressman Jamie L. Whitten (D–Miss.), who is accountable mainly to a Delta constituency in which the black majority was voteless during most of his career, "has held an iron hand over the Department of Agriculture's budget," Nick Kotz wrote in *Let Them Eat Promises: The Politics of Hunger in America.* Whitten consistently has used this power to back large federal subsidies for agriculture, prominently including the rich cotton planters in the Delta, and to oppose federal programs to feed the poor. "Each time a group of doctors, team of reporters, or other investigation produced firsthand reports of hunger in the South, Whitten launched his own 'investigation' and announced that parental neglect is largely responsible for any problems," Kotz wrote.

Like other committee and subcommittee chairmen on Capitol Hill, Whitten is an overseer who is not overseen. He "truly believes in his own fairness, his idea of good works," but "has anesthetized his soul to . . . human misery and indignity," said Kotz.

That Jamie Whitten should suffer from blindness to human need is one thing. But that he can use his blindness as an excuse to limit the destiny of millions of Americans is another matter, one which should concern anyone who believes in the basic strengths of this country's constitutional guarantees. The checks and balances of a reasonable democratic republic have gone completely awry when a huge bureaucracy and the top officials of an administration base their actions concerning the deepest human need on their fearful perception of what one rather limited man seems to want.

The system of seniority and temerity that gives a man such as Jamie Whitten such awesome power must come under more serious public scrutiny if the American system of government is ever to establish itself on the basis of moral concern about the individual human being.[7]

For ten years, Daniel Rapoport, as a reporter in the House for United Press International, did in fact scrutinize "[t]he system of seniority and temerity." In his book *Inside the House* he sensibly concluded that a drastic remedy was needed: House members should be permitted to serve no more than four consecutive terms. After a two-year break they could again stand for reelection, but if they won would return at the bottom of the seniority ladder.[8]

Since 1972, there has been, at last, a burst of important reforms, including, in the House, curtailment of the despotic power of committee chairmen, and dethronement of some of them. Both the House and Senate now operate with a degree of openness that, only a few years ago, would not have been believed. Uncommitted legislators have gotten onto committees once dominated by lawmakers allied with special interests, such as the oil industry, military contractors, and, in the taxation area, the rich. Arrangements are in place for much more oversight activity.

Heartening as such belated reforms are, they deal inadequately with many fundamental problems. The one we want to stress here is that the American people delegate much of their sovereign power to Congress but continue to lack the wherewithal to make Congress accountable for its exercise of that power. To be sure, as David R. Mayhew said in *Congress: The Electoral Connection,* "the reelection quest establishes an accountability relationship with an electorate . . ."[9] But, of course, it is standard procedure for a legislator to define accountability mainly or entirely in terms of good service to the personal needs and wants of his constituents or in terms of special benefits for them, such as useless military facilities, that cost the rest of us dearly. In the process, accountability to the whole people suffers.

To an extent, the clash of parochial and general interests is not only inevitable, but desirable: the wronged person, group, business, or other interest must have someone to whom to turn. Even here, however, there is a sharp imbalance that was illustrated in a 1965 survey which posed this question: "Have you written to your Congressman during the last 12 months?" The affirmative responses, broken down into income groups, show who has Congress' ear: $0–4,999, 4.8 percent; $5,000–9,999, 9.1 percent; $10,000–14,999, 19.5 percent; over $15,000, 21.0 percent. A breakdown by education was complementary: not completed high school, 3.8 percent; completed high school, 13.0 percent; completed college, 25.0 percent. Similarly, business executives—a relatively small proportion of the electorate—accounted for 19.4 percent, while the large number of unskilled workers accounted for only 4.7 percent.[10]

The root problem is that the people turn over power to Congress and then turn their backs; in a poll of adults in 1965, half were unable even to name their congressman. A delegation of power unaccompanied by the vigilance of those who delegate it becomes an abdication of accountability. With the abdication, Congress has been free to surrender "its enormous authority and resources to special interest groups, waste, insensitivity, ignorance, and bureaucracy."[11] "Congress is the great American default," Ralph Nader judged.

The popular explanation for this is that it is under the domination of the White House and relentless special interests. There is no question that this is true. Why? Because, in large part, Americans have failed to involve themselves in the activities of Congress, and they have failed to determine the direction these activities should take. Of the three branches of government, the executive and the judicial may get away with being insulated from the citizenry, but Congress is potentially the branch most exposed to democratic demand. And so turning Congress around for the people is the most practical and immediate priority in improving the executive and judicial branches as well.[12]

The telecasting of the House Judiciary Committee's Nixon impeachment proceedings showed, we believe, that the public, given the chance and time to do so, understands and appreciates the congressional institution and mission, and that congressmen can rise well to national responsibilities. How striking it is that some of the Judiciary Committee members who rose while being watched, lapsed back into agentry for assorted special interests almost as soon as the television cameras were turned off.

Existing mechanisms to enable the public to watch Congress deal with things that matter very much to each of us—taxes, prices, unemployment, crime, war, energy, the environment, and the Pentagon and other bureaucracies Congress created—are seriously deficient. The press, to take the principal one, slights not only a great deal that is important but also a great deal that is revealing. One day in late 1974, Colman McCarthy, a *Washington Post* editorial writer, went up to Capitol Hill to take his first look at the House Rules Committee in action—a few feet from the press gallery. He came away "benumbed by how this small band uses its immense power." McCarthy began an article this way:

"Zarb? Who's Zarb?" the 82-year-old congressman at the head of the table demanded to know. Rep. Ray J. Madden (D–Ind.), a lawyer since 1913, a member of the House for 31 years, and chairman of the House Rules Committee, was informed by a chorus that "Zarb" was Frank G. Zarb, the head of the Federal Energy Administration.

The latter's name had arisen as the committee's hearing wore on one recent afternoon. Madden's question was significant because of the snickers and muffled laughs it drew from many in the tiny committee room. It was also significant because the Rules members were dealing with a crucial energy bill—on strip mining—in a period when the nation faced an energy crisis. . . . Rep. James J. Delaney (D–N.Y.), was dozing in a postlunch nap. When he wakened, he heard a witness begin his testimony, "I'll be very brief, Mr. Chairman." Delaney snapped, "Aw, don't believe him." That drew laughs and Delaney looked satisfied.[13]

We venture that such performances would not long survive relentless exposure on the tube, and radio. Somehow, the government that has been able to turn over eighty-two television channels mostly to commercial exploitation has been unable to guarantee a few for televising of proceedings in its national and state and local legislatures, so that the people could see and hear for themselves—at any time, not merely on special occasions—how these bodies were wielding their delegated sovereign power.

"A legislative process carried out largely out of public sight cannot hope to challenge the executive with success," said the Twentieth Century Fund Task Force on Broadcasting and the Legislature.[14] The Joint Committee on Congressional Operations, led by Senator Lee Metcalf (D–Mont.) and Congressman Jack Brooks (D–Tex.), has proposed a one-year test of full-time audio and video coverage of sessions on the Senate and House floors. After a trial period of a few months, the coverage would be made available—live and on tape—to both commercial and public broadcasters, who would be wholly free, without congressional intrusion, to decide how to use it. This would be an important progressive step.

Consider two debates that occurred the week of May 19, 1975. One debate, lasting two days on the House floor, concerned a bill authorizing $32 billion in procurement by the Department of Defense. Proponents and opponents, Walter Pincus wrote in the *New Republic,* "debated specific issues as they came upon a series of amendments to the bill. Had radio and television been there, more of the public than the several hundred who came and went from the galleries could have had a quick education on key defense issues—troop strength abroad, the new ICBM reentry vehicle called MaRV and the B-1 bomber." On May 21, a debate on a proposal to increase allocations for members' staffs and perquisites "would have given the public a view of the House dealing with its own problems," Pincus said. "This was not an example of greedy old congressmen seeking to make their lives easier; the debate showed that the proposed increases originated with newly elected members who found it difficult to meet the expenses of their newly won offices." One of the things revealed was "the brutal debating techniques of

Rep. Wayne Hays, chairman of the House Administration Committee, which approved the increases in the first place. . . . When Republican Millicent Fenwick tried to get the microphone, Hays said, 'And as for that woman from New Jersey wanting to talk, I'll have something to say about her when she's through.' He did. Hays later spoke sarcastically of people who have five million dollars who oppose funds to help those without wealth to stay in office. Radio and television coverage would have caught that. History, as reflected in the *Congressional Record*, won't because Hays had deleted from the printed record his harshest remarks."[15]

The gist of the situation is this: A Congress out of sight is out of mind; out of mind it is unaccountable to the people; because unaccountable, it realizes but a fraction of its potential to make the Executive accountable. For this situation Alfred E. Smith wrote a splendid prescription: "The cure for the evils of democracy is more democracy."[16]

Yet it would be wrong to suggest that the whole problem of Congress is simply that it is out of sight and out of mind, or that, as some have suggested, it is a gutless branch. The problem is bound up with the nature of Congress. On Capitol Hill the competing interests of society find their arena—and that is where they should find it; Congress was intended to be a deliberative forum. It cannot easily be that and, at the same time, "where the action is." Deliberation, by definition, takes time; action, by definition, may be a mere product of visceral stimulation. Thus, a visceral President may sound as though he knows what is right but be downright absurd, or worse. After the Organization of Petroleum Exporting Countries, in September 1975, announced a 10 percent price increase, Gerald Ford stared manfully into the TV cameras and said, "When the price of gasoline goes up at the service station, I want the American people to know exactly where the blame lies." Congress, of course. This was nonsense, and it came with ill grace from a President who himself had put a $2-per-barrel import tax on oil. Richard L. Lyons, the *Washington Post*'s experienced reporter in the House, emphasized the contrast with Congress, which

often looks confused and squabbling, but that is its function—to argue, look at an issue from every side and hammer out a compromise that becomes national policy.

When a big new issue hits Congress—such as Medicare or federal aid to education, it usually takes five, 10 or more years for the consensus to form and the issue to become law.[17]

Issues more complex than Medicare or aid to education beset Congress with increasing frequency. These strain the mechanisms and structure of deliberation and compromise and make the legislative process ever more difficult, particularly because it is inherently too inflexible to cope with rapidly changing, intricate circumstances. Consequently, more and more legislation delegates more and more responsibility to administrative units with a capability for devising detailed and flexible implementing regulations that have the force of law. Furthermore, it is literally impossible for a legislator—any legislator—to be expert or even knowledgeable about all of the multiple problems which he faces each day. And Congress as an institution does not command the expertise and staff which, in the vast bureaucracies, are available to the President (this is not to excuse Congress' prolonged failure to take advantage of new information technologies to improve its expertise, or to give itself adequate staff and resources for adequate oversight).

During the Constitutional Convention the question arose whether the Executive should have three coequal leaders. James Wilson argued against such an arrangement, foreseeing "nothing but uncontrolled, continual and violent animosities which would not only interrupt the public administration but diffuse their poison thro' the other branches of government, thro' the state, and at length thro' the people at large."[18] The conclusion was that a President—one person—would be the most efficient decision maker.

Congress has no counterpart. President Kennedy viewed it as a collection of 535 skeptics, Theodore Sorensen, one of his top aides, has said. Surely skepticism is a preeminent quality when enlisted by Congress for its vital oversight function, but it is not necessarily the quality most needed for leadership. Congress, it is true, can through compromise of competing interests achieve a consensus, but the process of consensus decision making is poorly suited to situations that require swift responses to complex questions, or to long-term approaches to basic societal problems. Legislation requiring a substantial gestation period—civil rights, say—is appropriate to the peculiar processes of Congress; the energy crisis—an issue with so many separate components that no one committee can get a handle on it—is not. "Only the executive," one observer has said,

has the legions of administrators, investigators, fact-gatherers, evaluators, and the technological hardware necessary to respond effectively to the pressing and complex urban, energy, environmental, racial, and foreign crises that tumble over themselves in their demands for immediate attention.[19]

Partially in recognition of its congenital disabilities, Congress has abdicated much power to the White House. Presidential power, moreover, must and will grow even beyond what it is today. One reason for this is the domination of the economy by a relatively few corporations, the giant multinationals; this significantly paralyzes the marketplace, the intended regulator of the economy under a system of private enterprise. The paralysis is compounded by the cartels of exporting countries that control products as basic as petroleum and uranium. Until such time (if it ever comes) when the giants may be broken up and the marketplace restored to health, where but in government can the public interest hope to find a protector? In dealing with monopolies by foreign governments of raw materials essential to our survival, who but the Executive can substitute—to the extent necessary—for the marketplace and the antitrust laws?

Moreover, a President has no choice but to be the national leader in foreign affairs. His is the single voice that speaks for the nation. "Crises, both foreign and domestic, have enlarged the office," Rexford Guy Tugwell, a member of Franklin Roosevelt's "Brain Trust," has said. "When there has been the need for decisive action, Presidents have had to supply it. The situation of a suddenly compacted world is involved; so, too, is the existence of armed forces capable of undertaking the missions of enforcement often involved in bargaining. There is also our economy, and its growing inter-dependence with those of other nations; there are the special complications of international trade and monetary agreement."[20]

Given its congenital disabilities, Congress, no matter how it may reform its own procedures, never will be able to check and balance presidential power in the manner and to the extent intended by the Framers. Additional and more effective restraints must be imposed.

Separation and Division:
The Courts/the States

The federal judiciary is the third of the power centers that the Framers separated each from the other. Here we will deal briefly with the bench and, finally, with the last constitutional barrier erected against the concentration of power: the division of rule between the federal and state governments.

The judiciary has maintained substantial independence, but the benign effects of this should not be overstated. For the most part, the courts deal with specific and usually narrow issues. The courts are passive in the sense that they wait for cases and controversies to be brought before them. Before court processes even begin, consequently, liberties can atrophy, unconstitutional or illegal governmental actions can be implemented and become entrenched, sometimes permanently, justice can be denied and safety menaced. Essentially, the judicial process makes determinations after the fact; it generally looks backward. And some issues that might come before the courts never arrive, because potential plaintiffs lack either the money or the time (or both) to undertake litigation that, even after great expense and delay, may fail.

In addition to such aspects of its functioning as are inherent, unavoidable, necessary, or desirable, other factors impede the ability or willingness of the judiciary to review governmental actions. One is the requirement that a plaintiff have "standing"—be qualified in judicial eyes—to challenge such action. Another is the restraints under which the courts may rule on the constitutionality of an action, but not on whether the action was wise or appropriate. An additional point was made by George Reedy, who was press secretary to Lyndon Johnson in the Senate as well as in the White House: "Nearly four decades of experience have produced a rough form of parallelism between the executive and the judiciary, and court decisions in modern times are more likely to sustain than overturn national policy."[1] This is true, in part, because for the courts to venture too aggressively into fundamental political controversies is to jeopardize their power. It is, for example, difficult to imagine that the Supreme Court could have handed down the school desegregation decision in, say, 1940 without the justices possibly having to run for their lives.

Up to this point, we have dealt entirely with the separation of powers within the federal government. Now we turn to the *division* of powers. At the time of the Constitutional Convention in 1787, each of the then-existing states was still a repository of great governmental power and, in fact, genuinely a sovereign entity. In the fight for independence, it may be remembered, state militia had played a vital role. After independence had been won, the Continental Congress proposed, and the states ratified, the Articles of Confederation, "a firm league of friendship" in which" [e]ach state retains its *sovereignty*, freedom, and independence, and every Power, Jurisdiction and right, which is not by this confederation expressly delegated to the United States, in Congress assembled." (Emphasis supplied.) To be sure, the convention delegates agreed that some form of centralized direction was necessary, but they nevertheless expected the states to retain strong, independent governments which would be an effective counter to federal power.

This role for the states vanished a long time ago—done in by the same forces that made a strong Presidency a necessity. Insofar as basic national problems are concerned, state lines have become almost meaningless. Moreover, many states today retain governmental structures that are outmoded and unresponsive to modern needs. Without the billions of dollars dispensed to the states by Washington in such forms as grants, matching funds, and revenue sharing, state governments probably could not survive. The once-sovereign states largely have been reduced to being administrators of federal programs; seldom do they innovate or lead in such a way as to influence or inhibit federal actions. In October 1975, after the governor of New York State and the mayor of New York City had pleaded for federal funds to relieve the city's severe financial crisis, Joseph A. Califano, Jr., a former aide to President Johnson, granted that federal aid could be the only solution. But if it is, he said, "We may well be on the way to making the President the governor of every state and the mayor of every city."[2]

The third on the list of powers enumerated by the Constitution is, "The Congress shall have the power. . . . To regulate commerce with foreign nations, and among the several States, and with the Indian tribes; . . ." In the 1930s, the Supreme Court interpreted the commerce clause to mean that Congress has the power to pass almost any law affecting commerce so long as a link, no matter how tenuous, may be discerned to an interstate effect on economic activity. The Court's commerce clause decisions broke the ability of the states to retain basic power. Admittedly, this oversimplifies the matter—there were additional compelling reasons for the decline of state power.[3] Nevertheless, the federal government generally derived from its expanded power over commerce the legal means with which to act almost without restriction. In the future the influence of the states may rebound somewhat. But in terms of constitutional limitations on federal power this would matter little. The essential point remains that in curbing federal power, the states do not now and will not again play a significant role.

The evidence in this chapter and in the two that preceded it leads inexorably to the verdict that the separation and division of powers—the theory developed and elegantly refined by the Framers to preserve the safety and happiness of the people—is moribund. Some detect no vital signs. "The balance that the Founding Fathers ingeniously devised no longer exists," Abe Fortas, the former justice of the Supreme Court, has said.

It has been destroyed by the complexities of modern life; the vast expansion of governmental function; the decline of Congress due to the growth in the number of its members, and principally, to its failure effectively to reorganize its management and procedures; and the enormous increase in Presidential power and prestige. At the same time, we have permitted the erosion and obsolescence of the checks, the restraints upon the President in which the drafters of the Constitution placed their ultimate reliance.[4]

    5

Cities are not mentioned in the Constitution. Corporations and labor unions are not mentioned. I can't think of a single problem that agitates us now that was present in the minds of the framers with the possible exception of the freedom of the press, and even that is in entirely different form today with the electronic media and the monopolies in the print media.

Robert M. Hutchins
Center Magazine, Center for Democratic Institutions

Nongovernmental institutions affect our safety and happiness as profoundly as laws passed by Congress and directives issued by Presidents. These institutions *govern.* Yet the Constitution does not deal with them. This is its most glaring deficiency. The Founding Fathers, unaware that such centers of power were destined to evolve, understandably did not devise adequate checks and balances—and the Constitution remains barren of them two centuries later. No bill of rights is in place to curb excesses of nongovernmental power, although Jefferson, in 1787, protested to Madison the omission from the Constitution of a bill of rights that, he felt, should contain, among other things, a "restriction of monopolies. . . ."[1]

Foremost among the great nongovernmental power centers are the giant corporations whose decisions on pricing amount to taxation without representation, whose decisions on the safety of products determine whether people live or die, whose decisions affecting the environment shape the quality of life, and whose conduct of foreign affairs frequently overshadows the State Department's. Columnist Jack Anderson, in February 1972, published internal documents of International Telephone and Telegraph Corporation which indicated that ITT was collaborating closely with the Central Intelligence Agency to prevent Salvador Allende from becoming president of Chile, and then to subvert his government once he had been elected. This was a clear warning that there had been a secret merger of the two great superpowers of unaccountability, multinational corporations and the CIA. "The Anderson papers," said Senator Frank Church (D–Idaho), chairman of the Subcommittee on Multinational Corporations, raised the issue of multinationals "becoming a Fifth Column in international politics, using their home governments to destroy foreign regimes not to their liking."[2]

Much evidence can be adduced to support the assertion of Philip Agee, author of *Inside the Company: CIA Diary*, "that the CIA is essentially an instrument for the pursuit of the great transnational corporate interests in the name of 'national security.' " Laurence Stern, a *Washington Post* reporter who is highly knowledgeable about the CIA, has said, "This was never more clearly demonstrated than in ITT's special pleadings in Washington for intervention against the Allende government. ITT's offer of secret financing to reverse the popular election was submitted by John McCone, who played the dual role of ITT board member and former CIA director."[3]

Kings ruled by divine right. "We the people of the United States" established the government in Washington. The rulers of the multinational corporations can claim no comparable legitimacy. "It is high time that the repositories of economic sovereignty, the giant corporations and their financial allies, be recognized in constitutional theory and in our thinking about the separation of powers today," the distinguished constitutional scholar Arthur S. Miller has said. Miller got to the crux of the matter.[4] So did Edward S. Mason, the Harvard economist, when he asked, "Who selected these men, if not to rule over us, at least to exercise vast authority, and to whom are they responsible?"[5]

Giant corporations are by no means the only nongovernmental institutions that make significant impacts on our lives. Labor unions are another. Many are large because they must be, i.e., the corporations they deal with are large or even enormous. Most genuinely pursue basic equity for their members. However, some union bureaucracies—like other bureaucracies—become more accountable to self-serving ends than to the ultimate source of their power, which in this case is the dues-paying rank and file. Unions sometimes acquire excessive power with which, through featherbedding and other indefensible practices, they advance their members' economic welfare, but at the expense of equity to their employers and the public generally. And unions sometimes take on roles in foreign affairs that betoken unmistakable unaccountable power, as many AFL–CIO unions did when they accepted concealed funding from the CIA.

The legitimate public government entrusts large chunks of power to dozens of professions, semiprofessions, and crafts—legal, medical, accounting, optical, etc. Most all of these callings have become significantly unaccountable to the public the better to serve their own interests. They have done this directly by, say, illegal price-fixing, an activity in which lawyers, who are officers of the courts, have been pacesetters, or indirectly by tilting toward moneyed interests, such as pharmaceutical manufacturers in the case of physicians dependent upon advertising revenues and payola or any powerful client at all in the case of certified public accountants, the purportedly independent scorekeepers of society.

The Founding Fathers rightly exempted the press from accountability in any ordinary sense. "Congress shall make no law . . . abridging the freedom of speech, or of the press," they said in the First Amendment. They had no illusions. The press in the early decade of the republic was frequently atrociously dishonest and irresponsible. One of its principal victims was Jefferson. But, he said, "our liberty depends on the freedom of the press, and that cannot be limited without being lost."[6] Moreover, while various leaders have threatened the democratic process, the press has not—and, meanwhile, it has exposed most every great scandal of government that has come to light. However, the press—by omission at least as much as by commission—exercises great power. It is a power insufficiently assessed and audited. Press performance suffers—as does the performance of any great power center that eludes reliable, sustained monitoring. The press cannot be and must not be made accountable to government, and the First Amendment, of course, forbids this in any case. But nongovernmental mechanisms undertaking to assess and audit press performance are entirely consistent with the First Amendendment because they themselves are an exercise of free speech and free press.

Nongovernmental institutions have enlarged their power with the aid of technologies unimagined by the Founding Fathers. Some of these technologies themselves have truly staggering potentials for unaccountability. Nuclear reactors imperil all future generations with possible release of cancer-causing radiation. Scientists want to re-engineer our genes. Supertankers menace the oceans. Aerosol sprays threaten the stratosphere. Scientists in specialized roles—particularly when these roles are performed within governmental or corporate power structures—often suffer, as one observer said, "a commensurate narrowing of their range of accountability and their perceived duty."[7]

In the Virginia Bill of Rights, adopted in 1776, "the good people" of the state, "assembled in full and free convention," declared in Section 1:

That all men are by nature equally free and independent, and have certain inherent rights, of which when they enter into a state of society, they cannot by any compact, deprive or divest their posterity; namely, the enjoyment of life and liberty, with the means of acquiring and possessing property, and pursuing and obtaining happiness and safety.

The people made no compact with the nongovernmental institutions to "divest their posterity," but that has not prevented these power-wielders from intruding massively into the pursuit of happiness and safety.

33

The Fourth Branch:
Bureaucracies

*. . . I think it would be easy to show that the officials of a
seventeenth-century prince were more responsible, i.e., answerable, to him,
their sovereign, than the officials of any modern democracy are as yet to
the people, their supposed sovereign.*

Carl J. Friedrich
The Politics of the Federal Bureaucracy

*A $56,000 Federal study of 15 Government agencies has confirmed a
suspicion of many Americans: Government bureaucrats frequently pay no
attention to citizen complaints.*

David Burnham
New York Times

The Framers wrote the Constitution at a time when the nation's marketplaces were largely local, personal, simple, and, as a result, significantly
accountable to the people they directly affected. They also lived at a time
when technology was relatively benign, primitive, and accountable. They
had no way to foresee, and consequently did not provide for, marketplaces
that would become national and even international, impersonal, and complex. They had no premonition of technologies too arcane to be understood
by all but narrow specialists, and so volatile that each of several has the
capacity to menace a vast population if not all human life—sometimes with
little public awareness of peril. Partly to try to make the new marketplaces
and technologies accountable, Congress and the Executive together evolved
various modes of regulation.

Regulation often turned out to be itself unaccountable, wasteful, unresponsive, arbitrary, and even tyrannical. Some agencies, principal examples
being the Civil Aeronautics Board, the Interstate Commerce Commission,
and the Federal Maritime Commission, have operated mainly to put a
governmental seal of approval on cartels, to inhibit that essential competition
which makes for accountability in the marketplace, and thereby to waste
billions of consumer dollars a year.[1] Other units, the Federal Aviation Ad-

ministration, the Food and Drug Administration, and the Environmental Protection Agency being outstanding cases in point, have responsibilities— for the safety of airline passengers, foods, food additives, medicines, pesticides, the purity of air and drinking water—that society dare not abandon to the mercies and vagaries of the marketplace. But most of the agencies frequently turn out to be run by men—usually the President's men—who owe primary allegiance to the industries they nominally regulate. Their decisions are seldom reviewable in the courts. Their performance commonly escapes sustained, effective oversight, if subject to any oversight at all, by Congress and the press. Here again, the Constitution provides no specific checks and balances on their power.

Along with the regulatory agencies and operations, all government departments, bureaus, and assorted subdivisions exercise discretionary power and administer discretionary justice. This is a huge, growing, and insufficiently mapped jungle of unaccountability in which corporate elephants and other big game roam pretty much as they please, while the ordinary citizens are lucky to escape being trampled. On a single day in October 1975, for example, the *Washington Post* disclosed in one front-page story how Commissioner Donald C. Alexander and certain other senior officials of the Internal Revenue Service "have for more than two years successfully blocked tax audits and investigations of Sen. Joseph M. Montoya (D–N. Mex.) who heads a subcommittee that oversees the IRS," and in another page-one story that the Federal Power Commission "knew at least four years ago that natural-gas producers were failing to deliver gas to their pipeline customers in the amounts specified in contracts, but did nothing about it"—an exercise of discretion without which the threat of the natural-gas shortage of the winter of 1975–76 would not have occurred.[2]

The Department of Justice is often outgunned and outmanned when it takes on, say, International Business Machines in an antimonopoly suit. But when the department takes on an individual, "unreviewable discretion is often the norm and arbitrariness often the rule," Arthur S. Miller wrote in an article in the *Progressive* on politicalization of the department. Professor Miller gave this example:

Several years ago, a patient at a Veterans Administration hospital was erroneously injected with embalming fluid by an orderly who had the duty of giving injections. Result: total paralysis of the patient. The patient sued the Government, only to be met with the defense (from technical "agency" law) that the orderly acted beyond the "scope of his employment." Thus a weak, even silly, legal stratagem was used by government attorneys in an effort to stave off paying a few thousand dollars.

Multiply that case by thousands and the pattern of overzealous action by the

Department of Justice takes on added meaning. It is a proud tenet of the Solicitor General's office that the Government's case is won when justice is done, but all too often that precept is forgotten; the game is to win, by using every technicality and legal stratagem.[3]

Commonly, great discretionary power is rendered unaccountable by nonfeasance, which thrives in an atmosphere of secrecy, obscurity, or inattention at least until a catastrophe occurs or a scandal erupts. The Federal Aviation Administration, a unit of the Department of Transportation, provides an outstanding example. The FAA is the "someone" wishful thinkers assume is resolutely protecting them when they fly. To some extent, much of the time, it does. But authorities have imputed to the agency repeated failures —usually unnoted by a wide public until a crash occurs—to take necessary and even obvious precautions.

The worst disaster in aviation history occurred on March 3, 1974, when 335 passengers and 11 crew members were killed in a crash near Paris. They had been aboard a Turkish Airlines DC-10, an aircraft jointly manufactured, designed, and developed by McDonnell Douglas Corporation and General Dynamics Corporation. In subsequent, successful liability litigation against the companies, officers of both acknowledged that they had known that the plane had a potentially dangerous aft bulk-cargo door. The crash occurred shortly after takeoff when the cargo door opened at an altitude of about 12,000 feet. The resulting decompression was of near-explosive force; it collapsed the cabin floor and disrupted control cables beneath the floor.

After an extensive inquiry, the House Commerce Special Subcommittee on Investigations said in a report that the crash had "the same" cause as the near-crash over Windsor, Ontario, of an American Airlines DC-10 two years earlier.[4] On June 12, 1972, that aircraft also lost its aft-cargo door shortly after takeoff—and again at an altitude of about 12,000 feet. Thanks to extraordinarily skillful piloting, the plane made a safe emergency landing. Immediately, the subcommittee report said, the FAA staff, the vast majority of which is "dedicated and competent," properly undertook to have the agency issue an order—in legally binding form—that the requisite design changes be made in all DC–10's. FAA Administrator John H. Shaffer, in a demoralizing—and initially inexplicable—action, aborted such an order. He had, it turned out later, made a confidential "Gentleman's Agreement" with Jack McGowen, a top McDonnell Douglas executive, under which the company would send out "recommended," nonmandatory, nonurgent, stopgap service bulletins to the airlines flying DC–10's. "As a result of this departure from the clear and proper regulatory response which the agency should have made," the subcommittee said, the lives of thousands of air passengers were needlessly and unjustifiably put at risk for almost two years. During this period, dozens of DC–10's were flying with their cargo door mechanisms in the same vulnerable condition as the Turkish plane . . .[5]

On December 1, 1974, ninety-two persons perished in the crash of a TWA jetliner into a rock outcropping near Washington. Here again, any of several actions by the FAA could have prevented disaster.[6] The subcommittee said in its report that it had

found throughout its inquiry—from the DC–10 crash to its most recent investigation into the feasibility of requiring Ground Proximity Warning Systems—a tendency for the agency to avoid the role of leadership in advancing air safety which the Congress intended it to assume. This is manifested primarily by the FAA's willingness to let the industry engage in self-regulation when vital safety matters are concerned. In some instances this abdication of responsibility has been coupled with an administrative lethargy—a sluggishness which at times approaches an indifference to public safety. . . . In some instances, the agency action was forthcoming only after public announcement by this Subcommittee that hearings would be held on the subject matter in question. . . . in the case of the ground proximity warning system, an FAA period of inactivity extending over a year and a half was abruptly terminated immediately after Subcommittee hearings on the subject were announced.[7]

In the case of what Ralph Nader terms "silent violence," such as the exposure of multitudes of consumers or workers to chemicals that cause cancer, which may not be manifest for twenty or even thirty years, nonfeasance easily has escaped notice, in any useful sense, for long periods and possibly forever.

Excessive discretionary power is a problem not merely in regulatory agencies, but throughout the mammoth government bureaucracy. In the Department of Justice, Professor Miller has said, such power is "almost unrestrained."[8] This is of grave concern and importance. The taxpayers pay the attorney general's salary, but he is the President's lawyer. Representation of a President, of course, does not always coincide with representation of the broad public. The attorney general, Miller pointed out, is thus in "the ambiguous position of being a *political* officer charged with legal duties."[9] The position was surely ambiguous when it was held by John N. Mitchell, who had been Richard Nixon's law partner and campaign manager, but it was much more ambiguous when it was held by Robert F. Kennedy. Assuming that when the CIA was seeking to assassinate Fidel Castro it was doing so with the approval of or at the instigation of the Kennedy White House, what chance was there of an investigation and prosecution by a Justice Department headed by Robert Kennedy, his brother's liaison with the CIA? During the Nixon Administration, Attorney General Elliot L. Richardson resigned in protest against the firing of Watergate Special Prosecutor Archibald Cox. In what conceivable circumstances, one may wonder, would Robert Kennedy have resigned in protest?

"With top-level approval, the FBI carried out hundreds of illegal break-ins under an elaborate 'Do Not File' system that kept all traces of the burglaries out of regular bureau files," George Lardner, Jr., reported in the *Washington Post* in September 1975.

Members of the Senate intelligence committee, which began delving into the so-called "black bag jobs" yesterday, said they were shocked by the devious manner in which the burglaries of "domestic subversives" were authorized.
"It's really the perfect cover-up," declared Sen. Richard S. Schweiker (R–Pa.).
Under the system, which appears to have been discontinued, FBI officials, Schweiker pointed out, could even submit affidavits in court saying that bureau records contained no indication of this or that break-in.
"It would be technically telling the truth, yet it would be a total deception," Schweiker said.
"Pure frightening," Sen. Howard H. Baker, Jr. (R–Tenn.) agreed later.[10]

If we read the Founding Fathers correctly, they would be appalled by the evolution, under their grand design, of a scofflaw government. "Our government is the potent, the omnipresent teacher," Louis D. Brandeis, the great Supreme Court justice, said almost a half-century ago. "For good or ill, it teaches the whole people by its example."[11] The subject would be less worrisome were the FBI's "Do Not File" system a case of an isolated agency caught in an aberration. As lawless and unaccountable as the FBI and CIA have been (a subject we return to in a subsequent chapter), evidence abounds that lawlessness has been rampant also among agencies that lack the excuse, for whatever it may be worth, of being responsible for law enforcement or "national security." Most any day's newspaper is apt to report a new example. Jethro K. Lieberman found enough material for a book, *How the Government Breaks the Law.*[12]

The theory that the government has something known as an inherent power to wiretap in domestic criminal matters was enunciated by John Mitchell while he was chief law enforcement officer of the United States. Aiding and abetting him were William H. Rehnquist, now a Supreme Court justice, and Solicitor General Erwin N. Griswold, a former dean of the Harvard Law School. The notion was so extreme that the Supreme Court—

while dominated by appointees of Richard Nixon—outlawed it with a unanimous decision.

In addition to being the ultimate mockery of the ideal of a government of laws, government lawlessness has had profound adverse effects on public health and safety. The Food and Drug Administration (FDA), a unit of the Department of Health, Education, and Welfare, is the source of two cases in point. In one, which we detail in a later chapter, the FDA was discovered to have assured that residues of cancer-causing chemicals in animal feed would, without being detected, reach the nation's dinner tables for nearly twenty years. The second case involves prescription medicines. The bulk of those being sold had not been shown by "substantial evidence," a phrase precisely defined in a 1962 law, to fulfill the claims of effectiveness made for them by their manufacturers. The law required the producers to provide that evidence by October 1964; if they failed to do so, the law said, the FDA "shall" halt their sale. The companies were of course resistant; the FDA was, at best, lackadaisical. Not until mid–1966 did the FDA contract with the National Research Council (NRC), operating arm of the National Academy of Sciences, to evaluate the evidence of efficacy. The NRC delivered the last of its evaluations of the more than 3,000 products at issue in April 1969. The burden was then on the FDA to act.

But the agency moved with exceeding slowness. It repeatedly granted companies more time to provide evidence they were supposed to have provided in 1964. If a company requested a hearing, interminable delay followed —with sales of the suspect product continuing unabated. If a company did not request a hearing, the FDA permitted it to go on selling the product, anyway. One critically important group consisted of ninety antibiotic combination products that the NRC had condemned as irrational, and just one of which, the Upjohn Company's Panalba, was causing hundreds of thousands of needless injuries—a few of them fatal—each year. Finally, at the urging of Dr. Robert S. McCleery, an FDA official who had resigned in protest, the American Public Health Association and the National Council of Senior Citizens sued the FDA to compel it to enforce the law its officials had sworn to enforce. Ruling for the plaintiffs in 1973, United States District Judge William B. Bryant said he "cannot understand the solicitude of the FDA for the drug manufacturers in giving additional time to supplement the record" on evidence of efficacy. And, he said, the agency's behavior in permitting sales of suspect drugs to continue even when the manufacturer had not requested a hearing "constitutes agency action unlawfully withheld."

Colman McCarthy, in three editorial-page columns in the *Washington Post* on the government as lawbreaker, cited such additional cases as these:

at a cost to public-interest environmentalist groups of $15,000, the courts forced the Forest Service, a unit of the Department of Agriculture, to begin obeying the Organic Act of 1897; another successful case against the Forest Service cost them at least $40,000; the Department of Housing and Urban Development delivered a report—a useless one on removal of lead paint from homes where children, usually poor and more often black, eat it—two years after the deadline set by law; the National Environmental Policy Act of 1969, which requires federal officials to draft a statement forecasting the environmental impact of a proposed action, has been violated time and again. Indeed, Senator Philip A. Hart (D–Mich.) found that the Federal Power Commission had licensed fourteen hydroelectric plants without once filing an impact statement. By 1971, Hart said, other known violators included the Departments of Commerce, HUD, Interior, and Health, Education, and Welfare; the Civil Aeronautics Board, and the Army Corps of Engineers.[13]

In cases such as those against the Forest Service, in which citizens are driven to sue merely to get a government agency to obey or enforce a law, McCarthy said, a "startling irony is clear: citizens pay taxes for the salaries of government lawyers who then fight against private lawyers hired by citizens who can't get the government to obey the law in the first place. The costs of justice must be paid three times: first, to support a Congress to protect the public weal through passage of laws, then to pay the salaries of officials who break or defy the law and, third, to pay for private lawyers to have the law obeyed."

Former Supreme Court Justice William O. Douglas has suggested that all government regulatory agencies be abolished every ten years. Of course they will not be, if only because their expertise—narrow as it may be—is indispensable. They are much more likely to survive as relatively unchecked and unaccountable sources of governmental power.

The End of Government by and for the People

The saddest life is that of a political aspirant under democracy. His failure is ignominious and his success is disgraceful.

H. L. Mencken
A Mencken Chrestomathy

When campaigns do come to grips with "issues," the result is usually thundering piffle. In the Kennedy–Nixon campaign of 1960, famed for its so-called "debates," the great "issue" was what American policy should be towards Quemoy and Matsu. Anybody remember who they were?

Russell Baker
New York Times

Each fall season we are exhorted by editorial pontification to determine our own destiny by judicious use of the electoral franchise. This, I submit, is an exercise in futility. One needs only to examine the roster of knaves, fools and combinations of both that we manage to elect year in and year out to positions of authority where the incumbent is literally in control of our survival.

Arthur Darby
Letter to the Editor, *New York Times*

The Framers' ultimate check on unaccountable and unrestrained power was the reposing of sovereignty in the people, this being, as James Madison put it, "the primary control on the government . . ."[1] Along with the other carefully designed checks and balances, sovereignty in the people has proved to be significantly a mirage.

The country's growth, industrialization, and international involvements, and other developments, such as modern technology, have caused the number of important public issues to proliferate almost beyond human ken. Because of secrecy or inadequate mechanisms for debate and public enlightenment, some of these issues never reach the public at all, or reach it late or in unbalanced form. This aside, those issues that do come before the public are so numerous and so complex as to overburden or overwhelm the most informed and conscientious citizen.

Every four years, a voter enters a polling place and pulls a lever for a presidential candidate. This permits him only to say "yes" to one man and "no" to another, but it allows him no opportunity whatsoever to distinguish among those policies he wants to approve and those he wants to disapprove. All he can do, in the crudest way, is to cast a single vote on the basis of a mix of those actions and attitudes of the candidate that he happens to know about at that instant. Surely many of the voters who helped to reelect President Nixon in the 1972 "landslide" had but could not register serious reservations about him and certain of his policies, and, in some cases, essentially wanted no more than to try to assure the defeat of his opponent. Once reelected with what he loosely perceived as a mandate, Mr. Nixon was free to exercise power pretty much as he cared to. Had it not been for the Watergate scandal, which left him no choice but to resign or be impeached and convicted, the electorate would have had no recourse until 1976. At that time, because he would be ineligible for reelection under the Twenty-second Amendment, the people would have had no way effectively to hold him accountable for his performance.

The problems that beset people-sovereignty in the election of a President have counterparts for the voter when he pulls a lever for congressional candidates—once every two years for a representative, and once every six years for one of two senators. The voter commonly does not know much of what an incumbent does, because of secrecy on Capitol Hill and, often, insufficient press coverage. An incumbent, especially a senior one, usually cannot be reliably judged on the basis of his speeches, or always by his votes on the floor; his performance in the committees on which he serves is often the truest indicator. Throughout most of our history, many important committee proceedings have been secret except for occasional leaks to the press. This hardly could be viewed as the optimum safeguard of that citizen knowledge which is essential to the exercise of effective sovereignty. Professor Philip Kurland, of the University of Chicago Law School, has said that "there can be no real accountability, even at an election, when the actions of the administration have been shrouded in secrecy, so that the public never knows what miners and sappers have been at work at the substance of a free society."[2] The same applies to congressional secrecy.

Russell Baker, the *New York Times* columnist, has fairly suggested that the sensible thing might be "for people who are not well-informed about the candidates to abstain from voting and leave it to those who are, for what will make democracy work, if anything will, is not a mass electorate but an informed electorate." How does it get informed? Usually through political campaigns. But these, Baker said, are deliberately built to make judgments difficult for the voters. Commonly, they attempt to persuade the voters that the candidate is a good television performer and looks trustworthy. They also strive to show that the candidate has good teeth, a happy family, and a nondescript mind. None of this information is very interesting if you are trying to decide whether the candidate believes in a regressive tax structure, subsidies for the failing corporations, expanded health care programs or, any of the other dull nuts-and-bolts stuff he will have to deal with if elected . . .

In 1972 George McGovern spent months trying to defend himself on the "issues" of legalizing marijuana, amnesty for war evaders and abortion.

None of these had much to do with whether McGovern was qualified to deal with the foreign policy and economic problems he would have confronted as President in 1973, but the Nixon people had successfully turned them into "issues" which voters judged important.[3]

Another flaw in the concept of people-sovereignty in its preeminent expression, the ballot, is that it presupposes a reasonable responsiveness in elected officials to the electorate's opinions and interests. In reality, effective sovereignty over these officials often coalesces not in the many who elect them, but in the few with the cash to make campaign contributions, pay large "honorariums" for speeches, provide free travel in company aircraft, and the like. Thus, the influence of powerful institutions—corporations, mainly, but also labor unions, professional and trade associations, and other special interests—interdicts meaningful people-sovereignty. "If the lavish use of money is countenanced in politics, no poor man can win without truckling to the contributors of campaign funds," Edward Alsworth Ross said in 1907.[4] By then there already had been a long history of truckling, and since then there have been seven more decades of it.

The erosion of people-sovereignty has been dramatically evidenced by declining voter turnouts. In the 1972 presidential contest, only 55 percent of the eligible voters bothered to cast a ballot, while 45 percent—62 million voters —did not bother. Richard Nixon achieved his vaunted "landslide" with the votes of only about one-third of the potential electorate.

In the 1974 congressional elections, only 45 percent of a record 141 million voters went to the polls. This was the lowest turnout since 1958, a recession year when only 43 percent of the eligible voters turned out. According to the Census Bureau, which interviewed more than one hundred thousand eligible voters two weeks after the 1974 election, many of the estimated 76 million stay-at-homes said they either were uninterested or disliked politics in the post-Watergate era. Most significantly, perhaps, the Census Bureau found that four out of five Americans between the ages of eighteen and twenty-one did not vote. The only group bucking the pattern of massive apathy were those approaching retirement age.[5]

To be sure, more people would vote if, say, registration were to be made easier and elections were to be held on Sundays rather than Tuesdays. But such considerations fail to explain *declines* in turnout. What does significantly explain them, we believe, is the surmise of the Census Bureau and astute political scientists, a surmise backed by considerable evidence, that more and more voters feel it doesn't matter who is elected. After the 1974 elections, political scientist Arthur Miller, of the Center for Political Studies at the University of Michigan, said that voters "have a low confidence in government and they don't see how an election is going to cause much improvement."[6]

Such assumptions could be subjected to a revealing even if inconclusive test were each voter to be enabled to vote "no" to all the candidates, or at least to register conscientious objection by abstaining as a positive act—something legislators everywhere do.[7] Lacking such a test, we judge that people increasingly perceive people-sovereignty at worst as a farce or a myth, or at best as not worth the bother. No matter the cause of the malaise, the people are not achieving accountability in their elected officials in the manner contemplated by the Founding Fathers. Thus, the ultimate constitutional defense against unaccountable power has crumbled.

The Bill of Rights—the first ten amendments to the Constitution—was the last great bulwark erected against tyranny in the federal government and, through the "due process" and "equal protection" clauses of the Fourteenth Amendment, in state government.

James Madison, strongly influenced by Thomas Jefferson, worked hard to secure the guarantees in the Bill of Rights, which embrace, John Adams said, rights derived from "the great Legislator of the Universe."[8] In a letter to Madison in 1787, Jefferson said "that a bill of rights is what the people are entitled to against every government on earth, general or particular; and what no just government should refuse, or rest on inference." In contrast, Alexander Hamilton had thought a bill of rights to be superfluous, "for why declare that things shall not be done which there is no power to do and where the power is retained by the people?"[9]

While it is easy in hindsight to side with Jefferson, Madison, and Adams, the problem was not mainly in Hamilton's reasoning, but in the unforeseen weakening that would occur in the other safeguards erected by the Framers against unaccountable power. The country should cling to the Bill of Rights as to a raft after a shipwreck, but should be aware that giant waves of unaccountable government power have so bashed and battered it that it alone is not sturdy enough to save us. Our government has undermined, or allowed to be undermined, certain key protections of the Bill of Rights. To take a few cases in point:

The Fourth Amendment says, in full:

The right of the people to be secure in their persons, houses, papers, and effects, against unreasonable searches and seizures, shall not be violated, and no Warrants shall issue, but upon probable cause, supported by Oath or affirmation, and particularly describing the place to be searched, and the persons or things to be seized.

The Amendment is not (if anything could be) a formidable barrier to electronic surveillance which unreasonably searches one's home, and innermost confidences, without one even being aware that an invasion of privacy has occurred. In 1969 and 1970—before the Supreme Court unanimously struck down the practice—the government, without warrant, conducted more than 40,000 days of tapping and bugging of persons engaged in what the Nixon Administration expansively defined as radical activity.[10] President Nixon personally approved the undertaking of burglaries and wiretapping for purported "national security" purposes, although on taking office he had sworn a solemn oath to "preserve, protect and defend the Constitution of the United States."

The Fifth and Fourteenth amendments say, in part, that no person shall be deprived "of life, liberty, or property, without due process of law; . . ." The Fourteenth, in addition, forbids a state to "deny to any person within its jurisdiction the equal protection of the laws." For a very long time, however, the institutions of criminal justice routinely have been depriving very large numbers of people of life and liberty without according due process, and of the equal protection of the laws as well. A distinguished United States District judge, Marvin E. Frankel of New York, said in his book *Criminal Sentences: Law Without Order:*

The largely unbridled power of judges and prison officials stir questions under the clauses promising that life and liberty will not be denied except by "due process of law." The crazy quilt of disparities—the wide differences in treatment of defendants whose situations and crimes look similar and whose divergent sentences are unaccounted for—stirs doubts as to whether the guarantee of the "equal protection of the laws" is being fulfilled.[11]

In this connection, Frankel cited the 1972 decision with which the Supreme Court outlawed capital punishment, at least with the modes of administration which existed at that time. The way in which choices have been made as to who may live and who must die, far from according due process "smacks of little more than a lottery system," said Justice William J. Brennan, Jr.[12]

After a thorough investigation of what passes for justice in major courthouses around the nation, Leonard Downie, Jr., wrote in *Justice Denied: The Case for Reform of the Courts* that despite decisions in the Supreme Court and lower appellate tribunals strengthening the right to due process, civil as well as criminal trial courts deny it to citizens "every few minutes . . . in the rush to satisfy bureaucratic aims with savings of time and money—not, however, the citizen's time or money. The guidelines of Supreme Court decisions are ignored. Compromise and whim decide more cases than due process."[13]

The Sixth Amendment says, in part, "In all criminal prosecutions, the accused shall enjoy the right to a speedy and public trial, by an impartial jury of the State and district wherein the crime shall have been committed . . ." Downie, who spent two years investigating court operations in a half dozen major cities, and who is now an editor of the *Washington Post*, said:

But only one of every ten suspects convicted of a crime today receives a trial. The rest agree to plead guilty, usually after bargaining for what they think is a favorable sentence . . .

Justice is supposed to be swift; otherwise, according to legal theory, there is no justice at all. But suspects who insist on trial by jury must wait in crowded, filthy jails for as long as a year or more before their cases are called.[14]

As of 1975, the number of men and women being held in jails, on any given day, was 150,000. "The inescapable reality is that jail confinement of the accused is far more oppressive than prison confinement of the convicted," law professor Leonard Orland and lawyer Sue Wise wrote.[15]

Downie went on to say that auto-accident victims "must wait two to five years for a judge or jury to decide how much they may collect in damages to pay their medical bills."[16] His book was published in 1971. After that, "the right to a speedy and public trial, by an impartial jury" eroded further. In 1972, the Supreme Court ruled that, in criminal trials in state courts, jury verdicts need not be unanimous. In 1973, the Court sanctioned six-person juries in federal civil cases. Dissenting, Justice Thurgood Marshall said, "Today, the erosion process reaches bedrock . . . my brethren mount a frontal assault on the very nature of the civil jury as that concept has been understood for some seven hundred years."

The argument for weakening or abolishing the jury system, as was noted, is the pragmatic one that it saves the bureaucracy time and money. But in the case of rights that are, as Justice Marshall said, "so vulnerable to the pressures of the moment," they can end up being "not really protected by the Constitution at all."[17] This melancholy appraisal is bolstered by a conclusion reached by Professor Edward S. Corwin, the eminent historian: "If there has been one validated hypothesis which has served to characterize the courts' treatment of civil liberties it has been the proposition that the scope of those protections . . . has hung indeed on 'each wave of new judges blown in by each successive political wind.' "[18]

Despite the setbacks dealt to liberty by successive administrations, and most of all by the Nixon Administration, Harvard law professor Alan M. Dershowitz has correctly said that it would be "wrong to conclude—as many radicals have asserted—that we have become a repressive society, or even that we are on the road to becoming one. We are still among the freest and least repressive societies in the history of the world."[19] Still, the Bill of Rights is not the bulwark of our liberties many believe it is. Its application to the federal government has been diluted, its application to state governments was limited to begin with, and its application to the great nongovernmental institutions that so dominate our lives has been negligible.

For all of the reasons set out in this and the preceding chapters, the conclusion is inescapable that the Constitution is failing to fulfill the fundamental goal laid down by the Founding Fathers: to promote the safety and happiness of society by preventing power from concentrating, by safeguarding liberty, and by insuring justice. The devices in the Constitution that were designed to achieve this have broken down while mighty institutions not envisioned by the Framers have been building up. In consequence, governmental and nongovernmental rulers have become immensely unaccountable. Because unaccountable power is incompatible with proper democratic governance, public confidence in American institutions has declined—and this is not surprising. To restore that confidence, legislative solutions doubtless can accomplish much, and we mention such remedies as we go along. But legislation alone cannot suffice. We must also make innovative *constitutional* changes, such as we will suggest in the final chapter. These will, in the words of Professor Arthur S. Miller, "make power that is necessary as tolerant, decent and responsive to human needs as possible," and also will begin to restore effective sovereignty to the people—where the Founding Fathers intended it to be.

II
Government Secrecy

The Executive   8

We are a democracy, and there is only one way to get a democracy on its feet in the matter of its individual, its social, its municipal, its State, its National conduct, and that is by keeping the public informed about what is going on. There is not a crime, there is not a dodge, there is not a trick, there is not a swindle, there is not a vice which does not live by secrecy. Get these things out in the open, describe them, attack them, ridicule them in the press, and sooner or later public opinion will sweep them away.

Publicity may not be the only thing that is needed, but it is the one thing without which all other agencies will fail.

Joseph Pulitzer
Pulitzer

Secrecy is lethal to accountability. One constitutional scholar, Professor Arthur S. Miller, of George Washington University, considers secrecy "the ultimate weapon of those who are determined to exercise arbitrary and unbridled power."[1] The "great instruments of accountability" are Congress, the courts, the electoral process, and the press, says John W. Gardner, chairman of Common Cause, the citizens' lobby. "All . . . may be rendered impotent if the information crucial to their functioning is with-held. Thus does secrecy perpetuate abuses of power, diminish the responsiveness of government and thwart citizen participation."[2]

The incompatibility of secrecy and accountability would seem to be self-evident, a truism: accountability cannot be brought to bear on conduct the existence of which is concealed. It might also seem to be self-evident that there is a related antagonism between secrecy and the requirement of the American democracy that government must be with the consent of the governed. What kind of consent is it, and what kind of democracy, if the governed cannot know what those who govern are doing? Such questions rarely seem to trouble our Presidents and secretaries of state. They do trouble some rank-and-file citizens. One of them, Pat Riley, of Washington, D.C., poured out her frustration, after the end of the war in Vietnam, in a letter to the *Washington Post.* Secrecy, she wrote, "seems to be the by-word of American leaders. They now worry in public that other nations will not trust 'us' to uphold commitments—they who did not trust the American people enough to reveal what commitments were made in our name." In an eloquent passage she recalled a day shortly before Christmas in 1967. As she was walking out of a department store, a man pressed upon her,

for "just a small contribution," a button which said, "I'm proud to be an American." I put out my hand as if to ward him off and turned quickly. The enormity of it all crashed in upon me. I wasn't proud.

And now, we are told, it is all our fault. If only I, through my duly elected representatives, had authorized more money, more arms, more men, we could have "won"—the slow and tortuous disintegration of a demination could have been forestalled. . . .

I am tired, just plain tired, of being held accountable for events over which I have no control, and, moreover, don't want to control. . . .

I am tired of a foreign policy, crafted in an era of aristocrats and kings, which rests on the methods of tyrants and dictators rather than on democratic principles. . . .

Mine is but one voice, perhaps representative of many, that cries out not just to be heard but to be told. Explain it to me. Use simple words. Give me facts uncluttered by euphemisms. . . .

I don't have to be an expert to make a judgment—when I am told. If we the people err, we are mature enough to accept the consequences. But we are under no obligation to defend our leaders from the consequences of misguided policies conceived and executed in secrecy.[3]

"It is well to remember that every withholding of government business from the public is an encroachment upon the democratic principle that government officials are accountable to the people," Clark R. Mollenhoff wrote in 1962 in *Washington Cover-Up.*[4] Mollenhoff, a Pulitzer Prize-winner who is unique among reporters in his early perception of the uses of secrecy in concealing corruption and in his relentless, enduring, and invaluable crusades against it, went on to say:

It follows that citizens should regard all governmental secrecy with some suspicion as an encroachment on their right to know.

The American citizen should reject all arbitrary claims to secrecy by the bureaucracy as sharply as he would reject any claims to a right of the executive branch to by-pass Congress in levying taxes. A wise citizen should be as outraged at arbitrary secrecy as he would be at arbitrary imprisonment. Logically he should insist on the same safeguards against arbitrary secrecy that he would against unjustified arrest or taxation. The public's "right to know" is that basic.[5]

The wise citizen outraged at arbitrary secrecy was a rarity, and so it was with a justified expectation that he could get away with it that, among other illegal acts, Richard Nixon, less than two months after taking office in 1969, authorized a series of B–52 bombing strikes on Cambodia. Over the next fourteen months, B–52s flew 3,695 sorties and dropped 105,837 tons of bombs, at a cost of $150 million. All of this was concealed from Congress for more than four years. He instructed his top officials—the secretaries of the Departments of Defense and State, two chairmen of the Joint Chiefs of Staff, and the chief of staff of the Air Force—to make false and misleading statements to Congress, and they did; and to carry out his instructions, the Pentagon falsified its own classified records and, on the basis of these records, submitted false reports to Capitol Hill.[6]

"If the governed are misled, if they are not told the truth, or if through official secrecy and deception they lack information on which to base intelligent decisions, the system may go on—but not as a democracy," David Wise, former Washington bureau chief for the *New York Herald Tribune*, wrote in *The Politics of Lying: Government Deception, Secrecy, and Power.*[7] But even after saturation coverage of President Nixon's uses of secrecy to cover up secret wars and criminal activities, large numbers of Americans, even if appalled by such abuses of secrecy, do not seem to sense that secrecy is itself the enemy of democratic government. They will tell you "that politicians are crooks, or at least clowns and snake-oil salesmen," Tom Wicker wrote in the *New York Times.* "Yet, even in the wake of Watergate and Agnew and the infinite deceptions of the Vietnam years, let one of those supposedly tricky politicians become a Government official and classify a document, and those supposedly cynical voters begin bowing and scraping before his rubber stamp. Let one of those reputed clowns merely whisper 'national security' and otherwise sensible Americans put their fingers in their ears and close their eyes."[8]

The problem may lie less in our history than in the teaching of it. One of the early statesmen, James Madison, said, "Knowledge will forever govern ignorance, and a people who mean to be their own governors must arm themselves with the power knowledge gives. A popular government without popular information or the means of acquiring it is but a prologue to a farce or a tragedy, or both."[9] Another early statesman, Edward Livingston, said: "No nation ever yet found an inconvenience from too close an inspection into the conduct of its officers, but many have been brought to ruin and . . . slavery . . . only because the means of publicity have not been secured." Livingston taught "the over-arching lesson of the Watergate Scandal," Raoul Berger, a constitutional scholar at Harvard Law School, has said.[10] "The generation that made the nation," Henry Steele Commager, the historian, reminds us, "thought secrecy in government one of the instruments of Old World tyranny and committed itself to the principle that a democracy cannot function unless the people are permitted to know what their government is up to."[11] At times since World War II, the principle seemed almost to have been forgotten.

The tension between openness and secrecy was present from the beginning. Thus, the Framers of the Constitution held closed sessions—and Thomas Jefferson was distressed, as he made clear in a letter to John Adams:

I am sorry they began their deliberations by so abominable a precedent as that of tying of the tongues of their members. Nothing can justify this example but the innocence of their intents and ignorance of the value of public discussion.[12]

And on August 4, 1790, according to the *Journal* of the United States Senate, President Washington submitted to the Senate for its approval a secret proviso for inclusion in a treaty with the Creek Indians.

From these acorns of secrecy big oaks grew slowly. Not until World War I did the Army classify documents on an organized basis, although officers and officials had used such designations as *Secret* or *Confidential* during the Revolutionary War, David Wise recalled in *The Politics of Lying*.[13] In an Executive Order in 1940 President Roosevelt formally recognized the military classification system and authorized the Secretaries of War and Navy to stamp "Secret," "Confidential," or "Restricted" on documents. But until World War II, "There really was no classification system," William M. Franklin, director of the historical office of the State Department, told Wise.

With the advent of the "Cold War" and the Korean conflict the whole business crossed the line from rationality to madness. The crossing began in force on September 24, 1951, when President Truman, in an Executive Order, extended the secrecy system to civilian departments. The order allowed *any* agency of the Executive branch to put a classification stamp on what the agency deemed to be "official information the safeguarding of which is necessary in the interest of [now come, in terms of deceptions, two words of boundless fecundity] national security."

Two years later, President Eisenhower substituted Executive Order 10501, *Safeguarding Official Information*. Although Presidents Kennedy, Johnson, and Nixon amended it, it provided the basic framework for the classification system in effect today. By 1972, according to a study conducted by the Nixon Administration, more than thirty thousand persons in the Pentagon and some thirteen thousand in the White House and three major departments were empowered to classify documents.[14] Even these figures understated the reality: "Hundreds of thousands of individuals at all echelons in the Department of Defense practice classification as a way of life," William G. Florence, a retired Air Force expert on classification, once testified. In an article in 1971 he said:

Every day they sit in the Pentagon, thousands of workers with rubber stamps marked "Confidential" and "Secret" and "Top Secret," and they stamp this paper and that, with little regard for what they are doing. It is a mass exercise in wish-fulfillment, a giant attempt to keep secret what is already public knowledge, what is bound to become widely known, or what is so trivial that it cannot possibly be of use to anyone.

In the process, the buying of toilet paper for some military men becomes a national secret. Purchases of paper clips and paint and long winter underwear can turn into guarded statistics. The purpose and dimensions of a new aircraft, long trumpeted in congressional hearings, remain, to the Pentagon's way of thinking, "Top Secret" matters. Literally millions of documents are needlessly classified alongside the relatively few—I would estimate from 1 to 5 per cent in the Pentagon—which must legitimately be guarded in the national interest.[15]

By David Wise's calculations, classified documents in active government files as of 1971 conservatively numbered 100 million, with the Pentagon alone holding the equivalent of 2,297 stacks of documents each equal in height to the Washington Monument. It is 555 feet high. In addition, the National Archives has a vast trove of classified papers—some 458,500,000 pages for the period from the start of World War II through 1954.[16] Secrets are safe at the Archives. Donald Mac Millan, of Missoula, Montana, found this out in 1971, when he was in Washington doing research on pollution for a Ph.D. dissertation in history. The Archives denied him access to files on pollution from the first decade of the twentieth century because, he said, they were stamped "Bureau of Investigation."[17]

Junking the present classification system doubtless would throw hordes of classifiers out of work, but David Wise, for one, would not be deterred. "I doubt there is any need for a formal system of official secrecy in the United States," he says. "We have only had such a system for a bit more than two decades, and there is nothing in our tradition or history that requires its continuation. It is a relic of the Cold War. It breeds concealment and distrust; it encourages the government to lie. It is unrealistic, however, to think that Congress and the Executive Branch would agree to end all official secrecy. As an alternative, there could be substituted a system under which a sharply limited number of documents might be protected, for a much shorter period, solely by agencies directly concerned with national security and foreign policy."[18]

The classification system—a wholly presidential creation—was supplemented by "executive privilege." This is the flimsy doctrine, unsupported by any microscopic filament of the Constitution, or by any law, that a President has "inherent" power to keep certain matters secret when "the public interest"—as he defines it—requires confidentiality.

President Dwight D. Eisenhower fathered the doctrine, which emerged from the White House in the form of a letter dated May 17, 1954. He claimed that communications among *all* employees of the Executive branch must be privileged against disclosure "[b]ecause it is essential to efficient and effective administration" that they "be in a position to be completely candid in advising with each other on official matters, and because it is not in the public interest that any of their conversations or communications . . . concerning such advice be disclosed . . ." This was his rationale for ordering employees of the Department of Defense not to testify before Senator Joseph R. McCarthy (R-Wis.)—an order liberals applauded. He made the vertiginous claim that thus he was maintaining "the proper separation of powers between the Executive and Legislative Branches," this separation being "vital to preclude the exercise of arbitrary power by any branch of Government."[19] Clark Mollenhoff presciently perceived at the time that General Eisenhower had defined Executive privilege so broadly that it could be used to block any investigation into any Executive agency. But the press so idolized "Ike" that it failed to see that he was asserting arbitrary power in the name of precluding it. There was "hardly a ripple of criticism," Mollenhoff wrote. "On the contrary, most editorial pages praised President Eisenhower for expressing some fine new theory on the U.S. Constitution or wrote off the letter as an historically unimportant, one-shot claim of secrecy."[20]

One shot? Four years later, Attorney General William P. Rogers repeated the President's 1954 letter in paraphrase and went on to enlarge his assertion of raw Executive power without any showing whatsoever of constitutionality or lawfulness:

By the Constitution the President is invested with certain political powers. He is accountable only to his country in his political character, and to his own conscience . . . Questions which the Constitution and laws leave to the Executive, or which are in their nature political, are not for the courts to decide, and there is no power in the courts to control the President's discretion or decision, with respect to such questions. Because of the intimate relation between the President and heads of departments, the same rule applies to them.[21]

The anti-McCarthy liberals who had welcomed the doctrine in 1954 "as a necessary device to protect the integrity of the Executive branch," Arthur S. Miller wrote in 1973, would in the 1970s see it dramatically turned around, so that it now operates as a shield and a buffer to prevent Congress and the courts—and through them, the American people—from obtaining data both relevant and vital to their well-being. As people, we are asked to trust government officials because only they "have the facts" in the face of a long and dreary record of outright lying and examples of official mendacity that have become only too familiar.[22]

Thus Executive privilege, introduced as a tactic against McCarthyism, became in the Nixon Administration a central strategy for the defense of criminality in the White House.

In the spring of 1973, Attorney General Richard G. Kleindienst said that the President, should he care to, could put all 2.5 million Executive employees under the blanket of Executive privilege, which President Eisenhower had woven in 1954. Then, in a breathtaking extension of the Eisenhower doctrine, Kleindienst stunned a Senate committee by telling it not only that the President could keep from Congress facts it would need were it to consider impeaching him, but also that "You don't need evidence to impeach."[23] Mr. Nixon himself, also in 1973, invoked Executive privilege in trying to withhold evidence sought in the criminal proceedings arising out of the Watergate cover-up. The Court of Appeals for the District of Columbia rejected his claim, and the President did not seek Supreme Court review. Then, in June 1974, he refused to comply with subpoenas for tape recordings and documents, relating to his conversations with aides and advisers, which the House Judiciary Committee had issued in the course of its impeachment inquiry. The Supreme Court, in *United States* v. *Nixon*, said the President had to comply:

[W]hen the ground for asserting privilege as to subpoenaed materials sought for use in a criminal trial is based only on the generalized interest in confidentiality, it cannot prevail over the fundamental demands of due process law in the fair administration of criminal justice. The generalized assertion of privilege must yield to the demonstrated, specific need for evidence in a pending criminal trial.[24]

But there was a deeply troubling aspect to the decision. Despite the absence of an explicit reference in the Constitution to the claimed privilege of presidential confidentiality, the Court said that to the extent that it "relates to the effective discharge of a President's powers, it is constitutionally based." What a President may believe or claim to be related "to the effective discharge" of presidential powers conceivably could be most anything. Chief Justice Warren E. Burger, moreover, made the startling assertion that Executive privilege is "rooted" in the Constitution—startling because he was unable to cite a clause or a sentence from which Executive privilege draws its nutrients. "One is astonished," said Professor Raoul

Berger, who is the country's leading legal authority on Executive privilege, and who is author of *Executive Privilege: A Constitutional Myth,*

that the Chief Justice should seize on precisely this case—where it had become increasingly plain that Mr. Nixon was invoking the privilege in order to conceal a conspiracy to obstruct justice—on just this unsavory occasion to legitimate and anoint Presidential claims that "confidentiality" is indispensable to conduct of the office.

But seasoned "court-watchers"—a breed akin to Kremlinologists, who are accustomed to [reading] obscure portents—have pointed out that the opinion was stitched together in order to obtain a unanimous decision that would be "definite" enough for the intransigent Mr. Nixon to understand.

In addition to the classification system and Executive privilege, the Executive branch employs numerous other techniques to keep secret from Congress and the people whatever they want to keep secret. A study by the staff of the Senate Subcommittee on the Separation of Powers revealed at least 225 refusals by the Executive branch to produce either documents or witnesses requested by Congress. Arthur S. Miller wrote in the *Progressive:*

In all but a dozen of these cases, the refusal was based on reasons other than executive privilege. Excuses offered included these: (a) a reply would take too much time; (b) a reply would be "inappropriate"; (c) national security—which has become the new all-encompassing excuse—prevents disclosure; (d) the material is an "internal working paper," and (e) the material is classified. In addition, a number of Congressional inquiries often were simply ignored. Because of inadequate staffing and no reasonably sufficient desire for pursuing information, such inquiries are often simply dropped by Congress. . . . Only when it is driven to the wall, and all other techniques fail, is executive privilege invoked. The result, all too often, is that Congress gets only the information that the bureaucrats want to divulge.[25]

". . . there has been this feeling that perhaps the government is lying," Herbert G. Klein, director of communications for the Executive branch, said during the Nixon Administration's tenth month in office. The feeling dated back to 1960, when Americans in large numbers began to realize that their government would lie to them. A U–2 was shot down over the Soviet Union, which withheld the details. The Eisenhower Administration then claimed that the U–2 had been engaged in "weather research" for the National Aeronautics and Space Administration; that its pilot, Francis Gary Powers, was a civilian employee of the U–2's manufacturer, Lockheed Aircraft Corporation, and that the craft had been on a flight inside Turkey but possibly had drifted over the Soviet border. There had been "absolutely no—N–O—no—deliberate attempt to violate Soviet Air space," the government said.

Having waited until the United States had its foot firmly in its mouth, the

Soviet Union then disclosed that it had captured both the U–2 and its pilot. With that, the truth finally came out: The U–2 was a spy plane, and Powers was a CIA employee. In an interview two years later, General Eisenhower was asked what had been his "greatest regret" as President. "And he floored me," David Kraslow, of Knight Newspapers, wrote, "when he said, 'The lie we told about the U–2. I didn't realize how high a price we were going to have to pay for that lie.'"[26] The price essentially was that détente was wrecked for a decade.

As David Wise correctly emphasizes, it wasn't that the government hadn't lied before in such matters; it had lied, to take but one important case in point, when it claimed noninvolvement in the coup in 1954 against President Jacobo Arbenz Gutman of Guatemala, when in fact the CIA had run the whole operation. But now, as Wise put it, a wide public *knew* that the government they wanted to trust "does not always tell the truth." Yet the harm was perhaps not irreparable. Dwight D. Eisenhower was leaving office in January 1961, and there was in the public an enormous outpouring of goodwill and trust for his successor. But John F. Kennedy continued rather than tried to stop the lying that had begun to erode the confidence of people in the integrity of their government—an erosion which, Wise wrote in 1973, was "perhaps the single most significant political development in America in the past decade." When the electorate comes to exact a high price from leaders who lie there will be less likelihood of lying; but John Kennedy delayed the advent of such an era. "President Kennedy had his Bay of Pigs, which required Adlai Stevenson to read an official lie into the record of the United Nations," Wise said. "And it was under Kennedy that an Assistant Secretary of Defense proclaimed 'the right to lie.'"

Under Lyndon B. Johnson, lying, deception, and stealth became something like a governmental way of life. Johnson had promised in his 1964 presidential election campaign that he would not send American boys to fight Asian boys. He later got an effective abdication of war powers by Congress with what Wise generously termed an "official misrepresentation of staggering proportions" of the Tonkin Gulf episode. The first book to provide a comprehensive look at the enthronement of deceit in Washington was *Anything But the Truth: The Credibility Gap—How the News Is Managed in Washington.* In early 1967, the authors, William McGaffin and Erwin Knoll, "confided to a colleague in the Washington press corps that we were planning to write a book about the lies told by the government. 'Only one book?' he asked. 'My God, you could write a book a day.'"[27]

Richard Nixon during his 1968 presidential election campaign pledged "an open administration." Three weeks after his election, Herbert G. Klein, on being designated by the President-elect to direct communications for the

Executive branch, said, "I'm confident we will—truth will become the hallmark of the Nixon administration . . . We feel that we will be able to eliminate any possibility of a credibility gap in this administration."[28] Three years later—specifically, in October 1972, when relatively little was known about Watergate, historian Henry Steele Commager provided this assessment:

For the first time in our history we have an administration that lies systematically and almost automatically: it lies about the origins of the war, lies about casualties, lies about the treatment of the POWs, lies about the bombings, lies about North Vietnamese "aggression," lies about the nature of the blockade (publicly it excluded only military supplies, but actually it excludes food), lies about the nature of American "withdrawal," and from the famous day when L.B. Johnson called Diem "the Churchill of Asia" to the latest tribute to Thieu's "struggle for freedom"—lies about the client state on whose behalf we are presumably fighting the war. . . . No other administration in our history has practiced deception, duplicity, chicanery, and mendacity as has the Nixon Administration. Where totalitarian regimes invented the technique of the Big Lie, this Administration has developed a more effective technique, that of lies so innumerable that no one can keep up with them, so insolent that they confound refutation, and so shameless that in time they benumb the moral sensibilities of the American people.[29]

The citizen who makes a false statement to a federal investigator, even if the statement is unsworn, faces possible prosecution and five years in prison. The government official—starting with the President—who lies to the citizen is unaccountable. Not surprisingly, even the official inclined to be truthful may find himself in situations where the incentives to lie are more compelling than the incentives to tell the truth.

William J. Cotter provides a memorable case in point. During the 1950s he participated in a CIA program of opening other people's mail, expecially mail to and from the Soviet Union. He left the program in 1955, but, by the later account of CIA Director William E. Colby, it continued into 1973, as Cotter knew. After eighteen years in the agency, Cotter left it in 1969 to become Chief of the Postal Inspection Service—the person principally responsible for assuring the integrity of the mails. Despite this obligation he reportedly promised the CIA that he would not interfere with its mail intercepts without first consulting it. In 1971, the Federation of American Scientists inquired whether *any* federal agency was intruding in the normal mail-handling process in order "to obtain the information contained therein"—exactly what Cotter knew the CIA to be doing. He assured the federation, in writing, that there was no such irregularity.

Subsequently, Congressman Charles H. Wilson (D–Calif.) raised the question of possible CIA mail surveillance, but Cotter did not come forward to reveal the existence of the program. Moreover, he told another congressional panel that he had "no official awareness of the mail surveillance" after he left the CIA program in 1955. Meanwhile, prompted by the federation's inquiry, he began pressing the CIA in 1971 to abandon the surveillance; finally, apparently to save himself, he stopped it in 1973. In June 1975, Cotter acknowledged to the federation's Jeremy J. Stone that he had known in 1971, when he signed the letter saying there was no surveillance, that the letter was not truthful. The Rockefeller Commission report on the CIA, in addition, showed that Cotter had misinformed Congress. Asserting that Cotter's loyalty was "first and foremost to the CIA, not the Postal Service," Congressman Wilson in late July 1975 asked Postmaster General Benjamin F. Bailar to remove Cotter. Bailar than announced that Cotter was retiring, purportedly for health reasons.

Without knowledge of this episode, Congressman Paul N. McCloskey (R–Calif.) in 1971 wondered whether Congress should make it a crime for a government official "willfully" to deceive Congress (and, through it, the public). Four years later, Senator Edward M. Kennedy (D–Mass.) introduced a bill to make it a misdemeanor for any government official knowingly to make a false public statement "for the purpose of misleading Congress or the public on matters involving official policy or action of the United States." Here at last was a first step—albeit an inadequate one—toward recognition of something Walter Lippmann said long ago: "There is no more right to deceive than there is a right to swindle, to cheat, or to pick pockets."[30]

Light is the only thing that can sweeten our political atmosphere—light thrown upon every detail of administration in the departments—light blazed full upon every feature of legislation—light that can penetrate every recess or corner in which any intrigue might hide; light that will open to view the innermost chambers of government, . . .

Woodrow Wilson
"Committee or Cabinet Government," 1884

Unlike the Executive, Congress has no need to conjure up a claim of "inherent" power to conceal certain activities; the Constitution explicitly authorizes the Senate and the House of Representatives each not to publish such parts of the journal of its proceedings "as may in their judgment require secrecy." From the beginning, legislators have expressed their desire for secrecy principally in the closing of committee meetings. From 1965 through 1972, for example, between 36 and 43 percent of all committee meetings were closed.[1] But Congress began to open up, to the point that closed meetings in 1973 accounted for only 16 percent of the total and in 1974 only 15 percent.[2]

Until 1974, House and Senate conferees responsible for trying to resolve differing bills almost always met in secret. Often they have found the conference an ideal environment for rewriting legislation to their particular tastes, and sometimes for failing or refusing to uphold the position of their particular chamber. The late Senator George Norris (R–Neb.) protested in 1934 that the conference was so powerful that it was a third "House" whose members "are not elected by the people. The people have no voice as to who these members shall be. . . . No constituent has any definite knowledge as to how members of this conference committee vote, and there is no record to prove the attitude of any member of the conference committee."[3]

Again in 1974, even this began to change; twelve conferences were opened to the press and public.[4] Early in 1975, the House and then the Senate amended their rules so that conferences would be open unless a majority of either House or Senate conferees voted—in public—to close a session. "[W]e are accountable to the electorate and they have the right to know what we did and why," Senator William V. Roth (R–Del.), a sponsor of the open-conference move, said. "When Congress makes decisions in secret, that in itself becomes an issue."[5] Later in 1975, first the House and then the Senate passed resolutions requiring all meetings of their committees, and of conference committees as well, to be open, unless members vote to close them to protect "national security" and other specified types of information. Senators Lawton Chiles (D–Fla.) and Roth were principal sponsors.

Until 1971, the House did not permit recorded votes on amendments. "This was a hangover from 17th century England, when Parliament didn't want powerful kings to know how members voted," Richard L. Lyons wrote in the *Washington Post.*

In 20th century America it meant members of Congress could vote against their constituents' interests and not be found out. In 1970, the House decided the public was entitled to know how its elected representatives voted.

The first time this new rule was used in 1971 the House killed the supersonic transport (SST), a billion dollar federal aid project to build an airliner that would fly faster than sound. The House had been voting SST money for years—despite complaints that it would foul the environment and benefit only the rich—until members had to stand up and be counted.

Moreover, Lyons reported, the historic House vote on February 27, 1975, to end the oil depletion allowance "was a direct result of recent procedural changes" including the recorded vote.[6] In September 1975, House Democrats voted to open their caucus when they are debating and voting on legislative proposals, unless a majority votes—on the record and in public—to close it.

Until it improved its own procedures in the 1970s, Congress' contribution to greater openness in government was directed not at itself, but at the Executive branch and federal agencies. The contribution was mainly two laws: the Freedom of Information Act of 1966, which was sponsored principally by Congressman John E. Moss (D–Calif.), and which will be examined in a moment; and the Federal Advisory Committee Act of 1972. This law, of which the leading advocate was Senator Lee Metcalf (D–Mont.), opened up to public scrutiny the process by which the private sector advises the government. In hearings on the need for the legislation, Metcalf brought out numerous cases of conflict of interest and secretive dealings.

A bit of the flavor is conveyed by a situation created in 1970 by Secor D. Browne, chairman of the Civil Aeronautics Board (CAB). He established an Advisory Committee on Finance and named as its chairman James P. Mitchell, a vice-president of the Chase Manhattan Bank with primary responsibility for financial dealings with airlines. In 1969, Northwest Airlines had reported to the CAB that its biggest stockholder was Kane & Company, the "street name" for Chase Manhattan; Eastern Airlines had listed Kane & Company as its second-largest stockholder, and Trans World Airlines had named Chase Manhattan as the trustee of its largest single block of stock, amounting to 11.75 percent of outstanding capital. In addition, Metcalf disclosed, the bank was "the major creditor for five of the nine local service carriers." The sums involved in all of this were vast, as indicated by the nine local carriers' combined long-term debt, as of September 30, 1970, of $532 million. Chase Manhattan's Mitchell had indicated that the local carriers needed a federal subsidy of between $80 million and $90 million a year, compared with $58.1 million proposed by the CAB for 1971—and with only about $25 million urged by the White House Office of Management and Budget. When the committee held its organizational meeting on November 2, 1970, in Mitchell's office, it decided that all of its sessions "would be closed to the press and the public." The minutes of the meeting, which Senator Metcalf disclosed, went on to say that a verbatim transcript— required under its charter from the CAB—"was not necessary to the conduct of the committee's business." A few weeks after Metcalf aired all of this, Browne disbanded the Mitchell committee.[7]

Some advisory committees avoid public scrutiny by meeting at length over lunch or dinner. On May 7, 1975, the Organized Crime Task Force of the National Advisory Committee on Criminal Justice Standards and Goals met in open session with William T. Archey, an official of the Justice Department's Law Enforcement Assistance Administration. The transcript shows that considerable concern was expressed about how to get out from under the antisecrecy requirements of the Federal Advisory Committee Act. Aaron M. Kohn, managing director of the Metropolitan Crime Commission in New Orleans, had this exchange with Archey:

Mr. Kohn. We could have all our good, honest-to-goodness discussions over the lunch-hour while the stenographer is gone. (General laughter.)
Mr. Archey. I hate to be talking about how the hell we get around this because that puts me in a rather difficult position. But at the same time, I would suggest henceforth that you have dinner meetings which can be picked up as a result of the grant and which do not have minutes and are not of public record. . . .
    Now, I suppose if the dinner meeting would last seven or eight hours, that, you know, that is—I am not going to get into that side of it. . . .[8]

The Freedom of Information Act of 1966 originated mainly from complaints that news media and their organizations, such as the American Society of Newspaper Editors, had begun to press in the early 1950s against policies of the Eisenhower Administration that withheld news. The need for such a law was indeed great, not merely because of the policies of one or another President, but also because of the seemingly unquenchable lust for unaccountability through secrecy that characterizes bureaucracies, many of which elude serious press attention for years—elude it even when congressional hearings or other proceedings lay out their behavior in a public record.

The Department of Health, Education, and Welfare (HEW) has provided two durable examples. The first arose after a fire in a nursing home in Marietta, Ohio, in 1970 killed thirty-two persons. Mal Schechter, Washington editor of *Hospital Practice* magazine, then began a two-year effort to get the Social Security Administration (SSA) to give him access to its inspection reports on the Ohio facility and on several nursing homes in the Washington area that also receive financing under the Medicare program. The SSA and the department refused, on the ground that the Social Security law shields from disclosure any matters "specifically exempted" by HEW regulations, and that these regulations specifically exempted nursing-home inspection reports. In amending the law in 1972, Congress directed HEW to release Medicare records henceforth; but Congress having said nothing about earlier Medicare records, HEW continued to withhold the records Schechter wanted. Aided by two lawyers for Ralph Nader, Ronald L. Plesser and Alan B. Morrison, Schechter had to undertake two lawsuits, under the Freedom of Information Act, before finally winning his case in 1974.

The second example involves access to data on the testing of medicines in animals and humans. Knowledge of such testing is essential in therapy if it is to be prudent and rational. For obvious business reasons, however, drug manufacturers are advantaged if they can treat test data as trade secrets, these being exempt by law from disclosure. The Food, Drug, and Cosmetic Act of 1938 nowhere classifies test data as trade secrets. Yet, from the start the Food and Drug Administration (FDA) has imposed secrecy on test data as "a matter of policy."[9] Thus, a manufacturer may find a new chemical to be dangerous and so inform the FDA, which then subsequently is bound by its own policy to permit another company to try out the same chemical without forewarning it that additional innocent patients may be uselessly imperiled.

In 1962, the House Intergovernmental Relations Subcommittee was investigating the FDA's handling of certain new drugs including MER/29, a cholesterol-lowering agent that caused cataracts and other major adverse reactions in thousands of persons before the agency finally forced it off the market.[10] The FDA tried until the bitter end to deny access to its files to the subcommittee, using the trade-secret and other dodges. When the data was finally obtained, the evidence showed that the FDA had approved MER/29 for the market without having required its safety to be demonstrated. Later in 1962, in an effort to be legislated into secrecy, the FDA contrived to have included in amendments to the 1938 law an obscure provision which prohibited disclosure, even to Congress, of hazards in officially obtained data on drugs, foods, food additives, and pesticides, if such data purportedly would endanger trade secrets. Fortunately, a former FDA medical officer, Dr. Barbara Moulton, discovered in a close reading of the amendments, which had been passed by the House, what the agency was up to. Her discovery was aired in the press, enabling Senator Estes Kefauver to knock out the provision during a conference with the House.[11]

Although the FDA in recent years has significantly improved its information policies, and although those policies are in fact more open than those of numerous other agencies, classification as trade secrets of animal and clinical test data submitted by manufacturers continues.

How substantial a threat to bureaucratic secrecy did the Freedom of Information Act actually present, once the proper discount has been made for the exchange of congratulations among government and media leaders? Various omens suggested wariness, none more so than the warmth of the embrace given it by Lyndon B. Johnson, the President who around this time was enlarging American involvement in the war in Vietnam by stealth. He signed the act on the Fourth of July with an acclamation of the United States as "an open society in which the people's right to know is cherished and guarded." But there were substantive problems. The law put the burden not on the agency that was withholding information, but on the citizen who wanted it, and who, if he cared all that much, would have to undertake litigation that could be costly, lengthy, and futile. The burden was heavy enough that few newspapers, including the largest and most prestigious, ever assumed it. Thanks largely to the Justice Department, which, Robert O. Blanchard, of American University, has pointed out, had "opposed every attempt to enact even the most reasonable freedom of information statute," the law was weighted down with ambiguities and with nine categories of exemptions, mainly for national-security materials classified secret under a White House Executive Order, agencies' internal rules and regulations, investigatory files, and medical reports. According to Blanchard, each exemption category became, in effect, "a secrecy law."[12] Citing the national-security exemption, for example, the Atomic Energy Commission refused a request by Congresswoman Patsy T. Mink (D–Hawaii) for a report on underground nuclear testing. The dispute went to the Supreme Court; it ruled that if an agency stamps "Secret" on a document, it is immune under the Freedom of Information Act from being questioned about the validity of the classification. The law was no help, either, to Senator Howard H.

Baker, Jr., (R–Tenn.) and other members of the Senate Watergate committee when they tried to persuade the CIA to declassify its files on persons with knowledge of Watergate matters.[13] Such experiences testified to the soundness of the advice of Harold Cross, a First Amendment legal scholar, who had said the law should have but one exemption: "except as otherwise provided by law."[14]

Weak and as little used as it was, the law did make some breakthroughs possible, and each contributed significantly to accountability in a different area. Mal Schechter's court battles for access to government nursing-home inspection records were finally won under the Freedom of Information Act. Carl Stern, of NBC News, achieved a major victory when, after a twenty-month effort, he forced the FBI to disgorge the story of the counter-intelligence group it had set up to infiltrate domestic "new left" and "black militant" organizations, including one that had been headed by the Rev. Dr. Martin Luther King, Jr. Ralph Nader's Center for Study of Responsive Law compelled the Department of Labor to make public violations of job-safety standards by federal contractors. In an important advance for consumers, the center ended the Department of Agriculture's routine suppression of records on meat and poultry products it detains on the suspicion that they may be adulterated, unwholesome, or unfit for human consumption. And under threat of a Freedom of Information suit, as detailed later in this book, the Atomic Energy Commission (AEC) yielded documents showing that the AEC tried repeatedly for at least ten years to suppress its own scientists' studies showing dangers in nuclear reactors that the agency never had officially acknowledged.

In the early 1970s, Congressman William S. Moorhead (D–Pa.), who had succeeded John Moss as chairman of the House Government Information Subcommittee, held extensive hearings which prepared the ground for amendments to remedy the weaknesses in the 1966 law. Such amendments were proposed and pressed, most effectively by Ralph Nader and his associates, in the Administrative Practice and Procedure Subcommittee, headed by Senator Edward M. Kennedy (D–Mass.). The subcommittee was "responsible for the toughness of the amendments and the brilliant maneuvering that got them through the Senate and conference committee" despite the opposition of virtually every federal agency, one observer said.[15] Congress passed the amendments overwhelmingly. President Ford vetoed them on October 19, 1974, a little more than two months after promising an open administration. Congress, again overwhelmingly, overrode his veto about a month later. The amendments became law on February 19, 1975.

The amended Freedom of Information Act exposes much more of government to sunlight, even though the original exemptions remain. The essential reason is that the amendments make it far less burdensome, time-consuming and costly to get information out of government. The original law provided agencies with an incentive to classify papers they wanted to withhold for reasons unrelated to national security; the amended law imposes on the courts a duty to determine the validity of a claim that disclosure would endanger national security. Under the exemption of "law enforcement files for investigative purposes," the report on the cover-up of the My-Lai massacre was exempted even though no prosecutions were pending. "Now, under the new amendments," says Theodore J. Jacobs, then director of the Center for Study of Responsive Law, "law enforcement files such as those kept by the FBI would have to be furnished on request unless disclosure would interfere with a pending proceeding, violate an individual's privacy, or compromise a confidential source or investigatory technique." In addition:

Agencies are now required to publish indexes of materials to help the public know what the files may contain, they must process requests for information within ten working days, and they may charge only the direct costs of search and duplication.

Finally, agency personnel may be disciplined for arbitrary or capricious conduct, and the government may be required to pay attorneys' fees and other litigation costs in cases in which the complainant prevails.[16]

Regrettably, this proved to be overly optimistic. Reuben B. Robertson III, a lawyer for the Center for Study of Responsive Law, sought documents from the Federal Aviation Administration on certain safety and performance studies of commercial airlines. The FAA withheld the papers under the exemption in the Freedom of Information Act for records "specifically exempted from disclosure by statute." The law under which the FAA operates requires the agency to withhold data when "any person" objects to disclosure and when agency officials decide that disclosure would adversely affect the objector and "is not required in the interest of the public." The requested studies, the agency said, could not be released because they had been compiled from airline industry data supplied with pledges of confidentiality. Robertson sued, claiming that the Freedom of Information Act eliminated such vague "public interest exemptions" and required concrete justification for a refusal to divulge confidential information. He won—but the Supreme Court undid the victory. In a 7 to 2 decision in June 1975, the Court held that a federal official operating under a law permitting nondisclosure "in the interest of the public" can under the Freedom of Information Act withhold information. There are nearly one hundred such laws: they offer officials varying degress of discretion in withholding information. Congress allowed those laws to stand when it enacted the Freedom of Information Act and the amendments, Chief Justice Warren E. Burger said. Robertson said the decision left the FAA and the Civil Aeronautics Board, as well as other federal officials, with complete discretion to define the "public interest." His lawyer in the case, Alan B. Morrison, said the aviation agencies are "better off now than the FBI and the CIA. . . . The whole information act goes down the drain as regards the FAA and the CAB."[17]

Whether Congress will undertake to correct this situation by revising the one hundred laws is doubtful; indeed, Chief Justice Burger termed such revision "a virtually impossible task." Meanwhile, however, Congress is quite free to make itself more open and accountable.

Accountability of legislators requires that the public have a reasonable opportunity to determine *why* they behave as they do on various issues. In order to do this, it is essential that the public be able to find out—fully, reliably, and swiftly—whence came their election-campaign contributions. During most of the nation's history, Congress, usually in alliance with the White House, has made this difficult or impossible. This has been highly adverse to accountability. The first serious disclosure statute for federal candidates, with coverage of primary contests and with provision for enforcement mechanisms did not become effective until April 7, 1972.

Disclosure of the identity and activities of paid lobbyists is another essential clue to legislative behavior and accountability. Supposedly, the Federal Regulation of Lobbying Act of 1946 requires disclosure of lobbying receipts and expenses, but it is—in the phrase Lyndon Johnson once applied to the 1925 election-financing law—"more loophole than law." John W. Gardner, chairman of Common Cause, the citizens' lobby, correctly says that many of the most powerful lobbyists "mock the law through non-compliance," and that lobbying has become and remains "one of the most secretive and potentially corrupting ingredients in American politics." In making his case, he cited examples including one involving Congress in 1974:

the American Trial Lawyers Association set up an elaborate and devious lobbying system to oppose no-fault auto insurance. It secretly arranged for mailgrams opposing the legislation to be automatically sent to key Congressmen by Western Union offices around the country. Association members needed only to call Western Union and give the names of friends and associates, and for each name given, 10 messages were sent off to Capitol Hill. The Association even arranged for Western Union's sales force to encourage local trial lawyer associations and other interested groups to use the mailgram service. The result was a deluge of messages to key congressional offices protesting no-fault insurance, all seemingly sent by concerned constituents. In one case, 31 sets of 100 telegrams were all sent by the same individual.

The American Trial Lawyers Association was not registered as a lobbying organization.[18]

Despite its pretentious title, the Federal Regulation of Lobbying Act, while perpetuating secrecy and nonaccountability on Capitol Hill in the guise of combatting them, applies neither to aides to legislators nor to the Executive branch. "Only those who seek to influence *legislation* are covered," Gardner told the Senate Government Operations Committee. "This is a glaring inadequacy. Some of the most effective and secretive lobbying today involves personal contacts by corporate heads and special interest lobbyists with officials in executive departments and agencies."

Fewer than two thousand lobbyists are registered under the law, although the number in Washington is estimated at five thousand, according to Richard D. Lyons of the *New York Times*.[19] In reports to the registration agents, the Clerk of the House and the Secretary of the Senate, they report aggregate annual spending of about $10 million. The true amount of lobbyists' spending "is believed to be several multiples of this," Lyons said.

Congress' General Accounting Office (GAO), in an investigation requested by Senator Abraham A. Ribicoff (D–Conn.), the subcommittee chairman, found administration and enforcement of the law chaotic and concluded that it is "ineffective." The GAO studied 1,920 lobbying reports filed with Congress for the third quarter of 1974. Nearly half—917—had not been completed, the GAO found. Forty lobbyists ignored the requirement to say how much they had been paid for their services. Lobbyists filed 1,175 reports—nearly 60 percent of the total—late. Fifty were so late that the *Congressional Record*, which is required by law to print the reports each quarter, went to press without them. "The law as it presently operates is a disgrace," Ribicoff said. "This secrecy must stop."[20] Only an enforced law to bring lobbying out into the open can make lobbying—and, consequently, Congress—properly accountable.

The Supreme Court

*Everything degenerates, even the administration of justice, nothing is safe
that does not show it can bear discussion and publicity.*

> Lord Acton
> *Lord Acton and His Circle*

The critical point in the decision-making process of the Supreme Court is
the conferences of the justices. The secrecy is extreme. Professor Louis
Henkin, of Columbia University Law School, terms the proceeding "[t]he
most confidential . . . in all of government."[1] The Court's secrecy was already
entrenched in 1821, when Thomas Jefferson protested it:

Another most condemnable practice of the Supreme Court is that of cooking up
a decision in caucus and delivering it by one of their members as the opinion of the
court, without the possibility of our knowing how many, who, and for what reasons
each member concurred. This completely defeats the possibility of impeachment by
smothering evidence. A regard for character in each being now the only hold we
can have of them, we should hold fast to it. They would, were they to give their
opinions seriatim and publicly, endeavor to justify themselves to the world by
explaining the reasons which led to their opinion.[2]

A century and a half later, the Court still had failed to develop a comprehensive justification for secret deliberations. Strikingly, many—including
lawyers—have uncritically accepted weak rationales for this situation while
hotly protesting secrecy in the Executive branch. Yet "basic democratic
theory requires that there be knowledge not only of *who* governs but of *how*
policy decisions are made," Professor Arthur S. Miller, of George Washington University, and D. S. Sastri, a doctoral candidate there, said in 1974 in
a rigorously researched—but little noted—article.[3] "Only if it can be demonstrated that certain other fundamental values are jeopardized or transgressed
should secrecy continue to be the norm. We maintain that the secrecy which
pervades Congress, the executive branch and the court is itself the enemy."

They point out that the Supreme Court has enormous power. One justice
who holds the swing vote can validate or invalidate an action of any unit of

federal or state government. For statutory interpretation and administrative review it is the end of the line. And it makes law. What justifications have justices given for exercising such power in secrecy too impenetrable to be compatible with accountability?

The late Justice Felix Frankfurter once said that the Court's manner of operation "is not due to love of secrecy or want of responsible regard for the claims of a democratic society to know how it is governed." Rather, he said, if subjected to the full force of publicity to which the Executive and Congress are exposed, the Court could not function effectively.[4] This is the argument for secrecy that has won virtually unanimous approval, Miller and Sastri say. But, they point out, an argument against the full glare of publicity is no argument against accountability before "the bar of thoughtful public opinion and history." Because that which the justices do not put on paper is unknowable, the authors continue, we have no way of answering vital questions. For their point of departure in writing an opinion, did they choose one major premise but discard others? If they reached a compromise marked by ambiguity, did the ambiguity result from a felt necessity to blur sharp differences of opinion in original drafts? Did the justices "work back from conclusions to principles rather than 'forward' from principles to conclusions"? Miller and Sastri say:

Having made bland assertions that secrecy is absolutely essential for the performance of their tasks, the Justices have not proffered a cogent explanation of the reason for the essentiality. Justice Tom Clark [in 1956] maintained that without absolute secrecy, decisions would become prematurely known and "the whole process of decision destroyed." But this does not explain why maintenance of secrecy must be continued after the decision is taken or why judges suffer from "judicial lockjaw." Justice W.J. Brennan states that the conferences are carried out in "absolute secrecy" for "obvious reasons" and avoids any further elucidation of the matter. These assertions suggest that there is in the secrecy of the Supreme Court something of a semi-holy arcanum, something untouchable on which the very efficiency of the Court's functioning depends.

In challenging the validity of that notion, the authors trace the origins of secrecy in the Supreme Court's conferences to Chief Justice John Marshall, who instituted the practices "for reasons now lost in antiquity and . . . no longer germane to the United States." But their most powerful challenge to the purported need for absolute secrecy in making decisions comes from a study showing that other countries which do not maintain such secrecy do not threaten cherished values.

In Switzerland, the presiding judge of the Swiss Federal Court, the highest tribunal, appoints a colleague to summarize a case, the arguments of the parties (made through the mails), the issues, and his conclusions. His report is circulated to the other judges; they pass on their views to the presiding judge and comment informally on the report. On decision day,

the judges assemble in the courtroom, where newspapermen, lawyers, and the public are present. The judge-reporter reads his written report to the court. If any judge has communicated an opposing view to the presiding judge, he then states his views on the matter publicly, after which a discussion among the judges takes place. After all of the judges have expressed themselves, the reporter makes a reply to the opposing judge's remarks and the discussion then takes the form of questions and answers. At the end of the discussion, the reporting judge proposes a vote to be taken on his motion, and the presiding judge puts the proposition to vote by show of hands. The Registrar then prepares a written report of the conference to communicate to the parties—dissenting votes are not recorded. *The entire decision-making process takes place in public and dissent is not suppressed.* (Emphasis supplied.)

The Mexican Supreme Court also confers in public. "In a courtroom filled with spectators, the reporting judge is called upon by the presiding judge to read the draft of the decision he has prepared and to lead the discussion," Miller and Sastri say. "The various judges express their views openly and the reporting judge meets criticism by giving a final reply. Each judge then announces his vote. If the majority votes in favor, the draft opinion prepared by the reporting judge is adopted by the court. Otherwise, another reporter is appointed, a new draft prepared, and the process is repeated."

In the so-called flag-salute cases in 1942, Justices Hugo L. Black, William O. Douglas, and Frank Murphy changed their minds in public, i.e., engaged in decision making out in the open; and the sky did not fall. Behind the scenes, too, says Nina Totenberg, who covers legal affairs for National Public Radio, most shifts in votes "result from the ongoing efforts of the Justices to apply their best judgment and knowledge of the law to their best under-standing of subtle or ambiguous facts." But, she wrote in the *New York Times Magazine,* "Court insiders say that judicial minds are sometimes changed for less elevated reasons. Most recently such criticism has focused on Chief Justice [Warren E.] Burger." Critics of the chief justice, Ms. Totenberg reported,

cite his voting behavior in the Court's first big busing case—the 1971 Charlotte, N.C., case—in which he wrote the Court's unanimous decision ordering extensive busing to desegregate Southern schools. The first vote in conference was said to be 6 to 3 against busing. In an unusual move, each Justice went back to his chambers and drafted an opinion. Justice [John Marshall] Harlan's was said to have been the toughest pro-busing opinion. Then several Justices had second thoughts and switched their votes. Soon the vote was 6 to 3 for busing, with Burger, [Harry A.] Blackmun and [Hugo L.] Black dissenting. Eventually, the three capitulated—Black being the last holdout. And Burger, who had envisioned himself writing the opinion against busing, ended up writing the opinion for it and incorporating much of the language from the drafts of the more liberal Justices.

But why? Who chose and who discarded what major premises? Did any of the justices "work back from conclusions to principles rather than 'forward' from principles to conclusions"? All we have to go on is Ms. Totenberg's speculative account, which may be correct as far as it goes, but which necessarily is unattributed and not a substitute for open deliberation:

Some who know the Chief Justice well contend that he changed his vote for personal and political reasons rather than reasons of legal judgment. At the time, they speculate, Burger did not want to be part of a small minority if that stance would cause people to think of him as an automatic supporter of positions favored by then-President Nixon. Critics point to other examples of Burger's fighting hard to get a conservative position upheld, only to switch to the other side when he saw he had lost. This occurred, they say, in the Court's unanimous ruling in 1972 that the Government could not wiretap domestic radicals without first obtaining a court-approved warrant—a stunning rebuff to the Nixon Administration [which had appointed four of the nine Justices—Burger, Blackmun, Lewis F. Powell, Jr., and William H. Rehnquist]. In that case, Burger and Blackmun are said to have origi-nally supported the view that no warrant was necessary, though they eventually switched their votes. And in the abortion case, Burger is said to have fought doggedly for the position that the states have the right to prohibit abortions. But when it became clear that a majority would vote the other way, he voted with it.[5]

Arthur S. Miller and D. S. Sastri, in their article, went on to deal with the contention that secret deliberations tend, as they put it, "to preserve the independence of the Justices because they speak out frankly to their breth-ren, without the outside influence of groups or individuals." The argument is shallow, they said, because the justices "have no reason not to speak out frankly in open court and lay bare their minds. As lifetime appointees, they have security of tenure. If security is not their concern, then what is passing through their minds about the vital issues that are brought before them is a matter of which the public has a right to know. The ideas rejected by them are as important for public enlightenment as the ideas advocated in their opinions." If Ms. Totenberg's account is correct, Chief Justice Burger was against busing—until he saw he was going to lose; for warrantless wiretap-ping—until he saw he was going to lose, and for the position that the states could limit abortions—until he saw he was going to lose. Would he have been on both sides of these and other issues if the Court were not, in her phrase, "the least accountable branch of government"? There is a related point: "By deliberating cases in open court, the Justices would inform the public not only that that [outside influence] is absent but also that it is unwelcome. When deliberation is cloaked in secrecy, the public has no way of knowing who exerts influence over decisions."

Miller and Sastri do not challenge the *power* of the Court to protect the confidentiality of its internal operations, although they dismiss the claim of inherent power, made by Chief Justice Burger in a footnote in the Pentagon Papers case, as having "no warrant in logic, history or democratic theory." But they do question the wisdom of the Court in refusing to ventilate its deliberative process, except when "a pressing public need" for secrecy has been demonstrated. "Members of priesthoods traditionally wish to withhold their rituals and other arcanae from the public at large, perhaps as a way of maximizing their power," the authors say. "But that is scarcely a valid reason to support judicial secrecy in a nation that prides itself on being both democratic and enlightened." Positive gains would flow were the Court to opt for disclosure. It would set a peerless example for the Executive, Congress, and federal administrative agencies, not to mention other institutions throughout the land. It also would help achieve "a fuller understanding of the Court; and through that understanding, improve the process of judicial policy-making," the authors say.

More subtly, but of great importance, it would be a means of furthering the democratic ideal. Unless one believes with Alexander Hamilton that the people are a "great beast," then they should be considered to have the internal fiber and moral stamina to withstand knowing the internal operations of the governing process. As matters now stand, the federal judiciary stands *last* among the three branches of government in public esteem [according to a national opinion sampling by the Gallup Organization in 1972].

Another aspect of the Court's secrecy merits mention. The problem is illuminated by a case in which the issue was the right of libraries to photocopy articles in copyrighted scientific and technical journals without permission and without payment. On one side were the federal government, libraries, and some educators: they had argued successfully in the lower courts that unhampered dissemination of information was an overriding value and consequently justified the practice. On the other side were magazine and book publishers, writers, and societies that publish scientific and technical journals: they were appealing a decision that, they said, improperly deprived them of their property. When the Supreme Court voted to take the case, Justice Blackmun declined to participate, Warren Weaver, Jr., recalled in the *New York Times*. Then he "reversed himself and participated actively in the oral argument, only to reverse himself again at decision time." Why? It's a secret:

[T]here is no requirement that a Supreme Court Justice or Federal judge indicate what impelled him to recuse himself—the technical term—and the result, in the eyes of many lawyers and court observers, has been a kind of conspiracy of silence.

Ostensibly, a Justice bases his refusal to reveal his reasons for disqualification on personal privacy, a belief that he need not make public the fact that he owns stock in a corporation or that he had some past relationship with a party in a dispute.

But more often, this reluctance to explain an official act that can have important public consequences appears to be based on a sort of protective arrangement among the Justices of the high court, more an act of deference to his colleagues by the recuser than any attempt to shield personal facts.

For if each Justice who stepped aside in a case issued a brief statement of his reason, the Supreme Court inescapably would begin to compile an informal ethics code of its own. Within a year or two, it would become clear what sort of propriety guidelines some of the Justices, if not all of them, imposed on themselves.

And such a body of precedent, even though personal and unofficial, would almost certainly put increased pressure on Justices who seldom if ever excuse themselves from participating in a decision.[6]

The justices, by not giving reasons for disqualifying themselves, thereby build yet another secrecy barrier to accountability.

In the copyright case, the result of Justice Blackmun's unexplained reversal of his original recusal, followed by his unexplained reversal of his reversal of his recusal, was, in February 1975, a 4 to 4 decision—a tie that deprived "a major industry and a broad range of professionals of an important ruling with national implications," Weaver said. "A tie on the high court automatically affirms the decision of the court below but does not establish any national precedent on the issues involved. *No opinions are written, and the votes of the Justices are not disclosed*" (Emphasis supplied.)

In sum, the justices had conferred secretly on the case; one of them disqualified, qualified, and finally redisqualified himself for secret reasons, and in disposing of the case the remaining eight justices kept their opinions and their votes secret. To reiterate Lord Acton's position: ". . . nothing is safe that does not show it can bear discussion and publicity."[7] One wonders what the justices would say about that.

Secrecy is a disease as natural to government as sclerosis of the liver is to drunks. Bureaucracies hide their mistakes like an alcoholic hides bottles.

Louis Kohlmeier
Washington Columnist

President Ford's pledge of an open administration, followed shortly by his veto of strengthening amendments to the Freedom of Information Act, was but one of many indicators of the seesaw nature of the struggle between the openness that is a precondition of accountability and the secrecy that is a precondition of unaccountability. True, Congress overrode the veto; but such rare victories should not be permitted to blur the reality that they rest on shaky foundations.

Nothing evidences this more ominously than a key provision of the Federal Criminal Code Reform Act of 1976, a large and complex legacy of Richard Nixon accepted and supported by the Ford Administration. In perverse acknowledgment of the role of the press in exposing Watergate, and in perverse reaction to assorted subversions of the Constitution and their multitudinous scandalous progeny, the provision would subvert the First Amendment. The chief sponsors of S. 1 (as it is designated) are a pair of "conservatives" with a long history of conserving inequity, Senators Roman L. Hruska (R–Neb.) and John L. McClellan (D–Ark.). But at least initially, S. 1 also had numerous sponsors with liberal or, in a First Amendment context, conservative credentials. The sponsors included Senate Majority Leader Mike Mansfield, Minority Leader Hugh Scott, and, for several months, Birch Bayh (D–Ind.). To its credit, the House of Delegates of the American Bar Association, by nearly unanimous voice vote at the ABA convention in August 1975 registered its opposition.

The bill would impose censorship by enabling the government to prosecute reporters for "receiving stolen property" if they obtain or disclose contents of *any* government report without official permission, or if they are found to have or if they publish, without government approval, virtually any "national security" information. Under these preposterous provisions, there is not a reporter who deals with government activities, in Washington or elsewhere, who might not be confronted by a choice of risking prosecution and jail on the one hand, and defaulting his obligation to try to make government accountable on the other. As if to assure reporters that they would not have to face such a choice very often, the sponsors of S. 1 seek to cut off their sources with another provision that authorizes prosecution of government employees, former as well as present, who tip off reporters about federal officials who break the law or who lie about secret government activities.

William J. Eaton, a Pulitzer Prize-winning Washington correspondent of the *Chicago Daily News,* found it "incredible" that the Senate, "so soon after the Watergate revelations," should be "seriously considering a bill that would send reporters to jail for disclosing government documents without official permission. This bill could be called the Richard Nixon Revenge Act or the First Amendment Inoperative Act and it would be laughed to death," Eaton said in a column in the *Guild Reporter.* "This type of law not only would have what the lawyers term a 'chilling effect' on First Amendment rights, it would put them in a deep-freeze with no prospect of thawing."[1] The bill might also be called the Prosecution of Reporters and Non-Prosecution of Government Criminals Act, because violations by reporters obviously would be made public where everyone could see them, while officials who break the law could, more than ever, do so in secrecy.

Under existing espionage laws, the government can prosecute only if it can show that information was released with intent to harm national security. Under S. 1, disclosure of nearly any purported national security information would be punishable, even if disclosure were to do no more than embarrass a government official. Thus if Congress passes S. 1, it will give the country, on the bicentennial of the American Revolution, its first official secrets act. That is what S. 1 amounts to, in the expert judgment of two newsmen-lawyers who are leaders of the Reporters Committee for Freedom of the Press, Jack C. Landau, a Washington correspondent of Newhouse Newspapers, and Fred Graham, of CBS News.

William Eaton went on to say:

Newspaper investigations of the My Lai massacre, the Pentagon Papers, FBI and Army snooping and other scandals just would not be possible.

Those disclosures, along with many of the stories that broke open the Watergate case, were based on government memos, reports and other documents that would become sacrosanct.

In effect, reporters and the American people would be forced to rely on U.S. government handouts for their knowledge of what federal officials are doing for us or, to us.

After years of lying by those in power, from Presidents on down, that is hardly going to generate renewed confidence in The System. . . .

The pernicious theory behind S. 1 is that government reports are the private property of government officials, that public disclosure without government consent always is harmful and that anyone who tries to challenge the official line by revealing official reports is jailbait.

Could anything be more contrary to the American spirit or more reminiscent of the divine right of kings?

This bill would sanctify the official cover-up and turn a vigorous, robust press into a whimpering servant of the government authorities. And First Amendment be damned.

The more you think about it, the more it sounds like Communist doctrine that exalts the regime and forbids dissent, with the controlled press acting as a transmission belt for party bosses.[2]

This subversive bill misconceives what the Founding Fathers had in mind when they wrote the First Amendment, and this misconception, if it takes root and grows, will deal a terrible blow to governmental accountability. For centuries before the American Revolution, Potter Stewart, an associate justice of the Supreme Court, recalled in 1974, "the press in England had been licensed, censored, and bedeviled by prosecutions for seditious libel. The British Crown knew that a free press was not just a neutral vehicle for the balanced discussion of diverse ideas. Instead, the free press meant organized, expert scrutiny of government. The press was a conspiracy of the intellect, with the courage of numbers. This formidable check on official power was what the British Crown feared—and what the American Founders decided to risk." In guaranteeing a free press, Stewart said, the Founders' "primary purpose" was "to create a fourth institution outside the government as an additional check on the three official branches. Consider the opening words of the Massachusetts Constitution, drafted by John Adams: 'The liberty of the press is essential to the security of the state.' "

Stewart rejected the belief of some Americans that, as he phrased it, "the former Vice President and former President of the United States were hounded out of office by an arrogant and irresponsible press that had outrageously usurped dictatorial power." On the contrary, he said, "[i]t is my thesis that . . . the established American press in the past 10 years, and particularly in the past two years, has performed precisely the function it was intended to perform by those who wrote the First Amendment of our Constitution. I further submit that this thesis is supported by the relevant decisions of the Supreme Court."[3]

The decisions Stewart cited included the one on the Pentagon Papers, the hitherto secret Defense Department history of American involvement in the Vietnam war through early 1968. Three years later, the *New York Times* and then the *Washington Post* and other newspapers obtained the documents and began to publish them. The Justice Department went into the courts to restrain the newspapers from continuing. In a 6 to 3 ruling on June 30, 1971, the Supreme Court declined to do so.

Each justice wrote an opinion. Hugo L. Black's was an eloquent reminder of first principles. The Founding Fathers, he said, "gave the free press the protection it must have to fulfill its essential role in our democracy. *The press was to serve the governed, not the governors . . . The press was protected so that it could bare the secrets of government and inform the people. Only a free and unrestrained press can effectively expose deception in government.*" (Emphasis supplied.)

But as in the case of President Ford, who pledged an open administration and then vetoed the Freedom of Information Act amendments, and as in the case of the Senate, which overrode the veto while seriously considering S. 1, the Pentagon Papers decision underscored continuing volatile tensions between openness and secrecy. On its way to "losing" in the High Court, the Nixon Administration had "won" an unprecedented victory in the courts below: it had managed to prevent the newspapers from publishing the documents—for fifteen days, in the case of the *Times*. This was a prior restraint of publication, the first in the nation's history. In addition, the Court did not bar possible censorship in cases that might arise in the future; only Justices Black, who died soon after the decision, and William O. Douglas, who retired in November 1975, said that the Constitution barred injunctions against publication under *any* conditions. Notwithstanding the First Amendment guarantee of a free press, the other justices—including Stewart—made it clear that they could conceive of circumstances justifying issuance and enforcement of such injunctions. Out of the nine opinions written, says Melvin L. Wulf, legal director of the American Civil Liberties Union, "one standard emerges under which a majority of the Justices would have allowed information to be suppressed prior to publication: proof by the government that disclosure would 'surely result in direct, immediate and irreparable injury to the Nation or its people.' "[4]

Ten months after the Pentagon Papers decision, the government tried for the first time in the courts to censor a book before publication, *The CIA and the Cult of Intelligence* by Victor Marchetti and John D. Marks.[5] In the extensive legal struggle that ensued, the CIA ordered 339 deletions, but was cut back to 168; and of these, United States District Judge Albert V. Bryan, Jr., of Alexandria, Virginia, was able to say that only twenty-seven were classified. Alfred A. Knopf, Inc., published the book in 1974 with white space denoting the precise location and length of each of the 168 deletions. Afterward, however, the Court of Appeals for the Fourth Circuit upheld the lifelong restraint imposed by the CIA on Marchetti's free speech as it affects information he obtained while in the CIA. The court said that Marchetti could not disclose any information considered by the CIA to be *classifiable*, even if it had not actually been classified, and even if he were to learn of it from unofficial sources after leaving the agency. The Supreme Court refused to review this anti-First Amendment decision. In doing so, it contributed much as would S. 1 to secrecy, suppression, and unaccountable government.

In lower courts, meanwhile, Fred Graham, of CBS News, has discerned and documented a developing pattern "in which judges try to dampen publicity by gagging those most obviously under the judicial thumb—the lawyers, defendants and witnesses—and when that fails, there's a tendency to try direct action against the press, or—increasingly—secret proceedings." As a result, Graham said, there are

about a half-dozen major confrontations each year between judges and newsmen. Into that fractious atmosphere has been injected a new doctrine known as the Dickinson rule.

It got its name from a case in Baton Rouge, La., in 1972, when a judge ordered the press not to report a hearing in open court and then convicted two reporters for contempt after they wrote stories. The U.S. Fifth Circuit Court of Appeals said the order was unconstitutional, but upheld the conviction, saying the reporters should have obeyed the order and appealed it. *It was the first time in the history of this country that newsmen have been held in contempt for reporting a public hearing in the face of an admittedly unconstitutional order. But when the Supreme Court was asked to review the case, it declined, leaving other judges free, at least for the present, to invoke the Dickinson rule against the press.* (Emphasis supplied.)[6]

The High Court does not give its reasons for declining to review decisions from courts below, and so we are denied its thinking on how it could be that a judge who has sworn to uphold the Constitution can issue unconstitutional orders, how judges on an appeals court, who have taken the same oath, could uphold him, and how justices of the Supreme Court, who also have taken the oath, could ignore the situation.

Graham said that the Watergate cover-up trial, conducted by United States District Judge John J. Sirica, demonstrated that secrecy can be contagious "once it is injected into the judicial system in the name of fair trial-free press." He told how Sirica issued a gag order that did not completely exclude comments to the press—and followed it up with a gag order that itself was secret. Even after the jury had been sequestered, he kept sealed the transcript of much of the secret questioning done while the jury was being chosen. He denied a motion by defendant Robert C. Mardian for a severance, but sealed the reasons, presumably, Graham said, to spare the feelings of Mardian's lawyer, who was in ill health. Finally, Graham and George Lardner, Jr., of the *Washington Post,* "wrote a letter to Judge Sirica, protesting the growing secrecy and requesting that the records be unsealed. He refused, and—you guessed it—sealed our letter."

Washington's next big trial was of John B. Connally, the former secretary of the treasury and presumed presidential aspirant who had been charged with bribery in an indictment returned by the Watergate grand jury. When the jurors departed the United States District Court for the last time, "they left behind more than their verdict of acquittal," John P. MacKenzie wrote in the *Washington Post.* "They left behind their identities, their names sealed by a judicial order that apparently has no precedent. Chief Judge George L. Hart, Jr., who issued the order, doesn't know of a legal precedent and says candidly that he never looked for one." This was an exercise of raw judicial power undertaken in the confident—and correct—expectation that no one would try, or dare to try, to hold him accountable. Another arbitrary and unaccountable exercise of judicial power occurred in plea-bargaining between the Justice Department and Vice-President Spiro T. Agnew, who by then had resigned. United States District Judge Walter E. Hoffman, who presided, has refused even to have the stenographic record of a key session transcribed, let alone made public.[7]

Columnists Jack Anderson and Les Whitten said in a mid-1975 summary, "Attempts to muzzle the press have become worse since Watergate was supposed to have stopped the practice." Among their examples was this one:

• Six reporters in four states are appealing jail sentences imposed on them for refusing to reveal the confidential sources of their stories. In the past four months, 50 other reporters around the country have been subpoenaed. If they betray their sources, of course, the unauthorized sources will dry up, and the people will be able to get only the official version of the news.[8]

The seesaw struggle between openness and secrecy also goes on, often with disturbing results, in federal agencies and state and local governments.

The Federal Agencies

The Consumer Product Safety Commission in 1974, when it was one and a half years old, had promulgated impressive regulations for openness. Except when trade secrets or proprietary information are involved, all meetings between commission personnel and outsiders are open to the public; the agency's public calendar discloses in advance what meetings are scheduled; records of all meetings and significant telephone conversations are kept and are open to public examination, and, finally, the public is free to look at drafts of staff papers, and at all incoming and outgoing correspondence, including that with the Executive branch and Capitol Hill. In other federal agencies one or another such forward step has been taken occasionally. Dr. Alexander M. Schmidt, Commissioner of the Food and Drug Administration, for example, keeps public logs of contacts made with FDA officials. By and large, however, the commission's philosophy—"our business is the public's business," says Chairman Richard O. Simpson—is exceptional. Much more representative is the opposition of almost all of the agencies to the 1974 amendments to the Freedom of Information Act, or the Department of Health, Education, and Welfare fighting for years to keep secret inspection records on nursing homes; or the State Department keeping secret the names of some of the countries to which we give military aid, and in what amounts.

From a superabundance of examples of secrecy in federal agencies, this one: the Federal Reserve Board (Fed) systematically collects from banks data including some of direct concern to consumers. *Consumer Reports* asked the Fed to release the interest rates on consumer loans voluntarily reported by each of 370 banks each month. The Fed refused; Consumers Union, publisher of *CR*, sued under the Freedom of Information Act. That law obligated the Fed to specify what was confidential and why, and to release what was not confidential; but the Fed made a blanket claim of confidentiality. In December 1973, three months after the suit was filed, the board made a special survey showing that 73.7 percent of the 370 banks did not consider the data they gave the board confidential—but the Fed did not reveal the existence of the survey to the United States District Court trying the suit. Nonetheless, the court ruled for Consumers Union; but, on appeal by the Fed, the case was remanded for more detailed findings.

For an article in the March 1975 *CR*, Consumers Union managed to obtain information on rates charged by a number of banks for three types of consumer loans in each of eleven metropolitan areas. There were sharp differences. For example, while the First National Bank of Dallas was generally charging 17.97 percent for personal loans and 11.52 percent for auto loans, the Republic National Bank's rates generally were far lower—10 percent on personal loans and 7.51 percent on auto loans. Before publication, but too late to stop it, the board learned of the article, urged Consumers Union not to publish it, and, failing, broke off efforts for an out-of-court settlement of the litigation. Just as *CR* was reaching the subscribers, the *Washington Post* reported that Fed Chairman Arthur F. Burns had persuaded the FBI to investigate what Burns claimed to have been an "apparent theft" of government documents by Fed employees. Peter H. Schuck, director of Consumers Union's Washington office, wrote, "Relying on two criminal provisions—one had never been used in a prosecution and the other had been used (unsuccessfully) to prosecute Daniel Ellsberg for release of the Pentagon Papers—the FBI immediately dispatched agents to interview lower-level Fed employees with access to the data." This punitive expedition flushed out Consumers Union's source; threatened with criminal prosecution, he resigned.

Under pressure of the litigation and outrage on Capitol Hill, the board resumed settlement negotiations and—a year and a half after forcing Consumers Union into the courts—wrote to the 370 banks to ask each the extent to which it considered consumer loan interest rate data *in fact* confidential. Schuck wrote:

The survey was completed in April [1975] but its findings have never been made public by the board. And with good reason; they could hardly be more damaging to the board's position in this whole sorry affair. Of those banks with a single interest rate for a particular loan consumer category, *over 90 per cent* responded that *none* of the information reported to the Fed was confidential. Even in the case of banks that charged customers varying interest rates for consumer loans, more than 50 per cent stated that *none* of the information was confidential. It also turned out that despite all of the Fed's predictions that disclosure would cause large numbers of banks to drop out of the survey, only about 10 fewer banks had reported to the Fed *after* the public listings of banks and rates in *Consumer Reports* than had reported before the listings were published. . . .

These results are not surprising. Consumer loan rates are for the banker what price is to the retail merchant; neither can do business by keeping secret the prices they charge.

When board officials showed Consumers Union the results of their own survey, Consumers Union assumed it at last had made its point, albeit after an enormously long and expensive legal battle. But Consumers Union had not counted on the tenacity of the board, which, Schuck said, "intended to continue to withhold any of the interest rate information that a bank deemed confidential. Only after CU threatened to go back to court again, did the board back down and agree to make all of the data public beginning May 1, 1975."

In the end, Burns tentatively endorsed a proposal that regulated banks be compelled to post such rates on their premises—a step that would facilitate comparison shopping. But before "Burns got burned," as Schuck put it, to whom was the board's secrecy making it accountable? To the millions of consumers who were being denied the help of the Fed (which, by the way, is empowered to *compel* member banks to submit data) in paying exorbitant interest rates on loans and collecting inadequate interest on savings? Or was the board being accountable to the banks that without the sunshine of publicity can charge too much for loans and pay out too little for the use of other people's money?

"The *Consumer Reports* affair," Schuck wrote, "is not merely an example of the arbitrary exercise of power by bureaucrats; Dr. Burns obviously believed that an important principle—the integrity of the Fed's promises [to banks to keep data they supply confidential] and its files—was at stake. More fundamentally it shows once again that regulatory agencies will almost always perceive their bureaucratic interests as nearly identical with the economic interests of regulated industry and will act on that perception while regarding consumer interests as *terra incognita* on the regulatory landscape."[9]

In the fall of 1975, by a remarkable vote of 94 to 0, Senators Lawton Chiles (D–Fla.) and William V. Roth (R–Dela.) got through a bill to require some four dozen regulatory agencies to open their meetings to the press and public, although administrators were left free to invoke any of ten specified grounds to close them. The agencies that would be covered include the Federal Reserve, National Labor Relations, and Emergency Loan Guarantee boards, and the Civil Rights, Civil Service, Federal Communications, Federal Power, Federal Trade, and Interstate Commerce commissions. The House was expected to pass the bill in the summer or fall of 1976.

States and Cities

In the states and cities the trend also seems to be generally toward more openness. The State of Florida is an outstanding example. In 1972, his second year as governor, Reubin Askew decided to hear the budget requests of department heads "in the privacy of my capitol office." He had hoped thereby to make the budget process more candid, more productive, and speedier. "It quickly became apparent, however, that the hoped-for efficiency would not be worth the price," Askew said later.

Newspaper and television reporters crowded the reception area outside, angrily and persistently questioned the need for secrecy. Obviously, if the meetings were not opened, their reports could plant the seeds of doubt and suspicion in Florida's mind.

I told the press [Florida's is extraordinary] I was wrong [and so, obviously, is its governor extraordinary], and the meetings were opened.

And I have since found other ways to encourage more candid and productive budget presentations in public sessions. In fact, I believe the presence of reporters has helped achieve the kind of spending priorities which best serve the interests of the people.[10]

Askew's preference for accountability through openness has Robert Moses' preference for unaccountability through secrecy as its polar opposite. Moses operated in New York City through the Triborough Bridge and Tunnel Authority and other authorities whose records were as secret as those of a private corporation's. In this way, Robert A. Caro has written in *The Power Broker: Robert Moses and the Fall of New York,* he "could keep the public from finding out what he was doing . . . If, throughout his half century and more in the public eye, he displayed an eagerness and a flair for publicizing certain aspects of his career and his life, he displayed an equal eagerness and flair for making sure that only those aspects—and no others—were known." For operators on the take, Moses' authorities were safer sources than the city:

A politician or public official could accept a legal fee or an insurance premium from Triborough with assurance that no reporter or reformer would ever be able to discover that he had done so. . . . A politician considering accepting a Triborough fee could be assured that should some neophyte legislator ever attempt to open Triborough's books, Moses would assail the attempt as an attempt by a politician to interfere with an agency whose independence he didn't like and to get his hands on some of its funds—that the press would back up that argument, and that the public would be conditioned by years of praise for Moses and for public authorities to accept it. . . . *Robert Moses had $750,000,000 of Authority money to give away. In the ultimate analysis, it was the public's money. But Robert Moses was not accountable to the public. He was not accountable to anyone. He had $750,000,000 to give away. And no one would ever know to whom he gave it. And this made politicians and public officials—at least those . . . interested in retainers—all the more anxious to make sure that he gave some of it to them.* (Emphasis supplied.)[11]

Unaccountable power must be unacceptable power in the eyes of the citizens whose taxes pay for government agencies, whether these agencies are federal, state, county, regional, or local. The principle is no less valid in Dubuque than in Washington.

An acute shortage of currency led to the financial panic of 1907 in which there was a wave of bank failures. To prevent a recurrence through provision of "an elastic currency," Congress in 1913 created the Federal Reserve System (Fed).

The Constitution gives Congress exclusive power "To coin money, regulate the value thereof. . . ." In addition to delegating this vast power to the Fed, Congress also has given it extremely broad regulatory functions; increasing authority over areas of consumer credit including truth-in-lending and equal opportunity to get credit; indirect influence over much of the business community through the Bank Holding Company Act; and, through its dealings with central banks abroad, considerable influence in international monetary policy. Yet for more than sixty years Congress has failed to make the Fed accountable—either to itself or to the White House. Among the Fed's principal defenses against accountability is secrecy.

Money and Power

The Fed controls the money supply, expanding it by buying government securities in the open market, and contracting it by selling these securities. The Fed also sets the discount rate—the charge to member banks for borrowing from it. Finally, it is empowered to raise or lower the proportion of reserves member banks must have behind their deposit liabilities. With these principal monetary controls, the Fed determines interest rates and the availability of credit, as well as prices and employment. Thus it affects nothing less than the economic welfare of every person in the country. It is, said the late Representative Wright Patman (D–Tex.) "probably the most important single determinant of whether we will have prosperity or depression."[1] Patman was one of the critics who, among other things, blamed the Fed's refusal to increase the money supply for the Great Depression of 1929–1933.

The Fed's Unaccountability

All federally chartered banks must be, and many state banks voluntarily are, members of the Federal Reserve System. Collectively, the member banks are one of the system's three basic elements; the others are the twelve district (or reserve) banks, each in a separate region, and the board of governors.

In each region the member banks elect the district bank's president and six of its nine directors (the board names the other three and also has a veto over nominations for district bank presidencies). The directors elected by the private banks pay the salary of each district bank president out of the banks' funds without a by-your-leave from Congress. Thus, while board members in Washington were drawing $42,500, as were senators, representatives, and federal judges, district bank presidents were being paid from $50,000 (in Richmond, Virginia) to $95,000 (in New York City). Nominally, they are public officials; effectively, they are agents of the private banks that elect and pay them. This accountability in the district banks runs strongly to the commercial banks. Sometimes accountability also runs to major industries. In Seattle, for example, Malcolm T. Stamper is chairman of the Fed's district bank, and president of the Boeing Company. In San Francisco, Charles Dahl is president of the Federal Reserve Bank, and a director of Crown Zellerbach Corporation. In Dallas, John Lawrence is a director of the district bank, and chairman of the conglomerate Dresser Industries. For the most part, however, the district banks are accountable to the banks that own them—banks that benefit from high interest rates much as Exxon Oil benefits from high oil prices.[2]

In Washington, the President, with the advice and consent of the Senate, appoints the governors, of whom there are seven. Their terms run fourteen years and are staggered. Consequently, a vacancy normally occurs once each two years, and even a two-term President can expect to name only four governors. He does designate the board chairman—but the chairman's four-year term does not coincide with the President's four-year term. It is the informed judgment of Congressman Henry S. Reuss (D–Wis.), chairman of the House Banking and Currency Committee, that the Fed is "responsible to nobody."[3] The litany invoked to defend the various arrangements is that they assure the Fed's "independence." Actually they assure a schizoid economic policy in which an elected President and an unelected Fed are free to pull the economy in opposite directions.

The Fed's most powerful instrument for implementing monetary policy is the Federal Open Market Committee (FOMC), which buys and sells government securities in the marketplace. Its voting members are the seven governors, the president of the New York district bank, and under a rotation plan, four district bank presidents (the other seven attend FOMC meetings, however). An indicator of the FOMC's clout is that as of early 1975, it had in its portfolio government securities valued at an eye-popping $93 billion, and on this sum was drawing annual interest of about $6 billion—paid for by the taxpayers, but with the balance after operating expenses being turned over to the Treasury.[4] To recapitulate for a moment: The FOMC's members consist of seven governors essentially unaccountable to the White House and five district bank presidents accountable dominantly to the approximately 5,700 member commercial banks. Among these banks, it should be noted, the ten largest in 1971 held $343 billion in bank trust assets, about one-third of the nation's total.

What about accountability to Congress? Capitol Hill's principal instrument for making an agency accountable is control over its appropriations. The Fed escapes this control by drawing its operating funds, about $600 million a year, from the $6 billion it collects from the taxpayers in interest on government securities—what Congressman Patman called "this huge slush fund."[5] Since his election to the House in 1928, Patman had been a self-described "voice crying in the wilderness for the accountability of the Federal Reserve System." Even in 1975, when he was eighty-two, and after he had been forced out of the chairmanship of the House Banking Committee, he was pressing as hard as he could to achieve that accountability. One of the minimum steps he urged was to forbid the Fed to earn interest on government bonds; this would make it come to Congress for appropriations, as it ought to do. As things stand, Congress "has lost whatever control it may once have had," Professor Arthur S. Miller told the committee in 1964. "Congress, in short, has abdicated—in this, as well as many other matters of great public importance. . . . It is not extravagant to say that Congress is slowly bleeding itself to death—from self-inflicted wounds."[6]

Thanks mainly to Senator William Proxmire (D–Wis.), who became chairman of the Senate Banking, Housing, and Urban Afairs Committee in the Ninety-fourth Congress, a tourniquet in the form of passage of a concurrent resolution was applied in May 1975. The resolution requires the chairman of the Federal Reserve Board, currently Dr. Arthur F. Burns, to tell Capitol Hill a year in advance what its targets are for the growth of the money supply. Moreover, the chairman must appear quarterly before either the Senate or House Banking committees to be questioned about implementation of the targets, which are intended to implement the growth and strength of the economy. The resolution was at once a breakthrough and a step toward accountability so halting that Congress remains dependent on what Arthur Burns cares to tell it about monetary policy. As of December 1975, he had refused to supply Congress with the same staff analyses that are provided at each meeting of the Open Market Committee on the supply of money needed to reach particular economic targets.

The Fed's Secrecy

The Fed's shield of secrecy has three primary layers. The first is its freedom from dependence on congressional appropriations and, consequently, from the opportunities the appropriations process affords for penetrating secrecy.

The others are its immunity from auditing by Congress' General Accounting Office, and its concealment of the FOMC's decisions and reasons for the decisions.

Never since its creation in 1913 has the Fed—an agency which in 1972 handled 35 billion pieces of paper worth $24 trillion—been subjected to a complete, independent audit. Along with a very few other important agencies, principally the Federal Deposit Insurance Corporation and the Internal Revenue Service, the Fed refuses to consent to GAO auditing. The few publicly available clues to its operations suggest why the Fed enjoys the comforts of secrecy. To take a case in point, the Fed has built for its approximately six hundred employees a new Taj Mahal in Washington, which it has named after former Chairman William McChesney Martin. As of March 1975, it had cost more than $46 million and was far more expensive than the justly criticized Mussolini-modern Rayburn House Office Building and the incompetent Dirksen Senate Office Building. Even allowing for inflation, the cost differences are striking. The cost per square foot was: Rayburn, $36.56; Dirksen, $36.06, and Martin, $57.67. Per cubic foot: Rayburn, $2.45; Dirksen, $2.52, and Martin, $4.52.[7]

The staff of Patman's House Banking Subcommittee on Domestic Monetary Policy found a wide range of waste when it examined certain Fed expenditures during 1974, such as $13,969.24 to move Ralph Evans from Miami, Florida, to Atlanta, Georgia.

The Fed bars the GAO not only from looking at its expenditures, but also at other important doings behind its marble proscenium. Multibillion-dollar transactions in foreign exchange, for example, sometimes result in large losses, according to Professor Sherman J. Maisel, a former Fed governor. Congressman Patman, writing of the attempt to rescue the Franklin National Bank of New York in 1974, said a few months later:

it now appears that the Fed advanced $1,750 billion of the people's monies at 8 per cent interest against collateral of doubtful value. Some creditors of Franklin were paid who would not have been otherwise, for instance, banks which had advanced federal funds to Franklin in amounts upwards of $500 million, and some six thousand of its six hundred and twenty thousand depositors whose deposits were not insured by the Federal Deposit Insurance Corporation.

By what right, without consultation with the President and the Congress, do Dr. Burns and the Fed secretly dispense $1,750 billion of the people's money? . . .

There is more at stake here than meets the eye. It is an assertion of the right of complete independence from political accountability by Burns and the Fed to use the people's money in any way they see fit. It is arrogance we must not tolerate. No one man or institution should have this unbridled power. The people did not elect Dr. Burns, and he is not our king.[8]

In the summer of 1973 Patman asked Burns for a list of Fed employees paid $20,000 or more a year. Burns was still resisting a year later, going so far as to claim that disclosure of the list might lead to kidnapings or robberies of those employees, although the pay of every member and employee of Congress is a matter of public record. Burns finally provided the list—more than fifteen hundred Fed employees were on it—in December 1974.

Patman in 1974 got a bill for an audit of the Fed to the House floor. Only after watering it down so the audit would be limited to "administrative expenses" did the House pass it, by a vote of 290 to 58. "Dr. Burns personally lobbied against it among members of Congress and Manhattan bankers," Patman charged on the basis of voluminous documentation. The Senate failed to act, and even the weakened bill died.[9]

In 1975 Patman was trying anew. Again there was a powerful lobbying campaign against the bill. He said that it was "carefully orchestrated by the Federal Reserve itself," that it was "highly questionable" because it entailed the outlay of public funds to generate pressure on Congress, and that it would not be tolerated if any other federal entity had undertaken it.[10] Here are a few of Patman's disclosures:

• On Boeing Company stationery, President Malcolm T. Stamper wrote legislators to oppose the auditing bill, disclosing in the body of the letter, however, that he was acting "in my capacity as president of the Boeing Co., and as Chairman of the Federal Reserve Board of Seattle." Thus was the muscle of a $1.7 billion corporation combined with the muscle of the Fed.

• Telegrams opposing GAO auditing came to Capitol Hill from Thomas M. Meyersieck, a Crown Zellerbach executive who did not bother to disclose that the president of his giant company, Charles Dahl, is a director of the Federal Reserve Bank of San Francisco.

• John V. James, president of Dresser Industries, Inc., of Dallas, a $1.2 billion energy conglomerate with no more apparent reason than Crown Zellerbach to concern itself with the issue whether the GAO audits the Fed, sent members of Congress a two-page, single-spaced letter analyzing the bill and urging its defeat. On checking, Patman found that John Lawrence, chairman of Dresser, is a director of the Federal Reserve Bank of Dallas.

Where, Patman wondered, "does the Federal Reserve end and the private corporation begin? And where, in all this, is the public interest?" His questions will be seen as even more to the point if one knows that legislators got additional pleas to kill the audit bill from the American Bankers Association; from bankers who concealed their directorships on various district banks of the Fed; from former directors of these banks who used, Patman said, "amazingly similar language," and who were responding to pleas from present officials of the banks; from G. L. Bach, who wrote on a Stanford University letterhead without disclosure that he is a paid Fed consultant, and from that putative apostle of economy in government, the Chamber of Commerce of the United States. "These lobbying activities—more than anything else—are clear evidence of the need for a top-to-bottom audit," Patman told the House. "These efforts dramatize—in stark terms—the tremendous conflict of interest inherent in the entire Federal Reserve System."[11]

Under Arthur Burns in the period 1971–73, the FOMC, meeting every few weeks, increased the money supply when the economic indicators, in the view of economists of virtually all persuasions, believed it should have been held steady. This stimulated the economy in time to help the reelection of Richard Nixon, who had appointed Burns. In 1972 the supply of money rose 8.7 percent; after the election, the Fed reversed course and decreased the growth to 4.7 percent.[12] Thanks in part to these policies, we got double-digit inflation coupled with the worst recession since 1929.

The more that is publicly known about monetary policy *at the time it is made,* the better that policy is likely to be. That is the view of former board member Maisel, academics, and most everyone else except the Fed itself, which, Maisel says, pursues secrecy out of "fear of political attack and public criticism."[13] The FOMC's special technique of secrecy is to meet behind closed doors, with assorted conflicts of interest, internal disagreements, mistakes, and arrogance also conveniently out of sight. A decision is reached as to the policy to be followed on purchases of government securities. But there is no disclosure of the policy until ninety days later, when the Fed releases what Patman termed "an enigmatic summary" which by that time is nearly useless. The meeting minutes are published *five years later*—when they are of no use. This technique certainly keeps Congress and the public in the dark, but not, Patman said, "those who have the most to gain—the bankers."[14] The corrective is obvious: the FOMC's decisions and a transcript of the discussions underlying them should be released immediately.

Professor Miller, in 1964, found the Fed, "in all of its operations, . . . to be an independent organization, not responsible or accountable to any official, including the President. . . . To the extent that the Board operates autonomously, it would seem to run contrary to another principle in our constitutional order—that of the accountability of power." The Employment Act of 1946 requires the President to submit an economic program which to be serious must include recommendations on monetary policy. Miller said:

The heart of the matter is that the Federal Reserve's structural independence and so insulation from the President means that the Employment Act of 1946 is simply not enforceable. The President cannot, as he is required to do by the Employment Act, submit a program that is likely to be effective in achieving the goals of the law unless the Federal Reserve is willing to cooperate. There is no assurance that the required cooperation will be forthcoming. . . . Thus the President's program is really not a working program but a vision, the fulfillment of which depends on the policy of the independent Federal Reserve.[15]

If the Fed is to be made accountable to the people whose economic destinies it controls rather than to the bankers who profit from the high interest rates it sets, its operations must be brought out into the light of day.

III
Corporate Secrecy

Who Owns the Corporations?   **13**

Great corporations exist only because they are created and safeguarded by our institutions; and it is therefore our right and our duty to see that they work in harmony with these institutions. . . . The first requisite is knowledge, full and complete; knowledge which may be made public to the world.

Theodore Roosevelt
First Annual Message to Congress

"Corporate secrecy" is not merely an aspect of the power of giant corporations. It is the first and usually decisive obstacle to knowledge of and response to the abuses, illegalities, and injustices which corporations heap upon citizens, governments and environments. Without the ability to deny the government, the small businessman, and the ordinary citizen literally every kind and form of information about their activities, large business enterprises simply could not dominate—as they too often do— our economic and political life. For control of the process of information is control of the process of policy.

—Ralph Nader
Senate Testimony

There are approximately two thousand giant corporations which account for about half of this country's nonpublic business. The enormous economic power wielded by these corporations translates directly into political power and "[m]uch of what passes as governmental power is derivative of corporate power . . ."[1] Because of this, the great corporation must be regarded as a public institution, at least, as John Kenneth Galbraith once put it, "by any man of minimally untrammeled mind." Consequently, he said,

It follows from the public view of the corporation that there is no longer a presumption that it has private affairs that are protected from public scrutiny. It will still be wise to accord it managerial autonomy in its operations. This is necessary for effective administration and for efficiency. But this is a pragmatic decision. No principle is involved. On the safety of products; or the environment; or wage and price making; or profits; or executive compensation . . . there is no natural right to be free of public scrutiny.[2]

However, accountability has not been the hallmark of these corporations; secrecy has.

John D. Rockefeller was an exemplar of corporate secrecy. In her great *The History of the Standard Oil Company,* Ida M. Tarbell said that "the few malcontents [who] kept him before the public. . . . interfered with two of his great principles—'hide the profits' and 'say nothing.' "[3] One of his principal instruments for concentrating the oil business in his hands was the South Improvement Company. Those who were approached to engage in transactions with it were asked to sign either of two pledges to keep secret those transactions. Standard Oil in 1874 and 1875 bought three companies in a purchase so secret "that Mr. Rockefeller, five years after . . . dared make an affidavit that it had never occurred!"[4] He hatched secrecy plans which the CIA would emulate long afterward:

Men who entered into running arrangements with Mr. Rockefeller were cautioned "not to tell their wives," and correspondence between them and the Standard Oil Company was carried on under assumed names![5]

Theodore Roosevelt made his declaration of the need to open "mammoth" corporations to public view in 1901. At the time, there were actually very few truly big businesses. "The great trust movement of the period created only two industrial corporations with assets exceeding $500 million by 1909, and both of these, U.S. Steel and Standard Oil (New Jersey), were specialized to a particular industry," Professor Willard F. Mueller, of the University of Wisconsin, has said. Testifying, as did Harvard's Galbraith, at a hearing on corporate secrecy held by Senator Gaylord Nelson (D–Wis.), Mueller went on to say:

In contrast, by the first quarter of 1971, there were 111 industrial corporations with assets of $1 billion or more. Although there are about 200,000 corporations and nearly 200,000 partnerships and proprietorships engaged in manufacturing, by the beginning of 1971 the 111 largest of these held at least 51 percent of the assets and 56 percent of the profits of all corporations engaged primarily in manufacturing; the 333 corporations with assets of $500 million or more accounted for fully 70 percent of all industrial assets, excluding their unconsolidated holdings.

Indeed, by 1970, the two largest industrial corporations alone, had sales of nearly $40 billion, which is about as great (in constant dollars) as those of the over 200,000 manufacturing establishments operating in 1899.[6]

Merely on the basis of such awesome statistics, the plea of Theodore Roosevelt for "knowledge, full and complete" about the great corporations has incomparably more urgency than in 1901. But bloated size per se is not the key issue. One has but to read the newspapers or watch the tube to be suffused with awareness that "Big Business *is* government."[7] Conniving to topple the regime of Salvador Allende in Chile. Fronting for the CIA (or vice versa). Making decisions decisively affecting our safety, health, environment, jobs, taxes, culture. Running the oil embargo for the Arabs. And doing all of this behind shrouds of secrecy.

"There were some of the early heads of oil companies who felt they owned the oil companies," William W. Keeler, then chairman and chief executive officer of Phillips Petroleum, told CBS Television reporter Jay McMullen.

McMullen: Felt they owned the government, too, didn't they?
Keeler: Yes, I expect that's right.[8]

To govern, says the *Oxford Universal Dictionary,* is "to rule with authority . . . to direct and control the action and affairs (of a people, etc.) . . . to hold sway, prevail . . . manage, order . . ." In *America, Inc.: Who Owns and Operates the United States,* we made the case that the giant corporation—"an entity utterly unlike the ordinary business"—"rules, directs, controls, sways, prevails, manages, orders," and that it does these things, *governs,* largely unrestrained by reins of accountability.[9] This governance is conducted in much secrecy. The governed are thus deprived of reasonable opportunity to give or withhold informed consent. But as Dr. Mueller correctly pointed out, "In a free society, no institution vital to the public interest can maintain a claim to legitimacy if its affairs are shrouded in secrecy."[10]

"Say nothing," one of the sayings of Chairman John, was implemented by our nonsystem for chartering corporations. Irrationally, the states rather than the federal government are the chartering authorities for organizations whose activities have national and international impact. Paced in the nineteenth century by New Jersey and Delaware, which emerged as the alltime champ, the states competed for chartering business by trying to give away as much as possible. They tried, that is, to outdo each other in *not* burdening corporations with responsibilities, especially for disclosure, commensurate with their importance. New Jersey became the home of Rockefeller's trust, which the Supreme Court dismembered in 1911. The vestigial remnant, Exxon, exemplifies the excrescent paternal relationship with the state. The company's revenues in 1967, for example, were more than four times larger than the combined revenues of the State and all of its local governments.[11] Delaware's chartering standards being the lowest, it became the home of International Telephone and Telegraph, which, at about the same time was boasting that it "is constantly at work around the clock—in 67 nations and on six continents, in activities extending from the bottom of the sea to the moon . . ."[12]

Had the government wanted to impose on corporations responsibilities and disclosure requirements commensurate with their power and importance, it would have switched to federal chartering long ago. Even at the Constitutional Convention in 1787 James Madison proposed that the Constitution explicitly empower Congress "[t]o grant charters of corporation in cases where the public good may require them and the authority of a single state may be incompetent."[13] *Incompetent:* it was an adjective that would prove to be apt. In 1901, President Roosevelt told Congress, "The Government should have the right to inspect and examine the workings of the great corporations engaged in interstate commerce."[14] Inspecting and examining the workings of, say, ITT, is precisely what Delaware does not want to do and, in any case, is incompetent to do. In 1903, a bill for federal chartering was introduced in Congress, but like others later, got nowhere.[15] Thus, what Roosevelt termed "[t]he first essential in determining how to deal with the great industrial combinations . . . knowledge of the facts—publicly" has been constantly frustrated.[16]

Surprising though it may be, our requirements in some important areas of disclosure are less stringent than other countries'. Richard J. Barnet and Ronald E. Müller report in *Global Reach: The Power of the Multinational Corporations:*

In Japan, for example, corporations are required to give the tax collector and the shareholders the same profit figures. This eminently reasonable disclosure requirement, completely at odds with the ethic of the new alchemists [the "global-corporation executives"], has not put Japanese firms into bankruptcy. A similar requirement here would not bankrupt IBM either. Moreover, there is historical evidence that where the United States takes the lead in regulating global corporations in areas that frustrate fiscal or monetary policy, other governments, having similar interests vis-à-vis their own global corporations, follow suit.[17]

The first thing the public should be able to find out about the great corporations is, who controls them. The essential data in most cases are secret. This fact itself, while not a secret, dwells in the exurbs of public awareness. For years, Senator Lee Metcalf (D–Mont.) has worked assiduously to heighten that awareness, to establish who controls what, and to prod regulatory agencies to use their existing powers to compel large corporations —*public* institutions—to make basic data about themselves readily accessible.

With a form letter of inquiry, Metcalf in May 1972 asked each of 324 large corporations to disclose the identities of the thirty largest stockholders.

The letter went to 18 oil and 81 other industrial corporations; 17 airlines, 19 railroads, and 14 other transportation firms; 46 electric and gas utilities; 5 communications firms; 50 retailing enterprises; 50 banks; and 24 stock-company life insurance companies. Of the 324, only 89 responded fully—and fully 46 of these were transportation and utility enterprises that, being regulated, are required in any case to make public certain of the requested data. Among the 24 insurance firms, only one—Travelers Insurance Companies—replied in full, a rate of 4.2 percent. For miscellaneous transportation it was 14.3 percent; for retailing, 16 percent; for banks, 18 percent; for oil companies, 22.2 percent; for other industrials, 25.9 percent; for electric and gas, 34.8 percent; for airlines, 52.9 percent; for railroads, 78.9 percent; and for communications, 80 percent.

Fifty-eight firms did not so much as reply to Metcalf's letter; retailers were the worst offenders here, but others included General Foods Corporation, Aluminum Corporation of America, and 13 other industrial corporations. The number of corporations supplying partial or irrelevant data was 177—almost twice as many as responded fully. The commonest excuse was a professed need for secrecy, often politely phrased as a belief that the relationship between a company and its shareholders is "a private matter."

The privacy rationale collapsed under falling bricks of anomaly in January 1974, when two subcommittees of the Senate Government Operations Committee, one headed by Metcalf, and the other by Senator Edmund S. Muskie (D–Maine), published *Disclosure of Corporate Ownership*, a 419-page report on the inquiry with an analysis of the data by the Library of Congress.

Mobil Oil was "pleased" to respond fully. Ashland Oil, Atlantic Richfield, and Continental Oil also supplied the requested data with alacrity. How then could the same data be "confidential," as claimed by Standard Oil of California and Union Oil of California? Or "priviledged and confidential," as claimed by Texaco and Phillips? Or just "privileged," as claimed by Gulf Oil? Or "a fiduciary obligation" in need of asylum, as alleged by Shell? Or "private" matters, as asserted by Standard Oil of Indiana and Exxon, which may not have forgotten the Saying of Chairman John? The anomalies extended to other categories. For example: Ford Motor Company and Chrysler Corporation complied—General Motors refused. RCA and American Telephone & Telegraph complied—ITT and International Business Machines refused. Safeway Stores and Grand Union Company complied—Food Fair Stores and Great Atlantic & Pacific Tea Company refused. Bankers Trust New York Corporation and First National City Corporation complied—Morgan Guaranty Trust Company and Bank of New York refused.

To say that 89 firms replied fully to Metcalf's inquiry is not to say, unfortunately, that each was fully enlightening. In listing its 30 principal shareholders, Litton Industries, for example, four times recorded "An individual." The anonymous owners accounted for 1,930,956 out of 16,917,546 shares, "A private partnership consisting of 2 individuals" for 175,133, and "A private foundation" for 304,865. Three Swiss banks accounted for an additional 2,874,671 shares.

Another problem is the use of "street names"—an example being Cudd & Co.—which are not to be found in phone books and, standing alone, do not indicate the institution or the nominee behind them. To translate street names, one needs a copy of the *Nominee List.* The publisher, the American Society of Corporate Secretaries, reportedly refused in 1971 to sell copies to an official of a federal regulatory agency, a newspaper editor, and a lawyer. Metcalf then had the 1971 edition printed in the *Congressional Record* of June 24, 1971. The Society after that began selling copies. (The price—in 1975—was $25; the address of the Society is 9 Rockefeller Plaza, New York, N.Y. 10020.) Cudd & Co., incidentally, turns out to be a street name used by Chase Manhattan Bank.

In replying to Metcalf, some firms used an informative format for street names, such as "Pitt & Co., Bankers Trust Co., New York, N.Y." Others simply gave the street names. Such practices have serious consequences when followed in reports required by regulatory agencies which, needless to say, presumably regulate on a factual base. The Metcalf–Muskie report cites the example of Burlington Northern, Inc. (BN). As a railroad operator, this conglomerate is required by the Interstate Commerce Commission (ICC) to submit annually a listing of its thirty largest stockholders. In its report for 1973, BN's "Top 30" proved to include twenty-six street names, without a clue as to the institutions behind them. Eleven of these names were used by only four banks, of which Bankers Trust alone accounted for six. Further analysis of this deceptive document showed that the "Top 30" actually amounted to the top twenty. Moreover, BN had not so much as mentioned the four banks in the ownership reports for 1973 that it filed with the ICC and the Securities and Exchange Commission (SEC), although in the "Top 30" list they accounted for 25 percent of the voting stock. Such practices are "by no means uncommon," *Disclosure of Corporate Ownership* said.

The holdings of institutional investors, especially banks, are often hidden from view of regulators and the public through use of multiple nominees—"Hemfar & Co", "Lerche & Co.", "Kane & Co.", "Bark & Co.", "Pace & Co." and many more. In response to the Federal regulators' request for the addresses of these "security holders" the companies report simply "New York, N.Y.", "Boston, Mass." or "Pittsburgh, Pa.", occasionally adding a post office box number. These nominee names are not in the city directory. They are not in the telephone book. Letters to some nominees whose post office box is listed have not been answered.

The consequence of this continuing use of nominees in ownership reports to Federal regulators is a massive coverup of the extent to which holdings of stock have become concentrated in the hands of very few institutional investors, especially banks.

Senators Metcalf and Muskie reached these further conclusions:

• "Neither companies nor ordinary stockholders have information which they need, to protect their own interests, regarding stock ownership and the personnel and business relationships between portfolio companies and institutional investors, principally banks."

• "The Federal Government does not have sufficient information in these areas upon which to base reasoned public policy. Much of the information collected by Federal agencies regarding stock ownership, displayed in public files and shared with State agencies and the public, is meaningless or misleading . . ."

• "The information needed regarding the several levers of corporate control is held by a few institutional investors, principally six superbanks headquartered in New York. These institutional investors have the capacity to report their holdings quickly and fully."

• ". . . neither the Congress, nor the commissions, nor the executive branch, can fully evaluate the effect of concentration . . ."

• "Meanwhile, the portfolio companies in which a few banks have substantial influence make many decisions affecting public policy. Oil companies deal with foreign nations regarding oil supply and cost. Pipelines companies deal with the Soviet Union for natural gas. Utilities exercise the right of eminent domain. Milling companies and the Soviet Union arrange grain sales which sharply affect domestic price, supply, transportation, and storage. These are momentous public issues in which Federal officials play a minor role, much of it after basic decisions have been agreed upon by American companies and foreign governments."[18]

Corporations with multiple divisions and product lines are notably unwilling to disclose how each performs—the investment, costs, revenues, and profits. They hold tenaciously to the secrecy—and stonewalling of accountability—that comes from consolidating information, as, say General Motors does in a financial statement on products as diverse as home appliances and locomotives. These corporations and their legions of friends in Washington usually profess to be economic "conservatives." They are of course nothing of the kind. To be a genuine economic conservative is to believe businessmen and investors respond intelligently to profit opportunities by directing the flow of capital funds into the most efficient enterprises. To respond intelligently they must know what it is they are buying. Businessmen and investors do know "a great deal about small and medium corporations because, almost invariably, such firms are quite specialized," economist Willard Mueller said in 1971. "One need only glance at the annual report of almost any industrial company with annual sales under $50 million to learn its strengths and weaknesses in a line of business. But not so with a large conglomerate corporation whose annual report masks more than it reveals."[19]

Unlike a conglomerate corporation, says economist Walter Adams, Distinguished University Professor at Michigan State University, a professional football team "can't escape scrutiny and public accountability." The coach of, say, the Washington Redskins

may insist on secrecy with respect to strategy and tactics before his team enters competitive combat. But he cannot conceal the performance record after the game. The yards gained by rushing, the yards gained by passing, the fumbles, the interceptions and so forth. He cannot even deny to his competitors access to the game films. It seems that this is what we are talking about. Sure, a corporation has the right to privacy concerning market strategy, market tactics, but it has no right to conceal performance records of the past, if, indeed, it is an organism affected with the public interest.[20]

One could imagine the outcry if the Redskins were to try somehow to conceal their performance record while their rivals were under compulsion to continue to disclose theirs. Yet, Senator Gaylord Nelson (D–Wis.) has pointed out, General Motors, for example, is able to learn or infer much competitively sensitive information about its competitor Maytag's washing machine business by reading Maytag's annual report to stockholders and the SEC, while Maytag can learn nothing at all about GM's washing machine business by reading GM's annual reports.[21]

Nelson described the situation for which the SEC, through Democratic and Republic administrations alike, is dominantly to blame, as "simply not fair." For the broad public, however, the stakes reach far beyond fairness to the use of conglomerate secrecy about multiple lines of business to undercut and frustrate the mission of the Federal Trade Commission (FTC) to make the economy competitive.

In 1947, the FTC began compiling and issuing the *Quarterly Financial Report on Manufacturing*. Government agencies used it, especially for national-income accounting. Thousands of corporations also bought subscriptions. After a time, however, the usefulness of the report eroded seriously. The reason was that the individual categories of "industry" in the report became increasingly distant from the reality, which was that large corporations were increasingly entering multiple industries. In many cases, the "industry" data, Willard Mueller told Nelson's Subcommittee on Monopoly, became "worse than useless." He cited the example of ITT's profits, which are bunched

in a single FTC "industry" despite the fact that nearly half [of them] are earned from foreign operations, another substantial amount from nonmanufacturing industries, and the remainder from such diverse manufacturing industries as electronics, paper, baking, publishing and chemicals.

By 1974, the report had become so misleading that James M. Folsom, acting director of the FTC's Bureau of Competition, would assay it at "about one-third garbage."[22]

Why did it matter? Because the government—and therefore the investment community and the public—were unable to pinpoint the specific industries where sustained excessive prices and profits indicated a lack of competition. With such pinpointing, new competitors would be stimulated to enter lines where profits are abnormally high; without such information they have no such stimulus. Thus, reporting by line of business is procompetitive, to the extent that it is, in the judgment of former FTC Chairman Lewis A. Engman, "vital to the American people."[23] Commission member and former Chairman Paul Rand Dixon, similarly, considers line-of-business reporting "the greatest step forward in the antitrust field" in his lifetime.[24] Being powerfully procompetitive, line-of-business reporting is also proaccountability; consolidated reporting is anticompetitive and antiaccountability.

Congress in creating the FTC authorized it to direct corporations to furnish "such information as it may require as to the organization, conduct, practices, management, and relations to other corporations." Congress further authorized the FTC to require corporations to furnish the specified information in reports that were to take "such form as the Commission may prescribe . . ." The Office of Management and Budget (OMB) in the White House, however, asserted final authority over all federal reporting requirements, even those of nominally independent agencies. In matters of this kind, OMB considers conglomerate corporations, not the agencies, as its natural ally; indeed, President Nixon in 1972 plucked Roy L. Ash from the presidency of Litton Industries, a huge, hokey conglomerate, to be the director of OMB. Even before this, Mueller said, OMB often had been "the errand boy of the advocates of corporate secrecy." Admiral Hyman G. Rickover, blunter still, says OMB "does what big business wants."[25]

What big business wanted was to block the FTC's effort to require line-of-business reporting by the 500 largest corporations. When the FTC moved in late 1970 to require such reporting, OMB squelched it. Its technique was to submit the issue to the Business Advisory Council on Federal

Reports. Of the 29 council members who attended a meeting on the subject, 29—100 percent—were from the top 150 industrial corporations. They voted 29 to 0 against the FTC proposal.[26] Three years later, in 1973, an amendment to the Alaska pipeline law stripped the OMB of its authority over surveys made by all independent regulatory agencies. The Senate approved funds for the FTC to undertake a line-of-business survey of 500 top companies. The House Appropriations Committee then tried to cripple the program by specifying that only 250 firms—too few to be useful—could be surveyed. Finally, a compromise, 345 firms, was devised and added to an unrelated bill—which became the last bill to be vetoed by Richard Nixon. Congress overrode the veto. Then, however, 216 of the 345 firms—their identities secret until Consumers Union threatened to sue the FTC under the Freedom of Information Act—tried to compel the FTC to abandon the program. This failing, 120 of the opponents were fighting in 1975 in the courts.

A final point about this critical episode should be made. By any reasonable yardstick, it is *conservative* to try to give the FTC—and the Antitrust Division of the Justice Department, as well—the facts it needs to enlarge competition. To do the opposite is not to be liberal, either in a classic laissez-faire sense or in a New Deal sense, but simply to be an agent for GM, GE, ITT, Litton, and the rest. Throughout this effort, men commonly termed "liberals"—such as Senator Philip A. Hart (D–Mich.) and Congressman John E. Moss (D–Calif.)—led the fight for openness. Men who like to be and are called "conservatives"—such as Congressman Jamie L. Whitten (D–Miss.) and Senator Roman L. Hruska (R–Neb.), who spearheaded efforts to deny the FTC adequate funds for line-of-business reporting—led the fight for secrecy—or, more specifically, for the continued unaccountability of giant corporations.

The willingness of powerful units of government to work for corporate secrecy was more dramatically illustrated in early 1974, when the Senate Subcommittee on Multinational Corporations disclosed that the Departments of State and Justice actually had bestowed a national-security classification on an agreement among private companies. The classification was the first of its kind, to the knowledge of subcommittee chairman Frank Church (D–Idaho). There was a "second peculiarity," he said: the classification applied specifically only to the American companies that were parties to the agreement—although various foreign firms that also were parties had copies which were unclassified.

The agreement (formally, the Libyan Producers' Agreement) committed the world's major oil companies—American, Belgian, British, Dutch,

French, German, Japanese, Spanish—to a so-called safety-net arrangement: If the Libyan revolutionary regime were to shut down the operations of any of them, the others would make up the lost oil from their own supplies.

The agreement was executed and given a business-review letter—a Justice Department assurance that no antitrust action is contemplated—in January 1971. A news story about this in the *Washington Post* prompted Martin Lobel, a Washington lawyer who was then an aide to Senator William Proxmire (D–Wis.), to request a copy of the agreement from the Justice and State departments. Officials of each assured him he could have one at the conclusion of sensitive price negotiations then under way in Tehran between the companies and Middle East countries. The negotiations ended in February, but the departments stalled again. The phrase "national security" was invoked. Proxmire called a meeting to press for release; but, led by Nathaniel Samuels, a deputy assistant secretary of state, to believe that the agreement had been classified, he backed off. Actually, the agreement had not been classified. This was confirmed later by former Attorney General John N. Mitchell. In a deposition made for the Church subcommittee, Mitchell told staff investigator Jack A. Blum the situation had been simply that the State Department "was supportive of the oil companies' position that it would not be in the interest of the oil companies or in the national interest" for the agreement to be released.

Proxmire's withdrawal left the situation quiet for about two years. Then, in 1973, associates of Ralph Nader filed a suit under the Freedom of Information Act to compel the Department of Justice to disclose all agreements it had administratively exempted from antitrust challenges and the business-review letters attesting to the exemptions. This triggered developments noted in a memo made public by Senator Church. The writer of the memo was W. E. Jackson, a partner in Milbank, Tweed, Hadley and McCloy, a leading Wall Street law firm whose distinctions include the ability to represent twenty or so oil companies at once without seeing a conflict of interest. The recipient was John J. McCloy, *the* oil-industry lawyer and a senior partner in the firm. Writing on April 5, 1973, a few weeks after filing of the Nader suit, Jackson said he had just been told by Gordon S. Brown, an economic-commercial officer of the State Department, that the Justice Department would oppose disclosure of business-review letters and associated materials related to the oil industry. Jackson told McCloy:

The State Department, pursuant to its regulations, has classified the Libyan Producers Agreement and documents relating to it. He (Brown) asked that such documents in our files be so marked and that we ask the American companies involved to do the same with respect to such copies of documents in their possession.

He also asked us not to convey this information to the foreign companies involved unless he advised otherwise. . . .

Nine months later, seeing no point in continuing secrecy for the agreement, Church asked the State Department to declassify it. After some resistance it obliged. [27]

Theodore Roosevelt said, as was noted, that it is essential for the public to have knowledge about the great corporations. The public is denied such knowledge because big government and the big corporation each helps the other guard its turf of unaccountable power. And each is motivated to help the other by a perception that the unaccountability of one interlocks with the unaccountability of the other.

Corporate secrecy is now a formula for keeping the public in ignorance of the public business. The burden of proof is on the secrecy, not on the public access to the corporate information. That is how it henceforth should be.

John Kenneth Galbraith
Senate Testimony

Where should the line be drawn between that corporate information which sensibly should be public and that which properly should be confidential? Our rule-of-thumb is that corporations should not be permitted to keep the public ignorant of the public's business. Does a corporation have information that if not disclosed can be used significantly to imperil the safety or welfare of the public? Or does a corporation have information that if disclosed can be used importantly to advance the public interest? If a corporation has either kind of information, in our judgment, the general rule should be that it should be public, and that a corporation contending to the contrary must carry the burden of proof. The basic rationale is simple: the mission of corporate managers is to make the corporation prosper. The prosperity of the corporation may be either consistent or inconsistent with the public interest. The tendency is to keep secret those things that may profit the corporation but harm the public. Disclosure is therefore required. It is indispensable to corporate accountability.

The tension between corporate secrecy and the public interest seldom emerges in purer form than it did in an extensive correspondence almost a half-century ago between Lammot du Pont, president of E. I. du Pont de Nemours & Company, and Alfred P. Sloan, Jr., president of General Motors Corporation. The issue between them, which we have detailed elsewhere, was whether GM should equip its lowest-priced cars, Chevrolets, with safety glass. Over a period of years, Lammot du Pont tried unsuccessfully to persuade Sloan that GM should do so. His company being the potential supplier and the potential market being enormous, it goes without saying that he was acting in his company's best interest—but he also happened to be acting in the interest of that vast public which on no account should have been denied an elemental protection against preventable automotive death, disfigurement, and injury. Sloan emphatically did not see a congruence between the GM interest and the public safety: "Accidents or no accidents, my concern in this matter is a matter of profit and loss." He acknowledged "the comparatively large return the industry enjoys and General Motors in particular," but said he felt that GM "should not adopt safety glass for its cars and raise its prices even a part of what the extra cost would be. I can only see the competition being forced into the same position." He went on to say:

Our gain would be a purely temporary one and the net result would be that both competition and ourselves would have reduced the return on our capital and the public would have obtained still more value per dollar expended.

A few days later, Sloan dealt with du Pont's point that Ford by then had been using safety glass in windshields for years:

that is no reason why we should do so. I am trying to protect the interest of the stockholders of General Motors and the Corporation's operating position—it is not my responsibility to sell safety glass. . . . You can say, perhaps, that I am selfish, but business is selfish. We are not a charitable institution—we are trying to make a profit for our stockholders.[1]

Sloan really said it all. But he said it in correspondence that escaped public attention for almost forty years and, had it not been for a lawsuit, might have escaped it forever. The point hardly need be argued that a lot of blood would not have been spilled on the highways had there been timely public disclosure of the issues raised by safety glass and certainly by the du Pont–Sloan correspondence.

Since 1966 auto safety has been regulated by an agency of the Department of Transportation. Regulation does not alter the presumption that secrecy is the ally of corporate rather than public interest. Ralph Nader provided this example: "If the auto companies routinely come up to the Department of Transportation and make public speeches saying that they can't increase the safety of cars because it is going to increase the price of cars by x dollars, that should eliminate their claim to secrecy about their cost data, because what they are saying is: "We have information that lives cannot be saved unless the cost of cars goes up. But we are not going to tell the public what the information is, to see whether or not we are telling the truth."[2]

Since the du Pont–Sloan exchange, technology has opened up many new industrial frontiers. This has proliferated opportunities for corporate error and abuse. The impacts are potentially more devastating—consider, say, the damage potential of a supertanker on marine life. At the same time, secrecy has tended to become more rather than less pervasive. The reason is that the corporate dynamic is unchanged. It makes secrecy pay.

A pharmaceutical manufacturer, for example, has large stakes in the confidence of physicians that the benefits of its prescription medicines exceed the risks when they are used as recommended. It is, however, a commonplace occurrence for studies or wide usage to show that a medicine which has won a large market, or has been tried in numbers of humans, is unsafe, or less safe than had been assumed. The company, if it controls the information, then must decide whether to suppress it or report it. Suppression may well serve the company's interest, disclosure the public interest.

The decision often has been to suppress. That was the case with MER/29, a cholesterol-lowering drug which had achieved great popularity. Evidence began to accumulate that the drug caused cataracts and skin and hair afflictions in thousands of persons before sales ended in 1962. The manufacturer, Richardson-Merrell, Inc., suppressed (and falsified) the evidence, was indicted, and, in June 1964, pleaded no-contest. The company had been increasing its sales and profits each year—and it continued to do so after being prosecuted.[3] For the Food and Drug Administration this was an ominous signal, because, as Commissioner Alexander M. Schmidt has said, accurate animal and human test data are "the bedrock" of regulation, and, if not "impeccable," make fulfillment of the agency's consumer-protection mission impossible.[4]

Testifying in the summer of 1975, Dr. Schmidt told Senator Edward M. Kennedy (D–Mass.) that in the preceding five years the FDA had had before it cases of possible criminal withholding of test data by four more pharmaceutical firms. He named three of the firms and the drugs as: Lederle Laboratories—Triflocin, an experimental diuretic found, after being tried in prisoners and others, to cause bladder cancer in laboratory animals; Ayerst Laboratories—Practolol, an experimental heart drug; and Ciba-Geigy Corporation—Slow-K, a diuretic which the FDA judged to have benefits outweighing its risks and approved for sale.

The case of the fourth firm, G. D. Searle & Company, which dominated four days of hearings held by Kennedy's Senate Health and Administrative Practice subcommittees, left Schmidt "alarmed and upset." It is easy to see why.

One of the drugs involved, Flagyl, which is prescribed—or, more precisely, overprescribed—for trichomonas vaginitis, a minor vaginal infection, had been reported by July 1974 to cause tumors or to cause cancer in seven separate studies of laboratory animals. There is consequently a fully warranted scientific concern that it may be tumorgenic or carcinogenic in humans. The second drug in the case is Aldactone, which lowers blood pressure and inhibits salt retention and which causes cancer in rats. The third, Aldactazide, is an overprescribed combination of Aldactone and a diuretic. The FDA in 1976 compelled Searle to adopt a strict new warning label for Aldactone, and removal of Aldactazide from the market was being considered.[5]

All of these drugs entered the market in the early 1960s, have been prescribed millions or tens of millions of times, and are among Searle's "top ten" in sales. In 1972 alone, Aldactazide accounted for revenues of $17.8 million, Aldactone for $9.1 million, and Flagyl for $8.2 million, for a total of $35.1 million. As of 1975, physicians were writing prescriptions for Flagyl alone at a rate of 2.2 million annually. According to the respected *Medical Letter*, symptoms of trichomonas vaginitis often clear in response to such nondrug therapy as avoidance of panty hose, tub baths twice a day, and biweekly douches with a tablespoon of white vinegar in a quart of warm water.[6]

The FDA's concern with Flagyl (metronidazole) as a tumorgen or carcinogen was aroused in 1972, when the *Journal of the National Cancer Institute* published a study showing that the drug caused cancer in mice. The FDA asked Dr. M. Adrian Gross, one of its scientists, to review that study along with a report by Searle on two studies which it had done in rats, which had been submitted to the agency two years before, and which had drawn little or no attention. Gross concluded that Flagyl had "a highly significant" capacity to cause benign tumors or malignancies.

While reviewing the Searle report, Gross became aware of several discrepancies between raw data and the summary of those data. Summaries, of course, are what FDA scientists usually examine, and, as Commissioner Schmidt indicated, the operating assumption is that the data are "impeccable," no matter what differences there may be in interpreting data. Initially, Gross assumed the discrepancies would be readily explainable. The FDA pointed out the discrepancies to Searle representatives on May 31, 1972, when they came to a meeting. "The visitors promised to look into this and provide explanations where needed," the agency said in a memo prepared at the time. There followed in the summer of 1972 several additional meetings and exchanges of letters, partly because the FDA had decided to incorporate a mention of the rodent cancer studies in the labeling, or official prescribing instructions, for Flagyl. Despite the obvious importance of resolving questions about whether a drug used by millions of women might in some of them be carcinogenic, Gross said later in a fifty-six-page memo that Kennedy inserted in the hearing record, "the issue of the discrepancies was not explained to the FDA for nearly two years."

Actually, Searle did not really explain the discrepancies in an open, forthright way even then, and it has not explained at all why it dawdled so long before responding in any fashion. Instead of an explanation, Searle on May 16, 1974, submitted to the FDA an "amended" version of its original, massive, three-volume report. By examining it closely, Gross was able to ascertain that almost every page was identical to the original. But he made a discovery that, he testified, startled him: Searle had revised raw data—which scientists regard as close to sacred—to make them conform to the summary. The effect of the revision was to undergird the implication of Flagyl's safety conveyed by the summary.

Gross particularly emphasized the case of male rat CM 21, a control not treated with the drug. In the original report, a table of raw data listed a benign mammary tumor in CM 21, while a summary table listed a *malignant* mammary tumor—rare in males—in the same animal. Obviously, the more malignancies listed for untreated controls, the safer the drug appears to be. In the revised report, the table of raw data listed CM 21 with a malignant tumor. Searle would later say it had been wrong the first time and blame a typographical error.

The amended report having raised more questions than it answered, the FDA authorized Gross to make an investigation at Searle's plant in Skokie, Illinois. The FDA did not find the experience reassuring. At first, for example, the company claimed not to have key records; then it said they couldn't be found, and finally it produced them, "as if by magic." After some difficulties, Gross got to see a slide of mammary tissue from CM 21, but had reason to wonder if the tissue actually may have been taken from a female rat. In any event, FDA pathologists agreed that even an inexperienced practitioner of their specialty could not possibly have mistaken the malignancy for a benign tumor. Just such a mistake—if that is what it was—had been made by Searle's Dr. John W. Sagartz. In his own handwriting, he had said in postmortem records on most of the animals that various organs "appeared normal and unremarkable" under both gross, or visual, and microscopic examinations. The examinations had been done in the summer and fall of 1967. Sagartz did not come to work at Searle until May 1968. At the hearing, Kennedy released a letter in which a lawyer for Sagartz, by then an Army veterinarian, said that his client had yielded to, but should have resisted, pressures from his immediate superior at Searle, Robert McConnell. Other examples of secretive, furtive, obstructive, or puzzling behavior were cited by Gross and Nancy Ling, an FDA investigator based in Chicago, but they essentially are variations on the themes herein.

Testifying under oath, Gross said that Searle put on a similar "song and dance" in the case of Aldactone. He told, for example, of a presentation made by Searle to an FDA advisory committee in June 1975. The firm screened a transparent slide containing data on rats which had been given the drug. The transparency, Gross protested to Kennedy, showed "no malignant breast tumors whatsoever, when in fact there were tumors." Searle executive vice-president James A. Buzard—also under oath—pounced on Gross's testimony. He produced "the" transparency shown at the meeting and pointed out that it in fact acknowledged four malignancies—not enough, in the judgment of outside experts consulted by Searle, to be statistically significant, in any event.

But under questioning, Buzard made a damaging admission: he had failed to tell the subcommittees that, in addition to "the" transparency, Searle had shown the FDA advisers three other transparencies, none of which mentioned malignancies. He blamed the omission on an innocent keypunch error. He also resolutely denied that Searle ever had tried to mislead the FDA or had engaged in any impropriety. He also offered to help FDA investigator Ling get information which company subordinates had denied her.

More than Buzard's tricky performance about the transparencies hurt Searle's cause. The company previously had tarnished its reputation with questionable promotional activities, including misleading advertising to physicians, on behalf of its birth control pills.[7] There were the two-year silence about the discrepancies in the Flagyl rat data, the odd certifications of John Sagartz, and other gamy episodes. For those attending the hearing, what came through powerfully, even overwhelmingly, were the aromatics of concealment, secrecy, manipulation, and maybe worse—all in the service of an iron determination to further the corporate interest at Lord knows what human cost. Certainly, Senators Kennedy and Richard S. Schweiker (R–Pa.), both of whom listened to the whole story, found the solid, documented version of events given by the FDA's witnesses to be the credible one. On April 7, 1976, Commissioner Schmidt told Kennedy that the FDA would ask the Justice Department to consider convening a grand jury to determine if Searle's conduct of animal testing violated criminal laws.

Other cases involving other companies and other industries differ essentially only in form, particulars, nuance, and impact. With equal reliability, they, too, enlist secrecy to serve the private interest even when to do so is assuredly to dis-serve the public interest. The dynamics of the situation compel this: stockholders—and managements—come first.

Allied Chemical Company knew that workers at a chlorine-gas plant were dangerously exposed to toxic substances but did not tell them.[8] For at least a year, chemical firms in Europe and the United States, along with the Manufacturing Chemists Association, joined in withholding significant findings linking liver cancer to vinyl chloride, the gas used to make one of the commonest plastics, polyvinyl chloride.[9] Campbell Soup Company, backed by the Agriculture Department, refused to disclose the inspection process by which it detects botulism, a sometimes lethal food poisoning.[10] The Justice Department charged Abbott Laboratories with conspiring to sell, and with selling, contaminated intravenous fluids that were associated with 9 fatal and 150 nonfatal blood poisonings; in 1975, after a long legal battle, the firm pleaded no-contest to the conspiracy count in a sixty-count indictment, paid a $1,000 fine, and went about its business as the country's largest supplier of intravenous fluids.[11]

McDonnell Aircraft Corporation once contended to the United States Commission on Civil Rights that the company's affirmative-action plan to increase minority employment was confidential.[12]

The auto-safety law requires manufacturers to give the government copies of all "notices, bulletins and other communications" on safety problems that they send to dealers; General Motors, by using a system of *verbal* communications, long concealed knowledge of defective mounts for V-8 engines in 6.6 million 1965 through 1969 Chevrolet cars and trucks.[13] At Ford Motor Company, manufacturing slipups apparently made body rust a problem among 12 million 1969 through 1972 cars and light trucks. Rather than tell its dealers or customers, it offered free or cut-rate repairs in a confidential 1972 memo to consumer-service managers—an offer that most owners never heard of until columnist Jack Anderson revealed it in 1975, long after the offer had expired.[14]

The Truth in Negotiations Act says that a contractor must disclose costs and profits on contracts with the Pentagon that are obtained through negotiation rather than competitive bidding. In 1974–75, all of the major oil companies, and many smaller ones, refused to comply—and made the refusal stick by withholding fuel needed by the armed services.[15] During the summer of 1975, computer firms, steel and nickel suppliers, and pump manufacturers were among those also refusing to comply.[16] There is no mystery about the reason for noncompliance. It permits secrecy about excessive profits. A study by the General Accounting Office of Navy contracts where cost data were denied showed contractors earning up to 78 percent over costs.[17]

Under the tax laws, all men and corporations are created equal. The laundry worker may be assured that the Internal Revenue Service will show the same respect for the confidentiality of his tax return that it will show for Exxon's. That being the case, the IRS in 1971 naturally had to refuse reporters' requests to name the multinational oil companies that had settled liens for $1 billion for fifty cents on the dollar.[18]

Lawsuits against corporations pose a constant threat of opening closet doors on various and sundry skeletons. One way to keep the doors closed is to sign a consent decree, under which a firm promises the government never to do again what it does not admit ever having done before. This was the case when the auto industry and the government, in 1969, entered into a consent decree. The industry did not admit it had conspired for twenty years to retard development and installation of pollution-control devices, but pledged to engage in no such activity thereafter.[19] We have sampled types of evidence which alone are easily sufficient to overpower defenses of that corporate secrecy which is "a formula for keeping the public in ignorance of the public business." The case was essentially made long ago, and we would be content to rest with it. But two dramatic recent disclosures have pounded finishing nails into the coffin prepared for excessive corporate secrecy. The first disclosure was of massive, secret, and illegal tapping of corporation treasuries to finance domestic election campaigns; the second was of pervasive, systematic corporate influence-buying and outright bribery abroad.

The influence of wealth at elections is irresistible.

Benjamin Rush
Voices of the American Revolution

. . . no man in public office owes the public anything.

Marcus Alonzo Hanna
The History of the Standard Oil Company

The Founding Fathers knew the uses of money in political campaigns. George Washington, running in 1757 for a seat in the Virginia House of Burgesses, won votes in the manner customary for the time: he provided friends with 28 gallons of rum, 50 gallons of rum punch, 34 gallons of wine, 46 gallons of beer, and 2 gallons of cider royal. The voters in his district in Fairfax County numbered 391.[1]

In 1841, soon after taking office, President William Henry Harrison contracted a fatal illness—the presumed result of stress "induced by the press of contributors and workers seeking appointment to office," the late George Thayer said in his fine chronicle of campaign financing, *Who Shakes the Money Tree?*[2]

Writing before the full efflorescence of Watergate was known, Thayer said that the half-century following the election of 1876—approximately from Reconstruction to the Great Depression—was "America's Golden Age of Boodle. Never has the political process been so corrupt." Starting generally with the inception of the Age of Boodle, corporations engaged in the massive industrialization of America began, on a truly grand scale, to make secret election-campaign contributions. The Commonwealth of Pennsylvania became a bazaar for the sale of political power to private power. It produced three United States senators—Simon Cameron (remembered for his aphorism "An honest politician is one who, when he is bought, stays bought"), Matthew Quay, and Boies Penrose—who established that Big Business gladly would invest millions of dollars in campaign "contributions" because the payoff in profits would be enormously greater. Penrose, Thayer said, once spent a half-million dollars "to bribe the necessary members of the Pennsylvania Legislature." Standard Oil was reputed to have done everything to the same legislature except refine it. In the presidential campaign of 1904, a supreme Republican fund-raiser, Marcus Alonzo Hanna,

[w]ith his customary efficiency, . . . shook down the business world for $2.5 million. All major corporations were assessed and most paid with no argument. . . .
In 1905 and 1906, the Legislative Insurance Investigating Committee, or Armstrong Committee, uncovered evidence . . . that a number of large insurance companies had donated sizable sums to several campaigns as far back as 1896, and that such funds were concealed on their books as "legal expenses." Such firms as Aetna, Mutual, New York Life, Equitable and The Prudential, it was revealed, had long used funds belonging to policyholders for a variety of political purposes.[3]

The Framers of the Constitution, of course, had not known that the industrial revolution would hit the United States full blast many decades after they had done their work. They provided no mechanisms other than what Congress and the states might haphazardly devise to cope with concentrated economic power that could buy governments. We were, in a word, caught short.

In 1907, Congress enacted the Tillman Act, which made it a crime to contribute or receive corporate funds for political purposes. Over the following sixty-two years there was a grand total of *two* prosecutions of corporations under this and subsequent election laws. Thus, through the half-century of the Age of Boodle and for more than thirty years afterward there was nothing that remotely could be considered a deterrent to secret, illegal buying of candidates. Thanks to a major effort by former Internal Revenue Service Commissioner Sheldon S. Cohen in the Johnson Administration, sixteen prosecutions were undertaken in 1969 and the first seven months of 1970.

Through most of the twentieth century the principal election law was the Corrupt Practices Act of 1925, which endured until 1972. It appeared to have been designed to make enforcement unlikely and to make no one accountable for nonenforcement. It was no help, either, that honest words such as "bribe" increasingly came to be displaced by euphemisms such as "testimonial dinner." But there is a more fundamental point: until the New Deal began to swell the Washington bureaucracy, the government had—relatively—few "goodies" to dispense or withhold. Its impact on business across-the-board was therefore restricted. In the last four decades, however, as former Watergate Special Prosecutor Archibald Cox has said,

two developments have radically altered the entire context of election financing: The costs of running for office have multiplied geometrically; and more and more business activities have become vitally affected by Government decisions.

Few large donors can say today that they are not and will not be pretty directly interested in some Government decision. This reality confronts those who raise money and those who give it.[4]

The most systematic, relentless, ruthless exploitation of the reality occurred, of course, in the campaign to reelect Richard Nixon, for which at least $60.5 million was raised by the Committee for the Re-election of the President. Heading its money-raising arm, the Finance Committee to Re-elect the President, was Maurice H. Stans, a spiritual protégé of Marcus Hanna, a member of the Certified Public Accountants' Hall of Fame, and, until he became chairman of the Finance Committee, Secretary of Commerce.

One may wonder if his job was not made easier by publicity that, under normal circumstances, would be judged adverse. Newspapers carried stories indicating possible connections between large contributions by oil men and White House generosity to the oil industry, or contributions by the milk lobby and higher subsidies for dairymen, or contributions by steel executives and import quotas on steel, or a pledge by International Telephone and Telegraph to contribute up to $400,000 and the settlement of an antitrust suit against ITT. Surely it is reasonable to assume that numerous economic interests did not need cryptanalysts to decode the message, the White House was, or might be, for sale.

Clearly, contributions, large ones, were in order. But, some fatcats are squeamish. They want to or are willing to give, but crave secrecy—especially when the money they are giving is the corporation's. The problem was ameliorated, oddly enough, by passage of the Federal Election Campaign Act of 1971, the first law seriously designed to require full and timely disclosure of campaign contributions. Despite its title, Congress did not actually send it to the White House until January 19, 1972. It would take effect sixty days after President Nixon signed it. Therein lay his opportunity to provide Maurice Stans with the best possible environment for raising secret money.

The old financing law, the Corrupt Practices Act of 1925, which provided for *some* disclosure, even if inadequate, would expire the moment the new law went into effect. The old law's final reporting period ended February 29; and it would *not* require disclosure of any contributions made on March 1 or thereafter. The new law would not require disclosure until it became effective and would not apply retroactively. Consequently, the longer the President delayed signing the new law, the more time Stans would have to go out and tell the fatcats: Give now because you can give in secret. Had the President signed the law on the day he got it, this black hole of disclosure would have lasted only nineteen days, to March 19. But he delayed until February 7, thereby giving Stans an extra eighteen days. And during that bonus period from March 19 to 12:01 A.M., April 7, 1972, Stans raised many millions of dollars. This is clear in records obtained in a successful lawsuit brought by Common Cause, the citizens' lobby, on the ground that the Finance Committee and its affiliates were required to, but did not, register or file any reports under the 1925 law.

Like Marcus Hanna, Stans "assessed" corporations. He put on the necessary charade, of course, of asking executives to contribute personal funds. As an experienced certified public accountant, he had to know that many of them, while highly compensated, have an expensive lifestyle that does not permit them to write a personal check even for, say, $10,000.

Such men are not to be confused with the "super-rich," as Ferdinand Lundberg called them—William L. McKnight, for example, one of the founders of Minnesota Mining and Manufacturing Corporation. His wealth, as of 1975, was estimated at up to $1 billion. He could write a personal check for $50,000 "without missing it," said Joseph W. Barr, a 3M director who was appointed by the board to investigate illegal contributions of company funds. This was not the case with the professional managers who in the 1960s displaced the founders in running the company. "It sounds funny to people," Barr said in reply to a *New York Times* inquiry, "but a man making a quarter of a million a year is paying out close to $100,000 in taxes. He has $150,000 left over. He's supporting his wife and children and trying to build up an estate." The *Times* account continued:

Such men, Mr. Barr said, "can't write a check for $10,000 when somebody like Stans, or any political fund-raiser, Democrat or Republican, comes around and says, Hey, look boys, you used to give us a quarter of a million. What's happened to you?"

Barr's appraisal had strong support in testimony taken by the Senate Select Watergate Committee in 1973 from two oil executives who were asked by Stans for $100,000 each. Stans did not specifically ask for corporate money, Orin E. Atkins, chairman of Ashland Oil, Inc., and Claude C. Wild, Jr., Washington vice-president of Gulf Oil Corporation, said. But, for contributions of that size, the corporate treasury was, they said, the only realistic source. To assure secrecy, the contributions were made before the stricter disclosure law took effect on April 7, 1972.[5] Draws on the corporate treasury were standard operating procedure. There is no question that executives all over the country did it. William McKnight said, "I don't know that 3M did anything different than a great many other companies did."[6] Yet a few did resist. One was American Motors Corporation. A Stans emissary asked for $100,000, a standard Stans assessment. AMC said no, period.[7]

Stans in 1975, after several months of plea-bargaining with the Watergate special prosecutor, pleaded guilty to five misdemeanor counts involving illegal fund-raising, one of them at 3M. He was fined $5,000. Others who raised, hid, and misused secret cash for Richard Nixon were less fortunate. Herbert W. Kalmbach, the President's personal lawyer, went to prison.

"But what of the root of all this evil?" columnist Clayton Fritchey asked. "What has happened to the corrupters? What punishment has there been for the business executives who set out to subvert the government by trying to buy it with what they knew to be illegal, undercover corporation contributions running into millions?" Fritchey's incisive column went on to state:

For all practical purposes, the corporations and their heads have either gone free, or at most, suffered a slap on the wrist. Not a single tycoon has gone to jail for a single day.

Some, perhaps most, of the fault lies with Special Prosecutors Archibald Cox, Leon Jaworski and Henry S. Ruth, but the Justice Department, the courts, the Congress and some of the government's independent agencies are entitled to a share of the blame. The record of the press is nothing to cheer about either, for if it had been more demanding, the prosecution probably would have been more impressive.

Fritchey, writing in March 1975, emphasized that it is still not known how many corporations contributed to Nixon's $60.5 million, or how much. And, he said,

it doesn't appear that the Special Prosecutor's Office is ever going to find out, for after two years the results are, at best, quite limited.

Back in 1973, under Special Prosecutor Cox, several large companies were allowed to plead guilty to violating the criminal statutes against political contributions by corporations. Nobody would go to jail and the fines would be nominal. That seemed acceptable at the time because the theory was that this would encourage scores, if not hundreds or thousands, of other companies and company heads to come forward and confess their derelictions.

That, however, is not the way it worked out. After all this time, only about 20 or so companies have been charged by the Special Prosecutor and some of them would not have been flushed out at all had it not been for outside investigations by Common Cause, the Ralph Nader teams, the Securities [and] Exchange Commission, the Civil Aeronautics Board and others.[8]

The point deserves emphasis: corporations and executives by the "scores, if not hundreds or thousands," are believed to have violated the criminal code. By doing so they participated in the greatest scandal in the country's history. An extraordinary effort was made to bring them to justice. All but a few escaped accountability. The fervent atmosphere of Watergate reform long since has been transmogrified into a preoccupation with casting and other aspects of a movie about the fine reporters who broke the Watergate scandal, or otherwise has dissipated. Why should a corporate executive fear that, if he should make a secret, illegal contribution, he will be "flushed out"?

A hypothetical, reflective corporate executive might reason that in the unlikely possibility his contemplated violation would be "flushed out" he would need only to be publicly contrite and he would be out of the jam. And the corporation itself: would it suffer? Well, who stopped buying Gulf gasoline? Or flying American?

The executive might finally consider the case of George M. Steinbrenner, III, chairman of American Shipbuilding Company, and a partner in the New York Yankees. An indictment obtained by the office of the Watergate special prosecutor lodged fourteen felony counts against Steinbrenner. They charged him with making a secret, illegal contribution of $100,000 of American Shipbuilding funds to the Nixon reelection campaign; with covering up the use of company funds through a plan, set up in 1970, to pay bonuses to employees that would be kicked back to political campaigns; and with causing employees to cover up the cover-up when interviewed by FBI agents, and to engage in yet another cover-up before a federal grand jury. The charges were the most serious made in connection with illegal campaign contributions in the whole Watergate period. They exposed Steinbrenner to a theoretical maximum of fifty-five years in prison and $100,000 in fines. The prosecution case was powerful.

But what happened? Steinbrenner initially pleaded not guilty. Bargaining ensued. The prosecution, seeking to avoid a trial, agreed to let him plead guilty to one of the fourteen felony counts, making illegal contributions, and to a misdemeanor, devising a cover-up scheme. By so doing he reduced the maximum possible time he could spend in prison to six years. Probation officers for the United States District Court in Cleveland, Ohio, made a presentencing investigation. They found that Steinbrenner, forty-three, had no previous criminal record. Many phone calls were made in his behalf. The Yankees sent a telegram. "There were a lot of letters from quite prominent people—the people you read about in the newspapers," Dominick Lijoi, who prepared the presentencing report, told Bryce Nelson of the *Los Angeles Times*. "My understanding is that he (Steinbrenner) has done a lot of good for deprived kids. The public sentiment has to be taken into account." He also said that federal judges in Cleveland put four out of five first-offenders on probation for nonviolent crimes, that the company's counsel had merely been fined after pleading guilty to a misdemeanor, that the community did not need protection from Steinbrenner ("In fact, he's contributing, not stealing"), and that there was no purpose in sending a man of Steinbrenner's business and social status to prison. The upshot was that probation officials recommended neither prison nor probation—only a fine.[9]

In August 1974, Steinbrenner, accompanied by Edward Bennett Williams, a leading defense lawyer in criminal cases, appeared before Judge Leroy J. Contie, Jr. Since President Nixon had named him to the federal bench three years earlier, he had acquired a reputation for harshness in sentencing.

At the Steinbrenner sentencing proceeding, Thomas F. McBride, a member of Special Prosecutor Jaworski's staff, plainly expected a jail sentence to be imposed. He pointed out to Judge Contie that Steinbrenner's case was distinguished from others involving illegal corporate contributions: while Steinbrenner originally had pleaded innocent, the others had pleaded guilty at the outset—"took their medicine," McBride said.

Contie imposed the maximum allowable fine, $15,000, on Steinbrenner, but did not send him to jail; he did not even put him on probation. For this he offered no explanation from the bench. Bryce Nelson, in an interview, then asked for one. The judge was reluctant to say what it was—to be accountable. "Once you start explaining things," he said, "people start picking them apart. . . . I can't start explaining things to the public." Later in the interview, Contie did say he gives "great weight to the recommendations made by the parole department."

The moral is, the bigger you are, the softer you fall.

He cared nothing about candidates or issues—unless they had some effect on Howard Hughes.

And if they did he figured he could buy his way to favor. "Everybody has a price," he always said. And he was going to offer that price—to a city councilman or the President of the United States.

Noah Dietrich
Howard: The Amazing Mr. Hughes

In addition to industrial corporations, large contributors to political campaigns include a huge and growing array of organized economic interests. The circumstances, dedication, and scruples vary, but all share a common goal of trying to make elected officials dependent upon and beholden to them—and whether the broad public is served thereby is incidental.

For example, three giant co-ops—Associated Milk Producers, Inc.; Mid-America Dairymen, Inc., and Dairymen, Inc.—set out in 1968 to achieve a simple goal: to force up milk prices. One major strategy was to engage in anticompetitive practices (which led finally to successful antitrust suits against them). Another major strategy was to buy decisive influence from elected officeholders and candidates at both the federal and state levels. To this end, the dairymen poured several million dollars into the campaigns of those who might help or hurt them, Republicans and Democrats, state assemblymen, and Presidents. After the lobby pledged $2 million to Richard Nixon's reelection campaign, Agriculture Secretary Clifford D. Hardin, suddenly reversing a days-old decision, raised the level of government support for milk prices. The reversal added an estimated $300 million to dairy farmers' income. The farmers gave millions of dollars out in the open. The average between January 1, 1974, and October 24, 1974, the final day of the last preelection reporting period, was $3,232 per day. Between Election Day in November 1972 and May 31, 1974, they gave eighty-two senators and representatives—one out of seven members of Congress—$213,300. Almost half, $102,450, went to nine members of the House and Senate Agriculture subcommittees with responsibility for milk prices, and another $21,720 went to five other members of the full House Agriculture Committee. Congressman David R. Bowen (D–Miss.) was assigned to the House milk-price subcommittee in February 1973; by the end of May 1974, the co-ops had given him at least $30,000.[1] In 1972, the co-ops proved to be adept at timing legal contributions so that disclosure would be delayed until after the polls had closed. The open contributing aside, however, Associated Milk Producers, largest of the three co-ops, also gave hundreds of thousands of dollars secretly and illegally.[2]

Throughout the last century, a goodly number of persons and families have tapped private fortunes to buy what they wanted from elected officials. Secrecy has attended such transactions not only because of a generalized preference for it, but also because some contributors were seeking to buy appointments to public office, especially ambassadorships, in violation of the criminal code. Such sales peaked in the Nixon Administration, which nominated thirty-one known contributors as ambassadors.[3] The Senate Foreign Relations Committee, overcoming fitful nausea, confirmed them. Ruth Farkas, a department-store millionairess, secretly contributed $300,000 in full assurance that she would be named an ambassador—and was named ambassador to Luxembourg. Cornelius V. Whitney, president of Whitney Industries and operator of a racing stable, made a secret $250,000 contribution in the expectation that he would be named ambassador to Spain, but asked for and got a refund when President Nixon was prevailed upon by the State Department not to nominate him.[4] Herbert W. Kalmbach, President Nixon's former personal counsel and former vice-chairman of the Finance Committee to Re-elect the President, promised an ambassadorship to J. Fife Symington, Jr., in return for a secret $100,000 contribution. Symington became the envoy to Trinidad and Tobago. The late Vincent de Roulet had been a generous contributor to Richard Nixon, as had been his mother-in-law, the late Joan Whitney Payson, president of the New York Mets. He became ambassador to Jamaica. While in that post, he agreed to make a $100,000 contribution to Nixon's 1972 campaign in exchange for an ambassadorship in Europe, Kalmbach has testified.

Even if personal gain in any ordinary sense may not be involved, the desire for secrecy sometimes leads to intricate schemes for concealment. A *Washington Post* investigation established that oil tycoon Leon Hess, chairman and chief executive of Amerada Hess Corporation, routed $135,000 to the late Isidore (Irving) Warshauer, an obscure certified public accountant in New York. Warshauer, his wife, and thirteen other persons—relatives, friends, business associates, and a client's widow (who said later, "I never gave away any money to anybody for President")—then were credited by the Finance Committee to Re-elect the President with contributions of $9,000 each, or a total of $135,000.[5] The *Washington Star* subsequently reported that Hess earlier had used the same set of conduits to contribute $225,000 in personal funds to the bid of Senator Henry M. Jackson (D–Wash.) for the 1972 Democratic presidential nomination. In both cases, Hess reportedly was trying to head off Senator George S. McGovern.[6]

In a class by himself, however, was the late billionaire Howard Robard Hughes. His secrecy about his political investments was in keeping with his fanatic personal reclusiveness. But by firing a couple of his closest aides, Noah Dietrich and Robert A. Maheu, Hughes inadvertently assured that a huge amount of closely held information would surface.

Dietrich, Hughes' chief executive officer from 1925 to 1957, wrote a candid, revealing, and fascinating book, *Howard: The Amazing Mr. Hughes.*[7] In 1972, the year in which *Howard* was published, Hughes held a disembodied telephone news conference. Speaking of Maheu, whom he had fired in 1970 as chief of Hughes' Nevada Operations, Hughes said, "He's a no-good, dishonest son-of-a-bitch and he stole me blind." This struck Maheu as more than unkind. He filed a massive defamation suit. In a deft stroke, his lawyer, Morton R. Galane, named as defendant not Hughes personally, but Summa Corporation, which is wholly owned by Hughes, as was its predecessor, Hughes Tool Company. The suit succeeded. On December 5, 1974, a United States District Court jury in Los Angeles awarded Maheu a $2,823,333.30 vindication.

During the pretrial period, Howard M. Jaffee, a Hughes lawyer, took a deposition from Maheu. On July 4, 1973, brushing aside a firm warning from Maheu against exploring "the political world of Howard Hughes," Jaffee persisted in asking questions about that world. At Galane's instruction, Maheu answered. His story, revealed under oath in two days of direct and cross examination, was consistent with the story Dietrich had revealed in his book. Both stories were consistently astonishing.

Dietrich: "During the late 1940s and throughout the 1950s Howard's political contributions ran between $100,000 and $400,000 per year. He financed Los Angeles councilmen and county supervisors, tax assessors, sheriffs, state senators, and assemblymen, district attorneys, governors, congressmen, and senators, judges—yes, and Vice-Presidents and Presidents, too."[8] (Dietrich, whose story is too rich and full to be done justice in a summary, himself structured a Hughes Tool subsidiary in Canada so that its profits could be adjusted to produce whatever sums Frank J. Waters, a Hughes conduit, said he needed for political contributions in the United States.[9])

Maheu said he once told Thomas G. Bell, a Las Vegas lawyer who was a conduit for Hughes cash in Nevada, of "the desire of Howard Hughes to own all the officials in Nevada. . . . He wanted every politician, at whatever level, beholden to him." The cash flowed in underground rivers from the "proprietor's drawing account" at the Silver Slipper Casino, a Las Vegas gambling establishment of which Hughes was the sole owner, and consequently was not illegal corporate money. From time to time, Maheu said, Bell "would inform me that he had, pursuant to Mr. Hughes' instructions, covered all the bases in Las Vegas, the County of Clark and the State of Nevada." Bell himself, in a deposition detailed in the *Washington Post*, named eighty-two Nevada candidates who in 1969, the year before they ran for election or reelection, got $385,000—mostly in currency—from the "proprietor's drawing account." The recipients included the Democrat who ran for governor and won and the Republican who lost, two state supreme court justices, the state attorney general, the state comptroller, twenty-seven legislative candidates, aspirants to the bench in lower courts, and candidates for commissionerships of Clark County, regent posts at the University of Nevada, district attorney, city commissioner of Las Vegas, and justice of the peace.[10]

In 1967 or 1968, Maheu recalled, Hughes gave him a written directive to contribute, "I believe, $50,000," to Nevada's senior senator, Alan Bible (D), and in 1970 "authorized" for the reelection campaign of the state's junior senator, Howard W. Cannon (D), "at least initially," $70,000. In a sworn financial summary, Richard A. Ellis, a certified public accountant retained by Maheu, said that between January 1, 1965, and April 30, 1970, Maheu was the pass-through for more than $300,000 that flowed from Hughes' "personal account" in Los Angeles, which was administered by his secretary, Nadine Henley, and which also was identified as "Hughes Productions." The recipients were designated in phone calls to Maheu from "a fellow by the name of Bart Evans" at Hughes Aircraft, Ellis said. Alan Cranston (D–Calif.), a United States senator since 1968, was listed for $65,000. Sums of similar magnitude went to John V. Tunney (D), now the junior senator from California, and George Murphy (R), whom Tunney defeated in 1970; several senators from other states; and, in California, Democratic and Republican governors, congressmen, and mayors.[11]

Mainly from the "proprietor's drawing account" and "Hughes Productions," Hughes, in each case covertly, twice gave $50,000 in currency to Charles G. (Bebe) Rebozo that was "ear-marked" for Rebozo's intimate friend President Nixon. A few days after giving $50,000 to Nixon–Agnew committees for the 1968 presidential campaign, he had $50,000 in checks —signed by, and drawn on the account of, former Nevada Governor Grant

Sawyer—delivered to Nixon's opponent, then–Vice-President Hubert H. Humphrey.

Hughes didn't engage in secret political investments for the hell of it; he wanted things. He tried to get the Johnson Administration to cancel underground nuclear tests that might hurt the $300 million Hughes' Nevada Operations, which included the Silver Slipper and five casino-hotels. He wanted and got Justice Department antitrust clearance for acquisition of a sixth casino-hotel, although the deal fell through. The dangers to democratic process posed by the embodiment of nearly unlimited wealth, power lust, and secrecy in the late Howard Hughes may be indicated by an excerpt from the *Washington Post* story:

At a meeting in 1967 with Raymond M. Holliday, then chief executive of the Hughes Tool Co., "I [Maheu] showed Mr. Holliday a handwritten memorandum from Mr. Hughes where Mr. Hughes was asking me to make a million-dollar payoff to a President of the United States. Mr. Holliday fainted, dropped the yellow sheet of paper on the floor, and requested of me whether or not his fingerprints could be taken off the piece of paper."[12]

During most of America's industrial century, the threat of secret campaign contributions that corrupt the electoral process came mainly from corporations, banks, and fatcats. They had the money. Industrial unions generally were poor, oppressed, struggling, bloodied by Pinkertons and the police, trampled on by biased laws and Neanderthal judges. The New Deal began to change all of this drastically, especially with the National Labor Relations Act. Starting about 1936, unions became a counter-source of big political money and power. Sometimes they made secret contributions from union treasuries. When John L. Lewis was asked to divulge the source of nearly $500,000 for President Franklin D. Roosevelt's reelection campaign in 1936, George Thayer said, Lewis's reply was, "I'll tell you where it came from. Right here, from the coffers of the United Mine Workers of America. It came by request of the President of the United States through one of his trusted aides."[13]

In 1943, Congress made it a criminal offense to give or receive general union funds for political purposes. Despite this and subsequent laws intended to impose equal restraints on unions and corporations, violations have continued. Prosecutions have been few, but doubtless understate the reality. In addition, there are many highly questionable circumventions. But it must be said that the political arms of the AFL-CIO and the United Automobile Workers, in particular, frequently transcend parochial concerns, and push for legislation important to nonunion as well as union workers, such as occupational health and safety laws. Often, too, these political arms of labor provide truly critical muscle for *pro bono publico* causes, such as efforts to enact civil-rights, consumer, and health-insurance laws, and to prevent tax and other rip-offs.

Granted all of that, when government has a significant role in determining how a company fares, the company and the union tend to perceive a common interest that binds them together. Often both respond with political largess. This is emphatically the case in an extraordinarily parasitic industry, shipping. Shippers want lavish federal subsidies; shipping unions want them to have the subsidies. Consequently, politicians positioned to be influential rake in campaign contributions from both sides, while taxpayers rake in bills. Consider these events of the year 1970 and related *sequelae:*

• The House Merchant Marine and Fisheries Committee voted a subsidy for the shipping industry which exceeded the sum in the White House budget by $124.3 million. Of the thirteen members who voted for this, the *Wall Street Journal*'s Jerry Landauer reported, ten regularly got campaign contributions from the Seafarers International Union (SIU), AFL–CIO.[14] Few organizations are more proficient at handing out money to elected officials than the SIU. It pays a $1,000 honorarium, for example, to a congressman who comes to a SIU breakfast to read a SIU-prepared speech.[15] The SIU is also expert at raising the money it gives away, as Landauer also has reported. Its political arm, while getting $5 or $10 per person from SIU members who are American citizens, has extracted as much as $500 a year each from hundreds of foreign nationals who cannot vote in our elections but who want to work on high-wage American ships.[16]

The Justice Department obtained an indictment of the SIU for violating the prohibition on contributing general union funds—specifically, for contributing up to $750,000 from those funds through SPAD (Seafarers' Political Action Donation Committee) between 1964 and 1968. On the ground that the department had failed for two years to press the case, a United States district judge dismissed the case in May 1972; and for reasons that struck knowledgeable persons as lame, the Justice Department did not appeal. After the final preelection reporting deadline for campaign contributions had passed, but before the November election, SPAD contributed $100,000—which it had borrowed for the purpose—to the Finance Committee to Re-elect the President. Recipients of any contribution of $5,000 or more were required by law to notify federal election auditors by telegram within forty-eight hours of receipt. The committee disclosed the SPAD gift four months later, on January 31, 1973.

• American President Lines and Pacific Far East Lines pleaded guilty to having contributed—secretly, of course—a total of $8,200 to House and

Senate candidates, of both parties, in the 1966 and 1968 elections.[17] A lobbyist explained how simple it all was: "I'd have a Congressman to lunch and present him with a contribution."[18] A former chairman of House Merchant Marine, Albert Bonner, used to boast that when he played gin rummy with shipping executives, he rarely lost.[19]

• In Ottawa, Canada, the SIU was disclosed to have made campaign contributions—none exceeding $500—to four members of the cabinet of Prime Minister Pierre Elliott Trudeau. He said he himself had not received a SIU contribution, but "wouldn't be worried about if if I had." His wife, Margaret, turned out to have accepted a free trip to Japan, to participate in the launching of a tanker, as the guest of a ship owner.[20]

The electoral process in a democracy is subverted when the governed are unable to learn, fully and promptly, who gives how much to whom in campaigns to elect those who govern them. It has been seriously subverted for a century.

Belated but heartening steps forward have been taken in recent years. In addition to the 1971 strict-disclosure law, Congress, in 1974, enacted new legislation that limits contributions by individuals and expenditures by candidates. Several states, in addition, have reformed laws controlling elections for state offices. It would be misleading, however, to suggest that such reforms are a cure-all for the ills of election financing. For one thing, the provisions and mechanisms for disclosure are defective. Under the 1974 law, no contribution made ten days preceding an election, unless it is $1,000 or more, need be disclosed until after the election. More important, news media sometimes have failed to dedicate the resources needed to permit swift and full reporting of the voluminous records that become available.

Another defect in the new law, and a grave one, is that it fails to put adequate curbs on contributions by "political committees." These sometimes engage in what Brooks Jackson of the Associated Press, a Washington reporter expert in election financing, termed "quasi-bribery." He cited the example of the political committees of the maritime unions, principally the Seafarers and the Marine Engineers Beneficial Association (MEBA), also AFL–CIO. These unions wanted and were determined to procure passage of a bill that would require increasing proportions—eventually 30 percent—of imported oil to be carried in tankers flying the American flag and crewed by American seamen. This would add many billions of dollars to the costs of imported oil. Nonetheless, the House passed the bill in May 1974, and the Senate four months later—although President Ford vetoed it. Between January 1, 1974, and October 24, 1974, the last day of the final preelection reporting period, an unofficial tabulation showed that the political arms of the Seafarers and MEBA contributed nearly $800,000 to congressional races. Of the 266 representatives who voted for the bill, 138 received about $226,000; of the 42 senators who voted for it, 18 were listed for about $194,000. The 22 members of both bodies that voted against the bill together got only $28,400.

The principal beneficiaries included Senator Mike Gravel (D–Alaska), who got $21,300 plus a $25,000 "loan" (later "forgiven"); Senator Russell B. Long (D–La.), the bill's floor manager, and chairman of the Senate Finance Committee and the Senate Commerce Merchant Marine Subcommittee, $22,000; John Glenn, who unseated Senator Howard Metzenbaum (D–Ohio) in the primary, $20,000; Metzenbaum, $13,000; Senator Charles McC. Mathias (R–Md.), $19,000; Senator Alan Cranston (D–Calif.), $18,000; Senator Bob Packwood (R–Ore.), $13,000; Congressman Frank M. Clark (D–Pa.), a member of House Merchant Marine, $18,500, and Congressman Leonor K. Sullivan (D–Mo.), chairman of the House committee, $5,500.[21]

By 1975, benefits to the maritime industry—direct subsidies, various regulations, and tax advantages—were estimated to be flowing at a rate of $1 billion a year. As if this were not enough, the Senate Commerce Committee in June 1975 approved a bill empowering the Federal Maritime Commission to force independent ship operators to *raise* their rates to levels approximating those of established lines. The bill's principal sponsor and shepherd was Senator Daniel K. Inouye (D–Hawaii). He had introduced the bill in 1973, after the maritime unions had contributed $10,000 to his campaign organization, and reintroduced it in 1975, again after the unions had contributed $10,000. He insisted, predictably, that his introduction of the bills and the contributions were unrelated. He could also have said that he really didn't need the money, having had no opposition in the 1974 primary, having gone on to seek reelection without a Republican opponent, and having won with almost 83 percent of the vote.[22]

Federal law provides criminal penalties for an official convicted of taking "illegal gratuities." He must not, that is, take anything of value "for himself" "for or because of" an official act, even if he would have done the identical act in the normal course of his duties. Under the ban on "illegal gratuities," a tax accountant was convicted because he had made "Christmas gifts" of $25 and $50 to Internal Revenue Service agents for going easy in auditing his clients. Is a campaign contribution given "for or because of" an official act an illegal gratuity? Legislators legally receiving campaign contributions get them through committees they or aides set up for that purpose. According to a court decision cited by Brooks Jackson, a contribution made to such a legislator's committee cannot be an illegal gratuity unless the prosecution proves the committee was his "alter ego" or was used as a conduit to him. Jackson wrote in the *New Republic:*

If it is bad public policy to allow an IRS agent to take a $25 gift for a soft tax audit, is it not as bad to let a senator take $20,000 while helping to get more government subsidies for a maritime union that gave the money? It is probably worse, because the public treasury loses hundreds of millions of dollars in maritime subsidies but only a relative handful of dollars through the chiseling of a single IRA agent.

Jackson proposed a cure: "either to limit the size of special-interest donations or eliminate them entirely." The 1974 election law does neither. It permits any special interest calling itself a "political committee" to give a candidate $5,000 in the primary and another $5,000 in the general election. It should be noted that the American Medical Association and its affiliates in the states and the District of Columbia have more than fifty legally independent "political committees." Between Election Day in November 1972 and October 14, 1974, these units contributed approximately $1.5 million to more than 300 House incumbents—of whom 114 were sponsors of Medicredit, the AMA proposal for national health insurance. There were no strong countervailing pressures on these congressmen from sick people, Jackson pointed out.[23]

Conceivably, special-interest contributions could be eliminated were we to go to a system of public financing of congressional elections; the 1974 law provides public financing only for presidential elections. But election laws alone should not be expected to shoulder the heavy burden of eliminating the power and privileges of special interests in politics. "Until monopolies, polluting industries, price-fixers, closed-shop unions, lobbyists, elitist professions, and the like are brought to heel, it is unreasonable to expect them to be brought under control in our political process," George Thayer correctly said.[24]

Corporate Bribery

What was disturbing was not just the huge bribes themselves; but the fact that they could for so long, and so effectively, have been buried within the company accounts. The ability of a giant corporation, in spite of its auditors, thousands of shareholders and elaborate controls, to conceal such huge sums through underground routes, spotlighted the fact that the big oil companies were, in both the technical and general sense, unaccountable.

Anthony Sampson
The Seven Sisters:
The Great Oil Companies and the World They Shaped

In making illegal contributions to election campaigns in the United States, corporations essentially were making secret investments. They had at least a reasonable expectation that the investments would yield large returns. Abroad, political contributions, influence-buying and outright bribes also bring large returns. To assume that corporations making illegal contributions in the United States would not also be making corrupt payments abroad would be illogical on the face of it. Indeed, influence-buying and buying abroad have the advantage not only of apparently not violating the laws of the United States, but also of often being deductible as ordinary and necessary business expenses.

Another consideration for a large company is that it can easily hide and "launder" cash through one or another of its international operations. Such operations sometimes are already being used for other corporate purposes. Gulf Oil Corporation, for example, had a subsidiary in the Bahamas which it used to set artificial prices for crude; the same subsidiary was the source of $125,000 secretly and illegally contributed by the company's top lobbyist, Claude C. Wild, Jr., to presidential candidates in 1972.

The immorality of bribery is peripheral to our immediate case: when a large corporation, especially one that feeds from the public trough, such as Lockheed Aircraft, spends corporate funds to grease outstretched palms anywhere, the government, the public, and the stockholders—the nominal owners—have an undiluted right to know about it.

"The men who run global corporations are, as a group, neither more nor less moral than the politicians they seek to buy," Richard J. Barnet, co-author of *Global Reach: The Power of the Multinational Corporations,* has said.

Corporate planners have become a public menace not because they have no con-science but because they have too much power in the making of crucial public decisions. They are accountable to no one. (No proxies are solicited when corpora-tions contemplate investments in foreign elections or "destabilization" of foreign governments. No regulatory agencies are informed.) As long as the fundamental credo of the corporation remains grow or die and the global giants battle with one another for ever greater shares of the market, it is naive to expect that protection of the public interest can safely be left in private hands. . . .

When a corporation reaches the size and power sufficient to dominate the politi-cal life of whole communities, it is no longer just a piece of private property. It is a social institution and our laws must reflect that reality.[1]

Until the 1970s the American foreign policy clandestinely and corruptly conducted by giant American-based corporations was almost unknown to the American public. The global story began to come out in 1972 as a result of the investigation into the Watergate break-in. More disclosures followed over the next three years as the result of investigations by the press; federal agencies, including the office of the special Watergate prosecutor; and the Senate Select Watergate Committee, headed by Senator Sam J. Ervin, Jr. (D–N.C.). Initially, the Securities and Exchange Commission aggressively developed available leads, thereby carrying out its mission of trying to assure adequate disclosure of corporate activities, as did the Senate Subcommittee on Multinational Corporations, headed by Senator Frank Church (D–Idaho). Shortly, however, the SEC and Congress allowed to develop a system of voluntary "disclosure" in which more than one hundred large corporations (by May 1976) had acknowledged substantial illegal or improper payments but got away with absolute concealment of the vital facts: who paid how much to whom?

Our purpose here is a relatively narrow one: primarily to establish that corporations use secrecy massively and systematically to evade accountabil-ity. That purpose will be adequately served if we highlight a few major cases involving secret corporate funding of political candidates in the United States, where all corporate contributions in federal elections have been illegal for almost seventy years; secret bribing and political funding abroad; and influence-buying everywhere.

Lockheed Aircraft Corporation. Lockheed, the largest defense contractor and builder of the TriStar L–1011, a wide-bodied "Jumbo" jet airliner, began to emerge as a top bribe-payer in June 1975, when Thomas V. Jones, chief executive of Northrop Corporation, testified before the Senate Subcommittee on Multinational Corporations. In preparation for the hearing, the subcommittee had obtained a report which showed that Northrop had made a contract with a Swiss firm to get foreign customers, but to do so in ways Northrop preferred not to hear about. A Lockheed contract had been the model. "I simply inserted Northrop for Lockheed," Northrop consultant Frank J. DeFrancis said.

On June 10, 1975, four days after Lockheed's role as a model in bribery for Northrop had surfaced, Lockheed itself appeared onstage. The company was "not aware why Northrop compares itself to Lockheed," a spokesman primly told Robert M. Smith of the *New York Times.* Lockheed, he insisted, "carefully kept all dealings with consultants within the letter and spirit of foreign laws."

Lockheed's auditors refused to certify its financial statements, which the company had to send out to stockholders for the annual meeting on July 18, unless Lockheed acknowledged that bribes had been paid to foreign officials, and unless it defined the extent of such payments. Meanwhile, the loan board was talking with the auditors. By all accounts, neither the auditors, the board, the SEC, nor Congress' General Accounting Office, which under the loan-guaranty law monitored Lockheed, had known of the bribes. Finally, the pressures became too great for Lockheed, and it buckled.

On August 1, 1975, Lockheed issued a press release that stripped away its pretense of dealing with consultants always "within the letter and spirit of foreign laws." Since 1970, Lockheed admitted, it had paid out at least $22 million, which, to its knowledge or belief, went to officials and political organizations in numerous foreign countries. During the same period, it had obligated itself to pay consultants—legitimately or illegitimately retained to expand foreign sales—a mind-boggling $202 million. Moreover, Lockheed conceded, it had maintained a secret fund of some $750,000 from which it had paid $290,000 in commissions and "other payments." The fund was slush, an honest word understandably spurned by Lockheed in favor of mush: the fund was kept "outside the normal channels of financial accountability." Later, after Treasury Secretary William E. Simon characterized Lockheed payments to foreign officials as "bribes," Daniel J. Haughton, then chairman of Lockheed, choked on that precise word, saying that Roger A. Clark, an attorney in Rogers & Wells, the law firm of William P. Rogers, the former attorney general and secretary of state, preferred to call the payments "kickbacks." The preference possibly was based not on a fastidious taste for nuance, but on a theory that bribes are not tax-deductible while "kickbacks" might be.

While other company executives apologized or expressed a feeling of shame for conduct similar to Lockheed's, that corporation accentuated the positive. Foreign commissions and "other payments," Lockheed said, "were necessary in consumating foreign sales," and, moreover, were "consistent with practices engaged in by numerous other companies abroad, including many . . . competitors, and are in keeping with business practices in many foreign countries." If for any reason Lockheed should be unable "to conform to local competitive business practices," the result would be to "seriously prejudice the company's ability to compete effectively in certain foreign markets." And naming the recipients could have "serious adverse impact" on an unspecified share of foreign orders of $1.6 billion. These arguments amounted to an assertion of "a right to bribe in order to do business abroad and thus stay afloat," said the *Washington Post*'s Jack Egan.

The government itself was being edged toward the pit, having become a partner of Lockheed when, in 1971, it enacted the Emergency Loan Guarantee Act. "What are the government's interests in further protecting Lockheed . . . if it needs to resort to bribes to sell its products abroad?" Egan wondered.

The next developments came from an investigation made by Senator William Proxmire (D–Wis.), chairman of the Senate Banking Committee, and Richard F. Kaufman, an aide who specializes in defense procurement.

Proxmire set a hearing for August 25, 1975, on whether provisions of the emergency-loan law had been violated. The law is administered by a board consisting of the secretary of the treasury, Simon; the chairman of the Federal Reserve Board, Arthur F. Burns; and the chairman of the SEC, Ray D. Garrett, Jr.

At the hearing, Simon came down hard on Lockheed:

As a Government official who has spoken out about the importance of maintaining the free enterprise system, I find Lockheed's actions deplorable. . . . Practices such as bribes made to secure foreign business can only increase the distrust and suspicion that is straining our national institutions. To argue that bribes to foreign officials are necessary for effective competition is contrary to every principle under the free market system.

Furthermore, Simon was "distressed that the Government has been involved, even if indirectly, in the L–1011 program if, as intimated by Lockheed, that program is partially dependent upon bribes for its success."[2] But Simon did not match his rhetoric with action: the board continued as before to make good on the guarantee. Arthur Burns, testifying at an unrelated hearing on October 8, 1975, told Proxmire he regretted that he had endorsed the loan-guarantee legislation in the first place.

Lockheed, even aside from the loan-guarantee legislation, always seemed to have had extraordinarily close ties to the government. In documents made public on September 11, on the eve of a hearing, the multinationals subcommittee revealed a pattern of close cooperation between government agencies and Lockheed in promoting its sales—sales facilitated by bribes.

One set of papers involved Indonesia, where a coup deposed President Sukarno. Concerned about the status of its agent in Indonesia, a firm headed by Izaac Dassad, who had been close to Sukarno, Lockheed asked the United States Embassy in Jakarta to assess Dassad's standing with the successor government, headed by President Suharto. The checking was done by "embassy CIA personnel." The CIA found Dassad to be "in." Later, however, Dassad fell out of favor with the regime and, consequently, with Lockheed. Company officials then agonized over pressures to pay bribes to Indonesian Air Force officials. Drawing on the Lockheed memoranda, William H. Jones reported in the *Washington Post:*

"If such payments should some day become public knowledge," wrote Lockheed officials P.F. Dobbins and T.J. Cleland, "the repercussions could be damaging to Lockheed's name and reputation."

In addition, they wrote their superiors, Lockheed had no way of writing off such payments as deductions that would be permitted by the Internal Revenue Service. [Lockheed Chairman Haughton later revealed that the company had claimed direct bribes as business deductions.] But, if Lockheed failed to go along with the bribe payments, the firm would stand to lose some $300,000 in annual spare parts sales, and sales of eight airplanes in 1973–74 estimated at $40 million, they said. The superiors of Dobbins and Cleland later advised them that the Indonesian Air Force must be convinced of the need for an agent to pass through payments, because of the "significant protection provided for them as well as for us," and because there would be no reduction in the amount of bribe money going to the Air Force.

A "reasonable" scale of commissions was said to be 3 per cent for airplanes and 5 per cent on other sales, with a ceiling of 10 per cent on smaller parts.

In the Philippines, Lockheed agent Buddy Orara told in a memo of a requirement to pay off not only government officials, but also Army officers and journalists. "As you know, moving around in the local circles for this kind of objective (sales of planes) involves financial requirements," Orara said.

In Saudi Arabia, the government in 1969 issued a decree requiring all aerospace procurement contracts to contain a clause specifying that no agent had been used to make sales, and saying also that agents' fees, if any were discovered to have been paid, would be deducted from the final price paid by the government. But in one of the papers released by the subcommittee, a Lockheed official said that the company had "full intention of paying our representative his usual fees . . . and ignoring the . . . clause." At the subcommittee hearing on September 12, Lockheed's Haughton testified that during the preceding five years, the firm had paid $106 million to Saudi entrepreneur Adnan N. Khashoggi, with a substantial portion of the money going to Saudi officials—under the table—to approve purchases of Lockheed products. Khashoggi, whose firm, Triad, is the first multinational conglomerate in the Arab world, denied the charge. Other bribes went directly to Saudi officials through numbered bank accounts in Switzerland and Lichtenstein.

Senators questioning Haughton were sometimes angry, while he was calm and sometimes unresponsive. Referring to Lockheed's "dubious tax deductions," Senator Clifford P. Case (R–N.J.) expressed revulsion that tax deductions could be claimed for "corruption of people in power." He told Haughton, "I'm sorry for you." Haughton claimed, as would be expected, that bribes had to be paid in order to compete against aerospace firms based here and abroad. But when Senator Joseph R. Biden, Jr. (D–Dela.) pressed for details on how other manufacturers, including those in the Soviet Union, participated in a payoff system, Haughton and other Lockheed officials were unable to supply any. Biden accused Haughton of giving "phony" answers and of "reprehensible" and "lousy" conduct in paying bribes on the basis of mere "gossip" about competitors. Under Biden's questioning, moreover, Haughton pretty much admitted that Lockheed gets a bonus from bribery by computing its profits on the basis of total cost—which is simply inflated to include bribes.

Senator Church proceeded to establish a crucial point: Lockheed had paid bribes to sell aircraft for which no competition existed. Why had it done so? the senator asked William W. Cowden, a Lockheed sales manager. "Because we are competing," Cowden replied, "for the dollars that would be spent on something else." "Such as?" Church inquired. "Such as guns," Cowden answered. "Such as Kellogg's Corn Flakes," Church retorted. He went on to make one of the most telling and depressing points in the whole sordid business:

This is where the whole practice becomes so venal. You force these governments in the direction of arms purchases, whereas other purchases might be more advantageous to them and their people.

When you pass fat wads of money to these foreign officials, you greatly influence whether they are going to buy an airplane or whether they are going to buy some wheat.[3]

Early 1976 brought sensational new disclosures. On February 4, the Multinational Subcommittee revealed that Lockheed had paid commissions of up to $7 million to its secret agent in Japan, Yoshio Kodama. A convicted war criminal, he became, Senator Church said, "a prominent leader of the ultra right wing militarist political faction in Japan." Kodama even had come to play a role in the selection of several Japanese prime ministers after World War II. Much of the $7 million had been paid by Lockheed in connection with a $130 million deal for sale of its TriStars to Japan's domestic airline. "In effect," Church said in opening the hearing, "we have had a foreign policy of the United States Government which has vigorously opposed this [ultra right-wing] political line in Japan and a Lockheed foreign policy which has helped to keep it alive through large financial subsidies in support of the company's sales efforts in this country." In theory, the President was accountable for the official foreign policy, but where was the accountability for the contrary Lockheed foreign policy? "It is difficult to imagine how Lockheed could have done more harm to American-Japanese relations," Marius B. Jansen, professor of Japanese history at Princeton, said in a letter to the *New York Times* published eleven days after the hearing.

An embarrassed American Embassy in Tokyo is headed by a recent Lockheed vice president [James D. Hodgson]. A friendly government is hard put to answer the taunts of an indignant opposition. East Asia's sole democracy, the proud product of decades of American-Japanese cooperation, stands weakened—not by the left but by Lockheed.

All told, Lockheed's payoffs in Japan, over a period of twenty years, amounted to $12.6 million, and were made mainly through Kodama to top government officials. Many of the details of bribes paid in the late 1950s, in connection with the sale of Lockheed's F–104 fighters, were reported at the time to the CIA in Washington, Ann Crittenden reported in the *New York Times* on April 2, 1976. On the basis of information from former CIA officials and Japanese sources, she said that Kodama, while not identified as a CIA agent, "has had a long-standing relationship with American Embassy officials in Japan. In addition, Mr. Kodama was the recipient of American funds for covert projects on several occasions . . ." The implication was clear enough: a secret collaboration of two titans of unaccountability, Lockheed and the CIA, that undermined official American foreign policy. Where the President at the time, Dwight Eisenhower, was in all of this, was unclear.

The February 4 Church hearing also brought out that in addition to the $7 million it paid Kodama, Lockheed in the previous five or six years had paid commissions or bribes of $8 million more to agents in Japan, Germany, Italy, France, and Turkey. ". . . we will see that Exxon and the CIA haven't been the only ones making million dollar political contributions to parties and government ministers in Italy, thus providing the Italian Communist Party with its strongest election issue, corruption," Church said in his opening statement. Two days later, on February 6, A. C. Kotchian, president and vice-chairman of Lockheed, acknowledged payments of $1.1 million to, in Church's phrase, "a high government official" in the Netherlands. "What did you get for your money?" the senator asked. The money bought a "climate of good will," Kotchian replied. "Would you call it a bribe?" Church persisted. "I consider it more as a gift," Kotchian answered, "but I don't want to quibble with you, sir." Kotchian and chairman Daniel Haughton quit a few days later. The scandal kept growing.

Exxon Corporation. In dollar volume, Exxon appears to have outclassed all competition in the government-buying sweepstakes. From 1963 to 1972, its Italian affiliate, Esso Italiana, secretly contributed $27 million to Italian political parties, including $11,948,046 to the governing Christian Democrats (which also had been secretly financed by the CIA), $5,160,952 to the Social Democrats, $1,245,028 to the Socialists, and $86,000 to the Communists (!). In a report to Exxon directors in 1972, H. D. Schersten, then the company's general auditor, told of finding a "Special Budget" for the payments which, while secret, were legal under Italian law. All but $6 million of the total was covered up by fake invoices. "The principal factors which permitted the irregularities to occur and remain undiscovered for a long period of time was the fact that higher levels of management in both the Region [Esso Europe, based in London] and in Jersey [actually, head-quarters in New York], condoned the falsification of records to obtain funds for confidential special payments," the audit report said. As a result, "the internal control system was rendered ineffective." The report became public at a hearing of the Senate Multinationals subcommittee in July 1975. The company said that such practices long since had been halted. Strikingly, no evidence has been produced to show that Exxon contributed corporate funds to politicians or political organizations in the United States.

In addition to the $27 million contributed in Italy with the approval of "higher levels of management" in London and New York, Exxon disclosed that Vincenzo Cazzaniga, while chief of Esso Italiana, had taken $29 million to $32 million out of the subsidiary via concealed kickbacks, forty secret bank accounts, and other occult financial methodology. Cazzaniga paid $19 million to $22 million to Italian political parties. "I have never done anything not authorized," he was reported to have said. This seems most unlikely. Exxon and its auditors make a persuasive case that Cazzaniga had acted on his own authority in making the payments, which, in any event, raised Exxon's total to between $46 million and $49 million. Moreover, they don't know—and have started litigation against Cazzaniga to establish—what happened to the other $10 million.

According to the audit report, the payments to the political parties were camouflaged by, for example, the issuance of bogus vouchers for purchases, so that the company could charge off the costs on its Italian income taxes. Subcommittee chairman Frank Church called the practice "a fraud on the Italian Government." He also pointed out that the payments "not only relate to questions that were before the Italian Government, but they track [in time] with the issues that were under consideration then by the Government, all of which were of importance to the oil companies." The issues included tax legislation. This raised the question, of course, whether the payments were, as claimed, political "contributions." In any event, the purpose of the payments, an Exxon executive, Archie L. Monroe, said, was "to further democracy." When asked why $86,000 had been earmarked for the Communists—through a publishing house, Editrice Rinnovamento, which puts out dailies in Rome and Palermo sympathetic to the Italian Communist Party—Monroe said, "I don't know."

An issue crucial to accountability was whether Exxon's directors knew of the secret political payments. Monroe conceded to Church that they had not been told. Senator Church discerned a "pattern" in multinational corporations in which "management refrains from advising the board of directors of serious improprieties." Jerome I. Levinson, the subcommittee's brilliant staff director, did say that Exxon in 1972 had disclosed the payments to a State Department official. This made the government an accessory, in a sense. The official, understood to have been Graham Martin, a former ambassador to Italy, was said to have reacted blandly, saying that the Italian parties were getting "a nice slice of pie." Martin, our last ambassador to South Vietnam, was reported to have tried but failed to persuade the CIA in 1970 to resume secret financing of the Christian Democrats—jointly, it turns out, with Exxon.[4]

In Canada, Imperial Oil Company, Ltd., of which Exxon owns 70 percent, disclosed, also in July 1975, that it had contributed an average of $234,000 annually during the previous five years to Canadian political parties. Imperial Chairman J. A. Armstrong declined to specify recipients beyond a general reference to the Liberal, Progressive, Conservative, and Social Credit parties, or to say who got how much. He did say that Imperial's board "reviews and approves all political contributions" twice a year.

In a prospectus almost barren of details, Exxon on September 25, 1975, revealed an additional $849,000 in improper payments to government officials or political parties in foreign nations starting in 1963. The sum included $13,000 annually paid to a legislator of an unidentified country who was "serving in a consulting capacity" from 1969 to 1975. The $849,000 had been "improperly booked" in company tax records as legitimate business expenses, Exxon said.[5]

Gulf Oil Corporation. In March 1975, the SEC charged Gulf, smallest of the seven great multinational oil companies, and Claude C. Wild, Jr., its Washington lobbyist, with having falsified records and reports to hide a slush fund from which payoffs and political payments of $10.3 million were made between 1960 and 1974. To "launder" the money, Gulf processed most of it through Bahamas Exploration Company, Ltd., which was virtually a "dummy" subsidiary. More than half the $10.3 million, $5.4 million, went for illegal political contributions in the United States. The balance, $4.9 million, was distributed abroad. In testimony to the SEC, Gulf chairman Bob R. Dorsey said that the company had paid out about $4 million so it could continue to do business in an unnamed country. Although the testimony was sealed, it leaked to reporter Jerry Landauer, who cited it in the *Wall Street Journal* on May 2. More of the story emerged two weeks later when a contrite Dorsey told Senator Church's subcommittee that "the responsibility is mine, and I accept it." For "a sorrowful chapter in Gulf's long and productive history," he said, he was "basically ashamed."

In South Korea, where Gulf had invested $300 million in an oil refinery and other operations, the company came under "severe pressure for campaign contributions" from S. K. Kim, financial chairman of President Park Chung Hee's Democratic Republican Party. "He happens to be as tough a man as I've ever met," Dorsey testified. "I have never been subject to that kind of abuse." Kim, he said, "left little to the imagination as to what would occur if the company would choose to turn its back on the request." (One source said the Park regime could lower the price of fuel oil to intolerably low levels, for example.)

Shortly before two national elections, Gulf gave $4 million to President Park's party—$1 million in 1966, and $3 million in 1970, when $10 million had been demanded. In the election the following year, the party won with only 51 percent of the vote. Had the $3 million contribution provided the thin margin of victory? Senator Dick Clark (D–Iowa) asked. Dorsey replied that "statistically, I would have to admit you are right." Had Gulf's contributions constituted "an unwarranted interference" in another country's elections? "I would have to admit that," Dorsey told Clark.

Dorsey testified he had only recently become aware of payments made to Bolivia starting in 1966, when René Barrientos Ortuno was elected President. At Barrientos' request, Gulf made payments of $240,000 and $110,000 to his political party. In addition, Barrientos requested for himself a $110,000 helicopter, which Gulf first leased and then gave to him. He died in the crash of a helicopter in 1969, the year in which Bolivia expropriated Gulf's operations.

As was noted, Gulf had routed $125,000 through its subsidiary in the

Bahamas to Claude Wild, its Washington lobbyist, for 1972 presidential aspirants. Wild delivered $100,000 to the Finance Committee to Re-elect the President, $15,000 for Congressman Wilbur Mills, and $10,000 for Senator Henry M. Jackson (D–Wash.). Wild and Gulf each pleaded guilty to a single count of making illegal contributions; he was fined $1,000, the company, $5,000. Wild resigned in 1973, only to become a consultant who earned almost $90,000 in seven months before the connection was severed.

The Gulf story was quiescent until November 1975, when depositions were filed in United States District Court in Washington in the SEC case against Wild (the company meanwhile had settled). One of the depositions had been made, to SEC investigators, by Thomas D. Wright, a partner in Gulf's outside law firm in Pittsburgh who in 1973 had been asked by Gulf's directors to investigate its involvements. Wright proceeded to interview Wild and some members of the staff of forty-four that had accreted in his "governmental relations" department in Washington. In the deposition, Wright said Wild told him that he had passed out in excess of $5 million to scores of politicians over a twelve-year period, starting with $50,000 to Vice-President-elect Lyndon B. Johnson in 1960. Wild got the cash through the now-defunct subsidiary in the Bahamas at a rate of $300,000 to $400,000 a year. To get the cash from his personal safe-deposit box to politicians, Wild often relied on subordinates, particularly Frederick Myers and Thomas P. Kerester, both of whom also made depositions.

Myers said that starting in 1961, he made twenty trips outside Washington and numerous additional trips to Capitol Hill to deliver sealed envelopes into the outstretched hands of politicians, employees of politicians, or fellow workers at Gulf who presumably relayed the envelopes to politicians. In the case of then-Congressman Richard L. Roudebush (R–Ind.), now administrator of the Veterans Administration, Myers said, the hand was outstretched in the men's room of a Holiday Inn in Indianapolis. Roudebush said he has "absolutely no recollection" of such an encounter. In the case of then-Senator Edwin L. Mechem (R–N. Mex.), now a United States district judge, Myers said, the hand was outstretched behind a barn on a ranch near Albuquerque. Mechem said he thought he was receiving a legal campaign contribution.

Indeed, most everyone alleged to have Gulf cash either denied it, could not recall it, or claimed to have made the happy—but silly—assumption that it was Wild's own personal funds that he was generously contributing. An aide to Senator Russell B. Long (D–La.), who, in an interview with Morton Mintz, once volunteered that he is referred to as "the darling of the oil and gas industry," said the legislator has no record or recollection of alleged donations of $40,000 and $25,000 given to him for distribution to Democratic colleagues of his choice. If he had gotten the money, keeping a record or harboring a recollection of it would be precisely what he would be expected *not* to do.

Similarly, an aide to Wilbur Mills said the congressman has no record of $50,000 allegedly given to him for distribution among fellow Democrats in the House. If the chairman of the House Ways and Means Committee, which writes tax bills for the oil industry, had gotten money from a major oil company, why would he want to record it? Myers recalled delivering an envelope to Fred Harris when he was running for the Senate in Oklahoma; Harris denied that he knowingly accepted corporate funds. Myers also recalled giving an envelope to Senator Howard Baker; the Tennessee Republican doesn't recall such an incident.

According to Wright's deposition, Wild told him that since the early 1960s he had been giving $5,000 in the spring and $5,000 in the fall of each year to Senate Minority Leader Hugh Scott. Originally, Wright said he was told by Wild and Royce H. Savage, former general counsel of Gulf, that the company had paid an annual retainer of $20,000 to $25,000 to Scott's law firm in Philadelphia. After Savage tried to end that relationship, he said, Scott insisted that Gulf continue to pay the retainer "because of his association with the firm." Savage agreed to pay the fee for one more year, but then dropped it in favor of the twice-yearly $5,000 payments. These were intended, according to Wright, "for a personal matter, or some office matter, never in connection with political contribution matters." Scott not only denied ever having received a personal retainer from Gulf, but also, when he formally announced in December 1975 that he would not seek reelection from Pennsylvania, insisted that he used part of the money for his own campaign and part for other Republicans' election campaigns.[6]

In settling the litigation brought by the SEC, Gulf agreed to establish a special review committee to investigate the company's payments and payoffs, and to submit a report to the agency and the United States Court of Appeals for the District of Columbia. John J. McCloy, the Wall Street lawyer who has represented all of the major oil companies in international matters, headed the committee. After a ten-month investigation, the committee, on December 30, 1975, filed a 298-page report making these major findings and conclusions:

• "The illegal use of corporate funds for political purposes was originally instituted by the top management of Gulf," which in 1974 was the nation's seventh-largest industrial firm and fourth-largest oil company.

• The evidence on chairman Dorsey "falls short" of demonstrating that he was informed of Claude Wild's unlawful political activities, but shows that Dorsey had been sufficiently "involved" in those activities, as had E. D.

Brockett, a director and former president, that they should be excluded from any steps to implement reforms recommended by the McCloy committee.

• A succession of general counsel for Gulf, "up to the present incumbent," had been "going along with, if not actually planning, the program of illegal contributions." While general counsel, Royce Savage, who had joined the company in the 1950s, a year after dismissing a price-fixing indictment against twenty-nine oil companies, including Gulf, "was aware that [Wild] had a source of corporate funds available to him which he was probably using for political contributions and payments."

• Gulf's secretary, Herbert C. Manning, "failed to inquire as diligently and professionally as he should have into the source of funds he received" before making political contributions." Similarly, William L. Henry, an executive vice-president, and Fred C. Deering, former controller, did not make adequate inquiries.

• The company's domestic political payments were "shot through with illegality," being "generally clandestine and in disregard of Federal as well as a number of state statutes."

• Gulf's total political payout in the fourteen-year period ended in mid-1973 was at least $12.3 million—$2 million more than previously estimated. The discrepancy was accounted for by covert but legal political contributions in Canada, Italy and Sweden.

• The firm had a "gray fund" for gifts and tips to "relatively low-level governmental personnel in South Korea," and a "fondo nero," or black fund, out of which $10,815 was paid to Italian journalists."

In January 1976 the board forced the resignation of its chairman, Dorsey; its secretary, Manning, who had paid out political monies while associate general counsel; and Henry and Deering, who, as Gulf's controllers in the 1960s, when the slush fund was highly active, had been in charge of disbursing corporate monies.

Dorsey got a lump-sum payment of $1.6 million in retirement benefits, an annual pension of $48,158, and an option to buy 200,000 shares of Gulf at 20 percent below market price. His compensation in 1974 was $544,264.

Mobil Oil Company. Italian political parties that got payments from Exxon of $46 million or more in nine years meanwhile got more than $500,000 a year, from 1970 through 1973, from Mobil Oil Italiana. Everett S. Checket, executive vice-president of the parent company's international division, acknowledged this to the Senate Multinationals Subcommittee at a hearing on July 17, 1975. Mobil's justification was similar to Exxon's: "to support the political process." But it was a secret and unaccountable political process. Mobil listed the payments on its books as advertising, research, and other expenses. The recipient parties, Checket said, did not want the payments to be openly recorded. As in other cases, the chain of unaccountability was complete.

Unione Petrolifera, the trade association of privately owned oil companies in Italy, also had contributed to the parties, Checket testified. The technique used by the association's head, Vincenzo Cazzaniga, who at the same time had been chief of Esso Italiana, was to take out a bank loan to get the lira for the contributions, and then to assess the member companies to repay the loan. The basis of assessment was the amount of oil each company had sold EMEL, the government-owned power company, which was the conduit for the contributions. Mobil's share was $96,000.

Northrop Corporation. On February 18, 1972, in Los Angeles, Thomas V. Jones, Northrop's chairman and chief executive, received three visitors with obvious clout in Washington: Maurice Stans, chairman of the finance Committee to Re-elect the President; Herbert Kalmbach, President Nixon's personal lawyer, and Leonard Firestone, a Nixon fund-raiser in California (who himself gave $100,000, secretly, to the President's reelection campaign —and later was made ambassador to Belgium). The visitors made clear to Jones that persons in a status such as his were expected to be able to deliver $100,000 before April 7, when a new election-financing law would require disclosure.

Being solicited for political contributions was an old story to Jones and James Allen, a Northrop vice-president and director who, during the New Deal, had been an aide to William O. Douglas, then chairman of the SEC and later an associate justice of the Supreme Court. Allen in 1974 told Ernst & Ernst, a firm of certified public accountants, which outside directors of Northrop had retained, that Northrop years before had weighed "the risks attendant in making corporate political contributions against the probability of suffering corporate disadvantage." The company came down, in Allen's words, "on the side of the corporation and its shareholders."

To minimize the risks, Allen sought advice from Stanley Simon, a New Yorker described in the report of the Senate Select Watergate Committee, as a "doctor" for corporations. Simon suggested a "foolproof" technique, according to a letter that Jones' lawyer sent to Wilmer, Cutler & Pickering, a Washington law firm retained by the outside directors. The suggested method, said by the lawyer to have been "originally worked out by Joe Kennedy [Joseph P. Kennedy, father of President Kennedy] and used by numerous corporations for many years," was a foreign "laundering" operation. Simon proposed as launderer William Savy, a Frenchman, who also was to provide "intelligence and marketing services." Northrop worked out an arrangement with Savy under which, starting in 1961, it regularly drew money from its account in the Chase Manhattan Bank and deposited it in the accounts of two corporations that were alter egos of Savy, Wilco Holding at Banque International in Luxembourg, and Wilco S.A. at Crédit Suisse in Geneva. (In 1969, a third Northrop–Savy account, call Euradvice, was opened in Basel, Switzerland). When Allen asked him to do so, Savy delivered money to him, sometimes by dropping it at Simon's office, and sometimes by putting as much as $20,000 in each coat pocket and flying to New York to meet Allen.

At the meeting with the Stans delegation, Jones agreed to the request for $100,000 and then instructed Allen to get it. Allen, in turn, told Savy to write twenty $5,000 checks, made out to units of the Finance Committee, on the Luxembourg account. Jones also volunteered to the visitors that more cash was available should a "special need" arise. One did arise over the summer, when presidential aide John D. Ehrlichman asked Kalmbach to collect money for a special secret fund with which the White House hoped to buy the silence of the Watergate burglars about their ties to the Nixon Administration and to the Committee for the Re-election of the President (CREEP). On August 1, Kalmbach came to see Jones, an old friend; told him that a special need, which he did not specify, indeed had arisen, and left with either $50,000 or $75,000—it's not clear which.

A few days before the November election, the House Banking and Currency Committee, headed by the late Congressman Wright Patman (D–Tex.), announced its discovery that secret receipts of the Nixon campaign included $30,000 in checks written on the Luxembourg bank. Jones, knowing that the checks were among those written by William Savy, then undertook elaborate efforts to try to persuade Kalmbach, a CREEP lawyer, the outside directors, and even other Northrop executives, that only personal funds had been contributed. He also lied to a federal grand jury, later "correcting" his testimony.

On May 1, 1974, Jones, Allen, and Northrop each pleaded guilty to one count of making an illegal campaign contribution of $150,000. The company and Jones, whose violation was a felony, each was fined $5,000, and Allen $1,000. Jones reimbursed the company for its fine and $50,000 given to Kalmbach in August. The contributions to Mr. Nixon, the company said, were "an abnormal departure from the high business standards of business conduct of Northrop."

That this was another lie was established by the SEC less than a year later when, on April 16, 1975, it filed a complaint against Northrop, Jones, and Allen which the defendants immediately settled. The major allegations were these:

• During 1971, 1972, and 1973, Northrop disbursed approximately $30 million in corporate funds—a sum almost equal to its profits—to various so-called consultants and commission agents, most of them abroad. Despite the staggering amounts of money involved, the company made the outlays without the records and controls needed to assure either that payments actually were made for their intended purposes, or to document that the services being procured actually were provided. Certain of the middlemen refused even to confirm to the SEC that they had received money Northrop had given them for bribes and influence-buying.

• The company had transferred $1.1 million in corporate funds to William Savy, the French consultant, and his alter ego corporations. Savy had converted more than $476,000 into cash and returned it to the United States, where Northrop had disbursed it in political contributions, some of them illegal.

• Some monies from the secret source were routed to Frank J. DeFrancis, a Washington consultant who had a fifteen-year $100,000-a-year contract with Northrop although, he had said, "I don't know a damn thing about an airplane except the nose and the tail." On at least one occasion, he used the cash to retain another Washington consultant "who was simultaneously employed by a competitor of Northrop." This consultant proved to be John Russell Blandford, a former two-star Marine Corps general who was chief counsel of the House Armed Services Committee from 1965 to 1970, when its chairman was Congressman L. Mendel Rivers (D–S.C.), and for two years after Rivers died in 1970. Rivers had played an awesomely powerful role in building up (and covering up) the military-industrial complex, with major benefits to his own district. Because Blandford was Rivers' "blocking back, confidant, advisor and alter ego," he was "one of the most powerful men in the House," Daniel Rapoport wrote in *Inside the House.*[7] After leaving House Armed Services, Blandford offered his services in Washington to various defense contractors. Two that retained him were Lockheed Aircraft Corporation and Fairchild Industries. The latter produced a competitor to Northrop's F-5, a relatively inexpensive, easy-to-maintain fighter plane much used abroad, and an important factor in the international arms race.

The Pentagon never bought the F-5, but thanks to a strenuous lobbying campaign by Rivers, Congress paid the bill for development of an advanced F-5 that the United States donated to American allies in Asia.

As a condition of the settlement with the SEC, Northrop agreed to continue the investigation undertaken for the outside directors by Wilmer, Cutler & Pickering and the accounting firms of Ernst & Ernst and Price Waterhouse & Company. This investigation, newspaper reports, and a hearing by Senator Church's Multinationals Subcommittee produced this further information:

• Shortly after leaving House Armed Services in 1972, Blandford told Northrop's DeFrancis that he could be "beneficial" to the company. De-Francis agreed. The Pentagon, he noted, had picked Fairchild's combat-support plane over Northrop's F–5, and, wanting to avoid a recurrence, he decided Northrop should retain Blandford for five years, with Northrop giving DeFrancis a lump sum of either $40,000 or $60,000 to pay out to Blandford at the rate of $1,000 a month. To mask the connection with Northrop, Blandford made the contract not with it, but with United General Services, an air-charter enterprise operated by De-Francis.

• DeFrancis, who for twenty years had been legal counsel to West Germany through its embassy in Washington, said he had been told by a high German official and an American diplomat that Northrop's competitors were using illegal influence and actions to gain an unfair advantage in Bonn's defense procurement. He also said he had made cash payments to persons who were "of the type who would not want their names associated with Northrop."

• To promote the sale of aircraft initially in Iran, but later in other countries, Northrop, aided by DeFrancis, secretly set up in Zurich, Switzerland, an independent sales operation, which DeFrancis termed a "Lockheed-type arrangement." It was named the Economic Development Corporation (E.D.C.), and was headed by Andreas Froviep, a Zurich attorney. Northrop "is not interested in knowing how E.D.C. operates and who they are in touch with, but can only measure the benefit of E.D.C. by sales which occur," Ernst & Ernst reported.

• The Ernst & Ernst report told of a Northrop payment of $450,000 to Adnan Khashoggi, Saudi Arabia's best-known entrepreneur, who in 1972 and 1973 had been Lockheed's Middle East sales agent. This was bribe money earmarked for two Saudi generals. Northrop accused Khashoggi of having demanded the money for the generals and produced papers to back up the accusation. But Khashoggi turned the charge around. Northrop, he told the *Washington Post*'s Jim Hoagland, had "cooked up" the idea of buying influence. "I stopped the bribe," he said. "I put it in my pocket."

• In Washington, Northrop's top consultant for the Middle East was Kermit Roosevelt, grandson of President Theodore Roosevelt. He was responsible, by estimate of Chairman Jones, for contracts "running close to a billion dollars" in seven or eight years. As a top CIA operative in Tehran in the 1950s, Roosevelt played a leading role in the coup that overthrew Mohammed Mossadegh and restored the present shah, a personal friend. Northrop documents portray Roosevelt, *Washington Post* reporter Jack Egan wrote, moving among top Saudi and Iranian officials, and officials in the Pentagon, State Department and CIA—gathering intelligence for Northrop and pushing its products at the same time.

• Chairman Jones, at a subcommittee hearing on June 10, 1975, acknowledged that Northrop maintained a goose-hunting lodge in Maryland at which it entertained Pentagon officials.

Many more details, embarrassing not only to Northrop, but also to the Department of Defense, emerged from a draft report by the Defense Contract Audit Agency (DCAA). The report, dated August 6, 1975, but disclosed on October 6 by Peter Gruenstein in the *Washington Star*, showed that Northrop in the four-year period 1971–1974 had collected $5.5 million in "questionable" expenses incurred by seventy-two consultants. In violation of its own regulations, the Pentagon had reimbursed Northrop for some of these expenses without auditing them, the report said. In certain cases, documentation of expenses did not exist, was missing, was inadequate, or had been destroyed. The Air Force had "attempted to cover up" the report, said Gruenstein, of Capitol Hill News Service.

Among the more important of the report's disclosures and recommendations were these: Northrop's James Allen had instructed consultant DeFrancis to give at least a portion of the $40,000 or $60,000 to John Blandford, the former aide to Congressman Rivers, for "protection" in dealing with the company's competitors. Because DeFrancis' consulting activities for Northrop were unsatisfactorily documented, improper, or unallowable under regulations, Northrop's billing to the government of the more than $500,000 it had paid him in four years should not be permitted. Northrop paid $115,000 in expenses to Major General Winston P. (Wimpy) Wilson, former head of the Air National Guard, although his expense invoices "disclose substantial entertainment activities in connection with Northrop's hunting lodge," "lobbying," and $500 in illegal political contributions. Northrop paid $161,000 to General Adolf Galland, a former chief of the German Air Force, in 1971, while he was employed by United Aircraft Corporation. "According to Northrop," the DCAA report said, "all information pertaining to activity reports covering Galland have been destroyed." Northrop paid $824,000 to S. L. Sommer and Associates; its expense accounts, in addition to illegal political contributions for Northrop, indicate, "to a great extent, entertainment activities, including 'entertainment of congressional people' and entertainment at the [1972] Democratic convention in Miami." Northrop paid Anna Chennault, widow of General Claire Chennault, and a prominent Washington hostess with close ties to right-wing political leaders in Asia,

$161,000. Citing the entertainment that "appears to be a significant part of her duties," and the absence of evidence showing her services to be "bona fide," the report said her "consultant" fees are not legitimately billable to the government.[8]

Secretary of Defense James R. Schlesinger did not discipline Air Force officers who accepted entertainment or favors from Northrop. The relations between them and the contractor were, he said, a "customary exchange of amenities between personal friends." As of October 1975, the Department of Justice and the FBI were making an investigation. One may hope the investigators and their bosses have no friends at Northrop with whom they engage in a customary exchange of amenities, perhaps at the hunting lodge, or perhaps aboard the *El Commandante,* a yacht which Northrop operated at a cost to the taxpayers, in 1973 and 1974, of $273,000.

At Senator Church's hearings, Northrop had to peel away some of the secrecy of its operations, and Thomas Jones, the company chairman, found it expedient to apologize for the firm's foreign bribes. The record suggests that Northrop's behavior was in many ways routine for arms suppliers. Church said, "I'm afraid we had sufficient evidence . . . to suggest that a system of corruption is developing" in international arms sales.

In retirement, Jones, who was 55 in 1975, would have had a pension of $120,000 a year and stock options of $500,000. But the company first retained him as chief executive officer at $286,000 while removing him as chairman; then, in November 1975, the board passed a resolution praising Jones and his top aides for "continued excellent performance . . ."[9] and finally, having set the stage, the company in February 1976 returned Jones to the post of chairman.

Phillips Petroleum. Setting out to do a television documentary on "The Corporation," CBS reporter Jay McMullen in 1972 chose Phillips as the model because, he said, William W. Keeler, then its chairman and chief executive officer, had been "recommended to us by industry and trade associations as an 'outstanding corporate manager.' " Two days before the program was aired on December 6, 1973, Keeler and Phillips each pleaded guilty to having made an illegal, secret contribution of $100,000 in corporate funds to the Nixon reelection campaign. The firm claimed its directors had been unaware of the contribution. The board then ordered an investigation made. In July 1974, Phillips disclosed that a secret slush fund had been "maintained at the company's principal office" in Bartlesville, Oklahoma— by whom, it did not say. Money originating "in foreign transactions" had been put into the fund and spent "exclusively for political contributions." Over a ten-year period, $685,000 had been disbursed. Phillips identified no recipients other than the Finance Committee to Re-elect the President, to which Keeler had given $100,000.

As in numerous other cases, there had been far more secret cash than initially was indicated or admitted. This became known on March 6, 1975, when the SEC filed a complaint charging Phillips with having diverted in excess of $2.8 million, by means of false entries in its books, to two Swiss corporations. More than $1.3 million, converted to cash by these corporations, had been returned to the United States, where approximately half the sum had been distributed in political contributions, some of them unlawful. In a report filed with the SEC on September 26, 1975, the company listed fifty-three House and Senate candidates to whom it had given relatively small sums, from the corporate treasury, in 1970 and 1972. The recipients had no way of knowing the funds came from the company, Phillips said.

The SEC said that Phillips had distributed about $1.5 million—the balance of the $2.8 million not returned to the United States—overseas. In addition to the corporation, the agency's complaint named Keeler and his successor, William F. Martin; John M. Houchin, who between 1963 and 1974 rose from executive vice-president to board chairman; and Carstens Slack, Washington vice-president since 1968.

Keeler, in his last full year as chief executive, was paid $300,000. His estimated retirement benefits were worth $201,742 a year.

United Brands Company. In February 1975, Eli M. Black, board chairman of this food and meat-packing conglomerate, knocked out a window in his Manhattan office and plunged forty-four floors to his death. Not knowing what had driven Black to despair, the SEC routinely began an audit—the first of a global corporation to result in public charges of concealed payoffs to officials of foreign countries. The SEC found that with Black's authorization, United had paid $1.25 million to an official of Honduras, where the company had 28,000 acres of bananas, in an effort to lower the taxes on bananas.

A Honduran fact-finding commission said that Black had come to Tegucigalpa, the capital, in July 1974, to offer "several hundred thousand dollars" to President Oswaldo Lopez Areliano to "fix the banana problem," but that Lopez had rejected him. The "banana problem" was a tax of $1 per box, which cost United $30 million annually; it subsequently was reduced to 30 cents.

The recipient of the $1.25 million bribe was identified by the commission as Abraham Bennaton Ramos, former economics minister, who was said to have gotten the money at a meeting in Zurich, Switzerland, with John A. Taylor, United's senior vice-president for banana operations. Whether Bennaton passed some of the money to Lopez was not learned, because Lopez refused to allow scrutiny of his foreign bank accounts. As a result, he was ousted in April 1975. Bennaton denied involvement. Taylor declined to comment. United contended it was a victim of extortion.

The foregoing summary establishes that leading corporations, by their own admissions, have engaged in secret, routine, and systematic bribery in foreign countries, and in secret and illegal contributing for political purposes in the United States. The amount of money that we know they have corruptly spent is in the hundreds of millions of dollars. "These were not case of fawning subordinates trying to win executive suite favor," A. A. Sommer, Jr., a member of the SEC, has said. "Rather it was the executive suite itself which was engaged in deceit, cunning and deviousness worthy of the most fabled political boss or fixer." Speaking in July 1975, when many more shattering revelations were yet to come, he went on to say that "the suspicion grows that this disease may indeed be more widespread than any of us dared to suspect." It amounts, he said, to a "national crisis."[10]

The crisis is rooted in the very nature of the corporation. "It feels not the restraints that conscience and public sentiment lay on the business man," Edward Alsworth Ross wrote, in 1907, in his brilliant, almost forgotten book *Sin and Society.*

It fears the law no more, and public indignation far less, than does the individual. You can hiss the bad man, egg him, lampoon him, caricature him, ostracize him and his. Not so with the bad corporation. The corporation, moreover, is not in dread of hell fire. You cannot Christianize it. You may convert its stockholders, animate them with patriotism or public spirit or love of social service; but this will have little or no effect on the tenor of their corporation. In short, it is an entity that transmits the greed of investors, but not their conscience; that returns them profits, but not unpopularity.[11]

Ross, a University of Wisconsin sociologist, fully understood and pungently conveyed seventy years ago what few seem to grasp even now: "In enforcing the rules of the game the *chief problem is how to restrain corporations.*" (Emphasis supplied.) He continued:

The threat to withdraw the charter alarms no one, for corporations know they are here to stay. Fine the law-breaking officers, and the board of directors by indemnifying them encourages them to do it again.

Far from being eliminated in the cause of accountability, indemnification of corporate executives for criminal fines continued—and under standards that became increasingly lax. Writing long after Ross, in 1975, Christopher

D. Stone, in a book on corporations, pointed out that they now are able to buy liability insurance to cover officers and directors for a broad variety of offenses. Moreover, he said, "The new Delaware Corporation Code—the bellwether for other corporation codes across the country—specifically empowers corporations to purchase and maintain insurance against such liability for their executives 'whether or not the corporation would have the power to indemnify [them] under the provisions' of the rest of Delaware law." In short, Delaware deliberately designed the new code to enable executives to pass on criminal fines to someone else and thus to brush off accountability.

Ross continued:

Fine the corporation, and, if its sinning is lucrative, it heeds the fine no more than a flea-bite. Never will the brake of the law grip these slippery wheels until prison doors yawn for the convicted officers of lawless corporations. Even then you cannot fasten upon the officers legal responsibility for much of the iniquity they instigate.[12]

Why cannot responsibility be fastened upon the officers? Because corporations are marvelously adroit at diffusing and hiding it. This keeps public opinion impotent, meaning, Ross said, that

it allows itself to be kept guessing which shell the pea is under, whether the accountability is with the foreman, or the local manager, or the general manager, or the directors. How easily the public wrath is lost in the maze! Public indignation meets a cuirass of divided responsibility that scatters a shock that would have stretched iniquity prone. . . . Instead of playing hide-and-seek in the intricacies of the corporate structure, public opinion should strike right for the top. Let it mark the tactics of the Philadelphia mothers who, after vain appeal to underlings to put in a gate at a railroad crossing their children must make on the way to school, stormed the office of the president of the road.[13]

How on the mark! How Ross did get to the heart of the matter! This was his advice:

The directors of a company ought to be individually accountable for every case of misconduct of which the company receives the benefit, for every preventable deficiency or abuse that regularly goes on in the course of the business. Hold them blameless if they prove the inefficency or disobedience of underlings, but not if they plead ignorance.

Incisively, Ross assigned a role to the press, which routinely ought

to print along with the news of the exposure of corporation misconduct the names of the directors, in order that the public indignation may not explode without result, but find rather a proper target; for just indignation is altogether too precious a thing to be wasted. Consider the salutary effects of such severity. When an avalanche of wrath hangs over the head of a sinning corporation, no one will accept a directorship who is not prepared to give a good deal of time and serious attention to its business. Strict accountability will send flying the figurehead directors who, when the misdeeds of their proteges come to light, protest they "didn't know." . . .

Let it be understood that a man's reputation may be blasted by scandal within his corporation and we shall not see men directors on a score or two of boards. . . .

Make it vain for a director to plead that he opposed the wrong sanctioned by the majority of his colleagues. If he will keep his skirts clear, let him resign the moment he is not ready to stand for every policy of his board. In the board of directors, as in the cabinet of parliamentary countries, the principle of joint responsibility should hold.[14]

American society never would have turned so rancid had the sane and sensible advice of Edward Alsworth Ross been heeded in 1907. But now— in 1976—what incentives are there for business to be ethical? The firms that sinned for years, that profited thereby, and that were caught by the SEC, have gone free after promising to sin no more. Being corporations, they cannot in any event go to jail. The marketplace does not penalize them. The industrial executives who managed and concealed corrupt activities have overcome such ignominy as may have befallen them; even those who pled guilty to commission of a crime continue to draw huge paychecks, fees, or pension benefits. The Conference Board, an independent research organization financed largely by American corporations, surveyed seventy-three executives in the fall of 1975. In a story on the board's report, Michael C. Jensen said in the *New York Times* on February 13, 1976, "Large numbers of American businessmen believe they have not only the right but even the obligation to pay bribes and kickbacks abroad to win contracts for their companies." In sum, the inference many surely must draw is that corporate corruption continues to pay, although more elegant techniques to hide it would be welcomed.

For most of us, however, the essential message is that many of our largest corporations are rogue elephants, accountable to no one anywhere. There are tranquilizers that could be shot into them. Legislation should be enacted to make it illegal for a company based in the United States to pay bribes, or bribes masquerading as consulting, sales, or commission fees, wherever in the world they do business. Short of legislation, the SEC should require companies to reveal all such payments and to identify the recipients. And if large corporations were to be federally chartered, as they ought to be, their charters could provide for an array of strong sanctions against managements that paid bribes, or allowed them to be paid.

IV
Conflict of Interest in Government

The proper operation of a democratic government requires that officials be independent and impartial; that government decisions and policy be made in the proper channels of the governmental structure; that public office not be used for personal gain; and that the public have confidence in the integrity of its government. The attainment of one or more of these ends is impaired whenever there exists, or appears to exist, an actual or potential conflict between the private interests of a government employee and his duties as an official. The public interest, therefore, requires that the law protect against such conflicts of interest and establish appropriate ethical standards with respect to employee conduct in situations where actual or potential conflicts exist.

From the Preamble of an Executive Conflict of Interest Act proposed by the Special Committee on the Federal Conflict of Interest Laws of The Association of the Bar of the City of New York

Conflict of interest, while not as reliably lethal as secrecy, is toxic in the body politic. It makes the heart muscle of accountability go slack. The Gospel according to Matthew provided the quintessential warning: "No man can serve two masters: for either he will hate the one and love the other; or else he will hold to the one and despise the other. Ye cannot serve God and mammon." The Biblical admonition is embedded in conventional doctrine on public policy. This is not to suggest that conflicts do not exist; they abound. Rather, it is to say that the doctrine is a dike, albeit a leaky one, holding back a sea.

President Ford breached the dike as it never had been breached before when he nominated Nelson A. Rockefeller for Vice-President. In the number, variety, and magnitude of his conflicts he is alone on the mountaintop; except for other Rockefellers, possibly, no other person of wealth has ascended so far above the slopes and foothills. He is, as one congressman put it, "a walking, breathing conflict of interest."[1] In a government founded on the separation of powers he was, when Congress confirmed him in late 1974, a heartbeat away from combining in his person the greatest economic power with the greatest political power.

We do not expect Nelson Rockefeller to become President, whether by the death of Gerald Ford or by election. That does not erase or even diminish our concern about the significance of what happened: in nominating Rockefeller, a President ignored, scorned, or hopelessly misconceived the overriding determination of the Framers of the Constitution to prevent power from concentrating; even worse, Congress, in failing to request the President on this fundamental ground to rescind the nomination, effectively collaborated with Mr. Ford in sapping the tradition of resistance to conflict of interest which is an integral defense against unaccountability.

Rockefeller and his family have direct holdings of more than $1.4 billion in oil, banking, airlines, pharmaceuticals, and other enterprises. Rockefeller Family and Associates, which manages the assets of eighty-four living descendants of the founder, is, through nine employees, represented on the boards of forty corporations with combined assets of $70 billion. Chase Manhattan Bank, *the* Rockefeller bank and the country's second largest, holds in trust, for pension funds and other huge interests, stock sufficient to control numerous additional giant enterprises—many of which are in putative competition with each other in various sectors of the economy.

The conflict of interest laws are concerned with *appearance.* They are, the late Chief Justice Earl Warren once said, "directed not only at dishonor, but also at conduct that tempts dishonor. This broad proscription embodies a recognition of the fact that an impairment of impartial judgment can occur even in the most well-meaning men when their personal economic interests are affected by the business they transact on behalf of the government."[2] What happens to the concern for appearance when the Vice-President and his family own more than $300 million worth of stock in Exxon, Mobil, Standard Oil of California, and other oil companies—and when the Vice-President supports (as one would expect) White House policies toward the industry which are essentially Exxon's, Mobil's, and Socal's? And when those policies promise to increase the value of his holdings by millions of dollars? The appearance of conflict is unaffected even if Rockefeller may not want to benefit personally and may truly believe the policies to be in the national interest.

The oil companies have benefited enormously from tax loopholes, are targets of an antimonopoly complaint brought by the staff of the Federal Trade Commission, and have vast stakes in the Middle East, where foreign policy is presided over by Secretary of State Henry A. Kissinger, who had accepted a $50,000 gift from Rockefeller on leaving his employ. How could a President Rockefeller—setting tax policy, making appointments to and influencing the budget of the FTC, and guiding our foreign affairs—avoid actual, let alone apparent, conflict?

Oil conflicts are but the beginning. Rockefeller has, for example, an extremely high stake in the existing tax structure, not only because it is stacked to favor oil and other corporations in which he has holdings, but because it is stacked to favor him directly. Tax data released by Rockefeller for the ten years 1964 through 1973 showed that he paid total federal income taxes of $11.3 million on gross income of $46.9 million. The average tax rate, 24 percent, was about that paid by a family of four earning $30,000 or a single person earning $18,000. In 1970, when he reported gross income of $2,443,703, he paid no tax at all—the result, he said, of a mixup among his trust funds and personal accounts, with each source having made enough deductions to offset the tax. The Internal Revenue Service made an audit, however, that established a tax obligation of $104,180—a paltry 4 percent of gross income. But 1970's was not the only disputed return, Samantha Senger wrote in *People & Taxes*. The audit, made by the IRS only because the country's wealthiest citizen had been nominated for Vice-President, produced

a settlement with Rockefeller that he will pay a total of $903,718 in back taxes for 1969 through 1975—roughly 1/5 of the amount already paid for those years.

The IRS disallowed a deduction of a charitable contribution of $402,649 Rockefeller claimed for the expenses of an official tour of Latin America. The rest of the IRS assessment was based on another $824,598 of deductions Rockefeller claimed for office and investment expenses which were denied by the tax collection agency. In fact, for three of the five years in question, the deductions for office and business expenses exceeded the income from his personal investments and work.[3]

Reform of the tax structure would pose for Rockefeller, were he to become President, a conflict between his personal and family welfare and the welfare of tens of millions of families. Other conflicts would be posed by the antimonopoly suits brought by the Justice Department (sometimes called the President's law firm) against International Business Machines, in which Rockefeller and his wife have stock valued at $1 million, and against American Telephone & Telegraph, in which the family's holdings exceed $5 million. Yet other conflicts would arise from the controls a President Rockefeller would have over federal regulatory agencies that regulate airlines, the three television networks, banks, and chemical and drug companies, among other enterprises in which Rockefeller and his family have substantial interests. "As Vice President or President, he couldn't very well disqualify himself every time a policy decision affected Chase Manhattan Bank," *Washington Post* reporters William Greider and Thomas O'Toole wrote on the eve of congressional hearings on the Rockefeller nomination. "He would be out of work if he did." They went on to say:

Most people assume Rockefeller already has so much money, he wouldn't shave corners to get a little more. The problem is really the other way around: what impact would that great economic power have on government and politics if it were marshalled in tandem with presidential power?

What would a middle-level bureaucrat do, for instance, if he knew he was regulating the President's family fortune? Would a senator or congressman be able to resist the combined might of the White House and Wall Street's second largest bank, not to mention all the corporations that do business there?[4]

It is hard to imagine an appointment more perfectly designed to breed cynicism. We would make no such complaint if after a full political campaign the people had elected Nelson Rockefeller; but a President who himself had been appointed, nominated him.

Our complaint would be less insistent had the Senate Rules Committee and the House Judiciary Committee rigorously investigated the nominee before approving him, but unless time spent is mistaken for thoroughness, they did not. Congressman Robert F. Drinan (D–Mass.), a member of House Judiciary, protested that its chairman, Peter W. Rodino, Jr. (D–N.J.), did not honor requests to call more witnesses than the few who testified. "Requests for investigation into the impact of the interlocking corporate directorships were set aside," Drinan said. "Mr. Rockefeller's invisible and massive network of alliances, now virtually immune to ordinary accountability, were not subjected to that unique accountability required for a unique case."[5] In a letter to Congressman Rodino, Ralph Nader set out further facts about Judiciary's inquiry:

Not one subpoena was issued. Depositions made to the staff and submitted statements, with few exceptions, were not required to be sworn. The committee "relied totally on voluntary disclosure that was grossly incomplete and substantially unverified." By limiting each committee member to five minutes of questioning, the committee precluded "probing and piercing" of the nominee's "necessarily short and often general responses." Many received large gifts from Rockefeller when he was governor of New York and they held official posts, but only one of them was called. The seven days between the end of the inadequate hearings and the vote deprived congressmen and the public of "a decent interval" in which to review hearing transcripts. Finally, the committee kept secret all of the unpublished background materials.[6]

Our complaint again would be less insistent but for the many Republican legislators who, while loud in praise of Rockefeller, were silent about a conflict of their own. Thirteen of them since 1957 had accepted a total of $60,000 in direct contributions from Rockefeller, more had accepted undetermined sums from members of his family, and hundreds had benefited indirectly from large sums the nominee and his family had contributed to Republican committees for distribution to candidates. But none of their colleagues, even those making a brave, determined, and, they knew, hopeless battle against the nominee because of his conflict, said anything, either.

Our complaint also would be less insistent had the press, with a fraction of the vigor it brings to bear on any number of aspirants to and holders of high or lesser office, finally including Richard Nixon, undertaken to investigate and inform the public about Rockefeller's record and the implications of his nomination. The press on the whole did not fulfill this solemn responsibility. When not fawning over Rockefeller's purported leadership qualities, many editorial pages made the argument that simply because he was a man of wealth his critics would deny him public office. The argument was specious. To our knowledge, there was not a single critic who, privately or publicly, on any occasion, had urged wealth as a barrier to any public office. There never has been, and never should be, a barrier to the *election* of Nelson Rockefeller, or any person of wealth, by the people. Here, however, Congress was the electorate—acting in behalf of the public. Even without a political campaign in which Rockefeller's conflict of interest surely would be forcefully and repeatedly brought to public attention, there was no reliable indication that the electorate wanted Rockefeller to be Vice-President. A Harris poll conducted November 1–5, 1974, almost three months after Mr. Ford nominated him, showed the contrary: the public disapproved the nomination 43 percent to 39 percent. By a margin three times wider, 47 percent to 34 percent, the public believed that Rockefeller's wealth would create a conflict of interest.

So without adequate investigation or reporting of the conflict, without the benefit of the education about the conflict that would occur in an extended election campaign, and despite the pressure of repeated claims that a nation without a Vice-President was in peril, a plurality of the public appeared to be sending Congress a message that a majority of their surrogates would refuse to heed: Do not join Mr. Ford in arranging a marriage of colossal economic power to, potentially, the highest political power—a union possible uniquely in Nelson Rockefeller. The greatest irony was this: while the nomination was pending, Congress passed, and President Ford signed, a bill barring a federal judge who owns a share of, say, Exxon, from presiding at a proceeding involving Exxon.

Rockefeller was nominated and confirmed pursuant to Section 2 of the Twenty-fifth Amendment:

Whenever there is a vacancy in the office of Vice President, the President shall nominate a Vice President who shall take office upon confirmation by a majority vote of both Houses of Congress.

The burden the amendment puts on the President and Congress is unique: to act as surrogates for the entire electorate. The author of the amendment, Senator Birch Bayh (D–Ind.), said that Congress had "the awesome responsibility of participating in the election of a man to our Nation's second highest office. . . . I use the term 'elect' rather than 'confirm' advisedly . . ."7 The accountability of Congress ran to the people, not to the nominee of an unelected President. Inconsistently and hypocritically, knowing they had to consider the possibility that they were electing the next President, the majority voted for a conflict of interest.

Now to a cross section of conflict of interest in the Executive, the Congress, the Judiciary, and the independent agencies.

The Executive

As of mid-1972, Litton Industries, a leading defense contractor, was in dispute with the Navy over the fairness or legitimacy of claims for cost-overruns amounting to about $500 million. In addition, the corporation faced a financial squeeze in the coming months if the Navy released funds to Litton at the rate specified in a contract for construction of five huge landing-assault ships known as LHAs. Trying to get out of the bind, Litton president Roy L. Ash met with senior Navy officials at company headquarters in Beverly Hills, California. He proposed that the Navy "bail out" Litton, and said that if necessary he would go "on to the White House"—wherein resided Richard Nixon, friend and recipient of about $21,000 in Ash's reelection-campaign contributions—"to explain" Litton's problem. For good measure, he told of a grand plan envisioned by John B. Connally, then secretary of the treasury, for the rescue of all financially distressed Navy shipbuilders.

Several months later, President Nixon appointed Ash director of the Office of Management and Budget, the budgeting and management arm of the White House. The OMB's code of ethics for its employees admonishes them to try to avoid even an *appearance* of conflict of interest. In view of this, and in view also of the pending Litton claims for a half-billion dollars from the Navy, would Ash disqualify himself from dealing with the Navy budget? A sensitive man would; Roy Ash refused.

At a hearing of his Joint Economic subcommittee in December 1972,

Senator William Proxmire (D–Wis.) requested comment on the Ash appointment from Gordon W. Rule, the Navy's plain-speaking and honored top procurement official. In a reference to President Eisenhower's warning against the military-industrial complex, and objecting principally to Ash's high-handed conduct at the Beverly Hills meeting, Rule said that "old General Eisenhower must be twitching in his grave." Rule would say later that he intended "no disrespect" to the late President, which he certainly didn't, and he would generously apologize for what he termed a "verbal excess," although it struck others as merely piquant. The day after he testified, while he was in his sickbed, he was visited by Admiral Isaac C. Kidd, Jr., who, as chief of the Navy Material Command, must be presumed to have feared that the Navy's budget may have been imperiled. Kidd asked Rule to sign a request for early retirement that the admiral foresightedly had brought along. Rule refused. The next day, Kidd demoted and punished Rule by exiling him, without time limit, to a Siberia—the Navy Logistics and Management School—with the mission of updating the curriculum. Proxmire and Congressman Les Aspin (D–Wis.) said that this may have violated a law making it a crime to intimidate or harass federal witnesses. At a hearing on January 10, 1973, with Kidd sitting only a few feet away, Rule told Proxmire that the admiral "probably thinks I'm a burr up his ass, and he wants me out." Surprisingly, and maybe magnanimously, Kidd reinstated Rule a couple of months later. Rule had nothing but praise for the admiral.

The atmospherics of the episode should not obscure some significant points. In terms of immediate and real power as distinguished from potential and nominal power, the post of director of the OMB is at the summit—and far more important than the Vice-Presidency. By appointing to the OMB a man who would not renounce a massive conflict of interest, President Nixon in hindsight can be seen to have created a climate—inadvertently—for the larger transgression of President Ford in the Rockefeller case. The Ash appointment did set off a large fuss, indicating that the tradition of concern over conflict of interest was alive and well two years before the Rockefeller nomination and confirmation began to undermine it.

Most conflict of interest problems are more prosaic. In one variety, the government gives a sensitive post to an executive who has just left the affected industry and who in some cases later will return to it. This sort of thing has been notorious in the Federal Energy Administration (FEA), an example being its hiring of Melvin A. Conant, a former Exxon vice-president; the company gave him a $90,000 severance payment that was discretionary and that could have been withheld had he disagreed with Exxon's policies.[8] Another case, developed by Congressmen Charles A. Vanik (D–Ohio) and John D. Dingell (D–Mich.), involved Robert C. Bowen, an engineer who came from—and returned to—Phillips Petroleum. At the outset, the question was whether the Federal Energy Office (FED), predecessor to the FEA, properly could hire him. No, said Edward C. Schmults, general counsel to the Treasury Department. In a memo to William E. Simon, then head of the FEO and later secretary of the treasury, Schmults warned that hiring Bowen "would on its face constitute a conflict of interest." At this point, Simon could have signed a waiver certifying that Bowen's duties would not conflict with his interests, including a pension arrangement with Phillips, which had loaned him to the government in a questionable government plan to exchange executives with industry. Strikingly, Simon refused to take this "prudent course," G. Allen Carver, Jr., of the Criminal Division of the Department of Justice, said in a memo later released by Congressman Dingell; ". . . in any event, the failure of Simon to sign such a waiver was foolish." Carver went on to say:

A person of his experience and intelligence should have had the foresight to realize that at some point Bowen would do something which would be questioned as a possible violation of federal conflict of interest laws.

The "something" was suspected to be certain intricate regulations which underwent a mysterious, almost undetectable change in language, with the result that some oil companies were enabled in setting prices to claim costs twice—to take a "double dip." An investigation by Dingell's House Small Business Subcommittee seemed to implicate Bowen, but, back at Phillips, he denied having manipulated the language. In any event, Carver said in his memo, Bowen

is not the principal culprit here. Those who employed him and then sought his assistance in resolving policy questions were most to blame.

Prosecuting Bowen, therefore, would be unfair and oppressive. Simon and Johnson [William Johnson, then assistant administrator of the FEO] deserved to be criticized for allowing the situation to happen.[9]

Another conflict of interest problem involves what Ralph Nader terms the "deferred bribe." Here, the federal employee paid by the public to represent its interest in, say, procurement or regulation, looks ahead to the time when he will leave government—and begins to "buy" job insurance by tailoring his conduct to the needs of private interests that someday may employ him. This is often a subtle process, hard to prove and defiant of accountability. As director of the Bureau of Medicine in the Food and Drug Administration, Dr. Joseph F. Sadusk, Jr., made many questionable decisions benefiting many pharmaceutical houses, Parke-Davis among them. He later migrated into a vice-presidency at Parke-Davis.[10] If there was a connection, how could it be established? Anyway, why pick on him, the FDA being something like a cadet training school for the industries it regulates?[11] For that matter, why pick on the FDA, other government agencies also being major suppliers of trained manpower for companies and industries with which they deal?

At the Department of Defense, 27 percent of the employees who left to take jobs with Pentagon contractors were working in conflict of interest situations, the Council on Economic Priorities, a nonprofit organization funded by foundations, found in a study in March 1975. For example, the council said, Boeing, prime contractor for the Minuteman missile system, hired four former senior officials of the Minuteman procurement office between November 1968 and August 1971. Three months later, Michael C. Jensen of the *New York Times* reported that, in recent years, at least seven high-ranking military officers had, on their retirement, gone to the Northrop Corporation to perform a variety of sensitive and, in some cases, secret tasks. Drawing on a report that Ernst & Ernst made for Northrop's outside directors, and that was released by the Senate Subcommittee on Multinational Corporations, he cited Harvey J. Jablonsky, a retired Army major general who had opened a numbered bank account in Switzerland into which Northrop had deposited $600,000 in slush funds. The late Graves B. Erskine, who had been a four-star general in the Marine Corps, and had ties to the CIA, was said to have been retained to maintain "very sophisticated" liasion with the intelligence community in Washington. Bernard A. Schriever, a retired Air Force four-star general, and the architect of the nation's ballistic missile program, was in 1975 a consultant to whom Northrop guaranteed at least two days' work a month at $600 a day. Ernst & Ernst also named Hunter Harris, another retired four-star Air Force general.

In a second report in August 1975, the Council on Economic Priorities said that of 499 former Pentagon employees working for defense contractors in the 1974 fiscal year who had filed reports required by law, 61 were working for Northrop. One, Marvin E. Anderson, had quit the Defense Contract Audit Agency to become, at Northrop's principal plant at Hawthorne, California, supervisory auditor for dealings with the agency he had left. Ten days after retiring from the Air Force, Lieutenant Colonel Ronald E. Dudley, chief of testing of the Drone/Remotely Piloted Vehicle System Program Office, went to work for Lear Siegler, Inc., a major developer of the vehicle. Three days after retiring from the Navy, where he had been assigned to technical liasion at Gould, Inc., prime contractor for the Mk 48 torpedo program, Commander Thomas Poole became coordinator for Gould in its work for the Navy on the Mk 48 torpedo.[12]

Senator George S. McGovern (D–S.Dak.), in his 1972 presidential campaign, laid down a seven-point ethics-in-government program to which news media gave little attention. One of his suggestions was for legislation to require *any* government employee to wait five years before taking a job with a company he had dealt with in the government's behalf. In 1975, Senator Proxmire and Congressman Charles E. Bennett (D–Fla.) were trying to inhibit abuses with a bill to forbid any federal employee from taking any job that depended on acquisition of a contract he had participated in awarding. The bill also would forbid any employee playing any substantial role in a contract award from taking a job with any beneficiary of the award for two years afterward.

·Congress

The Constitution makes the House and Senate each the exclusive judge of the qualifications of its own members. This creates a persistent languor in Congress, seldom shaken off, about ethical issues, including conflict of interest, which involve members. Consequently, the soil of Capitol Hill is fertile for conflicts, and they spring up in luxuriant and wide variety. The public generally senses this, even while being uneasily aware that the precise extent and nature of such conflicts never can be fully exposed.

Some legislators get away with blatant conflicts because their power to dispense or withhold goodies deters colleagues from attempting anything resembling a challenge. From a recent crop, one might pluck the case of Congressman Robert L. F. Sikes, a "conservative" Florida Democrat. As chairman of the House Appropriations Subcommittee that passes on all military construction, he exercises the kind of power that can make valorous military men tremble. Predictably, his district, which includes Pensacola, the long-time site of a major Naval Air Station, is loaded down with military facilities. One of his close friends and co-venturers, Charles P. Woodberry, is founder and chairman of the American Fidelity Life Insurance Company, a source of overpriced policies for servicemen.[13] Sikes has been a director at least since 1960, and he and his wife own 16,500 shares of the firm's stock. Woodberry provided financing for the First Navy Bank, which opened at the Pensacola Navy Air Station in October 1973, and was the first full-service bank ever founded on the grounds of a Navy installation. Before the State of Florida granted a charter for First Navy in 1972, there appeared to be only five owners, and each said he intended to continue to own his shares. Later, however, the *St. Petersburg Times* reported that Congressman Sikes even then had shown "an unusual interest" in the enterprise. And by the time First Navy began operations, happily including among its accounts the Air Station's $200 million annual payroll, the stockholders had come to include Sikes and eleven of the Navy's highest-ranking officers. One was Admiral

Maurice F. Weisner, commander-in-chief of the Pacific Fleet. After the congressman sold eleven hundred shares, Vice Admiral Malcolm Cagle, ranking officer at the Air Station, bought fifteen hundred. Newspapers unearthed yet other unseemly conflicts involving Sikes, one of Capitol Hill's more proficient flag-wavers. But in the House, where a hapless outsider's peccadillo can produce reams of mimeographed outrage, all was predictably quiet until Common Cause complained and forced an investigation that led ultimately to an official reprimand for Sikes.[14]

Now a plucking from the Senate. The Pentagon had agreed to supply seventy-one F-5E fighters to the South Vietnamese Air Force, but was forced to abandon the plan when Congress, in 1975, refused to vote more military aid to South Vietnam. This left the Northrop Corporation, manufacturer of F-5Es, with an unfulfilled $77 million contract. A rescue operation was promptly and quietly mounted by the Senate Armed Services Tactical Air Power Subcommittee. Its chairman is Howard W. Cannon (D–Nev.), who also heads the Senate ethics unit responsible for investigating charges of impropriety—including conflict of interest—against senators, and the Rules Committee, which has jurisdiction over election laws. The ranking Republican on the subcommittee is Barry M. Goldwater (R–Ariz.), who was the GOP presidential candidate in 1964. To solve Northrop's dilemma, the subcommittee engineered a transfer of the seventy-one F-5Es to the United States Air Force, which previously had rejected the planes as unneeded. Strikingly, most of the planes will be stationed at Nellis Air Force Base, which is outside Las Vegas in Cannon's home state. More strikingly, *Newsday* reporter Patrick J. Sloyan discovered, Northrop had provided Cannon, Goldwater, and their families, including Congressman Barry M. Goldwater, Jr. (R–Calif.), with a total of $3,300 worth of free air travel in 1971, 1972, and 1973. Any inference that the travel influenced his decision making "is ridiculous and beneath comment," Cannon said. Senator Goldwater made a similar disclaimer. But neither could disclaim an *appearance* of conflict which resulted entirely from their free-and-easy acceptance of special favors. While the House was quiet about Congressman Sikes and the First Navy Bank, the Senate was quiet about Senators Cannon and Goldwater, and Northrop.[15] Such is the custom.

Conflicts do not always emerge on the Hill with such clarity. Is it a "conflict" for, say, a legislator who is a director of a savings and loan association to serve on a committee dealing with savings and loan legislation, particularly when he believes such legislation to be in the *public* interest? To accept a campaign contribution from the industry? Then to make a speech blessing that industry? Is it a "conflict" for advocates of a huge defense establishment, such as were the late chairmen of the Armed Services committees, Senator Richard B. Russell (D–Ga.) and Congressman L. Mendel Rivers (D–S.C.), to see to it that their states are saturated with defense facilities that provide jobs to grateful voters? In ethical terms, the answer to each such question must be "yes"; but we can conceive no way of trying to implement the ethic that would not pose insurmountable problems, and that ultimately would not do more harm than good.

Imperfect though it may be, the best approach is mandatory full disclosure to the public. This is not now required. House Rule No. 44 requires members and employees to file, with the Committee on Standards of Official Conduct, *confidential* disclosure reports listing each source of income exceeding $5,000, including any capital gain not derived from the sale of a residence; nongovernment reimbursements exceeding $1,000; the interest and position in business enterprises accounting for income of more than $1,000, and the names of professional organizations also accounting for income of more than $1,000. The House authorizes an extremely limited public disclosure—excluding, for example, the market value of business interests—and inhibits inquiries by requiring that a congressman be notified whenever a person asks to see his public filing.

The Senate is worse. With the exception of a public listing of gifts aggregating $50 or more, and of the source of each honorarium of $300 or more, specified financial information—such as debts exceeding $5,000, and real-estate holdings exceeding $10,000—is *confidentially* disclosed to the comptroller general. This is essentially a useless gesture.

The situation becomes still more patchwork when one takes into account the Executive and the Judiciary. All federal executives over Civil Service grade GS-13—but not the President and Vice-President—are required to report basically the same information as senators and their employees, although the rules are even less stringent for members of the President's staff and for consultants who are retained throughout the government. There is, however, no provision for public disclosure. Under a resolution of the Judicial Conference of the United States, all federal judges—Supreme Court justices excepted—file a *confidential* financial disclosure report with a special committee of the Conference, the conference of their circuit, and the clerk of their court.

Starting in 1971, Senator Birch Bayh sponsored a bill, the Omnibus Disclosure Act, based on the correct premise that "[i]f conflicts of interest exist, the public has a right to know . . ." The bill would cover all federal employees without exception, whether in the Executive, Legislative, or Judicial branches, whose annual income exceeds $18,000, and all candidates for federal office. They would be required to file yearly reports—open to public inspection—providing the following information:

First, the identity and value of interests in real or personal property worth more than $500; second, creditors to whom more than $1,000 is owed and the amount of each such debt; third, dealings in securities and commodities; fourth, transactions in real property; fifth, gifts of more than $100; sixth, the amount and source of each contribution to defray campaign or office expenses, and seventh, except in the case of a nonincumbent candidate, the identity of each client who pays more than $1,000 to a law firm with which the individual covered by the act is associated. [This finally would reach the many legislators—the late Senator Everett M. Dirksen (R–Ill.) was a notorious example—whose law firms attract industrial and other clients with interests the legislator is positioned to affect. Bayh's bill would require the public servant to specify *when* the client requested his law firm's services, and to identify any administrative or judicial action in which the government was a party and in which his firm was representing the client.]

Bayh has demonstrated his own good faith in the matter by making a voluntary disclosure of his assets, liabilities, and income each year since 1969, and by requiring since 1970 that each member of his staff earning $18,000 or more make a similar disclosure.[16]

The Judiciary

The Supreme Court said in 1955 that "to perform its high function in the best way 'justice must satisfy the appearance of justice.' " Conflicts of interest on the bench soil the appearance of justice and threaten the moral authority of the courts. Some conflicts take forms inimical to the separation of powers; mammon may be absent but the pitfalls of trying to serve two masters are certainly present. John Jay, the first chief justice of the United States, simultaneously held "a position at the top of the federal judiciary, a key ambassadorship, and the candidacy for a prestigious governorship," John P. MacKenzie recalls in *The Appearance of Justice*.[17] He tells us that we have indeed come a long way since then, but not so far that Abe Fortas, as an associate justice, did not restrain himself from functioning as the equivalent of a staff member in the White House of Lyndon B. Johnson.

Situations arise frequently in the lower courts in which mammon is palpably present. The *Wall Street Journal,* in a front-page story on October 20, 1970, summarized a bankruptcy case involving United States District Judge Frank Gray, Jr., of Nashville, Tennessee, under these headlines:

A Question of Ethics
Federal Judge Presides
Over a Case Related
To His Own Fortune

Friend Who Made Him Rich Is
Involved, as Well as Bank
In Which He Holds Shares

———

But He Sees No Conflicts

Despite this, fourteen lawyers, counsel to nearly that many parties to the proceeding, subsequently asked Gray, who had stepped aside following publication of the *Journal* story, to resume presiding. "No lawyer in any manner connected with this case has ever questioned, or thought of questioning the ethnics of the procedures to which Judge Gray adhered in presiding over the matters involved herein," the petition said. "It did not occur to any such lawyer that there could be, or would be any criticism of Judge Gray."[18] Possibly because he was more imaginative individually than the lawyers were collectively, Gray stayed out of the case.

In Oklahoma City, Oklahoma, Chief United States District Judge Luther Bohannon presided over the application of Four Seasons Nursing Centers and its affiliates—the source of what the government termed "the largest criminal stock fraud ever prosecuted"—for the protection of the bankruptcy court. At the outset, he had to appoint a trustee, required by law to be "disinterested." Bohannon appointed Norman Hirschfield, who previously, as a paid consultant to Four Seasons, had recommended the very proceeding that was now under way. Bohannon then named as co-counsel to Hirschfield Edward Barth; he was a partner in a law firm of Richard L. Bohannon, son of the judge, and of Bert Barefoot, once the judge's partner in Barefoot & Bohannon. John MacKenzie reported these and other irregularities in the *Washington Post* on August 22, 1970. The next day, at a meeting with Judge Bohannon, the lawyers proclaimed their faith and trust in him. However, the Four Seasons fraud had given rise to additional litigation, especially suits in behalf of shareholders whose lawyers contended that they had been victimized in New York City and that their cases properly should be tried there. In the end, the Judicial Panel on Multi-District Litigation, created by Congress to deal with precisely such jurisdictional disputes, delivered what MacKenzie, in his book, termed "a Solomon-like solution": it chose Oklahoma as the trial site, but selected an outsider for a judge.[19]

The Tennessee and Oklahoma cases each established, first, that for local lawyers to have knowledge of a judge's conflicts is not enough, because they may become part of the problem and in fact enlarge it, and, second, that outside intervention, primarily in the form of wide publicity, is potent therapy. These points are strongly reenforced in MacKenzie's illuminating chapter, "The Velvet Blackjack," where he shows that a judge subtly but effectively coerces a waiver of disqualification when he discloses that he has holdings in a company which is a party in a case before him, and then asks counsel—at his mercy then and in the future—if they object. MacKenzie details the best illustration—the "spectacle of one of the nation's most highly respected courts, the Fifth U.S. Circuit Court of Appeals, heavily involved in disqualifying business activity [ownership of oil and gas securities] while passing judgment on matters of great economic consequence in the area of judges' business interests and actively soliciting from more than two dozen lawyers a waiver of disqualification."

On October 6, 1969, three members of the Court of Appeals met to hear oral arguments on the Southern Louisiana gas rate case, involving at least $80 million a year in rate reductions and refunds merely for home-owners burning natural gas. Judge Warren L. Jones amiably disclosed that he and his wife owned "a few shares" in three companies affected by the proceeding. "If anybody thinks I'm disqualified, why, this should be the time for them to say so," he said. Nobody admitted to such a thought. Chief Judge John R. Brown was pleased about that. "I was going to say the court needed him badly," he said. A few days later, the court clerk, in a letter to counsel, revealed that in addition to the holding of "a few shares" announced from the bench, Jones held two trusteeships—in each of which he managed a portfolio in behalf of another person—with a com-bined value in oil and gas of about $500,000. Brown had said nothing from the bench about himself; but the letter made the stunning revelation that he had a portfolio of about $100,000 in oil and gas, about half of it person-ally held and about half held in trust for two families. Included was $35,000 in three firms that were parties to the pending case, Gulf Oil, Houston Natural Gas, and Tenneco. The letter went on to invite written questions about the possible disqualification of Jones or Brown. An order postponing rate reductions of $1.5 million a week appeared under the clerk's signature, in this startling form: "P.S. Also enclosed is a copy of a stay order this day entered by the court."

Four days before the deadline for receipt of written comments the court issued another communiqué: "The judges of this panel to which this case is assigned are not disqualified by prejudice. Neither are the disqualified by interest, whether individual, fiduciary or otherwise. *Kinnear-Weed Co.* v. *Humble Oil Co.*, 403 F.2d 437. . . ." To cite this case was to show, MacKenzie said, "how little chastened the judges had been by their embar-rassment of oil riches." That was the gentlest understatement. The plaintiff, Clarence W. Kinnear, claimed to be the inventor of one of the oil drill bits most widely used by the industry. His suit sought millions of dollars. The trial judge, Lamar Cecil, of Beaumont, Texas, ruled against him. Then Cecil died. Later, Kinnear learned of facts that had been easily available to the oil industry defendants while Cecil lived: Cecil had been a one-quarter owner, secretary, and treasurer of a drilling equipment repair firm whose best customer was Humble; the judge and his wife had leased thousands of acres to Humble and other oil companies, and Mrs. Cecil owned $9,000 worth of stock in Humble. A year before the Fifth Circuit phoned the aforementioned communiqué to counsel on the Southern Louisiana gas rate case, Judge Brown had ruled that Cecil had not been disqualified from presiding over the Kinnear case. Brown and his colleagues actually were citing this ruling as the authority for declaring that the gas and oil interests of Brown and Jones did not disqualify them in the pending gas case. But after reiterating that they "find no basis for disqualification of any judge," the judges concluded that it is "desirable" for them to step aside and for another panel to take over. This was done, although the litigation eventually was settled out of court.

The Canons of Judicial Ethics approved by the American Bar Association (ABA) in 1924, MacKenzie wrote, "held firmly to one useful and durable theme: judges must not only do justice, it must *appear* that they do justice." The theme is expressed in at least eight canons, including Canon 4: "A judge's official conduct should be free from impropriety and the appearance of impropriety . . ."[20] Obviously the canons did not prevent the violations cited here, not to mention the conflict of interest involvements that led the Senate to reject the elevation to the Supreme Court of Judge Clement F. Haynsworth, Jr., of the Fourth Circuit Court of Appeals. Most belatedly, reforms began to be generated. Chief Justice Earl Warren, at the close of his service on the Supreme Court took a strong initiative. The Judicial Conference cut it back to await action by the ABA. That organization, in 1972, then revised its canons; these now include Canon 2, which MacKenzie considers a major achievement because of its tone: "A judge should avoid impropriety and the appearance of impropriety in all of his activities." The commentary accentuates this: "He must expect to be the subject of constant public scrutiny. He must therefore accept restrictions on his conduct that might be viewed as burdensome by the ordinary citizen, and he should do so freely and willingly." A year later, the Judicial Conference adopted a toughened version of the ABA code. And a year after that, in 1974, Congress enacted legislation basically embodying the ABA and conference standards, and striking decisively at conflicts such as those in the Fifth Circuit. A judge or a Supreme Court justice who owns even a single share of stock in a corporation, for example, is barred from sitting in a case involving that corporation.

Independent Agencies

Any discussion of conflict of interest in independent government agencies must deal with the Federal Power Commission (FPC). There are two reasons: one, the General Accounting Office (GAO) made a ten-month investigation of conflict of interest in the FPC, resulting in a 115-page report in September 1974, and, two, the commission was the consumers' representative in the Southern Louisiana gas rate case. The GAO report, said Congressman John E. Moss (D–Calif.), who had requested the investigation, "makes a very strong case for concluding that . . . cumulative financial exploitation of consumers" by the oil and gas industry "was aided and abetted by the very federal agency charged with protecting the public against monopoly and profiteering."[21]

The report centered on the five-year period beginning in August 1969, when President Nixon named John N. Nassikas chairman of the FPC; Nixon eventually named all four of the other commissioners as well. The key findings included these:

• Seven administrative law judges and twelve other officials owned prohibited securities, some in natural-gas producers such as Exxon, Tenneco, and Texaco, and were ordered to divest only as a result of the GAO investigation. Five of the judges, who preside over quasi-judicial proceedings, had disclosed the holdings in forms filed four to seven years before the investigation.

(In a report on another investigation requested by Moss, the GAO charged that some officials of the United States Geological Survey [USGS], a unit of the Department of the Interior, owned stock in companies which hold mineral leases on federal lands the USGS administers. The examples included a supervisory mining engineer who since 1968 had owned stock in seven mining firms; a supervisory petroleum engineer with authority to suspend, or not to suspend, the operations of oil companies on lands leased to the government—and who since 1971 had owned stock in Exxon, Mobil, and Standard Oil of California; and another petroleum engineer who was receiving retirement income from Atlantic Richfield and owned 496 shares of its stock. All told, 49 out of 223 [22 percent] of the financial disclosure statements filed for the 1974 fiscal year "raised conflict of interest possibilities" or were violations of the law, the GAO said. As of March 1975, the USGS had required none of the officials involved to divest their holdings.)[22]

• Supposedly, every FPC official required to file a financial disclosure form also had filed a sworn affidavit affirming that he never had participated in a decision-making process involving a company in which he or a member of his immediate household had a financial interest. Contrary to Nassikas's assurances on this score, the GAO found that of 144 officials required to file affidavits, eleven (out of a total of eighteen) judges and eleven other officials had not. One of the nonfiling judges presided in a case in which General Motors was a major intervenor—but did not disclose until the proceeding was well under way that he owned GM stock. Several other judges had similar involvements, but Nassikas allowed them to preside, anyway.

• As of December 12, 1973, ninety-four upper-level officials required to file annual financial disclosure forms had not done so, seven had not done so correctly, and only twenty-four had fully complied; the record was similar for 1971 and 1972.

• The three officials responsible for carrying out the disclosure program—Executive Director Webster P. Maxson, General Counsel Leo E. Forquer, and Claudius L. Fike, head of the Office of Personnel Programs—had themselves not filed disclosure forms for 1971, 1972, and 1973.

In the cases we have cited the basic problem was the existence of a conflict of interest, a potential for exploitation, and an appearance of impropriety. Many of the persons involved—officials, legislators, judges, bureaucrats—saw their cases widely publicized and felt that they and their families had been embarrassed, if not humiliated or pilloried. The aftermath was sometimes even more unpleasant. In the cases of Robert Bowen, the Phillips Petroleum engineer, and of the Federal Power Commission, congressmen spoke publicly about possible criminal prosecutions. And sometimes the standard of purity seemed to go high indeed. Thus, as was duly reported by the *New York Times,* the wife of the FPC chairman was induced to dispose of an inheritance of fifty shares of stock in United States Steel because it owned a natural-gas pipeline subject to regulation—but so obscure and inconsequential that her husband reportedly had never heard of it.[23] The contrasts with Nelson Rockefeller could not be sharper. His conflict reaches "into every nook and cranny of our economy," Congressman George E. Danielson (D–Calif.) said. "It is congenital and it is insoluble."[24]

V
Conflict
of Interest
in the
Private Sector

Conflicts of interest are commonplace in the professions. Nowhere are the consequences more serious than in medicine. Here, conflicts lead directly to death and injury for which satisfactory accountability is usually nonexistent.

Plato saw so much avarice among doctors that he questioned whether the true physician is "a healer of the sick or a maker of money."[1] In the seventeenth century poet John Dryden was similarly concerned:

> So lived our sires ere doctors
>   learned to kill
> And multiply with theirs the
>   weekly bill
> The first physicians by debauch
>   were made:
> Excess began, and sloth sustains
>   the trade.[2]

Sloth continues to afflict the profession; it tolerates and even legitimates conflicts of interest which arise between healing the sick and personal enrichment. "As to the honor and conscience of doctors," George Bernard Shaw wrote in the preface to *The Doctor's Dilemma*, "they have as much as any other class of men, no more and no less. And what other men dare pretend to be impartial where they have a strong pecuniary interest on one side?"

Wise physicians, true professionals, avoid such an interest. They know, for example, that their patients, to whom they are primarily accountable, may or may not require a prescription. They are aware that overprescribing is rampant, and they are aware of the price it exacts. The overprescribing and misprescribing of antibiotics alone needlessly imperil the health and sometimes the lives of millions of patients, Senator Gaylord Nelson's Monopoly Subcommittee was told in December 1972 by three experts—Dr. Harry F. Dowling, a world-renowned specialist in the treatment of infections; Dr. Henry E. Simmons, then director of the Bureau of Drugs in the Food and Drug Administration, and Dr. Philip R. Lee, a former assistant secretary of the Department of Health, Education, and Welfare who led HEW's Task Force on Prescription Drugs. In hearings held by Senator Edward M. Kennedy (D–Mass.) in 1973, drug-induced fatalities in hospitals alone were reliably estimated at thirty thousand a year.

Sensitive to such realities, wise physicians abjure a financial stake in the decision whether to prescribe. By thus eliminating a conflict, they also are more likely to protect their patients. This is substantiated by more than the dictum of a great playwright. Studies have shown that physicians who benefit from prescribing are more wont to prescribe than physicians who do not benefit. A court case in Spokane, Washington, for example, brought out that four ophthalmologists who sold the eyeglasses they prescribed wrote 83 percent more prescriptions than four Spokane peers who left the selling entirely to independent opticians.[3]

The Senate Antitrust and Monopoly Subcommittee established in the 1960s that several thousand additional physicians had other conflicts which enabled them to profit from their prescribing. The bulk had set up private-label firms which repackaged medicines obtained from manufacturers, which charged extraordinarily high prices, which sometimes actually paid kickbacks to the physician-owners. In all cases, the private-label firms could prosper only if the physician-owners would prescribe the private-label products in preference to others. Other physicians owned pharmacies. Yet others were co-owners of medical buildings in each of which there was a pharmacy—the one most likely to fill their prescriptions. Sometimes, the pharmacist's rental was geared to his volume of business—which the physicians were best positioned to affect. Dr. James H. Sammons, of whom more later, warned in 1962 while a councilor of the Texas Medical Association that in the public eye physician ownership of drugstores appeared as "unequivocally greed of the worst sort."

All such practices violated the ethical code of the American Medical Association. Rather than act decisively against them, as would befit a professional organization, the AMA watered down the code to convert most of them into nonviolations. In the special case of the repackaging firms, the AMA without condoning them managed to do nothing effective about them. Senator Philip A. Hart (D–Mich.), the subcommittee chairman, tried repeatedly to attack medical conflcts of interest with legislation to bar doctors from profiting from their prescriptions, but couldn't get it even out of the subcommittee.[4]

"The greatest single curse in medicine is the curse of unnecessary operations," Dr. Richard Cabot, professor of medicine at Harvard, said in 1938. "[A]nd there would be fewer of them, if the doctor got the same salary whether he operated or not."[5] Since then the medical profession has done little to lift the curse, even that part of it attributable to conflict of interest. Indeed, if a conscientious hospital staff does bite the bullet on establishing that a colleague has shown an uncontrollable lust to cut, it might take the drastic step of throwing him out. Sometimes, however, such a surgeon simply moves the site of his butcher shop. But our concern here is with a large number of surgeons who are regarded in the profession as both competent and ethical. It is a concern made necessary by the continuing terrible toll taken by needless surgery—almost sixteen thousand deaths and a waste of nearly $5 billion annually, by the estimates of Dr. Sidney M. Wolfe, director of the Health Research Group.[6]

In deciding whether to operate, says Dr. George Crile, Jr., emeritus consultant of the Department of General Surgery at the Cleveland Clinic, the surgeon

is faced with a conflict of interest: he is paid if he operates and not paid if he doesn't. A further conflict arises if he has a choice between performing a major operation, for which he will receive a large fee, or a minor one, for which the fee might be only a fifth as much. Finally, if he knows that he is not expert in performing a certain type of operation and that others would be able to perform it better and more safely, his decision as to whether to do it himself is again subject to a conflict of interest. In short, there are many surgical decisions in which the best interest of the patient is in sharp conflict with the financial interest of the surgeon."

Writing in *Harper's* magazine, Crile cited evidence that "the overall mortality rate from appendectomies, including deaths resulting from the surgery itself, were highest in the areas where the most appendectomies occurred"; that "there will be more appendectomies (and other surgery) performed in areas of fee-for-service medicine [which Blue Shield plans provide] than in areas where patients subscribe to a prepayment plan [which has a financial interest in avoiding unnecessary operations, and in which doctors receive salaries]," and that twice as many operations per unit of population are performed in the United States, a bastion of fee-for-service, as in England and Wales, where that system has been displaced by the National Health Service.

Cancer of the thyroid is one of the rarest causes of death by cancer, although between 5 percent and 10 percent of all older women have lumps in their thyroids. Yet, "many surgeons advocate removing all thyroid nodules," Crile wrote. "If this were actually done by all surgeons, the number of deaths resulting accidentally from the operations would far exceed the number of patients whose lives were saved." By inserting a needle into the thyroid and withdrawing a very small specimen [in a small, inexpensive office procedure], physicians can determine if cancer is present. Consequently, Crile says, "[n]eedle biopsy of the thyroid has . . . gained wide acceptance abroad and in a few institutions in this country. Practicing surgeons, however, have been slow to accept it." Similarly, the radical mastectomy, which doctors in Europe and most of Canada have nearly abandoned in favor of less mutilating procedures, has held on tenaciously in the United States. Blue Shield plans that pay two to three times as much for a radical as for a simple operation, Crile suggests, "may" have something to do with this.

When he gave a newspaper interview indicating a relation between fees and practice,

> there was a sharp response from the local medical community. The Ethics Committee of the Cleveland Academy of Medicine (American Medical Association) asked me to appear, and then, disregarding the fate of 89,000 women who each year will be treated for new breast cancers, the committee concluded that I should not have informed the press of my belief that radical mastectomy was archaic and no longer necessary. It made surgeons who did radical operations subject to criticism by their patients, the committee explained. The committee took no official stand on the suggested relationship between the fee and the selection of operation.[7]

A profession pursues "a common calling as a learned art and as a public service—nonetheless a public service because it may incidentally be a means of livelihood," Roscoe Pound, former dean of the Harvard Law School, once said. And, he said, "[t]he medical society exists primarily for the purposes of medicine, not of the doctor of medicine, and for the advancement of the healing art." In a definitive essay on the professions, Pound further emphasized the "tradition of duty of the physician to the patient, to the medical profession, and to the public, . . . authoritatively declared in codes of professional ethics, taught by precept and example and made effective by the discipline of an organized profession . . ."[8]

Applying the dean's authoritative criteria, we find that Crile observed them fully. In the interview and in the *Harper's* article, he was clearly concerned with advancement of the healing art, and with the physician's duty to the patient, the profession, and the public—those 89,000 women treated annually for new breast cancers. What of the code of ethics? Crile's peers said, "Although the Committee felt your comments did not violate specific medical ethics, they are nevertheless reprehensible." Why? Because he had opened to criticism colleagues who had performed radical mastectomies, upset the women on whom they had operated, and had "had a deleterious effect" on the relation between patients and "all different specialities of surgeons." But nothing in the committee's letter, which Crile included in the article, indicates concern beyond the club and its immediate patients for the broad public and for the financial relationship which, as Crile suggested, could be an engine for continuing needless drastic surgery. Crile, concerned about the profoundly important results of an undeniable conflict of interest, was seeking to protect the public to which the profession is primarily accountable, while the committee, silent on the conflict, was preoccupied with making Crile accountable to his fellows.

. . .

Such ethical myopia is symptomatic. While the American Medical Association (AMA) and its affiliates throughout the country rightly maintain ethics committees, external checks on the ethics of the AMA (or other professional organizations) are generally only the fitful and wholly insufficient ones exerted by the press, and by government bodies, which in matters affecting the professions are often mere agents of the professions. Thus, for the immeasurable responsibilities entrusted to them by the public, they are usually effectively accountable only to themselves. The AMA has singularly abused the trust placed in it not only by the public, but even by its own members and, necessarily, by patients through their physicians. Nothing illuminates this more brightly than the relationship of the AMA to the pharmaceutical industry. This relationship entailed a conflict between the industry, a rich source of revenue, and the absolutely fundamental obligation to unite physicians in the pursuit of a learned art as a public service. For decades now, the AMA has been resolving the conflict in favor of the industry. The resultant injury and death to the public have been on an incalculable scale.

The lay person, even when not incapacitated, is in all but isolated cases incompetent to determine whether he needs a potent drug and, if he does, the appropriate dosage, and the preferred frequency, duration, and route of administration. He is, in short, helpless—wholly at the doctor's mercy. It follows inexorably that the physician in prescribing must not be given unbalanced, misleading, deceptive, or false information about the safety and effectiveness of medicines. It likewise follows that the principal organization of the medical profession, in fealty to its noble mission, must do everything within its power to assure the integrity of information about drugs which is disseminated to its members. In the early part of the twentieth century, the AMA was an admirable and at times inspiring organization. It maintained into the 1950s a program under which pharmaceutical advertising in the *Journal of the AMA (JAMA)* was limited to those medicines which had been given the justly coveted approval of the AMA's Council on Drugs, composed of distinguished independent experts.

Manufacturers have the overriding purpose of making a profit, not protecting patients. The courts have held that a company director "owes a loyalty that is undivided and an allegiance that is influenced in action *by no consideration other than the corporation's welfare."* (Emphasis supplied.)[9] If by deceiving physicians a company can seize a large share of a particular market, as has happened, the pressures on its competitors to do the same become well nigh irresistible.

With "wonder" drugs proliferating after World War II; with unprecedentedly large profits in prospect; with throwaway medical publications, which were entirely dependent for revenue on pharmaceutical advertising, springing up, and, most important, with the evidence incontrovertible that physicians—supposed scientists—prescribed largely on the basis of advertising and promotion rather than scientific literature, the stage was set for the industry to tell the AMA, in effect: Lower your standards, because if you do not we will shift much of our advertising away from *JAMA* and your speciality journals. Having become habituated to having the industry provide for as much as half of its revenues, the AMA complied.[10]

"It is no disparagement of honorable trades and callings, . . . to insist that an organized profession of physicians or of lawyers is not primarily analogous to a retail grocers' association and that there is a generic distinction between a medical society or an organized bar and a plumbers' or lumber dealers' association," Roscoe Pound said in his essay on the professions, which was published in 1949. "It is unhappily true that there was in the last century in America a tendency to deprofessionalize the old professions, to reduce all callings to the level of individual business enterprise, and to think of medical societies or bar associations as like trade organizations. But the root purpose is different. The trade association exists for the purposes of trade as a money-making activity. The medical society exists primarily for the purposes of medicine, . . . and for the advancement of the healing art."[11]

At least insofar as pharmaceuticals were concerned, the AMA became a trade association but lacked the saving candor to say so. In an early step in the transformation, it abolished the requirement that medicines advertised in *JAMA* had to be formally precleared by the Council on Drugs. This led to the appearance of misleading drug ads, a fact documented in the epochal hearings held over a two-and-a-half-year period, ending in 1962, by the late Senator Estes Kefauver (D–Tenn.), chairman of the Senate Antitrust and Monopoly Subcommittee. The AMA in these hearings took extreme hard-line positions against needed reforms. It opposed, for example, all efforts to stimulate physicians to prescribe drugs by generic names in order to save their patients from paying exorbitant prices for brand-name medicines that commonly were identical. Taking a position that on scientific and ethical grounds was preposterous, but that it continued to hold in 1975, the AMA fought a proposal to require manufacturers to demonstrate with substantial evidence that their medicines live up to the claims of effectiveness made for them. The AMA's performance—shameful is not too strong a word for it —fed suspicions that it had become, for practical purposes, an arm of the Pharmaceutical Manufacturers Association.[12]

The amendments to the Food, Drug, and Cosmetic Act of 1938 urged by Senator Kefauver would have died had it not been for the attention focused on pharmaceuticals by the birth in other countries of children who had seal-like flippers instead of arms and legs, and to the tracing of this catastrophe to the ingestion by their mothers, during the first trimester of pregnancy, of a sedative called thalidomide.[13] The Kefauver-Harris Amendments of 1962, as they came to be known, included a requirement that the advertising of prescription medicines accord with the official prescribing brochure approved by the Food and Drug Administration, especially that the advertising include a brief summary of contraindications for use, warnings, precautions, and other vital information. The FDA drew up and promulgated regulations to implement this provision and entrusted their administration to an extraordinarily dedicated physician, Dr. Robert S. McCleery.

He launched a criminal prosecution of Wallace Laboratories for having falsely advertised a prescription drug, Pree MT (previously Miluretic) in *JAMA*. A few months later, in January 1966, the firm pleaded no-contest and was given the maximum penalty—a fine of $1,000 on each of two counts. Since then, but especially in the years 1965 through 1968, the FDA has taken dozens more actions against false and misleading pharmaceutical promotion—criminal prosecutions, seizures of interstate shipments, remedial letters in which companies were compelled to apologize to the medical profession for misleading claims, remedial advertisements repudiating offending advertisements. Over and over, *JAMA* was a vehicle for these ads. To put a finer point on it, the *Journal of the American Medical Association* repeatedly, over a period of several years, was a conduit for biased, deceptive information about drugs with a potential to injure and kill, as well as heal —a conduit to the AMA's own members who, as a result, could, unawares, expose their patients to needless risk or to worthless therapy.[14] Unlike the manufacturers who on occasion were compelled by the FDA to repudiate their excesses, the AMA never apologized, never expressed chagrin or regret, never admitted to a need for reform, and never gave major publicity, when it gave any at all, to the dozens of crackdowns on misleading and false advertising. The circumstances would have made a cry of rape appropriate, but only the sound of the cash register could be heard.

All the while, each weekly issue of *JAMA* contained an assurance to AMA members, or at least to those who read the fine print, that the advertisements therein "have been reviewed to comply with the principles governing advertising in AMA scientific publications." Some AMA ads for itself claimed that "every statement" in accepted ads "must be backed by substantiated facts . . . or we won't run it!" And in April 1965, Glenn R. Knotts, director of advertising evaluation, asserted that *JAMA*'s "screening boards . . . enforce high standards for advertising" and confine claims in ads "for useful products to those which can be demonstrated by scientific fact."

The reliability of the AMA's assurances may be judged more fairly by a closer examination of the FDA's first criminal prosecution for false and misleading advertising of a prescription drug, the case already mentioned against Wallace Laboratories. The product, Pree MT, was promoted by Wallace for the relief of premenstrual tension. It combined meprobamate, a sedative/tranquilizer, with hydrochlorothiazide, a diuretic. In four successive issues of *JAMA* in mid-1964, the company claimed in ads, "Contraindications: None known" (a contraindication is a medical condition in which a medicine affirmatively should *not* be prescribed). For almost five years, however, the manufacturer, a division of Carter-Wallace, Inc., had listed contraindications for Pree MT millions of times—in the official prescribing brochure in every package; in the *Physicians' Desk Reference*, which is composed of prescribing instructions in space purchased by manufacturers, and which is the guide physicians most often rely upon; and in *New and Nonofficial Drugs*, published by the AMA's own Council on Drugs. Finally, someone in the FDA apparently leaked word to Wallace Laboratories that the FDA was working up a case. This led the company to request *JAMA*, for its issue of June 29, 1964, to chisel the phrase "Contraindications: None known" off the printing plate. *JAMA* complied.[15] Thus did the AMA, in this and numerous other shabby episodes differing essentially only in the details, make common cause with those having a financial interest in the deception of physicians and the victimization of their patients.[16]

It is a depressing fact that the medical profession did not try to make the AMA and other physician organizations accountable for such behavior. Countless doctors were too busy being good doctors, it is true; and by increasing thousands, physicians had declined to join the AMA, so that it represented less than half the profession by the early 1970s. In addition, physicians in large numbers, relying for information on *JAMA* and other publications dependent on pharmaceutical advertising, did not know what was going on. Still, it is a distressing statistic that in 1967, when the FDA sought comments on proposals designed to eliminate loopholes in the rules for drug advertising, not one physician in the United States was moved by the need to stop pharmaceutical firms from lying to the medical profession to write a letter of support to the agency. In 1973 alone, according to data twenty major manufacturers supplied to Senator Kennedy's Health Subcommittee, the companies had distributed to doctors more than 2 billion free samples—enough to provide each man, woman, and child in the United States with ten pills, tablets, capsules, bottles, or tubes. The companies also reported having given prescribing physicians, along with nurses, pharmacists, and others involved in health care, almost 13 million gifts at a cost of $5,534,426, as well as more than 45 million calendars, rulers, and other product "reminders" at a cost of $8,579,974. In addition, the firms provided

31,201 plant tours that cost $748,097, counting hotel, entertainment, and travel expenses, and sponsored 7,519 symposia, some of them at Caribbean resorts, which, with honoraria, came to $2,724,697.

The AMA's slide into decadence occurred on several fronts. In the 1960s, for example, its spokesmen had assured Senators Hart and Nelson that, the potential conflict being obvious, the AMA owned no stocks in pharmaceutical firms. But in 1973, Stuart Auerbach disclosed in the *Washington Post* that the AMA had invested almost $10 million from its members' retirement fund in drug companies. The acquisition would have conflicted with a long-standing ruling of the AMA's Judicial Council that it was ethically questionable for a physician to invest in drug companies. Predictably, the council resolved the dilemma by ruling that it was not unethical for the corporate body of the AMA to do what the physician alone should not do.[17]

After years of delay, the most complete, factual, and unbiased guide to drug-prescribing in history, *AMA Drug Evaluations: 1971*, prepared by the Council on Drugs with the aid of more than three hundred expert consultants, was ready for publication. Working with the Pharmaceutical Manufacturers Association, Dr. Max H. Parrott, the AMA board chairman, managed to delay publication for several months. He was, however, unable to get the council to delete its conclusion that each of dozens of widely prescribed—and widely advertised—medicines, especially combinations, were "irrational."

The council then began preparation of a second edition. The AMA gave the industry an advance look. This led to a demand by the organization's hierarchy to delete the phrase "not recommended" from the several drug evaluations where it appeared. The council rejected the demand. A month later, in October 1972, in what it said was part of a sweeping economy drive, the AMA abolished the council: the same council that had been advising physicians on the prudent use of medicines since 1906, attracting eminent medical scientists in every speciality, who served without pay.

The Senate Small Business Monopoly Subcommittee went into all of this on February 6, 1973, calling as witnesses Dr. John Adriani, who was chairman of the council from 1968 through 1970, and who had played a leading role in the singular achievement of having *AMA Drug Evaluations* published; his successor, Dr. Harry C. Shirkey; and a former vice-chairman, Dr. Daniel L. Azarnoff. With each testifying with the full assent of the others, they accused the AMA of being "a captive of and beholden to the pharmaceutical industry." In a press release, the AMA accused the three—each a highly respected specialist, teacher, and practitioner—of having made "inaccurate and irresponsible statements." A reader inclined to wonder whom to believe might take into account a Library of Congress survey, prepared at the request of Senator Nelson, the subcommittee chairman, which showed that in the preceding five years, *JAMA* had carried 14,830 pages of pharmaceutical advertising, but that there had been an ominous decline: the number of pages in 1972 were half as many as in 1968.

The witnesses also said that the AMA had assigned the task of completing the second edition to its paid employees. It will be "emasculated and worthless," Adriani testified. Shirkey, who had requested removal of his name from the book, said that the council unanimously refused to "accept this book as ours." The AMA, in its press release, said that the "once compelling" need for the council had disappeared with the FDA's assumption of its mission. Nelson and Adriani had perceived this correctly. The AMA, the resolute opponent of government involvement in medicine, was thrusting responsibility onto the government.[18]

The scientific and editorial content of *JAMA*, while continuing to the present to meet high standards in many respects, also suffered. The most blatant evidence came to light in 1969, when *JAMA*, which had found it possible to publish self-serving articles submitted by major advertisers including G. D. Searle & Co., Inc., and Upjohn Company, refused—incredibly— to publish a "white paper" submitted by the National Academy of Sciences– National Research Council (NAS–NRC). The "white paper" had been prepared by five internationally eminent specialists in the treatment of infectious diseases. Each had been chairman of an NAS–NRC panel which, under a contract with the Food and Drug Administration, had reviewed the evidence of efficacy for products that combine in fixed ratio two or more antibiotics or other anti-infective agents. Unanimously, the thirty panel members had condemned the combinations as irrational and dangerous as compared with the appropriate separate use of their ingredients. Widespread and indiscriminate use of products such as combinations of penicillin and streptomycin, one of the panel chairman, Dr. Calvin M. Kunin, testified, created not only needless hazards in patients, including irreversible deafness, especially in children, but a possible peril to "all society" by allowing bacteria resistant to treatment to proliferate.[19] In good part, the widespread and indiscriminate prescribing of combinations was attributable to extravagant spending on promotion. Some of this spending was going to *JAMA* at the same time it was refusing to accept the "white paper." Yet in 1961—eight years earlier—the AMA had told Senator Kefauver that, at the insistence of the Council on Drugs, the board of trustees had decided to put a gradual stop to advertising of the combinations "during the next two or three years."[20] The distinguished *New England Journal of Medicine* accepted the "white paper" without hesitation and published it May 22, 1969.

In an opening statement at a hearing on May 6, 1969, Senator Nelson recalled testimony a short time earlier in which the AMA's general counsel, Bernard Hirsh, had told the House Ways and Means Committee, "A tax-exempt organization by its very nature is dedicated and should be dedicated to performing things that are in the public interest." He also said that "drug advertisements often provide an important step in the process through which the physician becomes educated in the therapeutic value and risks of new drugs . . ."[21] Nelson then asked rhetorically whether a medical journal could consider ads for the combinations "educational." Behind this question another was implied, and it was fundamental: Was the AMA a professional organization, as it claimed to be, or an industry organization?

Authoritative answers to this and related questions finally came in the summer of 1975, when a disaffected former employee of the AMA with access to its files and a photocopying machine began feeding sensitive documents to reporters. The source did not disclose his identity; David Burnham of the *New York Times* nicknamed him "Sore Throat," a medicated variant of Bob Woodward's Watergate source, "Deep Throat." One memo showed that at least for political fund-raising purposes, the AMA was thought about, and thought of itself, as the spokesman for a major industry. The memo, prepared by AMA lobbyist Wayne Bradley, described a meeting held by Senator Paul J. Fannin (R–Ariz.) to raise funds in 1969 for his reelection effort in 1970. He is a member of the Senate Finance Committee, which makes decisions of enormous importance to industry, and which has jurisdiction over health legislation, as well, and he likes to be known as a "conservative." "About a dozen lobbyists representing all major industries attended," Bradley wrote Harry Hinton, of the AMA office in Washington.

The industries represented at the luncheon included *medicine*, drugs, tobacco, steel, oil, consumer goods, heavy industry, publishing and rubber. It was agreed that each of us would generally contact our friends and those within our own *industry* in behalf of the Senator's Oct. 2 [fund-raising] reception." (Emphasis supplied.)[22]

This was but the start of the public degradation deservedly inflicted on the AMA by "Sore Throat" and the damning and unrefuted internal memos he surfaced. One series of memos given to Stuart Auerbach, the *Washington Post* reporter, involved multimillion-dollar benefits the AMA was deriving from the treatment of its advertising revenues as tax-exempt, rather than as income from a business activity unrelated to the tax exemption—which was the kind of income it actually was. Fearing that the House Ways and Means Committee might knock out the existing arrangement, the AMA took certain precautions. It retained a Washington lawyer, Thomas Hale Boggs, Jr., whose father, the late Hale Boggs, was House majority whip, and whose law firm was said by William J. Colley, an AMA lobbyist, to be "very close to both the Senate Finance Committee and the House Ways and Means Committee." The firm has "not failed to deliver the desired results for their clients when it comes to legislation pending before either of these committees," Colley said. For Congressman Boggs' 1970 election campaign, Colley requested a "substantial contribution" from the American Medical Political Action Committee (AMPAC), on the ground that this would assure that Boggs would protect AMA interests in tax legislation. The AMA denied to reporter Auerbach that the contribution had been made. "Sore Throat" then supplied him with a 1969 memo showing that Mrs. Lee Ann Elliott, assistant director of AMPAC, had sent an AMPAC check for $7,500 to Harry Hinton, Colley's boss, with $5,000 earmarked for Boggs—half "to be used immediately," and half in 1970.[23]

The Boggs episode is revealing of the AMA's dishonesty and hypocrisy for a reason not immediately obvious. Being a tax-exempt organization, the AMA is not permitted to make political contributions. Consequently, it claimed to be separate from AMPAC. The money earmarked for Boggs was but one of the "Sore Throat" revelations to cast doubt on the claim. It turned out that AMPAC, which contributed $1.5 million in the 1974 congressional elections alone, was regularly sending contribution checks to the AMA office in Washington for both Democratic and Republican fund-raising events, and for congressional candidates. Generally, the couriers were, Auerbach wrote, "the same AMA lobbyists who seek political favors from them. This leaves no doubt in anyone's mind where the money is really coming from."[24]

Claiming to speak for the country's 380,000 physicians, two representatives of the AMA told the House Appropriations Committee in May 1970 that the organization was solidly behind proposed increases in federal health spending. But eight months later, after President Nixon vetoed the budget providing for that spending, AMA lobbyists on Capitol Hill covertly drummed up votes to uphold the veto—their purpose being only, said Auerbach, to store up goodwill at the Nixon White House.[25]

Also in 1970, the Pharmaceutical Manufacturers Association (PMA) was lobbying to defeat an amendment to the Social Security Act proposed by Senator Russell B. Long (D–La.). The amendment was designed to lower the costs of medicines in the Medicare and Medicaid programs by putting ceilings on the prices the government would pay. This was aimed at needlessly expensive prescribing by brand name. As reported by David Burnham in the *New York Times*, the AMA had lobbied—again covertly—alongside the PMA, but pretended in its best bedside manner that its concern was solely with the proper interests of physicians.[26] Any shred of wonder remaining about this kind of activity disappeared when "Sore Throat" surfaced memos showing that AMPAC from 1962 through 1965 secretly accepted $851,000 in political contributions from twenty-seven of the largest pharmaceutical houses in the country—the very companies from which the AMA always had claimed to be independent.[27]

Only because he and his organization were unaccountable to the community could Dr. James Sammons, who had left the problems of medical ethics in Texas to become executive vice-president of the AMA in Chicago, issue himself a license to hunt diabetics. The circumstances were these:

Over a ten-year period, the University Group Diabetes Program made a controlled study of unprecedented sophistication, size, duration, and cost. Twelve university clinics and more than one thousand patients participated. The National Institute of Arthritis and Metabolic Diseases paid the $7.3 million bill. Unexpectedly, the study produced a highly disturbing challenge to the generally accepted theory that lowering blood-sugar levels reduces the large risks of cardiovascular and kidney disease and blindness. The acceptance of this theory lay behind the prescribing to an estimated 1.5 million Americans of pills to lower blood sugar—mainly Upjohn's Orinase and Tolinase, Pfizer's Diabinese, Lilly's Dymelor, and Ciba-Geigy's DBI. The study's shocking finding was that the cardiovascular death rate in persons taking the pills over a period of several years was approximately two and one half times higher than in persons who relied on diet alone. The study also found that the ability of the hypoglycemic drugs to lower sugar levels vanished after as little as two years. Persons who supplemented diet restrictions with insulin injections had a survival rate no better than the controls relying on diet alone.

The study results were disclosed in 1970. Almost from the start they had the backing of the AMA. But among physicians there was a furor; indeed, the resistance to the findings was so great that, for example, doctors wrote 5.5 percent more prescriptions for the tablets in 1973 (an estimated total of 19,381,000) than in 1972.

The issue was put before the internationally prestigious Biometric Society, which upheld the basic findings and put the burden of proof on those who would prescribe the drugs. Now, for Upjohn and the other producers, there was a severe threat to a market of approximately $100 million a year. Nonetheless, *JAMA* arranged to publish in its issue of February 10, 1975, not only the Biometric Society report, but also an editorial by Dr. Thomas C. Chalmers, former associate director for clinical care of the National Institutes of Health, saying that the pills might be linked to between ten thousand and fifteen thousand unnecessary deaths a year in the United States alone.

Thanks to "Sore Throat," we know now that several days before *JAMA* was put in the mails, Dr. Sammons, the AMA's chief executive officer, undertook to send a letter to some four hundred executives of medical societies around the country. Alerting them to the contents of the upcoming February 10 issue of *JAMA*, he proceeded, with much arrogance, to disparage the study and the Biometric Society report. "A considerable body of expert scientific opinion contradicts these findings," he said. "Diabetic patients should not be influenced by press reports, and should continue on whatever diabetic management program their own physician has prescribed." The Upjohn Company then asked permission to reprint the letter for use by its eleven hundred salesmen who call on physicians and, obviously, who would use it to encourage them to continue prescribing Orinase and Tolinase. An AMA staff lawyer warned Sammons, "The policy of the A.M.A. is that the association's name may not be used for trade purposes." She also said, "Permission to reprint A.M.A. materials has not been granted if there is any indication that the name of the association or its materials will be used in any manner that might directly or indirectly be construed as an endorsement by the A.M.A. of a particular product or manufacturer." Upjohn has for years been a major advertiser in *JAMA*. Despite this legal advice, Sammons gave permission to reprint the letter.[28]

At Babylon, King Hammurabi's law code said in part:

If a physician performs a major operation on a noble with a bronze lancet and causes the noble's death or opens the eye socket of a noble and blinds his eye, the physician shall lose his hand. If a slave of a commoner dies because of an operation, the doctor shall make good slave for slave.[29]

Thus did Hammurabi make the physician accountable to the ancient community. Nothing seems to make a Dr. James Sammons accountable to the modern community.

Unaccountable Accountants

We in the accounting profession constitute one of the most important contributors to the decision-making process in the democratic system in this country . . . In the simplest sense, we are the scorekeepers in the game of producing goods and services and the distribution of their value among the various segments of our economy.

Leonard Spacek
A Search for Fairness in Financial Reporting to the Public

Nearly two years after Maurice H. Stans indignantly told the Senate Watergate committee to "give me back my good name,' he was convicted in United States District Court of illegal fund-raising activities on Richard M. Nixon's behalf. Following prolonged plea-bargaining between his lawyers and Watergate prosecutors, Stans, once president of the American Institute of Certified Public Accountants, and a member of the Hall of Fame of Accountancy, admitted his guilt on March 12, 1975, to five misdemeanor charges stemming from his work as chief fund-raiser for the Committee for the Re-election of the President.

The dapper, bushy-browed accountant got off lightly. His penalty was, and remains, quite simply, a $5,000 fine. Stans, whose so-called "profession," in the late 1960s, awarded him its highest honor—presidency of the Institute of Certified Public Accountants—three years in a row, is not likely to be drummed out of the corps. Officials of the institute dutifully told the press, in response to questions following Stans' conviction, that they were keeping an "open file" on their old colleague, but they also stressed that no action had been taken to initiate any sanctions. Then, in early 1976, they closed the file and ended any possibility of action.

Such complacency should not be at all surprising. The remarkable thing about the practice of accounting is not that it faces so many conflicts of interest, but that they are so dimly perceived. It has taken the courts to tell accountants where their duties lie. They are still trying to recover from the shock.

Judge Henry J. Friendly of the United States Court of Appeals in New York laid down the law just a few years ago with a decision that would strike a layman as nothing startling, just plain common sense. The case involved the Continental Vending Company, whose auditors had been found guilty of gross negligence for the financial statements they had prepared. Eight prestigious accountants testified on behalf of the defendants that the statements had, in fact, been prepared in accordance with "generally accepted accounting principles." But the jury decided, willy-nilly, that the statements had not been "fairly presented."

Affirming the convictions in 1969, Judge Friendly wrote:

The first law for accountants was not compliance with generally accepted accounting principles, but, rather, full and fair disclosure, fair presentation and, if principles did not produce this brand of disclosure, accountants could not hide behind the principles, but had to go behind them and make whatever disclosures were necessary for full disclosure.[1]

The decision, as *Business Week* later observed, "set off shock waves that are still shaking the accounting profession."[2] What should have been principle was now, quite suddenly, the law—without any tryout period as principle. The old rules of the game, the mumbo jumbo that could turn profits into losses and back again, were no longer good enough. It was startling. It was revolutionary. Accountants could be held accountable.

Despite the shock waves, accountants still retain much of their old-fashioned public image. Dull. Stolid. Reliable. People whom you can trust with your money. But are they? Listen to Leonard Spacek, recently retired chairman of Arthur Andersen & Company, one of the nation's "Big Eight" accounting firms, on the failures of his peers in a 1956 speech:

When we violate this trust by allowing major misrepresentations to appear in financial statements relied upon by the public, *then we are no better than common criminals* who by commission or omission have failed to live up to the responsibilities of membership in our social community. (Emphasis supplied.)[3]

Spacek is a maverick. Many of his colleagues found it more convenient, and profitable, to adhere to the rule that in business as in politics, to get along, you have to go along. In the 1950s, as Spacek saw it, the days of the robber barons and the moguls, the Jay Goulds and the J. Pierpont Morgans, were gone forever. The principal reason for that, he argued optimistically in that same 1956 speech, "is because accounting principles will not permit the misrepresentations, manipulations and secrecies by which they acquired positions of wealth and power with other people's money."

It was dismal prophecy. Times change and so do "generally accepted accounting principles," but not necessarily for the better. By the mid-1970s, accountants were being described not as the Horatios-at-the-gate that they no doubt could have been, but as "space-age alchemists" who had long since sold out to the conglomerates and multinational corporations that paid their salaries.[4] "GAAP"—generally accepted accounting principles—had, in the words of Abraham J. Briloff, professor of accounting at the City University of New York, become saturated with "CRAP"—cleverly rigged accounting ploys.

It was not until October of 1974, for example, that the profession's new rule-making body, the Financial Accounting Standards Board, acted to stop a systematic abuse that enabled many companies to mislead their stockholders—and the stock market—by recording substantial earnings when the companies were really losing money.

The cleverly rigged accounting ploy in this case dealt with the stretching out of research and development costs instead of charging them to expenses. Thus, as Robert Metz reported in the *New York Times,* if an aircraft company spent $50 million a year for five years in hopes of developing a new plane to peddle, it could "capitalize" the expenses over a period of ten years or even longer. It could, in short, deduct $25 million a year from pretax income over a ten-year period instead of $50 million a year for five years. Then, if the company earned, say, $30 million in a given year (apart from research and development), it would be able to report a net income of $5 million—instead of a loss of $20 million.

The gimmick led many investors to think their companies were operating at a profit when they were really reporting losses to the Internal Revenue Service. As a consequence, Metz pointed out, "not only were companies able to raise money in the equity market on their apparent profitability, their phantom profits helped keep stock prices at artificially high levels."[5]

Some of the most blatant cases have turned up in the courts, where they, and many more, so clearly belong. The most celebrated involves the National Student Marketing Corporation (NSMC), which was quite simply a gigantic fraud. It began in the bull market of the late 1960s, and it sounded—of course—like a great idea. NSMC was aimed at "the youth market"—which was said to spend more than $45 billion a year. NSMC's big claim on that money was a plan to set up a national network of campus "reps" who would sell or promote Product XYZ among their fellow students. NSMC went public less than three years after its creation in 1965. The original price of the stock was six dollars a share. Within six months, it was selling at eighty dollars.

"It was a shining example of capitalism in action—the old making way for the young, the Establishment opening its doors to the adventurous,"

Thomas Redburn reported later in the *Washington Monthly*. "Prudent investors like Bankers Trust, the Morgan Guaranty Bank, Harvard University, Cornell and the University of Chicago all bought shares in National Student Marketing."

The stock finally hit a mind-boggling high of $140 in late December of 1969. By then, the respected accounting firm of Peat, Marwick & Mitchell, another of the Big Eight, had given its stamp of approval to the company's claim of nearly $3.2 million in earnings for the fiscal year ending August 31, 1969. Yet a few days later, the company allowed that there would be a "charge against earnings" of some $510,000. And by February 1970, NSMC was reporting a $1.5 million loss for the first quarter. By July of that same year, the stock had plummeted to 3 1/2. It was to go lower, much lower.

It was to be sure a classic fraud. NSMC's founder, Cortes Randall, was finally sentenced in late 1974 to eighteen months in prison and a $40,000 fine for his part in the conspiracy and other illegalities. Two certified public accountants were also tried, convicted, and sentenced to brief prison terms for stock fraud in the NSMC case. Anthony M. Natelli and Joseph Scansaroli, both of Peat, Marwick & Mitchell, were each convicted by a jury of making false statements in a 1969 National Student Marketing proxy statement. It was apparently the first time that accountants from a major firm had been ordered to jail for fraud. The 1968 Continental Vending case had resulted in the conviction of three accountants from Lybrand, Ross Brothers & Montgomery, a third Big Eight firm, but they were later pardoned by President Nixon while he still had the power. United States District Judge Harold R. Tyler, Jr., of New York, ordered Natelli to pay the maximum fine of $10,000 and sentenced him to sixty days in jail with the rest of a year-long term suspended. Scansaroli was fined $2,500 and sentenced to ten days in jail, again with the rest of a year-long term suspended.

In sentencing the two men, Judge Tyler emphasized that he did not want to load them down with blame for something "which is really shared by many, many people in your profession, and, indeed, in other professions including my own—some sort of myopia as to what is really the public responsibility of an accountant who performs services as a public accountant." He immediately added: "I seriously doubt that you are any worse than many in your profession and, indeed, I suspect you are much better than they; certainly as individuals, I am almost sure you are." Both Natelli, who had been the partner in charge of auditing NSMC for Peat, Marwick & Mitchell, and Scansaroli, who was Peat, Marwick auditing supervisor for NSMC until he left in late 1969 to take a job with NSMC itself, were, the judge observed, both "extremely sympathetic figures."

What bothered the court was the insensitivity, the shortsightedness, the failure of the accounting business to recognize its duty to tell the truth. And that made it all the more important to impose sentences that might serve as a deterrent to all those other anonymous accountants interested only in pleasing their corporate clients.

The myopia, and the need to cure it, had already been painfully illustrated in the NSMC case when the jury returned its guilty verdicts on November 14, 1974. The work papers that the two CPA's had prepared in auditing NSMC, and then their own testimony on the witness stand, had, as Tyler said later, clearly led the jurors to their decision. The two men had allowed the padding of unbilled receivables or commitments from NSMC customers and the padding of sales figures, and they had condoned claims that NSMC had earnings in a period when in fact it had no earnings. Yet no sooner were the verdicts announced than a senior partner for Peat, Marwick unctuously protested: "We are shocked at the verdict. We don't believe the jury understood the accounting complications involved."

The remark appears to have bothered Judge Tyler more than anything in the whole case, and rightly so. He blamed it on "the mores of American legal and corporate life."

"Nothing could be further from the truth than alleged in that unfortunate press release," Tyler said at the sentencing. ". . . Nothing could be further from the truth in any respect during all of the proceedings in [the] case than that remark."

Yet not even the two defendants could claim any more perspicacity. ". . . I think you are absolutely sincere when you say that you do not believe that you did anything wrong in this audit or audits for National Student Marketing," the judge—now deputy attorney general of the United States —told them moments later. "After thinking about the matter for a long time, I think you honestly mean that. But the tragedy is that the jury found that this was an audit or audits done *with reckless disregard for what was really involved."* (Emphasis supplied.)

The impact of that recklessness—on investors, on taxpayers, on consumers, and on the unwitting public in its many guises—cannot be exaggerated. As Richard J. Barnet and Ronald E. Müller have written:

The institutional lag that cripples governments in their efforts to prevent global corporations from circumventing the spirit of tax, securities and banking laws is due in no small measure to the technological break-throughs of the accounting industry . . . Research and development in tax avoidance conducted in programs of international business at institutions of higher learning such as New York University and Columbia University is at least five years ahead of government research on loophole closing. . . . Skilled obfuscation is now an essential accounting tool. The challenge is to create a tidy world for investors, regulatory agencies, and tax collectors to scrutinize, which may have little or no resemblance to what an old-fashioned book-keeper might have called the real world. Indeed, it is often desirable to create a different world for each. Corporations give their stockholders one picture of how well they are prospering and the Internal Revenue Service another. (In 1966, for example, the oil industry showed profits of $3 billion on its own books, but reported $1.5 billion to the IRS. As Congressman Charles Vanik observes, ". . . for their stockholders they wear their wedding clothes; for the tax man, they wear rags."[6]

For accountants, footnotes are a favorite dodge, a crude, often dishonest way of hinting at the truth without really stating it. Lockheed Aircraft's auditors, for example, knew in 1968—two years before the word leaked out —that the company was facing difficulties because of the cost overruns on the C-5A. When Lockheed's annual report came out in 1968, even the Air Force expected Lockheed to lose at least $285 million on its contract to build the modern-day pterodactyls. But Lockheed gave its stockholders no such warning. Instead, they were told, in a footnote to the 1968 annual report, that "no loss is anticipated on the contract." The accountants then covered that outrageous remark by adding: "However, complete realization of the inventory is dependent on the accuracy of the estimated costs to complete and the legal interpretation of certain clauses in the contract."

The 1969 Lockheed report was even more discomforting, but the auditors still managed to bury their embarassment in a blizzard of small print. In a footnote that took up 180 lines of type, they allowed that there was a possibility of a loss of between $500 million and $600 million which had somehow been overlooked.

Charles Dickens never explained how Bob Cratchit kept his incorruptibility in keeping the books for Ebenezer Scrooge, but in England accountants are considered genuinely independent, their word above reproach, their findings beyond question. American accountants appear to be more interested in making money for their clients, and for themselves. As *Business Week* reported in 1972, "public accounting has become a big business—and a growth business" generating domestic revenues of $2.5 billion a year. The so-called Big Eight were responsible for at least $1 billion of those revenues all by themselves. Together, the Big Eight audit more than 80 percent of the corporations listed on the New York and American Stock Exchanges.[7]

That, in itself, leads to so many conflicts of interest that they defy counting. The incestuous possibilities within the oil industry offer a simple example. When the 1970s began, the outside accounting services for the thirty biggest oil companies in the United States were controlled by just seven accounting firms. Arthur Andersen audited the books of seven oil companies; Price Waterhouse had six under its wing; Ernst & Ernst, five; Arthur Young & Company, and Lybrand Cooper, four each, and Haskins & Sells and Peat,

Marwick & Mitchell, two each.[8] While all this leads to a certain uniformity of approach, such standardization also "begets habits and practices which could work to the disadvantage of the public or fall into the gray area of business morality," as Norman Medvin observed in *The American Oil Industry: A Failure of Antitrust Policy.*[9]

Back up now to the spring of 1955. The State Department has "arranged" with five big United States oil companies to have Price Waterhouse "pass upon the eligibility" of other Americans who want to participate in a proposed Iranian oil consortium. The five participating companies had agreed that each of them might transfer a piece of the action to outsiders, but only during the first six months of the venture. The six-month deadline was scheduled to expire April 29, 1955.

By March 10, the Antitrust Division of the Justice Department was understandably upset. In a plain-spoken, three-page memo to his superiors, one of the division's lawyers, W. B. Watson Snyder, pointed out that Price Waterhouse had "certified" eleven other oil companies as reliable applicants. But while these companies had asked for a total participation in the consortium of 36 percent, the setup was such that there was only 5 percent—1 percent from each of the original companies—to divvy up. Meanwhile, the memo noted, the American Independent Oil Company had complained to the attorney general that the majors and the secretary of state were denying it the right to participate in the consortium. The president of American Independent, Ralph Davies, protested that "he had a promise from the Secretary of State that he would be permitted to participate up to 5 percent on the consortium." Price Waterhouse, however, had not even included American Independent on its list of reliable applicants. Then, on March 7, 1955, three days after the list became public, an American Independent representative charged publicly that it had been left off the list because "Price Waterhouse imposed completely unrealistic conditions and conditions that we have not accepted."

By the time Snyder wrote his memo, American Independent was confident of getting the State Department to add its name to the approved list, but he was still concerned about all the clout that Price Waterhouse had been exercising. He thought its activities in putting the list of American participants together "may well be in violation of the antitrust laws." Price Waterhouse, the memo pointed out, was the accountant not only for many foreign oil companies, but also for most of the participants in the consortium. At times, Snyder wrote, Price Waterhouse had been found to be not only the accounting firm assigned to audit the operations of various oil cartel agreements, but also "the arbitrator of disputes between the companies."

"Whenever either the domestic or foreign branches of the petroleum industry carry out any joint operations, Price Waterhouse is chosen to do the accounting," the Justice Department memo reported. In fact, quite a furor was raised about the firm at the end of World War II when it turned out that big American [oil] companies were getting subsidies from the Office of Price Administration on the basis of audits by Price Waterhouse. Yet Price Waterhouse was at the same time "the official auditor for each" of the major oil companies clamoring for the subsidies.

Even a primitive sense of public morality would seem to have demanded an admission that such service for two masters carried at least the appearance of impropriety. Yet at Senate hearings on the controversy, one of the partners of Price Waterhouse baldly claimed that it could represent both the claimant and the government on every claim presented without any conflict of interest.

Hammurabi's Babylon would not have stomached such arrogance. But Price Waterhouse & Company is still doing quite nicely. A recent listing of its customers includes Exxon, Gulf Oil, Standard Oil of California, Standard Oil of Indiana, Shell Oil, IBM, DuPont, United States Steel, and Westinghouse Electric.

The lineups of some of the other big auditing firms is even more questionable. Ernst & Ernst represents not only Ashland Oil and Ling-Temco-Vought, but also the Bank of America. Peat, Marwick & Mitchell has Cities Service, General Electric, First National City Bank, and Chase Manhattan. What if the banks loan money to some of the corporations that the same accounting firm represents? An accountant is supposed to offer an opinion on the quality of loans in the bank's portfolio. What is he to do with inside information gleaned from the corporate borrower's books?

The only certain thing about accounting is that most practitioners would anxiously look for whatever answer that might make both bank and borrower happy, even at the expense of their shareholders. "Accountants are too worried about service to the client," one CPA told *Business Week*. "Most times they're too friendly with the client. I think there's simply got to be a mild adversary relationship there."[10]

"If" accounting is a profession, Leonard Spacek says, we must firmly establish the foundation of that profession on impartiality to all segments of society; but at the same time we must dedicate ourselves to the position that all segments are entitled to a fair accounting and that we as a profession shall insist on their getting it. But we cannot effectively assert this position unless we can also demonstrate it. Can or have we demonstrated it? No, we have not . . . Have we even shown a disposition or a desire to demonstrate it? Another No![11]

Indeed, far from asserting their independence, the big accounting firms have made a mockery of it by plunging headlong into management consulting work. "Like drummers with wagon loads of new wares," *Business Week* reported in 1972, "most of the big CPA firms are stocking a full line of management advisory services these days. Peat, Marwick will help clients find a new president or top financial officer, or tell top executives they should switch part of their pay into tax shelters. Lybrand will help a company set up a new pension plan; Touche Ross and Ernst & Ernst will undertake detailed marketing plan strategy. Arthur Young will help a corporation defend itself against a takeover."[12]

The potential for conflicts is mind-boggling. "What if a company should buy another company at our urging and it turns out to be a dog?" Ralph E. Kent, manager partner of Arthur Young, told *Business Week*. "Then there certainly would be the appearance of an unwillingness on our part to be able to say at the next audit: 'By the way, that was a lousy acquisition you made, and now we want you to write it off.' " "Someday," Harvey E. Kapnick, Jr., chairman of Arthur Andersen, added in warning, "this is going to come right down around the neck of the profession." If an accounting firm gives management advice to a corporation, Ralph Nader has pointed out, it can hardly be completely objective when it sits down to evaluate the advice which it furnished. The fault, as Abraham Briloff sees it, lies with the hierarchy of the American Institute of Certified Public Accountants, which seems determined to ignore dishonesty and deception in direct proportion to the prestige of its practitioners and the degree of subtlety they bring to the task. The morals of accounting, however, are such that subtlety is often not required.

The insensitivity reached full flower in the January 1975 *Journal of Accountancy* which contained a discussion draft on management advisory services called "Report of the AICPA Committee on Scope and Practice." Its central conclusion, as Briloff summed it up, was that the broad spectrum of management services should be wholly permissible for accounting firms *"since the committee saw no compromise of the auditor's independence resulting therefrom."* (Emphasis supplied.) Indeed, the committee even urged easier standards for admission to AICPA so that non-CPAs who were adept at management consultant services could qualify.

In making those findings, Briloff has charged in several forums, the committee chose to ignore not only material it had in hand, but also scholarly studies from at least half a dozen institutions "pointing to the impairment of independence in appearance, if not in fact." But what else could be expected, two members of the committee being former presidents of AICPA, and eight others being from the Big Eight? Briloff commented, "If a corresponding committee were formed from the food and drug industry to study the adequacy of their testing practices; or a committee corresponding-ly constituted from the cigarette industry were formed to study the hazards of smoking . . . would you expect them to come up with an objective evaluation which might be inimical to the economics of their respective industries? And if they did somehow come up with such a report, would anyone really believe it?"[13]

Unfortunately, the same skepticism has yet to spill over to the issuance of a corporation's annual reports. Some can no doubt be believed, but the plain, painful fact is that many cannot. That is one reason for what Stanley Marcus, chairman of Neiman-Marcus in Dallas, calls "a massive loss of faith in the business community by the American people—and perhaps a loss of faith on the part of businessmen as well." He asks, "Can free enterprise survive inaccurate, misleading, or 'unexplained' financial reporting?"[14] Possi-bly, but with the kind of distemper in which baseball would survive if pitchers who were calling the balls and strikes were to seek to remedy their unaccountability by forming an association. We don't see much difference between such pitchers and the scorekeepers of the economy who are biased toward large clients and who would have us believe that they can cure their unaccountability by congregating with like-minded CPAs in an institute.

Blue Cross and
Other Conduits of Private Power

21

Government routinely delegates enormous responsibilities and power to private contractors without making them accountable. This is the case on a grand scale with the Blue Cross Association, which has a massive conflict of interest and which is structured not to resolve it in favor of the public. Conflicts also flow into government through human conduits accountable to private power, such as advisory committees, consultants, and putative public servants.

Blue Cross

The United States spent $67.2 billion on health care in 1970. This was 7 percent of the gross national product—a larger portion than in any other country. Yet the health of Americans is, according to several indices, inferior. In 1969, for example, the infant death rate in the United States was 22.4 per 1,000 live births—higher than that of fourteen other industrial nations.[1] "It is widely acknowledged that the American health care crisis is primarily one of organization, administration, and accountability." Sylvia A. Law wrote in 1974 in *Blue Cross: What Went Wrong?* "Blue Cross is at the heart of the administration of the present medical care system."[2]

About one-third of the national health-care dollar—$22 billion in 1970—is spent in hospitals. Blue Cross is the biggest provider of hospitalization insurance, and is, consequently, a very big enterprise indeed. If it and its local affiliates were accountable to the subscribers, beneficiaries, and the public, they would try to assure that hospital costs are reasonable. Instead, they tend to pay whatever bills the hospitals submit and to pass on the costs in the form of higher rates. They have a built-in conflict, and they resolve it in favor of the hospitals and themselves. They are structured to do this.

Hospital representatives dominate Blue Cross boards. In 1970, 42 percent of the members of local Blue Cross boards represented hospitals and 14 percent the medical profession.[3] The boards perpetuate themselves, with the directors either reelecting each other, or nominating and electing replacements, and with private subscribers—80 million of them paying in more than $15 billion a year as of 1975—having no say in the process. In the same year, Blue Cross was designating 1,138—69 percent—of the 1,885 board members for all of its state and local plans as "consumer" representatives. The Associated Press reported, however, that "161 of the consumer representatives, or 14 per cent, are also hospital trustees. Most of the rest are corporate executives, bankers, and lawyers."[4] One would not seriously expect hospital representatives to enter like tigers into arm's-length negotiations with hospitals about hospital charges, and they don't.

What about external accountability? For the most part, there isn't any. "In most states," the AP reported, Blue Cross operates under special legislation giving it and Blue Shield, which has similar conflicts in the reimbursement of physicians' fees, "tax exemption as nonprofit, public service organizations. They do not have to answer to policyholders, as do mutual insurance companies, or to stockholders, as do profit-making private insurance companies."[5] Rate regulation by the states has been overwhelmingly ineffective, as indicated by a 197 percent increase in the cost of a one-day stay in a semiprivate hospital room in the ten-year period ending 1975. Only in Pennsylvania, under Insurance Commissioner Herbert S. Denenberg, was there a truly determined, imaginative, and reasonably successful effort to crack down on laxity and waste in Blue Cross plans. Overall, consumers are helpless, necessarily lacking even the power of decision over when and where they go to a hospital—their doctors decide that. And competition in the consumer context is insignificant.

How out of hand the whole thing can get was brought out in January 1971 at a hearing conducted by Senator Philip A. Hart (D–Mich.), chairman of the Senate Antitrust and Monopoly Subcommittee, on Blue Cross of Virginia (BCV). Based in Richmond, and sometimes referred to in national Blue Cross memos as "Richmond," it had 800,000 members and was affiliated with fifty-nine hospitals. During the late 1960s, its administrative costs for servicing claims soared over those of the seventy-three Blue Cross plans around the country. Waste and mismanagement—without accountability to the national Blue Cross or anyone else—were at the bottom of the situation. The subcommittee's and subsequent investigations turned up these items:

• BCV made a $156,000 gift to the Norfolk Data Center in the erroneous belief that it was a nonprofit data-processing venture owned jointly by eight hospitals. M. Roy Battista, a BCV vice-president, never revealed that he was a director of the center.[6]

• Four or five employees of BCV drove in BCV cars from Richmond to a resort at Hilton Head, South Carolina, but, as a matter of policy, charged BCV for first-class air fare plus taxis to and from airports.[7]

• BCV accepted a bid for rental cars $30,000 higher than another bid, and after renting 119 cars could not account for their use.[8]

• Robert C. Denzler, vice-president and general manager of BCV until he resigned under fire in June 1970, air-conditioned and furnished his home at plan expense; subsequently, he reimbursed the plan.[9]

• Setting itself up in an $8 million office building, BCV spent $1 million to decorate and furnish the building. The latter expenditure went in large part for purchases made without competitive bidding from a supplier whose sales manager was chairman of the BCV board's Building Committee.[10]

• BCV instructed some twenty to thirty of its in-house accountants to ferret out waste, but they did not detect items such as the foregoing.

In October 1968, while such mismanagement prevailed, the national Blue Cross dispatched a team to Richmond to make a "Total Plan Review." The team's final report said it was "particularly impressed with the overall corporate structure and organization of the plan" and was otherwise generally laudatory.[11] By early 1970, public complaints had alerted the national organization to trouble, but one Blue Cross official advised from Richmond that the national organization "refrain from moving in since we know the bad news that might erupt. . . . Richmond could blow up. It is a real 'can of worms.' . . ."[12]

Actually, Alden B. Flory, BCV's chief executive officer, told Senator Hart, Blue Cross has "no control. We are a separate entity, run the show our way . . ." What if BCV audits a hospital's books and finds "clearly wasteful practices?" Hart asked. "What do you do?" Flory replied, "Well, Mr. Chairman, I am not aware of our audits ever uncovering wasteful charges, and I really wouldn't know what we would do if we ran into them."[13] The senator further inquired, "There isn't any outside discipline, either the Virginia Corporation Commission [the state regulatory agency] or legislative body or the national Blue Cross, that could do other than sort of wonder. Nobody could correct, is that right, absent the internal discipline?" Flory: "Mr. Chairman, I would say you are absolutely right, but that responsibility rests purely on the boards of directors . . ."[14]

The national Blue Cross Association (BCA) is a prime government contractor under several government programs, particularly Medicare, which provides hospital insurance for the elderly. The American Hospital Association (AHA) and Blue Cross campaigned together to persuade Congress to let Blue Cross become the principal fiscal intermediary between the Social Security Administration and "providers"—hospitals and nursing homes. "The Blue Cross plans are hospital oriented and again I would say that I think that hospitals should have *the right* to select the method by which the program should be administered," an AHA witness once testified (emphasis supplied).[15]

"Throughout the congressional debate no distinction was made between the roles of the BCA and the AHA as technical experts, as self-interested parties, and as political organizations," Sylvia Law and her coauthors in the

Health Law Project said in their book on Blue Cross. Moreover, "Congress never considered the basic issue of whether it was a good idea to use Blue Cross to perform . . . critical administrative functions under the Medicare program."

Under the prime contract between the Department of Health, Education, and Welfare and Blue Cross, which was negotiated in 1964 and renegotiated in 1970, Blue Cross subcontracts with local plans actually to carry out the responsibilities assigned by the law to intermediaries. Medicare regulations allow Blue Cross, as well as providers, to claim as "administrative" expenses pretty much what they please, including the costs of conducting antiunionization campaigns, and secretive lobbying on Capitol Hill to give Blue Cross a prominent role in a national health insurance program if one evolves.

Blue Cross reimburses for "reasonable costs." The AHA defines these as costs attributable to "allowable" items but does not call for inquiry into whether the price of an "allowable" item is reasonable. Sylvia Law wrote:

Thus if a salary is "allowable" for a particular position, it is a reasonable cost whether the amount paid is $10,000 a year, $50,000 a year, or $200,000 a year. This concept of reasonableness, under which most of the income of American hospitals is received, has had a significant effect on hospital suppliers. . . . since the establishment of Medicare, the surplus of revenues over expenses in voluntary hospitals has grown enormously, as have the profits of hospital supply and drug companies. Investment analysts believe that hospital suppliers and drug companies are operating in a sector of the economy that is virtually recession-proof.[16]

The Social Security Administration specifies that a provider tries to assure that "allowable" items are bought at reasonable cost through the "Prudent Buyer Concept." This is nearly useless except possibly in the event of outright fraud. It does nothing, for example, to prevent a small rural hospital from paying a radiologist working fifteen hours a week $50,000 a year.[17] In the basement of Washington Hospital Center in Washington, D.C., are the relatively modest quarters of the pathology laboratory. The man who runs it, Dr. Vernon B. Martens, was making about $200,000 a year in 1972. Many of his counterparts make $300,000. One in the Washington area makes $500,000. They and other such specialists have monopolies. Independent laboratories provide the same services for far lower prices. Merely to give Martens his $200,000 a year cost each patient entering the Hospital Center an average of 79 cents a day, Ronald Kessler reported in the *Washington Post*.[18] The picture that emerges from all of this, Sylvia Law and her associates said,

is one of total unaccountability. Hospitals are paid in advance for whatever they claim. Books are audited, often years later, by commercial auditors with no particular expertise in health services and no capacity to judge whether or not a cost is reasonable; they note only whether it was properly catalogued in the books and represents a payment actually made. This procedure makes application of the prudent buyer concept impossible.[19]

What difference does it make if Medicare and also Medicaid (which provides federal matching funds to the states to finance health care for the poor) pay more than a fair share of hospital costs? The principal difference is that the elderly and the poor get fewer and lesser services. This is a direct result of the resolution by Blue Cross of its conflict of interest in favor of hospitals, to which it is structured to be primarily accountable. A system of national health insurance that eliminates Blue Cross and other private intermediaries would be one way to cure the situation.

Conduits of Private Power

The National Academy of Sciences. Congress chartered the National Academy of Sciences (NAS) in 1863 to serve the government as an official adviser. Federal agencies regularly ask the NAS to make judgments and give advice on crucial issues of health, safety, and technology. The government pays the bills for the undertakings it requests, but the status of the NAS is unusual—"close to the government but not fully part of it," Philip M. Boffey wrote in *The Brain Bank of America: An Inquiry into the Politics of Science.* "It granted the Academy the power to make its own rules and elect its own members, thereby rendering the Academy independent of direct supervision by the government. But it also required the Academy to serve the government . . ."[20] The NAS is prestigious. "For the American scientific community, it is, in part, the Established Church, the House of Lords, the Supreme Court, and headquarters of the politics of science," Daniel S. Greenberg once wrote in *Science* magazine.[21] But while all of these things, the NAS is also sometimes a unique bridge for conflict of interest.

The Food Protection Committee of the NAS provides an especially important case in point, partly because the regulations of the Food and Drug Administration require the commissioner of the FDA to "be guided by the principles and procedures for establishing the safety of food additives stated in current publications" of the academy and the National Research Council, its operating arm. Yet the committee has regularly gotten financial support from the food, chemical, and packaging industries to help pay for its permanent staff, and to pay for studies that the committee undertakes on its own.[22] In fiscal 1972, this support amounted to $78,000, or about 40 percent of its budget.[23] "They're biased as heck for industry," Dr. Marvin Legator, the FDA's former chief for genetics toxicology has said.[24] Dr. Jacqueline Verrett, an FDA scientist who is a leading authority on using chick embryos to detect toxins, has termed it "a joke that these people are being passed off as unbiased experts. They go overboard in their effort to whitewash."[25] In addition to the imputed bias, Boffey points out, committee panels "have seldom, if ever, included anyone primarily expert in mutagenesis (the production of genetic defects) or teratogenesis (the production of birth defects), and the members expert in carcinogenesis (the production of cancer) have been a small minority. Yet in many cases the most alarming evidence of hazards associated with a particular chemical has involved precisely these long-term effects."[26]

The committee's disposition to see things industry's way and the lack of expertise on long-term effects merged in the appointment of a special task force to devise and recommend guidelines for determining when chemicals can be present in the food supply at "toxicologically insignificant" levels. Of the nine task-force members, five worked for food or chemical companies. In addition, Bernard L. Oser headed Food and Drug Research Laboratories, which has such companies as its clients; Dr. William J. Darby, chairman of the committee from 1953 to 1971, "was one of the most intemperate critics of Rachel Carson"; Dr. Julius M. Coon "had openly derided contentions that food additives may cause cancer, birth deformities, or genetic defects," and the ninth member, the late Henry F. Smyth, Jr., "had had long experience in industrial hygiene."[27] Thus, the task force included neither a specialist in the causation of cancer, genetic changes, or birth defects, nor, unless one makes an exception for Dr. Smyth, a member who sensibly could be regarded as an unencumbered representative of consumers—in this case, the large number of people who eat.

The task force in 1969 issued an astounding report. It put forth the theory that so long as the amount is small enough, "every chemical" can be allowed in food "without prejudicing safety." While this was good news to food and chemical companies, it was alarming news to specialists in carcinogenesis, because they never have been able to determine a safe level for a cancer-causing agent. They have not found an amount of a carcinogen so tiny as to be innocuous. Building on the fatally flawed theory, the task force went on to suggest guidelines which, fortunately, the FDA did not adopt. One of them was that at the level of 0.1 part per million, a chemical should be deemed "toxicologically insignificant" in the human diet if it was not in certain groups of dangerous substances, and if commercial sources had produced it without evidence of hazard for at least five years. *Five years?* That may seem a long time, but for cancer, which is irreversible, the latency period

—the period before it is known to be present—is commonly twenty to thirty years. As for the other guidelines, they were comparably misconceived and need not be explored here.

To review the report, Dr. Jesse P. Steinfeld, then surgeon general of the Public Health Service, and a cancer specialist, appointed a committee of eight government and academic specialists in cancer causation; the chairman was Dr. Umberto Saffiotti, associate scientific director for carcinogenesis of the National Cancer Institute. The committee report set off a furor because it contained a rare if not unprecedented indictment, by distinguished scientists, of an NAS report, and because the indictment was publicized (in the *Washington Post*).[28] The Saffiotti committee said that parts of the task force paper were "scientifically unacceptable" and of "absolutely no validity in the field of carcinogenesis," and concluded, "No level of exposure to a chemical carcinogen should be considered toxicologically insignificant for man." Furthermore, "[t]he principle of a zero tolerance for carcinogenic exposures should be retained. . . . Exceptions should be made only after the most extraordinary justification." Finally, the Saffiotti committee made a recommendation to test some 20,000 compounds for carcinogenic effects. This was based on the recognition that most human cancers are caused by exposure to carcinogens in the environment, including industrial chemicals and cigarette smoke. The testing would go far toward making for accountability in the use of carcinogens, and would be a major step toward prevention of cancer.

The Food Protection Committee was not unique in having obvious conflicts of interest, as Boffey documents in his book. Another example involved the use of defoliants in Vietnam, which the Pentagon began in late 1961. Pressure began to build up in the scientific community for an independent review—in the field—of possible long-term effects. Through a series of adroit maneuvers, the Pentagon managed for nearly three years to stave off just such a review, which finally was made, under the auspices of the American Association for the Advancement of Science, by Harvard biologist Matthew S. Meselson and others in August and September of 1970. The NAS was the Pentagon's instrument in this affair. The NAS had expressed no interest in the herbicide issue until the Department of Defense (DOD) made an arrangement with its then president, Frederick B. Seitz, who, as chairman of DOD's Defense Science Board, himself had a conflict of interest. The arrangement was that the NAS would review a report to be made by the Midwest Research Institute to say whether the MRI had competently examined the scientific literature, which was all it was authorized to do under a Pentagon contract.

The academy put its review of the review in the hands of a committee headed by A. Geoffrey Norman, who had helped the Army Chemical Corps father the very herbicide program at issue. Apparently sensitive to the conflict, Norman declined to play that role, but did assume leadership in choosing members of the review panel. Of the six chosen, none was a critic of military defoliation, only one had an ecological perspective, and one was an official of Dow Chemical Company, a principal producer of military defoliants. The panel's report turned out to be a two-page summary memorandum, prepared by Norman, which whitewashed essentially by saying nothing. With that, Boffey wrote, "the Academy lapsed into silence until, once again, it proved useful to DOD and its allies on Capitol Hill to bring the Academy into play in another effort to blunt criticism of the herbicide program."[29]

In the early 1960s, after the late Rachel Carson's *Silent Spring* had awakened the country to the environmental dangers of pesticides, the Academy convened an assessment committee. "It was dominated by scientists who would tend to support the use of chemical pesticides to control insects as opposed to those who would be sensitive to deleterious side effects,"[30] Boffey said. Miss Carson asked, "What does it mean when we see a committee set up to make a supposedly impartial review of a situation, and then discover that the committee is affiliated with the very industry whose profits are at stake?"[31]

What it means, clearly, is unaccountability through conflict of interest. Yet, despite conflicts such as those cited here, the NAS many times has done exemplary work. Boffey is scrupulous in pointing this out; and elsewhere in this book we cite—and now praise—the quality and integrity of the review of the effectiveness of medicines which the NAS did under contract to the FDA. Moreover, Boffey credits NAS president Philip Handler with undertaking reforms. But it is dismaying to say the least that Boffey should reach this conclusion about "the Established Church, the House of Lords, the Supreme Court" of science (as Daniel Greenberg called it):

considered as a whole, *the reforms do not provide a fundamental solution to the Academy's major weakness: its servant-master relationship to the government agencies and industrial interests which provide financial support.* (Emphasis in the original.)[32]

The American Health Foundation. Many scientists believe high levels of blood cholesterol induce coronary heart disease and advise patients to lower their intake of saturated fats by, for example, substituting margarine made with polyunsaturated fats for butter. Both the belief and the advice are open to severe question, as Edward R. Pinckney, M.D., and Cathy Pinckney make clear in *The Cholesterol Controversy.*[33] To attack the disease, the American Health Foundation in November 1971 appealed to Congress to declare as "national policy" a need for extensive changes in the "average American diet," including greater reliance on polyunsaturated fats. The chairman of the foundation was David J. Mahoney, president of Norton Simon, Inc., maker of polyunsaturated Wesson Oil. In developing its "position paper," the foundation expressed grateful acknowledgement to Dr. Dorothy Rathmann, director of research of CPC International, maker of polyunsaturated Mazola Oil. Along with others from CPC, Norton Simon, other affected interests, and unaffiliated scientists, Dr. Rathmann is a member of the foundation's Committee on Food and Nutrition. In July 1972, the National Cancer Institute awarded $2 million to the commercially supported foundation "to assist in the construction of a new Health Research Institute." A month later, the National Heart and Lung Institute, which long had been supporting research intended to substantiate the preconception of a causative association between high serum cholesterol and coronary heart disease, awarded research funds premised on the need to lower elevated blood cholesterol. One of the principal recipients was Dr. Ernest L. Wynder, president of the American Health Foundation.[34]

The Anthracite Advisory Committee. The Federal Coal Mine Health and Safety Act of 1969 provides that in setting up advisory committees under the law, the Interior Department shall see to it that in no case shall the chairman and a majority of the members be "persons who have an economic interest in coal mining." In September 1974, the Department of the Interior, headed by Rogers C. B. Morton, established the Anthracite Advisory Committee to advise the department's Bureau of Mines on "improvements" in regulating safety in the hard-coal mines of central Pennsylvania. Assistant Secretary Hollis M. Dole chose the seven members. Four—a majority—were connected with the coal industry, including the president of one coal company and the vice-president of another. Congressman Ken Hechler (D–W.Va.) asked the General Accounting Office (GAO) to investigate. In a letter to Hechler, Comptroller General Elmer B. Staats, director of the GAO, confirmed that Dole indeed had formed a majority "from persons who have an economic interest in coal mining." The congressman, who consistently had imputed to the Nixon Administration a desire to undermine the law, "at the expense of human life," drew the obvious conclusion that the committee had been "in violation of the law." A department spokesman, without directly acknowledging a conflict of interest, told Ben Franklin of the *New York Times* that the committee's composition would be changed to conform with the law.[35]

The Office of Oil and Gas. On August 16, 1973, during the Nixon Administration, Secretary of Interior Rogers Morton went to the White House to brief oil-industry executives. Speaking of a unit of the Department of the

Interior which had been established to develop national energy policy, and which evolved into the Federal Energy Administration, Morton said:

I would just like to say at the outset that the Office of Oil and Gas is an institution which is designed to be your institution, and to help you in any way it can . . . Our mission is to serve you, not regulate you. We try to avoid it. . . . I pledge to you that the Department is at your service.[36]

The secretary's brother, former Senator Thruston B. Morton (R–Ky.), was at the time a director of Texas Gas Transmission Company. It had interests in offshore leases, which were the Department of the Interior's responsibility, and was one of the firms in the natural-gas industry that stands to benefit from higher gas prices. Rogers Morton—in unison with President Nixon, the industry, and the Federal Power Commission, one of whose members, Albert B. Brooke, Jr., was a former aide to the senator—favored raising gas prices through *de facto* or *de jure* de-regulation.

The foregoing only hints at the interlocks between the industry and the government. Senator Lee Metcalf (D–Mont.) in December 1973 listed the number of members various oil companies had on federal advisory committees: Mobil, 33; Exxon, 23; Phillips, 21; Texaco and Gulf, at least 20 each; and the Standard Oil Companies of California, Indiana, and Ohio, a combined total of 54. Examining the table of organization of Interior's Emergency Petroleum and Gas Administration, which is kept in readiness to operate the industry in behalf of the government in event of a national emergency, he found slots for 476 persons. Of these, Exxon accounted for 24, Shell 22, Texaco 20, Mobil 15, Atlantic Richfield 14, Sun 12, Northern Natural Gas 11, and Gulf 10—128 in all merely from these eight firms. At the Office of Oil and Gas, which Rogers Morton pledged to the industry "is at your service," Metcalf found an example of "the revolving door interlock, by which a Government official retires to the energy industry and is succeeded . . . by someone else from the industry." The director of the office, Metcalf said, had left for a post with Lone Star Gas Company, only to be succeeded by an executive of Continental Oil Company.[37]

If a man is in a position of conflicting interests, he is subject to temptation however he resolves the issue. Regulation of conflicts of interest seeks to prevent situations of temptation from arising.

The Association of the
Bar of the City of New York
Conflict of Interest and Federal Service

The laws are explicit about the duties of trustees of trust funds to the beneficiaries or owners of the money. The most fundamental duty is "undivided loyalty."[1] This duty entails investment of trust funds "so that they will be productive of income."[2] To permit excessive accumulations of cash to remain uninvested is to engage in "a continuous and serious violation of the trustees' fiduciary obligation . . ."[3] Their "undivided loyalty" being required, trustees by definition cannot have conflicts of interest. Thus do the laws assure that they will be accountable. The same ethic applies, even if the laws do not, to public officials responsible for public funds. But fiduciary conflicts —and resultant unaccountability—are often found in government, unions, Blue Cross hospitalization insurance, and hospitals, among other areas.

Government

The Treasury Department receives about 80 percent of all federal revenues through so-called tax and loan accounts maintained in 95 percent of the nation's commercial banks. The biggest single source is weekly employee payments for income taxes withheld from employee paychecks. The sums in the accounts are vast. The average for the years 1965 through 1974 ranged between $3.9 billion and $5.6 billion. None of this money drew interest for the taxpayers. It did earn profits for the banks, especially the largest. Treasury statistics show, for example, that on February 14, 1975, when the tax and loan accounts totaled $468,950,440, $93,992,300—20 percent—was in only fifty banks.[4]

In 1974, when taxpayers' money in no-interest accounts averaged $3,913,000,000, they were losing potential interest income at a rate exceeding $1 million a day, or $428 million for the year, Ronald Kessler reported in the *Washington Post.* He calculated that this could pay for a year's operation of the Supreme Court, the Senate, the Federal Trade Commission, the Federal Communications Commission, the Securities and Exchange Commission, the Smithsonian Institution, and the Secret Service.[5] The taxpayers' loss is the banks' gain. They invest 82 to 92 percent of the money and reap what the late Congressman Wright Patman (D–Tex.), chairman until 1975 of the House Banking and Currency Committee, termed a "bonanza." Bank profits in 1973 averaged 12 percent of revenues after taxes.

The Treasury Department's traditional explanation was that the expenses incurred by the banks in handling the accounts exceeded the investment income derived from them. Congressman Patman and Congress' General Accounting Office repeatedly questioned the claim. Finally, Treasury concluded in the summer of 1974 that on the basis of the banks' own estimates of their expenses, the cost of maintaining the accounts amounted to only about 5 percent of the potential interest lost to the government.

A Treasury Department official, Sidney Cox, told reporter Kessler that in order to put funds in the tax and loan accounts in interest-bearing accounts, the department would need either a change in the regulations of the Federal Reserve Board, which the board had refused to make, or new legislation. Writing on November 17, 1974, Kessler said, "Although the department promised to prepare such a bill, no legislation has yet been introduced by the Ford administration. In the meantime, the government's loss of income since the announcement was made has exceeded $150 million—enough to pay for about a year's operation of the House of Representatives." Possibly because of the publicity and concern on Capitol Hill, the average balance in the accounts declined sharply—from $3.9 billion in the year ended June 30, 1974, to $2 billion in the next seven months, to $469 million on February 14, 1975. Fearing that a relaxation of the pressure would cause a rebound, Patman early in 1975 introduced legislation to require payment of interest. Treasury finally sent its own bill to Congress in May 1975, the House passed it in December of that year, and it was pending in the Senate Banking Committee in mid-1976.

The States

Matthew S. Quay held one political office or another in Pennsylvania or Washington, D.C., from the 1850s until he died in 1904, and for fifteen years was the absolute boss of his state. The late George Thayer says that

Quay "developed the technique of 'shaking the plum tree,' or making deposits of state money in certain banks in return for advantageous loans or good investment tips. It was an inexpensive way to raise campaign funds and, at the same time, to line one's own pocket."[6] Plum trees continued to shake across the land long after Quay died. In Missouri, for example, the state in both Democratic and Republican administrations deposited tens of millions of idle dollars in interest-free accounts in favored banks. The banks then invested the funds, sometimes in small loans on which they charged usurious rates as high as 28 percent. At campaign time, the banks could be relied upon to make the necessary but relatively small campaign contributions, discreetly and without narrow partisanship. This long-standing cozy arrangement collapsed in the late 1950s as the result of the exposure given it by the *St. Louis Globe–Democrat,* for which reporters Carl E. Major and Ray J. Noonan made a model three-month investigation. The voters adopted a constitutional amendment requiring investment of idle funds. In the first year in which it was in effect it yielded the taxpayers about $1 million, which, as a practical matter, otherwise would have been stolen from them.

Similar efforts by the *Washington Post* in the 1970s accomplished major reforms in Maryland and Virginia. In May 1975 a federal grand jury indicted the state treasurer of West Virginia, his assistant, and four bankers on charges of extortion, bribery, fraud, and embezzlement. In return for depositing millions of dollars in state funds in noninterest-bearing accounts, the indictment said, the bankers delivered bribes, gifts and "political contributions" to the state officials.[7] Except for one of the bankers, all were convicted. The state treasurer was sentenced to five years and his assistant to two. The three bankers each got off with probation.

The United Mine Workers

In 1950 the United Mine Workers of America (UMWA) and fifty-five operators of soft-coal mines reached an agreement under which a royalty on every ton of coal mined would be paid by the operators into the UMWA Welfare and Retirement Fund. The receipts were large—$168.1 million in the year ended June 30, 1968. The purpose of the fund was to draw on "principal or income or both" to pay benefits to miners and their families —medical and hospital care, pensions, and compensation for work-related injuries or illness, death and disability, wage losses, etc. Administration was entrusted to three trustees—one from the union, designated in the agreement to be chairman; one from the operators; and a "neutral party" chosen by the others.

From the start, the fund did its banking business exclusively with the

National Bank of Washington and was its largest customer. The union owned the bank. Several UMWA officials were directors of the bank. W. A. (Tony) Boyle, after succeeding the late John L. Lewis as president of the union, also became chairman of the fund trustees and a director of the bank. The conflicts of interest were inherent and obvious. Also obvious—in the Labor-Management Relations Act, in other legislation, and in statements by Lewis, who had been dominant in developing and administering the fund —was the obligation of the trustees to act solely in the best interests of the fund.

Until he died in 1969, Lewis dominated the fund's affairs. Josephine Roche, the "neutral" trustee, never once disagreed with him. United States District Judge Gerhard A. Gesell, the fount of all the foregoing facts, presided over a class action brought on behalf of coal miners with a present or future right to benefits from the fund. He did not find that the obligation to act solely for the fund had been fulfilled. In his findings of fact and conclusions of law in an opinion in April 1971, he stated:

Over a period of years, primarily at Lewis' urging, the Fund became entangled with Union policies and practices in ways that undermined the independence of the trustees. This resulted in working arrangements between the Fund and the Union that served the Union to the disadvantage of the beneficiaries. Conflicts of interest were openly tolerated and their implications generally ignored. Not only was all the money of the Fund placed in the Union's Bank without any consideration of alternative banking services and facilities that might be available, but Lewis felt no scruple in recommending that the Fund invest in securities in which the Union and Lewis, as trustee for the Union's investments, had an interest. Personnel of the Fund went on the Bank's board without hindrance, thus affiliating themselves with a Union business venture. In short, the Fund proceeded without any clear understanding of the trustees' exclusive duty to the beneficiaries, and its affairs were so loosely controlled that abuses, mistakes and inattention to detail occurred.

The fund put staggering accumulations of cash into no-interest demand deposits. The balance at the end of 1966 was $50 million; 1967, $75 million; 1968, $70 million. These figures represented 34 to 44 percent of total resources. Judge Gesell found that only a fraction of such sums was needed to meet the fund's obligations, that liquidity could have been maintained in interest-bearing government securities "redeemable on one-half hour notice," that the trustees knew these things, and that Lewis (and, at the end, Boyle) and Miss Roche, who "idolized" Lewis, continued to deprive the fund of millions of dollars in interest "in spite of suggestions from successive Operator trustees that the money should be used to earn income for the beneficiaries." The trustees, Gesell said, "well knew that cash deposits at the

Bank were unjustified. It was a continuous and serious violation of the trustees' fiduciary obligation for them to permit these accumulations of cash to remain uninvested."

Shortly after acquiring the National Bank of Washington in 1949, Lewis solicited Barnum L. Colton to become its president. The two men and Miss Roche made an agreement to use the bank as its sole depository and, Gesell said, "to maintain large sums in interest-free accounts at the Bank without regard to the Fund's needs." By April 30, 1950, the fund had put $36 million into these accounts.

It is striking that it was the original trustee for the operators, the late Charles A. Owen, who saw that the banking arrangement entered into by John L. Lewis, a larger-than-life hero to the miners, was inimical to the miners, their families, and their dependents. In August 1950, only five months after the fund was established, he demanded at a trustees' meeting that all monies in the bank be withdrawn. He said:

It is undoubtedly the law that a trustee should not deposit trust funds in a bank which he controls or in which he has a substantial participation. Amongst other criticism, he may cause the dividends upon his stock to be enhanced by the Bank's use of a large deposit of his trust's funds for loan purposes. Also, conflicting interests may arise; or losses may occur.

But, said Gesell, "The trustees' minutes through 1950 and 1951 reflect that Lewis and Roche, rather than replying to Owen's repeated complaints on this score, ignored his protests altogether. . . . The conclusion is clear that Lewis, in concert with Roche, used the Fund's resources to benefit the Union's Bank and to enhance the Union's economic power in disregard of the paramount and exclusive needs of the beneficiaries which he was charged as Chairman of the Board of Trustees to protect." As for the bank, it "knowingly accepted and participated in a continuing breach of trust that redounded substantially to its own benefit."

The relief ordered by the judge included the removal of Miss Roche ("naiveté and inattention cannot excuse her conduct") and Boyle (he "violated his duty as trustee in several particulars"); a directive to successor trustees to obtain independent professional advice on investments; an end to all business between the fund and the National Bank of Washington; a ban on doing business with any bank in which the union, any coal operator, or any trustee has a substantial stock interest, or with which anyone in the fund has an official connection, and a prohibition on the fund maintaining "non-interest-bearing accounts . . . which are in excess of the amount reasonably necessary to cover immediate administrative expenses and to pay required taxes and benefits on a current basis."

The Teamsters

In the miners' case, Judge Gesell found in the evidence "no suggestion that Lewis personally benefited"; rather, "he allowed his dedication to the Union's future and penchant for financial manipulation to lead him and through him the Union into conduct that denied the beneficiaries the maximum benefits of the Fund." This contrasts sharply with the corruption that has infested the Central States, Southeast and Southwest Areas Pension Fund of the International Brotherhood of Teamsters, which is responsible for the pensions of some 400,000 Teamsters members.

In his definitive *The Fall and Rise of Jimmy Hoffa*, investigator Walter Sheridan wrote in 1972 that despite a series of successful prosecutions eight years earlier, "the fund continues to operate in a manner that violates established sound investing standards, enriches a small group of cronies, and permits substantial cash kickbacks to racketeers, and an accountant, a consultant and a trustee of the fund."[8] In the year ended January 31, 1971, contributions totaled $153 million, and receipts a staggering $314 million. Yet, the fund reported, its assets somehow increased by only $90 million. Sheridan said:

The simple conclusion is that although the rate of contributions and the number of members covered has increased steadily, the fund has consistently lost money. For some reason, perhaps because the fund is so big and has grown so steadily, the fact that it is losing money each year does not seem to bother anyone. Administrative expenses for 1971 were over $2,000,000, of which $800,000 was for salaries, $600,000 for fees and commissions and $700,000 for "other administrative expenses." Another $210,000,000 was for "purchase of assets and real estate," but there was no explanation as to what that means.[9]

By 1975 the fund had a net worth of about $1.5 billion and had become one of the country's leading sources of loans. "The list of Nevada borrowers . . . reads like a list of Las Vegas hotels and casinos," Wallace Turner said in the *New York Times*.[10] But some claimants for pensions, meanwhile, were being barred on technical grounds from collecting, according to a series in the *Wall Street Journal*.[11]

Health Care

"I cannot conceive of any prudent businessman keeping literally millions of dollars for years at a time in non-interest-bearing accounts," Congressman L. H. Fountain (D–N.C.), chairman of the House Intergovernmental Relations Subcommittee, said at a hearing on May 21, 1970. But that was precisely what had been done over an eight-year period by the national Blue

Cross Association and its local affiliate in Washington, D.C., Group Hospitalization, Inc. (GHI), with a resultant loss of possibly $5 million in potential interest income. The essential reason was the absence of mechanisms to make Blue Cross accountable to consumers. The gist of the story developed by the subcommittee and the General Accounting Office was this:

Until January 1, 1968, when it limited deposits in no-interest accounts to $280,000, Blue Cross for eight years had kept an average daily balance in such accounts of up to $15 million; even in 1967, the final year of this profligate policy, the daily balance averaged $10 million. The Civil Service Commission has responsibility for overseeing the $45 million per month the government deducts from federal employees' paychecks and appropriated by the government as a contribution to health benefits, but it never questioned the policy, Joseph Harvey, a Blue Cross vice-president, testified.

GHI managed the deposits. It put the bulk of the money in the National Savings & Trust Company, a Washington bank that was its "investment custodian." The president and chairman of National Savings, Douglas R. Smith, was simultaneously a trustee of GHI, GHI's treasurer, and a member of its executive and finance committees. F. P. Rawlings, Jr., a director of National Savings, was president of GHI from 1964 to 1967, and became chairman, at $50,000 annually, in 1968. Also receiving GHI no-interest demand deposits were three other Washington banks. Two, American Security & Trust Company and Union Trust Company, were represented on the GHI board; Riggs National was not. The banks enjoyed "unjustified enrichment," Congressman Fountain charged. But it was of course the banks rather than the subscribers to which Blue Cross, through conflict of interest, had made itself accountable.[12]

Finally, the Associated Press in August 1975 reported on a broad survey of Blue Cross and Blue Shield plans (the latter pays fees to nearly two hundred thousand individual private physicians). Twenty of these plans, the AP's William Stockton reported, had bank officials as directors—and Medicare funds deposited in the banks of these directors. "There also were at least 20 cases in which funds collected from private subscribers had been deposited at banks with representation on Blue Cross and Blue Shield boards," Stockton said. "In each case, other banks also received money from the health organizations." He also reported that at least eleven banks held Blue Cross or Blue Shield no-interest checking accounts in which excessive Medicare balances were found.[13]

Hospitals

The failure of the Blue Cross Association and its affiliates to collect interest on its deposits reflects a *modus operandi* which helps to explain why its operating expenses per enrollee increased at an average annual rate of 16.5 percent from 1965 to 1969. But there is a closely related factor: hospitals across the country also deposit large sums interest-free in banks run by their trustees. These cozy arrangements help to explain why hospital charges between 1965 and 1972 increased by 110 percent, compared with only 27 percent for other consumer goods and services. By and large, hospitals simply pass on their charges to Blue Cross, which then passes them on to consumers. Neither competition nor government regulation provide accountability.

In a series in the *Washington Post* in 1972, Ronald Kessler explored the situation at Washington Hospital Center (WHC), the largest private, non-profit hospital in the national capital area, and, with nearly nine hundred beds, one of the largest hospitals in the country. He found numerous blatant conflicts of interest, involving ten of the thirty-eight trustees, and other abuses inflating costs to patients. One of the most important conflicts was in the person of Thomas H. Reynolds, who managed WHC's financial affairs for many years and who also was a vice-president of American Security & Trust Company, the second-largest bank in Washington. Until 1970, WHC maintained no-interest accounts at American Security with balances averaging around $1 million, but rising as high as $1.8 million. "Using the most conservative assumptions, the hospital lost at least $50,000 a year in interest it otherwise would have received," Kessler wrote. "An annual $50,000 loss of interest amounts to an extra $1.50 on the average patient bill at the center."[14]

Later, Kessler turned to another charitable hospital in Washington, the 355-bed Sibley Memorial, which, during the preparation of the series, had refused to disclose the identities of its trustees. After the reporter prodded for several months, Sibley relented by releasing a list of the trustees—a list that omitted their business affiliations and addresses. In February 1973, Kessler wrote a story that might explain why Sibley had been secretive. It began:

Bankers who are trustees of Sibley Memorial Hospital have been keeping more than $1 million of the hospital's money in interest-free accounts at their own banks without paying off a mortgage the hospital owes to the same banks, costing the hospital and its patients more than $100,000 a year in interest payments.

The balances in the interest-free accounts—which have been criticized by the hospital's independent accountants—have risen and fallen as the influence of Sibley's most dominant trustee, who is connected with the bank where the most money has been kept, has gone up and down.[15]

The "most dominant trustee" was Stacy M. Reed, a director and member of the executive committee of Security National Bank. Another trustee, Fred W. Smith, was an advisory director of Riggs National Bank. A single interest-free checking account usually containing more than $250,000, but growing on one occasion to almost $1 million, was maintained alternately at Security and Riggs. Trustee Edward K. Jones was a director and board chairman of Interstate Building Association; trustee Lanier P. McLachlen was board chairman of McLachlen National Bank. Their institutions also had substantial no-interest Sibley deposits. Such tie-ins are no coincidence, True Davis, chairman of the National Bank of Washington, told Kessler.

Davis said one of the reasons bankers go on boards of nonprofit organizations is to try to get their primary accounts.
    The reason the balances in the accounts soon grow is equally simple: "The reason generally for the large balances is that bankers' first responsibility is to their banks," Davis said.[16]

Kessler's story gave rise to a class action in behalf of patients and naming as defendants the hospital, its nine trustees, and six financial institutions.[17] On July 30, 1974, United States District Judge Gerhard Gesell ruled that each of the five trustees—those named, plus George M. Ferris, senior partner and board chairman of a stock brokerage firm—had "breached his fiduciary duty to supervise the management of Sibley's investments," had "failed to exercise even the most cursory supervision over the handling of Hospital funds," and had, "at one time or another, affirmatively approved self-dealing transactions." Gesell went on to lay down clear lines of accountability:

The management of a non-profit charitable hospital imposes a severe obligation upon its trustees. A hospital such as Sibley is not regulated by any public authority, it has no responsibility to file financial reports, and its Board is self-perpetuating. The interests of its patients are funnelled primarily through large group insurers who pay the patients' bills, and the patients lack meaningful participation in the Hospital's affairs. It is obvious that, in due course, new trustees must come to the Board of this Hospital, some of whom will be affiliated with banks, savings and loan associations, and other financial institutions. The tendency of representatives of such institutions is often to seek business in return for advice and assistance rendered as trustees. It must be made absolutely clear that Board membership carries no right to preferential treatment in the placement or handling of the Hospital's investments and business accounts. The Hospital would be well advised to restrict membership on its Board to the representatives of financial institutions which have no substantial business relationship with the hospital.[18]

Harry Huge, a Washington lawyer in the firm of Arnold & Porter who represented the miners in the successful class action against the mineworkers' retirement fund and others, told Kessler, "The public is only beginning to realize that whether bankers steal money directly from the treasury of a hospital or take it by keeping large sums in interest-free accounts, the loss to the hospital is the same."[19] The importance of this may be judged from a survey in which Congress' General Accounting Office found that of nineteen unidentified hospitals, thirteen of them in Missouri—in the Kansas City, St. Louis and Springfield areas—and the rest in the Washington metropolitan area, all but two had overlapping interests between trustees and the hospitals they served.[20]

"The best way to avoid potential conflicts of interest and to be assured of objective advice," Judge Gesell said in his ruling, "is to avoid the possibility of such conflicts at the time new trustees are selected." His advice has broad application: the best way to avoid potential conflicts, in any situation, is to abort them. Accountability merely to one's self will not do; conduct must be able to withstand challenge in another place.

The legal right inherent in the First Amendment carries with it a moral obligation, a kind of moral compact between press and people. This is not something that can be enforced; but it is something that the press will ignore at its own and the country's peril.

John B. Oakes
New York Times

In an article in *Collier's* in 1905, Mark Sullivan revealed what is probably the worst known example of the press resolving the conflict between advertisers and the public in favor of advertisers. The revelation was the "contract of silence" that almost all dailies and weeklies in the country had signed with the Proprietary Association of America, the trade group of patent-medicine manufacturers. George Seldes, the grand old muckraker, recalled the article in *Media & Consumer* in 1974:

The contract of silence was a short paragraph, usually in red ink, threatening cancellation of advertising if any city or state legislative body took any adverse action to the always harmful and frequently criminal activities of the drug industry—those merchants of death. Time after time when a city ordinance or a bill in the legislature anywhere in the country proposed limiting or even investigating the deadly industry, telegrams from the Proprietary Association immediately blackmailed the local or statewide press into defeating the general welfare of the public. . . .

The result was that all public health bills from the 1900s to the 1930s were almost unanimously opposed by the press.[1]

Seldes went on to cite other press horror stories, particularly his finding that for decades after the Federal Trade Commission was established in 1915, "no one could produce evidence that even 1 per cent of the daily newspapers" reported the fraud orders issued by the FTC at a rate exceeding 400 per year "because the releases invariably named an advertiser." But the press has become incomparably better. FTC staff complaints, not merely commission orders, routinely get prominent, even front-page attention, in many newspapers, including the *New York Times* and the *Washington Post.* Drug manufacturers long since have learned to live with sustained critical exposure on television and in print media. No one possibly could have more credibility in evaluating the change in the American press than Seldes:

The press deserved the attacks and criticisms of Will Irwin (1911) and Upton Sinclair (1920) and the muckrakers who followed, and it needs today the watchdog and gadfly activities of the new critical weeklies, but all in all it is now a better medium of mass information . . . The 1972 Watergate disclosures, it is true, were made by only a score of the members of the mass media, but I remember Teapot Dome when only one of our 1,750 dailies *(The Albuquerque Morning Journal)* dared to tell the truth about White House corruption. We have come a long way since.[2]

No one has come further than the *Louisville Courier–Journal* and its sister paper, the *Louisville Times.* In 1972, the ownership established an advertising ethics unit. It shortly recommended that the papers bar ads for mail-order health insurance until truth--in-advertising standards could be formulated and effected. The papers thereupon imposed the ban—at an estimated revenue loss of $100,000.[3] This is certainly not to imply that the press as a whole has resolved persistent conflicts between the interests of advertisers and the interests of readers, as is immediately evident from any overview of the state of reporting of consumer matters. Indeed, regular monitoring of consumer reporting—and nonreporting—is so much needed that Francis Pollock, a dedicated consumer advocate, developed it into a unique and excellent enterprise, the monthly *Media & Consumer,* only to see it fail for want of capital in the fall of 1975. Repeatedly, Pollock found cases in which news persons who fought for decent coverage of consumer issues—anything from poor sanitation in restaurants to fraud in auto repair—faced wearying struggles and sometimes have been found expendable. Usually having no choice, readers in large numbers buy newspapers without great regard for content; no wonder publishers find it lucrative to publish advertiser-oriented real-estate, food and other special sections. But it must be said that many reporters and editors do not try in their own organizations to push out the news frontiers. Indeed, managements have initiated some of the best consumer reporting, either out of a sense of responsibility, out of a desire to build audiences advertisers cannot afford to ignore, or both.

A pioneer in consumer reporting, and an outstanding one, is the *Minneapolis Star.* A few years ago, it established a three-member consumer-reporting team that has undertaken a series of impressive projects that have commanded great reader interest. In one of the first, the paper engaged a laboratory to do bacteria counts on hamburger sold by markets and fast-food chains. After the *Star* publicized the results, a check of readers showed that their interest and retention of the story had been phenomenally high. In another project, the team took a dented car to several body-repair shops; their widely varying price estimates then were printed. Despite the success of such sensible efforts in Minneapolis and elsewhere, many news organizations never undertake them, or undertake them with an infrequency or timidity that fails to acknowledge their genuine importance and news value.

The press can sacrifice or slight the public interest for the benefit of news sources as well as for advertisers, whether the sources are officeholders, businessmen, sports promoters, or whatever. Many major news media have come to ban staff members from accepting gifts, junkets, or other "freebies" from news sources. The Louisville papers have gone much further, to preclude even the appearance of impropriety. They insist on paying rent for space they use in government buildings, for copies of books they review, and for tickets for film, music, and theater performances attended by their critics. They do not accept free tickets to sports events. Not until after Norman E. Isaacs, the papers' former executive editor, made a speech denouncing the sports department of the *New York Times* as a veritable "whore's den" of writers beholden to sports promoters, did the *Times* ban free tickets for reporters.[4]

In 1971, the Kentucky papers forbade members of the editorial, news, and photographic staffs from doing professional work for pay for any company or organization, profit or nonprofit, in their circulation area (Kentucky and southern Indiana). In subsequent eradications of possible conflicts of interest, the papers formally forbade all corporate officers, department heads, and other managers and administrators from having business involvements with any enterprise within the circulation area that has news, advertising, or entertainment-business connections with the newspapers. The policy is so strict that, for example, it bars the executives from owning any stock in any company that advertises in the papers, or even that prepares copy for, counsels, or rents to advertisers. The policy also forbids executives from making contributions to local or state political candidates in the circulation area.

A big and complicated urban society, Walter Lippmann once said, "cannot be governed, its inhabitants cannot conduct the business of their lives, unless they have access to the services of information and of argument and of criticism which are provided by a free press."[5] A good deal of the argument and criticism comes from a handful of syndicated columnists, among whom Lippmann had unique stature. They pose some special accountability problems, aside from their striking ability, in certain cases, never to write about matters as compellingly important as, say, the unaccountability of corporations or defense contractors, or never to write critically of such entities. One of the problems is that, with the exception of Ralph Nader and possibly a couple of others, major columnists and their syndicates refuse to provide lists of the newspapers that publish them. The practical effect is that a person reasonably may hope to correct an error or dispute an interpretation of events by sending a letter to the particular newspaper in which he saw an offending column, but will have the devil's own time if he tries to root out the error from dozens or even hundreds of papers. Columnists thus assume an omniscience denied lesser mortals. Reed J. Irvine, board chairman of Accuracy in Media, Inc., has proposed that the columnist or his syndicate "assume responsibility for seeing that valid corrections of erroneous statements are published in all the papers" that buy the column. This goes too far. We agree with Charles B. Seib, who is the internal ombudsman of the *Washington Post*, and who writes a column of press criticism from time to time, "that a columnist and his syndicate should see that letters from responsible sources taking issue with a column are distributed to subscribing newspapers," but that it must be left to the editors of the papers involved to decide whether to publish such letters.

The more pertinent accountability problem with columnists is conflict of interest. A principal case in point is "Inside Report," written by Rowland Evans, Jr., and Robert Novak, and appearing, as of late 1974, in 253 newspapers. "The authors insist they blend hard news and commentary," Stephen E. Nordlinger, a member of the Washington bureau of the *Baltimore Sun*, wrote in a splendid analysis in [*More*] in December 1974. "More often than not, however, the column reads these days like a propaganda sheet, castigating 'left-wing activists' like Ramsey Clark (28 October) and promoting such favorites as 'Mr. Taxation,' Wilbur Mills (23 October). By year's end, Evans and Novak were also carrying a new tag. After they depicted the Democrats on the House Judiciary Committee during the impeachment inquiry as 'divided and demoralized' (20 June), some began calling the column 'Errors and No Facts.' "

Twice a year, subscribers to an Evans and Novak twice-monthly newsletter, which is made up, Nordlinger said, of "column leftovers," attend closeddoor "seminars" in Washington. Top administration and political figures are the guest speakers. "To hear notables give off-the-cuff, off-the-record insights, the businessmen and others who attend—about 65 or 70—pay $200 each," Nordlinger said. "Some of those who have appeared at the request of Evans and Novak have been accorded exceedingly favorable treatment in the column, although there are exceptions . . ." The speakers at the six seminars held by late 1974 included Congressman Mills, then chairman of the House Ways and Means Committee; William E. Simon, deputy secretary and then secretary of the Treasury Department, and Robert Strauss, chairman of the Democratic National Committee. The columns built up all three, especially Mills, until he fell victim to a sex scandal.

In 1972, Nordlinger recalled, the "canny," "powerful" Mills was waging a presidential campaign—one which never got off the ground; yet, Evans and Novak portrayed Mills as "the only port in the political hurricane now besetting the Democratic party." Two years later, Mills faced his first Republican challenger, Mrs. Judy Petty, in thirty-six years. "Evans and Novak again rose to the occasion in a column which said that a visit to Mills in Arkansas by Secretary Simon ("dynamic," "highly visible") served as a "dramatic demonstration that the President has no interest whatsoever" in the GOP challenger. "This column on the Mills race made no mention of the Senate Watergate Committee's charge that Mills received $75,000 in illegal milk producer contributions for his presidential campaign," Nordlinger pointed out. He questioned Novak, who denied favoritism to Mills.

"William Simon also gets the same royal treatment," the reporter found. After Simon became secretary of the treasury in the summer of 1974, Nordlinger said, "Evans and Novak 'began pushing for budget trimming to fight inflation,' against the desires of his 'bitter personal rival,' budget director Roy Ash. When Simon seemed to be meeting resistance in reaching this goal, Evans and Novak said he was the 'target of guerilla warfare' from the Ash forces." Robert Strauss emerges like an egg yolk, "hard boiled" and "centrist." Similar simplistic compliments fall on Evans and Novak news sources and seminarians: "backroom Republican super-power" Melvin R. Laird; "shrewd" Clarke Reed of Mississippi, "the real power among the Southerners." Columnistic lightning bolts strike "aggressive" Roy Ash with his "lack of political sensitivity and contempt for Congress," Ramsey Clark, a "Texas emigré" "now resident in Greenwich Village," and George McGovern, "super-liberal darling of the Democratic left."[6] Evans and Novak ought to be accountable for writing such stuff, to be sure; but what of the newspapers that print it, often to the exclusion of pieces by a broad spectrum of the public, such as grace the Op Ed Page of the *New York Times,* and by informed staff members?

The question became more acute in January 1975, when the *Washington Post*'s Charles Seib, in a column on "The News Business," discussed the question whether columnists should "be expected to abide by the same conflict of interest standards most newspapers expect of their editorial staffs?" Seib provided these examples of cases that recently had come to his attention, including that of Evans and Novak, which we here omit:

• Tom Braden . . . strongly supported Nelson Rockefeller during the hearings on Rockefeller's financial largesse. It wasn't until later that he revealed—with some reluctance—that he had received over $100,000 in loans from Rockefeller back in the 1950s.

• William F. Buckley . . . defended Rockefeller in the matter of the campaign book about Rockefeller's 1970 gubernatorial opponent, Arthur Goldberg, but did not disclose that he was chairman of the firm that published the book for the Rockefellers.

• Ann Landers, who writes a personal advice column, accepted a free trip to China from the American Medical Association. Some editors felt that she didn't clearly disclose that AMA picked up the tab.

• Victor Lasky, best known as the author of the Goldberg book mentioned above, received $20,000 from Richard Nixon's Committee [for the Re-election of] the President while writing a syndicated column. The $20,000 deal was a secret until it came out in Watergate testimony. And nine months passed before Lasky's syndicate notified editors of it.

Seib noted the defenses entered in each case:

Braden asserts that a legitimate loan, properly repaid with interest, cannot be construed as an involvement amounting to conflict of interest. Buckley said that he assumed most people knew of his connections with the publishing house, but he has indicated that if he had to do it over again he would mention it. . . . Ann Landers' syndicate says that she adequately disclosed that the AMA paid for her China trip when she informed her readers that she went there as an AMA delegate. Lasky maintains that, as a freelance writer, he had every right to make an undisclosed deal with the CRP . . . and that the CRP connection didn't influence his views, which were pro-Nixon in the first place.

Seib granted that there was "something to be said for each of these defenses. But the fact remains that no self-respecting editor would permit a reporter on his staff to do any of the things listed and a self-respecting reporter would not do them in any case. (Which is not to say that some editors have not permitted such things and some reporters—and editors, for that matter—haven't done them.)" He went on to say:

The offenses listed, if all can be called offenses, differ in degree. But they all show an insensitivity to the need to avoid even the suspicion of conflict of interest.[7]

Under prodding from the NCEW, the National News Council, a watchdog over press performance and threats to press freedom, has sounded a warning to syndicates and to the writers and artists whose work they distribute: "Awkwardness for them is certain to grow unless there comes a general recognition that all communicators are under obvious obligation to live under the same standards they demand of those who hold public office."[8]

Conflicts of interest in commerce erode competition, which is society's primary instrument for making trade accountable. Consider ground transportation. One passenger train can carry as many persons as one thousand automobiles, one subway car as many as fifty autos, and one bus as many as thirty-five. Yet, the government allowed General Motors to dominate production of diesel locomotives and diesel buses as well as of automobiles. Thus, GM has had a truly staggering conflict of interest which it has resolved in the most obviously profitable manner: by doing everything within its power to push the sale of automobiles—until recently, it may be added, big, fat automobiles enormously wasteful of fuel and resources.

General Motors in 1949 was convicted of having conspired, mainly with Standard Oil of California and Firestone Tire and Rubber Company, to replace highly efficient urban electric-transit systems with bus operations which would contract never to buy new equipment "using any fuel or means of propulsion other than" petroleum. The conviction was upheld on appeal. The penalty inflicted on GM for this massive criminality was a fine of $5,000. GM's treasurer, also convicted, was fined a dollar.[1] Not surprisingly, GM continued through September 1955 to acquire electric rail and bus properties and to dieselize them. While railroads throughout the world electrified when they abandoned steam, ours switched to much less efficient diesel locomotives—because GM, the biggest single shipper, forced them to.[2]

The issue lay generally dormant until early 1974, when Philip A. Hart, the senior senator from Michigan, had the rare courage to hold hearings on the need to restructure the auto industry—which GM dominates, and which happens to be the keystone of his state's economy. On the opening day of the hearings, Bradford C. Snell, then an assistant counsel of the Senate Antitrust and Monopoly Subcommittee, which Hart heads, testified that GM played a dominant role in destroying more than one hundred electric surface rail-transit systems in fifty-six cities, including Baltimore, Philadelphia, New York, St. Louis, and Los Angeles, between 1932 and 1956. Based on an extensive study, *American Ground Transport*, which was financed by the Stern Fund of New York, Snell said the principal instrument of destruction was National City Lines (NCL), a holding company which GM and two suppliers of products used by buses, Socal and Firestone, formed in 1936. In 1950, NCL's owners gave it $9 million with which to finance the conversion of transit systems in sixteen states to GM buses. By the mid-1950s, motorization of electric transit systems was virtually complete.

In the study, Snell provided a case history of Pacific Electric System, which served Southern California with the world's largest electric railway system. A $100 million enterprise, it operated three thousand trains through fifty-six incorporated cities and annually carried 80 million passengers. In 1938, GM and Socal formed an affiliate of NCL that began to buy and scrap electric rail systems in Fresno, San Jose, and Stockton. In 1940, the affiliate began to acquire and scrap portions of Pacific Electric. Finally, it motorized the heart of downtown Los Angeles. Snell, in a portion of the study which was later supported in a statement to the subcommittee by Tom Bradley, mayor of Los Angeles, said:

Motorization drastically altered the way of life in Southern California. Today, Los Angeles is an ecological wasteland: The palm trees are dying from petrochemical smog; the orange groves have been paved over by 300 miles of freeways; the air is a septic tank into which 4 million cars, half of them built by General Motors, pump 13,000 tons of pollutants daily. . . . The substitution of GM diesel buses, which were forced to compete with automobiles for space on congested freeways, apparently benefited GM, Standard Oil, and Firestone, considerably more than the riding public. . . . As early as 1963, the city already was seeking ways of raising $500 million to rebuild a rail system "to supersede its present inadequate network of bus lines." . . . A decade later, the estimated cost of constructing a 116-mile rail system, less than one-sixth the size of the earlier Pacific Electric [which had extensive private rights-of-way], had escalated to more than $6.6 billion.[3]

In his testimony, Snell concluded that the Big Three—GM, Ford Motor Company, and Chrysler Corporation—"used their vast economic power to restructure America into a land of big cars and diesel trucks," making it into "a second-rate nation in ground transportation." He continued:

Unlike every other industrialized country in the world, we rely on cars and trucks for virtually all of our transport needs.

At the same time, in every city and suburb, our rail and bus services are either dead or dying. American travelers returning from Europe, for example, say there is a "bus gap." Even in Moscow, they say, the buses and subways look better than anything made in the United States. Travelers back from Japan tell the same story. Having ridden on 150 mile-per-hour bullet trains, they ask, "What ever happened to America's railroads?"

Let me suggest an explanation: The Big Three companies eliminated competition among themselves, secured control over rival bus and rail industries, and then maximized profits by substituting cars and trucks for every other competing method of transportation, including trains, streetcars, subways, and buses. . . .

Now we are running out of gas. And there are no public alternatives. No high-speed trains. No rapid rail transit. No decent, fume-free buses [in Germany and other countries, buses that burn diesel fuel in outlying areas operate entirely on self-generated electricity in built-up areas]. Nothing but 100 million gas-guzzling cars.[4]

In a sixty-seven-page reply to these and other charges by Snell, GM said that it "did not generate the winds of change which doomed the streetcar systems," but did, "through its buses, help to alleviate the disruption left in their wake." Referring to the 1930s, GM said, "Times were hard and public transportation systems were collapsing. . . . GM was able to help with technology, with enterprise, and in some cases, with capital. . . . The buses it sold helped give mass transportation a new lease on life which lasted into the postwar years." With similar vehemence, the company denied that it had coerced railroads into buying its diesel locomotives, saying in part that the Justice Department had twice investigated the charge and concluded it "had no case."

That last point had an especially hollow ring. When Ramsey Clark was attorney general in the Johnson Administration, he made a special point of trying to keep abreast of Antitrust Division activities. Yet, he didn't know until 1966, when he read it in a newspaper, that the division had developed plans to try to split GM into six companies and Ford into two, and to end the franchised-dealer system for them and for Chrysler as well. The plans had been drawn up at the direction of Donald F. Turner, a Harvard law professor and economist, soon after he took charge of the division in 1965. But Turner not only never made a recommendation to Clark, but, said Thomas R. Asher, a former division attorney who testified before Hart, "totally refused to address himself" to the issue. Eight weeks after resigning in 1968, Turner, in a confidential, twelve-page memo that the senator obtained for the hearing record, urged his successor to file an antimonopoly suit against the Big Three, including "an individual monopolization count against GM." The Turner memo, Asher said, "was quietly buried after one relatively brief meeting" of high division officials.[5]

Conflicts of interest that erode competition—which, to reemphasize the point, we rely upon to make commerce accountable—are the *raison d'être* of a law, enacted in the mid-1930s, that prohibits a person from serving bigamously as a director of two competing companies.

For nearly forty years, the prohibition—section 8 of the Clayton Act—went pretty much unenforced. This was yet another entry in the catalogue of abuses of discretionary justice. In 1972, however, the Federal Trade Commission (FTC) forced the resignations of directors who were serving at once on the boards of Aluminum Corporation of America and Kennecott Copper Corporation in one case, and on the boards of Alcoa and Armco Steel Corporation in another.

In 1972, the FTC forced the resignation of a director of two makers and sellers of air conditioners, Chrysler and General Electric Company. Also in 1974, Senators Adlai E. Stevenson, III (D–Ill.), and Floyd K. Haskell (D–Colo.) uncovered and protested numerous conflicts in the oil and gas industry. The FTC then alleged violations of the law by an even dozen members of the industry, led by Standard Oil of Ohio (Sohio), Amerada Hess Corporation, El Paso Natural Gas Corporation, Transcontinental Pipeline Company, and Kerr-McGee Corporation, and seven men, each a director of a pair of supposedly rival firms. Nine months later, in April 1975, the companies settled, and the seven directors resigned or agreed to resign. The companies, in addition, consented to pre-clear prospective directors for possible illegal interlocks, and to obtain disclosures from current and prospective board members of the names of other corporations for which they also are directors. Joining in the settlement were the following pairs of firms, cited with the director who interlocked them and the activities involved:

Sohio and Diamond Shamrock Corporation, purported competitors in exploration, production, refining, transportation, and sale of crude petroleum and natural gas, Horace A. Shepard; Amerada Hess and Newmont Mining Corporation, purported competitors in all of the aforementioned activities except transportation, William B. Moses, Jr.; Dixilyn Corporation and Austral Oil Company, purported competitors in all of the listed activities except transportation and refining, William H. Johnson; General American Oil Company of Texas and Pauley Petroleum, Inc., purported competitors also in all of the listed activities except transportation and refining, Paul A. Conley; El Paso and Transcontinental, exploration, production, processing, and sale of natural gas, Alfred C. Gassell, Jr., and Franz Schneider; Kerr-McGee and Oklahoma Natural Gas Company, all of the just-mentioned activities except processing, Dean A. McGee.

The FTC renewed its drive against illegal director interlocks in July 1975, when it issued complaints accusing Kraftco, Inc., and the SCM Corporation, producers of edible oils, margarine, and related food products, and Kane-Miller Corporation and United Brands, Inc., producers and sellers of rival foods including meat items of having illegal director interlocks—Richard C. Bond for the first pair, Joseph M. McDaniel, Jr., for the second. The pervasiveness of the phenomenon was further indicated a month later, when Ralph Nader's Corporate Accountability Research Group uncovered and asked the FTC to investigate the cases of eight industrialists each serving two companies producing competing products, as follows:

John T. Connor, Allied Chemical and General Motors corporations, each a producer of automotive safety equipment; Dean McGee, Kerr-McGee Corporation and General Electric Company, nuclear fuels; Silas Cathcart, Illinois Tool Works and GM, electrical components; Henry S. Wingate, International Nickel Company of Canada and United States Steel Corporation, iron ore, and nickel and other metals; John Harper, Aluminum Company of America and Goodyear Tire and Rubber Corporation, chemical and metal products; Charles McCoy, E. I. du Pont de Nemours & Company and Bethlehem Steel Company, plastic and steel parts; J. Mark Hiebert, Sterling Drug, Inc., and W. R. Grace and Company, household cleaning products, and E. R. Rowley, N. L. Industries and Borden Company, paint and coating products.

In a letter to the FTC's Bureau of Competition, the center's Mark J. Green said a study also showed that "the nation's ten largest banks have interlocking directors with the fifty largest industrial firms and twenty indirect interlocks. The latter were defined as two or more competitors sitting on one bank board."[6] The greatest objection to such interlocks was defined long ago by Louis D. Brandeis, the great crusader against monopoly who became a justice of the Supreme Court: They enable bankers to acquire "extraordinary power." He told how bankers who controlled the railroads were enabled also to control the issue and sale of securities. "Being bankers, they bought these securities at a price which they had a part in fixing or could have a part in fixing," he said.

They sold these securities, as bankers, to insurance companies in which they were able to exercise some control as directors. They got the money with which to buy these securities from railroads through their control of the great banking institutions, and then, in their capacity of having control of the railroads, they utilized the money to purchase from the great corporations, like the [United States] Steel Corporation, what the railroads needed, and in their capacity as controlling other corporations they bought from the Steel Corporation again, and so on until we had the endless chain.[7]

In recent years, two congressional investigations have established that giant banks, through holdings of their trust departments and through interlocks, have retained the "extraordinary power" of which Brandeis spoke in 1914. The staff of the late Congressman Wright Patman's House Banking Subcommittee on Domestic Finance surveyed the investments held by the trust departments of forty-nine commercial banks mainly for institutional investors, principally insurance companies, mutual funds, and pension funds, during 1967. The holdings totaled $607 billion, of which six New York City banks alone accounted for $64.4 billion. Each of the six, in addition to holding stock in the others, along with major banks elsewhere, held stock in and shared directors with firms in the same lines of business. All told, the staff said in a report in 1968, the forty-nine banks had together 768 director interlocks with 286 of the 500 largest corporations, or "an average of almost three directors for each corporation board on which bank director representation is found." The propulsion toward super-concentration in such arrangements was enlarged by another staff finding: the same banks held at least 5 percent of the common stock of each of 147 of the 500 largest industrial corporations.[8] Under guidelines set by Congress, control is "presumed" at 10 percent, although as little as 5 percent may suffice. The subcommittee staff said that a mere 1 or 2 percent confers potential "tremendous influence."

Major new findings were cited in *Disclosure of Corporate Ownership*, the report which the subcommittees headed by Senators Metcalf and Edmund S. Muskie issued in 1974 and which was discussed in the final chapter on secrecy.[9] Some of the most important data concerned control of putative competitors. The oil industry offers a leading case in point.

As of 1972, Bankers Trust Company held 6.1 percent of the *voting* stock of Mobil Oil (1.1 percentage points more than may be needed for control); Chase Manhattan Bank, 5.2 percent; and Morgan Guaranty Trust Company, 2.9 percent. Bankers Trust also held 5.8 percent of Continental Oil and Morgan Guaranty, 2.2 percent (the House subcommittee staff, it will be recalled, judged that 1 or 2 percent may confer "tremendous influence"). Chase Manhattan, in addition to its 5.2 percent of Mobil, held 4.5 percent of Atlantic Richfield, while a fourth Manhattan bank, First National City, held 2.7 percent. Morgan Guaranty, in addition to its 2.9 percent of Mobil and 2.2 percent of Continental, held 2.1 percent of Ashland Oil.

The four oil companies and two of the banks, Bankers Trust and First National City, were among 89 corporations that responded fully to a questionnaire (58 did not reply at all, and partial or irrelevant replies came from 177, including Exxon, Texaco, Standard of Indiana, Chase Manhattan, and Morgan Guaranty). In addition to oil and banking, the 89 firms replying fully were engaged in a cross section of economic activity—industry, transportation, communications, utilities, retailing, and insurance. Chase Manhattan held at least 2 percent of the voting stock in fully 46 of the 89 firms, Morgan Guaranty in 29, First National City in 28, Bankers Trust in 21, Bank of New York in 17, and State Street Bank of Boston in 16.

Overall, the patterns of control by giant banks were similar to that for oil. Thus, Chase Manhattan held 3.5 percent of Ford Motor Company—and 4 percent of Chrysler Corporation; 3.6 percent of General Electric—and 2.1

percent of Westinghouse; 7.4 percent of Monsanto Company (chemicals) —and 2 percent of Dow Chemical; 10.5 percent of Safeway Stores—and 2.5 percent of Grand Union. At the same time, Morgan Guaranty, with an investment portfolio of $27.4 billion compared with Chase Manhattan's $16.2 billion, held 2.7 percent of GE—and 5 percent of Westinghouse; 3 percent of Safeway—and 3.3 percent of Grand Union.

Disclosure of Corporate Ownership also provided enlightening data on director interlocks, again as of 1972. One centers on Atlantic Richfield. Its chairman and chief executive officer, Robert O. Anderson, was a director of Chase Manhattan, while Ellmore C. Patterson, chairman and chief executive officer of Morgan Guaranty, was a director of Atlantic Richfield. Another centers on General Electric. Ralph Lazarus, chairman of Federated Department Stores, was a director of Chase Manhattan, which held 3.6 percent of GE's stock, and a director also of GE. Other directors of GE included Thomas S. Gates, a director of Morgan Guaranty, which held 2.7 percent of GE's stock, and J. Paul Austin, chairman and chief executive officer of Coca-Cola Company, a director of Morgan Guaranty and also of GE. In passing, it may be noted that First National City Bank held 2.7 percent of the voting stock of Chase Manhattan and 2 percent of Morgan Guaranty.

Banks compete with insurance companies in several areas. Banks offer loans; life-insurance companies make loans to policyholders. To cite a specific example, Prudential Insurance Company, the nation's largest insurer, had at the end of 1974 $1.6 billion in real-estate loans in California, while Bank of America, which is based in California, and which is the largest bank in the country, had $5 billion in real-estate loans outstanding. Yet, during the sixty-year life of the Clayton Act, the government never had claimed that a director of a major insurance company who sat on the board of a major bank violated section 8. In consequence, hundreds of such interlocks came into being without being challenged. On October 6, 1975, however, in what Congressman Patman praised as "a giant step forward in an area that has been too long overlooked," the Department of Justice invoked section 8 in an effort to lay down the principle that a director of a major bank who is also a director of a major insurance company violates the antitrust laws. The department's mechanism was two lawsuits filed in United States District Court in San Francisco. One involved Prudential and directors of that insurance company who sit on the boards of Bank of America and Bankers Trust Company, the nation's seventh-largest bank. The second involved interlocks among Crocker National Bank, the fourteenth-largest, and Metropolitan Life Insurance Company, Equitable Life Assurance Society, and Mutual Life Insurance Company of New York—the second-, third-, and eleventh-largest insurance companies, respectively. The cases had not been resolved as of mid-1976.

Does it matter, say, that Chase Manhattan is the largest shareholder in Atlantic Richfield and the second largest in Mobil, an ARCO competitor? Yes, because there is in such circumstances something that, if not an outright conflict of interest, is a reasonable-enough facsimile to enfeeble competition and therefore accountability. "Clearly it is not in Chase Manhattan's interest to promote vigorous competition between them" (ARCO and Mobil), the Bureau of Competition of the Federal Trade Commission has said.[10] Yet common rather than independent ownership is but one of numerous deeply rooted joint undertakings and arrangements that knit ostensibly independent oil companies together, make each the confidant of others, and substitute community of interest for aggressive competition. There is, the FTC staff said, "no level of operation . . . free of strong ties" among the majors.

That assessment rests on a base of solid documentation. For example, the multinational oil companies engage in at least one hundred international joint ventures, from Aramco on down. If each of these ventures has only one board meeting annually, the sum of the opportunities for the American-based participants to exchange information—and possibly to take anticompetitive actions—with one or more rivals has been computed at 1,062.[11] It is illegal for firms able to bid independently to meet in advance of an offering and decide which one should bid and which should refrain. But this is gotten around in the sale of federal offshore petroleum leases by joint bidding that accomplishes the same result: two or more firms each able to bid independently combine to submit a single bid. In recent years, combinations of two or more large petroleum companies, colluding in ways that would be illegal if explicit, have accounted "almost exclusively" for the purchase of offshore leases from the government, John W. Wilson, former chief of the Federal Power Commission's Division of Economic Studies, has said.[12] This is a circumvention similar in spirit to that which permits, say, Morgan Guaranty Trust to put employees on the boards of Continental Oil, Cities Service, ARCO, and four other firms which, like them, engage in the oil and gas business, while section 8 of the Clayton Act prohibits a single human being from serving on the boards of even two competing firms.

Ida M. Tarbell concluded from her classic study of John D. Rockefeller's Standard Oil Trust that free and equal access to transportation was the crucial question. "So long as it is possible for a company to own the exclusive carrier on which a great natural product depends for transportation, and to use this carrier to limit a competitor's supply or to cut off that supply entirely if the rival is offensive, and always to make him pay a higher rate than it costs the owner, it is ignorance and folly to talk about constitutional amendments limiting trusts," she said.[13] All that's changed since the early twentieth century, essentially, is that domination of the pipeline industry has passed from the Standard Oil Trust to joint ownership by the integrated majors, which is to say, from a monopoly to a shared monopoly. "It is still true today that independent producers must sell their crude to these pipelines before shipment and that independent refiners, with no other source of supply, must purchase crude from pipelines owned by the integrated majors," Dr. Wilson told the Senate Subcommittee on Antitrust and Monopoly. The production and processing operations of the pipeline's owners must be coordinated, requiring, Wilson testified, "a close association and collaboration" that "cannot help but spill into their other activities."[14]

A "close association" is enhanced, too, by joint production ventures. Beyond this, the majors have agreements to exchange substantial quantities of crude oil and gasoline among themselves. And they further inhibit or utterly prevent workable competition by being vertically integrated—owning everything from the oil well to the gasoline pump—and by acquiring substantial interests in coal, uranium, and other sources of energy.

VI
Unaccountable Language

A person may shut out feelings of blameworthiness and remorse for his acts by separating himself from their consequences. Even General George S. Patton, Jr., who acclaimed his love of war, did this. He once confided, in his personal papers, that a soldier who was "a horrid bloody mess . . . was not good to look at, [because] I might develop personal feelings about sending men to battle. That would be fatal for a General."[1] More commonly, however, a person wishing to escape ethical accountability does so with one or another use or abuse of language.

One may say that everybody is guilty—meaning that nobody, including the speaker, is guilty. Such an incantation was used for a time by Richard N. Goodwin after he resigned from the Johnson Administration. If Vietnam were to turn into an apocalypse, he wrote in the *New Yorker*, "there will be no act of madness, no single villain on whom to discharge guilt; *just the flow of history.*"[2] (Emphasis supplied.) In this way, Edward Weisband and Thomas M. Franck have said, "Goodwin tried to disassociate himself from Johnson's Vietnam policy without attacking his former boss—for whom he continued to be a freelance speechwriter."[3]

One may invoke abstractions. They always have been available to serve both exalted and low purposes. The war in Vietnam was launched, was prolonged, and was finally ended on a sea of abstractions—"the domino theory," "peace with honor," "the integrity of our alliances," "moral commitment." These blotted out realities of national behavior that were as irrational as they were awful. Contrary to the abstractions that deluded us, John Kenneth Galbraith said in 1966, "Vietnam is not important to us. Nor is it a bastion of freedom. Nor is it a testing place of democracy. It is none of these things. Had it been lost in 1954, no one would now be thinking of it."[4]

On the personal level, men always have used abstractions to dehumanize other human beings and thus to excuse bestiality. In Southeast Asia, Americans who tagged Vietnamese and Cambodians as "gooks" were, a Marine in Cambodia said in 1970, "killing our own humanity." In one of hundreds of such stories, he wrote Senator Charles McC. Mathias, Jr. (R–Md.) of having "heard my men describe with excitement and pleasure the killing of a young woman with a 50-calibre machine gun, detailing how they laughed when the woman was knocked thirty feet by the impact. To many Americans, Vietnamese long since have ceased to be people."[5] The 347 men, women, and children massacred at My Lai 4 by American troops in 1968 were not "people."

John Leonard, while editor of the *New York Times Book Review*, contended that statistics are an abstraction which explain why "our ethical systems haven't caught up with the social fact of the way we live now," an example being the jailing of a father who beats his child *v.* the mere fining or reprimanding of "[a] company that distributes spoiled milk to thousands of children and is therefore responsible for killing—according to statistical analysis—several of those children . . ." The key words are "statistical analysis." Leonard believes that Americans refuse to believe such statistics apply to them and that this refusal explains the lag in our ethical systems:

If accountability is abstract, a random sample, a scatter curve, it means very little to us, because we are first and foremost individuals, not citizens. To quantify us is to enslave us to likelihoods, probabilities. . . . We haven't grown up at all from "I" to "we," and our childhood is hazardous to all of us.[6]

An abstraction can be doublethink, George Orwell's word for "the power of holding two contradictory beliefs in one's mind simultaneously, and accepting both of them. . . . The process has to be conscious, or it would not be carried out with sufficient precision, but it also has to be unconscious, or it would bring with it a feeling of falsity and hence of guilt." The unforgettable examples in Orwell's great novel *1984*, in elegant lettering on the glittering white concrete face of the Ministry of Truth, were:

WAR IS PEACE

FREEDOM IS SLAVERY

IGNORANCE IS STRENGTH

It is doublethink to speak of the "Free World" and mean by it, in addition to the United States and Britain, Chile, South Korea, and Spain. It was said in the late 1940s that the United States had "lost China." This was an astounding feat of doublethink, one that struck columnist Russell Baker as "comparable to losing a bull elephant in a studio apartment. Many Americans did not even know we had China until we lost it."[7] The same Americans probably didn't know we had Cuba and Cambodia to lose until we lost them, either.

The deeply ingrained notion of the moral superiority of the United States, and of her institutions and way of life, is an abstraction, a myth, and doublethink all rolled into one. It enabled us, Henry Steele Commager said in 1968, to maintain a double standard of morality in international relations. Thus communism is by very definition aggressive, but not capitalism: intervention in Hungary proved that, and intervention in Santo Domingo proved nothing. . . . When Communist countries carry on clandestine activities abroad, their conduct is subversive, and indeed they are engaged in an "international conspiracy"; but when our CIA engages in clandestine activities in sixty countries, it is a legitimate branch of foreign policy. . . . If Russian or Chinese planes should fly over American soil we would regard that as an intolerable violation of international law; but we make daily flights over China without troubling ourselves about the law. . . . When, in the last war, Germans destroyed villages because they had harbored snipers, we were justly outraged; but any Vietnamese who so much as fires a gun at one of our planes invites the instant destruction of his village by our outraged airmen. We looked with horror on the concentration camps of the last war; but we set up "refugee" camps in Vietnam which are, for all practical purposes, concentration camps. . . .

Only a people infatuated with their own moral virtue, their own superiority, their own exemption from the ordinary laws of history and of morality, could so uncritically embrace a double standard of morality as have the American people.[8]

The modern era has speeded the corruption of language into an instrument of deception and therefore of unaccountability. George Orwell wrote in 1946:

In our time, political speech and writing are largely the defence of the indefensible. Things like the continuation of British rule in India, the Russian purges and deportations, the dropping of the atom bombs on Japan, can indeed be defended, but only by arguments which are too brutal for most people to face, and which do not square with the professed aims of political parties. Thus political language has to consist largely of euphemism, question-begging and sheer cloudy vagueness. Defenceless villages are bombarded from the air, the inhabitants driven out into the countryside, the huts set on fire with incendiary bullets: this is called *pacification*. Millions of peasants are robbed of their farms and sent trudging along the roads with no more than they can carry: this is called *transfer of population* or *rectification of frontiers*. People are imprisoned for years without trial, or shot in the back of the neck or sent to die of scurvy in Arctic lumber camps: this is called *elimination of unreliable elements*.[9]

Advances in technology have facilitated the ability of the government to defend the indefensible. "Television has not only increased the impact of news and the speed of communication, it has also increased the ease and effectiveness of information distortion," David Wise wrote in *The Politics of Lying: Government Deception, Secrecy, and Power*. A President can request, and almost always get, time on the television the networks,

as Nixon did in 1972 to announce the mining of Haiphong harbor and other Vietnamese ports, and rally substantial public support for military actions that may lead to war. In many such cases, the President completely controls the version of events that he chooses to tell his audience. In the nuclear age, when mankind lives less than thirty minutes away from destruction, this is a truly frightening power.[10]

The techniques of political language so precisely captured by George Orwell—"euphemism, question-begging and sheer cloudy vagueness"— were perfected during the war in Southeast Asia and then were televised into our very living rooms. Pentagon flacks, never flinching, never flicking an eyebrow, spoke of "protective reaction" (bombing); "surgical strike" (precision bombing); "pacification center" (concentration camp); "incontinent ordinance" (bombs falling outside a target area); a "military structure" (anything from a villager's hut to a Viet Cong hospital[11]); "waterborne logistics craft" (sometimes just a sampan carrying supplies[12]); "smoke" (white phosphorus rounds frequently used in naval gunfire support).

In Phnom Penh in 1973, Air Force Colonel David H. E. Opfer, air attaché at the United States Embassy, complained to reporters in Cambodia: "You always write it's bombing, bombing, bombing. It's not bombing. It's air support." The Committee on Public Doublespeak, established by the National Council of Teachers of English to honor those who make signal contributions to semantic distortion, gave Opfer one of its first annual "Doublespeak Awards."[13] Another award went to Ronald L. Ziegler, who as President Nixon's press secretary made this statement about the safeguarding of Watergate tapes:

I would feel that most of the conversations that took place in those areas of the White House that did have the recording system would, in almost their entirety, be in existence, but the special prosecutor, the court, and, I think, the American people are sufficiently familiar with the recording system to know where the recording devices existed and to know the situation in terms of the recording process, but I feel, although the process has not been undertaken yet in preparation of the material to abide by the court decision, really, what the answer to that question is.[14]

Ziegler's is an extreme example of what Richard Gambino, of Queens College, describes as a pervasive "language of nonresponsibility."

An error in planning or prediction is not a "mistake," for this term raises depressing questions of personal competency and accountability; it is a "shortfall." . . . Evil people cover up, lie and bribe. Our leaders "contain situations" like so many protective dams. This is particularly true when they are involved in a "game plan" (conspiracy). Politicians and bureaucrats are too pure of soul to use provocative expressions or loaded terms. They would never deprive children of school funds or poor people of proper housing. They merely "trade off" highways for schools and missiles for slums. . . .

No bureaucrat deals with patterns, ways, means, values and numbers but with "norms," "parameters," "variables," "inputs," "outputs," "context fields" and "quotas.[15]

The "language of nonresponsibility" includes an additional phrase of surpassing importance to propagandists in their many guises. The phrase is the undefined or vaguely defined or inadequately defined "better than . . ." The phrase is a mainstay of the food industry, which is the world's biggest concentration of financial power, and of its yodelers on Capitol Hill and in the canyons of the bureaucracy. William Robbins, in *The American Food Scandal: Why You Can't Eat Well on What You Earn*, said:

Better than what? Our food is grown, processed and impregnated with chemicals, with hardly a passing thought from the industry about their effect on the consumer's health. . . .

"Let them eat the Delicious," say the buying officials of the supermarkets if we want apples. And where are the Rome Beauties, the Northern Spies, the Grimes Goldens, the Baldwins and Yellow Newtons of yesteryear? Their delightful flavors, like the tart sweetness of a fresh blackberry or the exotic tang of a ripe persimmon, have been sacrificed to a mythical god of efficiency, and our children may never know the riches of which they have been robbed.

Our tomatoes have become hard, grainy and tasteless because government researchers, serving agribusiness rather than the consumer, breed them for toughness rather than quality.[16]

The food industry's "better than . . ." stool rests on another wobbly leg: the claim that it gives us a bargain. Robbins put down the appeal diverted from tastebuds to pocketbook:

And how can we believe that our costs are lower when we are bled by hidden costs, both financial and social? We have paid billions in subsidies to wealthy farmers and giant agribusiness corporations and billions more because their prices were artificially supported by the Government. And we pay additional billions to be bombarded by advertising messages designed to persuade us that worse is really better.

Our food costs also include the billions spent for unnecessary processing that diminishes both quality and taste, for extravagant packaging and for preparation of "convenience" foods that offer us the flavor of cardboard . . .

The hidden costs include, in addition, hundreds of millions of dollars in extra taxes. Consumers must pay more because of tax dodges that let wealthy farming corporations pay less, while wealthy absentee investors in farming schemes often pay no tax at all. We pay, as another hidden part of our food bills, the billions in welfare costs brought on as small farmers and farm workers are driven from their fields. And still higher and more devastating are the social costs of our desolated rural villages and country lanes, left behind by the dispossessed people who crowd our slums.

Americans are told that at the food counters they pay out 16 percent of their income while consumers in other countries pay a higher proportion. "That, too, is deception," Robbins says.

Which Americans? The poor? A family of four at the poverty level . . . spends nearly half its earnings for a meager subsistence. The average wage-earner? That family of four, if moved up to the median tax bracket, would pay nearly a third of its income for food, and if it should advance to the relatively higher income average of suburban-ites, it would still pay over 25 percent. Only among families with relatively high incomes do we reach a level where less than a fifth of spendable earnings goes for food.[17]

Consumers of prescription pharmaceuticals are peculiarly vulnerable to manipulations of arcane language which are intended to influence not them, but their physicians, and which may determine quite literally life or death in certain situations. The Pill provides an example.

The Food and Drug Administration in 1960 allowed birth-control pills to go on sale without bothering to require adequate testing to determine if they might cause, among other things, disabling and fatal blood-clotting dis-eases.[18] Belatedly, retrospective studies of highest quality were undertaken —not first in the United States, it may be noted, but in Britain. In 1967, when oral contraceptives were being used by millions of women, and after millions more had used them, British scientists established that the pills do in fact cause blood-clotting diseases. Specifically, they concluded that the fatality rate in the 20-to-34 age range was 1.3 per 100,000 per year among users as compared with 0.2 among nonusers, and in the 35-to-44 age range 3.9 among users and 0.5 among nonusers. Hospitalization of women 20 to 44 for treatment of thrombotic disease was 47 per 100,000 per year among users as compared with 5 among nonusers.

Learning of these results in late 1967, and finding them solidly based, the FDA in Washington approved a draft of a proposed official revision of the labeling which would tell physicians: "A cause and effect relationship has been established for the following: thrombophlebitis, and pulmonary embo-lism." The British researchers said that "cause and effect" was scientifically the same as "a statistically significant association." Manufacturers knew, however, that in the ears of many physicians "statistically significant" sounds equivocal. Consequently, at a confrontation with FDA officials in May 1968, they insisted that that phrase be used. To blur and soften the impact of the British studies still more, they insisted that the clause here italicized be deleted: *"Because of the increased risk of thrombotic disorders observed in patients taking oral contraceptives,* the physician should be alert to the earliest manifestations of [thrombotic] disorders . . ." Finally, the companies insisted that the final prescribing instructions incorporate a suggestion that studies done with British women might not apply to American women, although the principal firm, G. D. Searle & Company, Inc., long had claimed universal relevance for studies on its Enovid done years earlier in Puerto Rico and Haiti.

Over the bitter protests of Dr. Robert S. McCleery, then director of the agency's Medical Advertising Branch, the FDA gave in to all three demands. In the official labeling which became effective for all brands on July 1, 1968, a mushy "statistically significant" had displaced a straightforward "cause and effect"; "Because of the increased risk . . ." had disappeared, and it was suggested to physicians that data on British women "cannot be directly applied to women in other countries." Thus did a message of esoteric language to sustain or increase sales of the pills occur unbeknownst to doctors and at the peril of women who hadn't an inkling what was happening. The diluted labeling was still in effect in 1973, when McCleery, in sworn court-room testimony in the case of a young woman who after sixteen months on the drugs had suffered a serious stroke, revealed the FDA's cave-in to indus-try pressure.[19] Not until mid-1976 did the FDA move to make the requisite changes. But the agency's obfuscatory skills were unimpaired, as was shown in 1975, when British scientists established that pill users run increased risks of fatal and nonfatal heart attacks. In the 40-through-44 age bracket, a study showed, the annual incidence per 100,000 persons was 111, compared with 21 among nonusers; in the 30-through-39 bracket, 11 among users, 4 among nonusers. Although the risk clearly increases with age, although there is no measurable difference in risk for a woman when she is, say, 39 as against 41, and although the health and safety of millions of women were at stake, the FDA repeatedly urged women 40 and over to seek other forms of contracep-tion while de-emphasizing the risk to women under 40 to the point that one might infer there was none.[20]

At Vladivostok in 1974 the United States and the Soviet Union reached an agreement which Secretary of State Henry A. Kissinger hailed as a "break-through" for arms "limitation." Secretary of Defense James R. Schlesinger acclaimed the agreement as "a major step forward." Toward what? Well, Schlesinger explained, the agreement probably would require twelve Trident missile submarines rather than the ten that had been planned; ten Poseidon missile submarines would be kept operating longer than had been planned; a new strategic bomber would be built and deployed, and a larger interconti-nental ballistic missile than we now have would be built and deployed. Tom Wicker asked, "This is arms 'limitation'?"[21]

For the stated purpose of helping them defend against a possible attack by China or the Soviet Union, the United States gave military aid to India and Pakistan. "But the Pakistani government used that aid to put down the independence movement in East Pakistan (Bangladesh)," Senator William Proxmire (D–Wis.) has said.

Through the force of arms, much of it supplied by the United States, they killed, burned, raped, tortured and devastated an entire countryside. They drove ten million people from their homes. They murdered and slaughtered others. Some were driven into the sea. Others escaped to refugee camps in India, where thousands remained uncared for. India retaliated and drove the West Pakistan Army from Bangladesh. Weapons for both sides had been supplied by the United States. In the budget we call that "international security assistance."[22]

E. Howard Hunt, one of the Watergate burglars and a former CIA agent and consultant to the Nixon White House, appeared before a federal grand jury in April 1973:

Q. Well, in your terminology, would the entry into Mr. Fielding's [Daniel Ellsberg's psychiatrist] office have been clandestine, illegal, neither or both?
A. I would simply call it an entry operation conducted under the auspices of competent authority.[23]

Hunt would not say that a crime is a crime is a crime because that would make him accountable; saying that a crime is "an entry operation" was a quest for unaccountability. Euphemisms questing for unaccountability permeate American life. "Everybody else says they want more money, but let David Rockefeller speak for higher interest rates and, boy, that's statesmanship," John Kenneth Galbraith has remarked.[24] Similarly, columnist Russell Baker has wondered, "How come it's a subsidy when Pan American [World Airways] asks the Government for a hundred million dollars to keep flying, but when people ask for considerably less to keep going it is a federal handout?"[25]

"Something drastic is needed, for while language—the poor state of language in the United States—may not be at the heart of our problems, it isn't divorced from them either," Edwin Newman says in *Strictly Speaking: Will America Be the Death of English?* For starters, we could replace "pollution" with Ralph Nader's phrase, "domestic chemical and biological warfare."[26] Newman, who is known as the in-house grammarian and dry wit at NBC News, reinforced his point this way: "It is at least conceivable that our politics would be improved if our English were, and so would other parts of our national life. If we were to be more careful about what we say, and how, we might be more critical and less gullible. Those for whom words have lost their value are likely to find that ideas also have lost their value. Maybe some people discipline themselves in one and not in the other, but they must be rare."[27]

Author Gore Vidal has been more scathing. "The use of language really offends me deeply and terrifies me," he has said. "The language has absolutely been so euphemized, so corrupted, so *burgered* that it just doesn't mean anything any more. It isn't just the politicians; it's any American with the 'likes,' the 'ahhs,' the 'you knows,' the inability to say *anything*. . . . the kids can't talk, they cannot arrange sentences in their heads. . . . They can't ask a question. Well, language is what defines intelligence. Language is what a civilization is all about."[28] But while "the kids" were like, ah, you know, not saying anything, others with regard for precision were using language as an alchemy to transmute accountability into unaccountability.

Dr. A. Dale Console had done this before he resigned, in 1957, as medical director of E. R. Squibb & Sons. "I reached a point where I could no longer live with myself," he said. "I had compromised to the point where my back was against a wall and I had to choose between resigning myself to total capitulation or resigning as medical director." One of the reasons he gave up a job that had taught him "the meaning of loneliness and alienation" was that a drug-company doctor "must learn to word a warning statement so it will appear to be an inducement to use the drug rather than a warning of the dangers inherent in its use . . ."[29]

Sometimes the aim of unaccountability alchemy is to make a document unreadable or incomprehensible. The Globe American Casualty Company of Cleveland, Ohio, did this in an exceedingly unimaginative way: it printed automobile insurance policies in a size of type so small, a judge ruled, that it "would drive an eagle to a microscope."[30] More commonly the language of insurance policies is incomprehensible no matter the size of the type. Herbert S. Denenberg, during his dedicated service as insurance commissioner of the Commonwealth of Pennsylvania, sought to make insurance policies readable by applying a technique, developed by Rudolph Flesch, which is based on the number of words per sentence and the average number of syllables per word. The standard family auto policy "is substantially less readable than Einstein's basic work on relativity," Denenberg told the Senate Antitrust and Monopoly Subcommittee in 1973. He said a readability analysis of an Insurance Company of North American (INA) homeowners policy showed it to be "less readable than Einstein's Theory of Relativity." On a scale ranging from zero (impenetrable) to 100 (crystal clarity) the Theory ranked at about 18 and a standard auto policy at 10; but the INA policy "had a negative readability quotient," Denenberg said. "That was going too far."[31]

Doubtless lawyers write all such language. They have been doing it for a long time. Thomas Jefferson believed that involved and technical legal language was conducive to miscarriages of justice. In 1817, he prepared a draft of *An Act for Establishing Elementary Schools.* Offering the draft to Joseph C. Cabell, he apologized for having spurned legal jargon in favor of simple terms.

You, however, can easily correct this bill to the taste of my brother lawyers, by making every other word a "said" or "aforesaid," and saying everything over two or three times, so that nobody but we of the craft can untwist the diction, and find out what it means; and that, too, not so plainly but that we may conscientiously divide one half on each side.[32]

"[T]he language of The Law seems almost deliberately designed to confuse and muddle the ideas it purports to convey," Fred Rodell, a law professor at Yale, has complained. "It ranges only from the ambiguous to the completely incomprehensible" and is carried on "in a foreign language . . . a jargon which completely baffles and befoozles the ordinary literate man, who has no legal training to serve him as a trot."[33]

Whereas any lawyer can make himself unintelligible to laymen with words such as "trover" and "assumpsit," and whereas there is (Rodell said) in the law books "no single rule that makes as much simple sense as 'Anyone who spits on this platform will be fined five dollars,' "[34] it takes a higher order of skill to con other lawyers. No one had it in greater abundance than Robert Moses, possibly the trickiest drafter of legislation the country has ever seen.

Robert A. Caro, in his Pulitzer Prize-winning biography of Moses, cites several examples of how bills drafted by Moses to give himself vast unaccountable power went through the New York State Legislature without a single lawyer detecting what was happening.[35]

A truly momentous use of definitional manipulation to achieve unaccountability occurred ninety years ago. The manipulated language was in the Fourteenth Amendment. Congress had passed it, in 1866, and the states had ratified it, in 1868. Its purpose was to protect the civil liberties of Negroes who had been freed from slavery only to find the Southern states enacting laws that nullified their new freedoms. The Supreme Court soon all but swept away the high purpose of the Amendment with a feat of judicial alchemy that converted it into an instrument to protect corporations.

"The records of this time can be searched in vain for evidence that this Amendment was adopted for the benefit of corporations," Hugo L. Black, the late justice of the Supreme Court, said in 1937. "The history of the Amendment proves that the people were told its purpose was to protect weak and helpless human beings and were not told that it was intended to remove corporations in any fashion from the control of state governments." In 1886, however, the Supreme Court, for the first time, contrived to amend the Amendment so that the word "person" in some cases would embrace flesh-less and bloodless corporations.

The Amendment says in Section 1, ". . . nor shall any State deprive any person of life, liberty, or property, without due process of law." Being an inanimate cluster of assets, a corporation has no life or liberty to lose; but the High Court managed so to distend "person" as to forbid a state from depriving a corporation of *property* without the due process intended for flesh-and-blood. Section 1 also says that no state shall "deny to any person within its jurisdiction the equal protection of the laws." Here the manipula-tion of "person" to include a corporation was touched by irony: it provided an even-handed assurance that in any legal dispute it might have with you, Texaco could count on equal protection.

"The judicial inclusion of the word 'corporation' has had a revolutionary effect on our form of government," Black said. This single act of judicial sleight-of-hand has also had a revolutionary effect on accountability. It made the corporation a first-class citizen and the human being a second-class citizen. "It is difficult to pretend any longer that there is 'Equal Justice Under Law,' or even that this is an ideal destined someday to be achieved," Jerry S. Cohen said in 1972. "The law simply cannot bestow equal justice so long as there are two separate and unequal classes of citizens—one that cannot be imprisoned and another that can, one for whom the most severe penalty is the punishment of its capital, and another that can receive capital punishment."[36]

In the federal government one of the simpler alchemies makes our economic condition look better than it really is; as a result, there is less for which it can be held accountable. Thus, the government cultivates the notion that we enjoy "full" employment when 4 percent of the work force is unemployed ("unemployed," it should be noted, under an official definition which ex-cludes many unemployed; moreover, Britain, among other countries, regards a 3 percent unemployment level as intolerable).[37] A related gimmick is the claim that only 37.5 percent of the work force is "blue-collar." Andrew Levison, in *The Working Class Majority*, showed that other Bureau of the Census categories conceal numerous manual-labor jobs, such as farm labor-ers, all service workers (including guards, housekeepers, hospital attendants, sweepers, and dishwashers), postmen, office-machine operators, typists, and cafeteria helpers. Levison's calculation is that probably 60 to 62 percent of the work force do rote manual labor.[38]

The Renegotiation Board is an agency which news organizations generally ignore, although it is the last checkpoint against rip-offs by defense contractors. Its mission, in more elegant prose, is to recover excessive profits from these contractors, or, if you will, to hold them accountable. This requires precise definitions of terms, starting with "excessive." The board on occasion has been willing to devise contradictory definitions, when that is what it took to let contractors retain excessive profits. Witness the board's contrasting treatment of McDonnell Douglas and Northrop corporations.

McDonnell Douglas was formed by a merger. McDonnell's principal product, F-4 Phantom aircraft, was so profitable that the company refunded $27 million to the government in 1966 alone. Douglas, meanwhile, was producing mainly spacecraft, had low profits or actual losses, and for this reason was for tax purposes highly desirable as an acquisition. McDonnell acquired Douglas in 1967. The board's staff made a study which concluded that the agency was empowered by law to define profits by product line or profit centers. In this case, the meaning was that aircraft and spacecraft should be treated separately. But the board, a political dumping-ground in all administrations, voted 4 to 1 to treat aircraft and spacecraft as a single product line. The result was a computation that McDonnell Douglas's excessive profits were a relatively trivial $5 million in 1967 and zero in 1968 and 1969. The dissenter, Goodwin Chase, a truly rare member who took his responsibilities seriously, disclosed that had aircraft and spacecraft been defined properly, as separate entities for board purposes, the firm would have had to refund at least $15 million for 1967, at least $16 million for 1968, and a large but undetermined sum for 1969.

Northrop, meanwhile, was producing aircraft—the F-5 "Freedom Fighter" and the T-38 supersonic trainer—which yielded high profits. The company also made utterly dissimilar products, including chemicals, which yielded low or moderate profits. Under the definition the board applied in the McDonnell case, that aircraft and spacecraft were for accounting purposes a single entity known as aerospace, Northrop could not conceivably combine products as diverse as planes and chemicals to avoid refund of excessive profits made on the aircraft alone. But in June 1974, a few months after laying down the McDonnell Douglas doctrine, the board, over Chase's outraged dissent, contradicted it, thereby letting the Northrop conglomerate escape with substantial if unspecified excessive profits.[39]

That McDonnell Douglas, Northrop, Lockheed, and other giant defense contractors are able to get away with such thefts, with the Renegotiation Board, the Pentagon, and even the White House and much of Capitol Hill as accessories, has its roots in the definition of them as "private" corporations. They are not, John Kenneth Galbraith has testified. He cited the example of Lockheed:

Much of the fixed plant of that corporation is publicly owned; even the shop in which it is building the Tristar [a wide-bodied commercial jet transport] belongs to the Government. Working capital comes from the Government. Its business comes all but exclusively from the government. Its cost over-runs are socialized. Its capital needs, even those resulting from the mismanagement of its civilian business, have now been guaranteed by the government.

Only its earnings, when it makes them, and the salaries of its executives are strictly in the private sector.

One asks is such a firm private? Under the Constitution a man is permitted to believe anything. The line between public and private enterprise is obviously so exotic here as to be ludicrous. It is, in fact, a device for diverting the attention of the public, that of congressional committees, and that of the Comptroller General from managerial error, lobbying for new weapons systems, political activity by executives and employees, all of which in the case of a public bureaucracy (or a full-fledged public corporation) would be of the greatest concern. *It is a way for hiding the public business behind the cloak of corporate privacy.* [Emphasis supplied.][40]

A homely example of the power of definition to make either for accountability or unaccountability involves peanut butter. A consumer buying a jar labeled "peanut butter" sensibly might think he is getting what *The Random House Dictionary of the English Language* (1966) defines as: "a smooth paste made from finely ground roasted peanuts, used as a spread or in cookery." The consumer might further assume that a producer should be accountable if the "peanut butter" contains a substitute.

In 1958, The Food and Drug Administration took a look at Jif "peanut butter," the brand promoted by Procter & Gamble with a picture of children playing on a "mountain of peanuts." The FDA found that the peanuts in Jif were only a molehill of 75 percent, less than in all other brands. The agency's analysis also showed that Jif was at least 20 percent hydrogenated vegetable oils. Procter & Gamble is the largest producer of these oils, which cost less than peanuts and consequently could be sold to other firms for use in nearly all brands of peanut butter.

The FDA tried to straighten out the situation by issuing a standard under which any product identified as "peanut butter" had to be at least 95 percent peanuts. This incited a titanic legal attack (the hearing transcript fills 24,000 pages, and related documents close to 75,000 more) which continued the *status quo*. The point man, counsel for Procter & Gamble, was H. Thomas Austern, of Covington & Burling, Washington's most influential law firm. Twelve years elapsed before a final FDA order became effective. It defines "peanut butter" as being at least 90 percent peanuts—a come–down from the 95 percent originally proposed, but a triumph over the Peanut Butter Manufacturers Association, which had fought for 87 percent.

In the end, Kraftco, Inc., proved once again that one never must under-rate the ability of American industry to strew banana peels in the consumer's path. Kraftco's peel was Koogle, a peanut "spread" which many consumers naively would trust to be not inferior to peanut "butter." Of course it was. Koogle was only about 60 percent peanuts, *Consumer Reports* found in an analysis (and, in comparison with peanut butter, has less niacin and iron, but more fat that is highly saturated, and three times as much sodium). But the price of blarney Koogle is about the same as other national brands—and much more than store-brands—of peanut butter.[41]

In its simplest form, the point of this chapter is: Sticks and stones may break your bones, but words can really hurt you.

Conservatives, Liberals, Criminals 26

Conservative . . . adj. *1. disposed to preserve existing conditions,
institutions, etc., and to agree with gradual rather than abrupt change.*
Liberal . . . adj. *1. favorable to progress or reform, as in religious or
political affairs.*
Criminal . . . adj. *1. Law. of or pertaining to crime or its punishment.*

The Random House Dictionary
of the English Language

Value judgments are of necessity inseparable from concepts and definitions
of accountability. In defining "progress," say, or "efficiency," one cannot
help but invoke value judgments, although these are often implicit or unperceived.

The adjective "conservative" is especially troublesome in this regard. The
dictionary definition is not particularly helpful, because it is the *choice* of
"existing conditions, institutions, etc.," to be preserved that matters. It is,
it seems to us, striking, that a person who characterizes his outlook as
"conservative," even one who seeks elective office, rarely is asked to spell out
precisely what it is he would conserve. This sacrifices our opportunity to learn
with some precision whether there is some correspondence between his
"conservative" values and one's own.

Many politicians, columnists, and other public figures whose appeal to the
electorate is that they are "conservative" support the corporate state. It is
difficult to see what is "conservative" about that. Indeed, says Ralph Nader,
"If radicalism is defined as a force against basic value systems of a society,
then the corporate state is the principal protagonist."[1]

In American society, basic values are set out in the Declaration of Independence, the Constitution, and the Bill of Rights. The Declaration says it
is a self-evident truth "that all men are created "equal"; but "conservatives"
have been principal barriers in the struggles for equality of opportunity, The
Creator endows all men "with certain unalienable rights," the first of which
is "life"; but many "conservative" spokesmen expend an extraordinary share
of their energies preserving capital punishment and demanding harsh prison

sentences, unless the convicted person is from their own ranks (e.g., former Attorney General Richard G. Kleindienst).[2] Until it becomes politically suicidal, moreover, they almost never initiate and almost always oppose legislation intended to assure safe environments for workers, consumers, and future generations. Such legislation, even if flawed, at least is related to a key purpose of the Constitution, stated in the Preamble: to "promote the general welfare." Whose welfare is being promoted by "conservatives" who oppose industrial-safety and antipollution measures?

Another enumerated right is "liberty." It takes no more fundamental form than in the First Amendment's guarantee of freedom of the press. "The press is the enemy," Richard Nixon used to tell White House aides. In an incident almost forgotten amidst other signs of his hatred of the press, the *New York Times* in May 1972 ran an advertisement in which a particular group called for his impeachment. Misguided? Possibly. But such a call was in a constitutional sense conservative, the Founding Fathers having provided for impeachment. For the *Times* to publish the ad (or, if one had been placed, *against* impeachment) was also conservative. But *Times* pressmen, denouncing the ad as "traitorous," tried to interfere with its publication, anointing themselves as censors. That was radical; and the "conservative" President sent an emissary to congratulate them. From the time of the first attacks on the networks by Vice-President Spiro T. Agnew in November 1969, the Nixon Administration waged almost unrelenting war on press freedom. Three years later, historian Henry Steele Commager would say, "Never before in our history, it is safe to say, has government so audaciously violated the spirit of the constitutional guarantee of freedom of the press."[3] Even during the Pentagon Papers case, few were the "conservative" voices who spoke out for the First Amendment or against Richard Nixon's subversion of it.

The Fourth Amendment guarantees "[t]he right of the people to be secure in their persons, houses, papers, and effects, against unreasonable searches and seizures." Nixon subverted it, claiming an inherent right to wiretap without a warrant and authorizing burglaries. His administration sponsored a crime bill for the District of Columbia, which was generally understood to be a prototype for national legislation. It contained, for example, a "no knock" provision to permit policemen, without a warrant, to break into houses—an act the Fourth Amendment would appear to forbid. In all, said Senator Sam J. Ervin, Jr. (D–N.C.), who had exalted status in the Senate as a constitutional lawyer and as an authentic conservative, the bill was a "garbage pail" of "repressive" powers. "This bill might better be entitled 'A Bill to Repeal the Fourth, Fifth, Sixth, and Eighth Amendments to the Constitution,'" he said.[4] Almost no "conservatives" and too few genuine conservatives or genuine liberals stood up for him. The rest carried the garbage pail to the White House, where Richard Nixon, the arch-"conserva-tive," signed it into law.

With the enactment of the first antitrust law in 1890, it became government policy to protect and promote competition as the regulator of the economy by making it illegal for businessmen to conspire in restraint of trade. On Capitol Hill, a leading "conservative," Senator Roman L. Hruska (R–Neb.), rather than seeking to conserve this policy, has made a part-time career of battling almost every procompetitive initiative taken by the Senate Antitrust and Monopoly Subcommittee, of which he is the ranking minority member.

What could be more conservative than to allow such victims of misman-agement as Lockheed Aircraft and Penn Central to fail? That's what private enterprise is supposed to be about. But it was largely "conservatives" in Congress who rescued them. The point here is not whether they were right to do so, but that they could profess to be "conservatives" while implement-ing welfare for corporations. Such behavior is of a piece with support of Pentagon boondoggles and implacable opposition to those who try to end such waste.

There is nothing "conservative" about secret wars, be it President Ken-nedy's against Fidel Castro or President Nixon's against Cambodia, and there is nothing "conservative" about voting on Capitol Hill to support such wars or not trying very hard to stop them. What is "conservative" about rolling power down Capitol Hill to the White House? About delegating vast secret power to the CIA, the FBI, and the National Security Agency, and then opposing every effort to oversee the use of that power? About what columnist Nicholas von Hoffman accurately termed a "jingo passion to show the flag in every remote armpit of the globe?"[5]

What is it these "conservatives" want to conserve? The power of the corporate establishment, for one thing. This is not always something they particularly care to advertise. And so when necessary they undertake divert-ing crusades for, say, prayer in the schools.

In the House of Representatives in 1975, the leader of Southern conserva-tives was Congressman Joe D. Waggonner, Jr., a Democrat from Plain Dealing, Louisiana. He had won their trust by demonstrating over the years that he was "steadfastly opposed to civil rights" and otherwise "thoroughly conservative," Roy Reed said in the *New York Times.* But with civil rights no longer much of a legislative issue, Reed defined Waggonner's "conserva-tism" so one could discern what he wants to conserve:

He approves of higher defense spending. He opposes funds for environmental work such as cleaning up water pollution. He favors sending jets to Taiwan and opposes giving unemployment compensation to migrant farm workers.[6]

Another vital sign flashed in September 1975, when the House Ways and Means Committee, of which Waggonner is a senior member, explored the "tax shelter," a device used to create paper losses that reduce or even wipe out large amounts of real income. The committee heard, for example, about a physician with an income of $105,000, who, thanks to a shelter, paid no income tax whatever; of a stockbroker with an income of $181,000, who paid $1,000, and of a business executive with an income of $448,000, who paid a trifling $1,200.[7] Next day, September 4, the committee voted virtually to end the shelter game. The *New York Times* account included this paragraph:

The key test in the committee came after one of the leaders of its conservative bloc, Representative Joe D. Waggonner, Jr., Democrat of Louisiana, offered an amendment to the basic proposal that would have cut its impact by more than two-thirds.[8]

In his emphasis, priorities, tone, and values, the congressman from Plain Dealing is typical of many "conservatives" about whom there is too little plain speaking, particularly in the press. They have only tenuous connections to a true and honorable conservative ethic which, as we see it, would include: conservation of the environment, the culture, civility, civilization, and fairness—including fairness in taxation—always; dedication to the checks and balances of the Constitution and to the freedoms set out in the Bill of Rights; relentless opposition to delegations of unaccountable power to the CIA, the FBI, or any other agency, to excessive secrecy, to a bloated military establishment, and to foreign adventuring; compassion for the poor, migrant farm workers being near the head of the list; vigorous support of antitrust activity, and a vigilant concern that majorities not be enabled to trample on minorities.

Men such as Waggonner are nonconservative or even anticonservative. They conceal this by labeling themselves "conservatives" while trying to conserve special interests and not much else. Thus do they escape accountability for the mutilation of the conservative ethic they pretend to cherish.

The adjective "liberal" raises essentially similar questions. Liberal about what? With what? For what? Some "liberals" were apologists for Joseph Stalin, and there was nothing genuinely liberal about that and certainly not about him. Some "liberals" are liberal about throwing good money after bad, about building and protecting vast paper-factory bureaucracies that don't do enough for the people they supposedly exist to help, about attacking tax loopholes for oil companies while protecting capital gains taxes, about supporting their leaders rather than the Constitution they have sworn to uphold, about equality in education, employment, and housing that doesn't get too close to home, about being—disastrously—more "anti-Communist" than "conservatives." They have "kept busy protecting their sinecures in government, the unions, and the wonderful world of non-profit institutions where tenure is king and ever-escalating salary without regard to performance the rule," Charles Peters commented in the *Washington Monthly.*[9]

The relationship between such "liberal" stigmata and valid liberal attitudes is, or ought to be, strained. The philosopher Charles Frankel, who has grappled with the dilemma, says that a liberal stands first of all "for parliamentary institutions and civil liberties." He seeks "to correct imbalances of power and to correct social institutions in such a way that no one has too much power. For the major source of injustice is the monopoly of power by any group, political, economic, or ecclesiastical; and the only way to prevent social injustice is to counter power with power."[10] It is to such fundamental principles that liberals ought to hold "liberals" accountable.

"Crime" is behavior that the state regards as socially harmful and for which it provides penalties in law. The penalties are the accountability. But the penalties often make no sense and, being senseless, mock accountability. Steal a dog in Colorado and you can get up to ten years; *kill* a dog in Colorado and you can get six months and a $500 fine. Burn an empty building in Iowa and you can get up to twenty years; burn a school or a church in Iowa and you can get no more than ten.[11] Such irrationalities should not obscure the point that someone's value judgments shape the definitions of crime, and, as well, of the emphasis on one crime as against another. This, too, is significant, because where emphasis is heavy accountability is more likely to be sought.

The FBI's annual crime report, to take a case in point, covers murder, forcible rape, aggravated assault, robbery, burglary, larceny-theft, and auto theft. "But what about citizens who are not victimized by the hoods and thugs who spring from dark alleys but by the crimes of business interests, labor unions, government officials and even some of the law enforcers themselves?" Colman McCarthy asked in the *Washington Post.* "Because no government agency has the mandate to report on the totality of America's crime, the citizen is on his own so far as learning what thieves and killers are out to get him is concerned."[12]

We have it on the authority of a recent attorney general, William B. Saxbe, that "white collar" price-fixers "can rob thousands of citizens of hundreds of millions of dollars," and are "not better than the car thief or the robber." Yet such crime draws relatively little attention and arouses relatively little indignation. For seventy years after the Sherman Antitrust Act was adopted in 1890, federal judges did not once send to prison a violator who was an executive of a large corporation. Saxbe, in ranking price-fixers with thieves and robbers, added, "And it is about time that all of the federal judges begin realizing that."[13]

Saxbe's assumption was that punishment of white-collar criminals, by making accountability personal, deters price-fixing and similar conduct. It's an obvious point. But it requires at the start that the Justice Department, when it decides to prosecute rather than file a civil complaint, seek indictment of human beings as well as corporations. The department in fact often has been unwilling to prosecute flesh-and-blood price-fixers. Sometimes they are needed to make the case against the corporations. Sometimes they blow the whistle on a conspiracy in which they were the principal conspirators; it then may become awkward to prosecute them or, if they are immunized, to prosecute the underlings who carried out their orders.

Even as Saxbe spoke, the department's Antitrust Division was about to wind up a prosecution in which the defendants were nine major chemical companies but no human beings. A federal grand jury in Newark, New Jersey, in July 1974, returned a one-count indictment which charged the firms with having conspired since some time in early 1970 to fix dye prices. The conspiracy began when unnamed officials of E. I. du Pont de Nemours & Company, the nation's sixteenth-largest industrial corporation in sales in 1973, "undertook discussions of a proposed across-the-board increase . . . with each of the other defendants," the indictment said.

By the end of 1970, the indictment continued, the other firms had signaled du Pont that they would follow a price increase by that company, "and accordingly, on January 7, 1971, defendant du Pont announced a 10 per cent increase [effective] March 1, 1971." The others followed with increases in "substantially the same amount." In 1971, the firms' combined sales were $300 million. Thus, the conspiracy in that year alone apparently produced excess revenues—or stole from the public—up to $30 million.

On October 18, 1974, eight of the companies entered pleas of no-contest, which for sentencing purposes are the same as verdicts of guilty. David I. Shapiro, counsel for dye customers seeking treble damages, pointed out that since 1954, three of the firms had built antitrust records "as long as your arm." Indeed, he filed a tabulation showing that the government in the preceding twenty years had filed twenty-two civil and criminal antitrust cases, fourteen of them for price-fixing, against five of the firms, with the following dispositions: guilty pleas or verdicts and imposition of fines—Allied Chemical Corporation, three; American Cyanamid Company, one (in another dye case); consent decrees—Allied, three with and three without admission of liability; BASF Wyandotte Corporation, one, and CIBA-Geigy

Corporation, one (in another dye case); dismissal—Cyanamid, one; acquittal on re-trial—Cyanamid, one; cases pending—CIBA, three, and Allied, Cyanamid, and du Pont, one each.

The Justice Department did not oppose the no-contest pleas. Chief United States District Judge Lawrence A. Whipple accepted them on the spot. Neither commented on Shapiro's disclosure of corporate recidivism. In contrast, persons who are caught in repeated offenses may face extreme consequences. Consider New York State's Second Felony Offender Act, which Governor Nelson A. Rockefeller pushed through in 1972. It requires judges to impose prison sentences of specified minimum duration on any offender convicted of a second felony regardless of the particular crimes committed. The Rockefeller law also bars a person accused of a second felony from pleading guilty to a misdemeanor. "This means that relatively minor crimes, such as joyriding, must be punished with substantial prison terms if the offender is a convicted-felony repeater," Nicolas F. Hahn and Scott Christianson, of the Institute for Public Policy Alternatives of the State University of New York, have pointed out.

Moreover, by extending the felony definition to cover any offense committed in *any* jurisdiction that *could* have resulted in a prison sentence of more than a year, the legislature includes blasphemy in New Jersey, miscegenation in Georgia, vagrancy in Rhode Island, fornication in Alabama, theft of a library book in North Carolina or turkey-stealing in Arkansas.

Less than two and a half years after the law became effective, New York State's daily prison population had risen by approximately 3,350, to more than 15,600. Depending on the accounting procedure used, Hahn and Christianson said, each prisoner annually costs the state between $13,000 (far more than the cost of a year at Harvard) and $26,000.[14]

Moving on to Washington, Rockefeller as Vice-President became chairman of the Commission on C.I.A. Activities Within the United States. Serving with him was Ronald Reagan of California, another former governor who had earned a "hard-liner" reputation for implementing "conservative" —read brutal—attitudes toward the common variety of criminals. Commendably, the commission with admirable candor found that CIA officials had committed a great many felonies, some of them truly shocking.

Now, however, Rockefeller and Reagan, and their colleagues, were understanding, compassionate, forgiving, just plain *soft*. Second felonies, tenth felonies, maybe, for anyone knows, hundredth felonies, should not be punished, they said. Their leader felt the same way. So attuned to the Rockefeller-Reagan approach was Gerald R. Ford that he—the President who had pardoned Richard Nixon of crimes not yet charged—shortly thereafter asked

Congress to require judges to impose mandatory jail sentences for violent crimes and habitual offenses.

In the case of the CIA officials' crimes, the commission's logic, applied in a hypothetical case entitled *State* v. *Bluebeard,* would have resulted in a decision like this:

The defendant is charged with, and has confessed, murdering one wife after another. These acts, while illegal and subject to criticism, should be viewed in proper perspective. The defendant should be judged on his whole record, and not on a few isolated overreactions to external pressures. Our review of Bluebeard's life shows that the great majority of his actions fully complied with the law. There is no evidence that he ever robbed, raped, cheated, or lied. A court of justice cannot condemn a man whose conduct has otherwise been so exemplary. The defendant is admonished to go and kill no more wives. Case dismissed.[15]

In the case of the convicted chemical corporations, the imposed penalties, especially in the case of the recidivists, make sense if *Bluebeard* makes sense. After receiving a probation officer's report, Judge Whipple in December 1974 imposed the maximum penalty, a $50,000 fine, only on du Pont and Verona Corporation. Then came CIBA and GAF Corporation, $45,000 each. A touch less culpable, under the judge's financial ratings, were Allied, BASF, and Cyanamid, $43,500 each, followed by Crompton & Knowles Corporation, $40,000. The ninth and last firm, American Color & Chemical, changed its plea from innocent to no-contest in March 1975, and was fined $35,000. For a conspiracy that had generated revenues of tens of millions of dollars, the aggregate of fines was $395,500.

What seems to come through from all of this is that while conduct such as price-fixing is defined as crime, and while it steals enormous sums from the public, the collective value judgment is manifestly that it somehow really isn't *serious* even when the offenders are repeaters. That is why the prisons are filled with men who have been held accountable for thefts and robberies and empty of men exempted from accountability even though they are, as Saxbe judged them, "not better."

The same sort of assessment applies to crimes of violence. Rape is a most serious crime to women who know of its physical and psychic horrors; but only lately have many police and prosecutors come to so regard it. Murder is the most serious violent crime. The FBI recorded 19,510 murders in 1973. This is a terrible toll by any count; and yet it is a foothill against the mountain of lives taken or shortened, not to mention damaged, by preventable hazards in the workplace. In 1972, the *President's Report on Occupational Safety and Health* said, "There may be as many as 100,000 deaths per year from occupationally caused diseases." Each year, the report added, "at least 390,000 new cases of disabling occupational disease" occur. Even these figures, shocking as they are, deal only with disease, not accidents, and they are widely considered to be gross understatements of the reality. Rachel Scott, who spent three and a half years on her fine *Muscle and Blood: The Massive, Hidden Agony of Industrial Slaughter in America,* visited the plants of major corporations whose executives are, as the phrase goes, pillars of society, and which have

the resources to measure and control industrial hazards. Yet now as throughout American history, companies such as these shrug at the pleas of workers whose health they destroy in order to save money. They hire experts—physicians and researchers—who purposely misdiagnose industrial diseases as the ordinary diseases of life, write biased reports, and divert research from vital questions. They fight against regulation as unnecessary and cry that it will bring ruination. They ravage the people as they have the land, causing millions to suffer needlessly and hundreds of thousands to die.[16]

In seeking out the victims of industrial slaughter, columnist McCarthy said, Rachel Scott was "as much a crime reporter as the journalist covering the homicide beat. The victims killed by inhaling chemicals like vinyl chloride, beryllium or silica, are as dead as they would be if killed by a handgun or butcher knife."[17] The crusades for capital punishment—the supreme personal accountability—are always aimed at those who kill with handguns and butcher knives, and never at those who engage in industrial slaughter.

Probably no one brought more insight and understanding to the whole area of definitions and values, and brought them earlier, than Edward Alsworth Ross, a University of Wisconsin sociologist. In his great but neglected *Sin and Society: An Analysis of Latter-Day Inequity,* published in 1907 with a letter of glowing praise from President Theodore Roosevelt, Ross drew a sharp distinction between *vice*—"practices that harm one's self"—and *sin* —"conduct that harms another"—and then brilliantly used the distinction to show that unaccountability has no truer friend than public misperception of sin.

As Ross saw it, the principal problem was that the public, in reacting against wrongdoing, "lays emphasis where emphasis was laid centuries ago. It beholds sin in a false perspective, seeing peccadillos as crimes, and crimes as peccadillos." Consequently, in the war against sin the reactions of the public "are about as serviceable as gongs and stink-pots in a modern battle."[18]

In modern society each of us must entrust vital interests to others—"the water main is my well . . . the banker's safe my old stocking. . . . My own eyes and nose and judgment defer to the inspector of food, or drugs, or factories, or tenements, or insurance companies. . . . I let the meat trust butcher my pig, the oil trust mould my candles, the sugar trust boil my sorghum . . ." This interdependence—vastly greater today—"ushers in a multitude of new forms of wrongdoing"—murder with adulteration instead of a bludgeon, burglary with graft instead of a jimmy, cheating with a company prospectus instead of a deck of cards. But the latter-day sinner "does not feel on his brow the brand of a malefactor." Why not?

First, because modern sin is "not superficially repulsive. . . . How decent are the pale slayings of the quack, the adulterator, and the purveyor of polluted water, compared with the red slayings of the vulgar bandit or assassin." Second, modern sin "lacks the familiar tokens of guilt"; it requires "no nocturnal prowling with muffled step and bated breath, no weapon or offer of violence. . . . The modern high-power dealer of woe wears immaculate linen . . . sins with a calm countenance and a serene soul, leagues or months from the evil he causes. Upon his gentlemanly presence the eventual blood and tears do not obtrude themselves." Third, modern sins are impersonal, passing their hurt "into that vague mass, the 'public,' and is there lost to view. . . . The purveyor of spurious life-preservers need not be a Cain. The owner of rotten tenement houses, whose 'pull' enables him to ignore the orders of the health department, foredooms babies, it is true, but for all that he is no Herod."

But the overriding problem is that "[i]t never occurs to the public that sin evolves along with society, and that the perspective in which it is necessary to view misconduct changes from age to age." In the seventy years since Ross wrote that, the word "never" has become overstatement; that said, his analysis remains essentially valid. Ross attributed the static definition of sin in the public mind to certain crude errors "which lie at the base of [the public's] moral judgments and lead astray its instinct for self-preservation."

The first such error is the assumption that "sinners ought to be graded according to badness of character"—that "the wickedest man is the most dangerous. This would be true if men were abreast in their opportunities to do harm. . . . But the fact is that the patent ruffian is confined to the social basement, and enjoys few opportunities. . . . He is the clinker, not the live coal; vermin, not beast of prey."

The highwayman with his alternative, "Your money or your life!" does less mischief than the entrenched monopolist who offers the public the option, "your money or go without;" but he is, no doubt, a more desperate character. . . . The life insurance presidents who let one another have the use of policy-holders' funds at a third of the market rate may still be trusted not to purloin spoons. . . . The embezzler who guts a savings bank, the corrupt labor-leader who wields the strike as a blackmailer's club, is virtually the assassin of scores of infants and aged and invalid; yet he has sensibilities that make him far less dangerous in most situations than the housebreaker or sandbagger. . . .[19]

To grade sinners "according to the harm they inflict upon particular individuals" is another error the public makes, according to Ross. A man who steals $2 in change from a pay phone may be sent to jail. But a phone company executive, who, more likely than not, engages in community activities, and who can get "an unwarranted rate increase that permits him to take $2.00, every month, from every telephone, can steal hundreds of millions of dollars from the American people and be sent, instead, to the White House for dinner," said Nicholas Johnson, a former member of the Federal Communications Commission. The thief had the coin of disadvantage, the executive "the coign of vantage," as Ross called it.

The proper grading of sinners is further skewed when the public takes into account "their education, breeding, manners, piety, or philanthropy. . . . How often clean linen and church-going are accepted as substitutes for right-doing! What a deodorizer is polite society!" Sexual transgressions bring a public lashing, these having been "recognized and branded" long, long ago; not so the new sins that are "[o]verlooked in Bible and Prayer-book" and "lack the brimstone smell."

The immunity enjoyed by the perpetrator of new sins has brought into being a class for which we may coin the term *criminaloid*. By this we designate such as prosper by flagitious practices which have not yet come under the effective ban of public opinion. Often, indeed, they are guilty in the eyes of the law; but since they are not culpable in the eyes of the public and in their own eyes, their spiritual attitude is not that of the criminal. The lawmaker may make their misdeeds crimes, but so long as morality stands stock-still in the old tracks, they escape both punishment and ignominy. . . . The criminal slinks in the shadow, menacing our purses but not our ideals; the criminaloid, however, does not belong to the half world. Fortified by his connections with "legitimate business," "the regular party organization," perhaps with orthodoxy and the *bon ton*, he may even bestride his community like a Colossus. In his sight *and in their own sight* the old-style, square-dealing sort are as grasshoppers. . . . Too squeamish and too prudent to practice treachery, brutality, and violence himself, he takes care to work through middlemen. Conscious of the antipodal difference between doing wrong and getting it done, he places out his dirty work. . . .

Secure in his quilted armor of lawyer-spun sophistries, the criminaloid promulgates an ethics which the public hails as a disinterested contribution to the philosophy of conduct. He invokes a pseudo-Darwinism to sanction the revival of outlawed and by-gone tactics of struggle. Ideals of fellowship and peace are "unscientific." To win the game with the aid of a sleeveful of aces proves one's fitness to survive.

Thus did Ross in 1907 paint such as "the adulterator, the rebater, the commercial free-booter, the fraud promoter, the humbug healer, the law-defying monopolist. . . . the corrupt legislator, the corporation-owned judge, the venal inspector, the bought bank examiner, the mercenary editor." But as Ross listed more and more characteristics and qualifications of those he was certifying for admission to his criminaloids' gallery, one began to experience the first flush of discovery: He had captured the very essence of a particular man who had not yet been born, but who in time would be known to every present reader.

Within his home town, his ward, his circle, he is perhaps a good man, if judged by the simple old-time tests. Very likely he keeps his marriage vows, pays his debts, "mixes" well, stands by his friends, and has a contracted kind of public spirit. . . . He is unevenly moral: oak in the family and clan virtues, but basswood in commercial and civic ethics. . . .

Seeing that the conventional sins are mostly close-range inflections, whereas long-range sins, being recent in type, have not yet been branded, the criminaloid receives from his community the credit of the close-in good he does, but not the shame of the remote evil he works. . . . he is often to be found in the assemblies of the faithful. . . . Onward thought he must leave to honest men; his line is strict orthodoxy. The upright may fall slack in devout observances, but he cannot afford to neglect his church connection. . . .

Likewise the criminaloid counterfeits the good citizen. He takes care to meet all the conventional tests,—flag worship, old-soldier sentiment, observance of all the national holidays, perfervid patriotism, party regularity and support. . . . The criminaloid must perforce seem sober and chaste, "a good husband and a kind father." . . .[20]

We could go on reciting Ross and giving clues to the identity of the prominent American born in 1913, but surely many readers would have guessed by now who it is. For those who may need one more clue:

When the revealing flash comes and the storm breaks, his difficulty in getting the public's point of view is really pathetic. Indeed, he may persist to the end in regarding himself as a martyr to "politics," or "yellow journalism" . . .

Thus did Ross portray the first criminaloid President of the United States. He was the Chief Executive "often to be found in the assemblies of the faithful"; indeed, he convened the assemblies in the very White House. He met "all the conventional tests," that of "flag worship" with a pin always conspicuous in his lapel. He always seemed "sober and chaste, 'a good husband and a kind father.' " At last the "revealing flash" came. The storm broke. Then, painfully, reluctantly, slowly, that public which had beheld his "crimes as peccadillos" began to perceive them as crimes; and having updated its definition of sin, it began to disown him and finally did so, crushingly.

However, Richard Milhous Nixon persisted "to the end in regarding himself as a martyr to 'politics,' or 'yellow journalism' . . ."

VII
Tricks of the Unaccountability Trade

Americans justly admire Harry S Truman for unequivocatingly accepting accountability for his actions. On his desk in the White House the late President had a sign saying, "The buck stops here." According to Stuart Schram in Chairman Mao Talks to the People, *Chairman Mao Tse-tung was earthier about it. After the economic disaster of the Great Leap in 1958, he said, "The chaos caused was on a grand scale and I take responsibility. Comrades, you must all analyze your own responsibility. If you have to shit, shit! If you have to fart, fart! You will feel much better for it." We don't know whether Mao caused the incidence of dyspepsia to decline in China, but we do know that Mr. Truman's example is so seldom emulated in the United States that the buck more and more often seems to stop nowhere. This is not an accidental development; it has occurred in part because those who seek to defeat, evade, or obscure accountability, and they are numerous, find it rewarding to devise, refine, and deploy a bewildering and endless variety of artifices, dodges, manipulations, stratagems and techniques.*

Someone wanting to discourage or defeat a program or project may do so by overstating the costs. Someone wanting to get a program or project started may do so by understating the costs. Both techniques erode and undermine accountability.

Ordinarily, understating costs, generally known as the come-on, or wedge-driving, is far and away the more serious problem. But the advent of severe inflation and high unemployment in 1974 was accompanied by an escalation of cost overstatement—mainly by industries seeking to slow, stop, or even reverse federal regulatory programs to protect the environment and the health, safety, and pocketbooks of consumers. The Ford Administration encouraged such efforts.

In March 1975, Congressman Benjamin S. Rosenthal (D–N.Y.) released a study which, he said, "strongly suggests that business attacks on federal consumer and environmental regulations are little more than self-serving attempts to use federal requirements as a scapegoat for deeper economic problems or managerial shortcomings. Our study shows that where federal regulatory programs are inflationary, they are invariably designed to protect one segment of the business community against another, not to foster consumer and environmental protection."

Much of the study concerned the automobile industry. Lee Iacocca, president of Ford Motor Company, claimed in a speech on November 13, 1974, that federal consumer and environmental regulations accounted between 1971 and 1975 for $530 of the $1,010 increase in the price of a Ford Pinto. But on the basis of data collected from the auto industry by the Bureau of Labor Statistics, the composite price increase of safety and emission standards for sixteen domestic makes was $414 ($116 less); and this was for the seven-year (not four-year) period ending in 1975. Iacocca claimed in the same speech that an air-bag and lap-belt system proposed for 1978 models would increase a Pinto's price by $290; but John Z. DeLorean, a former General Motors vice-president and safety engineer, put the maximum, in mass production, at $162.50, or $128.50 less. He allowed $100 for purchased parts, $14 for tooling and installation, $16 for manufacturer's profit, and $32.50 for dealer's profit. Iacocca, again in the same speech, estimated that proposed emission controls would increase the 1978 Pinto's price by $450; but the Environmental Protection Agency put the cost

The Rosenthal study was reenforced in June 1975, when Senate and House Democrats presented a policy statement on regulatory reform to President Ford. Warning against efforts to make regulation the scapegoat for management failures, the statement implicitly mocked Iacocca by recalling that "[i]t was not government that built the Edsel . . ." In 1970, the auto industry, in an earlier assault on pollution standards, predicted that the requirements scheduled to take effect that year would increase the average purchase price of a car by $150. "The actual increase amounted to $8," the policy statement said. And of the average price increase of $500 for 1975 American cars, "only $10.70 is attributable to safety standards."

Two more points may be quickly made. The first is that after bitter and prolonged resistance to pollution controls, GM in 1975 ran a mammoth advertising campaign saying, "Primarily because of the catalytic converter, gas mileage on GM cars has been increased by 28% on a sales-weighted average, according to EPA figures. The converter gives GM car owners the best of both worlds: emissions of carbon monoxide and hydrocarbons are cut by about 50% from the already lowered levels of 1974, and it is possible once more to tune engines for economy, drivability and performance. . . . when you think of the cost, think of the reduction in fuel consumption over the life of that average GM car; and don't forget the use of unleaded gas lowers maintenance costs by greatly increasing the life of spark plugs, engine oil and exhaust system components."

The second point is that the positive cost benefits of safety, environmental, and health regulation are rarely taken into account in the attacks on such regulation made by most any industry or its propagandists—"conservatives," usually—on Capitol Hill. Lee Iacocca did not balance his (dubious) Pinto cost figures, for example, with a statistic about the highway death toll. It fell from 5.7 per hundred million vehicle-miles in 1966, when the Motor Vehicle Safety Act became law despite auto industry opposition, to 4.2 in 1973. "In simple terms," the Democratic policy statement said, "the lives of thousands upon thousands of potential automobile crash victims have been spared and hundreds of thousands of disfiguring injuries prevented." What dollar value should be assigned to this? To the prevention of cancer through regulation that bars carcinogens from his work site or from food? To regulatory restraints on noise levels that shatter hearing and nervous systems?

Wedge-driving—*understating* costs as a come-on—pays off. This unaccountability technique usually wins salary increases, promotions, or other benefits for those who use it, while the person who may try to expose and halt wedge-driving may reasonably expect to get kicked around. At the local and state level, Robert Moses excelled in wedge-driving as in much else. Robert

A. Caro, in *The Power Broker: Robert Moses and the Fall of New York,* told how Moses constantly deceived New York City's Board of Estimate:

To obtain permission to construct a stadium on Randall's Island, he had assured the Board that the "PWA" [federal Public Works Administration] project would cost the city "not a penny." Then, with permission obtained and work under way, he announced that he would need $250,000 additional for materials the PWA would not buy, but assured the Board that this was the only contribution the city would have to make for the "whole Triborough Bridge project," in return for which the federal government was making a contribution of $46,200,000. The Board allocated the money. Within a month, he was back again, asking for a special bond issue of $8,000,000 to pay for the right-of-way for the bridge approaches. He blandly told the Board that when he had spoken of the "whole Triborough Bridge project," he naturally hadn't meant the land for the project.[2]

More recently, although probably with less deliberateness and more incompetence, the federal government has amassed a staggering record of wedge-driving even in the civilian sector. In February 1975, the General Accounting Office, in a report to Congress, said that 269 federal construction projects which originally had been estimated to cost $76 billion now were going to cost $133 billion—a 75 percent increase. The explanation given most often by federal agencies was not, as might be thought, inflation, but engineering changes made after projects had been authorized. Of the $57 billion in cost overruns, the Federal Highway Administration alone accounted for $38.7 billion, and the Army Corps of Engineers for $9.7 billion. The Metro rapid transit system in Washington, originally figured at $2 billion, was up to $4.5 billion (and rising). The Federal Bureau of Investigation Building, constructed to the elephantine tastes of J. Edgar Hoover, and named after him, was up from $60 million to $126 million.[3]

In 1970, West Virginia University in Morgantown proposed a "space age" mass transit system. It was to have one hundred cars operating on a 3.2 mile concrete guideway linking six stations on three campuses. The system was to cost $18 million. *Consumer Reports* told what happened after the federal Urban Mass Transportation Administration became enamored of the plan and took it over as a demonstration project:

But costs took off, and the UMTA official in charge of the program recommended abandoning it. The official, who was later fired, concluded that it would be cheaper to give every student in the university a free electric golf cart to use on the guideway.

They've gone about as far as they can go in Morgantown. Next month [April 1975] a 2.2 mile system will start operation with three stations instead of six, and 45 cars instead of 100. The scaled-down system has cost $63-million rather than the $18 million projected for the full system.[4]

The UMTA and the university drove the wedge deeper in May 1975, after the university threatened to exercise a contractual option to have the government tear the system down. The agency agreed to provide an additional $4.3 million "for a year-long start-up and debugging program, and may eventually grant up to $53.8 million more for expansion," the condition being assurance of "more economical future construction." Two more stations, for a total of five, are to be built.[5]

All of this is *petites pommes de terre* alongside the Department of Defense. Its current budget is $92.8 billion. Much of the money is for weapons systems. Some of these make no contribution to the defense of the United States because they turn out not to work, or to work unreliably. Others work only under favorable conditions. "We're lucky the North Vietnamese ran such a poor war," a squadron commander in South Vietnam volunteered to Stuart H. Loory, author of *Defeated: Inside America's Military Machine*.[6] "Any Air Force with one tenth the power of ours, if they used it wisely, could cripple us. I've often wondered why the North Vietnamese did not. All they had to do was send one plane a week over Danang with area type munitions like the CBU-24 [the canisters of white phosphorus cluster bomblets used by American pilots], and they could have kept us out of action."[7]

The F-15 fighter ultimately will cost an estimated $20 million per copy —so much that Air Force Colonel John Boyd says the Air Force would be "reluctant to commit [it] to any kind of wartime situation."[8] The XM-1 tank, costing more than $1 million, is naked to new hand-held weapons. The Soviet Union is down to 150 bombers of B-52 vintage, but the Pentagon wants to spend $6.7 billion on surface-to-air missiles to knock down bombers, and to spend possibly $50 billion or more to replace B-52s with B-1 bombers. The Air Force wants thirty-one so-called Aircraft Warning and Control System (AWACS) radar planes at a cost estimated in 1975 at $118 million each—the most expensive aircraft ever built. The final price tag may be $150 million. Since 1972, Senator Thomas F. Eagleton (D–Mo.) has been investigating AWACS. One of the questions he has pressed—an elementary question if there is to be accountability for expenditure of vast sums—is, why is the plane necessary? Driven to what Peter J. Ognibene, a contributing editor of the *New Republic* termed "desperation tactics," the Pentagon changed the original mission twice in three years. In 1970, the Air Force wanted the planes to defend this country against Soviet bomber attack," Michael Getler recalled in the *Washington Post.* "As that threat lessened, the primary mission changed to a tactical role over a European battlefield. More recently, the Air Force has put less emphasis on [the plane's] ability to control U.S. jets over enemy territory, a mission which would require it to get close to the front lines where, critics argue, enemy electronic jamming equipment could easily black out the AWACS radar. Instead, the Air Force is now emphasizing the planes' early warning role and their ability to control an air battle over NATO [North Atlantic Treaty Organization] territory. Similarly, though the missions have changed, the number of planes remains at 31 [compared with the fifteen the Air Force had set as its minimum need], a phenomenon that has caused some skepticism even in the Pentagon."9

The big numbers—the projected total cost of thirty-one AWACS planes, for example, is $3.7 billion—tend to become so familiar a part of the landscape that one needs now and then to have them put into some perspective. The organization SANE did this in December 1974, with an adaptation of figures provided by Seymour Melman in his book *The Permanent War Economy*.10 For example, one of the AWACS planes, as noted, would cost $111 million if thirty-one were to be built (but $180 million to $200 million if only fifteen). The cost of a vetoed plan of the Environmental Protection Agency to depollute the Great Lakes was, SANE said, $141 million; of unfunded 1973 rural health care, $22 million; of a funding cut in child-nutrition programs, $69 million; of medical school construction left unfunded in 1973, $250 million; of federal housing funds impounded in 1972, $130 million, and of eliminating hunger in America, $4 billion to $5 billion.

The last item, eliminating hunger, might be compared to the cost of the B-1 bomber program, which, according to Peter Ognibene, a student of these matters, ultimately could exceed $50 billion, or at least ten times as much as the cost of filling bellies. In return for the $50 billion, we would get 241 bombers capable of dropping nuclear weapons on the Soviet Union (although an already massively redundant capacity to do this is present in the existing fleets of B-52s and missile-carrying submarines), approximately 300 tankers, and maintenance and associated gear. On Capitol Hill, where the B-1 was being heavily promoted in 1975, Ognibene pointed out in the *Washington Monthly*, talk of the B-1 was almost inaudible; all the emphasis, instead, was on the program as a creator of jobs in one congressional district after another across the land:

The genius of the B-1 promoters was to realize that these monumental costs, which had proven such an impediment to weapons proposals in the past, could actually be turned into the plane's strongest selling point. In the offices of Rockwell International, the primary contractor for the B-1, someone discovered that the offending word "cost" could be restated as "jobs," and that the B-1 could be portrayed as the $50-billion solution to the unemployment problem. The $2 billion already spent on the plane has meant contracts and jobs for businesses in 48 states, and more money would mean more wealth for all.11

Ognibene told how the contractor's lobbyists tailored the approach in a vain effort to persuade Congressman John F. Seiberling (D–Ohio) that the B-1 would bring prosperity to his district, which includes the city of Akron. Unfortunately for Rockwell, Seiberling calculated not only that the B-1 program would take $84 million from his district in taxes while spending $70 million, or $14 million less, for jobs, but also, and more importantly, that defense procurement "does not produce many jobs . . . except for California and Texas, most states suffer unemployment as a result of defense spending."

Behind Seiberling's contention lies evidence including "The Empty Pork Barrel," a study made by the Public Interest Research Group in Michigan (PIRGIM). Ognibene reported:

Using a means of analysis conceived by Bruce Russett, a professor of economics at Yale, the group calculated that each additional billion dollars spent on the military results in a *net loss* of 10,000 jobs nationwide. A billion dollars spent in the defense industrial sector produces about 55,000 direct and supporting jobs; but if that billion had been left in the private sector, it would have created 65,000 jobs. So, spending, say, $5 billion a year on the B-1, its operation, and its support, would mean 50,000 fewer jobs in this country. Coincidentally, Rockwell's calculations of direct and supporting jobs per billion dollars spent on the B-1 closely approximate the PIRGIM figure.[12]

Thanks to a suggestion of Senator Proxmire's, the General Accounting Office periodically reports to Congress on the cost and status of selected major weapons systems. Few seem to pay much attention, partly because major news media often have ignored the reports, or have given them the space and prominence due a petty larceny, and also because powerful "conservatives" on Capitol Hill are generally disinclined to conserve taxpayers' dollars destined for defense contractors.

With Capitol Hill, in fact, eager to help out defense contractors who on occasion encounter difficulty at the Pentagon, it should not be especially surprising that the General Accounting Office, in its periodic reviews of major weapons systems, finds immense cost increases. A GAO report issued in February 1975 on forty-nine major weapons systems showed that the increases merely in the six-month period ended June 30, 1974, had been $17 billion. This sum would have been sufficient in 1971 to raise the income of all impoverished Americans above the poverty line and to have $6.6 billion left over, according to the SANE compilation.

Like Robert Moses, the Pentagon had started out with the thinnest edge of the wedge, called planning estimates. For the forty-nine weapons systems the planning estimates were $59.7 billion under the June 30, 1974, cost estimates—which, of course, were only thicker parts of the wedge. The

Pentagon later drove the wedge in further when it supplied Congress with so-called development estimates. These were $42.9 billion less than the cost of completion as figured in mid-1974. Moreover, said Proxmire, then chairman of the Joint Economic Committee's Subcommittee on Priorities and Economy in Government, and one of the rare legislators who actually tries to curb defense waste, deliveries are at least one year behind schedule for twenty-two of the forty-nine weapons, and planned performance characteristics have been significantly cut back in twelve.[13] John W. Finney of the *New York Times* provided a footnote in July 1975. The Defense Department, he said, had concluded that the Navy, instructed to come up with a "low-cost" fighter for its carrier squadrons, the F-18, had understated the cost of the program to build the planes by at least $1.6 billion.[14] To be sure, inflation was a significant factor in the cost increases, but far from the whole cause. With a budget of nearly $93 billion, the Pentagon will when necessary hold accountable with ruthless methods those who would give the taxpayers fair value. At the same time, it will go to nearly any length to shield, reward, and exempt from accountability the team-players who perpetuate the world's biggest boondoggle.

A. Ernest Fitzgerald, an industrial engineer, was for twenty years a part of the arms-buying process. Eventually he was appointed deputy for Management Systems in Air Force Headquarters in the Pentagon. He made up his mind to try to solve the mystery of why costs of the big, expensive weapons projects seemingly could not be decreased. "Gradually the answer unfolded," Fitzgerald wrote in *The High Priests of Waste*. "Waste was the Pentagon's policy."[15] Stuart Loory reached a related conclusion in finding that "[t]he American military machine today is not qualified to protect the nation's vital interests in situations short of nuclear exchange."[16] American military officers "suffer ruined careers for opposing the development of new weapons systems," he said. "Career advancement depends not on resistance to the purchase of new weapons, no matter how dubious their utility, but on participation in the campaign to urge ever more purchases."[17]

During one phase of his career at the Pentagon, Fitzgerald focused on the Autonetics Division of North American Aviation, which was building the Mark II avionics (electronic and electrical) system for the F-111 fighter-bomber that Defense Secretary Robert S. McNamara had willed into being. Autonetics had gotten the contract with a "Golden Handshake"—a come-on bid made with the understanding that the Pentagon would go along later with price-kiting in one form or another. Each unit was to cost about $750,000—but by late 1971 was costing $4.1 million. Trying to hold down the soaring costs of the Mark II, Fitzgerald met at one point with Major General "Zeke" Zoeckler, the F-111 Systems Program director, and his deputy, Brigadier General John Chandler, for more than half a day. Zoeckler became increasingly uneasy and, Fitzgerald said, finally

played his trump. He simply countermanded my instructions regarding . . . attempts to minimize inefficiency. "Inefficiency is national policy," the General proclaimed. He then went on to explain that inefficiency in the operations of military contractors was necessary to the attainment of "social goals." He said that contractor inefficiency provided for such things as (1) equal employment opportunity programs, (2) seniority clauses in union agreements, (3) programs for employment of the handicapped, (4) apprentice programs, (5) aid to small business, (6) aid to distressed labor areas, and (7) encouragment of improvements to plant layouts and facilities.[18]

"Was our prime purpose to buy necessary weapons at the lowest sound prices, as Secretary McNamara had so eloquently proclaimed, or was it run the world's biggest boondoggle?" Fitzgerald was asking during the first half of 1968. The clearest single answer came in 1971, when Senator Proxmire questioned Secretary of the Treasury John B. Connally at a hearing on the government guaranty of a $250 million loan to Lockheed Aircraft Corporation. When Proxmire protested the lack of a *quid pro quo* in the form of a requirement on Lockheed to be efficient or productive, Connally said:

What do we care whether they perform? We are guaranteeing them basically a $250 million loan. Why for? Basically so they can hopefully minimize their losses, so they can provide employment for 31,000 people throughout the country at a time when we desperately need that type of employment. *That is basically the rationale and justification.* (Emphasis supplied.)[19]

With the government not caring whether Lockheed performed, cost overruns were assured. On the C-5A, a giant transport plane, the overrun was a staggering $2 billion. The government never seemed to care whether the C-5A itself performed, either. It was intended to have an air life of thirty thousand hours, but Air Force fatigue tests concluded in 1974 proved that the plane would last only sixty-five hundred to ten thousand hours. The wing was supposed to hold up for one hundred twenty thousand hours aloft; cracks began showing up at two thousand.[20] In 1975 the congressional Armed Services committees approved an Air Force request for $1.1 billion for new wings for seventy-eight C-5As. But the General Accounting Office figured that the final bill for the wings and repairs of related defects would be $400 million more, or $1.5 billion, and that even with the repairs cargo capacity would have to be reduced from 110 tons to 87 tons so as not to overstrain the wings. For $1.5 billion, Proxmire pointed out, the Air Force could buy thirty Boeing 747s and "might be better served" by doing so.[21] There was this further dismaying chronology:

1972: The GAO found that on the average, a C-5A suffers a major technical breakdown during each hour it is airborne. A randomly selected C-5A had forty-seven major defects, including fourteen that "impair the aircraft's capability to perform all or a portion of six missions" it is intended to carry out.[22]

1973: After the Arab invasion of Israel, the Air Force undertook an emergency airlift of supplies to Israel, but "discovered that 36 of the C-5As couldn't be used because they needed repairs and 10 other planes were grounded because they lacked parts. In addition, mechanical malfunctions caused the termination of 29 flights and delayed the departure of 40 other flights."[23]

1975: Outside of Saigon, a C-5A crashed. More than one hundred Vietnamese orphans bound for the United States were killed.

The instructive thing is to see who was rewarded and who was punished as the result of the C-5A debacle. Connally, in the spring of 1976, was still being talked about as a possible Republican presidential candidate. At Lockheed in the year after Congress approved the $250 million loan guaranty in 1971, Congressman Les Aspin (D–Wis.) pointed out, the only changes in the C-5A management teams were occasioned by "promotions, death or retirement. No one has been fired or demoted for their part in one of the largest and surely best known procurement disasters in Pentagon history."[24] The Pentagon lavishly rewarded Lockheed: in 1970 and 1971, it restructured various contracts so as to achieve an immediate giveaway of at least $1 billion —"the largest single theft in history," Ernest Fitzgerald called it";[25] and in the first eleven months of fiscal 1972, Aspin said, the Pentagon "funnelled a total of more than $1.5 billion into Lockheed's coffers—$43 million more than last year." Just as Lockheed was rewarded for failing, so were the high civilian and military officials—including Defense Secretaries Clark M. Clifford and Melvin R. Laird—who were against Fitzgerald and for the policy of waste and for cover-ups to escape accountability.

Fitzgerald, replying to a question at a hearing in 1968, "committed truth," in his phrase: he allowed that there indeed had been a $2 billion cost overrun on the C-5A. He thus assured that he would be fired. The man who actually did the firing was Robert C. Seamans, secretary of the Air Force. At a hearing before Proxmire, he did not commit truth. He claimed that Fitzgerald had not been fired—rather, his job had been eliminated. Deservedly, Seamans became probably the first official of his exalted rank to elicit derisive, raucous laughter in a public congressional appearance.[26] This did not slow his progress. The National Academy of Engineering made him its president. Then President Ford nominated and the Senate confirmed him as head of the new Energy Research and Development Administration.

Fitzgerald had a harder time. Even before he was fired, he was subjected not only to harassment, but to opening of his personal mail by Air Force investigators. Brigadier General Joseph Cappucci, director of the Air Force Office of Special Investigations, launched an investigation intended to dig up the kind of material useful in character assassination—and found that he was a "pinchpenny type of person," as evidenced by his old car, a Rambler. Fitzgerald fought his firing, for six years, in the Civil Service Commission and in the courts, while the taxpayers paid the salaries and expenses of the lawyers for the Pentagon, the Commission, and the Justice Department whose mission in life was to use every possible legal tactic to make the firing stick. Fitzgerald finally was vindicated and returned to the Pentagon. There, Defense Secretary James R. Schlesinger, backed by the Nixon and Ford administrations, carefully insulated Fitzgerald from any duties in which he might find and obstruct waste by giant defense contractors. Thus waste as a Pentagon policy was preserved. At the same time, and, for that matter, even after President Ford dropped him from his Cabinet, Schlesinger never missed an opportunity to lament publicly that Congress wasn't giving the Pentagon enough money. He never lamented the cost of litigating against Fitzgerald, who, during those six difficult years, had been represented by three Washington lawyers at the request of the American Civil Liberties Union. These lawyers—John Bodner, Jr., John F. Bruce, and William L. Sollee—ran up legal fees of more than $400,000. Bodner, of the law firm of Howrey and Simon, told the *Washington Star,* "Major litigation like this literally eats the little guy alive. How can he be expected to fight all this legal talent the government can bring to bear? They're getting paid yearly salaries to do what they do. What does it matter to them?" It began to matter on December 29, 1975, when United States District Judge William B. Bryant ruled that the Civil Service Commission must pay the costs Fitzgerald incurred in fighting his unjust dismissal. Unless overturned on appeal, the ruling was of high importance because of its potential to encourage other civil servants to air abuses.[27]

Well before Bryant's decision, Senator Proxmire saw in the Fitzgerald case the clearest evidence that federal employees who put the public interest ahead of a strongly opposed bureaucratic interest routinely face intimidation and punishment. Subsequently, Senator Edward M. Kennedy (D–Mass.), chairman of the Senate Health and Administrative Practice and Procedure subcommittees, subpoenaed numerous staff physicians and scientists in the Food and Drug Administration so as to get sworn testimony from first-hand sources on such crucial matters as whether medical officers whose decisions aided the drug industry were rewarded or not punished (they were), while those whose decisions were adverse to the industry commonly were harassed or banished to outer precincts (they were).[28] (At first blush, Kennedy's action in subpoenaing staff-level employees may seem unsurprising and merely sensible, but it happened to have been an innovative and invaluable precedent in congressional oversight to subpoena government employees to testify under oath.)

Nader and two associates, Robert Vaughn and Peter J. Petkas, proceeded at Proxmire's request to draft a reform bill, which Nader told Kennedy in September 1974 addressed "the central problem of the Federal Government today."

The draft bill would express these intents of Congress:

• Public employees would be made personally accountable for failure either to enforce the laws or for negligence, incompetence, or improper performance of public duties.

• The rights of employees to expose corruption, dishonesty, incompetence, or administrative failure would be protected.

• The rights of employees to contact and communicate with Congress would be protected.

• Employees would be protected from reprisal or retaliation for the performance of their duties.

Henry Durham worked for Lockheed for nineteen years in Marietta, Georgia. This is where the C-5A was built, and, likely, *had* to be built; the commitment to a site for constructing the transport, the world's biggest, was made while Georgia's senior senator, the late Richard B. Russell, was chairman of the Senate Armed Services Committee and, as well, of the Defense Subcommittee of the Senate Appropriations Committee.[29] In July 1969, Durham was given production-control responsibilities that led him to discover that C-5As which were, according to Lockheed records, virtually complete were in fact missing thousands of parts. Durham made an investigation which quickly established that by falsifying the records, and through related fraudulent devices, Lockheed with the toleration if not the connivance of the Air Force had collected more than $1 billion in payments for fake construction progress.

Making himself as unwelcome at Lockheed as Fitzgerald was at the Pentagon, Durham complained through company channels—finally to board chairman Daniel J. Haughton. In the end, Durham was forced out. While the proposal to bail out Lockheed with the $250 million loan guaranty was gestating on Capitol Hill, he sent letters to eighty-six senators and representatives offering to come to Washington to present evidence of "disastrously rotten management," of corruption, and of collusion between the Air Force and the company. Not even an acknowledgement came from most, including the chairmen of the Armed Services committees, Senator John C.

Stennis (D–Miss.) and Congressman F. Edward Hébert (D–La.), and the chairman of the Senate Banking and Currency Committee, Senator John J. Sparkman (D–Ala.). Finally, Durham wrote to Morton Mintz, who, after an investigation in Marietta, wrote a long story which was published by the *Washington Post* and the *Atlanta Constitution* on July 18, 1971. Three years later, when the American Ethical Union honored Henry Durham with its Elliott-Black Award for "translation of the highest ethical and moral values into significant social actions in the public interest," he recalled what had happened after, in Ernest Fitzgerald's phrase, he "committed truth":

I began to receive serious threats on my life and the lives of my wife and children. The telephone rang day and night. Anonymous callers not only threatened to kill me but viciously threatened to disfigure my daughter. Lines of automobiles drove slowly past our home. Signs saying "kill Durham" appeared on bulletin boards and restroom walls in the plant and around town. The local press fanned the flames. I had to stand armed watch at night to protect my family.

Finally, when the threats and vicious calls intensified instead of abating, I appealed to Senator Proxmire for federal protection for my family. For over two months, federal marshals guarded my family around the clock.

We have been ostracized by the community and even our church. People stopped their children from associating with mine.

Proxmire, a leading opponent of the loan-guaranty bill, had asked Durham to testify before his subcommittee. "Kill Proxmire" signs appeared alongside the "Kill Durham" signs; and the Marietta paper classified each man as a "Public Enemy." The senator did not actually convene a hearing until September 1971, which was well after Congress, by a narrow margin, had enacted the bill to bail out Lockheed. Essentially repeating the charges made in the *Post* story, Durham put into the record voluminous documentation of twenty-three specific charges. Proxmire asked the General Accounting Office to investigate them. The GAO's auditors in Atlanta did so and, in March 1972, made a report that, Proxmire said, "corroborates nearly every aspect of Mr. Durham's charges." Durham himself obtained and released a copy of the report; had he not done so, it probably never would have gotten out of GAO headquarters in Washington.

The boss of the GAO, Comptroller General Elmer B. Staats, then had his headquarters staff review the Atlanta report. The review made a softer case. Indeed, Durham, in a thirty-three-page, point-by-point analysis, denounced it as "a whitewash" and criticized Staats personally. When Proxmire straddled the fence on the issue, Durham suggested an explanation: lacking adequate investigative staff of its own, the subcommittee must call upon the GAO for help. It may be said that Proxmire need not have hesitated to join Durham in criticizing the GAO, because the agency is the servant of Congress. But Proxmire and other critics of the defense establishment are not Congress; the chairmen of the Armed Services, Appropriations, and Government Operations committees, along with other agents of the military-industrial complex, pretty much are.[30]

A short time before Durham left Lockheed, a company official visited him to express concern that Durham might tell his story "outside." The official warned Durham that Ernest Fitzgerald "will never be able to get a good job as long as he lives," and indicated, Durham said later, "that anyone who bucks Lockheed, the Pentagon, or the Nixon Administration is in for a rough time the rest of his life." For two and a half years thereafter, Durham was unable to get a job commensurate with his abilities, although one might think that American industry would compete for the services of a man as determined to cut costs as Henry Durham. Thanks to a person who took a special interest in him and who prefers not to be named, Durham finally went to work. Few know for whom or where, which is the way Durham wants it.

Ernest Fitzgerald and Henry Durham had the rare courage to try to make the system accountable, rather than to go along with those public and corporate leaders who make it unaccountable. When the system punishes rather than rewards such men, it indicts itself.

The name of this game is to conceal true authorship or sponsorship. This makes it difficult to find the donkey to which the tail of accountability should be pinned. The Central Intelligence Agency, while without peer in playing the game, did not invent it and does not play it alone.

In 1961 before thalidomide was discovered to cause the birth of deformed children in women who had taken it in the first trimester of pregnancy, an article about the sedative appeared in the *American Journal of Obstetrics and Gynecology*. The article said that if the drug is taken by a pregnant woman and passes the placental barrier there "is no danger to the fetus." The listed author was Dr. Ray O. Nulsen, of Cincinnati, Ohio. The actual author was Dr. Raymond C. Pogge, medical director of the William S. Merrell division of Richardson-Merrell, Inc. It was this enterprise which at the time was seeking permission from the Food and Drug Administration to market thalidomide.[1]

It would be misleading to imply that this kind of thing was unique to Richardson-Merrell when in fact it was common in the pharmaceutical industry. Dr. Haskell J. Weinstein, who for a time in 1959 was acting medical director of J. B. Roerig Company, a division of Chas. Pfizer & Company, Inc., told the Senate Subcommittee on Antitrust and Monopoly in 1960

that a substantial number of the so-called medical scientific papers that are published on behalf of . . . drugs are written within the confines of the pharmaceutical houses concerned. Frequently the physician involved merely makes the observations and his data, which are sketchy and uncritical, are submitted to a medical writer employed by the company. The writer prepares the article which is returned to the physician who makes the overt effort to submit it for publication. The article is frequently sent to one of the journals which looks to the pharmaceutical company for advertising and rarely is publication refused. The particular journal is of little interest inasmuch as the primary concern is to have the article published any place in order to make reprints available. There is a rather remarkable attitude prevalent that if a paper is published then its contents become authoritative, even though before publication the same contents may have been considered nonsense.[2]

The subcommittee, then led by Senator Estes Kefauver, also produced abundant evidence of "salting" of lay publications by drug houses with articles intended to generate a demand to physicians for prescriptions for particular products.³ This practice has continued and is on an international scale. In October 1967, in an intra-company memo, an official of G. D. Searle & Company in Beirut, Lebanon, commented to a colleague about " 'Al Tabibak' Medical Magazine." Here is what D. A. Evans wrote to C. Evan Pilgrim:

Under separate cover I have sent to you a specimen of the above independent (!) lay medical journal. The pages mentioning our products [principally oral contraceptives] are marked by the page corners being folded.

This magazine recommends "impartially" products to the public for specific common illnesses. Obviously we have to pay for such "impartiality".

It is my intention to use this publication during 1968.

In 1953, the Center for International Studies at the Massachusetts Institute of Technology published *The Dynamics of Soviet Society*. The principal author was Walt Whitman Rostow, who would later be President Johnson's assistant for national security affairs. "[T]here was no indication to the reader that the work had been financed with CIA funds and that it reflected the prevailing agency view of the Soviet Union," Victor Marchetti and John D. Marks reported in *The CIA and the Cult of Intelligence*. "MIT cut off its link with the center in 1966, but the link between the center and the CIA remained . . ."⁴ The CIA "attaches a particular importance to book publishing activities as a form of covert propaganda," the Senate Select Committee on Intelligence Activities said in April 1976 in its final report on the foreign and military intelligence activities of the United States. By 1967, the CIA had "sponsored, subsidized or produced over 1,000 books, approximately 25 percent of them in English," the report said. "In 1967 alone, the C.I.A. published or subsidized over 200 books . . ." The committee also found that "an important number" of the books actually produced by the CIA "were reviewed and marketed in the United States." Describing the domestic "fallout" of such covert operations, the report revealed that "a book written for an English-speaking foreign audience by one C.I.A. operative was reviewed favorably by another C.I.A. agent in The New York Times." The reviewer was not a member of the *Times'* staff. One of the pre-1967 books in which the CIA had a hand was *The Penkovsky Papers*, which purportedly was based on the reports of a Soviet spy who was executed. Unknown to the publisher, Doubleday, CIA agents had written it. The book became a commercial success and was serialized in many newspapers, including the *Washington Post*. The Russians called the book a fraud, and they were right.

Similarly, the public had no way of knowing that the United States Information Agency had sponsored two books written in the 1960s, by Jay Mallin, a *Time* magazine correspondent: *The Truth About the Dominican Republic*, and *Terror in Vietnam*. The USIA, it turned out, had a $6 million "book development" program. "Why is it wrong to let the American people know when they buy and read the book that it was developed under government sponsorship?" Congressman Glenard Lipscomb (R–Calif.) asked USIA Director Leonard Marks at a House hearing. Marks' reply was one of those statements of the obvious that nonetheless is welcome because it is on the record: "It minimizes their value. . . . if we say this is our book, then the author is a government employee in effect. It changes the whole status of the author. . . ."[5] Moreover, as Senator J. William Fulbright (D–Ark.) pointed out at a hearing of the Senate Foreign Relations Committee, the USIA "is not authorized to propagandize the American people. If you'd said that the books were published by USIA," he told agency officials, "it would be one thing—but not to do so is doubly subversive of our system."[6]

The late Rachel Carson's best-selling *Silent Spring*, published in 1962, warned eloquently against excessive use of pesticides. This upset true believers, including the industry, of course, but also Congressman Jamie L. Whitten (D–Miss.). He is chairman of the House Appropriations Subcommittee with responsibility for the Agriculture Department, which had jurisdiction over government pesticide regulations and program until 1970, and until early 1975, also over the Environmental Protection Agency, to which regulation was subsequently transferred. He is knowledgeable, powerful, and easily and consistently reelected. While the Department of Agriculture was responsible for pesticides, and while he held decisive control over the department's funding, it ignored hundreds of challenges to pesticide safety. In 1964, the Velsicol Chemical Corporation was under criticism on Capitol Hill: one of its pesticides, endrin, was being blamed—wrongly, the company insisted—for a massive fish kill in the lower Mississippi River. Samuel Bledsoe, of Velsicol's public-relations firm, Selvage, Lee and Howard, suggested to Whitten that he write a book to counteract alleged gross inaccuracies in *Silent Spring*. The congressman's *That We May Live* was published in 1966 by D. Van Nostrand Company of Princeton, New Jersey—but only after a pledge to subsidize sales of several thousand copies had been made by at least three chemical companies, Velsicol, Shell Chemical, and what is now Ciba-Geigy Corporation. Commercially, the book did not do well.[7]

The Continental Oil Company had at its world headquarters in Stamford, Connecticut, in 1972, an editorial staff that included four writers. One of them, Wilbur Cross, felt himself to be under ethical constraints, he said in a letter to about forty members of the Society of Magazine Writers. "I obviously cannot write up company-oriented pieces for profit," he said. But Continental Oil would like to help you do that very thing . . .

We'll even do typing, editing and proofing for you, if you like. And in certain instances we'll arrange transportation. . . .

We have an excellent editorial staff here, as well as in other parts of the world and abroad, and can provide a really solid assist, including ideas, data, documentation, interviews, photos and other visuals, and similar material.

Cross listed various subject areas in which "we have much to offer," including "almost any topic relating to oil, gas, coal, uranium and chemicals," land reclamation, and environmental problems.[8]

Continental Oil's generosity to writers thankfully stopped short of offering to pay them; not so Negative Population Growth, Inc.'s. In a mailing to writers in 1975, Donald W. Mann, president of NPG, said: "We are offering a $1,000 bonus to the first writer who writes a major article (2,000 words or more) about Negative Population Growth, Inc. and its concepts and gets it printed in a major national magazine (with a circulation of at least 300,000). I would be more than happy to cooperate in the writing of the article."[9]

"American correspondents often have much broader entrée to foreign societies than do officials of the local American embassy, which provides most CIA operators with their cover, and the agency simply has been unable to resist the temptation to penetrate the press corps," Marchetti and Marx observed.[10] As of February 1976, the Senate Select Committee said in its final report on foreign and military intelligence activities, the CIA had about fifty "U.S. journalists or personnel of U.S. media who were employed by the C.I.A. or maintained some other covert relationship with it . . ." At that time, the CIA's new director, George Bush, indicated he was going to end such use of news personnel. "Effective immediately," he said, "the C.I.A. will not enter into any paid or contractual relationship with any full-time or part-time news correspondent accredited by any U.S. news service, newspaper, periodical, radio or television network or station." But the committee, in its report in April 1976, revealed that the CIA, by interpreting the word "accredited" to apply only to those whose formal press credentials authorize them to represent themselves as correspondents, was continuing to employ as agents more than twenty-five news executives, free-lancers and others.

In 1966, the CIA secretly created Forum World Features, a news service based in London, to supply newspapers around the world with political and other articles, Bernard D. Nossiter reported in the *Washington Post* in July 1975. This long-concealed sponsorship was in addition to previously disclosed hidden financing of political and propaganda activities, such as Radio Free Europe and, Nossiter also has reported, of CIA subsidizing of private political organizations that had promoted European unity.

At Forum World Features, Brian Crozier, a right-wing British writer, supervised day-to-day operations, which, according to an apparently authentic CIA memo, were intended to provide "a comprehensive weekly service covering international affairs, economics, science and medicine, book reviews and other subjects of a general nature." The original owner of record was John Hay Whitney, former United States ambassador to Britain and chairman of the *International Herald Tribune*. Replacing him in early 1973 was Richard Mellon Scaife, who has major interests in the Mellon family's banking and Gulf Oil enterprises, and who gave $1 million to Richard Nixon's reelection campaign. Whitney's office had no comment on Nossiter's story, which was based on a disclosure in *Time Out,* a left-wing London weekly. The *Post* made an unsuccessful three-day effort to reach Scaife. The CIA "quietly closed down" Forum World Features in April 1975. Some London editors said it had been highly professional.[11]

Long before the CIA, or even its World War II predecessor, the Office of Strategic Services, had come into being, various industries, companies, and other special interests were gaining entrée to the editorial pages of hundreds of weekly and small daily newspapers without readers—and sometimes even editors—being aware of what was happening. The interests contracted with one or another of the so-called editorial services, such as E. Hofer and Sons, Publisher, of Portland, Oregon, to supply free "canned" editorials. What was "canned," needless to say, was the message the buyer wanted disseminated; but the source of the message being in no way identified, the reader would be disposed to think it was his hometown editor.

During the 1960s, as part of its fight against what became Medicare, the American Medical Association published a 171-page booklet, *U.S. Newspapers Comment on Health Care for the Elderly,* which contained a purported "cross-section" of newspaper opinion which reflected "the viewpoint of a majority of the American people." But Senator Pat McNamara (D–Mich.) discovered that eleven newspapers had used the same editorial, usually without changing a word, that ten each had used two others, and that, all told, fifty newspapers had published more than six "AMA-slanted" editorials. Thus, for example, McNamara found that the views of the editor of the *Modesto Tribune* in California appeared to "coincide precisely" with those of the editor of the *Roanoke Times* in Virginia. The editorials had been canned for the AMA by the E. Hofer firm in Oregon.[12]

A variant on the canned editorial is the phony letter-writing campaign. One was conducted by the nation's largest producer of electric power in the course of a five and a half year effort—ultimately unsuccessful—to acquire the Columbus and Southern Ohio Electric Company. The would-be acquisitor, American Electric Power Company, Inc., a holding company operating in seven East Central states, needed the approval of the Securities and Exchange Commission. An SEC administrative law judge, Irving Schiller, held and completed hearings in 1968, but reopened them in 1969 at the request of American Electric Power. In hopes of "improperly influencing" the proceeding, according to Bernard E. Nash and Gary N. Sundick, who represented the SEC's Division of Corporate Regulation in opposing the merger, the company generated an "unprecedented outpouring" of several hundred letters from mayors and other public officials. Some of the letters were identical—a dead giveaway of a common source.[13]

The approximately twenty-five thousand members of the American Trial Lawyers Association (ATLA) stood to lose more than $1 billion a year in fees if a 1972 bill for no-fault auto insurance were to be enacted. Consequently, ATLA mounted a major effort to defeat the bill, which had been introduced in the Senate by Senators Warren G. Magnuson (D–Wash.) and Philip A. Hart (D–Mich.), and which would have provided federal standards for the states to follow in enacting their own legislation to assure prompt compensation of victims and survivors no matter who—if anyone—had caused an accident. The trial lawyers' effort to defeat the bill, which ultimately failed by a vote of 46 to 49, involved setting up a $100,000 lobbying effort in Washington, election-campaign contributions offered or withheld, as circumstances indicated, and the mail drive.

In Salt Lake City in July 1972, six constituents of Senator Frank E. Moss (D–Utah) each wrote him to ask that he oppose the Magnuson-Hart bill. Their main complaint was that the bill threatened states' rights and was anticonsumer. Each letter was typed, apparently on the same machine, on a sheet of plain white paper; each was mailed in a similar envelope; and each text was identical to one or another of the "suggested letters" that the Utah Trial Lawyers Association had circulated to its members. Much more industrious was a Salt Lake City judge, Robert C. Gibson. He sent Moss a letter which evidently was a piecing together of five paragraphs from four of the association's texts. At the offices of the San Francisco Trial Lawyers Association at about the same time, a parallel letter-writing campaign was under way. In this case, however, there was a refinement: persons willing to send anti-no-fault letters were provided with stamped envelopes addressed to the United States senators from California, Democrats Alan Cranston and John V. Tunney.[14]

The purposes of drug companies may best be served when letters to government agencies in their behalf are signed by physicians and pharmacists. An outstanding example involves medicines for the treatment of infections that combined, in fixed ratios, two or more antibiotics or other anti-infective agents. Introduced in the 1950s, they were condemned from the start by specialists in the treatment of infectious diseases. They said it is unwise to administer two or more agents, each potent enough to kill or stultify bacteria and therefore capable of doing harm as well as good, when one suffices— the rifle shot *v.* the shotgun blast. They also said that a combination obviously makes it impossible to increase the dose of a needed component without also increasing the dose of an unneeded one.

But the manufacturers lavishly promoted the combinations, which were more profitable than the components sold separately. Cravenly, medical publications, including the *Journal of the American Medical Association,* accepted advertising for the products at the same time that the AMA's scientific leadership, speaking through the Council on Drugs, condemned them as a significant threat to public health. Eventually, the AMA hierarchy would deal with the council by abolishing it, even if this meant that the two last chairmen of the council would accuse the AMA of being "a captive of, and beholden to, the pharmaceutical industry." It was not merely the advertising revenues, but drug-company gifts to the American Medical Political Action Committee (AMPAC)—$851,000 merely in the four years 1962 through 1965—that made the AMA beholden (read accountable) to the industry.[15] During these same years, fixed-ratio combinations were accounting for approximately 40 percent of all prescriptions, so gimmick-minded and pharmacologically ignorant was much of the medical profession—especially those doctors who found it natural to mix a taste for reactionary politics with a taste for radical drug therapy.

One of the combinations most popular with a large, gullible segment of the medical profession was the Upjohn Company's Panalba, a recipe of 250 milligrams of tetracycline and 125 mgs. of novobiocin per capsule. It was the tetracycline that was effective and essential in the treatment of a broad spectrum of infections. The inclusion of novobiocin, a promotional stunt, was literally responsible for hundreds of thousands of needless injuries, a few of them fatal, each year. Yet, Upjohn not only undertook a letter-writing campaign to try to keep Panalba on sale, but enlisted approximately 1,200 physicians to carry it out.

Although the medical profession (and, of course, the public) didn't know it, Upjohn in 1960 had received and, with questionable legality, suppressed reports of studies showing Panalba's ingredients to "antagonize" each other, which made the combination *inferior* to the components ingested separately. Specifically, the amount of novobiocin entering the bloodstream was either zero or markedly—and sub-therapeutically—less than it would have been had tetracycline not been present; and the serum level of tetracycline was slightly lower than it would have been had novobiocin not accompanied it. Thus, the combination eliminated the therapeutic potential imputed—questionably—to novobiocin at the same time that it decreased the therapeutic potential of tetracycline, its essential ingredient. But Upjohn continued for almost ten years after receipt of the reports to promote Panalba to doctors who had no way of knowing that it had a negative rationale; and the drug, introduced in 1957, came to be regularly prescribed by an estimated twenty-three thousand physicians and to account for 12 percent of the firm's domestic income; its contribution in 1968 alone exceeded $18 million.

The studies finally were brought to light as a result of a review of fixed anti-infective combinations made for the Food and Drug Administration by five expert panels of the National Research Council, the operating arm of the National Academy of Sciences. Unanimously, the panels held at least fifty of the combinations, Panalba included, to be therapeutically irrational —not only no more effective than their ingredients used singly, but dangerous as well. The FDA could have ended the matter then and there by declaring these combinations a legally "imminent" hazard to public health. Instead, it went on certifying them, batch by batch, as safe and effective antibiotics while it moved to get them off the market with other methods which, while ultimately successful, opened the door to litigation. Upjohn, represented by Stanley L. Temko, of the prestigious Washington law firm of Covington & Burling, and supported by the Pharmaceutical Manufacturers Association, represented by Lloyd N. Cutler, of Wilmer, Cutler & Pickering, another leading Washington law firm, did litigate. By doing so, it kept Panalba on sale for well over a year after the FDA could have removed it —with hundreds of thousands of needless injuries resulting.

In March 1969, during preparation for trial of Upjohn's lawsuit, an FDA inspector discovered in Upjohn's files the 1960 studies showing that Panalba was less than the sum of its parts. An FDA scientist then made an analysis of the records which in May 1969 was disclosed on Capitol Hill—first by Congressman L. H. Fountain's House Intergovernmental Relations Subcommittee, and then by Senator Gaylord Nelson's Senate Subcommittee on Monopoly.

In testimony before the Nelson subcommittee, Dr. Herbert L. Ley Jr., then commissioner of the FDA, and himself a specialist in antibiotic therapy, reported both the consequences of the uses of Panalba and details of the letter-writing campaign to keep it on the market.

In the twelve years since it went on sale, 47.5 million persons, by Upjohn's estimate, had been treated with Panalba, Ley testified. He calculated that the worse-than-useless novobiocin component caused an allergic or hypersensitivity reaction in approximately one out of five, or 9.5 million. Most such reactions are "merely irritating," he said. "You can't sleep for several nights or a week, or you may break out in a very unpleasant, uncomfortable rash." A smaller proportion of Panalba users, Ley continued, "experience temporary but very severe liver damage as a result of the novobiocin component," and "a still smaller number" suffer blood disorders. These accounted for eleven of the twelve fatalities among Panalba users reported by the company. The agency emphasized, however, that adverse reactions to most any potent drug generally are grossly underreported.

Shortly after the Department of Health, Education, and Welfare had published the National Research Council report on Christmas Eve, 1968, but before the FDA inspector found the studies in Upjohn's files, the company started its campaign to get physicians to pressure the government not to deny them the combination with which they were innocently inflicting massive preventable injury on their helpless patients. At about the same time, E. R. Squibb & Sons, Inc., producer of Mysteclin-F, which combined tetracycline with an antifungal drug, amphotericin B, and which also had been condemned, launched a similar campaign in behalf of its mixture. Within a brief period, Upjohn and Squibb together had generated 3,500 letters, of which one-third were in behalf of Panalba.

Upjohn began its drive with a "Dear Doctor" letter in which J. C. Gauntlett, a vice-president and director, said, "In principle, if the physician's right to prescribe is denied for one category of useful [sic] drugs, it is conceivable this same right may be denied for others. We believe the decision as to whether these drugs are used should rest in the hands of the practicing physician." There was of course no mention of the profits to be obtained. Dr. William L. Hewitt, a professor of medicine at the University of California in Los Angeles who chaired one of the National Research Council panels, told Senator Nelson that the letter "represents, in my opinion, a bold, unscrupulous and selfish attempt to raise the spectre of Government regulation against the inalienable right to and, indeed, duty of every physician to manage his patient's problems to the best of his ability." He pointed out that novobiocin, "a very poor drug" therapeutically, and one seldom prescribed alone, had astonishing financial curative powers when incorporated into Panalba—because the combination, at the retail level, commanded a price approximately triple that for tetracycline. Panalba's "net theft from the public," Hewitt calculated, was about $12 million annually.

Dr. Ley, in an exchange with Benjamin Gordon, the Nelson subcommittee's staff economist, said that most of the letters supporting Panalba "took the form: I have been using this product for ten years, and it does a good job for my patients. . . . These are testimonials. There was nothing in the way of a considered judgment, or substantial evidence . . ." Gordon asked if any of the letters were worded similarly. "Yes," Ley replied. "We noted in both the Panalba and the Mysteclin situation that many letters followed roughly the same wording. Even paragraphs were identical in letters coming from institutions that were not necessarily close together. There appeared to be something that made the letters very similar. Finally, we received a handwritten note on a letter which a physician had received from the firm requesting that the physician write to the FDA. It then became apparent that the firms had been active in stimulating the response." Squibb, for example, prepared guidelines for letters in behalf of Mysteclin-F which the Maine Medical Association then paraphrased and circulated to its membership. In another example, doctors at the Oak Forest State Hospital in Oak Forest, Illinois, spoke up for Mysteclin-F in letters identical in language to that used by physicians at Chicago State Hospital. In the end, the letter campaigns failed, as did last-minute intervention, procured by Upjohn, by Robert H. Finch, then Secretary of HEW, and an unusually generous interim court ruling by United States District Judge W. Wallace Kent of Kalamazoo, Michigan, Upjohn's home city.[16] But, in keeping with standard practice in matters of this kind, Upjohn continued to sell Panalba abroad, under the name Albamycin-T.

Six years later, Senator Nelson disclosed that at least one drug house, Ayerst Laboratories, a division of American Home Products Corporation, had structured another massive but unsuccessful letter-writing campaign from behind the scenes. This time, the purpose was to force HEW Secretary Caspar W. Weinberger to rescind a proposal to limit federal payments for drugs prescribed for Medicaid and Medicare patients to medicines that have the required therapeutic benefits, that are the lowest in price, and that are generally available to pharmacists. The drug industry tirelessly tried to defeat the proposal because of a justified apprehension that it would stimulate prescribing by generic rather than brand name not only in the government, but, more important, in the private sector. The taxpayers and consumers would save hundreds of millions of dollars—substantially at the expense of the major drug companies.

HEW received twenty-three hundred letters on the proposal. Most came from doctors and pharmacists and opposed the plan. At a hearing of his Subcommittee on Monopoly in March 1975, Senator Nelson read from a letter in which William F. Appel, a Minneapolis druggist who favored the proposal, said that Ayerst Laboratories had ordered two hundred of its salesmen each to solicit letters of opposition from five druggists. Appel quoted one of the salesmen as saying the letters would be presented to Secretary Weinberger by William L. Davis, president of Ayerst, "as evidence of the opinion of the nation's pharmacists." Appel then requested Davis specifically to include his letter endorsing the HEW proposal in the packet he later gave to Weinberger, but the executive omitted it. Davis had agreed to testify but decided not to. American Home Products refused to comment. Its other prescription drug division, Wyeth Laboratories, and Warner-Chilcott Laboratories, a division of Warner–Lambert Pharmaceutical Company, also used their salesmen to stir up opposition to the HEW plan, according to the subcommittee's Benjamin Gordon.[17] At the time of this writing, HEW had held fast and was scheduled to put the plan into effect in August 1976.

Potpourri

29

There follows a collection of miscellaneous examples of unaccountability. Each is brief. Each is intended to be illuminating in a different way.

Unportable Pensions

For 35 years, Murray Finkelstein was a shoe salesman in New York City. One day his long-time employer went out of business. The Retail Shoe Employees Union arranged for Finkelstein to get a new job at a firm that was covered by the union's pension plan. But it was also a firm whose quality Finkelstein did not respect. He felt he was given a choice of surrendering his self-respect or his pension rights. He chose to give up the latter, forfeiting benefits built up over nineteen and a half years.

In another case, an employee of a Midwest meat packing company was sent to work during World War II at a second plant of the same firm in the same city because of the need to fulfill government contracts. He stayed there until 1965, when the second plant was closed. He was paid $231.55 in pension benefits and was sent back to the first plant—not as a regular employee, but as a casual laborer, ineligible for pension benefits. Five years later he was dismissed for being overage. As a result, at age sixty-six, after forty-three years of continuous employment with the same company, this employee's total pension benefits amounted to $231.55. If he had been allowed to carry his pension credits from one plant to the second plant of the same company he would have been eligible for a pension upon retirement.

Both of these cases, and others like them cited in a 1972 report of the Senate Committee on Labor and Public Welfare, illustrate some of the problems associated with what is known as pension "portability." The term refers simply to an employee's right to transfer his accrued pension rights from one employer to another. Millions of employees do not enjoy that right, even, as in the case of the meat packer, within the same company, or, as in the case of Finkelstein, within the same industry. When a person dare not leave one job for another because he would lose his pension, he is deprived of an essential freedom that, in most cases, is more meaningful than the freedom to vote.

There are other, equally severe problems associated with vesting provisions —or the lack of them—in many pension plans. For example, Stephen Dane worked for the Great Atlantic and Pacific Tea Company (A&P) for thirty-two years. When the New Jersey plant he worked in was closed in 1970, Dane was out of a job at age fifty-one. He was also without a pension, despite his thirty-two years' service, because the A&P pension plan required employees to be at least fifty-five years old to qualify for benefits.

Whether the problem is portability, vesting rights or something else, the end result is the same: an employee, often with years of loyal service to the same employer, is left with nothing at retirement. He or she is discarded, in short, like a used tool. Yet, no one seems ready to be responsible for that, to be held accountable for what is owed to such an employee.

Nonprofitability

The country's largest membership organizations for the elderly are the American Association of Retired Persons (AARP) and the affiliated National Retired Teachers Association (NRTA). Their combined membership as of January 1976 exceeded 9 million and was growing rapidly. Their broad appeal depends significantly on the ambiance they create for themselves with the use of a magic descriptive phrase: not-for-profit. The appeal is greatly enhanced by the modest dues of two dollars a year, or five dollars for three years.

The dues buy various benefits, services, and publications, especially *Modern Maturity*, a bimonthly, full-color, glossy magazine. It seems a bargain. But few members are aware that dues revenue is insufficient to pay the bills of the associations, which make up the deficit with a subsidy, called "allowances". The subsidizer is the Colonial Penn Group, Inc., a highly profitable operator of insurance (life, health, auto), travel and other enterprises. The "honorary president" of the AARP–NRTA, Leonard Davis, is, with his wife, Sophie, the largest single stockholder in Colonial Penn. As of July 26, 1974, when the couple owned 4,177,153 shares, the listed price on the New York Stock Exchange was $25⅛; the total value, at least on paper, was nearly $105 million.

In exchange for the subsidy, first disclosed in 1972, Colonial Penn has exclusive access to the association's membership lists—the key to low-cost merchandising through computerized mass-mailings—and to the columns of *Modern Maturity* and other AARP–NRTA publications. A balance sheet published in the June–July 1974 issue of the magazine shows that Colonial Penn paid the associations $5,782,987 in 1973 for "administrative expenses, joint services to members, membership development and promotion of the welfare of members." Elsewhere in the same issue is a box which says, in small type, that Colonial Penn provided the "administrative allowances" as "compensation for advertising space . . ." The box was tucked into the lower left corner of a page in which appeared material in editorial format headlined, "How Much Life Insurance Is Enough?" At the bottom of the page is a line in boldface type saying, "Advertising material prepared for AARP by Colonial Penn Life Insurance Company." This relative candor, it ought to be noted, followed disclosure by the *Washington Post* in 1972 of the Siamese-twin connections between the company and the associations.

The arrangements between Colonial Penn and AARP–NRTA exclude mention of the wares of any competitor of the company, making the membership of the associations significantly a captive audience. The claim of the company and of the AARP–NRTA is that no better values than Colonial Penn's are to be had. But is that so? Consider the travel service. It offers tours at standard prices—the prices one would pay a typical agency. But inexpensive charter flights are not offered. As for group health and hospital policies, the Wyatt Company, an independent firm of actuaries and employee-benefit consultants, compared two policies sold by Colonial Penn to AARP–NRTA members with a policy offered by the National Council of Senior Citizens —and judged the latter to be the superior value.

The life insurance sold through the associations to men fifty-five and older was compared with similar insurance offered by 118 other companies in a massive, unique computerized study directed by Dean E. Sharp, assistant counsel of the Senate Antitrust and Monopoly Subcommittee. Colonial Penn's best-selling policy ranked consistently near the bottom in value as measured by several yardsticks. The company claimed the comparison to be unfair. Uniquely, it said, Colonial Penn sells policies to the elderly without requiring a physical examination, or even filling out a health questionnaire. This results in the insuring of an abnormally high proportion of high-risk persons and accounts for a policy price 38 percent higher than it otherwise would be, the company contended; but it never complied with Sharp's request to substantiate the 38 percent higher price. Sharp, who has left the subcommittee to practice law in Washington, had good reason to be skeptical. Colonial's Penn's rivals pay the face amount of a policy to the beneficiary no matter how soon after purchase of the policy the insured may die. In contrast, Colonial Penn's policy has an "unlevel" death benefit under which the beneficiary of an insured who dies in the first year in which the policy is in effect gets a benefit of only $58 per $1,000 face value, or only $8 more than the premium. The pay-out in the second year after a policy is issued is only $117 and in the third year a mere $168. Only if the insured dies more than three years after buying a policy does his beneficiary get the full face amount of that policy.

The AARP and NRTA are in many ways useful and innovative organizations which have done much to help the elderly. But a problem lies in their legal classification as not for profit. They are that in a technical sense, but they also are the prime money-making instrument for an insurance enterprise that, in terms of return on capital, for several years has been the most profitable large corporation in the United States. It is a defective accountability that ties the associations' service to their millions of members to their production of multi-million-dollar profits for Colonial Penn.[1]

Experiments

Once upon a time, physicians used to bleed patients. Some survived. The physicians credited the bleeding. During the 1930s pellagra, a disease caused by a deficiency of niacin in the diet, was widespread in the South. If at a certain stage of acute pellagra a victim was put to bed he would show a short-lived improvement even if put on a pellagra-producing diet. The remission would occur whether he took no medicine or whether he took most any medicine. Consequently, physicians prescribed most every drug in the pharmacopeia and ignorantly credited each with the unrelated improvement that followed.

A well-controlled clinical trial, in contrast, is designed to eliminate bias on the part either of the investigator or the subject, and thus, Sir Peter Medawar has said, "to test the hypothesis that one treatment is better than another and express the results in the form of the probability of the differences being found to be due to chance or not." In sum, says Dr. Paul D. Stolley, the randomized, controlled clinical trial advances rational therapy, "substituting tentative truths for cocksure error."[2] This makes for accountability in medicine.

The Anglican Church service traditionally ended with a prayer to the long life of the Royal Family. To find out if prayer was effective, Sir Frances Galton compared the mean age at death of males in the Royal Family with that of other Englishmen whose social and economic status was comparable. For the period 1758–1843, Galton reported in 1872, men in the Royal Family who had survived their thirtieth year achieved a mean age of 64.0. Clergymen did slightly better, 64.5, and Army officers better still, 67.0. But physicians did best: 67.3. Galton concluded that prayer was not shown by evidence to prolong life. "No one of Galton's stature has conducted a statistical enquiry into the efficacy of psychoanalytic treatment," Sir Peter said. "If such a thing were done, might it not show that the therapeutic pretensions of psychoanalysis were not borne out by what it actually achieved?" He continued:

It was perhaps a premonition of what the results of such an enquiry might be that has led modern psychoanalysis to dismiss as somewhat vulgar the idea that the chief purpose of psychoanalytic treatment is to effect a cure. No: its purpose is rather to give the patient a new and deeper understanding of himself and of the nature of his relationship to his fellow men. So interpreted, psychoanalysis is best thought of as a secular substitute for prayer. Like prayer, it is conducted in the form of a duologue, and like prayer (if prayer is to bring comfort and refreshment) it requires an act of personal surrender, though in this case it is to a professional and stipendiary god.[3]

The Kefauver-Harris Amendments of 1962 to the Food, Drug, and Cosmetic Act require a manufacturer seeking to market a new drug first to provide substantial evidence of safety and effectiveness based upon well-controlled clinical trials done by experts in the particular field. Only after performing animal testing, and only after submitting an experimental protocol to the Food and Drug Administration, can a pharmaceutical manufacturer begin human testing. At the same time, no similar requirements exist for surgical techniques which may be intended to treat the same conditions as medicines and which may have drastic impacts on patients. The result is what Dr. David H. Spodick, professor of medicine at Tufts University, terms a "schizoid double standard" which makes for less accountability in surgery than in medicine. He has cited the example of patients with a heart condition known as hypertrophic obstructive cardiomyopathy. A surgeon undertook replacement of the mitral valve, claiming this to be "the surgical procedure of choice." Nine months later, an editorial in the *American Journal of Cardiology* termed the technique "at best premature and potentially dangerous." Who was correct? No one can say for certain. There having been no controls in the experiment, there was no standard for comparison and, consequently, for accountability. Had the surgeon proposed to treat the patients with a new pill or injection with the same uncontrolled protocol, Spodick says, the FDA or the human-trials committee of his hospital would have "squelched" it.[4]

Specifications

To bar competition in procurement without appearing to do so, agencies at all levels of government frequently invite bids on one or another item, but write specifications for the item that only favored suppliers can meet. This technique was adapted by the tomato industry in the late 1960s, when Mexican growers began selling in the United States large quantities of tomatoes that were higher in quality but lower in price than tomatoes grown in Florida. The Florida Tomato Committee, a group of twelve growers

TRICKS OF THE UNACCOUNTABILITY TRADE

nominated by the industry and "appointed" by the secretary of agriculture, had a ready response: a regulation that it proposed and that the Department of Agriculture immediately approved. Simon Lazarus told about the rule and its impacts in *The Genteel Populists:*

This innocuous-seeming rule forbade the sale of "mature green" tomatoes unless they are 2 9/32 inches in diameter; at the same time it forbade the sale of "all other" tomatoes unless they are ¼ inch larger—2 17/32 inches in diameter. The effect of the rule was to exclude virtually all Mexican-grown tomatoes from the American market. The reason is that Florida tomatoes are green at maturity (and have to be gassed to look red on supermarket shelves). Mexican tomatoes are pink at maturity; very few of either kind of tomato, which are botanically identical except for their color, grow to boast a 2 17/32-inch diameter.

The minutes of the committee meeting at which the rule was adopted show a member saying, "It will eliminate our competition, and that's what we're trying to do." They were notably successful, Lazarus found.

Within one month after the regulation went into effect in the spring of 1970, Mexican tomatoes, which had gained up to 70.6 percent of the American tomato market, slipped to 24.0 percent. The impact of the regulation also was felt by consumers. By the winter of 1971, the Consumer Price Index showed that prices for tomatoes had jumped 40 percent more than prices of all other foods consumed at home.[5]

Thanks to a lawsuit by Consumers Union and other consumer groups, the Department of Agriculture in October 1975 agreed to rescind the regulation.

Policy Statements

An agency's pretense that it is doing something about a problem often gets it off the hook indefinitely. One of the more effective pretenses available to federal agencies is the issuance of a policy statment which, in high-sounding language, suggests conduct that cannot be enforced; this is in lieu of the promulgation of rules providing penalties for violations. The Federal Communications Commission has been using this dodge since Congress created it in 1934. "Broadcasters have unfailingly ignored such statements, knowing they pose no threat to their licenses," the Rev. Everett C. Parker, director of the Office of Communication for the United Church of Christ, has pointed out.

The FCC took the policy-statement route in 1974, when it refused to set and enforce standards for children's television programming by rule-making. The first opportunity to challenge broadcasters who may not adhere to the policy—an expensive, difficult task in any case—won't come until 1977, and some stations will be insulated from scrutiny until 1982. Normally, it takes the FCC six to eight years to act on a license challenge. Consequently, Mr. Parker said, some stations cannot be held accountable "for today's unconscionable exploitation of children for as long as twenty years—an entire generation of children."[6]

Loyalty

In a large organization, a person's loyalty commonly tends to divide between the organization itself, which is remote, and the smaller components of which he is a more intimate part. When the goals of the organization do not coincide with the goals of the components, accountability becomes ambivalent. Roy L. Ash, director of the Office of Management and Budget in the Nixon administration, provides a striking case.

Ash, in the early 1950s, was assistant comptroller of the Hughes Aircraft Division of Hughes Tool Company, which, in turn, was wholly owned by Howard Hughes. He reported several times each week not through his nominal boss but directly to Charles B. (Tex) Thornton, whose title was assistant general manager, but who actually ran the division. Hughes Aircraft was building weapons-control systems for the Air Force. The contract held the company to a 10 percent profit. At the same time, Thornton, aided by Ash, wanted to impress the parent company and its owner with his ability to earn a much higher rate of profit. As a consequence, Ash ordered division accountants to post false entries in division books in order to show a low profit to the Air Force. At the same time, he ordered division accountants to post other false entries to show a high profit to Hughes Tool.

James O. White was one of the accountants who first protested and then joined in a revolt. In litigation that surfaced all of this, White testified that Ash once told him "that I ought to take my orders like a good company man does and like he did." He also recalled Ash saying, "You should be loyal to the division" and to Thornton. White couldn't swallow that. Ash denied in court that he had said such things, but this claim was impeached by testimony he had given in pre-trial depositions. As a result of the accountants' revolt, Noah Dietrich, who was Howard Hughes' chief executive officer, and was himself a certified public accountant, learned what was going on. Thornton, Dietrich testified, admitted to him that he had juggled the books to hold Hughes Aircraft profit to appear to be only 10 percent, but contended that all defense contractors did the same thing and that it was not wrong. Actually, the juggling was not only wrong, but, according to an audit by Haskins & Sells, an independent firm of CPAs, had caused the Air Force to be overcharged—or defrauded—of $43.4 million. Under pressure from

Dietrich, Hughes Aircraft refunded the money. Thornton and Ash went on to found the conglomerate Litton Industries.[7]

Bigotry

Throughout history, men have escaped accountability for evil acts by using, ignorantly or deliberately, prejudice of all kinds—racial, religious, chauvinistic, ethnic, sexist. This is too well known to require elaboration here. But something should be said about Robert Moses. Perhaps no other man was as clever as he was in deploying a personal bigotry toward the poor, especially blacks, with such devastating effect, but with so little public perception of what was happening. Robert A. Caro, in his *The Power Broker: Robert Moses and the Fall of New York,* tells how Moses

had restricted the use of state parks by poor and lower-middle-class families in the first place, by limiting access to the parks by rapid transit; he had vetoed the Long Island Rail Road's proposed construction of a branch spur to Jones Beach for this reason. Now he began to limit access by buses; he instructed Shapiro [Sidney M. Shapiro, an engineer in his employ] to build the bridges across his new parkways low —too low for buses to pass. Bus trips therefore had to be made on local roads, making the trips discouragingly long and arduous. For Negroes, whom he considered inherently "dirty," there were further measures. Buses needed permits to enter state parks; buses chartered by Negro groups found it very difficult to obtain permits. . . . Moses was convinced that Negroes did not like cold water; the temperature at the pool at Jones Beach was deliberately icy to keep Negroes out.[8]

Moses was endlessly inventive in making the Henry Hudson Parkway a thing of beauty. "From Seventy-second to 125th Street, for example, he lined the roadway with trees and shrubs and faced the walls along its sides with granite and marble and expensive masonry," Caro says. But between 125th and 145th streets, this being twenty blocks of Harlem,

he lifted the roadway into the air—on a gaunt steel viaduct. There is not a tree or shrub on the viaduct. There is not a foot of granite or marble or masonry. The only ornamentation whatsoever on the starkly ugly steel is the starkly ugly cheap concrete aggregate with which it is paved.[9]

In the slums, reformers said, parks meant more than even beauty or play space, because they were a sign to the urban poor "that society cared for them, that the city in which they had been trampled so brutally low was holding out a hand to help them to their feet."[10] But, Caro reported,

Robert Moses built 255 playgrounds in New York City during the 1930s. He built one playground in Harlem.

An overspill from Harlem had created Negro ghettos in two other areas of the city: Brooklyn's Stuyvesant Heights, the nucleus of the great slum that would become known as Bedford-Stuyvesant, and South Jamaica. Robert Moses built one playground in Stuyvesant Heights. He built no playgrounds in South Jamaica.

"We have to work all day and we have no place to send the children," one Harlem mother had written before Robert Moses became Park Commissioner. She could have written the same words after he had been Park Commissioner for five years. After a building program that had tripled the city's supply of playgrounds, there was still no place for approximately 200,000 of the city's children—the 200,000 with black skin—to play in their own neighborhoods except the streets or abandoned, crumbling, filthy, looted tenements stinking of urine and vomit; or vacant lots carpeted with rusty tin cans, jagged pieces of metal, dog feces and the leavings, spilling out of rotting paper shopping bags, of human meals.[11]

Investigations

Accountability can be ducked by not investigating, or underinvestigating, problems for which one is responsible; by going to the other extreme, to wit, studying problems to death; or by ignoring the results of a good investigation.

The Department of Health, Education, and Welfare (HEW) in fiscal 1976 was spending $118.4 billion, or more than one-third of the federal budget, on a total of 322 programs. HEW is accountable for administering these programs so as to detect and deter chiseling and fraud. It defaulted by having absurdly few criminal investigators—thirteen to watch over Social Security and Medicare health insurance for the aged, which consume in excess of 60 percent of the budget, and ten for all of the other programs, including guarantees of student loans, welfare, Medicaid, and the Food and Drug Administration. The ten investigators had about one hundred fraud cases—a four-year backlog—under or awaiting investigation. Long after Congressman L. H. Fountain (D–N.C.) had exposed all of this, HEW in December 1975 formed a new criminal investigations unit with seventy members.[12]

Richard M. Helms, while director of the Central Intelligence Agency, provided a masterly lesson in how to study a problem to death. At the urging of his staff in 1967, he authorized a review of intelligence collection. Months later, he got a report beginning, "The United States Intelligence community collects too much information." Much waste and duplication was found. A glut of trivia sometimes obscured important data. Too many reports were being written. Obviously, the taxpayers' money was being dissipated. But some of his deputies were offended. Worse, the report harshly criticized some of the Pentagon's intelligence programs. Helms met the challenge by locking up the report within the CIA. Then, Victor Marchetti and John D. Marks say in *The CIA and the Cult of Intelligence,* he

resorted to the time-honored technique of forming another special study group to review the work of the first group. He organized a new committee, the Senior Executive Group, to consider in general terms the CIA's managerial problems. The SEG's first job was to look over the . . . study, but its members were hardly fitted to the task. They were the chiefs of the agency's four directorates, each of which had been heavily criticized in the original study: . . . After several prolonged meetings, the SEG decided, not surprisingly, that the study was of only marginal value and therefore not to be acted on in any significant way. A short time later Cunningham [Hugh Cunningham, who had made the study] was transferred to the Office of Training, one of the CIA's administrative Siberias. The SEG never met again.[13]

President Truman in January 1951 foresightedly created the Materials Policy Commission. William S. Paley, the Columbia Broadcasting System executive, headed it. In mid-1952 the commission filed an extraordinary report which, among other things, predicted scarcities by 1975. Truman praised the report, telling Congress, "I do not believe there has ever been attempted before such a broad and farsighted appraisal of the material needs and resources of the US in relation to the needs and resources of the free world." During the quarter-century that followed, the report was all but ignored, and the predicted scarcities arrived pretty much on schedule.[14]

Reorganizations

Reorganizations are sometimes necessary to correct structural deficiencies or to meet changed conditions. It was wise of Congress in 1974, for example, finally to separate the antagonistic functions of promotion and regulation of nuclear energy which had been combined in the Atomic Energy Commission. At the same time, many reorganizations are merely reshuffles which, while underway, are a distraction from one or another glaring need for accountability. At the Pentagon, Admiral Hyman G. Rickover many times commented on the propensity of bureaucrats to fake corrective actions with reorganizations. "Every time they have trouble," he said, "they change the organization. Generally, they change the telephone numbers."[15]

Wired Competition

A fair and open competition is inherently equally accountable to all competitors. A fixed or "wired" competition, then, is automatically unaccountable to some. It is an ordinary event for a newspaper somewhere to report that one or another government agency has rigged a bidding competition to favor a particular business enterprise. But it was extraordinary when the prestigious National Institutes of Health (NIH) was caught doing it.

The NIH wanted the country to have more "centers of excellence" for research and training in the health sciences. It had $1 million in hand for this high purpose. And so it set up the Health Sciences Advancement Award. A total of 128 leading educational institutions filed initial applications. A panel of nongovernmental consultants reviewed them, the NIH said, "for overall compliance with the guidelines . . . and for the quality of the proposal." The panel eliminated 113 applicants. The fifteen remaining were invited to become finalists by filing detailed proposals.

The NIH announced the competition in April 1966. To all appearances it was fair and open. The House Intergovernmental Relations Subcommittee established, however, that the NIH—secretly—had started to solicit, receive, and actually approve applications at least one year earlier. It had committed to Cornell University and the University of Virginia funds that innocent applicants understandably had assumed were in escrow. The fifteen finalists, unbeknownst to them, were competing for money that had not been appropriated. Eventually, Congress came to the rescue by making the money available; and in July 1966, the NIH announced the winners of the Advancement Award: the universities of Colorado and Oregon, and Purdue, Vanderbilt, and Washington universities.[16]

A subtler but much more important wired competition is what William Raspberry, a *Washington Post* columnist, calls "the merit trap." It is based on the assumption that objective tests discover merit among applicants for jobs, promotions, school admissions, and the like. Raspberry doesn't question that low test scores fairly may weed out incompetents and losers; he does dispute the notion that high test scores are a fair and reliable guide to the relative merit of the survivors:

Take, for instance, an examination for postal clerks. Experience may show a high correlation between those who score less than, say, 69 per cent on the exam and those who turn out to be inadequate mail carriers, and in that sense it makes sense to disqualify those applicants who score less than 69 per cent.

But be careful of the trap. For what seems to follow does not follow: that a person who scores 83 on the exam will be a better mail carrier than one who scores 80, that one who scores 94 will be markedly better at the job than either of the other two, and that the applicant who scores 100 will be best of all.

That's the merit trap, and while it may be more obvious in the case of postal clerks, it is no less real in the case of most screening tests, excepting only those that measure specific job skills.

An official of the United States Civil Service Commission told Raspberry of an experiment in which a "B" average from any accredited college was held to be sufficient to enter government employment. The experiment showed that it was impossible to distinguish between the on-the-job performance of those who had earned their "Bs" at prestigious Ivy League schools from those who had attended small, third-rate, land-grant colleges. The official "doesn't doubt that if the applicants had been given written exams, the Ivy League grads would have won most of the jobs," the columnist said. "On 'merit,' of course."

The connection with unaccountability is this: any device, tests and examinations included, that discriminates unfairly, even if inadvertently, against any segment of the citizenry is inherently unaccountable to that segment. The merit trap tends to discriminate against members of minority groups, often by tending to define merit in terms of verbal agility rather than ability to perform on the job. The United States Court of Appeals for the District of Columbia found, for example, that the now-abandoned Federal Service Entrance Examination, which was supposed to measure mental abilities, including verbal skills, reasoning, and conceptualizing, probably was biased against black applicants. One reason was a lack of job-relatedness, that is, a lack of correlation between examination scores above the failure level and the quality of performance on the job.[17]

Uses of Ignorance

Now and then the government sells off an asset. If there is no way of knowing what a fair price is there is no way of holding officials accountable for possible gross miscalculations. Nowhere has this kind of ignorance been more carefully tended than in the Department of the Interior, the custodian of millions of acres of offshore oil and natural gas fields and of oil shale fields in the West. Interior's practice has been to sell leases to the tracts without knowing their worth, and without knowing how much it may cost to produce oil or gas from them. No other country has raised ignorance to this level. The particular sales technique is known as bonus bidding and essentially involves leasing to the highest bidder. Under a royalties approach, in contrast, the government would share in whatever revenues were earned, thus substantially overcoming the disadvantage of initial ignorance.

Interior's preposterous *modus operandi* drew useful attention in 1974 from the Subcommittee on Activities of Regulatory Agencies of the House Permanent Select Committee on Small Business. At one hearing, subcommittee chairman John D. Dingell (D–Mich.) brought out that the department secretly had appraised eighty-nine tracts in the Gulf of Mexico at a grand total of $146,051,000—only to see them bring $1,491,617,000, more than ten times as much—at an auction on December 20, 1973. Among the tracts were thirty-five that the department appraised at an identical $144,000 each—but one brought $91,617,000, or 637 times as much; another brought $76,827,000, or 533 times as much. It may appear that the department did well and that the bidders overpaid. Possibly. But Congressman Dingell suggested that the opposite may have been true. Among the eighty-nine tracts, for example, were nineteen on which only one bid each was received —and was accepted despite the proved unreliability of the department's secret pre-sale appraisals. Dingell also noted that on the relatively few occasions when the department has rejected initial bids and put out new invitations to bid three months later, it has gotten prices averaging thirteen times higher the second time around.[18]

Dingell's suspicions were reenforced by an investigation made by subcommittee investigators William F. Demarest, Jr., and Peter D. H. Stockton of the lease of an oil shale tract in Colorado in January 1974. Gulf Oil and Standard Oil of Indiana won the lease with a joint high bid of $210.3 million. This was indeed a lot of money, especially when compared with the secret valuation which the Department of the Interior had put on the tract. At a hearing after the leasing, the valuation turned out to have been a paltry $5.6 million. But wait. Dingell had a computer analysis made showing that the tract actually could be worth up to $1.5 *billion*, or 268 times more than the department had calculated. "An immensely valuable public asset was turned over to oil industry control for a fraction of its real value," the congressman said.[19]

Interior Department officials admitted to Dingell that they have always relied completely on the oil and gas industry for vital figures on production and have never asked Congress for funds to audit the industry data. Congressman Silvio O. Conte (R–Mass.) likened this reliance to "putting a fox in to watch the chicken coop." "You have a legitimate statement there," replied John B. Rigg, the department's deputy assistant secretary for minerals. He noted that it was long before he joined the department that it had begun to adopt as official government statistics the data supplied by the American Petroleum Institute and the American Gas Association. The AGA and other industry sources consistently and sometimes drastically have underestimated the extent of natural-gas reserves. In March 1974, for example, the staff of the Federal Power Commission reported on a study showing that fields discovered in Louisiana in 1971 and 1972 contained new reserves of 4.8 trillion cubic feet—54 percent greater than the AGA estimate of 3.15 trillion. Such underestimates, on which the FPC relied in increasing wellhead prices, served the industry well: the synthesized shortages at once helped to force up prices and to increase pressures for de-regulation in a noncompetitive industry.

Expertease

In government and corporate bureaucracies, in news media, and in numerous other areas of life, reliance on the putative expert is a perennial cop-out on accountability. If his advice turns out to be bad, the person who asked for it and relied upon it has someone besides himself to blame (and if the advice turns out to be good, the expert may find himself shouldered aside). Experts are at times indispensable and at other times catastrophic; they are manipulated and manipulable. The problem always is to know which experts to believe, about what, and when.

"The government economists were just dead wrong about the rate of inflation, the budget deficit, the price of oil, the price of food, and dozens of other vital economic predictions," Senator William Proxmire (D–Wis.) said in July 1974.[20] At about this time, the Pentagon's experts were saying that they needed a budget of $95 billion and not a dime should be cut by legislators who could not possibly judge such arcane matters. But other experts—including a former secretary of defense, two assistant secretaries, two admirals, and a general—were saying the budget could be cut $14.9 billion without any weakening at all of the national defense.[21]

Experts in World War I insufficiently appreciated the terrible power of the tank against troops unequipped to cope with them. Experts in World War II were confident the Germans could be bombed into submission; instead, their will to resist was strengthened. Experts told President Kennedy the Bay of Pigs would succeed. Experts said the war in Vietnam would end in 1966 . . . 1967. Sir Robert Thompson, known as "the British expert on guerilla warfare," once declared, "Now, in March 1963, I can say, and in this I am supported by all members of the mission, that the (South Vietnamese) government is beginning to win the shooting war against the Viet Cong." In June 1965, Sir Robert made another pronouncement: "If the United States is resolute the prospects could be transformed in a year or two." And in 1975, when the war in Vietnam was all but over, he was raging at those who would refuse further military aid to South Vietnam.[22]

It is unfair to single out the military. True, war is much too serious a matter to be entrusted to them, as Georges Clemenceau said. But is it not also too serious a matter to be entrusted to "the best and the brightest"?[23] Indeed, most any really serious matter should not be uncritically entrusted to those who purport to be experts in it. In medicine, for example, physicians —supposed experts—needlessly prescribe and overprescribe lethal drugs, while surgeons remove healthy organs. In the legal system, expert justices of the Supreme Court frequently split five to four. Expert witnesses—psychiatrists, appraisers, hand-writing specialists—give contradictory opinions. In communications, a story that one editor will put on page one will be deemed totally unnewsworthy by another.

The pitfalls of uncritical reliance on experts were hilariously illustrated in a paper presented in 1972 by Dr. Donald H. Naftulin, John E. Ware, Jr., and Frank A. Donnelly. They hired an actor to pose as a fictitious "Dr. Myron L. Fox," equipped him with a phony but impressive *curriculum vitae* appropriate to his distinguished appearance and authoritative manner, and coached him to deliver a one-hour lecture and answer questions "with an excessive use of double talk, neologisms, *non sequiturs*, and contradictory statements. All this was to be interspersed with parenthetical humor and meaningless references to unrelated topics."

The title of the lecture was "Mathematical Game Theory as Applied to Physician Education." Dr. Fox had three audiences. The first consisted of eleven psychiatrists, psychologists, and social-work educators gathered for a teacher-training conference. A videotape was made and shown to eleven mental health educators—psychiatrists, psychologists, and psychiatric social workers—and finally to thirty-three educators and administrators, including twenty-one with master's degrees. Each person who listened to Dr. Fox's mutterings and ramblings about game theory was at the end given a written questionnaire to fill out anonymously. In all three audiences the favorable responses far outweighed the unfavorable. A person in the second audience actually claimed to have read the lecturer's publications. None detected the lecture for what it was.[24]

Advisory Committees

The federal government has about 1,500 advisory committees. Some are simply arms of a particular industry. An extreme example is the National Petroleum Council. The secretary of the interior appoints its approximately 155 members. Of this number, as of early 1975, 140 had ties to the petroleum industry which, in fact, paid for its $1.3 million budget. Its chairman, John E. Swearingen, was also chairman of Standard Oil Company (Indiana). Its mission is to advise the Department of the Interior and the Federal Energy Administration on national energy policies. Senator Lee Metcalf (D–Mont.), who has done more than any other legislator to straighten out the whole advisory committee situation, has cited two other extreme examples of government-sponsored infiltration of itself by industry:

1. The National Industrial Pollution Control Council. President Nixon

created it in April 1970 to advise him and the chairman of the Council on Environmental Quality, through the secretary of commerce, on industrial pollution problems. His appointees were top executives of sixty-three major polluting companies; none represented public interest groups of any kind. The council set its first meeting for October 14, 1970, but did not announce it, denied entry to environmental groups that had heard about the meeting, and refused to release a transcript. "The next gathering, in February, 1971, convened in the State Department building, where security regulations prohibit entry of non-employees without special arrangements," Metcalf said.[25]

2. The Defense Industry Advisory Committee, as it was called when Secretary of Defense Robert S. McNamara established it in 1962, but the Industry Advisory Committee (IAC) since 1968. The defense secretary is chairman; all of the other twenty-three members are defense contracting executives. Little is heard about the IAC, which forbids members to talk about it publicly without the secretary's consent.[26]

In the Food and Drug Administration and in its parent Department of Health, Education, and Welfare, the use of outside advisory committees has been closely examined by the House Intergovernmental Relations Subcommittee. The findings are mixed. On occasion, an advisory committee has taken an advanced, courageous stand and has either won or been denied support by the government. On other occasions, an advisory committee, either on its own initiative or under pressure from HEW or the FDA, put a prestigious imprimatur on an unwise action or policy. In 1965, in a pointed reminder that an advisory committee can make it easy for an official to avoid accountability, William S. Warren, dean of the Columbia University Law School, said that an FDA commissioner was likely to adopt the advice of an expert panel "without the soul-searching critical analysis to which he would subject the same recommendations from his own official staff, even if that staff consisted of the very same experts."[27] In 1970, the subcommittee's parent Committee on Government Operations, in a report on subcommittee hearings on HEW's use of an advisory panel on cyclamates, the artificial sweeteners, said that the department had improperly used the advisers "to make recommendations on matters that had already been decided, involving a basic issue which the advisory body was not qualified to decide."[28] Congressman L. H. Fountain (D–N.C.), the subcommittee chairman, said in summing up, "Excessive and/or improper use of advisory committees is wasteful, illegal, and may well destroy the incentive and morale of an agency's career personnel. It is important, also, that a regulatory agency such as the FDA not use advisory committees for the purpose of diffusing executive responsibility for difficult regulatory decisions, or as a means of having someone ratify a decision they have already made."[29]

The FDA provided a case history of how an agency that has made a highly questionable decision can go about trying to get it ratified by outside advisers who doubt the wisdom of doing so. The agency in 1967 approved the sale of Inderal (propranolol) for the treatment of irregular heartbeat. Physicians in growing numbers then began prescribing it for angina pectoris, a manifestation of severe heart disease. By 1972, they were prescribing the drug more often for this use, which the FDA had *not* approved, than for the use the agency had approved. What troubled doctors was that without FDA approval of Inderal for angina they faced heightened liability to claims of malpractice that might be brought by injured patients. As a result, cardiologists built up pressures to have the FDA change the labeling of Inderal to recommend its use in angina. Finally, the manufacturer, Ayerst Laboratories, formally asked the FDA to legitimize the use of Inderal in angina.

The FDA was legally free to comply only if Ayerst were to supply substantial evidence of effectiveness in the form of at least two well-controlled studies done by qualified experts. The company agreed to seek such evidence in 1970—and hadn't produced as of mid-1975. Meanwhile, however, it supplied thirty-three studies which the FDA's Bureau of Drugs gave to its six-member Cardiovascular and Renal Advisory Committee for evaluation. Dr. J. Richard Crout, director of the Bureau of Drugs, told the committee he believed Inderal to be effective in angina—a way of asking it to ratify a decision he had already made. But the conscientious committee found that the thirty-three studies, neither singly nor in their totality, met the requirement for substantial evidence. There was also concern in the committee about Inderal's safety, because of data indicating that users had a higher rate of congestive heart failure than nonusers, and also because of evidence that chemically related drugs—so-called beta blockers—might be carcinogens. At the same time, the committee was concerned about the pressures from the FDA and cardiologists to legitimitize Inderal's use in angina, and also about the fact that physicians were persisting in using the drug in angina patients without the benefit of any well-considered advice on how to do so. The FDA did not tell the committee that it would be legally impermissible, in the absence of well-controlled studies demonstrating effectiveness, to revise the labeling for Inderal to recommend it in angina. Not knowing, the committee gave the FDA all the ratification it needed: it said the labeling should be changed so as to guide doctors in the proper use of Inderal in angina, if they insisted on using it in the absence of proof of efficacy.

The committee took this action at a meeting on April 13, 1973. Its views and concerns were recorded. Congressman Fountain obtained a transcript and put it in the record of a subcommittee hearing. He and the subcommittee's investigators, Delphis C. Goldberg and Gilbert S. Goldhammer, established with the transcript that the minutes of the meeting—prepared by an official of the Bureau of Drugs—were incorrect and misleading, because of their erroneous claim that the advisory committee had concluded that the data available to it "establish" Inderal to be "safe and effective under certain conditions of use for the treatment of angina pectoris." The Bureau of Drugs followed up in January 1974, by misrepresenting the committee's views to the medical profession, saying in a bulletin to doctors that the committee "has now recommended approval and the agency has accepted the recommendation."[30] In this way, the FDA made an able and well-meaning advisory committee accountable for what truly was the agency's own decision to circumvent the drug law.

Disarming Consumers

A consumer product commonly carries a label or tag saying that it meets the standards of, or is approved by, Underwriters' Laboratories (UL) or some other similar organization. The intent is to impart assurance that the item meets rigid standards, particularly for safety. Then, if the product turns out to create an electrical or fire hazard, the user is more inclined than he might have been otherwise to blame the fates, rather than to hold accountable a manufacturer who had complied with UL's criteria. The National Commission on Product Safety, which looked into UL, found that this nonprofit standard-setting organization had a "generally constructive record," but that it was significantly flawed. In its final report to Congress and the President before it disbanded in June 1970, the commission said:

Thousands of television sets which caught fire were manufactured to meet UL standards. The Hankscraft vaporizer, cited for scalding children, bore the UL label. A charcoal igniter described as lethal at our Chicago hearing was UL certified. The Little Lady toy oven, described in our Interim Report as reaching temperatures of 660° on the inside and 300° on top, was made in conformity with UL standards. Consumers Union tested 29 portable electric heaters certified by UL and rated 15 of them "Not Acceptable" for . . . safety reasons . . . (Footnotes omitted.)[31]

The commission said that in some of the cited cases UL "had tried to upgrade the applicable standard but had met with opposition from affected manufacturers." Moreover, UL has been "relatively independent of the manufacturers who finance its work. . . . Nonetheless, its president says it must 'successfully walk the tightrope of responsibility' between setting standards too high to be acceptable to manufacturers and permitting an unacceptable number of injuries. The problem of drafting an acceptable standard is also locked into the capacity of the manufacturer to produce and the willingness of the consumer to pay."[32]

Automobile owners in the early 1970s were spending $25 billion to $30 billion annually on maintenance and repairs. Much of this spending was occasioned by rip-offs for which no effective accountability seemed to be generally available. One case in point is "captive" parts—those for which the sole sources are the car manufacturers, who use annual model changes and other anticompetitive devices to deter potential rivals from entering the market. When a Chrysler Airtemp home air conditioner was retailing for $148 in a competitive market, one had to pay almost as much mainly for a piece of sheet metal in the form of a hood for a 1968 Chrysler Newport— an uncompetitive $101.90 for the hood itself, plus $37.30 for hinges and other parts. When you could buy an intricate Frigidaire (General Motors) dishwasher for $229, you had to pay $236 for a bumper assembly for a 1969 Buick. When you could buy an upright Philco (Ford Motor) freezer for $166, you had to pay $238.85 for a front door for a 1969 Mercury.[33]

How to Pay Others to Make You Happy
When They Take Your Money

As a boy, one of the authors worked in a grocery. Beer and soda then were sold only in reusable bottles. A customer made a deposit of two cents per bottle; the store paid two cents per bottle brought in. The empties thus acquired were held for beer and soda dealers in a garage at the rear of the store.

A time came when a couple of youngsters with large numbers of empties appeared for refunds several times in a couple of days. They collected relatively substantial sums. The proprietor became suspicious. He began to keep an eye on the garage. Finally he caught the boys stealing bottles for which refunds already had been paid and carrying them around to the front of the store for further refunds.

Various modern enterprises have refined the boys' crude technique. They first extract excessive sums from the public for whatever product they happen to provide. Thus enriched, they shrewdly invest a portion of the excessive income in propaganda to persuade the public not only to be content with its lot but even to welcome the opportunity to part unwisely with still more money. It is as if the bottle thieves had been able to persuade the proprietor to make them more efficient.

Public utilities play an old version of this unaccountability game. Their goal is to charge high rates to customers, who, of course, have no other source of electricity. At the same time, the power companies do not want to stir their customers to anger lest they make trouble with regulatory agencies. The utilities traditionally have resolved the problem by spending tens of millions of dollars a year on institutional, or "good will," advertising campaigns, although the rationale is opaque for monopolies promoting services for which no competition exists. Thus, consumers who have paid too much end up paying more for propaganda designed to influence them to pay still more.

If such advertising can be justified at all, the stockholders ought to pay for it. This sensible pro-accountability view in fact was adopted by the Oklahoma Corporation Commission in December 1973, although broadcasters and others benefiting financially from the advertising overturned the ruling in the Oklahoma Supreme Court. In Iowa, the state Commerce Commission in January 1975 ruled that power companies could run promotional campaigns, but that the stockholders—not the customers—must pay for them. This ruling was final. Later in 1975, the State of Connecticut did by legislation essentially what the Iowa Commerce Commission had done by regulation.

Within reasonable limits, brand names serve a legitimate and useful role in commerce. Frequently, however, they inflate prices unjustifiably. Part of the excessive revenues thus generated pay for the advertising that undergirds and perpetuates the inflated prices. Consider bananas. "The consumer does not know United Fruit bananas from any other kind of bananas and, therefore, doesn't care whose bananas she buys," the advertising agency of Batten, Burton, Durstine and Osborn said in a report apparently prepared for United Fruit Company. "Assuming that the quality of bananas is comparable, the lowest price bananas get the sale." The report went on to say that United Fruit (later United Brands) must "build consumer preference for its own brand" of bananas to make them "bring a price higher than they would normally get."[34]

United settled on the brand name "Chiquita." Advertising copy was written. Jingles were composed. A Chiquita label was affixed to each promoted banana. And higher prices were charged—*and paid.* For 1964, the Chiquita advertising budget was set at $6 million. The target price premium was 20 cents per box over unbranded bananas. The first seven months of 1964 "bore out the company's hopes," William Robbins wrote in *The American Food Scandal.*

Its Chiquita bananas were selling for 14 to 23 cents a box more than all other, unbranded United Fruit bananas. At retail, for the full year, Chiquita bananas were getting about 30 per cent of the market at about 10 per cent higher than other bananas.

For 1965 the company set a still higher goal: increased volume and 50 cents a box extra for the branded bananas. . . .

The results were even better than United Fruit had dared hope. It was getting 84 cents a box more for Chiquitas that year than for its other bananas, compared with 63 cents for the full year of 1964. The reason, of course, was the effectiveness of the device of brand-name promotion, as a consumer survey showed. Of women interviewed, 49 percent said they looked for Chiquitas when shopping for bananas; 27 percent said they would ask for Chiquitas by name, and 25 percent said they would even go to another store looking for Chiquitas if the store in which they were shopping did not have them in stock. . . .

Some of the results were disquieting. Consumers who were most receptive to advertising claims were among those who could least afford to pay a premium price for a product that had no essential advantage of quality. Among the most ill-used victims, those who tended most often to buy the Chiquita brand when they bought bananas, were low-income blacks in the inner cities.[35]

In 1967, United's branded bananas were bringing 97 cents more per box at wholesale than unbranded—and a consumer survey showed that 53 percent of shoppers looked specifically for Chiquitas.[36]

Clientism

Clientism is the process by which a person who is accountable to one interest transfers his loyalties to another interest with which he supposedly has an arm's-length adversary relationship. It sometimes springs from pure motivation, but frequently it silently frays what should be taut lines of accountability. The classic example is the regulatory agency that regulates in behalf of the regulated rather than the public.

But the problem reaches into private organizations affected with public-interest responsibilities. News media are an important example. James H. McCartney, of the Washington Bureau of Knight Newspapers, has told of a dispute that arose in Chicago between the Federal Bureau of Investigation and the Chicago Police Department. Each thought it was owed the principal credit for the capture of a notorious narcotics peddler. "City editors all over town were getting two distinctly different versions of what happened from their men in police headquarters and those on the federal beat," McCartney said. "The late Clem Lane, city editor of the *Daily News*, finally threw up his hands in exasperation. 'Haven't we got anybody around here any more who hasn't got an ax to grind?' he cried." His frustration was occasioned by the police reporter siding with his friends, who considered FBI agents to be overpaid "glory hunters," and by the federal reporter siding with *his* friends, who felt that "the police were 'dumb cops' who would have let the peddler escape."

McCartney correctly saw parallels throughout the news business, certainly including Washington, where "[s]ome of the most influential reporters

... have deep vested interests in their beats or in their specialities—so deep that they have as much difficulty in presenting objective views as the two Chicago reporters." Some of the examples McCartney gave, in 1963, have become dated, but his point certainly has not. Washington reporters in significant numbers are still permitted or subtly encouraged or pressured by their organizations to be cronies of the powerful, to feed softball questions to the President or the secretary of defense or the secretary of state, and to be "ins" who play along with news sources, rather than "outs" who when necessary run the risk of being ostracized.[37]

The toilers in the laboratories of unaccountability, as we have shown, are fecund and tireless. Those who seek accountability, in contrast, become preoccupied with yesteryear's problem while new and sometimes graver ones accumulate unnoticed. There is much groping in the dark. If a remedy is conceived, the gestation period is likely to be extremely long; and even if born, remedies frequently prove to be frail, inadequate, or regress masquerading as progress. Witness:

Over the decades, millions of persons were killed or injured in automobile accidents. A large proportion of this toll was avoidable—the result of needlessly unsafe vehicle design. But the accidents were not a cost to auto manufacturers. Consequently, they had scant incentive to adopt safety features made possible by various technologies. With all other institutions turning their backs, there was no accountability for the vast bloodshed. Finally, in 1966, the government intervened with the National Motor Vehicle Safety Act. But there is doubt whether such a law would have come into being until much later had it not been for the bizarre circumstance that General Motors was caught snooping into the private life of Ralph Nader for having dared to demonstrate that the Chevrolet Corvair was unsafe.

It took a twenty-five-year fight to win enactment of the Pure Food and Drugs Act of 1906. Huge loopholes swiftly were opened. For example, an amendment in 1912, which had been advocated by Parke-Davis, said that to be violative, patent-medicine labels had to be false *and* fraudulent. This effectively legalized the false statement, because establishing fraud requires the proving of something very difficult: *intent* to deceive.[1] We coasted along until the late 1930s, when an "Elixir of Sulfanilimide" caused 108 deaths, including the suicide of its developer.[2] Only then did Congress at last enact a law—the Food, Drug, and Cosmetic Act of 1938, which, for the first time, required manufacturers of prescription medicines to provide evidence of safety in advance of marketing. Not until massive publicity a quarter-century later attended thalidomide, the sedative that caused the birth of thousands of limbless babies around the world, did Congress tighten the 1938 safety requirements and finally require manufacturers to provide "substantial evidence"—derived from adequate and well-controlled investigations—that their 1938-and-after medicines were effective in the uses for which they were recommended. The National Academy of Sciences–National Research Council later found that only 12 percent of all of the 1938–1962 products fulfilled all of the claims made for them, while 15 percent fulfilled none.[3]

On September 26, 1969, on a volleyball court at the Indiana State Reformatory, 208 inmates—all but one of them black—were staging a sit-in in protest against the refusal of authorities to meet certain demands. Guards opened fire with 12-gauge shotguns, killing two and wounding forty-six of the inmates. Eleven victims filed a civil suit accusing nine guards and two prison officials of having used undue force. On November 26, 1974, a jury returned a verdict in favor of the prisoners. An account in the *New York Times* the next day included these paragraphs:

Experts in the prisoners' rights movement say that only *in the last year* have juries across the country begun to award damages to inmates who have been the victims of brutality by prison officials or employees. . . . Last February, in one of the first cases involving the award of damages to inmates, a Federal jury ordered two Baltimore City Jail guards personally to pay $8,000 in damages to four former inmates.

The jury had found that the guards had stripped three of the inmates before handcuffing them to overhead pipes and had beaten the fourth inmate as punishment for being noisy during the jail's sleeping hours.
(Emphasis supplied.)[4]

With disturbing frequency, remedies for unaccountability are put forth and adopted that prove to be significantly regressive, but become entrenched, anyway. The prisons again provide a case in point. The notion caught hold that prisons should be denominated "correctional institutions." These would "rehabilitate" an inmate and thus deter him, on his release, from relapsing into "a life of crime." Most states then empowered judges to sentence a convicted man not to a fixed term, but to an indeterminate one, say, one year to life. Prison and parole officials then must decide when the convict has reformed and should be let go. This was held out to be humane and progressive—and it was, in theory. In practice, however, it turned out to be inhumane and repressive.

The indeterminate sentence, Jessica Mitford said in *Kind and Usual Punishment: The Prison Business*, is "the perfect prescription for at once securing compliance and crushing defiance, because the prisoner is in for the *maximum* term and it is theoretically up to him to shorten the time served."[5]

Roosevelt Murray is a living example. He was joy-riding in a stolen car in Baltimore, was arrested, was tried and convicted, and could have been punished with a harsh but fixed sentence of four years. Instead, a judge sentenced him, in 1958, when he was seventeen, to an indeterminate sentence in Maryland's Patuxent Institution for "defective delinquents." This category, says Joseph Whitehill, a novelist and long-time volunteer teacher of a "Great Books" course at Patuxent, is "so loose and impressionistic that one could remove the entire present population tomorrow, scan and select from the main body of men in Maryland prisons, and come up with 500 *new* 'defective delinquents.' "

Whitehill long had advocated the indeterminate sentence, believing it to be logical and humane. "But," he told Jessica Mitford, "by the time I had talked man-to-man with some hundreds of inmates who were under it, I began to hear what was wrong. Logical or not, the inmate hears 'forever' and despairs. The indeterminate sentence is a frank statement of the naked, absolute power of the state. In this it differs in no significant way from the gas chamber. The man under indeterminate sentence has all the negotiating options of a cornered rat."

Roosevelt Murray was cornered in Patuxent for sixteen years. While there he was convicted and sentenced for assaulting a social worker. In February 1974, a Baltimore County jury held that Murray was no longer a "defective delinquent," and so he was transferred to the Maryland state penitentiary to serve the balance of his sentence for assault. The state freed him on September 2, 1975, three days after his thirty-fifth birthday. He had served half of his life as a prisoner.

"Nowhere has the indeterminate treatment model been carried to greater sophistication than in California, where the prison system is larger and more complex than in any other state," Leroy Aarons wrote in the *Washington Post.*

And perhaps, nowhere else is its failure more apparent.

California pioneered the indeterminate sentence system, creating in the process a massive treatment establishment. In the forties and fifties the state was hailed as a model of progressive prison administration, an image that still lingers.

The real picture is less flattering.

California has the largest adult prison population, the longest terms, and more prison violence than almost any other state in the nation. Much of that record can be traced to the indeterminate sentence and its ramifications.

California in the mid-1940s pioneered a parole process overseen by the Adult Authority (AA), which Aarons called "a glorified parole board appointed by the governor and traditionally composed of ex-policemen and prosecutors. . . . The AA has the autonomous power to judge prisoners' rehabilitation progress or lack of it and the power to set or not set release dates—all of it accomplished behind prison walls with no right of appeal." This is of course unaccountable power, ceded in the name of liberal reform. The result, Aarons said, is that the AA

is the most hated and feared body in the system. It is not unheard of, for example, for an inmate serving five years to life for robbery to wait 15 years without having his final release date because of his failure (often unexplained) to impress the AA with his progress, or for being what that body concludes is a "troublemaker."

A dramatic example of its power occurred in 1970, when, in a reform mood, AA began setting release dates at a high rate. The state's prison population dropped from a high of 28,000 in 1968 to 19,000 in 1972.

In that same year, the Reagan administration, responding to the Attica rebellion in New York and growing turmoil within California's prisons, ordered a "get tough" policy on releases. The AA abrubtly reversed course, driving the prison population back up. As of early this year, [1975] California prisons held 25,000, roughly one in every 10,000 residents in the state—a per capita level 1½ times as high as New York's and twice that of Pennsylvania.[6]

The assumption on which the AA for thirty years had exercised its terrible politically influenced power over the lives of thousands of human beings was, it will be remembered, that vocational and psychological "rehabilitation" would have benign effects on prisoners and, by extension, on the society to which they would return. But an important study in 1970 by sociologist Robert Martinson produced the unexpected conclusion that "with few and isolated exceptions, the rehabilitative efforts . . . have had no appreciable effect on recidivism." In reporting this, Aarons noted that New York State, which had commissioned the study, suppressed Martinson's report "for five years before it was dislodged by court order."

By the late 1960s, the Post Office Department was swiftly deteriorating. The public was justly dissatisfied because it was constantly being asked to pay more for less. Politics infested Post Office operations: Congress was appointing postmasters, through patronage, at the rate of 3,000 a year. Presidents chose postmasters general but cared little what they did. Finally a presidential study commission was appointed. Much thought was given to reform. What finally emerged, in 1970, was a law creating the United States Postal Service, a government-sponsored enterprise with many of the freedoms of a private corporation and with politics—in the form of patronage appointments of postmasters—eliminated. But politics in other forms remained. When the time came to issue the first quarter-million dollars in Postal Service bonds, part of the business went to Dillon Read & Company, whence came Peter M. Flanigan, a fixer in the Nixon White House. Certain high-paying legal work had to be done: the Postal Service picked Mudge Rose Guthrie & Alexander, the law firm whence came Richard Nixon and Attorney General John N. Mitchell.[7]

Congressman Morris K. Udall (D–Ariz.), who played a major role in bringing the Postal Service into being, and who had high hopes for it, said in 1974, with anguished disappointment, "the system we created isn't working." One reason is that it is a monopoly—and monopolies "tend to do as they please when they discover they have no real competition . . ." Another reason is that the employees also have a monopoly:

They know, on one hand, that they can put tremendous pressure on public executives and legislators when they want to, usually when they want their way in a dispute over a labor contract. At the same time, given the lack of competition, they have no really effective source of outside pressure to make them perform in the most responsive manner for the public. The only way they can be brought to act responsively and responsibly is by making them feel motivated to do so.[8]

Udall's disappointment was shared by, among others, James H. Rademacher of the National Association of Letter Carriers. "The federal postal monopoly should be earned," he said, and "we, and by we I mean the Postal Service, are not earning it. You now have the situation where 90 per cent of the letter boxes in the nation are uncollected between Friday noon and Monday morning. . . . We are acting like monopolists and not getting any better."[9]

Some of the consequences of abandoning a postal operation with minimal accountability for one with near-zero accountability were reported in 1974 in the *Washington Post* by reporter Ronald Kessler after a searching investigation:

1. The Postal Service "has deliberately slowed delivery of first class mail and has overcharged first class mail users by an apparent $1 billion a year while undercharging commercial mail users . . ."

2. "Delivery of first class mail—the class used by most Americans for letters—has been slowed by a Post Office policy of putting aside mail arriving from out of town during the night for sorting during the day."

3. There is no way of knowing whether a letter you mail one day will reach its destination the next day or the next week, partly because sorting machines have error rates as high as 17 percent.

4. By changing its method of calculating costs, the Postal Service transformed a $152 million loss on third-class ("junk") mail into a $407 million profit—and thus was enabled to claim that first-class mail was not subsidizing third-class. But the new method system failed to show true costs, according to the General Accounting Office and the chief administrative law judge of the Postal Rate Commission.

5. The Postal Service "is spending $1 billion to build parcel sorting facilities that promise slower and more damage-prone service than the agency's parcel post competitor, United Parcel Service," and it has spent $49 million developing a mechanized system for sorting letters that, by its own account, is slower than hand sorting.

6. After adopting purportedly cost-conscious policies, the Postal Service

incurred cost-overruns of more than $140 million on contracts that were awarded mostly through negotiation rather than competitive bidding, which is generally the most inexpensive technique for procurement. The 1970 law does not require competitive bidding.

Under the old system, postal revenues went into the Treasury. Congress —535 bosses—then annually appropriated monies needed by the Post Office Department. Whatever may be said of it, the system at least had some residual *potential* for accountability. Under the new system, Congress will be making appropriations, without having control, until 1984, when the Postal Service is supposed to become self-sustaining. One way or another, Congress must take responsibility for making the Postal Service accountable. This, in turn, requires, first of all, a drastic reorganization of the present board of directors, one which recognizes that ability and dedication do exist outside the corporate executive suites that until now have been overrepresented.

Developments such as the Postal Service raise a perturbing question: Do we learn? We do, occasionally, but never, it seems, enough—and rarely with the essential speed, scope, reliability, or permanence. Yet it would be wrong to leave the impression that all is gloom. Important progress *is* being made in certain areas. No more important pro-accountability development could be cited than public-interest law, which is practiced in behalf of protection of the environment, of equitable taxation, of public health, and of other necessitous causes, including the poor. "Rather than dream of taking power," Simon Lazarus said of public-interest lawyers, "they are working on mechanisms to check power."[10]

Early in this century, Henry L. Stimson left a Wall Street law practice to become a United States attorney and, under new regulatory laws, prosecute corporations. From what he had seen of the law, he said, "wherever the public interest has come into conflict with private interests, private interest was more adequately represented than the public interest."[11] Lazarus, in his book *The Genteel Populists*, said, "The same speech could easily have been made by any of the young lawyers clustered with [Ralph] Nader and in satellite 'public-interest law firms' around Dupont Circle in Washington, D.C., or by their more cautious colleagues who have induced private law firm employers to work on individual public-interest projects."[12]

The traditional social landscape has been heavily populated by those who pursue wealth and thinly by those who forswear it to serve God. With Nader to inspire them, even though no one matches his twenty-hours-a-day, rooming-house, solitary, ascetic dedication, a corps of public-interest lawyers— and other professional and lay persons—has emerged. These people, predominantly young, sacrifice material advantages not in religious orders, but in endeavors to help an amorphous public. They provide a priceless offset to the interests that have millions of dollars to spend on lobbying, campaign contributions, publicity campaigns, and other techniques designed to continue pollution, to fight mass transit, or to engage in other dubious activities. For their work and achievements, the public-interest organizations—and the foundations and citizens that support them—are owed an incalculable debt. No brief listing can do justice to them, but here are some of the areas in which they have been effective: the safety of products, ranging from automobiles to medicines; the safety of the environment, ranging from pesticides to nuclear power; safety on the job, ranging from mine accidents to the dangerous decibel levels of newspaper presses; the professions, ranging from promiscuous use of X-rays to anticompetitive practices of lawyers; and freedom of information, ranging from secret reports on unwholesome meat to secret reports on emergency cooling systems in nuclear reactors. The persistent difficulty is in finding a constant source of funds to represent the unrepresented in a society in which fortunes are made representing the overrepresented.

One of the most important innovations, which came into being under Nader's tutelage in 1970, and which does have a steady source of funds, is the Public Interest Research Groups (PIRGs). These now operate on dozens of college campuses. Tens of thousands of students each permit ear-marking of a fee of two dollars or so for a PIRG. While relying on student funding and on student volunteers, each PIRG hires full-time supervisory professionals. The PIRGs take on a huge variety of projects that reflect the special needs of the particular state in which each is located. Environmental concerns and inequities in public-utility rates have been among PIRG preoccupations.

Most states have delegated regulation of the occupations they license wholly to the practitioners—doctors, lawyers, dentists, real estate brokers, morticians, optometrists, and the like. The results were predictably abusive of accountability, particularly price-fixing. In recent years the Antitrust Division of the Department of Justice has been attacking this particular evil with impressive success. A case in point involved the Oregon State Bar, which quite typically issued uniform fee schedules, in particular, the 1969 "Schedule of Minimum Fees and Charges," and the 1973 "Schedule of Suggested Fees and Charges." Oregonians needing legal services had no choice but to pay fees which at the very least were influenced by the state bar and the thirty-seven hundred members who were collecting in excess of $150 million annually for legal services. This was "an ideal factual situation for application of the most basic antitrust principle—that any tampering with price is illegal, per se," the division said in a suit attacking the schedules. Responding to the suit, which was filed in May 1974, and which was the first to accuse a state bar organization of denying the public the benefit of competitive pricing, the state bar claimed to be "not amenable to charges of violating the Sherman Act." Why? Because, it said, it is "an instrumentality of the State." Unable to sustain a claim that the state had licensed the "instrumentality" to engage in professional price-fixing, the state bar pledged to issue no more fee schedules, and the case was dismissed.

A variation on the basic theme was played by the Alabama Optometric Association. This estimable organization managed to persuade the Alabama Legislature in 1965 to change the law so that an optometrist who examined eyes or fitted eyeglasses *as an employee* automatically was engaging in "unprofessional conduct" and, by action of the Alabama Board of Optometry, could lose his license. The Lee Optical Company employed thirteen optometrists who were not members of the Association. In October 1965, the association accused them of practicing their profession illegally. Two days later, the board went to court for an injunction to enjoin Lee Optical from engaging in "the unlawful practice of optometry." The real issue underlying such grotesqueries was of course the lower prices charged by outfits like Lee Optical as compared with those charged by independent optometrists. In litigation that eventually went to the Supreme Court, Lee Optical and the employee-optometrists finally prevailed.

By estimate of Consumers Union (CU), merely the restrictions on price advertising imposed on optometrists by state regulatory boards cost consumers, in 1974 alone, $457 million. On March 17, 1976, CU took a major step in behalf of consumers victimized by such practices. It filed a suit in United States District Court in Philadelphia under which optometrists and all others in licensed occupations no longer would be permitted to monopolize their particular state regulatory boards. The key claim in this test case was that consumers have a constitutional right to be eligible for membership on such boards. Opening up the boards to consumers could not help but advance accountability.

In a mountain hollow in West Virginia, the Pittston Company, which is the largest independent coal operator in the nation, mined coal, processed it to separate out impurities, and dumped the refuse into a pile across a stream. The pile grew into a crude massive dam 400 to 500 feet long, 450 to 650 feet wide, and 44 to 60 feet high. Behind the dam the company impounded a sea of black muck—coal-waste water and sludge. Below the dam lay the narrow, nineteen-mile-long Buffalo Creek Valley. Spread across it were sixteen small communities, or "coal camps," with a combined population of approximately 5,000.

At 8 o'clock in the morning of Saturday, February 26, 1972, without warning to the people of the Valley, the dam collapsed. A black wave twenty to thirty feet high surged down toward the coal camps. Sometimes traveling at thirty miles per hour, 130 million gallons of rampaging water became engorged with crushed and splintered homes, telephone poles, automobiles, and other debris. Immediately below the dam was Saunders, a hamlet of twenty homes and the Free Will Baptist Church; it was totally demolished. Many persons died immediately when the rampaging water and sludge engulfed their homes. Many others died when the debris to which they clung was slammed into railway trestles and highway bridges that crossed the Valley floor. At Crites, homes trapped by a trestle splintered into stakes that impaled several; more than twenty bodies eventually were found there. The final death toll was 125. Most of the victims were women and children who had been unable to struggle out from under the debris and thick muck.

Few among the valley people suffered serious physical injuries; they either were killed or escaped to high ground. But the deaths of relatives and friends and the destruction of the close-knit Buffalo Creek community inflicted severely disabling emotional and mental injuries on survivors. Gerald M. Stern, a partner in the Washington law firm of Arnold & Porter, and author of *The Buffalo Creek Disaster,* explained why:[13]

First, there were horrible scenes of death which these men, women and children saw around them as the waters receded and the mangled bodies of the dead appeared. In many cases, the survivors at first could not even identify members of their own family because the slimy black coal waste made them unrecognizable. Bodies of three young children were never identified. . . .

Many of the 4,000 uprooted and homeless survivors were so isolated by the disaster that they did not know for days whether their relatives and friends had survived. For many days thereafter, small groups of survivors huddled around isolated fires on the sides of the Valley trying to find warmth and shelter, waiting for rescue. Other survivors found temporary shelter in schoolhouses at the end of the Valley or even further away.

Once the immediate rescue efforts had been completed, most survivors were moved into temporary trailers . . . Life in these trailer camps, or "concentration camps" as they were called by the survivors, only exacerbated their feelings of loss, particularly loss of community. The trailer camps were not formed so that inhabitants of a former village would be living side-by-side with the same members of that hamlet. Rather, the surviving families were randomly placed, by number, in trailers next to families who were often strangers to them.[14]

The survivors had a clear legal right to sue Pittston for traditional damages —for the death of family members, for physical injuries, for the loss of their homes and property, and for the loss of their possessions. In the bloody annals of corporate negligence, few companies were more vulnerable than Pittston. In building the refuse pile, Pittston had disregarded federal and state laws, proper engineering practices, and the lessons of the failure of three of its own black-water dams since 1955 (including one in which a man and his three children were trapped in a house). After a slag dam at Dola, West Virginia, failed in 1967, Pittston's own insurers refused even to consider renewing its policies for damage by its dams unless it would get a report and opinion on the dams from independent engineers. This would have cost $500; Pittston never bothered.[15]

Thirty-six hours before the collapse at Buffalo Creek, the mining operations had been visited by three top Pittston officials: John Kebblish, executive vice-president—coal; Irvin Spotte, president, Pittston Coal Group, and James Yates, chief engineer of the Coal Group. Despite heavy rains, they neither inspected the dam nor ordered an emergency spillway installed. Some of the residents, in contrast, had become exceedingly fearful that because of the rains the dam would fail. They were so concerned that they sought to have the National Guard called in to warn people who were in peril. But Stephen Dasovich, the Pittston Coal Group vice-president in charge of the Buffalo Division, thwarted their efforts, assuring residents and county sheriff that the dam was sound. Later, when he saw the dam fail and a hamlet wiped out before his eyes, he broke down. He had to be taken to a hospital in an ambulance.

The majority of survivors settled their claims for traditional damages in a traditional way at the coal company's claims office. Ultimately, they collected more than $826 million. But a community of 625, made up of 160 families decided to seek legal aid from outside of West Virginia and asked Arnold & Porter to represent them. Gerald Stern, the partner who took charge of this public-interest case, was one of the lawyers who went immediately to Buffalo Creek to begin interviewing survivors. He quickly found that they had deep emotional and mental injuries, the magnitude and significance of which were awesome. Small children refused to let their mothers bathe them because they feared drowning.[16] Older children insisted on sleeping with their clothes on because they feared they might have to flee their beds for high ground.[17] A young man who was in the county jail when he learned that his entire family had been wiped out, became uneasy at the first sound of rain and developed a chronic skin rash and a severe drinking problem.[18]

Stern decided to try and expand a traditional lawsuit to include damages for mental agony. With the help of psychiatrists, particularly Dr. Robert J. Lifton, who had studied the survivors of Hiroshima, Stern and his associates devised the concept of "psychic impairment." This embraced not only the psychiatric injuries suffered by survivors, including the man who had been in jail, and others who had been in hospitals and even in other states, but also their loss of communality, which had been identified by sociologist Kai Erikson.

The most difficult legal question was whether Pittston was legally accountable to the survivors, even if a jury were to find that the disaster for which Pittston was to blame had caused their psychiatric injuries. "Traditionally, the law does not permit recovery for psychiatric injury *merely* because that injury can be proven to have been caused by another person or persons," Stern explained.

For example, a mother who sees and hears a truck run over and kill her child may suffer severe psychiatric trauma, but the law traditionally has denied the mother recovery for her own suffering, terming her a mere "bystander." Needless to say an individual seeing a friend killed has even less chance of recovery in the courts for mental suffering.[19]

Stern argued that "each resident of the Valley, even those not there that day, were direct victims of the coal company's reckless conduct, and not mere bystanders." United States District Judge K. K. Hall agreed. All survivors, even those outside the Valley at the time of the disaster, he ruled, could collect for mental injury if their lawyers could convince the jury that the coal company's conduct was reckless—more than merely negligent—and that the recklessness caused their mental suffering. With the legal precedent established under which the court would not be bound by concepts of space and time in cases of mental suffering, and with Pittston recognizing that the court would dismiss none of the psychic impairment claims, the company agreed to settle for $13.5 million, with the allocation of the money among the 62 survivors to be decided by their lawyers. After making payments for wrongful deaths, property losses, and the like, the lawyers had $6 million left for distribution to the plaintiffs for psychic impairment. Using a point system based on each survivor's immediate involvement in the disaster, his mental disability, his loss of community ties, and the disruption of his way of life, the lawyers, after deducting expenses and legal fees, were able to give each survivor between $7,500 and $10,000 net, and to put approximately $2 million in a trust fund for the 224 plaintiffs who were children under 18. The money was distributed in August 1974. Pittston's profits in the preceding five years exceeded $136 million.

For Pittston to be unaccountable—to disregard federal and state laws, proper engineering practices, past dam failures, and its underwriters—was easy. Indeed, Stephen Dasovich had "designed" the dam by drawing a rectangle on a piece of paper.[20] To make Pittston accountable required not only a catastrophe, but the devising and acceptance of a legal breakthrough.

VIII

The Press:
Unaudited Power

Setting the Agenda

The only way that democracy can be made bearable is by developing and cherishing a class of men sufficiently honest and disinterested to challenge the prevailing quacks. No such class has ever appeared in strength in the United States. Thus the business of harassing the quacks devolves upon the newspapers. When they fail in their duty, which is usually, we are at the quacks' mercy.

H. L. Mencken
Minority Report: H. L. Mencken's Notebooks

But I suppose in the end newspapers cannot be free, absolutely free in the highest and best sense, until the whole social and economic structure of American life is open to the free interplay of democratic processes.

William Allen White
Address at Wharton School of Finance,
University of Pennsylvania

Newspapermen have a special obligation to retain public confidence through conscious and deliberate effort to open ourselves to the public, to pay particular attention to complaints of unfairness, inaccuracy, bias, vindictiveness—that is, to make ourselves voluntarily accountable.

John B. Oakes
New York Times

News, like beauty, is in the eyes of the beholder. News, to strip the point of euphemism, is what the press—publishers, broadcasters, editors, reporters—say it is. We do not suggest that the death of a President, say, conceivably could be defined as non-news, just as Charles Evans Hughes, when he said the Constitution is what the Supreme Court says it is, did not mean to suggest, for example, that the State of New York conceivably could be entitled to three United States senators and each of the other states to only two. Hughes was looking to the vast expanse between absurd extremes, and so are we. The Supreme Court has a charter to interpret, and so does the press. It decides what news is, what to report and what to ignore, what to play up and what to play down, what story to stay with and what story to abandon. There is in the press a tendency to pretend otherwise. The pretense is encapsulated each morning on the front page of the *New York Times:* "All the News That's Fit to Print." The implication is that the news is a package that has but to be wrapped and delivered as if by United Parcel Service. This notion, in addition to assaulting reality, diverts attention from an absolutely crucial fact: to decide what news is, is to exercise substantial power.[1]

Was it news that the air we breathe was being poisoned by the exhausts of tens of millions of motor vehicles? In most cities the press paid no serious attention until the poisoning was far advanced.[2] Was it news when modern, properly functioning treatment plants were discovered to be letting disease viruses into tap water? Precisely one radio and one print reporter were present when the Environmental Protection Agency disclosed this in March 1972, at the first hearing on the purity of drinking water held by the Senate since 1893; on the same day, the *New York Times,* unrepresented at the hearing, had a staff of about eighteen in Wisconsin for the presidential primary.[3] Was it news that ten million Americans were hungry? A great many of their fellow citizens learned of this only because CBS decided it *was* news and produced "Hunger in America," a television documentary, which was shown May 21, 1968. With an average of one thousand Americans per day dying of cancer, was it front-page news when government data showed that the rate of increase in cancer mortality was 5.2 times normal in the first seven months of 1975 (this was, it turned out, a peak in a trend toward abnormally high rates of increase over a period of a few years)? Not in the *Washington Post,* which broke the story.[4]

Was it news that some three million Americans migrated from farm to city between 1957 and 1964? The mass media paid little heed.[5] Was it news in 1961 when twenty-nine defendants in the price-fixing conspiracy case against General Electric, Westinghouse, and twenty-seven other manufacturers of heavy electrical equipment pleaded no-contest or guilty? Of twenty-two major newspapers examined by the *New Republic,* only four thought the story worthy of page one, while four carried nothing about it.[6] Was it news when two scientists discovered that Freon propellant in aerosol sprays might be having a calamitous effect on the ozone layer in the upper atmosphere? The University of California at Irvine thought so and sent a press release to, among others, the Los Angeles bureaus of three nationally circulated newspapers and three nationally circulated news weeklies. None printed a word, with the result that the findings did not become public knowledge for about two months, until the scientists reported them in person at a scientific meeting.[7]

Air. Water. Food. Cancer. Migration. Corporate Crime. The ozone layer. These examples suffice to make the point: the press determines what news is. Walter Lippmann said the press is "like the beam of a searchlight that moves restlessly about, bringing one episode and then another out of the darkness into vision."[8] To operate the searchlight is to exercise substantial power.

Whoever in a democracy exercises substantial power must be answerable. This is our central contention. The press cannot be exempt. Under the First Amendment, which is priceless, the press cannot be—must not be—answerable to government. But to assess or audit press performance is merely to exercise First Amendment rights, which are no one's monopoly. The great problem in assessing and auditing the print and electronic media that, for most Americans, are the predominant sources of news, is the inadequacy of existing mechanisms, within and without news organizations. These mechanisms turn a generally dim light on the searchlight operators. The public sees what the searchlight sees, but is itself poorly equipped to pierce the surrounding darkness.

How can an assayer assay the handling of news of which he is unaware? Can the public sensibly entrust total responsibility to press owners and managers? Imputing to them nothing but good faith, are their perceptions and judgments that sound? Consider: The first recorded automobile fatality occurred in September 1899. Over the next fifty-seven years, the number of motor-vehicle deaths exceeded 1,125,000, not to mention many, many million injuries. Press coverage consisted overwhelmingly of nothing more than episodic reports of accidents—"Three persons were fatally injured yesterday when their car [the make and model usually unidentified] went off a road and crashed into a tree. . . . "—and of endless and virtually useless exhortations to drive safely. On July 16, 1956, Congressman Kenneth A. Roberts (D–Ala.), showing more curiosity than the press establishment, opened public hearings—the first of their kind—on the role in the slaughter played by automobile design. Expert witnesses testified that the auto industry had the capability to design cars so that occupants could survive crashes that were routinely fatal, and to lessen the severity or eliminate injuries. Lay news media gave the hearings absolutely negligible attention.

In 1965—some 450,000 highway deaths later—Senator Abraham A. Ribicoff (D–Conn.) opened hearings that generated much excitement because they included an unexpected development: General Motors had been caught "snooping" into Ralph Nader's private life. Only then did the importance of safe vehicle design begin to be reported forcefully enough to make it sink into public awareness—and to produce the auto safety law of 1966. "To

THE PRESS: UNAUDITED POWER

enlarge the audience on a congressional issue can be to change the outcome,"
David R. Mayhew said in his perceptive *Congress: The Electoral Connection.* [9] But the press fails even to try to enlarge the audience for dozens of
important issues while managing quite well to expand it for various entertain-
ments that preempt news resources. Like most business organizations, news
enterprises are generally organized along authoritarian lines, although their
special nature—and the nature of many of the people in them—leavens and
softens the situation in many cases. Internal accountability runs upward—
from reporter to editor, from editor to manager, from manager to owners.
The owners' first concern is to make the enterprise survive and prosper.
Frequently, in the past, this concern got so out of hand as to make many
owners accountable to their advertisers at high cost to their readers. This is
understandable. One need but realize that many news and editorial operations which are low in quality pay off in huge profits in a largely recession-
proof business.

In 1974, for example, pretax profits of television networks and stations
were reported by the Federal Communications Commission to be $737.1
million—12.9 percent ($84 million) more than in 1973. That year's $653.1
million, in turn, was 18.3 percent higher than 1972; and 1972 profits were
41.9 percent higher than 1971. The networks alone did even better. After
enjoying profit increases of 106.5 percent in 1972 and 66.6 percent in 1973,
the three commercial networks enjoyed profits in 1974 of $225.1 million, up
21 percent ($40.3 million) from 1973. "The 13 publicly owned newspaper
companies [which also have broadcast and other interests] last year [1974]
earned an average of 8.5 per cent of their revenue after taxes, compared with
a little over five per cent for industry at large," Lee E. Dirks, a leading analyst
of newspaper stocks, pointed out. [10] Also in 1974, the financial performance
of ten publicly held newspaper companies was among the top five hundred
companies in all industrial classifications, and an unnamed big-city daily,
regularly monitored by *Editor & Publisher,* enjoyed a profit margin before
taxes two and a half times that of American industry as a whole. Executive
compensation also is impressive. The combined income of the chairman and
president of the Times Mirror Company, the conglomerate owner of the
Los Angeles Times, was $558,078; of the Gannett Company, the chain that
owns more American newspapers than any other, $455,000; of Dow Jones
Company, which publishes the *Wall Street Journal,* the *National Observer,*
and *Barron's,* $391,214; of Knight-Ridder Newspapers, the circulation
leader among American newspaper chains, $340,000, and the Washington
Post Company, owner of the *Washington Post* and *Newsweek,* $405,000.

Over the years, the *New York Times* has spent enormous amounts of
money on its news operations that, in a purely commercial sense, were

wasted. That the *Times* has done this, and that partially in consequence it has consistently shown one of the smallest profit margins in the industry, is a high tribute to its president, Arthur Ochs Sulzberger, and members of his family who preceded him in *Times* management. This record surely licensed managing editor A. M. Rosenthal to charge that "American journalism is not spending enough time and space—which means money—to report properly on the world, or the nation." In a lecture in April 1975, in which he referred to radio and television stations as "usually gold mines," Rosenthal said, "Constitutionally and pragmatically there cannot be a limit on the amount of money a business can earn, except in certain windfall situations." But, he said, "I do believe that since they have constitutional protection under the First Amendment, that publishers, stockholders, and owners of TV stations and networks have a moral or ethical obligation to define for themselves how much is enough."[11] Few will do it. What reason is there to think otherwise when, in 1975, after two world wars, the Korean conflict, and the debacle in Southeast Asia, "only a half dozen or so" newspapers, by Rosenthal's own count, had foreign reporting staffs?

Wars and their prologues and aftermaths aside, many foreign countries, the Scandanavian being foremost, have for many, many years been on the frontiers in dealing innovatively and often successfully with some of the most vital problems that face us in the United States. Had there been adequate comparative journalism we might have had forewarning against approaches that failed elsewhere, and we would have had some targets to shoot at.

The problems we have in mind include housing (no slums in Sweden); the environment (the Scandanavian countries have a unique treaty under which a citizen of one who is damaged by pollution originating in another acquires, for litigation purposes, citizenship in the country that was the pollution source);[12] occupational health and safety (coal-mine safety advanced far more rapidly in several countries, including Czechoslovokia and Poland, than in the United States);[13] mass transportation (fine new subway systems serve Mexico City, Munich, Montreal, Toronto, and Budapest; some German buses burn diesel fuel in uncongested areas, but switch to electricity in congested ones);[14] delivery of health-care services (we heard much about Britain's problems, little about Scandanavia's successes); day care of children (East Germany is said to have one of the best systems);[15] prescription medicines (Norway minimizes confusion among physicians by restricting marketing of redundant medicines); title insurance (in Britain, the government keeps the records, certifies titles, and charges small fees which accumulate in a public insurance fund that pays off for any mistakes that may occur);[16] anticompetitive conduct (in West Germany, enforcement of antitrust laws sometimes makes our own seem like weak tea);[17] health insurance (under a plan later copied in other Canadian provinces, Saskatchewan established and administers and subsidizes universal health insurance);[18] the elderly (British Columbia established a guaranteed income for persons sixty and older, and for the handicapped);[19] automobile insurance (British Columbia, again, set up a provincial government agency with the exclusive right to sell auto insurance—at cost, and under the no-fault concept; Saskatchewan and Manitoba also have province-owned auto insurance corporations);[20] treatment of criminals (the brutality that pervades our system, starting with long, long sentences, is in sharp contrast to the much more humane practices in numerous countries of Western Europe); and the humanization and democratization of work (much pioneering work has been done in Scandanavia, England, Germany, and Yugoslavia).[21]

In 1976, as in past presidential-election years, major American news organizations are spending large sums interviewing voters to find out what they think. Not enough will be spent on the primary mission of the press, which is to provide voters with the facts they need to know—including facts on how other countries cope innovatively with problems that here seem intractable.

The pressures first to survive, and then to prosper and then (questionably) to acquire other enterprises, are relentless and universally understood. But what of First Amendment responsibilities, such as not skimping on money for news, or not flinching from antagonizing advertisers should need arise? Here, as A. M. Rosenthal made clear, the pressures are seldom relentless, and, indeed, the need often goes unperceived. Among the pressures that may be truly countervailing, none are more important than the conscience and dedication shown by some—too few—owners and managers. Among large news organizations, none are more justly noted for consistent courage, high ethical standards, and sustained and progressive innovation than two sister newspapers in Kentucky, the morning *Louisville Courier–Journal* and the afternoon *Louisville Times.* They are a privately owned monopoly operation, enhanced by television and radio stations, and so they closely mirror the personal qualities and standards of two men, Barry Bingham, Sr., board chairman, and Barry Bingham, Jr., editor and publisher. The Binghams have been the country's pacesetters in devising and implementing safeguards against conflicts of interest in the press.

In 1967, the Louisville papers became the first in the nation to appoint a readers' advocate, or ombudsman, to investigate complaints of bias, inaccuracy, or omission with editors and reporters. When warranted, John Herschenroeder, a former city editor of the *Courier–Journal,* writes a correction that is promptly and conspicuously printed. Not until five years later did the *New York Times* begin to publish corrections in the same prominent place.

Herschenroeder handles 4,000 complaints a year for his papers, which in 1975 had an average daily circulation of 214,000 in the morning and 168,000 in the afternoon.

In 1974, the *Louisville Times* named a full-time media critic, Bob Schulman, who had had almost thirty years' experience in newspaper, magazine, radio, and TV journalism, who is known for his balanced but tough judgments, and who has a highly refined sense of ethics. "What better combination of talents for a person to evaluate the performance of your chosen profession?" Barry, Jr., said in a personal letter to William J. Miller, a former editorial executive of *Fortune, Life* and the *New York Herald–Tribune.* "And yet most publishers cringe at the very thought. Little do they know that their readers are, daily, tearing their hair and vomiting up their breakfast coffee in rage over some inaccuracy, or misrepresentation. . . . Those people have the adrenalin but probably not the expertise to criticize us in the most productive ways. What can be more useful than having it done by an expert?" Bingham also saw in the arrangement clear advantages to management—a commentary on how enlightened one can be about self-interest: "And, believe me, as good as [an owner thinks his] newspapers or broadcast stations are, a good critic can find faults which is exactly what he should be doing. As a management tool for improving your product, it has few equals. As a way of telling your reading or viewing public about the quality of your product and [that] you welcome reasoned criticism from any source (and have hired a source to perform that function) it is unparalleled."[22]

Bingham wrote the foregoing letter in March 1975, about a year after Schulman began writing his twice-weekly column, "In All Fairness," in which he has taken his own newspaper and the *Courier–Journal* to task. He also has taken Bingham himself to task. Soon after the column began to appear, two reporters for the papers were arrested at a motel for snooping outside a closed meeting of the Fraternal Order of Police (FOP), of which most local policemen are members. Barry, Jr., waffled. He said the reporters' tactic had been "morally wrong. Period." But in assuming responsibility, Bingham praised their "vigorous enterprise and competitive spirit," qualities he associated with journalistic excellence. Moreover, Bingham said, the public had a vital interest in the purpose of the closed meeting—to discuss with the police chief his improper and possibly illegal bugging of a police car as part of an investigation of possible police corruption. Consequently, he reasoned, the public's right to information "at least" rivaled the FOP's right to privacy. Schulman did a column on this. Running with it was a staff-drawn cartoon showing Barry, Jr., at a podium carrying a sign saying, "Message Snooping Is YUK," while behind him two reporters sneakily eavsesdrop at a door marked "FOP." Schulman's tone was no less acerbic.

Summing up Bingham's position as, "The end justifies the means," Schulman said: "Does that sound right coming from newspapers that have consistently rated the Nixon White House as 'sleazy and amoral' for having excused improper acts to achieve the ends sought?" Bingham, the *Wall Street Journal* reported, had a "characteristic response . . . that Mr. Schulman wasn't tough enough on him. 'Instead of asking a rhetorical question, he should have come right out and said I was wrong,' he says."[23]

The bottom line on conscience and dedication is a willingness to accept, consistently, a low rate of return. In Louisville they run at about 3 percent of sales—a rate most owners, particularly in publicly held corporations, would view as unacceptable.

The Binghams—who have not expanded outside of Louisville—are of course not alone in showing courage and dedication. In the face of clear and present dangers to the valuable broadcast properties of the Washington Post Company, Katharine Graham, the chairman, made the brave and supremely important decisions to publish the Pentagon Papers and to support the *Washington Post*'s continued investigation into the Watergate scandals.[24] In Alabama, the *Montgomery Advertiser* and *Journal* for years have been digging out major scandals involving or touching Governor George C. Wallace. Other outstanding newspapers include the *Des Moines Register,* and the *Minneapolis Tribune.* Many others are excellent in certain areas. If quality and financial success were to correlate in some sensible way, which they do not, many more of the eyes of Texas would turn to the *Texas Observer* and to other fine monthlies, such as the *Progressive* and the *Washington Monthly,* and to the weekly *Nation* and *New Republic.*

Internal accountability that relies preponderantly on the conscience and dedication of owners and managers is simply not good enough, and not only because too few owners and managers have enough conscience and dedication enough of the time. Many if not most of them, honorable persons, to be sure, tend to become insensitive to the cares and concerns of ordinary people. This is less true of news staffs. They ought to have a voice in the selection of top editors. This is not to impute to staffs superior wisdom or superior anything, but merely to say that accountability for professional performance should not, as it does in most news enterprises most of the time, run so heavily to those who are primarily businessmen with the formidable power to hire, fire, demote, promote, and transfer, and so lightly to news persons whose true status is that of employees, but who in most cases try to conduct themselves *as if* professionals.

Meanwhile, many owners and managers comfortably insulate themselves from the tonic stimulus of knowledgeable questioning on fundamental issues, such as the allocation of resources to the inconsequential, possible kow-towing to advertisers or special or political interests, definitions of news (blacks might be especially sensitive to this, because their plight was long considered to be non-news), and the handling of news about one's own enterprise that concerns the outside community. Repeatedly, for example, networks and broadcasters have ignored hearings on, objections to, and the course of legislation designed to immunize them from effective challenges to their licenses to use the public's airwaves. Writing in 1974 about a bill that would extend the duration of a license from three years to five, and that also would reduce the potential for license challenges, John J. O'Connor of the *New York Times* began: "If all goes according to the plan of the National Association of Broadcasters, chief lobbying arm for the broadcast industry, the script might make an interesting TV series called 'the Great American Ripoff Machine.' It could be the program that asks the question: How do you make a powerful industry almighty?"[25]

As things stand, the condition of internal accountability is generally parlous. Most news establishments, including some of the best, refuse even to undertake serious and systematic two-way communication with staff. They leave to divination such basic questions as: How does the organization define its mission? How well is the mission being performed? Could performance be improved? Yet the prevailing shortages of working mechanisms for internal assays would matter much less were the press to be subject to external audits and assessments. A. M. Rosenthal explicitly recognized this in his lecture. Each day, he said, large quantities of significant news flow into newsrooms across the country but are never aired or printed—the result of conscious decisions by editors "to throw the news away . . . because time and space are money and they can get away with it." Rosenthal emphasized that readers and listeners let them get away with it:

The consumer who would raise hell if he were short-changed at the supermarket or who found himself buying watered milk says nothing and does nothing to try to persuade the local editor or publisher or broadcaster that he does want to know what is going on in the world or the country even when there is not a disaster or crisis taking place.[26]

In a scattering of communities, conscientious publishers have launched news councils as vehicles for citizens' appraisal of their performance. To our knowledge, however, nowhere have rank-and-file citizens, on their own initiative, established mechanisms for sustained and systematic assays—untainted by the evils of ax-grinding or attempted intimidation—of how their newspapers and broadcasters perform their news missions; nowhere (to our knowledge) have members of unions or churches, say, increased dues slightly to pay some competent, independent person to be their media assayer.

To be sure, such mechanisms could harbor seeds of nasty threats to press freedom and independence. Bigots might take them over. Complaints might be pressed by those who want to close their eyes to unpleasant facts or views. Those who do not understand the role of a free and independent press may be annoyed at the refusal of a news medium to "get on the team." Those who want mainly to be entertained may weary of a fibrous diet of news— but presenting the news is what the press is supposed to do. On balance, however, we believe that, in most communities, press performance would improve if, for example, public television stations each were to engage an experienced, fair-minded, and independent former news person to critique press performance, once or twice a week. Public officials submit to questions from the press. Should press owners and managers—who also exercise substantial power—be immune from audit? Why should they remain, as Arthur E. Rowse, a long-time press critic, put it, "essentially unexamined by anyone, including themselves"?[27]

"One thing I just don't understand about the press is its sensitivity," Barry Bingham, Jr., has said. "If publishers would only garb themselves in the hide which most politicians have developed after years of press treatment, we wouldn't be so annoyed by the occasional rocks which will come crashing through our glass houses."[28]

In recent years, it is true, there have been notable improvements. Press criticism has become routine in some newspapers, including the *Washington Post*, the *Washington Star*, and the *Los Angeles Times*. The press has become a reporter's beat at the *New York Times*. Press criticism in magazines, once the almost exclusive province of *Time* and *Newsweek*, now is standard fare in the *Village Voice*, the *Washington Monthly*, *New York*, *Philadelphia*, and the *Washingtonian*. On television, the CBS Morning News now features regular press criticism; so do some radio stations, including WTOP in Washington. The *New Yorker* carries incisive critiques of television. Publications devoted entirely to press evaluation, especially *Columbia Journalism Review* and [*More*], have won growing audiences outside as well as inside journalism.

Commendable as they are, all such efforts are too little, too late. Few publishers have started press councils, as was noted, although the idea has been around a long time. Some news organizations, including the *Washington Post*, are cooperating with the new National News Council, which studies complaints about news coverage and publicizes its finding, and which is supported by foundation money; but the *New York Times* and the *Chicago Tribune*, among other powerful media, oppose it.[29] Few news organizations have ombudsmen. Few show interest in commissioning critics who are free to indulge in even-handed criticism of their own news products.

Press evaluation in magazines seldom focuses on the large numbers of newspapers and television stations that, for tens of millions of Americans who live outside the great metropolitan areas, constitute the primary source of news. Journalism reviews have highly limited circulation outside the news business, some have died for want of money (including, in the fall of 1975, the important and most useful *Chicago Journalism Review*), and others are in financial peril. Few newspapers assess TV news performance, and such assessments, overall, have tended to center on coverage of catastrophes or extraordinary events rather than on matters of special concern in the states and communities. Local television stations that audit newspapers—which give reams of free publicity to TV fare—are fewer still. If there is a common denominator that may be stressed, it is that one of the most fundamental issues is one of the most neglected: How and for what purposes are news resources—manpower, space, time, money—used? Much is written about how various stories are covered; little is said about stories that are not covered at all. Yet the omitted stories are frequently far more important, and to readers, although not necessarily to news executives, more interesting.

The uses to which a newspaper puts its front page (or a television network its news headlines) is a guide to the degree of fealty it gives its high trust. A paper may have the most able, conscientious, and educated reporters, but this is of "no use if editors play their output down," Jonathan Power, an economist and journalist who lives in Britain, has said.

When The Guardian two years ago [in 1973] decided to lead on its front page with the story of the wage levels of South African black workers it created a furor whose course has not yet run.

A parliamentary committee was established. The Cabinet, both in Britain and South Africa, discussed it. And in many cases wage levels moved dramatically upward. However, it was not a new story. The essential facts had been known for decades. Yet its presentation was such as to force the issue to the top of the agenda.[30]

After many years of press-watching, one of the authors was moved to formulate Mintz's Mass Media Proposition. In unveiling it, in 1974, at the A. J. Liebling Counter–Convention, a media event sponsored by [More] he left himself numerous escape hatches, saying that the proposition is not an axiom, not a law; that it is full of loopholes; and that it should not be carried to extremes. Despite the qualifiers, he said (and still believes), the proposition has a hard core of validity. Here is the proposition in unexpurgated form:

If it's really important, it doesn't get the attention it deserves, or gets it late, or gets it only because some oddball pushes it. Nuclear power plants. Filthy food plants. Cancer-causing food additives. Pesticides. Auto safety. Occupational health and safety. The safety of consumer products. Medicines. Oral contraceptives. The safety of IUDs and other medical devices. Fire prevention. The purity of drinking water. Pollution of public waters. Air pollution. The environment. Subversion of the Constitution. Secret wars. Government secrecy. Corporate secrecy. Election-campaign financing. The poor. Pensions. No-fault auto insurance. Health insurance. Life insurance. Welfare for corporations. The tax structure. Defense contracting. Economic concentration. The costs of monopoly. Administered pricing. Multinational corporations. The professions. The news media. Congress. And the regulatory agencies.[31]

During the thalidomide catastrophe in the early 1960s, British women who had taken the sedative in early pregnancy gave birth to 425 children who were armless, legless, or without limbs altogether, and otherwise deformed. The drug had been marketed in Britain by a subsidiary of the Distillers Company. Initially, suits for damages were filed by parents of sixty-two of the children, acting together and retaining a single firm of solicitors. Once legal action commenced, the case was *sub judice*, i.e., subject, under British common law, entirely to court control. Public reporting or comment beyond the texts of complaints, responses, and open-court proceedings was prohibited. Such restrictions on publicity are the rule in England; the intent is to protect the right to a fair trial. As is customary, settlement negotiations were undertaken behind the scenes. These went on intermittently for four years while evidence was assembled and other trial preliminaries were taken care of. In 1968, on condition that the plaintiffs would withdraw allegations of negligence, and taking into account ambiguities in English common law about fetuses, Distillers offered to settle for 40 percent of the sum that might be awarded were there to be a verdict of negligence. The parents' counsel advised acceptance of the offer. Distillers then agreed to divide $2.8 million among the sixty-two families—an average of $45,162.

In an account in the *Columbia Journalism Review*, Alfred Balk told how reports of the settlement stimulated the filing of 370 additional claims—"perpetuating *sub judice*"; how "the press generally remained behind its wall of self-censorship, carefully avoiding stories about matters before the courts"; and how the London *Daily Mail*, in December 1971, did carry two investigative stories about the travails of parents, including a father who contended he was being "legally blackmailed" into accepting inadequate compensation for his limbless nine-year-old daughter. "Distillers had just announced six-month profits of £35 million ($87.5 million), and was offering to establish over a ten-year period a trust fund of £3.25 million ($8.1 million)," Balk said. This figured out to a crude average of $22,000 per child—a pathetically meager sum. Balk continued:

According to the father, art dealer David Mason, [plaintiffs'] lawyers had presented the offer in strictest secrecy, warned that no money would be paid unless every parent agreed, allowed only ten days to decide, and provided only a half-hour for parents to ask questions. When the Masons and five other sets of parents held out, the lawyers threatened to request appointment of substitute legal guardians who would sign on their behalf.

"I call this legal blackmail," Mason told Longmuir [Harry Longmuir, the *Daily Mail* investigative reporter]. "I refuse to accept that British justice will allow a massive company to push people around like this."

A day after that story, the *Daily Mail* was threatened with contempt of court on grounds that publicity might lead Distillers to withdraw its offer. When the Attorney General followed with a threat of a formal complaint, the *Daily Mail* was silenced.

At the *Sunday Times* of London, Harold Evans, the young editor, was, he has said, "really galvanized" by the meagerness of the settlement, and by the threat to Mason by the parents' own lawyers. In 1967, at his direction, the *Sunday Times* already had done much—paying a pharmacological expert to advise thalidomide parents, paying another source $12,500 for documents that German authorities had obtained in connection with a prosecution of the German manufacturer, Chemie Grunenthal, and publishing a 7,000-word story on Chemie Grunenthal's role in the marketing of thalidomide. Now, Evans said, "I sent for David Mason, and I was impressed with him. I said past legal advice be damned, we must find a way to go ahead." The way—devised by James Evans (no relation to Harold), the brilliant young counsel for Lord Thomson's Times Newspapers, of which the *Sunday Times* is an independently edited unit—was, Balk wrote,

the ingenious approach of campaigning on moral—not legal—grounds: *legal* negligence (denied by Distillers and still to be resolved in court) aside, did not the corporation even if vindicated have a *moral* responsibility to children its products had harmed?

On September 24 [1972] the paper crossed the Rubicon: it published a story headlined, OUR THALIDOMIDE CHILDREN: A CAUSE FOR NATIONAL SHAME, along with an editorial, CHILDREN ON OUR CONSCIENCE.

The article and editorial pointed out that the Distillers offer amounted to less than 10 percent of 1971 after-tax profits, a sum "grotesquely out of proportion of the appalling injuries the thalidomide children suffered." The drug was "a symbol of the havoc that a technically complex society can wreak," the paper said. And the case revealed an urgent need for "major reforms in our legal system. . . . It shames our society that a decade should have passed. . . . It shames the law that the compensation proposed should be so low . . . The Government must act. The adversary system will not do."

A footnote promised a "future article" on how the tragedy had occurred. The paper never printed it because of a formal complaint made by Distillers' counsel to the attorney general. Editor Evans got a warning that publication of anything more bearing on the litigation could result in a contempt action. The attorney general asked to see, and was shown, the "future article"—and then got an injunction to prevent publication; he also got a High Court censure of a television station that covered Evans' campaign. Since then, litigation over injunctions has involved the *Sunday Times* almost continuously. But Evans helped to bring about a full-scale debate on the issues in Parliament, where members repeatedly castigated Distillers and the government. To increase the pressure, the paper published a list of Distillers' major institutional shareholders and other owners who might have preferred to be at a distance from Distillers sufficient to disinfect their dividends. Balk wrote:

About the same time individual stockholders began requesting a special meeting. Some of Distillers' largest shareholders—Britain's two biggest insurance companies, a major bank, and other institutions—publicly endorsed the idea, a supermarket chain banned Distillers products from its shelves; a Labor M.P. introduced a bill to impose an implicit safety warranty on all drug manufacturers, distributors, and sellers. In nine days Distillers' shares fell $70 million on the London Stock Exchange.

The pressures were too much for Distillers. Finally, in 1974, it increased its offer to $50 million—eight times more than originally had been offered —with each family to get $12,000 at once and with the balance to go into a trust designed to assure the children a lifetime income. Evans and the *Sunday Times*, in a country with what he terms a "half-free press," had persevered in the face of the gravest risks. Their achievement was magnificent. In the United States, where there are no comparable risks, rarely does a major unit of the American press take up a comparable cause against a great corporation. The necessary moral sensitivity often seems to be lacking.

The press commonly exposes some atrocity and then stops, failing to explore deeper ramifications, disdaining commitment, and tiring quickly of an issue. Evans didn't rest; he led the *Sunday Times* to far frontiers, including examination of how medicines get to be marketed, how handicapped persons of all kinds are treated, corporate secrecy, and the awful disabilities of the legal and judicial system. "The four or five people who worked on the case at the *Sunday Times*—admittedly a high order of journalists—have prepared a better case against Distillers in twelve months than was prepared by the Queen's Counselors, lawyers, and solicitors over a whole decade," he said.

Evans and the *Sunday Times* were able, as he put it, to force the thalidomide children "into the conscience of the country." That is to say, they exercised the "real power" of the press: to "create an agenda for society." This is an exquisite formulation of what the press is always doing, whether by commission or omission, by emphasis or deemphasis. The power to create an agenda is substantial. It should be clearly understood. That is a prerequisite for useful auditing and assessment.[32]

32   Overseeing the Overseer of the Overseer

In the time of Calvin Coolidge and Herbert Hoover, "the Federal Executive, business and the press were united," John Kenneth Galbraith said in *The Liberal Hour.* "These are the times in our democracy when all looks peaceful and much goes wrong."[1] Philosophically, this is an endorsement of the separation of powers, of which the press is *de facto* one. When it identifies with Presidents, governors, or local politicians, or with any special interests, as it is too often wont to do, it is poorly situated to seek accountability, or even to provide essential support to others who may seek accountability.

This takes us to a peculiarly important point: with the attention it gives or withholds, the press can profoundly affect how well or how poorly existing mechanisms for accountability perform. Uppermost in our minds is Congress, which has oversight responsibility over the Executive branch.

We need not emphasize here that Congress has gravely defaulted on its oversight responsibilities, this being glaringly obvious in regard to the CIA, the FBI, and the Internal Revenue Service, for example. Our immediate concern, rather, is with press neglect of the oversight Congress *does* perform.

A brief scene-setting: The President is one person, the initiator, perceived as *the* leader of the nation; Congress is 535 persons, the reactor, perceived as a conglomeration. The press fell into a "habit of worshipping Presidents [that] is hard to break," columnist Anthony Lewis has observed. "After Vietnam and Watergate and all the warnings about the Imperial Presidency, the networks still build up a White House press conference as if it were going to produce tablets from Sinai. The newspapers give massive display to what the President says. The magazines weigh his every word."[2] In contrast, a few committees and subcommittees on Capitol Hill consistently do arduous, solid, important, well-researched oversight, only to find that if one or two faithful reporters happen to have another assignment, a cold, or a day off, their hearings may go entirely or largely unnoted. One of the authors said in a lecture in 1972:

For more than a decade, the House Intergovernmental Relations Subcommittee, headed by Representative L.H. Fountain, has audited the performance of the FDA [Food and Drug Administration] in assuring the safety and efficacy of all sorts of medicines—antibiotics, antidepressants, oral contraceptives, intravenous solutions, diuretics, the cholesterol-lowering agent MER/29, muscle relaxants—prescribed for tens of millions of us. My memory could be betraying me, but I do not remember seeing at a single one of these hearings a reporter for the news weeklies, the networks or the Washington bureau of any major newspaper chain or principal newspaper other than the [then] *Washington Evening Star.*[3]

Similar examples of limited coverage could be cited in regard to a host of other important matters, including hearings on oil-import quotas that cost the motorist five cents per gallon of gasoline, auto safety, pesticides, drinking water, multinational corporations, and de-regulation of natural gas. Sometimes stories on such hearings are written, but are waylaid on their way to readers or viewers by editors who judge them less important than other material. Their reasons are rarely explained and in many cases appear to be inexplicable, but often induce reporters to move to greener pastures.

The net effect on congressional oversight is chilling because Congress, Walter Pincus pointed out in the *New Republic,* "tends to think that nothing happens unless it appears in the press . . ."[4] Indeed, some of the ablest legislators say privately that they tire of holding hearings that produce useful information that the press ignores. For that reason, Capitol Hill aides sometimes schedule hearings only after trying to ascertain that at least one or two interested reporters will be free to attend. Thus the circle closes: the Executive, caparisoned in unaccountable power, attracts reporters in packs; Congress, which has been busy rolling power down Capitol Hill into the White House, defaults on its responsibility to oversee the bloated monster it has helped to create; the press by its indifference to congressional oversight aggravates the malaise on Capitol Hill, and the public, which does have rather large stakes in all of this, cannot assess press handling of congressional oversight that is nonreported.

How well or how poorly Congress monitors the Executive, the independent agencies, and the laws—"It has been more than 20 years since a congressional committee took a look at the U.S. tax code and how it operates," Pincus said—is a matter of supreme importance in our public life. It is not, news managers confide, a sexy story. Maybe not: it is merely a vital story. It doesn't seem to get written. Here, however, the circle closes from the opposite direction: "The truth is," Pincus said, "that little serious thought has been given by legislators on all committees to how *any* federal agency or program ought to be monitored." Indeed, he said, "neither Rep. Wilbur Mills during his 15 years as chairman of the House Ways and Means Committee, nor Sen. Russell Long, chairman of the Senate Finance Committee, has had any interest in the supervisory function of Congress."[5] Because they didn't, major programs have escaped congressional oversight altogether; the Social Security Administration, which supervises distribution of more than $80 billion a year, has escaped it for more than twenty years. If powerhouses like Russell Long and Wilbur Mills had undertaken a fraction of the oversight that duty required, or if the putative leaders on Capitol Hill had ever criticized them for their derelictions, doubtless the press would have shown some interest in the oversight function.

The press was obligated to be skeptical of Wilbur Mills, at least now and then. Was it? Walter Shapiro, an editor of the *Washington Monthly*, wrote tellingly about this in December 1974:

Over the last 15 years Mills was consistently described as "the second most powerful man in Washington," but he was somehow never held accountable for the results of his use of that power. *The New York Times* would praise him editorially for sponsoring "every major law on . . . tax reform, foreign trade, Social Security and health insurance," but would neglect to mention that our tax system continues to be notoriously unfair, our foreign trade legislation has done little to help our balance of payments, Social Security continues to be one of our most regressive taxes, and Medicare has turned out to be as much of a bonanza for the medical profession as it is for the elderly.[6]

The *Wall Street Journal* reported in June 1973 that Mills, prodded by a lobbyist who had contributed heavily to the congressman's corruptly financed campaign for the Democratic presidential campaign in 1972, had gone to the Internal Revenue Service "to stop massive tax investigations of several big shoe companies." Reporter David McClintock, who wrote the story, estimated that in doing this small favor for Mills, the IRS cost the public an estimated $100 million in uncollected taxes. But, Walter Shapiro noted, "the story was never picked up by any other major paper." A month after the *Wall Street Journal* story, in fact, the *Washington Post* depicted Mills as "a towering figure" who

has dominated the [Ways and Means] committee and the House with his detailed knowledge of the complex issues he handles. . . . The power of Wilbur Mills is something that goes beyond his formal role as committee chairman, and something that defies easy definition. It is something in the personality of the man, his calm self-assurance, his firm command of the committee that handles the critical issues that touch all Americans, a feeling that if Mills says the bill is a good one, then it is.[7]

This was not merely the way a veteran *Post* reporter perceived Mills, but the way virtually all of the mass media saw and presented him. *Fortune* in 1968 described him as "a kind of de Gaulle of the Ozarks."[8] *Time* in 1963 gushed over a grasp of the intricacies of taxation which "often astonishes expert witnesses," and his humble abode in Kensett, Arkansas—"a little one-bathroom house that might be the home of a factory hand." Columnist Joseph Kraft genuflected because "no other man in this country has [his] mixture of talent, outlook and power."[9]

Kraft's colleagues in the columning business, Rowland Evans and Robert Novak, mourned that Mills' "once majestic authority has dwindled close to mortal dimensions."[10]

The root of the problem was not Mills, but the seemingly unquenchable lust of the press to canonize selected public figures. Shapiro cited a "perfect example," a column Kraft wrote in 1971 after President Nixon chose as secretary of the treasury, John B. Connally, a king of wheeler-dealers whose catering to special interests—and brazenness in doing so—seldom has been matched:

It must be understood that Connally is one of the most able and effective men in American politics. He is a born leader, intelligent in his analysis of problems, full of poise and public presence and with great force. . . . He is in close touch with the impressive young man sure to lead the Texas delegation at the convention in 1972 —Lt. Governor Ben Barnes.[11]

Subsequently, Connally was indicted in the milk-lobby scandal; a jury acquitted him. Barnes, Shapiro noted, was "so totally discredited that he was denied renomination in 1972."

The point here is John N. Mitchell's point, somewhat revised: the press watches most anything but what they *do*. "It can be argued that no role played by the press is more important than that of illuminating the character of public officials," Shapiro wrote.

The canons of objective journalism insure that newspapers and television are full of stories which begin, "Wilbur Mills, the chairman of the powerful Ways and Means Committee, announced yesterday that. . . ." For the intelligent reader to evaluate news like this he needs to have some sense of what kind of man Wilbur Mills is. . . . If the public has been led to believe that Mills is a dedicated man whose entire life shines with integrity, the average reader will probably conclude that whatever Mills does is motivated by his concern for the public interest. If, however, the reader has been given an impression that many of Mills' dealings are shady, he is likely to look at a Mills statement and wonder, "What's his angle?" In the 17 years since Mills took over as chairman of the House Ways and Means Committee, there have been too few hints in the press that this sort of skepticism would be justified.

To the credit of a few reporters, including Eileen Shanahan of the *New York Times*, hints that Mills engaged in trading special favors to lobbyists for power, say, to control the flow of their campaign contributions to other congressmen, did appear in the press now and then. "But rather than being treated as front page news, they generally were buried within stories with off-putting headlines like 'Tax Reform's Chances,' " Shapiro said. Far more influential were the hosannas that flowed from columnists, editorialists and profile-writers.

·   ·   ·

Mills' reputation drowned in Washington's Tidal Basin at 2 A.M. on October 7, 1974, when his good friend Fanne Fox, known in strip joints as the Argentine Firecracker, left his car, which had been stopped for speeding, and jumped in. Police said both were intoxicated. "There is little comfort to be found in the way this journalistic honeymoon ended," Shapiro commented.

Because something is seriously wrong with the press when it requires a full-blown sex scandal for newspaper editors to take an interest in the behind-the-scenes legislative activities of the man who writes our tax laws and shapes our health legislation. Sadly, it is all too easy to envision what the press would still be writing about Wilbur Mills today if he had not run for President and if he still curled up each evening with the tax code.

If the press won't oversee the overseers, who will?

One bit of progress deserves mention. It involves news media with small or middling circulation, particularly the approximately one thousand two hundred dailies that lack a Washington correspondent of their own. Thus cut off, they make heavy use of self-serving press releases from their congressmen and senators, often publishing them as "news." In 1973, Ralph Nader's Public Citizen, Inc., provided $40,000 in start-up money for the Capitol Hill News Service (CHNS). Operating independently of Nader, CHNS, under its founder, Peter Gruenstein, had acquired by July 1975 approximately seventy clients—newspapers and broadcast stations in seven states that paid modest fees for reporting on the activities of their particular legislators in Washington—and was "largely self-sufficient." The staff of twelve provides, in addition to the usual fare, a film service for television stations.

Working for low pay, but enjoying the pleasures that come from watching the great unwatched, CHNS, among other things:

• Reported on the extensive use by congressmen of House recording studios for campaign purposes, although the studios—which charge token fees—are supposed to be used only for communication with constituents.

• Disclosed that a reporter for the *Scranton Tribune* was "moonlighting" at $5,000 a year for Congressman Joseph M. McDade (R–Pa.).[12]

• Disclosed that of thirty-nine congressional committees surveyed by the CHNS staff, only five had rules prohibiting members of the committee staff from accepting gifts from lobbyists or special-interest groups.

• Played a probably decisive role in the defeat in 1974 of Congressman Frank M. Clark (D–Pa.), merely by digging out the facts—which then were printed by the *Beaver County Times* in Clark's home district—about his acceptance of more than $25,000 in campaign contributions from maritime unions and shipping interests, and about his support of legislation favored by those groups.

"The American body politic is hemmorhaging from Executive people unwatched," Ben H. Bagdikian said in an article on CHNS. "But the remedy, a responsive and daily accountable Congress, has also gone largely unwatched in any way significant for local voters. Most members still do not have to answer pertinent questions for the voters back home, and most continue to propagandize their constituents at the constituents' expense with the cooperation of the local news media. This process started a long time ago but the price of an immobilized government has now come due."[13]

When the press in any community fails to try to hold accountable those who wield substantial power, and when there are neither "alternative" media nor mechanisms to monitor press performance, unaccountability is bound to flourish. Newspapers and broadcasters who neglect their accountability mission are slighting their ethical obligation under the First Amendment, as Walter Lippmann put it, "to provide, even at a commercial loss, an adequate supply of what the public will in the longer run need to know."[14] They numb what the late Hannah Arendt, the philosopher, termed "the sense by which we take our bearings in the real world"; they seem to recognize dimly if at all that survival requires "men willing to do what Herodotus was the first to undertake consciously, namely, *legein ta eonta,* to say what is."[15] On the basis of hard experience in Appalachia, Tom Gish, who with his wife, Pat, publishes the *Mountain Eagle,* whose offices in Whitesburg, Kentucky, were destroyed by arsonists in 1974, expressed the "need to be skeptical, to be suspicious, to ask a million questions, and to demand answers of all who would come to save us, no matter what cloak they wear." He went on to say:

Had we asked the right questions and insisted upon the right answers at the right time, we might have been saved from a TVA that devastates an entire area for its strip coal; from a Corps of Engineers that builds dams simply to build dams; from a Forest Service that serves only the lumber industry; from an Appalachian Regional Commission that seeks not to assist but to eliminate an entire culture rich in its own heritage. We might even have been saved from our own folly in turning over the greatest wealth in the nation to a few moneymen from the outside who wanted our minerals.[16]

The performance of the press in holding power accountable in regions, states, counties, and cities surely if subtly influences the performance of the national press in holding power accountable on Capitol Hill and in the White House and other power houses of Washington. And because news organizations around the country are clients and affiliates of the news services and networks, i.e., paying customers, they significantly affect what those very large and very important enterprises report—how, that is, they define news.

The problem is in the legitimacy an exalted office with access to unaccountable power and secrecy can bestow upon the darker intimations of human character. It is a problem and a danger, and the best safeguards against it are strict laws rigidly observed and constant public scrutiny.

Bill Moyers
Newsweek

Sunlight is said to be the best disinfectant . . .

Louis D. Brandeis
Other People's Money

Since the start of the Cold War, systematic deception, manipulation, and intimidation of the press have been inevitable and indispensable concomitants of presidential secrecy and lying, especially that secrecy and lying whose intended victims have been the American people. The Soviet Union knew why Francis Gary Powers had crossed their borders in a U-2; but to keep the facts secret from the American people (and others) the Eisenhower Administration, until its hand was forced, lied to them through the press. When, shortly before the 1962 elections, Secretary of Labor W. Willard Wirtz asserted that the number of unemployed had declined by two million in the twenty-one months John Kennedy had been President, he was using the press to try to deceive the voters; once the election was over, he admitted that the figures had not been adjusted for seasonal variations and thus contained "invalid" statistical comparisons.[1]

Trying to justify his military intervention in the Dominican Republic, President Johnson on June 17, 1965, told a news conference that "some 1,500 innocent people were murdered and shot and their heads cut off." "It made fine newspaper copy," William McGaffin and Erwin Knoll recalled. "The true figure, when it was finally ascertained, was not 1,500 or 150 or even 15—in fact, there was no evidence that any heads had been cut off— and most of the atrocities committed in the Dominican revolt were the work, not of the rebels, but of the junta which the United States secretly supported."[2] The Cambodians on whom American bombs were falling did not have to be told by the Nixon White House that they were being bombed; but to keep the American public ignorant the President obviously had to keep the bombing secret from the press.

The White House used varied techniques to bring or keep the press in line. One was abuse of the trust placed in the word of the government, a trust that the press widely shared with the public especially during the Eisenhower and Kennedy administrations. A second was abuse of the patriotic unwillingness of the press to do anything that possibly could endanger "national security." A third was the granting of favors—exclusive interviews, tips, access—to friendly newsmen whose careers thereby were advanced, and the denial of the same to independent or unfriendly newsmen, who then faced a possible judgment by their employers that they were no longer useful.

The Nixon Administration, uniquely driven by a President's sick hatred of the press, finally tried to destroy it as an institution by using Vice-President Spiro T. Agnew as a boo leader against the networks, the *New York Times*, and the *Washington Post;* by subpoenaing newsmen and their notes and film; by having the FBI, using a cover story supplied by Mr. Nixon himself, make a full field investigation of CBS correspondent Daniel Schorr; by trumping up charges for the arrest of columnist Jack Anderson's colleague Leslie H. Whitten, Jr.; by wiretapping columnist Joseph Kraft; by putting numerous newspersons on an "enemies list"; by converting the Federal Communications Commission into an instrument for intimidation of broadcasters; by instituting the Pentagon Papers case, in which the Supreme Court, for the first time, ruled that newspapers could be restrained *in advance* from printing information that the government had found objectionable; and by a host of other power plays, including a shrinkage of the frequency of press conferences to record lows.

But it must be said that there is in the foregoing, and in similar recitals, the grave fault of tending to depict the press wholly as a victim, a monolith, or a tiger. It is overall none of the three. In the 1972 election campaign, 93 percent of all daily newspapers reporting a presidential endorsement endorsed Mr. Nixon, the President who had created the biggest threat to freedom of the press. The Scripps-Howard chain teletyped an editorial to its papers headlined, "WE CHOOSE NIXON AGAIN," and beginning: "Four years ago when the editors of (Name Your Paper) . . . met in editorial conference, they decided . . ."[3]

Press critic Ben H. Bagdikian, in a detailed analysis, showed that "pro-Nixon papers had a much higher tendency to suppress damaging Watergate stories than papers making no endorsement."[4] He also found that the Nixon Administration's three-year war against the news media had succeeded, the evidence being that during the campaign there was a demonstrated "retrogression in printing newsworthy information that is critical of the Administration and a notable decline in investigation of apparent wrongdoing when it is likely to anger or embarrass the White House." In Washington, Bob Woodward and Carl Bernstein, the *Washington Post* reporters who broke the Watergate scandal, were lonely for months; Bagdikian said it is "possible that more man-hours of investigative journalism were put into the 1962 rumor that John F. Kennedy had been secretly married in 1947 than were assigned to investigate the Watergate affair."[5]

It is true that successive administrations abused the trust of the press in the name of government; but it is also true, and more important, that this trust remained too large for too long; and this, in turn, reflected the continuing predilection of the mass media to report what leaders and their flacks say (announcements, handouts, statements) rather than to pay sufficient attention to what they do. Richard Reeves wrote:

The President [Nixon] goes to a customs station in Laredo, Texas, to "dramatize" his commitment to ending the flow of narcotics into the country—and a hundred of the best reporters in the country are there with him, even if they're 100 feet away behind Secret Service barricades. Is there one reporter in Washington or one in Newark with the smarts, the time and the money to figure out whether the Nixon Administration is really doing anything effective about drugs? . . . I suspect that President Nixon would have been glad to expose himself to the people and the White House press corps if that would have diverted public attention from a couple of hundred reporters crawling through the agencies and corners of the Federal Government.[6]

The reporters "accompanying" Mr. Nixon to Laredo were in one plane and he in another, his campaign plane. En route, White House flacks gave them a press release; and, on landing, with no opportunity to speak with the President, they immediately dictated stories based on the handout and nothing more. The handout attacked judges for worsening the drug problem, without saying which judges or how they were doing this. The stories "made headlines all over the country, (NIXON SAYS JUDGES HINDER DRUG WAR, Baltimore *Sun*, page 1, Sept. 23)," Ben Bagdikian recalled. It developed that what the Nixon Administration was doing about the drug problem was building a bureaucratic disaster called the Drug Enforcement Administration, whose administrator, John R. Bartels, Jr., would resign in 1975 under fire.

On innumerable other occasions, the media served up one or another Nixon Administration handout without seasoning the hogwash with a few grains of skeptical salt, facts, or follow-up. At the White House, Mr. Nixon and his publicists, such as press secretary Ronald L. Ziegler and speech-writer Patrick J. Buchanan, were pressing whines from sour grapes; the media were treating the President unfairly, they cried. The fact was that the Nixon crowd was also constantly decanting the whines into the very vessels they most viciously clubbed, including the networks, which unfailingly granted their requests for air time (and then often found themselves and their reporters subjected to undocumented attacks); the *New York Times*, in whose Op Ed page Buchanan, say, seemed to appear when he wished, and the *Washington Post*, which when savagely and unfairly attacked by Ziegler for its one serious slip-up in its Watergate coverage (a story saying that Hugh W. Sloan, Jr., who was treasurer of the Finance Committee to Re-elect the President, had told a grand jury that H. R. Haldeman controlled a secret fund) led the paper with Ziegler's attack.[7] Indeed, the major media were so generous of their energies and resources in trying to be fair to the Nixon men that inadvertently they may have been unfair to the public by neglecting the claims on their attention of the cloutless—consumers, ripped-off taxpayers, the poor, the elderly.

In protecting "national security," major news media on several occasions concealed from the American people information that must be presumed to have been known to the other side. Before the Bay of Pigs, the *New York Times* toned down a dispatch on the impending invasion by, among other things, omitting mention of the CIA's role; yet, President Kennedy would later tell *Times* managing editor Turner Catledge, "If you had printed more about the operation, you would have saved us from a colossal mistake."[8] Long before Gary Powers was shot down, the *Washington Post* and the *New York Times* knew, but did not inform the public, that U-2 flights were being made over the Soviet Union.

Did such episodes lead the press to forswear collaboration in similar circumstances? Obviously not, as shown by the bizarre story of the CIA's secret $350 million project with Howard Hughes, the billionaire recluse, to raise a seventeen-year-old Soviet submarine that sank in the Pacific Ocean in 1968. A specially built ship, the *Glomar Explorer*, succeeded in the summer of 1974 in raising a portion of the sub. Subsequently, some thieves and blackmailers broke into the offices in Los Angeles of the Summa Corporation, Hughes' wholly owned company, and stole documents some of which described Project Jennifer, as the CIA called it. Later still, the *Los Angeles Times*, following up on various bits and pieces of information, assembled a story, albeit a somewhat inaccurate one. The paper broke the story on February 8, 1975. In the first edition the story was prominently displayed on page one, where it obviously belonged. Twenty minutes after the presses began rolling, the CIA phoned to ask—on national security grounds—that the story be killed. Unwilling to go that far, the paper moved the story in later editions to page eighteen. The central point to be remembered from this background, not to mention the involvement of thousands of persons in one or another phase of Project Jennifer over a seven-year time span, is that as of February 8, 1975, and quite probably earlier, the Russians must have known the essential details of the project.

Over the ensuing weeks, investigations were begun or renewed by several major news organizations, including the *Los Angeles Times,* which assigned eight reporters and put their story in type, to hold in the event someone else would break it; the *New York Times,* whose reporter Seymour Hersh had been looking into Project Jennifer on and off since late 1975; the *Washington Post;* CBS; NBC; *Time; Newsweek; Parade,* and National Public Radio. CIA Director William E. Colby personally appealed to top executives of each of these organizations not to report the story. "Colby's argument with all the editors and publishers he called was that other publishers had withheld, that the CIA wanted time to attempt to complete its operation [mainly to recover nuclear torpedoes and codes], and did not want the Soviets to learn of it," Stephen Isaacs would report in the *Washington Post.* But how could the Soviets *not* have known of it, at least since the February 8 story? So as not to interfere with what the CIA indicated to be an ongoing military operation, each news organization independently consented to publish only if someone else were to do so first, or to publish only after Jennifer would be either completed or abandoned. The intention was to hold the story, not to suppress it forever.

The voluntary suppression began to crumble in March 1975, when Charles Morgan, director of the Washington office of the American Civil Liberties Union, who had begun to hear talk almost a year earlier of a connection between a Hughes ship ostensibly built to mine the ocean floor for minerals and a CIA project, told the ACLU board that "if the American press is controlled by the CIA, I was going to have the ACLU publish the story, not only on the CIA venture, but on its control of the press." Columnist Jack Anderson, who knew of Morgan's intention, then broke the story on the Mutual Broadcasting radio station in Washington at 9:30 P.M. on March 18. News executives had been in touch with him beforehand. Consequently, the *New York Times,* in all of its editions that same night, was able to carry the most detailed account, which Seymour Hersh had submitted three weeks earlier. The *Washington Post* missed its first edition because it chose to wait to hear precisely what Anderson would disclose.

The press in conscience must on occasion voluntarily keep information secret while always taking a hard, show-me-why attitude toward those (certainly including the CIA) who seek a delay in publication or suppression.

Anyone who would say that there is never a justification for either is foolish, ignorant, or irresponsible; and allowance must be made for the difficulty of making decisions in this area without full knowledge of the facts, which is usually unavailable, and with the speed that is usually required. These things said, it seems to us that all of the major news organizations involved made the wrong decision in the Soviet sub case; and it is precisely that *all* of them did it that is deeply troubling. The suggested explanations are deeply troubling, too.

". . . the Russians knew," Jack Anderson and his associate, Les Whitten, wrote.

We knew they knew. They knew we knew they knew. But, as Colby told us, it would be 'rubbing their noses in it' to let the American people know. What was at stake in publishing, then, was not national security but international etiquette, not American secrets but Soviet face, not the sabotage of a second Glomar mission but the ruffling of Russian tail feathers if we should go ahead with it. These are considerations not to be mocked, but we hold them to be insufficient reasons for renewing the dread precedent of cutting off the news—the windpipe of the American system.

All right. If there is no compelling reason to suppress, is there a public need to know a story that might inconvenience the conduct of our diplomacy? We think so. An estimated $350 million was spent outside of the legitimate appropriations process—in a gamble to recover an archaic diesel sub, obsolete missiles and outdated codes. No doubt this submerged museum piece would have been of some intelligence value had it not fallen apart. But was it worth a sum that, for instance, could have financed the down payment on 100,000 new homes? Was it a national necessity or was it an admiral's toy?

Anderson also said, "I talked to Navy people of the highest possible rank who said that this obsolete sub had no real military significance." The *Washington Post*'s ombudsman and press critic, Charles B. Seib, was acid:

On balance, and from hindsight, it appears that the media gave in too easily to Colby's national security argument. Little weight seems to have been given to the fact that a Feb. 8 story in the Los Angeles Times, although sketchy and partly in error, must have alerted the Russians to the sub-raising mission. Also, there is something disturbing in Colby's success in achieving a sort of group agreement that 'we won't print unless somebody else does.' Aside from its other implications, it put the media executives in the uncomfortable position of having one man—Jack Anderson—decide whether the story would be printed and when.

Finally, there appears to have been no aggressive effort to check out Colby's arguments for secrecy on Capitol Hill, at the White House or at the highest levels of the Defense Department.

We lost our national innocence in the matter of official lying, you will remember, in 1962 when Arthur Sylvester, the Pentagon's spokesman, said that it was the government's right "to lie to save itself." The Watergate experience later established the breadth and flexibility of that phrase "to save itself." Further, most editors would agree that by the very nature of his job Colby has a license to lie. Yet they seem to have accepted his plea with a readiness they would have found naive in one of their reporters.

Why the ready acceptance? Leaving aside Colby's motives in running around from one editor to another and leaving fresh details—a possible hint that he wanted the story out, for his own reasons, but with his self-serving imprint on it—columnists Anderson and Whitten offered a plausible hypothesis.

There have been signs of late that the press—battle-scarred from its jousts with two Presidents and shaken by the enormity of its victory over them—has begun to wear a hair shirt.

The older blather about "responsibility" to keep secrets instead of exploding abuses has begun to creep back into press parlance.

The old pre-Watergate, pre-Vietnam ideals of partnership with government, of cozy intimacy with the high and mighty, of a camaraderie of secrets shared by this peerage but kept from the public, begins to appeal once more to a press concerned that its abrasive successes have earned it a bad name and a hostile reception.

A professor of constitutional law, Arthur S. Miller, of George Washington University, was no less perturbed. "We are being governed in part by *diktats*, issued in secret with the willing collaboration of the 'free' press and the government," he said. "That's hardly what the First Amendment is all about. Who appointed that informal board of censors?"[9]

Soon after the *Glomar Explorer* episode sank out of the news, there was a flurry in the press about allegations that the CIA had plotted to assassinate certain foreign leaders. But Harry Howe Ransom, an early student of the CIA, thought that "greater attention and higher priority" was owed other issues, "such as the assassination of America's reputation in the world resulting from ill-conceived 'intelligence' missions; the assassination of entire governments (e.g., Guatemala, Iran and Chile) or the assassination of the Constitution by excessive secrecy and the use of intelligence agencies for explicitly prohibited purposes." He went on to say, "Democracy's assassination is the top news story of this generation."[10] It will not be treated as such if news managers receive secrecy pleas from the CIA with, as Charles Seib put it, "a readiness they would have found naive in one of their reporters."

To return to our examination of the techniques used by the White House (and others) to try to bring the press into line, or to keep it there: when high officials grant favors such as exclusive interviews, the presumption naturally must be that the grantor wants to peddle something or that he is hoping in some way to be canonized; and the presumption further must be that the particular purposes of the grantees and their employers also are being served. None of this excludes the possibility that the result will be news of interest to the public whose interests thereby also are served. But it is also a fact that in situations where the press is in a dependency status, hard and necessary questions which could make a return engagement improbable seem with remarkable consistency not to get asked. Thus, a friendly relationship between press and President tends to constrict the flow of useful information. "A President and his Administration are invaluable sources of information for any journalist," Lewis J. Paper, legislative counsel to Senator Gaylord Nelson has observed. "If these sources are made available to a reporter, he may be reluctant to do anything which will antagonize the President and result in decreased access." Sooner or later, an unwillingness to antagonize a President is bound to translate into an unwillingness to try to hold a President accountable. Paper, in an article adapted from his book on the Kennedy Presidency, recalled that John Kennedy's

relations with the press were generally marked by accessibility, friendship and good cheer. But beneath the veneer of amiability was a President anxious to manipulate that relationship to his political advantage and to control what was said about him and his Administration. Journalists who failed to reciprocate the Presidential friendship with favorable stories frequently were "exiled" from Administration news sources—including, and most especially, the President himself. Virtually no one was immune from this rule of reciprocity.

Any doubt as to the accuracy of those observations was removed with the publication of *Conversations with Kennedy,* in which Benjamin C. Bradlee, now editor of the *Washington Post,* disclosed his close relationships with the President while chief of the Washington bureau of *Newsweek.*

Lewis Paper, in his article, told of an episode in which a television network granted a request by a top aide in the Kennedy White House to cancel scheduled interviews with two high administration officials about steel prices, then an especially sensitive subject. According to Paper's source, the cancellation was motivated by the network's concern that proceeding with the interviews would jeopardize its access to administration news sources. The press cannot readily prevent a President from trying to pressure it to withhold information, but, as Paper correctly points out, "the press should recognize that it cannot remain independent in the long run if it is more concerned with scoops in the short run. It's all a matter of remembering that one good turn by the President does not deserve another by the press."[11]

Too often, the press substitutes for necessary reporting all sorts of gushy personality stuff that tells little about an officeholder's record and perform-ance, but much about his ties, suits, drinks, honeymoon itinerary, and other inconsequential distractions and gossip. In recent times, few have benefited more from this kind of obsequious puffery than Nelson A. Rockefeller on the occasion of his nomination to be Vice-President. Nicholas von Hoffman, in a careful analysis of eighteen issues each of *Time* and *Newsweek,* discovered a pap blizzard which reduced to near-invisibility assorted wretched aspects of his *curriculum vitae,* starting with his massive and pervasive conflicts of interest, the approximately $20 million he and his family, over a period of seventeen years, contributed to his four gubernatorial campaigns, his three quests for the Republican presidential nomination, and various politically oriented projects, a super-hawkishness that leaves even Barry Goldwater agog, his circumvention of the New York State Constitution in order to finance huge projects which elude accountability to the taxpayers, his bar-baric—but futile and expensive—anticrime and antinarcotics legislation, his dereliction of duty in refusing to go to the scene of the Attica Prison uprising, and, as a last item, his grandiose and wasteful $1 billion mall in Albany.

Gerald Ford would have us believe that he is a latter-day Harry S Truman, but if in similar circumstances Mr. Truman had nominated for Vice-Presi-dent a man with a record remotely like Rockefeller's, Mr. Ford might well have been in the vanguard of those making an attack on the issues; and the news magazines probably would have done the fine reporting jobs they often do. In Rockefeller's case, they told us that he drinks Dubonnet on the rocks and, so just like you and me is he, that he has "an ever-present cache of Oreo cookies."[12]

It is true that Spiro Agnew made phony speeches vilifying the networks and the *Washington Post* and the *New York Times;* but it is also true that it was almost a secret in most of the press that the Nixon White House tried its best to make it easy for broadcasters generally—including the networks—to secure their station licenses in perpetuity against effective challenge; and the press did not, or feared to, tax Agnew with the impossibility of reconciling his attack on newspaper monopolies with President Nixon's support of the Newspaper Preservation Act, which his own Justice Department had warned would entrench monopoly.[13]

It is true, finally, that Mr. Nixon held few press conferences (twenty-two in his first thirty-four months in office, for example; President Kennedy held sixty-five in a comparable period. President Truman averaged better than three a month, and Presidents Eisenhower and Johnson each had two a month). The infrequency of Nixon press conferences caused unexamined issues to accumulate in large numbers and then be dropped in favor of preemptive crises of the moment. The crowds were sometimes ludicrously big. The format was incoherent; even an arrangement for follow-up questions, something of square-one sensibleness, did not gain a foothold until—and thanks to—the Ford Administration. Mr. Nixon usually recognized a handful of White House "regulars," but for most reporters getting recognition was difficult if not impossible. And at least one reporter who managed to ask a tough question while the President was on camera never got a second chance to do so. Acknowledging the full force of such obstacles, and others that could be cited; and acknowledging, too, that some doubt the usefulness in enlightening the public of the presidential press conference as an institution, it remains our conviction that a great many questions which should have been asked could have been asked; that the press defaulted in not asking them, and that the public, on balance, lost.

In one of his better put-ons, which somehow drew scant attention then or later, Richard Nixon went to the annual dinner of the White House Correspondents Association in May 1971 with this wryly fraudulent message:

Don't give me a friendly question. Only a hard, tough question gets the kind of an answer—you may not like it—but it is only that one that tests the man. And it is the responsibility of the members of the press to test the man, whoever he is. You have done that. . . . I benefit from your probing, from your criticism, and if I succeed . . . it will be . . . due in great part to the fact that members of the press examined searchingly everything that I suggested, every recommendation that I made, and made it necessary for me to come up to the mark. . . . So thanks for giving me that heat. And remember, I like the kitchen. Keep it up.[14]

For an unpublished article, Morton Mintz in 1972 assembled dozens of "hard, tough" questions that might have been but were not asked of Mr. Nixon on the infrequent occasions when he exposed himself to any press questions at all. One arose from the case of General John D. Lavelle, who as head of the Seventh Air Force had commanded four hundred fighter-bombers and 40,000 men. Without the standard authorization required for an activity so freighted with implications for the war in Vietnam and American foreign policy generally, his pilots between November 1971 and March 1972 bombed North Vietnam 147 times. Lavelle having made it clear that they could report air strikes only if there had been enemy provocation, the pilots' frequent cover story was the false claim that they had been fired upon. The Senate Armed Services Committee summoned Lavelle to explain the bombings for which there had been no clear accountability. He insisted he had not fought a private war; rather, his superiors including the Joint Chiefs of Staff (who denied it) had given his deputies tacit encouragement. It was the White House with its policy of systematic deception and lying that had been pulling the strings, and so it was not in a position to treat the Lavelle bombings as the terrible scandal they were. Instead, the White House tried to cover up by having the Air Force announce that Lavelle had retired for reasons of "health." Later, General John D. Ryan, chief of staff of the Air Force, said he had relieved Lavelle because of the raids. Ryan testified that his recommendation was that Congress be told the truth, but was overruled by Secretary of Defense Melvin R. Laird.[15]

The pithy question suggested by *Washington Post* reporter George C. Wilson was of the kind that, in Mr. Nixon's phrase, "tests the man":

As Commander-in-Chief, why did you let the Air Force allow General Lavelle—our air war commander in Vietnam—retire with no disciplinary action after violating your orders about restricting the bombing of North Vietnam?

Another question developed from the 1968 election, when twenty of the twenty-one Nixon-Agnew fund-raising committees were found by W. Pat Jennings, clerk of the House of Representatives, to have failed to comply with the Corrupt Practices Act of 1925, which was the election-financing statute then in force, and which provided criminal penalties for violations. Early in 1969, Jennings certified the violations to the Justice Department. Shortly thereafter, Mr. Nixon's campaign manager, John N. Mitchell, took office as attorney general. The question, which would have been most timely in 1969, was:

Having run on a law-and-order platform, did you reprimand Mr. Mitchell for the failure of twenty Nixon-Agnew committees to comply with the Corrupt Practices Act; and do you believe the Justice Department should prosecute?

To be sure, Mr. Nixon could be adept at dealing with tough questions, possibly even one involving a hypothetical prosecution of John N. Mitchell by John N. Mitchell, if only by giving false or misleading answers. And it is possible that the paucity of hard, educational questions (i.e., questions that impart useful information even if left unanswered) spared the public more confusion, deception, and lies than it already was getting. But there was too little real probing, in our judgment; and this was adverse to presidential accountability.

President Ford is far more open and forthright, and, at least in his first year or so in office, he held many more press conferences than had his predecessor. But it didn't make much difference, because very few hard questions about very many important subjects were asked. Here are a few brief examples, from among hundreds that were possible:

Mr. Ford repeatedly urged deregulation of natural gas, which happens to be mainly in government lands. No one asked him to explain why he wanted the price of gas owned by the American public to be equivalent (in energy terms) to the price of oil owned by the Arabs—a price he denounced as too high. No one asked him why producers already earning, say, 46 percent on equity should be allowed to earn two or three times that.

In November 1974, Mr. Ford pledged to "re-invigorate" the Renegotiation Board, which has the mission of recapturing excessive profits from defense contractors, "so as to expand its role in the fight against inflation." The White House then refused to let the board expand its ludicrously small staff by so much as one person; and Mr. Ford let six months go by before moving to fill a vacancy. He nominated Richard G. Holmquist, an out-of-work Lone Star Industries executive with invisible qualifications—he was not an accountant, auditor, or lawyer, and he had no significant experience in government procurement. To fill another vacancy, the President nominated Christopher U. Sylvester, who for almost twenty years had been administrative assistant to Senator Milton R. Young (R–N.Dak.), and who wanted a change of scene. To overcome his aide's ennui, Young suggested to Mr. Ford that "something appropriate" be found for Sylvester. Asked why the President might favor a request from him, Young replied, "I'm the ranking Republican on Appropriations" (the powerful Senate Appropriations Committee) and added, "Maybe it's because I asked him."[16]

Admiral Hyman G. Rickover, in testimony on Capitol Hill the day after a docile Senate confirmed Holmquist, and while the Sylvester nomination was pending, charged that "political hacks" sometimes are named to the board; that board members are "open to—and comply with—political pressures," and that the board is "subject to big business," because the Office of Management and Budget in the White House "does what big business wants." What is lost in all of this is the opportunity—the *obligation*—to recapture excessive profits of several hundred million dollars a year, said Rickover, who is known as the father of the nuclear Navy, and who has had an important role in defense procurement since 1939.[17]

Mr. Ford was not asked how he would square his reinvigoration pledge with his (belated) nominations of a couple of hacks, his refusal to expand the board's staff so it could save sums approximating those he had tried to squeeze out of the food-stamp program, and his views on the brave, blunt, and expert testimony of Admiral Rickover. But it was the kind of subject that usually doesn't interest the press very much. Most of the columnists and commentators don't trouble themselves about such things, and assorted scandals at the Renegotiation Board, over a long period, failed to incite a word of editorial comment at major newspapers, including the *Washington Post* which had reported the scandals. The board situation should not be overemphasized: Mr. Ford was available to be questioned, but was not, on a host of vital matters, ranging from the dangers of excessive reliance on nuclear power, to his opposition on a bill intended to reduce the cancer toll of one thousand deaths a day by requiring chemicals to be shown safe before marketing, to colossal waste by the Pentagon.

In his first speech to Congress in August 1974, Mr. Ford promised that his administration would engage in "hot pursuit of tough laws to prevent illegal invasion of privacy." This seemed to be supportive of the unanimous decision by the Supreme Court in 1972 that the government did not have the "inherent" power claimed by the Nixon Administration to wiretap domestic organizations and persons, even on purported national security grounds, without obtaining a judicial warrant to do so. Subsequently, the United States Court of Appeals for the District of Columbia ruled that the Constitution forbade the government, without a court order, to wiretap domestic agents that were not agents or collaborators of a foreign power. In fact, Judge J. Skelly Wright said in the majority opinion, "Our analysis would suggest that absent exigent circumstances, no wiretapping in the area of foreign affairs should be exempt from prior judicial scrutiny, irrespective of the justification for the surveillance or the importance of the information sought."

With this background, Mr. Ford's new attorney general, Edward H. Levi, disclosed in June 1975 that the Justice Department had authorized warrantless wiretaps in 1974—the year Mr. Ford became President—on 148 persons and organizations. The number was significantly higher than the average during the preceding five years. Although the number may seem small, it isn't. As columnist Tom Wicker explained, most of the taps were of substantial duration, and each of them recorded each of dozens or hundreds of conversations indiscriminately as it occurred. Consequently, he said, "there is no way to know how many thousands of persons, most of them entirely innocent, were overheard and recorded in the conduct of their private affairs."

Levi's justification for warrantless wiretapping did not seem to be compatible with the President's promise of "hot pursuit of tough laws to prevent illegal invasion of privacy." In a letter to Senator Edward M. Kennedy (D–Mass.), the attorney general said, "It is the position of the Department of Justice that the Executive may conduct electronic surveillance in the interest of national security and foreign intelligence, and in aid of his conduct of the nation's foreign affairs, without obtaining a judicial warrant." This is the kind of excessive claim that could have been expected from John N. Mitchell, Mr. Nixon's first attorney general; that the Supreme Court had rejected 9 to 0 in 1972; that President Ford seemingly had repudiated in

1974; and that was hopelessly incompatible with the Court of Appeals opinion. Wicker said:

If anything could be broader than "national security and foreign intelligence," it is "in aid of his conduct of the nation's foreign affairs." Taken together, those justifications would give a President power to tap just about anyone without a warrant, since almost any activity could be claimed to have some relationship to "his conduct of foreign affairs."

In the hands of a determined President, Mr. Levi's assertion of power might even be used to evade by indirection territory definitely proscribed by the Supreme Court.[18]

On June 25, 1975, the day after Senator Kennedy made Levi's letter public, President Ford held a press conference. No one asked him if he supported Levi's assertion of power and, if he did, how he could square it with his speech to Congress; no one inquired if he would favor or oppose legislation to require the government to get a court order before placing any electronic surveillance on anyone; indeed, no one asked him any questions whatever on the subject. It does not mitigate this performance that more than two weeks later, on July 12, Levi put out a statement that no warrantless wiretaps were currently operating on American citizens, and that he would permit such surveillance only "in cases where the target of surveillance is an agent or a collaborator of a foreign power." At the President's press conference, no one asked about the crime program Mr. Ford had just announced, or about reports of CIA-sponsored assassinations or attempted assassinations, or, except peripherally, about the then-fresh report by the Rockefeller commission on the CIA.

It is not Mr. Ford's fault that so many serious questions don't get asked, or, certainly, that press owners and managers don't seem to mind and have the good luck by and large not to be asked why they don't mind. Accountability suffers.

IX
Consequences of Unaccountability

Decency, security and liberty alike demand that government officials shall be subjected to the same rules of conduct that are commands to the citizens. In a government of laws, existence of the government will be imperiled if it fails to observe the law scrupulously. Our government is the potent, the omnipresent teacher. For good or ill, it teaches the whole people by example. Crime is contagious. If the government becomes a lawbreaker, it breeds contempt for law; it invites every man to become a law unto himself; it invites anarchy.

Louis D. Brandeis
Olmstead v. U.S.

The Bicentennial Year was to be the occasion for the people to become reacquainted with their unique heritage of liberty and freedom. They would experience a nourishment of the spirit. They would feel a new pride in their country that would help to heal the wounds of Vietnam and Watergate. But for many Americans, there was a nagging worry about their government, a fear that it, secretly and systematically, had not heeded the warning written almost a half-century earlier by the late Supreme Court Justice Brandeis. And before 1976 was half over, a cascade of revelations had confirmed and reconfirmed the fear in overwhelming detail: The "omnipresent teacher" had transformed itself into the supreme lawbreaker.

With Presidents starting with Franklin D. Roosevelt leading the Typhoid Marys of government officialdom, crime had become contagious among the law-enforcement and intelligence agencies, particularly the Central Intelligence Agency, the Federal Bureau of Investigation, the National Security Agency, and the Internal Revenue Service. William C. Sullivan, a retired assistant director of the FBI in charge of intelligence, gave the Senate Intelligence Committee this testimonial to the infectious new pragmatism:

The one thing we were concerned with was this: Will this course of action work, will it get us what we want, will we reach the objective that we desire to reach? As far as legality is concerned, morals or ethics, [these were] never raised by myself or anyone else. I think this suggests really in government that we are amoral. In government—I am not speaking for everybody—the general atmosphere is one of amorality.[1]

Similarly, retired FBI supervisor William Branigan told the committee:

It was my assumption that what we were doing was justified by what we had to do . . . the greater good, the national security.[2]

Here was the magic key: the incantation of "national security" to escape the checks and balances created in the Constitution to limit abuses of governmental power, and ultimately to escape almost totally from accountability. Congress, the supposed overseer, didn't oversee, and didn't care that it didn't. That was the crucial failure: had it performed the oversight mission intended by the Founding Fathers, accountability mechanisms elsewhere in government would not have failed, or would not have failed so calamitously. Not only has Congress "often declined to exercise meaningful oversight," the committee said in April 1976 in its report, *Intelligence Activities and the Rights of Americans,* but it also "on occasion has passed laws or made statements which were taken by intelligence agencies as supporting overly broad investigations." Moreover, Congress ignored early warnings, such as *The Invisible Government,* a 1964 best-seller in which David Wise and Thomas B. Ross pointed out how the National Security Act, the 1947 law creating the CIA, had invited abuses. The invitation was in language authorizing the CIA, in addition to its information-gathering mission, to perform "such other functions and duties related to intelligence affecting the national security as the National Security Council may from time to time direct." As Ross and Wise made clear, a phrase as elastic as "such other functions" could be stretched around most anything—and it was.

The Constitution, in one of its exquisite accountability mechanisms, says, "No money shall be drawn from the Treasury, but in consequence of appropriations made by law; and a regular statement and account of the receipts and expenditures of all public money shall be published from time to time." With the questionable excuse that even a generalized, limited disclosure of the CIA's budget would imperil national security, Congress allowed the Executive to conceal agency funding in the budgets of the Department of Defense and other agencies. By letting go of the pursestrings, Congress all but nullified the possibility of effective oversight. The spending is enormous —more than $10 billion a year, according to the House Intelligence Committee report that leaked in February 1976, and about 8 percent of all *controllable* federal spending, according to the Senate unit's April 1976 *Report on the Foreign and Military Intelligence Activities of the United States.* To be sure, a few trusted senators and congressmen supposedly reviewed the CIA budget, but they were mostly aging cold-warriors—putative "conservatives" who prided themselves on circumventing the Constitution and on being know-nothings, see-nothings, and say-nothings.

The CIA's belated, forced disclosure that it had spent some $13.4 million between 1963 and 1973 on covert activities aimed at Salvador Allende of Chile—first to prevent his election as President, and then, after he was elected, to "destabilize" his government—came as a shock to the Capitol Hill "watchdogs" supposedly privy to the CIA's most significant secret operations. This particular operation had spanned a decade and was an acknowledged interference in the absolutely internal affairs of a country with which we had no legitimate quarrel whatsoever. "You can say that I was surprised," said Senator Stuart Symington (D–Mo.). Reporting Symington's reaction to the Chilean involvement, the *Washington Post*'s Laurence Stern, in a story on September 11, 1974, characterized him as "a loyal supporter of the Agency in the past." Stern went on to say that Symington's surprise apparently was shared by the venerable Senator John C. Stennis (D–Miss.). This was revealing because Stennis, as chairman of the Armed Services Committee, and as a member of the Appropriations Committee's CIA subcommittee, was presumed by virtually everyone to have access to more intimate knowledge of the agency than any other legislator—if he wanted such access.

"You have to make up your mind that you are going to have an intelligence agency and protect it as such and shut your eyes some and take what is coming," Stennis said during a Senate debate on November 23, 1971. When the debate reached the issue of CIA operations in Laos, a memorable exchange occurred between Senators Alan Cranston (D–Calif.) and the late Allen J. Ellender (D–La.), the late chairman of the Senate Appropriations' intelligence subcommittee:

Cranston. The chairman stated that he never would have thought of even asking about CIA funds being used to conduct the war in Laos. I would like to ask the Senator if, since then, he has inquired and now knows whether that is being done?
Ellender. I have not inquired.
Cranston. You do not know, in fact?
Ellender. No.
Cranston. As you are one of the five men privy to this information, in fact you are the number one man of the five men who would know, then who would know what happened to this money? The fact is, not even the five men know the facts of the situation.
Ellender. Probably not.

In a skeptical assessment of Congress' intention to deal with the round of CIA misadventures exposed in 1975, David E. Rosenbaum of the *New*

York Times wrote, "Congress screamed when the U-2 plane was shot down over the Soviet Union in 1960, when the CIA bungled the Bay of Pigs invasion in 1961, when the agency was shown in 1967 to have infiltrated the National Student Association and countless other organizations, when the agency's unauthorized operations in Laos were disclosed in 1971 and when its role in ousting the Communist government in Chile was exposed last year." The screaming diverted attention from congressional inaction. "More than 200 separate measures designed to make the CIA more responsive to Congress have been introduced in the last quarter-century," Rosenbaum noted. "None has been enacted."

The reporter proceeded to nail down the essential reasons why Congress had not exercised control of the CIA. They added up to this: Congress failed to control the agency because it didn't know—*and often didn't want to know*—what the agency was doing. Rosenbaum cited this statement by Senator Howard H. Baker, Jr. (R–Tenn.), who had become knowledgeable about the CIA during his service on the Senate Watergate Committee: "I do not think there is a man in the legislative part of the government who really knows what is going on in the intelligence community."

Rosenbaum ran a revealing count on the number of times Capitol Hill's four intelligence oversight subcommittees had met in 1974. House Armed Services' panel led the pack—with six meetings. Senate Appropriations' followed with five, and Senate Armed Services' with two. House Appropriations' unit "reported no records of its meetings," Rosenbaum said.[3] This dismal showing, it should be noted, occurred in a year when charges against the CIA were abundant in the press.

The demolition of Congress as an effective overseer of the government intelligence and law-enforcement (and law-breaking) community had multiple sources. Presidents, for example, decided that they, and only they, had the authority to determine what government-held information Congress should have and what could be made public. Implicitly, Congress had no rights in the matter. The "government," as *New York Times* columnist Anthony Lewis put it, somehow had come to be defined as the Executive branch alone. "Congress is a second-class branch, which gets information—and thus a share of power—only by the executive's charity," he said.[4] Subtle methods also were used to lull Congress into lying down and rolling over. Soon after he assumed chairmanship of the House Intelligence Committee in 1975, Congressman Otis G. Pike (D–N.Y.) told a witness what he had learned, in fourteen years on the Armed Services Committee, of the relationship between Congress and the holders of government secrets. "For decades committees of Congress have not done their jobs and you've been loving it. You could come up here and whisper in one friendly congressman's ear and in my opinion that's why we're in the mess we're in now."[5]

The well-aimed whisper neutralized Congress during the days when a handful of senior members ran Congress. Confiding a few secrets to the chairman and ranking minority member of a subcommittee would guarantee for an agency immunity from harassment—or difficult questions—by that subcommittee. The senior members, in turn, considered themselves honored and privileged to be cut in on the nation's deepest secrets. Apparently, it never occurred to them to question the substance of the policies that produced those secrets. Probably in most cases they uncritically endorsed the policies.

From the point of view of the Executive branch, it was often a toss-up whether to toy with Congress or to level with it. After stepping down as director of the CIA, the late Allen W. Dulles said he had felt obliged to be forthright with only one person, the President of the United States. He suspected, he added, that J. Edgar Hoover operated the same way.[6] Dulles' perception of his relationship with Congress has been described by Tom Braden, now a columnist but once a CIA official. During the early 1950s, Braden recalled, Dulles was fretting at an agency meeting because he was due to appear later that morning before Senator Richard B. Russell (D–Ga.), chairman of the Senate Armed Services Committee. Braden wrote:

The question he is pondering as he puffs on his pipe is whether to tell the senators what is making him fret. He has just spent a lot of money on buying an intelligence network, and the network has turned out to be worthless. In fact, it's a little worse than worthless. All that money, Dulles now suspects, went to the KGB.

Therefore, the questions are somber and so are the answers. At last Dulles rises. "Well," he says, "I guess I'll have to fudge the truth a little."

His eyes twinkle at the word *fudge*, then suddenly turn serious. He twists his slightly stooped shoulders into the old tweed topcoat and heads for the door. But he turns back. "I'll tell the truth to Dick [Russell]," he says. "I always do." Then the twinkle returns and he adds, with a chuckle, "That is, if Dick wants to know."[7]

Years of exposure to the blandishments and charms of a succession of CIA directors naturally took its toll on the congressional sense of perspective. Congressman Michael J. Harrington (D–Mass.) was rebuked by the House Armed Services Committee, and denied further access to its files, for seeing to it that the American public—and the Congress, for that matter—learned of their government's clandestine, destructive interference in the internal affairs of Chile. What outraged senior and conservative members of Armed Services was Harrington's violation of committee rules: in an unsuccessful effort to get someone in Congress to follow up, he had passed to outsiders paraphrases of portions of "secret" testimony in which CIA Director William E. Colby, in 1974, had revealed the CIA's Chilean operation to Armed Services' intelligence subcommittee.

It wasn't the revelations that shocked the elders of Armed Services. Neither were they disturbed by the subcommittee's months-long burial of Colby's testimony, which came to light on September 8, 1974, through investigative reporting by the *New York Times'* Seymour M. Hersh. What angered them was Harrington's breach of the classification system. For them, *that* was the real—and perhaps only—outrage.

Even when Congress displays a will to exercise its oversight responsibilities, the Executive often thwarts it by the direct, simple technique of denying truth. On occasion, a witness lies outright. On other occasions, an official misleads a congressional panel by carefully constructing answers to be unreasonably narrow or literal. And on still other occasions, officials deny an action has occurred—and may honestly believe such to be the case. In those instances, they themselves either have been deceived or deprived of relevant information.

In 1973, members of the House Foreign Affairs and Senate Foreign Relations committees questioned State Department officials about United States activities in Chile. The officials, some testifying under oath, left the clear impression that the administration was denying unconfirmed rumors that the CIA had engaged in covert political activities in Chile. Obviously, those officials either were lying, or were purposely misleading the committees; or else they were baring abysmal ignorance of matters in which they were paid to be expert and current. Among those witnesses were the American ambassador to Chile, his deputy, and superiors in the State Department. As of May 1976, the contradictions between the testimony and actual events had not been resolved. And Senate Foreign Relations had yet to act on a one-and-a-half-year-old staff recommendation that the Justice Department investigate for possible perjury.

Doubtless the Executive branch and its allies would howl in anguish should Congress actually cite for perjury a government official who had lied for what he claimed were reasons of "national security"; but thereafter the Executive might be more likely to level with Congress. Currently, what incentive is there to do so?

For Congress to play such hard ball with the Executive is almost unheard of; for the Executive to use intimidation to have its way with Congress is not, even if specific cases are rare and hard to prove.

In the case of the FBI, the public relations genius of the late J. Edgar Hoover, its first and long-time director, made genuine congressional oversight difficult. By endlessly feeding the press, film-makers, television, and favored writers a diet rich in the hokum and pablum they were pleased to purvey, he built an image in the public mind of an incorruptible, supertough, superefficient, gangster-exterminating, Red-hunting G-man. It was a "super-human image," Clarence M. Kelley, the current FBI director, acknowledged in a remarkable speech in which he said that the bureau was "truly sorry" for past abuses of its power. Strikingly, Kelley, the former police chief of Kansas City, Missouri, linked the bloated image, "and the power and glory that accompanied it," to "a unique position that permitted improper activity without accountability." With the image at last "greatly diminished," the FBI will "never again" be unaccountable for improper actions, Kelley said. Indeed, he said, "no man should again serve as Director for more than ten years. No Director of the FBI should abide incursions upon the liberties of the people." In another passage, Kelley cut Hoover down from godlike to human scale:

Amid the thunder and lightning of criticism, the FBI has descended from Mount Olympus. And, as it turns out, we are mere mortals, with human imperfections, and we always *have* been.[8]

That Kelley finally dared to utter such truths was in good measure a tribute to the effectiveness of the congressional oversight provided by the Senate Intelligence Committee, headed by Senator Frank Church (D–Idaho), which in 1975 began a fifteen-month investigation of the intelligence and law-enforcement agencies. But in the preceding fifty-one years since Attorney General Harlan Fiske Stone appointed Hoover acting director of the old Bureau of Intelligence with a mandate to limit its activities "strictly to investigations of violations of the law, under my direction or under the direction of an Assistant Attorney General regularly conducting the work of the Department of Justice," there has been nothing but nonoversight, or parodies of oversight.[9] Few lawmakers were bold enough to do anything that might dim Hoover's image. And some, perceiving him as the nation's foremost protector of law-and-order and "national security," wanted him under no such restraints as those put on him by Stone, who was out of office ten months after issuing his mandate. "When in November, 1939, Hoover told the House Appropriations Committee that he had set up a 'general intelligence division' under presidential proclamation, no questions were asked," Laurence Stern said in a *Washington Post* story derived from *Intelligence Activities and the Rights of Americans,* the Church committee report.

Nor did any member of Congress challenge Hoover's assertion the following year that he was empowered to investigate espionage, sabotage, neutrality violations and "any other subversive activities."

In the words of the Senate report, "Congress was simply choosing to avoid the issue of defining the FBI's intelligence jurisdiction."

Even though these events took place in the security-conscious atmosphere of impending war, they set the basic pattern of Hoover's relation with Congress on not only legislative but budgetary matters over the remaining 32 years of his tenure. He died in 1972.[10]

For about twenty years, until his retirement in 1973, the chairman of the House Appropriations subcommittee with responsibility for the FBI was Congressman John J. Rooney, a Brooklyn Democrat who groveled before Hoover when he was not petulantly tyrannizing the State Department, which also was in his bailiwick. The Rooney subcommittee and its Senate counterpart were the only congressional forums in which the haughty Hoover deigned to appear—and then only on condition that the public be excluded. Only after Congress meekly had given Hoover all the money he wanted did the subcommittees release the transcripts of his testimony. The transcripts evoked the atmosphere of a lovefeast. Hoover would tick off statistics intended to prove the FBI's efficiency in recovering stolen cars. If it was a Rooney hearing, the chairman, after being praised by the director for providing indispensable support, would praise Hoover. Then each would denounce do-gooders, radicals, and subversives. Rooney would not ask—and would not allow anyone else to ask, if anyone was inclined do so—any potentially embarrassing questions.

The depravity of the Rooney approach was captured in Hoover's vicious effort to ruin the Rev. Dr. Martin Luther King, Jr., the black civil rights leader who, at the March on Washington in August 1963, had told the nation of his "dream" that a day would come when "all of God's children, black men and white men, Jews and Gentiles, Protestants and Catholics, will be able to join hands and sing in the words of the old Negro spiritual, 'Free at last, free at last, thank God Almighty, I'm free at last.' " In 1964, the FBI "anonymously" mailed to King a "sterilized" tape recording apparently containing compromising, sexually explicit excerpts of conversations in King's hotel rooms. Mailed with the tape was an anonymous letter that King apparently regarded as a suicide suggestion. The purpose of the mailing, former FBI Assistant Director William Sullivan told the Senate Intelligence Committee, was "to blackmail King into silence . . . to stop him from criticizing Hoover . . . to diminish his stature. In other words, if it caused a break between Coretta [Mrs. King] and Martin Luther King, that would diminish his stature. It would weaken him as a leader.' " Eight years later, in 1971, Rooney was interviewed by NBC News about FBI offers of King tapes and transcripts to news media:

Rooney. Now you talk about the FBI leaking something about Martin Luther King. I happen to know all about Martin Luther King, but I have never told anybody.

Interviewer. How do you know everything about Martin Luther King?

Rooney. From the Federal Bureau of Investigation.

Interviewer. They've told you—gave you information based on taps or other sources about Martin Luther King?

Rooney. They did.

Interviewer. Is that proper?

Rooney. Why not?

Others on Capitol Hill who were not Neanderthal footservants such as John Rooney helped Hoover by keeping silent, sometimes out of fear. If they did not know from the grapevine that Hoover and his experts in snooping had been gathering information for a long time on congressmen and senators, they knew it from columnist Jack Anderson, who is of course widely read in Washington, and who had been saying for years that the information-gathering on legislators had been under way since 1950. In 1972, W. Patrick Gray, Hoover's interim successor, claimed that the FBI really had no dossiers or secret files. In a column on November 6, 1972, Anderson disclosed that, six months earlier, he had offered to show Gray where some of the files were stashed, recalled that he had printed the file numbers of some of the dossiers, and suggested he might start a search with the file on House Speaker Carl Albert. In that file, Anderson said, Gray would find a report—many years old now—"based upon a conversation picked up by an FBI listening device, about Albert's relationship with lobbyist Fred Black." It hardly can be doubted that knowledge of such activities on Capitol Hill had a chilling effect on prospective critics of the FBI; and it is open to no doubt whatsoever that while Hoover was in charge of the FBI it was almost never criticized by a lawmaker. Not until 1975 was there official confirmation of the existence of the dossiers—along with a disclosure that the CIA kept files of its own on legislators who, for one reason or another, crossed its path.

The Internal Revenue Service, which knows the finances of every American, is empowered to audit tax returns, can select particular citizens it may care to investigate and prosecute, and has a large potential for illegal and improper harassment. But until the Senate created the Church committee, Congress did not bother to set up a unit with the specific assignment of monitoring possible abuses by the IRS. Heavy responsibility for this grotesque congressional nonfeasance falls on Congressman Wilbur D. Mills (D–Ark.), who until caught in a dalliance with a stripper had an adulatory press. As chairman of the House Ways and Means Committee, he insisted that it operate as a single unit, with no subcommittees. This mode of operation, a rarity on Capitol Hill, not only enabled Mills to maintain tight control, but also to tie down members in lengthy legislative hearings. They had no time left to monitor the IRS, even if they had wanted to do so. One consequence, Senator Church said in early 1976, was that the IRS—"the largest intelligence agency in the country"—had given copies of twenty-nine thousand taxpayers' returns to other federal agencies in 1975 alone, and had done so "to assist them in intimidating citizens." The recipient agencies included the CIA and the FBI. Between 1969 and 1973, the Church committee said in *Intelligence Activities*, the IRS had created intelligence files "on more than 11,000 individuals and groups" and had started tax investigations "on the basis of political rather than tax criteria."

The CIA, FBI, and IRS each has a legislative charter that Congress was remiss in monitoring. In the case of the National Security Agency (NSA), however, Congress was even more remiss, because it permitted the NSA to come into being and grow like Topsy, not under authority of law, but under an Executive Order; and not under an ordinary Executive Order, but under one that never has been made public. President Truman issued the directive in 1952. It told the NSA to "obtain foreign intelligence from foreign communications or foreign electronic signals," General Lew Allen, Jr., the current director of the NSA, is said to have told the House Intelligence Committee.[11] But under "a secret arrangement" with ITT, RCA Global Communications, and Western Union, the NSA obtained "millions of cables which had been sent by American citizens in the reasonable expectation that they would be kept private," the Senate Intelligence Committee said in *Intelligence Activities*. Of the approximately one hundred fifty thousand messages taken each month, several thousand were distributed by the NSA to other government agencies. This supersnoop operation ended in May 1975 after Congress got wind of it.

The NSA was not subjected even to pseudo-oversight on Capitol Hill until 1975, by which time it had twenty thousand employees, was spending about $1 billion a year directly, and had at its disposal the services of about eighty thousand servicemen and civilians who serve the Army, Navy, and Air Force cryptologic agencies at a cost of possibly $14 billion.[12] "The N.S.A.'s place on the organizational chart is ambiguous: It is 'within but not a part of' the Defense Department," David Kahn, author of *The Codebreakers*, has said. "It gets its assignments from other elements of the Government. They tell the United States Intelligence Board what information they need that the N.S.A. can probably provide."[13]

In the early 1960s, General Allen told the Church committee, domestic law-enforcement agencies asked the NSA for information on United States citizens traveling to Fidel Castro's Cuba, and two attorneys general and a secretary of defense approved the request. In 1970, the Bureau of Narcotics and Dangerous Drugs, worried about the legality of tapping a limited number of pay phones in New York City, submitted the names of 450 Americans to the NSA for inclusion in its "watch list." This resulted in the NSA intercepting "thousands of international phone calls" between New York and Latin America, *Intelligence Activities* disclosed. The FBI provided the names of 1,000 Americans (and 1,700 foreigners) for the "watch list," and the CIA, the Secret Service, and the Pentagon added others, for a grand total, Allen said, of 1,650 Americans. Allen said he abolished the list when he took command in 1973.

The gist of what we had here was this: the NSA, a huge establishment using electronic equipment of almost unimaginable sophistication, was massively invading the privacy of thousands of persons and businesses. The NSA was engaging in this activity without the knowledge or authorization of Congress, and at the request of other agencies that Congress had authorized but didn't oversee. The NSA has the capability "to monitor anything," Senator Church has warned. That capability "could be turned around on the American people," he said. "And no American would have any privacy left. There would be no place to hide. If a dictator ever took charge in this country, the technological capability that the intelligence community has given the Government could enable it to impose total tyranny."[14]

"Presidents and other senior executive officials, particularly the Attorneys General, have virtually abdicated their constitutional responsibility to oversee and set standards for intelligence activity," the Senate Intelligence Committee said in *Intelligence Activities*. The abdication began with Franklin Roosevelt in 1940, when he overturned a brief ban on wiretapping imposed by Attorney General Robert H. Jackson and ruled the practice necessary against "persons suspected of subversive activities . . ." When the press in 1941 reported that labor leader Harry Bridges had discovered a FBI tap on him, J. Edgar Hoover gave FDR a full briefing, according to an account by Francis Biddle, who was attorney general at the time. Then, grinning broadly, the President slapped Hoover on the back and said, Biddle recalled, "By God, Edgar, that's the first time you've been caught with your pants down.' "[15] With that kind of ho-hoing fortifying FDR's official go-ahead for wiretapping "persons suspected of subversive activities," Biddle in the same year, 1941, approved a tap on the Los Angeles Chamber of Commerce, difficult to believe though that may be. He did provide a caveat: Unless the FBI turns up "some evidence connecting the Chamber of Commerce with espionage, I think the surveillance should be discontinued."[16] With the gates opened wide, here is what FDR and his successors in the White House and their attorneys general did in the snooping field, as summarized in *Intelligence Activities:*

• Mr. Roosevelt asked the FBI to file "the names of citizens sending telegrams to the White House opposing his 'national defense' policy and supporting Col. Charles Lindbergh."

• "President Truman received inside information on a former Roosevelt aide's efforts [the aide was Thomas C. (Tommy the Cork) Corcoran, now a Washington lawyer] to influence his appointments, labor union negotiating plans and the publishing plans of journalists." Such tidbits of political intelligence came to Mr. Truman from Hoover labeled "Personal and Confidential."

• "President Eisenhower received reports on purely political and social contacts with foreign officials by Bernard Baruch, Mrs. Eleanor Roosevelt and Supreme Court Justice William O. Douglas." [In 1954, shortly after the Supreme Court had denounced "the indecency of installing a microphone in a bedroom," Mr. Eisenhower's attorney general, Herbert Brownell, Jr., took issue with the Court. Reversing a ban by Howard McGrath, his predecessor in the Truman Administration, on microphone surveillances requiring break-ins, Brownell asserted that bugs in a bedroom might be necessary occasionally. He urged a blank check for "unrestricted use of this technique in the national interest."][17]

During the Kennedy Administration, when the Dominican Republic was campaigning for a larger share of the United States quota for foreign sugar, the FBI bugged a New York hotel room occupied by Congressman Harold Cooley (D–N.C.), chairman of the House Agriculture Committee, and also bugged a Washington law firm, two registered lobbyists, Capitol Hill staff members, and, on the specific authorization of Attorney General Robert F. Kennedy, Cooley's secretary. Kennedy, in 1963, authorized phone taps on Martin Luther King, Jr., requested but never got an evaluation of the results although he got "unattributed information . . . from which he might have concluded that microphones were the source," and never requested termination of the taps. The FBI thus was left free to, and did, install additional taps on King by invoking Kennedy's original authorization.

• "President Johnson asked the FBI to conduct 'name checks' of his critics and of members of the staff of his 1964 opponent, Senator Barry Goldwater. He also requested purely political intelligence on his critics in the Senate, and received extensive intelligence reports on political activity at the 1964 Democratic Convention from FBI electronic surveillance." In late 1964, *Washington Post* executive editor Benjamin C. Bradlee told Attorney General Nicholas deB. Katzenbach and Assistant Attorney General Burke Marshall that a reporter in the Washington bureau of *Newsweek*, of which Bradlee was chief at the time, had been approached by the FBI with an offer to hear some "interesting" tapes on Dr. King. In testimony to the Church committee, Katzenbach said he had been "shocked" and had informed President Johnson, who promised to inform Hoover. But the committee "discovered no evidence . . . that the President made any further effort to halt the discrediting campaign at this time or at any other time; indeed, the bureau's campaign continued for several years after this incident."

• "President Nixon authorized a program of wiretaps which produced for the White House purely political or personal information unrelated to national security, including information about a Supreme Court justice."

Among other personal uses made of the law-enforcement and intelligence agencies were President Kennedy's deployment of the FBI and IRS to harass steel-company executives in 1962, and President Nixon's manipulation of the CIA to try to defame Daniel Ellsberg for releasing the Pentagon Papers. But no known episode was more disquieting than the four-year paramilitary operation that the Kennedy Administration had the CIA mount against Castro's Cuba. Apparently intended somehow to avenge the Bay of Pigs fiasco, the operation developed into a secret war. Writers Taylor Branch and George Crile III, who made an extensive investigation, said that the secret war involved thousands of Cuban exiles and other persons who, operating out of bases in the United States, staged commando raids, destroyed industrial and power facilities, and made numerous attempts to assassinate Castro—all at a cost of about $100 million a year to unknowing taxpayers. The war remained secret not only for tactical reasons, but also because Congress, on which the Framers had conferred exclusive war-making authority, had authorized no such enterprise. But Branch and Crile cited a third and more sophisticated reason for secrecy: President Kennedy (they contend) wanted to perpetuate the illusion that the Bay of Pigs had so eroded his faith in the CIA that he no longer would trust it as he had before. He "summoned forth his much admired charisma to present himself as a man who had learned the hard lessons of history and who was deeply suspicious of the CIA," they wrote in *Harper's* magazine.

Word seeped from the White House into the newspapers that Kennedy had inherited the CIA's Cuban plan from the Eisenhower Administration, that he never had put his heart in it, that he had been pressured into action by Agency officials with a personal interest in the scheme who coerced the young and inexperienced President before he even had time to redecorate the Oval Office. The President was said to have grave doubts about advancing the cause of free, democratic societies by secret and devious means. He was known to be seething with anger at his advisers and especially at the CIA, which he told his aides he would like to "splinter . . . into a thousand pieces and scatter to the winds.". . .

But instead of "splintering" the Agency, the President moved to control and strengthen it by assigning Robert Kennedy to supervise its clandestine operations.

The Attorney General protected the President's interest by forcing the CIA to adhere to the chief political lesson of the Bay of Pigs—that clandestine operations should never expose American leaders to the risk of spectacular failure. Within this restriction, the Kennedys placed more, not less, of the free world's defense in the hands of the CIA. Rather than shriveling up in the disgrace of its Cuban failure, the overt action side of the Agency grew faster than it ever had before, receiving a new lease on life and a new infusion of confidence from the White House."[18]

In late 1975, the Church committee, in a report on alleged assassination plots against foreign leaders, did not lay the death of any of them directly to any President or to the CIA. The committee found, however, that American officials had initiated and participated in plots to assassinate the Congo's Patrice Lumumba and Fidel Castro, and that these officials had encouraged or been privy to coup plots which resulted in the deaths of the Dominican Republic's Rafael Trujillo, South Vietnam's Ngo Dinh Diem, and Chile's General Rene Schneider. "Whether or not the Presidents in fact knew about the assassination plots, and even if their subordinates failed in their duty of full disclosure, it still follows that the Presidents should have known about the plots," the Church committee said in a report. "This sets a demanding standard, but one the committee supports. The future of democracy rests upon such accountability." But accountability there was not. "The whole thing strains credulity . . . even the Director of the CIA didn't know what was going on for long periods of time," Senator Church said.[19] Senator Walter F. Mondale (D–Minn.), a member of the committee, compared the effort to ascertain who was in charge of murder plots to "pinning jelly to a wall."[20] The committee itself said that the "ambiguity and imprecision leaves open the possibility that there was a successful 'plausible denial' and that Presidential authorization was issued but is now obscured."[21]

In addition to assassination plots, the government engaged in all sorts of other covert activities in which we took sides in other countries. In Chile, for example, the CIA financed *El Mercurio,* an anti-Allende newspaper, and in Guatemala, Iran, Indonesia, and numerous other nations with which we supposedly were at peace the CIA conducted operations against leftists—which is to say, against the right of other peoples to choose their own leaders. The peaks of hypocrisy in all of this are high, but President Nixon scaled them with surpassing ease when he gave this answer to a reporter's question about the possibility that the United States had intervened against Allende:

For the United States to have intervened in a free election and to have turned it around, I think, would have had repercussions all over Latin America that would have been far worse than what happened in Chile.[22]

As he knew, the United States in fact had intervened—covertly. "If there had been no CIA to do the job covertly," Victor Marchetti and John D. Marks said in *The CIA and the Cult of Intelligence*, "the U.S. Government almost certainly would not have tried to involve itself in the Chilean elections, since it was obviously not willing to own up to its actions."[23] The authors make a point we want to underscore: Presidents frequently have readily or even casually approved foreign-policy initiatives covertly that they would never approve overtly. When they have acted covertly, they have escaped the constraints of the Constitution, particularly the appropriations and oversight powers vested in Congress. Had they acted overtly, they would have found, and knew they would have found, little or no support, for, and perhaps strong opposition to, their meddlesome ventures abroad. The penchant for secrecy has continued even into the Ford Administration, one case in point being President Ford's directive to the CIA to pass $6 million to non-Communist politicians in Italy. He did not ask, and would not have gotten, advance approval from Congress for pouring the money down an Italian drain.

No inference should be drawn that the CIA and the FBI did only what Presidents told them to do. The Church committee's *Intelligence Activities* report cited a stunning example to the contrary: the CIA's program, carried out for about twenty years, of indiscriminately opening citizens' first-class mail. The FBI also had a mail-opening program, but cancelled it in 1966. "The bureau continued, however, to receive the illegal fruits of CIA's program," the report said.

In 1970, the heads of both agencies signed a document for President Nixon, which correctly stated that mail opening was illegal, falsely stated that it had been discontinued and proposed that the illegal opening of mail should be resumed because it would provide useful results. The President approved the program, but withdrew his approval five days later. *The illegal opening continued nonetheless. Throughout this period CIA officials knew that mail opening was illegal but expressed concern about the "flap potential" of exposure, not about the illegality of their activity.* [Emphasis added]

With Presidents using the agencies for their own often illegal purposes, with the agencies undertaking illegal actions on their own, and with congressional nonfeasance aiding and abetting the whole process, it would be improbable that other accountability mechanisms could amount to much—and they didn't. The Justice Department had been ignoring allegations of criminal conduct by CIA officials for more than twenty years and was guilty of "an abdication of its statutory responsibilities," said the Rockefeller commission in June 1975 in a report on the CIA's "plainly unlawful" conduct over its twenty-eight-year history. The White House set up the Forty Committee, composed of top national-security officials, to review CIA covert-action projects, but the Church committee, in its report on *Foreign and Military Intelligence Activities*, said that the Forty Committee actually reviewed only a "small fraction" of the projects, frequently did not bother to meet formally to consider them, and instead gave or withheld approval in phone calls. The Office of Management and Budget, which is supposed to police federal spending for the White House, provided only "a handful of people with little independent supervision, with inadequate controls, even less auditing and an overabundance of security" in the case of the CIA, which was getting an estimated $10 billion annually, the House Intelligence Committee found.[24] The General Accounting Office, the congressional watchdog, found itself locked out when it tried to audit the performance of intelligence agencies; they invoked secrecy to elude this routine accountability. Finally, what of the Postal Service, supposedly the preserver of the sanctity of the mails? In 1961, Postmaster General J. Edward Day told the Church committee, CIA Director Allen Dulles confided that he had something "very secret" to divulge. Day said he interrupted to ask, "Do I have to know about it?" Dulles answered, "No."

With no accountability anywhere, here are just a few of the things that happened, as reported by the Senate and House Intelligence committees and the Rockefeller commission. The FBI developed more than five hundred thousand domestic intelligence files. The CIA indexed at least three hundred thousand individuals and, during its Operation CHAOS (1967–1973) created separate files on seventy-two hundred Americans and more than one hundred domestic groups. The IRS created intelligence files on more than eleven thousand individuals and groups. The CIA enlisted underworld figure John Roselli in its campaign to kill Castro. The FBI sent an anonymous letter to the wife of a Ku Klux Klansman, asserting the adultery of her husband, that was intended to break up her marriage. The FBI disrupted meetings, ostracized persons from their professions, and provoked target groups into rivalries that could have resulted in the death of some of their members. During the 1960s alone, the FBI and CIA conducted hundreds of break-ins, sometimes to install bugs or to steal membership lists. The National Security Agency eavesdropped on the conversations of antiwar protesters, including pediatrician Benjamin Spock, actress Jane Fonda, and the Rev. Ralph Abernathy, successor to Dr. King. The FBI spent twenty-five years monitoring the wholly legal activity of the National Association for the Advancement of Colored People. For nine years starting in 1954, CIA employees went into bars in one city on the

THE CIA, FBI, NSA, AND IRS

East Coast and another on the West Coast, randomly picked up unsuspecting patrons, and slipped LSD into their food and drink. All of these things—and others cited elsewhere in this book—were done (again) in the name of "national security".

The trigger for the congressional investigations and for President Ford's appointment of Vice-President Rockefeller to chair an investigatory commission was a story in the *New York Times* on December 22, 1974, in which Seymour Hersh reported on massive domestic spying by the CIA, and earlier accounts of covert efforts to overthrow the Allende government in Chile. The Rockefeller commission, in its report in June 1975, called for stringent controls of the CIA. In February 1976, Gerald Ford announced a plan to control the agency by Executive Order. It boiled down to nothing more than trusting whatever President may be in office, and legitimatizing domestic spying. "I would hope," he told a press conference, "that the American people will elect a President who will not abuse [his] responsibility." Columnist and author Garry Wills pointed out a slight defect in the Ford plan: the CIA has been most dangerous when controlled by a President because it became the "action arm of the Imperial Presidency. . . . In other words, in a form of government where legitimacy arises only from accountability the CIA was formed expressly to escape accountability."[25]

Meanwhile on Capitol Hill, the House Intelligence Committee under Congressman Pike, after a late start, began to hold *public* hearings. This was crucial, because it provided the clashes, the confrontations, the drama, and the other ingredients essential for a thorough education of the public. Sadly, the Pike effort foundered with the assassination by unidentified assailants of Richard S. Welch, who had been the chief of the CIA station in Athens, and with the furor which resulted when CBS correspondent Daniel Schorr obtained a copy of the committee's final report and secretly arranged for its publication. "Both incidents gave the enemies of reform fresh red herrings to raise in the name of national security," the *Washington Post*'s George Lardner, Jr., wrote in the July 1976 *Progressive*.

The Senate Intelligence Committee did much to make "assassinations almost tedious, burglaries boring, and eavesdropping old-hat," Lardner said.

It is, to be sure, not easy to make so little of so much. But it was a failure that has yet to be appreciated. Quite simply, the system broke down amid face-saving pretexts about how well it was working. The investigators mimicked the investigated. The corruption of secrecy prevailed. . . .

Careful handling was required. Not even the American Revolution was brought on by popular demand. But instead of the exquisite sense of timing and flair for drama that gave us 1776, the would-be reformers of the nation's intelligence community insisted on closed-door hearings, counterproductive extensions of announced deadlines, and elaborate courtesies for the abusers of power. . . .

John N. Mitchell, the convicted felon who was Nixon's Attorney General, was asked for his avuncular advice on how to make the system work. Henry Kissinger, the resident Secretary of State who has been accused in some quarters of being less than truthful was . . . spared the rigors of public interrogation [except by the Pike committee, which voted several times to ask the House to cite him for contempt; nothing came of it].

Instead of a Senator Sam Ervin wiggling his eyebrows and waving his dog-eared copy of the Constitution in front of the television cameras, as he did in the Watergate investigation, the public saw (or did not see) a strung-out series of closed sessions and heard (or tuned out) a string of "no comments." Lardner pointed out that chairman Church "was in a fix no matter which way he turned. Had he insisted on sticking to the committee's original September [1975] deadline, he would have been accused of giving the investigation short shrift so he could run for President. As it was, he kept slogging ahead until the headlines began to read like warmed-over news leaks, until the public began to yawn."

With the public starting to yawn, reform—*real* reform—at times seemed almost hopeless. Indeed, Senate "conservatives" such as chairman John Stennis, one of the blindest and deafest of the CIA watchdogs, came within an ace of maintaining the status quo. Finally, Church and Senators Abraham A. Ribicoff (D–Conn.) and Howard W. Cannon (D–Nev.) developed, and the Senate adopted, a compromise between resolutions proposed by the former's Government Operations Committee and the latter's Rules Committee for a permanent Senate select committee to monitor the intelligence agencies.

The Senate beat back, 63 to 31, an effort by Stennis and Senator John G. Tower (R–Texas), a member of the Church committee who refused to sign its final report, as did Senator Goldwater, to leave the new committee with control only over the CIA. Then, on May 19, 1976, the Senate adopted the resolution for the new select committee 72 to 22.

The committee has fifteen members, exclusive jurisdiction over any legislation affecting the CIA, and power to subpoena information from the agencies. In addition, the committee will share legislative jurisdiction with the Armed Services Committee over the Defense Intelligence Agency, the National Security Agency, and the military intelligence agencies, and with the Judiciary Committee over the FBI.

To be sure, this was an important step forward. But it would be erroneous to assume that it was sufficient. On the day the Senate approved the compromise resolution, Senator Gaylord Nelson (D–Wis.) pointed out that it undercut the committee in deeply disturbing ways. The paramount issue was "how to curb the abuses of the intelligence agencies, and not how to maintain secrecy," he said in a floor speech. The resolution, however, put the emphasis on secrecy. Once someone in the Executive with a rubber stamp classifies some material—under a system that to this day has "no basis in law or reason"—the Senate is required by its resolution to impute validity to the classification. Rather than authorizing the select committee to examine whether the classification is genuinely needed to protect national security and, then, under careful procedures, to decide whether the material should be disclosed, the resolution says that if there is a presidential objection to disclosure the issue can be decided only by vote of the full Senate. This "makes it likely that decisions on classified information will reflect undue deference to the executive's classification system," Nelson warned.

Moreover, he said, the resolution does not substitute for "legislation telling the intelligence community and the public what surveillance techniques are legal and which are not and defining the jurisdictional limits of each agency." For Congress not to enact prohibitions on such practices as "warrantless wiretapping, politically motivated tax audits, or attempted assassinations of foreign leaders" is, Nelson said, a "serious abdication of congressional responsibility."

Corporations exist because of a societal decision that in pursuing their own interests they will, even without seeking to do so, advance the public interest. The corporation is "a creature of the state," the Supreme Court has said. "It is presumed to be incorporated for the benefit of the people. . . . Its rights are only preserved to it as long as it obeys the laws of its creation."[1]

The essential problem always has been government's seemingly chronic failure to make corporations accountable, in reasonable measure and in reasonable time, for activities adverse to the public interest. To be sure, government has made a stab at it with criminal, antitrust, environmental, tax, and other laws, with regulatory agencies, with disclosure and fiduciary requirements, and with a grab-bag of other devices. But when it comes to megacorporations, particularly the multinationals, we simply have failed to equip ourselves to cope with the mega-unaccountability of which they repeatedly have shown themselves to be capable.

There is first of all the question of the degree of loyalty that the United States can count upon from multinationals which in pursuing their self-interest may necessarily look upon this or any country merely as another haven in which to do business.

The question arises even as to General Motors, which, unlike, say, International Telephone and Telegraph, always has done the bulk of its business in the United States. In 1929, GM acquired the largest automobile company in Germany, Adam Opel, A.G. This predestined the subsidiary to become important to the Nazi war effort. In a heavily documented study presented to the Senate Subcommittee on Antitrust and Monopoly in February 1974, Bradford C. Snell, an assistant subcommittee counsel, wrote:

GM's participation in Germany's preparation for war began in 1935. That year its Opel subsidiary cooperated with the Reich in locating a new heavy truck facility at Brandenburg, which military officials advised would be less vulnerable to enemy air attacks. During the succeeding years, GM supplied the Wehrmacht with Opel "Blitz" trucks from the Brandenburg complex. For these and other contributions to wartime preparations, GM's chief executive for overseas operations in 1938 was awarded the Order of the German Eagle (first class) by Chancellor Adolf Hitler.[2]

GM, in a reply to Snell's paper that the subcommittee published at the company's request, did not deal directly with these particular charges. The company did say that up until 1939 Adam Opel "had produced only its traditional products—cars, trucks and spare parts." Heatedly denying any wrongdoing, and vigorously asserting its loyalty to the United States, GM went on to say, "After the German invasion of Poland in 1939, the American personnel resigned from management positions rather than participate in the production of war materials, even though at this time the United States was neutral"; however, "[t]he last of GM's American employees who had been assigned to Opel departed from Germany in [or, did not leave Germany until] early March 1941."

Snell continued:

Ford [Motor Co.] was also active in Nazi Germany's war preparations. In 1938, for instance, it opened a truck assembly plant in Berlin whose "real purpose," according to U.S. Army Intelligence, was producing "troop transport-type" vehicles for the Wehrmacht. That year, Ford's chief executive received the Nazi German Eagle (first class).[3]

In a statement to the *Washington Post,* Ford said, "It should be obvious that the policies and direction of any company in Germany, regardless of its ownership immediately before and during World War II, were dictated by the German Government."[4]

GM, Standard Oil of New Jersey (now Exxon), and I. G. Farben entered into a joint venture called Ethyl G.m.b.H. that, Snell said,

provided the mechanized German armies with synthetic tetraethyl fuel. During 1936–39, at the urgent request of Nazi officials who realized that Germany's scarce petroleum reserves would not satisfy war demands, GM and Exxon joined with German chemical interests in the erection of the Ethyl tetraethyl plants. According to captured German records, these facilities contributed substantially to the German war effort: "The fact that since the beginning of the war we could produce lead-tetraethyl is entirely due to the circumstances that shortly before the Americans had presented us with the production plants complete with experimental knowledge." *"Without lead-tetraethyl,"* the wartime document added, *"the present method of warfare would be unthinkable."* (Emphasis supplied.)[5]

Four months after the United States entered World War II, the Justice Department obtained an indictment of Exxon and its principal officers for having made arrangements, starting in the late 1920s with I.G. Farben involving patent sharing and division of world markets. Jersey Standard agreed not to develop processes for the manufacture of synthetic rubber; in exchange, Farben agreed not to compete in the American petroleum market. After war broke out in Europe, but before the attack on Pearl Harbor, executives of Standard Oil and Farben, at a meeting in Holland, established a *modus vivendi* for continuing the arrangements in event of war between the United States and Germany—although the arrangements interfered with the ability of the United States to make synthetic rubber desperately needed after it entered the war in December 1941. Rather than face a criminal trial, Exxon and the indicted executives entered no-contest pleas—the legal equivalent of guilty pleas—and were fined the minor sums which were the maximum amounts permitted by law. A few days later, on March 26, 1942, the Senate Special Committee Investigating the National Defense Program held a hearing at which Thurman Arnold, chief of the Antitrust Division, put into the record documents on which the indictment had been based, including a memo from a Standard Oil official on the *modus vivendi* agreed to in Holland. After the hearing, the committee chairman, Harry S Truman, characterized the arrangements as treasonable.[6]

". . . on August 4, 1933, the *New York Times* reported in a small news item that the new Chancellor of Germany, Herr Hitler, had for the first time received a delegation of American businessmen at Berchtesgaden," Anthony Sampson wrote in *The Sovereign State of ITT*. "It consisted of two men: Colonel Sosthenese Behn [the late founder and president of ITT] and his representative in Germany, Henry Mann. The meeting was the beginning of a very special relationship between ITT and the Third Reich." Sampson provides rich detail about this relationship, but we shall focus on one aspect:

Behn also had meetings with Hermann Goering, the head of the German Air Force, and it was not long before ITT did Goering an important service. In 1938 Lorenz [a German electrical company Behn had bought] acquired a 28 percent share in the Focke-Wulf company, whose bombers were to wreak havoc on Allied convoys: . . .[7]

Subsequently, Behn began to enlarge his base in the United States. In September 1942, Sampson wrote:

he announced a great new ITT plant in New Jersey. ITT laboratories in America, helped by a contingent of refugee French engineers from Paris, achieved some valuable inventions, including the High Frequency Direction Finder, nicknamed Huff-Duff, which was used to detect German submarines attacking the Allied convoys in the Atlantic. Thus while ITT Focke-Wulf planes were bombing Allied ships, and ITT lines were passing information to German submarines, ITT direction finders were saving other ships from torpedoes. . . .[8]

Whether Behn was ultimately more helpful to the Allies than he had been to the Axis may never be known, even after the intelligence records are available; perhaps only he knew whether he was ultimately an agent or a double agent. But certainly there could be no doubt where his first loyalty lay; the only power he consistently served was the supranational power of ITT.[9]

The company managed to bury its history "in a mountain of public relations, so that scarcely anyone on its staff now [1973] knows that it was ever associated with Focke-Wulf bombers or with Hitler's SS," Sampson wrote.

Most remarkable of all, ITT now presents itself as the innocent victim of the Second World War, and has been handsomely recompensed for its injuries. In 1967, nearly thirty years after the events, ITT actually managed to obtain $27 million in compensation from the American government, for war damage to Focke-Wulf plants—on the basis that they were American property bombed by Allied bombers.[10]

The compensation decision was made by the Foreign Claims Settlement Commission. Sampson termed the decision "surprising." Earlier, he noted, Behn's "important Nazi ally," lawyer Gerhardt Alois Westrick, had insisted on making Focke-Wulf and Lorenz (likewise a chief supplier of German war materiel, and the holder of a citation from the Nazi party for its outstanding contribution to the war effort) German companies. Banker Kurt von Schroeder, "the safeguarder of ITT's progress in Germany" who was to become "a general in the SS and the crucial channel of funds into Hitler's Gestapo," had insisted on the same thing. Behn had connived with them to secure a favored status for ITT plants in Germany.[11] Moreover, before World War II ended, Nazi officials themselves made large payments to ITT subsidiaries "to compensate for war damage and promote a quick resumption of the war production. The Focke-Wulf manufacturing company, for instance, received about 185 million [reichsmarks]."[12] Mark J. Green, writing about ITT's representation in the Settlement Commission matter by Covington & Burling, the prestigious Washington law firm, said a former Covington lawyer told him:

The case was a perfect example of the nonadversary process in action. . . . There was no one representing the public saying "disallow!" or cross-examining ITT. The agency was very helpful to us, since all were on one side. Their job was to give away the money and our job was to get it.[13]

The commission having been set up to compensate United States nationals for damage done to their property in enemy countries, the $27 million was, Sampson said, "a notable reward for a company that had so deliberately invested in the German war effort, and so carefully arranged to become German. If the Nazis had won, ITT in Germany would have appeared impeccably Nazi; as they lost, it reemerged as impeccably American."[14]

We turn now to the large oil companies, particularly the five American-based enterprises among the "seven sisters": Exxon (formerly Jersey Standard), Texaco (the Texas Co.), Mobil (formerly Socony-Vacuum), Standard of

California (Socal), and Gulf. On *Fortune's* list of the 500 largest industrial corporations in sales in 1974, they ranked first, fourth, fifth, sixth, and seventh, respectively.[15] Their combined sales were $117.9 billion, their assets $87.7 billion, and their net income $7.8 billion. The foreign "sisters" are the Royal Dutch/Shell Group (Dutch and British) and British Petroleum (formerly Anglo-Iranian, and, before that, Anglo-Persian Oil Company). On the *Fortune* list of the 500 largest industrial corporations *outside* the United States in 1974, they ranked first and second, respectively. Their combined sales were $51.3 billion, assets $45.3 billion, and net income $3.9 billion.

Such figures speak (deafeningly) for themselves. Awesome size, however, merely introduces questions about how to make such behemoths accountable to some entity other than themselves. Is Exxon (1974 sales of $42.1 billion, assets of $31.3 billion, and net income of $3.1 billion) viably accountable to New Jersey, the state that chartered it? The larger question is whether Exxon and the other American-based "sisters" are viably accountable to the United States. That was essentially the issue raised by the *Washington Post's* Hobart Rowen with Frank N. Ikard, president of the American Petroleum Institute, on NBC's "Meet The Press" on January 27, 1974:

> Rowen. Mr. Ikard, in your view are Exxon, Mobil, Texaco, Standard of California and Gulf American companies, or are they international companies with some other kind of obligation or loyalty?
>
> Ikard. It is my view there is no question but what they are American companies loyal to the United States of America and would always be governed by whatever they thought this country's best interests were.

Ikard surely knew better. For one thing, one of the institute's member companies, Phillips Petroleum, had given the game away only a month earlier, on December 27, 1973, when its president, W. F. Martin, appeared on "CBS Reports: The Corporation." Pointing out that American oil companies "are not increasing their exploration in the United States, despite our government's pleas to do so in order to ease our energy crisis and unfavorable balance of trade," CBS reporter Jay McMullen asked Martin, "Should the corporation be expected to serve the national interests of this country by accepting less profit in the U.S. than it can obtain abroad?"

> Martin. I don't think we should be expected to.
>
> McMullen. In general, should an international corporation licensed in the United States be expected to hold the nationalistic interests of the United States above the interests of the other countries where the corporation does business?
>
> Martin. Yeah, well, I th—I think not, from this standpoint: that if we were expected to do that, we couldn't operate in those foreign countries. I think it's just that simple.

One of the authors cited the McMullen-Martin exchange to Z. David (Zeke) Bonner, president of Gulf Oil-United States, when he was the guest on "Face the Nation," a CBS News' program, on February 17, 1974. Pointing out that Gulf is a much bigger international company than Phillips, the reporter inquired, "does Gulf put the national interests of the United States above the interests of other countries in which it does business?" Bonner's reply was lubricated by equivocation: "I think the answer to that really is yes, although we have to be good businessmen, we have to be fair in every country we operate in. . . . We're loyal Americans. We're good Americans."

Loyalty and goodness in large corporations are qualities easier to proclaim than to measure. Yardsticks must be devised. We offer but three—arbitrary and possibly simplistic, to be sure, but, we believe, sufficient. The first is respect for the antitrust laws of the United States, these being the expression of the country's philosophic opposition to vast monopolistic concentrations of economic power that translate into political power. The second is willingness to bear a reasonable share of the tax burden. The third is fair dealing in sales to the armed forces and the government.

It is only thanks to the Senate Subcommittee on Multinational Corporations, its chairman, Frank Church (D–Idaho), and its staff that we have, for the first time, an abundance of evidence against which such yardsticks may be laid. Not until 1974, at Church's request, did the Departments of Justice and State declassify numerous documents, thus illuminating hitherto secret strata of vital information. The papers are but part of a cornucopia of valuables in the subcommittee's published hearings and reports. These are exemplars of how the congressional oversight function ought to be, but rarely is, exercised. We here want to express our admiration for the staff work particularly of Jerome I. Levinson, the subcommittee counsel, Jack A. Blum, associate counsel, and John B. Henry, II, and William C. Lane, assistant counsel. For the account that follows, in addition to the subcommittee publications, we rely also on *The International Petroleum Cartel,* a classic staff report to the Federal Trade Commission.

In the early 1920s there were fears in the United States of a possible oil shortage. The major companies, however, shortly became aware of a different impending reality: a glut. With this, they pursued in concert two natural cartelist objectives: limiting the output of crude resources from the Middle East, and limiting competition among themselves in world markets.

In 1925, the Near East Development Corporation (NEDC), owned entirely by American companies but principally by Exxon and Mobil, acquired a 23.75 percent share of the Iraq Petroleum Company. The IPC was then, and long would be, with Iran, the most important source of Middle East oil. Shell, British Petroleum (BP), and the quasi-governmental Compagnie Française des Petroles (CFP) each held an identical share, and Armenian tycoon Calouste Gulbenkian held the remaining 5 percent. This joint venture united four of the sisters for the first time.

David I. Haberman, who from 1953 to 1968 was a Justice Department antitrust attorney on the trial staff that prosecuted the *International Oil Cartel Case,* as it came to be known, told the Church subcommittee how, in 1928, the companies moved to achieve the complementary objectives of limiting output and limiting competition. They

fashioned a complex of what may best be characterized as private "nonaggression treaties," complete with "spheres of influence" and "peacekeeping machinery" for their mutual protection and defense. These 1928 arrangements became the corner- stone of a vast new supra-national system whose quasi-sovereign powers, policies, and programs were for a half-century to transcend national boundaries, and political and legal barriers.[15]

The first of these treaties was the "Red Line Agreement," named after a red line the French had drawn on a map essentially around the old Ottoman Empire. This was an enormous geographic area embracing Iraq, Saudi Arabia, the lesser states bordering the Gulf of Aden and the Arabian Sea, Syria, Lebanon, Jordan, Israel, and Turkey. Excluded were Iran, where Britain had held a petroleum concession since 1901, and Kuwait, on the Persian Gulf. The parties to the agreement, executed in Ostend, Belgium, on July 31, 1928, were BP, Shell, CFP, the private Gulbenkian interests, and NEDC, the American instrument which by the early 1930s was owned in equal shares entirely by Exxon and Mobil (Atlantic Refining, Gulf, Sinclair Oil, Standard of Indiana, and Texaco by then had sold out their interests). The signatories agreed "to share and share alike all oil discovered and pro- duced" inside the red line, Haberman testified. They made it "practically impossible for [themselves] to compete in production, refining, or securing concessions," the FTC staff report said. "Indeed, *the prevention of competi- tion was the sole purpose of many of the principal provisions.*" In sum, Red Line was a device designed by the American, British, Dutch, and French companies "primarily to control for themselves at the *source* the vast new crude *supply* potential of the Middle East," Haberman said.

To implement Red Line, the IPC joint venture produced and apportioned crude among the partner-owners. IPC was not permitted to compete in world markets against its owners. But Red Line did leave the companies free to compete in important markets outside of its perimeter. This they did not want to do, having seen a price war between Shell and Mobil erupt in India in 1926, and having seen its competitive effects spread to the United States and Europe. Consequently, thanks to an initiative of Exxon and BP, the freedom to compete survived only about two months, until September 1928. Then the Achnacarry ("As Is") Agreement was reached at Achnacarry Castle in Scotland. There, executives of BP, Exxon, and Shell ostensibly had gathered to shoot grouse. Achnacarry was of extreme importance. It prevailed up to World War II, subject only to intervening pacts reached to reflect changed circumstances.

Achnacarry incorporated seven basic "As Is" principles. Foremost was the principle that the companies accept and agree to maintain their relative shares of the world petroleum market as they were at the time, i.e., 1928. The six other principles, in Haberman's summary,

dealt with matters essential to maintaining effective international control through the pooling of company resources. These called upon the companies to (1) mutually share among themselves on a preferential cost basis; (2) to avoid unnecessary duplication of new facilities; (3) to maintain for each geographic producing area its natural financial advantage with respect to its nearby geographic markets; (4) to draw supplies for a given market from the nearest producing area; (5) to avoid use of surplus crude production from any geographic area to upset the price structure in any other area; (6) to eliminate measures that would materially increase costs and prices.

In short, then, "As Is" principles constituted a grand policy blueprint for a corporate world government of petroleum industry dominated by a handful of companies, notably, Exxon, BP, and Shell.

"Because of Standard's fear of the American antitrust laws, the parties purposely refrained from signing the final agreement," Assistant Attorney General H. G. Morison said in a memorandum for Attorney General James P. McGranery on June 24, 1952.[16] The Achnacarry price mechanisms are of particular interest because, as will be made clear, they functioned to merge obedience to the antitrust laws and support of the armed forces into a single test of the loyalty and goodness imputed to oil companies by "Zeke" Bonner of Gulf. The key here was the price of crude on the United States Gulf Coast. Because of various federal and state conservation and other governmental policies this was a high price. Under Achnacarry, the price of crude sold by one cartel member to another was the Gulf Coast price plus phantom—and relatively high—freight charges from the Gulf to the port of import no matter how close it was to the true port of export. By 1952, the Justice Department has said, the Gulf Coast pricing gimmick had "netted the parties to the conspiracy [an honest word for what it was] hundreds of millions of dollars of profit."[17] The parties by then long since had included the Arabian American Oil Company (Aramco).

Aramco

Gulf Oil had an option to buy from a British venture an oil concession of about one hundred thousand acres on Bahrein Island, which adjoins Saudi Arabia in the Persian Gulf. As a member of the cartel, however, Gulf would have had to share with the other cartelists any oil it might develop in Bahrein. Consequently, Gulf in December 1928 decided to transfer its option to Socal, then an outsider. Because of direct intervention by the State Department, the British Foreign Office let the deal go through without political interference. Surely Socal thereby incurred a debt of gratitude to the government of the United States.

In 1932 Socal discovered oil in Bahrein. It began development rapidly. The crude was low-cost, abundant, and required a pipeline only twelve miles long to get it to the tanker-loading terminal. Thus, Socal created the first serious potential threat to the stability of the cartel's marketing and pricing arrangements. The company greatly aggravated the potential in 1933, when it obtained for sixty years a concession—the size of the states of Washington and Oregon combined—in the new desert kingdom of Saudi Arabia. In 1936, because it needed more investment capital as well as more market outlets, Socal took Texaco in as its partner. The Justice Department's Antitrust Division unsuccessfully attacked the joint venture.

In 1939, the California-Arabian Standard Oil Company—also known as Casoc, but hereafter referred to as Aramco, which it would become—made its first exports. So impressed was King Ibn Saud that he expanded the Aramco concession to 444,000 square miles. This gave the company the world's most valuable oil monopoly—"a piece of real estate," the Church subcommittee said, "the size of Texas, Louisiana, Oklahoma and New Mexico combined." Now Socal and Texaco were destined to be welcomed into the cartel, if they chose to enter it. Too big to be licked, they had to be joined.

The companies from 1933 onward tried to persuade the Roosevelt Administration that their Saudi Arabian concession had potential strategic importance to the United States. The outbreak of war brought Nazi submarine and other military operations that curtailed Aramco's operations and hence the revenues it paid to Saudi Arabia. Ibn Saud pressed the company for cash. In turn, the owning companies and then the king himself pressed the White House to give him money. The obvious vehicle was the Lend-Lease Act. Except for one catch: Congress had restricted Lend Lease to our "democratic allies." "The solution President Roosevelt finally arrived at was to have the British divert a portion of their $400 million U.S. Lend Lease loan to help King Saud stabilize his country," the subcommittee staff said. "During 1941, 1942, and 1943, as Aramco reduced its Saudi payments the

British Government advanced $5,285,000, $12,090,000, and $16,618,280, respectively."[18] Thus, American taxpayers picked up a $33.9 million tab for Aramco in just three years.

Meanwhile, fuel shortages here worsened. Our vulnerability became obvious and frightening. Aramco lobbied for direct and larger Lend Lease to the Saudis and offered a *quid pro quo:* an interest in a reserve in the ground of 300 million barrels of oil (the Aramco concession was then estimated to contain 20 billion barrels, or 6,607 times as much; the estimates as of March 1976 was 180 billion barrels—nine times larger.[19]) In February 1943, President Roosevelt formally declared "that the defense of Saudi Arabia is vital to the defense of the United States." Thanks mainly to Secretary of the Interior Harold Ickes, however, the government developed an alternative *quid pro quo* which Mr. Roosevelt fully endorsed in June 1943. The proposal —bold and foresighted—was for a Petroleum Reserves Corporation that would buy out Aramco and build and operate refineries, pipelines, and other essential collateral facilities. Had this plan actually materialized, it is fair to say, the United States never would have found itself at the mercy of Saudi Arabia and the other producing countries and their cartel, and at the mercy of the putatively American companies that are members of that cartel. But even though the government reduced its proposal for ownership of the concession from 100 percent to 33 1/3 percent, Socal and Texaco refused to sell an acre of it. Finally, in November 1943, a despairing board of the Petroleum Reserves Corporation voted to end negotiations with Aramco because it refused to "present a reasonable or workable arrangement or the basis of a fair agreement."

While the negotiations were under way in supposed secrecy, word of them leaked to the press. The oil industry reacted with angry attacks on the Roosevelt Administration and the Petroleum Reserves Corporation. The industry made the argument that "[o]il in the hands of nationals of the United States [i.e., loyal and good Americans such as Socal, Texaco, Exxon, Mobil, and Gulf] is equally available for national security with oil owned or financially shared in by the government of the United States."[20] The argument was catastrophically mistaken, even if it took us thirty years to find that out. Nonetheless it was an argument adopted by the State Department.

After the stock-purchase plan failed, Ickes, in early 1944, launched a new plan under which the government would help to assure adequate oil supplies for the United States by building a major pipeline from the Persian Gulf to the East Mediterranean. This, said the Independent Petroleum Association, would be a reversion "to the hated procedures of the Nazis and Fascists. . . ." Mr. Roosevelt shelved the plan in the spring of 1944. The proposed corporation faded away.

The government of the United States clearly had been good to Aramco.

How good was Aramco to the United States? The answer appears in Assistant Attorney General Morison's June 1952 memorandum:

In 1944, the United States Navy attempted to buy petroleum products on the Persian Gulf for fueling the American fleet. Aramco offered to supply the Navy, for delivery in Navy tankers at the Persian Gulf, petroleum products *on the basis of the United States Gulf Coast price.* Navy procurement officers attempted to negotiate a price on the basis of lower Aramco costs but were unable to get Aramco to agree. Finally, on September 15, 1945, at a time when petroleum products were in critically short supply, a contract was entered into with Aramco to purchase motor fuel, Navy fuel oil and Diesel oil *at the minimum U.S. Gulf Coast prices for products of similar grades in tanker lots.* Prior to this date, other American companies had sold to the Navy at lower prices on a negotiated basis.

The pricing arrangements entered into between the companies operating in the Middle East removed any competitive effort. These privately negotiated purchases by the Navy resulted in the exaction of high prices without any relationship whatever to the low cost of producing oil in the Middle East area. While the United States was being charged $1.05 per barrel [for oil produced at a cost of 40.6¢, including a royalty of 21¢], sales were being made by Aramco to both affiliated companies and to the Japanese at 70¢ and 84¢ per barrel. The Special Senate Committee Investigating the National Defense Program, in its report entitled *"Navy Purchases of Middle East Oil"* (1948), found that, between January 1942 and June 1947, the subsidiaries of Standard Oil Company of California and The Texas Company sold $70,000,000 worth of petroleum products to the United States Navy, which total price was about 38½ million dollars higher than prices charged to other purchasers.

The Federal Trade Commission has collected information to show that, while these prices were being charged to the Navy, the Standard Oil Company of California was making a net profit of 84¢ to 95¢ a barrel on its share of oil produced in the Middle East and was able to do so because of the aforementioned series of agreements which eliminated any threat of competition from any company in the world.

Again in February and May 1950, when all the above arrangements were in full effect, the United States Navy requested bids from five subsidiaries of the American companies. In response to this invitation for bids, identical prices were quoted. *The pricing arrangements entered into between the companies operating in the Middle East prevented these companies from competing with one another even for Government business.*

Following Pearl Harbor the Petroleum Administrator for War [Ickes] set up the Foreign Operations Committee to work out oil supply arrangements for foreign areas not controlled by the enemy and for meeting the requirements of United Nations armed forces. Such committee consisted of 14 members, 12 representing American companies and two British nominees representing Shell and Anglo-Iranian. Eighteen sub-committees were appointed. The same individuals whom the record shows to have been most active in carrying out the [As Is"] arrangements were members of these committees. Allocations of supplies were worked out on a percentage basis to the second decimal point and were identical in character with those found in the files of the companies for operations prior to Pearl Harbor.[21] (Emphasis in original.)

The same pricing arrangements were brought to sales of oil to the Mutual Security Agency (MSA) for delivery in Europe. "At least three of the American companies have 'over charged' the MSA approximately 70 million dollars in approximately a 3-year period, on the basis of lower prices they charged on sales 'among themselves,' " Attorney General McGranery said.

During the 1940s, Aramco—still owned entirely by Socal and Texaco—was making Exxon and Mobil, the original American members of the cartel, increasingly uneasy. For one thing, Aramco was able to market a barrel of crude for as little as 90 cents, while the cartel had to charge $1.30 and more. Furthermore, Exxon and Mobil concluded that without an opportunity to share in the immense low-cost reserves of Aramco they would have, over the long term, unfavorable marketing prospects in Europe. Even gaining access to these reserves, while helpful, would not be enough, however, because the original owners still would be able to undersell Exxon and Mobil in world markets. To prevent this from happening, the Exxon/Mobil strategy—not candidly disclosed to Socal and Texaco until they were in the web—was to have the expanded Aramco sell oil exclusively to its four owners, not at cost as was normal cartel practice, but at the "world market price." This was a price the cartel itself of course controlled. Over bitter resistance from Socal and Texaco, Exxon, like them a 30 percent owner, and Mobil, which acquired 10 percent, relentlessly forced the price at which the four owners bought oil from Aramco upward until it matched that of BP, Shell, and the Gulf Coast. Aramco thus could not possibly engage in price-cutting. It paid out its swollen earnings as dividends to its owners, supposedly on a pro rata basis, but actually on a basis that Exxon and Mobil cunningly had skewed to favor themselves because they lifted less than their 30 percent share of Aramco oil but still got their 30 percent share of the profits.

For Socal and Texaco, the lure of inviting in the predators was that Exxon and Mobil would supply them with needed capital and markets, to the extent that the 30 percent share of each in an engorged Aramco would be more remunerative than a 50 percent share in the old Aramco: less would be more. But when Texaco and Socal discovered—too late—that they had been ensnared in an arrangement under which they would be buying Aramco oil at "world market prices," they said in a futile and memorable memo, "Texaco and Socal are unalterably opposed to cartels or to the countenancing of circumstances which may give rise to cartels or which would in any way restrict trade."[22]

A Socal director, Ronald C. Stoner, had suggested an altogether different route: arrangements with independent American oil companies that needed Arabian crude, such as Phillips, Atlantic, Standard of Indiana, and Sinclair. Generally his idea was that Aramco would contract to supply the independents, and they, in turn, would agree to advance the capital Aramco needed to grow. That is to say, production levels in the Middle East would have been set under the Stoner plan not by a cartel with two American members, but by multiple American companies without cartel affiliations and with motivation and opportunity to compete strongly with the giants. As the Church subcommittee staff said, this would have "radically changed the international oil industry." And in terms of the national interest, drastically for the better.

But how were Exxon and Mobil to escape the pricing and sharing obligations of the Red Line Agreement? The key was a piece of legal sophistry: because two of the signatories, CFP and Gulbenkian, had been in France during its occupation by the Germans, they had become "enemies"; that being the case, Red Line could be pronounced null and void. Blessed by the State Department and the British government, Exxon and Mobil then won over Shell and BP to a plan under which the existing Red Line arrangements in Iraq would be retained intact in a substantially similar new agreement—except that Shell and BP would not share in Exxon/Mobil's participation in Aramco, and except also that the French and Gulbenkian would be brutally and cynically frozen forever out of Saudi Arabia. During short-lived litigation initiated in Britain by CFP, supported by Gulbenkian, Exxon and Mobil had the gall to say—correctly—that the Red Line agreement to which they happily had been parties for almost twenty years "was in restraint of trade and contrary to public policy and void and unenforcible in law."[23] So, of course, was the successor to Red Line. The success of the Exxon/Mobil strategy was another most fateful development, because it meant that with a joint interest in the immense reserves of Saudi Arabia, as well as Iraq, the companies would seek to develop neither with maximum speed; instead, they would manipulate production in both to serve the interests of a newly expanded cartel.

Procompetitive or Procartel?

The Exxon/Mobil approach had antitrust implications that concerned George V. Holton, vice-president and general counsel of Mobil. He explained why in a forthright and incisive memo to the Mobil Executive

Committee on October 28, 1946, in which we have italicized portions for obvious reasons:

The arrangement would place practical control of crude reserves in the Eastern Hemisphere in the hands of seven companies. Five of them would be American owned and all of the latter have substantial reserves in the Western Hemisphere also. Obviously this concentrated control would lend itself to arrangements which could affect the import and export trade of the United States [thereby raising acute antitrust questions] . . . *there is, of course, possibility that the mere existence of the potential control might under the American Tobacco Company decision be construed as an antitrust violation.*

I cannot believe that a comparatively few companies for any great length of time are going to be permitted to control world oil resources without some sort of regulation. This is a political question. What restraints will be imposed and by what authority falls within the realm of conjecture. Our job seems to be to play the game as best we can under the rules now in force.[24]

Exxon, Mobil, and Texaco informed Attorney General Tom Clark of the negotiations in 1946 and delivered copies of the joint venture contract to him on March 12, 1947, the day they were signed. But Antitrust Division records indicate that it did not begin to analyze the documents until 1948, when the Senate special committee investigating the National Defense Program, in a report, cited "a predilection on the part of the State Department to consider international oil as a part of foreign policy." The report went on to say:

Obviously, antitrust policy must be consistent with overall Government policy and the promotion of national security. For these reasons, it is recommended that no action be taken at this time.[25]

The report would have better served the country had it said that overall government policy must be consistent with antitrust policy which by definition is anticartel and, we would argue, consequently supportive of national security.

In their losing struggle to prevent Exxon and Mobil from converting Aramco into a venture that would make a profit on the product it sold to its owners, Socal and Texaco correctly had predicted that the change would trigger demands for a bigger share of the take from King Ibn Saud. He, after all, was not being cut in on those profits. Aramco increased the royalty from 20 cents to 30 cents per barrel, but he was not satisfied and continued to insist that he share in the profits. Tensions increased; Aramco even experienced incidents of sabotage.

The State Department was much concerned, because at the time—

1950—it considered the Middle East to be "highly attractive and highly vulnerable" to the threat of Communist aggression. State perceived the oil companies as vital to American foreign policy: "their royalty payments provided the economic base on which the governments of the Persian Gulf states rested," the Church subcommittee staff said in a summary of State's position. And the companies' "control over that oil supply underwrote the economic, political, and strategic security of Europe which depended upon an uninterruptable petroleum flow outside of Russian control."[26]

As in the case of the need of Socal and Texaco for more capital and marketing outlets, there was a choice to be made between a procompetitive and a procartel resolution. The procompetitive approach was suggested by Richard Funkhouser, a State Department official. It was that Aramco relinquish some undeveloped portions of its immense concession (bigger, it will be remembered, than Texas, Louisiana, Oklahoma, and New Mexico together) to the Saudi Arabian government, which then would take competitive bids for tracts from American firms that lacked assured sources of Middle Eastern crude. This was a lovely concept because Ibn Saud would have gotten his money by advancing competition—which was sufficient reason for the majors to oppose it and for State to reject it. Hypothetically the majors again could increase royalties—but then they would have to increase prices. This they didn't want to do. The French, angry at being frozen out of Saudi Arabia, surely would accuse them of monopolistic abuse, and, in addition, it was the policy of the American Economic Cooperation Administration to keep product prices low. Finally, raising prices could lead to loss of a share of the market. Ultimately, the solution would be a lavish subsidy from American taxpayers who were kept completely ignorant of its existence, and who, of course, never were asked if they wanted their money used to finance the continued health and prosperity of the international oil cartel.

The key to the solution was the difference in the true costs to the company of a royalty and a tax on income. The first substantially increases costs, while the second increases them little if at all. On a visit to Saudi Arabia, a representative of the United States Treasury Department suggested to Ibn Saud that he could levy an income tax, although the original concession agreement with Aramco exempted it from such a levy. Yet, an Exxon official noted in a revealing internal memo in February 1949, "The painlessness of such a tax [to Aramco and its owners, i.e.] is an insidious argument for increasing SAG's [Saudi Arabian Government's] income."[27]

On November 2, 1950, senior executives of Aramco discussed Ibn Saud's demand for more money with State Department officials, including George C. McGhee, a multimillionaire oil man who served in several high posts from

1947 to 1970, and who then became a director of Mobil. The king wanted, through the income-tax device, a 50–50 split of Aramco profits. The State Department thought this might assure a long period of stability. Two days later, without negotiations, Ibn Saud by royal decree imposed a 20 percent tax; but there was no doubt that this was only his first step toward getting 50 percent.

Aramco's proposal was that instead of continuing to treat royalties paid to foreign countries as business expenses, the Treasury Department should rule that the oil companies could take each dollar of royalties, now labeled "income taxes," as a dollar credit against American taxes on foreign income. "It was evident that Aramco officials preferred retreating in this direction since it might involve no additional cost to the company," a State Department memo said.[28]

In passing, it should be noted that the secretary of state at the time, Dean Acheson, and his successor, along with many other high State Department and Pentagon officials, came from and sometimes returned to law firms whose clients included giant oil companies: Covington & Burling in the case of Acheson, Sullivan & Cromwell in the case of Dulles. The fair and sensible inference to draw, we think, is that such men tend to identify their old clients' interests with the country's, much as does the President who tends to think *he* is the United States. State urged the National Security Council (NSC) to approve the plan. The NSC did so, and the Treasury Department drafted the necessary ruling. All of this occurred, needless to say, in secrecy. On December 30, 1950, the taxpayers having been committed to paying the bill, Aramco agreed to a 50–50 split with Saudi Arabia.

Naturally a precedent was set. It soon was followed, for example, in Kuwait, a British protectorate. There, Gulf, which had withdrawn from the Iraq Petroleum Company, was a party to a cartel-type agreement—similar to Red Line—with BP. These equal partners owned and operated this fabulously rich concession. But Gulf had made a twenty-two-year contract to sell to Shell, a party to the 1928 agreements, approximately half of the oil—1.25 billion barrels—it owned in Kuwait, thus enabling Shell to maintain its "As Is" position in world markets. Similarly, BP, in a twenty-year contract, agreed to turn over to Exxon and Mobil 1.3 billion barrels of oil from Kuwait and Iran. "Thus," the commission staff said, "these contracts result in the division of the production of Kuwait and Iran between the buyers and sellers . . ."[29]

The Subcommittee on Multinational Corporations heard McGhee's account of all this on January 28, 1974. Senator Clifford P. Case (R–N.J.) termed the ruling "a gadget." Senator Charles H. Percy (R–Ill.) termed it "a gimmick." They do the inventors an injustice. In truth it was a marvelous pickpocket, possibly the greatest of all time. Year after year, silently, efficiently, it slit the taxpayers' pocket and lifted mammoth tax payments by American oil companies out of the treasury of the United States into the treasuries of kingdoms in the Persian Gulf. Neither the taxpayer-victims nor the Capitol Hill cops even knew about it. Ultimately, billions of dollars were secretly transferred without, Senator Church pointed out, "any appropriation or authorization from Congress," and indeed without the knowledge of Congress.

All of this was done in pursuit of a dual-track foreign policy that was overtly pro-Israel but at the same time covertly pro-Arab. The "national security" invoked in pursuit of the covert policy was bottomed on the notion that ownership of Middle East oil reserves by American-based participants in a cartel was equivalent to ownership by the government. This concept of national security never failed to enlarge the profits of the multinational oil companies, including those of non-American cartel members, particularly BP and Shell; it always excluded procompetitive strategies that might jeopardize cartel profits, entail no subsidiaries, and strengthen small- and medium-sized American oil companies.

The theory about the Saudi income tax that the Internal Revenue Service had adopted was that it was a levy on "realized proceeds of business operations." Such a theory was tenable only so long as the tax was related to market prices. But it wasn't: it was figured on fictitious, mandatory "posted" prices. Starting in 1957, posted prices were regularly and sharply higher than market prices—and consequently were unrelated to "realized proceeds." The producer-country levies then became taxes not on profits, but on sales. With that, the companies' payments to these countries no longer were eligible to be credited against income taxes in the United States. Internal Revenue did nothing about it. In 1965 Libya adopted a new tax law that incorporated the posted-price provision prevailing in the Persian Gulf. "Without comment or explanation," the staff of the Church subcommittee said, "the Service approved this law as a legitimate income tax whose payments were eligible to be credited against U.S. income tax." Cable traffic in 1971 between oil-company tax experts in New York and executives in London, the site distant from Washington deliberately selected almost a half-century ago for management of the cartel's affairs, actually acknowledged the phoniness of the suspect IRS position:

The essence of credibility of the income tax under existing arrangements is that companies agree that export sales will be made at the prices on which the tax is to be based and sales are so made even though market values might be lower. . . . *The artificiality of this system is obvious and well known, but it has not been challenged by I.R.S.*[30] (Emphasis supplied)

"The failure of IRS to reverse its original revenue ruling after 1957 when 'posted' and 'realized' prices diverged has cost the U.S. Treasury *billions* of dollars of revenues, and has permitted the major intentional oil companies to pay the lowest average rate of U.S. income taxes of any major industrial grouping," the Church subcommittee staff said.[31]

In 1974, for example, Exxon paid taxes to the United States amounting to 5.6 percent of worldwide income of $10.95 billion. Socal paid 4.3 on $1.76 billion; Texaco, 1.6 on $2.83 billion; Mobil, 1.6 on $3.60 billion; and Gulf, 4.9 on $3.90 billion. Tax Analysts and Advocates, an expert public-interest tax law firm, estimated that in permitting tax credits for what actually were either royalties or nonincome taxes, the IRS was costing other taxpayers about $3 billion *in 1974 alone.* At the same time that the Brobdingnagian oil companies were paying Lilliputian taxes to the United States, a family of four earning $15,000, and taking standard deductions, paid $1,820, an effective tax rate of 12.1 percent, or seven and a half times the rate paid by Mobil and Texaco.

In the mid-1960s, IRS auditors were questioning the artificial pricing practices of the industry and seeking to audit the returns of the five American majors (finally doing so, it filed liens for a record-breaking $1 billion, and settled—in the usual secrecy—for 50 cents on the dollar).[32] In a letter on January 11, 1967, to Secretary of State Dean Rusk, John J. McCloy, the former World Bank president who became the preeminent attorney for the oil majors, had tried to block the audit by cashing in their chips:

I believe that the Department of State has a particular responsibility to make known to the Treasury Department the implication of its proposed attack on crude oil prices because the present system . . . was recommended to the oil companies and to the foreign governments involved by the Department of State and the Treasury Department.

McCloy has an earned reputation, among those who know of his work for the oil companies, for cleverness. That it may be well-earned is suggested in the foregoing by his implication that the oil companies had been simple obedient soldiers in the service of our foreign policy to whom the system "was recommended." Resuming the interrupted passage:

These departments recognized that it was in the national interest of the United States to keep such nations stable and friendly to the United States and thereby ensure American access to the vast oil reserves there located. If the oil companies did not provide the necessary revenues by paying substantial taxes to producing countries large amounts of direct foreign aid might well be required.[33]

McCloy did not bother to note that these "substantial taxes" had been credited against income taxes in the United States and therefore had cost the companies—which had proposed the scheme to begin with—not a dime.

The Antitrust Case Against the Oil Cartel

In 1944 the Federal Trade Commission, by resolution, directed its economics staff to conduct a long-range investigation of international cartels (and by 1950 it had issued reports on cartels in seven major industries—phosphates, copper, sulphur, electrical equipment, steel, fertilizer, and alkali; except for the one on copper, the reports were virtually ignored by the press and virtually everyone else.)[34]

On December 2, 1949, the commission passed a resolution to investigate "agreements entered into by American petroleum companies among themselves and with petroleum companies of other nations in connection with foreign operations and with international trade in petroleum and petroleum products." Under the direction of chief economist Corwin D. Edwards, John M. Blair, and other staff economists, armed with subpoena power, worked for almost two years. The result was a magnificently informative report that Anthony Sampson correctly assayed as "of historic importance."[35] Entirely factual, and almost 400 pages long, *The International Oil Cartel* drew no conclusions and made no recommendations, but contained overwhelming evidence of gross antitrust violations.

The staff submitted a tentatively final draft to the commission in October 1951. This was a tense period in the Middle East. The Iranian Parliament in 1947 had passed a law requiring renegotiation of the terms of BP's oil concession. This resulted, in 1949, in a proposed new agreement. Its terms were the most favorable in the region. In 1950, however, the Oil Commission of the Parliament, headed by Dr. Muhammed Mossadegh, recommended rejection. Efforts at compromise failed. In March 1951, the Parliament unanimously passed a law to nationalize the concession. By May, Mossadegh was in as Prime Minister and the British were out as concessionaires.

The government then organized a national oil company to exploit the concession, refine crude in the refinery at Abadan, which it had seized, and sell the oil. As a practical matter, the only potential buyers with sufficient tankers and markets were BP's fellow cartelists—and they, for various reasons, wouldn't buy it. Immediately the American members of the cartel took the position that the Iranians had caused a "tremendous world shortage" which imperiled the defense of the United States. They should be immunized from the antitrust laws so that they could relieve the shortage, they argued. Actually, Iran had accounted for a mere 7 percent of world production in 1950. In that same year, Exxon, Mobil, Gulf, Socal, and Texaco all had submitted identical bids—$1.75 a barrel, or at least four times their cost —for crude oil delivered at Persian Gulf ports to the Armed Forces Petroleum Purchasing Agency.[36] Clearly they were loyal and good—to each other.

Lacking markets, Iran had to stop producing oil. The country fell into economic and political disarray. The Tudeh party, which had close ties to the Soviet Union, apparently increased in strength. In Washington and other world capitals, fears mounted that Iran now might fall into the Soviet orbit.

It was in the foregoing context that the Federal Trade Commission decided to withhold the staff report and to classify it "secret," meaning that anyone who released it without FTC authorization would be committing a criminal offense. Having done this, the commission sent copies to some forty senior officials in the government who had routine responsibility for international oil matters. Over the next several months many of these officials praised but none criticized the report.[37]

One of the agencies that got the report was the Justice Department. It had undertaken investigations of the cartel even before World War II. Through grand jury subpoenas issued in 1940 and 1941 it had obtained many promising leads, but suspended its investigation with the attack on Pearl Harbor. The department resumed its investigation in 1946, but deferred it in 1949 to avoid duplication of the FTC inquiry. Now the commission had given it what David Haberman, the Antitrust Division trial attorney, would term "a most exquisite blueprint" for a criminal antitrust prosecution.

In a memo in June 1952, requesting that a grand jury be empaneled to investigate the cartel, Assistant Attorney General Morison said that the agreements among the seven largest oil companies—"to divide markets, to distribute on a quota basis, to fix prices and to control the production of oil throughout the world"—"are in violation of the antitrust laws of the United States."[38] He went on to say that he believed the continuance and extension of the 1928 agreements "to establish a world cartel in oil" had resulted in:

(1) control of all major oil producing areas of the world; (2) control of all refining operations in the world; (3) control of all patents, know-how and technology covering refining processes; (4) division of world markets; (5) maintenance of non-competitive prices for oil and its products throughout the world; and (6) control of oil transportation by oil pipeline and tanker.[39]

Attorney General McGranery and then-President Truman agreed with Morison that a grand jury should make an investigation. Mr. Truman on June 23, 1952, directed that proceedings go forward immediately. On July 17, McGranery made a public announcement that a grand jury had been empaneled in New York City.

The FTC, meanwhile, had talked to Mr. Truman about its still-secret report. He asked the commission not to publish it but said it could be made available, as a classified document, to congressional committees. Thereupon, the Senate Select Committee on Small Business requested Mr. Truman to approve release of the report. He did. After consulting with responsible agencies and deleting perhaps 5 percent of the text for security reasons, the committee published it on August 22, 1952.

The combined effect of a public announcement of the grand jury investigation and the release of *The International Oil Cartel* that underpinned it was that "all hell broke loose," Stephen J. Spingarn, then acting chairman of the FTC, said shortly afterward.[40] In a two-and-one-half-month period ending January 15, 1953, for example, the *Washington Post* published ten editorials attacking the government for starting the grand jury investigation.[41] Bruce K. Brown, a Standard of Indiana executive, characterized the members of the FTC as "haters of free enterprise."[42] The *Oil Forum* of September 1952 said—this was the era of Joe McCarthy—"We all know how Alger Hiss was able to influence Government policies in favor of Russia, so one is justified in wondering if there were any communist-inclined officials in the Federal Trade Commission responsible for the 'Secret' international oil industry report. . . . it might be well to play safe, and have the FBI investigate every man who participated in its preparation and writing." Spingarn told a press conference, "I don't mind if they go a trifle below the belt, but they are below the ankles on this one."[43]

Hill and Knowlton, Inc., the international public relations firm, incorporated this gutter attack in a thirty-two-page booklet consisting of newspaper and magazine articles and editorials on the report and the antitrust case. The firm's client was the California-Texas Oil Co., Ltd. (Caltex), a joint marketing enterprise of Socal and Texaco which at that moment were accused in a civil suit of having overcharged the government more than $25 million for oil purchased under the Marshall Plan. Caltex distributed about eight thousand copies of the booklet, *National Petroleum News* reported, "to government officials, editors and molders of public opinion in 67 countries."[44]

The State Department from the start had opposed initiation of the grand jury investigation. In a memo to the Justice Department on April 16, 1952, for example, Secretary of State Dean Acheson tried to head it off with a warning that it possibly could seriously impair achievement of the foreign-policy aims of the United States in the Middle East. And no sooner had the grand jury investigation begun when, David Haberman, the Justice Department trial lawyer, recalled, it became clear that internal government disputes over security and foreign-policy aspects would hobble the litigation:

Indeed, defense counsel, who seemed to have ready access to inner councils of the Government, were quick to exploit these inter-agency conflicts in court. [The] Special Assistant to the Attorney General, Leonard Emmerglick [in charge of the prosecution], was put in the anomalous position of having to persuade the court that he and not defense counsel—was the duly authorized legal spokesman for the policy position of the U.S. Government with respect to security and sensitivity.[45]

Finally, in late 1952, the National Security Council obtained "Top Secret" reports on the issue from the State Department, joined by the Defense and Interior departments, and the Justice Department. Here are highlights:

State

"Oil is vital to the United States and the rest of the free world both in peace and war," the State Department report said. "Since the United States is the greatest consumer of petroleum and its products in the world (60% of total world consumption) now and for the foreseeable future, it is vastly important that the operations of the great oil fields of the world remain as far as possible in the hands of American-owned companies." "The operations of American oil companies abroad have profound effects on the conduct of American foreign relations. . . . *American oil operations are, for all practical purposes, instruments of our foreign policy toward* [the] *. . . oil producing countries . . . on or near the borders of the Soviet Union.* For this reason and because of certain local conditions the Middle East comprises one of the most explosive areas of the world. The oil companies are in a position of great influence upon our relations with the people and governments of these countries. *What they do and how they do it determine the strength of our ties with the Middle Eastern countries and our ability to resist Soviet expansion and influence in the area."* (Emphasis supplied.)[46] The document repeatedly reinforces the point, as in these striking passages:

The activities of the United States Government in petroleum must be handled in such a way as to avoid giving strength to the claim that the American system is one of privilege, monopoly, private oppression, and imperialism.

　20. In this struggle of ideas [e.g., "Freedom of competitive enterprise . . . This American Way of Life"] on which our security depends, the oil companies of the United States play a significant role. . . . In many foreign countries, they are the principal contact of the local inhabitants with American enterprise. What such

people think of the oil companies, they think of American enterprise and the American system; *we cannot afford to leave unchallenged the assertions that these companies are engaged in a criminal conspiracy for the purpose of predatory exploitation.*[47] (Emphasis supplied.)

State then turned to the impact of the announcement of the grand jury investigation and the release of the FTC report in other countries. State's assessment was unrelievedly grim, e.g.:

31. In both Venezuela and the Middle East a wave of economic nationalism which might endanger American interests is entirely possible. Once such powerful political and emotional forces are unleashed, it is difficult or impossible to restrain them.[48]

The paper went on to make the point that foreigners often overlook the presumption of innocence which in our country is imputed always to an indicted person or corporation. Thus, the department said, an indictment springing from a complaint by the government would be "almost as effective in foreign propaganda terms as a decision finding the oil companies guilty as criminals and conspirators." State then suggested termination of the grand jury proceeding and substitution of a civil complaint.

Justice

The Justice Department reviewed the history of the cartel, of its impacts, and of its record of collusive bidding and overcharging the Navy and the Mutual Security Agency. Emphasizing the country's vital need for petroleum, and its great insufficiency of reserves in event of a war more serious than the Korean conflict under way at the time, the paper said that imports of crude

are not free and subject to the natural competitive forces of our economy but are regulated by contracts and agreements between American companies. A cartel program for agreed upon imports is supplanting domestic production and retarding the drilling of new wells to find and earmark *proven* reserves as an underground stockpile. . . .[49]

There followed these charges:

7. *The international petroleum cartel is a serious threat to our national security.* . . .

11. *The cartel arrangements are in effect private treaties negotiated by private companies to whom the profit incentive is paramount. The national security should rest instead upon decisions made by the Government with primary concern for the national interest.* . . . the cartel members, by their control over dominant segments of the domestic industry, regulate and determine the extent to which this nation

shall be dependent on foreign supplies which could be cut off in time of war.[50] (Emphasis supplied.)

The department argued against a civil case: it would take four to six years to complete and, if won, "would put responsibility upon a judge to reorient a world industry by decrees acceptable to foreign governments."[51] In contrast, "indictment and trial could be concluded within twelve to fifteen months" and would "leave correction of the conditions found to be illegal to the companies by renegotiation."[52] In addition, the secrecy of a grand jury proceeding "will avoid the possibility of public, inflammatory exposures."[53]

Finally:

16. The Sherman Act was described by Chief Justice [Charles Evans] Hughes as our charter of economic freedom. The Supreme Court has repeatedly rejected proof of public benefit and business necessity as justification for cartel operations and has emphasized the primacy of economic freedom as the highest value for our economy. Our concern for an adequate future supply of petroleum is a concern ultimately for the preservation of freedom for ourselves and the free world. *Free private enterprise can be preserved only by safeguarding it from excess of power, governmental and private.* . . . *The world petroleum cartel is authoritarian, dominating power over a great and vital industry in private* [hands]. *National security considerations dictate that the most expeditious method be employed to uncover the cartel's effects and put an end to them.* The urgency of these considerations requires that the grand jury investigation go forward even though it might ultimately appear that indictments would not be warranted. *The facts presently available strongly suggest that the high policy represented by the Sherman Act has been consciously and persistently violated by activities long since determined by the Supreme Court to be illegal. The cartel should be prosecuted criminally if there is to be equal justice under the law and if respect for the law and its evenhanded administration is to be maintained. Far from hurting us abroad, the investigation and prosecution of this cartel's activities will authenticate our protestations.* . . . We cannot promote free enterprise abroad unless we are seen to conscientiously enforce our laws designed to preserve them for our own economy and foreign commerce.[54] (Emphasis supplied.)

The distillate of the disagreement was, Were they (the oil companies) us (the United States)? The State Department said they were; the Justice Department said they weren't. The disagreement went to what this country is supposed to be about. Abraham Lincoln once told us, but State had a tin ear. He had not said, "government of the people, by the cartel, for the cartel." Justice heard him aright.

The National Security Council met on January 9, 1953, a Friday, to discuss whether to advise President Truman to end the grand jury investigation. On Sunday evening, January 11, Mr. Truman summoned Leonard J. Emmerglick, the prosecutor, to the White House to tell him that he had decided to drop the grand jury proceedings on the condition that the documents being sought by the grand jury would be produced by the companies in a civil proceeding. Emmerglick told the subcommittee:

His purpose was to tell me and Charles Bohlen of the State Department, who was present, two things, first, that he had reached his decision with great reluctance and that he was constrained to take that decision, not on the advice of the Cabinet Officers who attended the Security Council meeting, but solely on the assurance of General Omar Bradley [then Chairman of the Joint Chiefs of Staff] that the National security called for that decision; and second, that he wished the civil action to be vigorously prosecuted.[55] [Bradley, through an aide, told one of the authors, "I do not remember discussing the issue with President Truman at any time."][56]

Carrying out the instructions of Mr. Truman, Emmerglick obtained from the companies a stipulation that they would produce the documentary material. On April 21, 1953, the Justice Department went into United States District Court in New York to file a strong civil complaint against the five American firms. The department charged that these companies, joined by the two foreign cartel members which were nondefendant coconspirators, had conspired to restrain and monopolize interstate and foreign commerce of the United States, principally by dividing foreign production and markets, fixing domestic and world prices, curtailing domestic production as necessary to prop up world prices, excluding lesser American companies from foreign production and from imports, preventing sales of foreign oil to competitors, and controlling a major part of the world's tanker fleet. As relief, the department sought the breakup of Aramco and similar enterprises and injunctions against marketing arrangements which enabled the companies to fix prices and engage in other illegal conduct.

Eight days after Mr. Truman made his decision, Dwight D. Eisenhower became President. In one of his first actions, General Eisenhower, who in all regards was one of the warmest friends the oil companies ever had in the White House, named Herbert Hoover, Jr., as his special representative within the State Department to deal with the worsening crisis in Iran. There, Mossadegh was unable or unwilling to settle with BP. His nationalized oil had no buyers. The economy was in an uproar. He insisted on continuing to govern by decree. In August, when Parliament said he couldn't, demonstrations broke out. He directly challenged the shah, ordered a plebiscite on the dissolution of Parliament, and won it with more than 99 percent of the votes cast and counted. The shah tried but failed to oust Mossadegh by decree, and fled the country with Queen Soroya while the mobs of the Premier's supporters—many of them Communists—demonstrated in the streets.

Hoover, undercutting the Justice Department from the start, proceeded on the assumption that, as Senator Church put it, "the only solution to the Iranian problem lay in the utilization of the major oil companies as a vehicle for restoring Iranian petroleum production." This kind of "solution"— intended to assure a flow of revenues for the shah's regime—had been urged all along by Dean Acheson. Being cartel-oriented, he predictably had rejected a Justice Department alternative proposal: rather than rely on the cartel, let noncartel American oil companies form a consortium to lift oil from Iran.

The American cartel companies expressed reluctance to accept part of the old BP concession—they could produce all the oil they needed elsewhere. But finally they did agree to go along. Their first *quid pro quo,* agreed to by President Truman, was abandonment of the criminal prosecution. Now the Eisenhower Administration could bring about the solution only if certain conditions would be fulfilled:

• *That the intransigent Mossadegh be overthrown and the shah restored to his throne.* The American and British governments secretly agreed to help accomplish the overthrow. They succeeded with the clandestine aid of the Central Intelligence Agency, which assembled a pro-shah mob of its own. In 1962, Allen Dulles, by then retired as director of the CIA, was asked whether it was true that "the CIA spent literally millions of dollars hiring people to riot in the streets and do other things, to get rid of Mossadegh. Is there anything you can say about that?" "Well," Dulles told Eric Sevareid, his interviewer on CBS television, "I can say that the statement that we spent many dollars doing that is utterly false."[57] (Although Iran remained pro-West, David Wise and Thomas B. Ross wrote in *The Invisible Government,* "little was done to alleviate the terrible poverty. . . . Somehow, the oil wealth of Iran never trickled down to the people. A total of $1,300,-000,000 in United States aid poured in during twelve years since 1951, but much of it appeared to stick to the fingers of the hopelessly corrupt officialdom.")[58]

• *That the civil antitrust suit be undermined and finally destroyed, so that the cartel, rather than being broken up, could extend its hegemony to Iran and thus become more powerful and entrenched than ever.* How, after all, could the cartelists be prosecuted—even civilly—for having done what Acheson had wanted them to do, and what the Eisenhower Administration was now asking them to do?

The Antitrust Division trial lawyers found themselves subjected to agonizing restraints and relentless pressures. Each of them, for one thing, had to get top-secret clearance, even though many of the documents were even then ancient history. "This seemed to us at the time and still seems to me at least to be utterly ridiculous," said Barbara J. Svedberg, who after three years on the case "simply reached a point of utter frustration" and asked the division to reassign her. She told the subcommittee:

There were certain approaches that were taken by the oil attorneys that were contrived to alarm everyone. . . .

"You are upsetting the whole Middle East structure. You are going to invite the Communists to come in and take over."

It was scare tactics. . . . [but such techniques] were very effective.[59]

On August 6, 1953, the White House National Security Council (NSC) laid out the "Terms of Reference" for prosecution of the cartel case, including these:

c. *It will be assumed that the enforcement of the Antitrust laws of the United States against the Western oil companies operating in the Near East may be deemed secondary to the national security interest* to be served by:

(1) Assuring the continued availability to the free world of the sources of petroleum in the Near East, and

(2) Assuring continued friendly relationships between the oil-producing nations of the Near East and the nations of the free world. In the event of a conflict between any proposed legal relationships and the enforcement of the Federal Antitrust laws, the proposed solution will include, without recommendation, appropriate legislative, executive or administrative action required to remove such conflict.[60] (Emphasis supplied.)

The NSC had no basis in law for deeming the Sherman Antitrust Act "secondary" to a cartelist or other definition of "national security." If Secretary Dulles, his brother Allen, of the CIA, and other NSC members perceived a true conflict between national security and the Sherman Act, they were morally obligated to consult Congress. Neither Secretary Dulles nor Acheson before him, nor others of imperious style who had ascended with them to the peaks of unaccountability, cared to consult Congress, and never did so. Or, if they truly had thought it necessary to immunize the cartel from prosecution, they might at least have been honorably straightforward about it. They had but to ask the President to invoke pertinent provisions of the Defense Production Act. They didn't; they preferred that the Justice Department case, and with it the antitrust laws, be, in Emmerglick's word, "subverted."[61]

On October 29, 1953, the NSC directed its dominant member, Secretary Dulles, to assume direction of the cartel case—"to protect the interests of the free world," etc. Church asked Emmerglick if he knew of "any legal basis" for putting the secretary of state in charge of an antitrust case. "I know of none whatever," the former prosecutor replied.

Meanwhile, Hoover, having rejected the Justice Department proposal for a consortium of noncartel companies, proceeded to facilitate formation of the first consortium of all seven cartel companies. Hoover and the companies both wanted to keep Iranian oil out of Russian hands—he so the West would have it, they so that it could not be "dumped" on the market and the cartel undersold.[62]

In January 1954, the companies met in London. Knowing they had Hoover over a barrel, they told him that progress toward an agreement on a consortium "would be prejudiced if while the antitrust phases were being explored the pending suit against them was actively pressed."[63] Under pressure from Hoover and the council, Attorney General Herbert Brownell, Jr., on January 21, 1954, rendered an opinion to General Eisenhower that the consortium as proposed "would not in itself constitute a violation of the antitrust laws . . ."[64]

Brownell, in his letter to Mr. Eisenhower, had specified certain premises on which his clearance was based. One of them was violated by a device called Aggregate Programmed Quality (APQ), which was kept secret for twenty-eight years—from the Iranians and everyone else—although it was, as Anthony Sampson put it, "really to be the arbiter of Iran's future growth."[65] The APQ functioned to hold production down to the level desired by the member of the consortium that wanted the least Iranian oil. The American cartel members, for example, had an abundance of oil in Saudi Arabia and Kuwait, and so if they desired to restrict production in Iran (as they routinely did), BP and Shell automatically—and covertly—had to restrict their production in Iran.

In a memo on August 19, 1954, to Stanley N. Barnes, the assistant attorney general in charge of the Antitrust Division, Emmerglick pointed out that the plan for the Iranian Consortium as revealed by the final agreements, which Hoover had supplied, "goes beyond" Brownell's premises.

In another memo to Barnes on September 15, Emmerglick pointed out that the cartel, although it had worked out everything else in great detail, had supplied no documents detailing how it intended to *market* the oil to be lifted from Iran. This, Emmerglick said,

tends to confirm the conclusion that nothing new or different has been devised, as a system of marketing which will depart from the cartel pattern.
It seems to me that the Attorney General would have to stultify himself to give an opinion that the agreements would be lawful.[66]

The same day, Brownell immunized the Iranian Consortium from the antitrust laws—i.e., he stultified himself. Yet, exempting anyone from the antitrust laws, whether in the name of "national security" or because of pressure from the President or the NSC, was something he simply was not empowered to do. No less a personage than John J. McCloy, *the* lawyer for the cartel, has emphatically affirmed that the Justice Department "does not have the authority to waive the application of the antitrust laws . . ."[67]

Brownell—again on the day he signed the letter—had conceded to Kenneth R. Harkins, an Antitrust Division attorney, that approval of the consortium was inconsistent with the cartel case and that necessarily the case must proceed with emphasis on the marketing aspects *and not on the production control aspects.*[68] (Emphasis supplied.) With the case under the direction of another cartel-oriented secretary of state, Dulles, and the NSC, that secretive body issued directives which, trial lawyer Haberman told the subcommittee,

precluded the Justice Department from challenging the legality of joint production, joint refining, joint storage, and joint transportation ventures among the seven companies, the very joint arrangements, as I have heretofore indicated, which were among the most significant features of the post-war supply cartel. So that what was still left open for prosecution were the older "As Is" market cartel arrangements which by then had become relatively incidental to the basic joint venture supply control system.

Thus, in practical effect, early national security constraints imposed by the National Security Council, and accepted by Attorney General Brownell, had cut the very heart out of the *Oil Cartel Case.*[69]

The case dragged on. About 1957, the NSC laid on additional restraints making it impossible for the Justice Department to seek such relief as would break up the joint enterprises. In 1961, Exxon and Gulf, taking advantage of the department's weakness, obtained out-of-court settlements which gave them, Haberman testified, *"carte blanche* . . . to continue salient features of their joint venture cartel system . . ."[70] Haberman refused to sign the consent decrees. Later, Texaco and Social initiated negotiations with the Justice Department looking toward similar decrees. By that time the staff consisted of Haberman alone. To cut his losses, he signed a decree with Texaco in 1964. Socal, however, submitted a study contending that since World War II there had been no cartel—a contention Haberman rejected without difficulty.

Finally, recognizing that the whole case had become an "exercise in futility," Haberman recommended that Socal and Mobil be dismissed without prejudice, meaning that the government was legally free to sue again. "Being denied the right to operate upon the head and body of the beast, we were left with the dubious option of trying to lop off the tail," he said in a memo. The District Court in New York, on Haberman's motion, dismissed

Socal and Mobil, without prejudice, in 1968. Thus, the cartel case ended after fifteen years.

Instruments of Foreign Policy—Whose?

Senator Church has said that the NSC's decision to place the American cartel members in the Iranian Consortium "effectively killed any chance of the Cartel Case being successfully prosecuted. But the Council in making this decision did so without statutory authority." A reader perusing the subcommittee's published collection of documents on the consortium, Church said,

will note a glaring omission: nowhere is there any reference to consultation with the United States Congress. The decisions reflected in this record were taken in secrecy, debated in secrecy, and never exposed to public debate and inquiry. Yet, these decisions helped seal the basic structure of international oil for 25 years.[71]

In fact, if not in intent, the NSC, in saving Iran from Communism, but not from poverty, corruption, or tyranny, was to give the cartel control of the world's richest oil deposits through layers of interlocking ventures. In a summary of the subcommittee's findings, Church said:

(4) *Since the United States national interest was considered identical to the companies' interest, for the next sixteen years [after 1953], international oil decisions were left to the companies. The U.S. Government lacked the capacity to arrive at independent judgments in this critical area. The companies pursuing their own interests had no strategic overview for the United States.*

(5) But during the decade of the '60s, two events occurred: first, the producing countries joined together in a producer country cartel, the Organization of Petroleum Exporting Countries (OPEC). Second, spare producing capacity in the U.S. was lost at a time when demand for oil soared in the industrial world.[72] (Emphasis supplied.)

A chart prepared by Exxon itself showed that demand for crude oil in non-Communist countries had increased annually from 1965 forward. But spare capacity stayed level from 1958 to 1965; then it dropped steadily to near-zero in 1974. At a subcommittee hearing on February 1, 1974, Exxon executive George T. Piercy admitted that the company year after year had underestimated demand, but denied that the repeated error was deliberate. Other cartel members made similar miscalculations. Thanks to these fortuitous underestimates the American "sisters" had a $2 billion upsurge in profits in 1973. Resuming Church's summary:

In 1971, the companies joined together, with the approval of the Departments of State and Justice, to bargain with OPEC over the price of oil. The resulting Tehran and Tripoli Agreements raised the price of oil to the consumers $11 billion over five years, but both the companies and State Department justified them on the grounds that they ensured five years of price stability and security of supply.[73]

The $11 billion left out the inflationary ripples. In April 1974, Senator Philip A. Hart (D–Mich.) calculated that price increases for gasoline and other petroleum products were costing consumers more than the war in Vietnam. The war had cost $26 billion to $30 billion annually. But on an annual basis, price increases for petroleum products over the preceding fifteen months exceeded $30 billion, Hart said.[74]

Church, in his summary, went on to say that the Tehran and Tripoli agreements in fact had ensured neither price stability nor security of supply:

The Tehran Agreement was a house of cards which came tumbling down even before the Yom Kippur War under an avalanche of ever-escalating demands by OPEC. The precipitate OPEC-imposed price rises thus accelerated a process of deterioration in company and consumer-country bargaining power which was well underway even before that war and the Arab embargo. The ensuing petroleum crisis thus should not have come as a surprise. . . . Yet the U.S. Government had no strategy to cope with it, nor even an institutional capacity to formulate one. *It relied upon the companies.* . . .[75] (Emphasis supplied.)

Had the companies not been "instruments of our foreign policy," in the affectionate phrasing of the State Department in 1953? Presidents Nixon and Ford, and their secretary of state, Henry A. Kissinger, never have given the least sign of recognizing it, but something profound had happened: the companies had become instruments of *Arab* foreign policy.

On May 23, 1973, King Faisal, who had succeeded Ibn Saud as ruler of Saudi Arabia, was in Geneva. So were members of Aramco's executive committee who represented each of the four owning companies. The directors paid a "courtesy visit." Socal vice-president, W. Jones McQuinn told what happened in an internal memo, one among two and a half file drawers of Socal documents subpoenaed by the subcommittee. Faisal issued instructions to the companies to undertake an extensive lobbying and propaganda campaign designed to dilute support of Israel by the United States. McQuinn wrote that the king warned that the Aramco concession, in his country, was in peril, saying, "You will lose everything." The memo then listed:

Things we must do (1) inform U.S. public of their true interests in the area (they are now being misled by controlled news media) and (2) inform government leaders —and promptly ("Time is running out" and "You may lose everything").[76]

The companies followed Faisal's marching orders and reported back to him on their activities. On their return to the United States, the directors, the subcommittee staff said,

went to Washington to present the King's message to a succession of high officials at State, Defense and the White House. But the company officials failed to persuade Washington policy-makers that U.S. Middle East policy endangered their concession.[77]

The point here is not to imply that they were disloyal or even wrong in trying to influence American leaders and American public opinion—through speeches, advertisements, statements to stockholders, and well-placed contributions—in favor of Faisal's cause. Rather, the point is simply the incontrovertible one that they were instruments of the foreign policy of the monarch of a desert kingdom where they had a lot of oil.

On October 12, 1973—six days after Egypt and Syria attacked Israel—the chief executives of Aramco's owners—Exxon, Socal, Texaco, and Mobil—sent a memo, carried by John McCloy, to President Nixon. They told him "that any actions of the U.S. Government at this time in terms of increased military aid to Israel will have a critical and adverse effect on our relations with the moderate Arab producing countries."[78] Not just for old times' sake, the executives once again equated their ownership of Middle East reserves with possession by the United States—while admitting that "[t]he bulk of the oil produced in the Persian Gulf goes to Japan and Western Europe."[79] The executives then entwined the Aramco and American flags as closely as the snakes on a caduceus, saying that Japan and Western Europe

may be forced to expand their Middle East supply positions at our expense.

Much more than commercial interests in the area is now at hazard. The whole position of the United States is on the way to being seriously impaired, with Japanese, European, and perhaps Russian interests largely supplanting United States presence in the area, to the detriment of both our economy and our security.[80]

The letter drew no response.

The companies' renewed identification of the interests of the United States with their own, not to mention the McCloying bluster about "Japanese, European, and perhaps Russian interests largely supplanting U.S. presence," came under severe trial only six days later, when the Arabs started their oil embargo.[81] The Socal documents obtained by the subcommittee by subpoena, and questioning of company officials about the papers at a hearing on June 20, 1974, showed that the interests of the companies coincided primarily with those of the Arabs.

James E. Akins, the American ambassador to Saudi Arabia, had tried through regular diplomatic channels to bend our foreign policy more toward the Arabs. Failing, he then tried to change the policy through Aramco. Frank Jungers, executive of Aramco, reported this to Aramco directors on October 26:

... Akins agreed with our assessment entirely and urged that industry leaders in USA use their contacts at highest levels of USG [United States Government] to hammer home point that oil restrictions are not going to be lifted unless political structure is settled in manner satisfactory to Arabs.[82]

The Saudis recognized that they lacked the capacity to administer the boycott effectively—and relied on Aramco to run it for them. Jungers made this clear in a cable to four Aramco directors—A. C. DeCrane, Jr., of Texaco; C. J. Hedlund, of Exxon; H. C. Moses, of Mobil; and W. J. McQuinn of Socal—on October 21:

A discussion of the complexities evolved with the Saudis entirely aware that this program would be very difficult to administer *but they are looking to Aramco to police it.* Yamani [Sheikh Yamani, the Saudi oil minister] at one point also remarked that any deviations by the Aramco offtakers [the owners in their capacity as movers of oil from Saudi Arabia] from the ground rules would be harshly dealt with.[83] (Emphasis supplied.)

At the subcommittee hearing, George M. Keller, vice-chairman of Socal and also a director of Aramco, said "that the only alternative was not to ship the oil at all. . . . Obviously it was in the best interests of the United States . . ."[84] True enough, but it did not make Aramco any less the instrument of Arab foreign policy.

Also in the October 21 cable, Junger disclosed that the embargo applied to shipments to the armed forces of the United States. Listing the terms of the cutback in exports required by the Saudis, he cited this one:

(2) In addition. . . . we must subtract all shipments to the United States either directly or indirectly including military . . .[85]

Keller acknowledged that in addition to cutting off oil to the United States, the Saudis had ordered the owners of Aramco to cut off oil they supplied outside the United States to the American armed forces. "And the instrument through which they reached the parent shareholders . . . was, of course, Aramco?" subcommittee counsel Jerome Levinson asked. "Yes," replied Keller. "And so Aramco was their handle?" "Yes."[86]

McQuinn acknowledged to Jack Blum, the subcommittee associate counsel, that Aramco's owners during the embargo had supplied the Saudis with information about shipments of Saudi oil to the American military indirectly, i.e., from places such as the Bahamas and Trinidad. "Do you feel that there was anything inappropriate about passing that information along to the Saudis?" Blum asked. "We did not feel that there was," McQuinn answered.[87]

There was also this exchange:

Senator Church. Given Aramco's status in Saudi Arabia and the dependency of Aramco upon Saudi Arabian consent, in order both to obtain oil and indeed to operate at all, doesn't it really follow that when the Saudi Arabian Government lays down certain strictures, Aramco is really in the position of a hostage?

Mr. Keller. Yes, sir, I think that is correct, Senator.[88]

A few more points bearing on whose interests coincided with whose:

• The more Saudi Arabia and the other OPEC countries charged for oil, the larger were the profits enjoyed by the cartel companies. Thus the combined after-tax income of the five American majors increased from $5,-397,400,000 in the year ended September 30, 1973, a few days before the embargo began, to $8,422,300,000 in the year ended September 30, 1974. This was an increase of $3,024,900,000, or 56 percent.

• Despite the numerous extremely costly tax and other favors conferred by the United States on the American sisters, they did not during the embargo favor the United States. The oil they supplied to their mother country was relatively less abundant than to Japan.[89]

• The United States is 70 percent sufficient in crude oil, greatly exceeding Europe in this regard; remarkably, though, the retail prices of gasoline from summer 1973 to summer 1974 increased 17 or 18 cents per gallon in the United States (with each cent of increase costing motorists $1 billion), compared with, say, 9.5 cents in Switzerland and 13 cents in Germany.[90]

• In 1976, negotiations were completed for the sale of Aramco to Saudi Arabia. Essentially this changed nothing. Saudi Arabia is a member of a cartel of producing countries, OPEC, which have in the cartel of oil companies, with their great refineries, tankers, pipelines, and marketing mechanisms, the perfect mate. Each is indispensable to the other. Each is the instrument of the other. Neither is the instrument of the United States.

From our account of the evolution of the cartel a few central points emerge. First, the United States even before World War II had genuine reason for concern that it have in the Middle East major and secure reserves of oil. Second, the United States after World War II had genuine reason for concern that Middle East countries with major oil reserves not gravitate into the Soviet orbit. Third, in pursuit of those legitimate objectives, the United States at every crucial juncture could have injected competition into noncompetitive situations, or, during World War II, it could have protected its interests *directly*, through a government corporation. Instead, the government each time violated the national commitment to competition and against restraint of trade by adopting a procartel approach and even tortured to death an antitrust suit intended to break up the cartel. Fourth, in strengthening the cartel, the government spent tens of billions of taxpayers' dollars for Lend Lease and, far more importantly, for tax breaks. Fifth, the government did its work for the cartel always without consultation with Congress, always in darkest secrecy, and always in the name of a "national security" that coincided with the enrichment of the cartel. Sixth, the cartel by way of thanks ripped off the American public throughout. Seventh, the government left it to the companies to build sufficient spare capacity, but they didn't. Eighth, the government left it to the companies to try to deter the OPEC countries, starting in 1971, from embarking on a course of explosive price increases; saw—or should have seen—that the companies had no bargaining power (or, in terms of a hindsight view of profits, no incentive), and did nothing about it. Ninth, when the crunch—the embargo—came in 1973, we found that they (the oil companies) were them (the Arabs). Tenth, they were them for one reason and one reason only; it served their interests. That seeming truism is fundamental: as corporations with American roots, their interests and the interests of the United States did run parallel at times, but *had to* diverge when they (with our help) could survive and prosper by becoming partners of (or hostages to) the Arabs. The spectacle astonishes when seen from the perspective of a growing distance: the country's leaders —Presidents, secretaries of state, the defense establishment—entrusting the destiny of the United States and much of the world to the agents of a foreign power—the kingdom of oil.

How to make the oil companies, and by extension all multinationals, accountable? Of course we must, as Senator Church has said, "ensure that spurious claims of national security are not again used to shut off public inquiry and debate," although it is not clear just how this would be done.[91] Of course we should not provide tax incentives to multinationals (as we do) to build abroad what otherwise would be built at home.[92] Of course Congress should empower the government to approve or veto long-term supply contracts between multinational oil corporations and producer governments. Certainly it's a good idea to create a federal corporation to buy foreign oil directly and then allocate it equitably among domestic refiners. And certainly we should institute federal chartering so that we can rationally set the terms under which all multinationals do business in the United States.

Nothing is more important than to cut the multinationals down to a size at which the forces of competition will come genuinely into play, because competition with all its faults is by and large strongly proaccountability. The great oil companies should be the first to be domesticated. To enable competition to flower, the priority for Congress should be to enact laws that permit companies neither to be integrated from the oil well to the gasoline pump, nor to control the energy sources that compete with petroleum. Such laws would extract from the industry an Aramco-size concession to accountability.

The rights and interests of the laboring man will be protected and cared for by the Christian men to whom God in his infinite wisdom has given control of the property rights of the country. Pray earnestly that right may triumph, always remembering that the Lord God Omnipotent still reigns.

George F. Baer,
as quoted in *American Capitalism*

I believe the power to make money is a gift of God . . . to be developed and used to the best of our ability for the good of mankind. Having been endowed with the gift I possess, I believe it is my duty to make money and still more money, and to use the money I make for the good of my fellow man according to the dictates of my conscience.

John D. Rockefeller
John D. Rockefeller: A Study in Power

Can the "inalienable" rights proclaimed in the Declaration of Independence —"life, liberty, and the pursuit of happiness"—ever be fully achieved without a reordering of the workplace? For tens of millions of men and women, to enter a polling place at four-year intervals to vote for President, or at two-year intervals to vote for a congressman or a governor, is an optional diversion; to enter a workplace five days a week to earn a living is a matter of, if a short phrase will do, vital importance. In the classroom, one may learn and perhaps be inspired by "life, liberty, and the pursuit of happiness"; but in the workplace one may learn that occupational accidents and disease endanger life, that the absence of due process when one faces arbitrary firing or punishment abrades liberty, and that malaise impedes the pursuit of happiness. To be sure, about one-fourth of all workers are members of unions. Too often, however, they find their unions unresponsive when they try to achieve some measure of control over their lives in the workplace.

By the doubtless conservative estimate made in 1972 by Elliot L. Richardson, then secretary of the Department of Health, Education, and Welfare, occupational diseases annually kill "as many as 100,000" persons and newly disable "at least 390,000." At the same time, work accidents, which are widely recognized to be grossly underreported, were said by James D. Hodgson, then secretary of labor, to account for 14,200 deaths and for 2.2 million temporarily or permanently disabling injuries.[1] Despite the extent of this assault on life, sane efforts toward prevention have moved at a snail's pace. Many businesses, feeling more accountable to the balance sheet than to workers, have neglected health and safety. Many leaders of large unions, while adept at securing more money in negotiations, and becoming entrenched partly through their success in bargaining for more money, have downgraded issues of health and safety. And government agencies with responsibilities in this field frequently have been negligent, because they have been captives of the industries they nominally regulate.

Nowhere is this lack of concern for the worker better illustrated than in coal mining. Each year, more than 200 miners are killed and thousands more injured by accidents in the mines. Additional thousands are exposed to the risks of various types of lung disease, the most widely known of which is black lung. Had the industry been concerned about anything other than maximum profits, had the union been truly concerned about the miners' welfare, and had the government been diligent in enforcing mine health and safety, such slaughter could not occur. Taken by itself, the American record in the mines would be horrible enough. The real proportion of the scandal over mine health and safety can be seen when comparing the United States to Europe. In a striking, well-documented report prepared for Ralph Nader's Center for Responsive Law, J. Davitt McAteer chillingly concluded:

American coal miners are killed at a much higher rate than European coal miners, and they suffer injuries at a higher rate underground than their European counterparts. This is despite the fact that European coal mines operate in inherently more hazardous conditions than American mines.[2]

There is no mystery about how European countries cut down on mine deaths, injuries and diseases. The know-how is available, but our mining companies, our unions and our government, in an unholy alliance, have continued to allow mining techniques that amount to nothing less than legalized killings.

In Europe, coal miners rely almost exclusively on the Longwall method, in which a lathe with a sharp blade moves across the coal face and slices off coal which drops onto a conveyor belt parallel to the face. The Longwall machine is pushed forward automatically by a series of hydraulic jacks that walk behind the conveyor belt.[3] As the lathe slices through the coal, the area behind it either collapses or is filled in with excess rock. This filling process decreases the stress on the unmined area and reduces the likelihood of cave-ins.[4]

In the room-and-pillar system used in the United States, coal removal is incomplete, and gaps are not filled in, thereby creating more pressure and increasing the possibility the mine will collapse.[5] The coal-recovery rate is only 45 to 65 percent, compared with 80 to 95 percent for the Longwall method.[6]

The Longwall method, according to McAteer's report, virtually eliminates the biggest single killer in the mines—roof falls—and also provides better ventilation and controls dust more effectively, thus reducing the possibility of lung diseases.

European mines also have other more humane methods for protecting miners from lung diseases. In West Germany, for example, miners' masks are much more effective in keeping out dust than those here; indeed, the American-style mask is unacceptable under German law because of its inefficiency.[7] In addition, a West German miner receives additional protection from dangerous dust by working in high-dust areas for only limited periods, and being rotated to less dusty and less dangerous jobs.[8] Every West German miner must have a physical examination at least once every three years. Here, under a recent law, a miner must have a physical every other year. But when a German miner is found to have some lung problems, he is immediately moved from the dusty area into a less dusty one—or is given work outside the mine. If the lung problem persists, he is retrained at government expense and receives government payments until he finds another job.[9] In most cases in our mines, the miner who is found to have lung problems is, as a matter of policy, not moved to a less dusty area, but merely given the option of moving to a less well-paying job to ease his lung problem.[10]

Another mine hazard, deadly methane gas, also is routinely dealt with more safely in European mines. Here, methane is either ventilated into the air or left to accumulate in the mine. This is the biggest single cause of explosions in our coal mines. In 1968, a single spark exploded methane in a mine at Farmington, West Virginia, and killed seventy-eight men. Only to a limited degree is the European method, known as outgassing, used here. Under this procedure, methane is sucked out from the mine with rubber tubes, is transported to a refining plant, and is then sensibly sold for heating or cooking.[11] Where many European nations have sophisticated monitoring systems to locate methane gas levels (some of them computerized), United States mines use safety lamps or hand-operated monitors to detect methane.

And so it goes. No wonder the United States has a far worse mine-fatality rate than European countries, even though most European mines, because they generally are deeper than ours, are inherently more dangerous. Figures for 1965–1969 show that the fatality rate per million man-hours was twice as high in the United States as in the European Economic Community (Common Market nations), and three times as high as in Great Britain, Czechoslovakia, and Poland.[12]

But does it have to be this way? Mine owners say some of the systems in Europe—such as the Longwall machine—are too expensive. Obviously greed, not worker safety, is the overriding consideration. But this scandalous situation could not have come about without the cooperation, or collusion, of the Department of Interior's Bureau of Mines and the United Mine Workers of America. For decades, they combined with the mine operators, 'to do' little or nothing to improve mine safety. As a 1971 article in *Fortune* magazine said in reference to the 1950s and 1960s, "the aims, interests and policies of the union and the companies became inextricably intertwined . . . and the threat of a strike in the coalfields disappeared from the land."[13] As the UMW's president at the time, W. A. (Tony) Boyle, put it in the same article: "The UMWA will not abridge the rights of the mine operators in running the mines. We follow the judgment of the coal operators, right or wrong." Boyle's attitude, combined with that of the coal operators and the Bureau of Mines, amounted to nothing less than a death-sentence for hundreds of miners and injuries for thousands more.

The miners began taking matters into their own hands through a series of wildcat strikes beginning in the late 1960s. One of the most effective of these, begun in February 1969, in West Virginia, put 42,000 of the state's 44,000 miners out of the mines within five days. The issue was health and safety conditions—particularly the devastation caused by pneumoconiosis, or black-lung disease.[14] The strike ended after twenty-three days when the West Virginia state legislature passed a bill to compensate victims of black-lung disease.[15]

The shameful role that Tony Boyle and the Bureau of Mines played in the denial to miners of the basic right to health and safety in the workplace has been vividly described by Brit Hume in his book *Death and the Mines.*[16] From the time Boyle took over from John L. Lewis in 1960 as president of the UMW, he did virtually nothing to improve safety standards, Hume says. Instead, Boyle devoted most of his time to his duties as a leader in the National Coal Policy Conference, a joint union-industry lobbying organization that Lewis had formed a decade earlier. On the matter of mine safety, the only testimony anyone on Capitol Hill could remember coming from Boyle had to do with a bill to remove an exemption in the 1952 mine safety act for mines with fewer than fifteen employees. The bill became law in 1965; after that, Boyle was silent on mine safety.[17]

The union leadership's interest in mine safety was also evident in its "safety division"—which consisted of just one person. The union obviously considered this sufficient to deal with a problem which, in Boyle's heyday, amounted to 1.3 million reported violations of the Federal Mine Safety Code between 1960 and 1968. Of these, only 231,000 were corrected.[18] Even this astounding number of violations appeared to understate the problem, because in many cases mine owners got advance notice of inspection or were so cozy with inspectors that an objective evaluation of hazards was impossible. As miner Ernest Porter of Boonville, Indiana, told the 1968 UMW convention, ". . . the Bureau of Mines sends a schedule to the company informing them when their inspectors will be there, and a day or so before their arrival, we undergo a cleanup campaign. Even coal dust is wiped off the hand rails. When that inspector comes on the job, you will invariably find an assistant superintendent or the superintendent accompanying him, showing him the things they want [him] to see."[19] And Charles Shawkey, a West Virginia miner, told the same convention that when state safety inspectors are met by the mine operators, "they act like old friends, like they are having a reunion."

After the Farmington mine disaster of 1968 in which seventy-eight persons were killed, Congressman Ken Hechler (D–W. Va.), summed up the case against the companies, the union and the government:

Coal miners don't have to die. In a civilized society it is nothing short of criminal to allow the present conditions to continue in the coal mines. Federal and state mine-safety laws are weak, most coal companies seem to know when the inspectors will appear, enforcement of safety standards is weak and entangled in red tape, the union leaders seem more interested in high wages than in health and safety, there is no aggressive attack on the health hazards of coal dust which cause black lung, the coal miners and their families have been steeled to take a fatalistic attitude toward death and injury and both Congress and the general public have been complacent and apathetic.[20]

After the Farmington disaster, Congress did pass strong new legislation, but enforcement of it has been weakened by the appointment of political hacks to positions of trust. And, after a bitter struggle, Arnold Miller, a long-time coal miner dedicated to democratic reforms, took over the presidency of the UMW from the corrupt Tony Boyle, who is serving three consecutive life sentences for ordering the assassination of a union challenger and his family. Regrettably, there appeared to be no spill-over of such progressive insurgency to other unions.

The mines are far from being the only worksite where corporate greed and union and governmental indifference or negligence have prevailed over workers' health and safety. As was noted, an estimated one hundred thousand workers or more die each year of occupationally related diseases, most of which are believed to result from exposure to dangerous chemicals. Present federal standards, even if enforced strictly, would cover less than five hundred workplace chemicals—compared to the fifteen thousand to fifty thousand chemicals that scientists estimate are commonly found in the workplace.[21] Moreover, cancer resulting from exposure to toxic substances may take twenty to thirty years to become manifest.[22] Reports linking cancer with certain types of jobs go back two hundred years, but until recently their significance has been distant from the public consciousness.

"Until now, society as a whole, industry in general, labor unions in particular have not accepted the notion that things in the workplace can cause cancer," according to Dr. Edward F. Radford, of Johns Hopkins School of Hygiene and Public Health in Baltimore.[23] "By and large," Radford said, "when you proposed that something in the workplace is producing cancer, the reaction you got was: 'It must be something else . . . smoking or it's in the community. But it's not in the workplace.'"[24] Many commonly used chemicals, such as chloromethyl methyl ether (CMME), bischloromethyl ether (BCME) and polyvinyl chloride weren't identified as cancer-causing agents until twenty to thirty years after they came into widespread use.[25] Thus, according to Dr. Irving J. Selikoff, of Mt. Sinai School of Medicine, who has done more than any other person to show asbestos to be a major industrial cause of cancer, "To prevent cancer in the year 2000, we have to identify the problem chemicals in 1975."[26] But an estimated 250,000 new substances are synthesized each year, making it impossible to catch up with the backlog and identify which new substances are safe and which are dangerous. Until systems are perfected to screen the new substances immediately, instead of the several years that such tests now take, the only sure proof that something causes cancer is to wait fifteen or twenty years and then count the dead bodies.[27]

At a March 1975 meeting on cancer in the workplace, sponsored by the New York Academy of Science, doctors and scientists reported that in addition to harm coming to workers exposed to dangerous chemicals, the families of workers also were being affected.[28] Dr. H. A. Anderson, of the Mt. Sinai Medical School, reported that asbestos workers carrying fibers home in their clothing and hair spread fatal lung cancers and lung abnormalities to their wives and children.[29] Anderson and a team from Mt. Sinai studied the families of 354 asbestos workers and found that 35 percent of them showed lung abnormalities on X rays that were comparable to those of men who had worked in asbestos factories.[30] In addition, Anderson said, a study of the death certificates of 252 members of the families of asbestos workers showed two deaths from mesothelioma, a rare form of lung cancer.

427

This disease occurs only about once in 10,000 deaths in the general population, but causes about one death in twenty among asbestos workers.[31]

The agency in the Department of Labor that enforces the Occupational Health and Safety Act of 1970 is the Occupational Health and Safety Administration (OSHA). In 1972, when the Nixon White House initiated its infamous "responsiveness" program to raise campaign contributions, OSHA's particular bargaining chip was nonenforcement of the health and safety law. Because of inadequate regulations issued by OSHA, Dr. Selikoff predicted in a speech in June 1972, tens of thousands of workers exposed to asbestos would die. Selikoff charged that George Guenther, then assistant secretary of labor in charge of OSHA, had created a situation in which "workers exposed to asbestos in any trade are required to work under conditions which permit them to inhale 20 million or even 30 million fibers in a working day."[32] If Guenther showed comparable disregard for safety in setting exposure standards for other toxic substances, Selikoff warned, we would "face an unparalleled disaster" in the workplace. Guenther, with the blessing of then-Labor Secretary James Hodgson, set an asbestos exposure level two and a half times higher than had been proposed by the National Institute of Occupational Safety and Health; and even the NIOSH recommendation turned out to have been based on information supplied by something less than an objective source—a physician and industrial hygienist employed by the British asbestos industry.[33]

The Guenther-Hodgson action was a continuation of industry-government policy to allow the slaughter of workers who are exposed to asbestos. Paul Brodeur, in his book *Expendable Americans*, focused on an asbestos-insulation factory in Tyler, Texas. By 1972, according to a study financed by the National Cancer Institute, 875 employees had been massively exposed to inhaled asbestos fibers, and an estimated 260 of them "will develop cancer, mainly bronchogenic carcinoma, and die from this disease . . ."[34]

Even when the warning signals of cancer hazards have been around for decades, workers have gone unprotected. Dr. Joseph K. Wagoner, head of field studies for NIOSH, has said that 200 years ago an English doctor reported an increase in cancer of the scrotum among chimney sweeps in London who breathed carbon products from the burning coal. Despite this, thousands of coke-oven workers in American steel mills are today inhaling similar carbon products—and are dying of lung cancer at fifteen times the rate of the general population, Wagoner said.[35] He also noted studies earlier in this century which showed that miners in the Erz mountains of Central Europe were dying of lung cancer caused by radioactivity. Yet, he said, in 1971 "thousands of American uranium miners were still working in radiation concentrations of such magnitude as to triple their prospects of dying of cancer."[36] American dye workers, Wagoner said, "are literally sloshing" in chemicals called aromatic amines that were found to cause cancer eighty years ago.[37] "As a result, these workers are now, and will continue to be, afflicted by bladder tumors at an epidemic rate."[38]

In certain types of industry, another kind of carnage goes on. In 1973 in Michigan alone, workers operating huge power presses that stamp out metal parts suffered 307 amputations of hands.[39] The AFL–CIO and the machine-tool-building industry claimed that most of these accidents could be eliminated by enforcing a rule barring a worker from putting his hands in the die —the part of a power press that shapes metal or other material, and the part that causes the amputations and manglings in accidents.[40] The National Machine Tool Builders Association told the Occupational Safety and Health Administration on June 4, 1974, that 3 out of every 500 power-press workers could expect to lose a hand or a portion of a hand every year. Over a period of thirty years, almost one in five workers would suffer such an injury.[41] But OSHA, the enforcement agency, decided that the "no-hand-in-dies" rule was unnecessary, unfeasible, and too costly, because many existing machines would have to be modified so that they could be operated by hands outside of the dies. OSHA revoked the rule in late 1974 after the "no-hands-in-dies" regulation was opposed by the Chamber of Commerce and the Organizations Resources Counselors, Inc. (ORC) which represent tool users. OSHA said that certain protective devices would adequately safeguard workers. OSHA also relied heavily on the fact that there are no good national statistics on the accident rate involving power presses.[42]

Although unions have dragged their feet or combined with management to bar tough safety standards in many industries, such was not the case here. Both the AFL–CIO and the United Auto Workers pushed to keep the "no-hands-in-dies" regulation. Said George Taylor, executive secretary of an AFL–CIO board on safety standards: "OSHA caved in to the Chamber of Commerce. It's as simple as that, . . ."[43] And, said UAW vice-president Douglas Fraser in support of the "no-hands" regulation:

Logic tells me that if you never exposed your hands to the die, it has to be safer . . . The fact that you don't put your hands in the dies at any time, it seems to me, makes it impossible to suffer an amputation."[44]

In Rachel Scott's 1974 book, *Muscle and Blood,* she noted that many state governments have joined industry, the unions and federal enforcement agencies in allowing unsafe conditions to persist in the workplace. For example, Scott said, in then-Governor Nelson A. Rockefeller's New York 228 deaths from industrial accidents were reported in 1968. The State Labor

Department investigated only 140 of the 228 deaths and initiated no prosecutions—even though an official memo said that 58 of the 140 fatalities investigated involved "violations of the industrial code of the New York State Labor Law . . ."[45]

There are some hopeful signs on the horizon for occupational health and safety as the issue gets more emphasis from some union leaders—notably Sheldon W. Samuels, director of health, safety and environmental affairs for the AFL–CIO's Industrial Union Department; Steve Wodka, legislative aide for the Oil, Chemical and Atomic Workers International Union; and Wodka's boss, Anthony Mazzocchi.

Because only about one-fourth of the nation's work force belongs to unions, some 60 million workers lack the security and grievance procedures built into most union contracts. Yet, even for union workers, the form of due process they are accorded under union contracts runs contrary to the Bill of Rights. As labor historian Staughton Lynd put it, workers are denied the basic rights of a presumption of innocence until proven guilty and trial by jury in situations where they are fired or disciplined in some way.[46] "Even in unionized shops the usual way of things is first the discipline and later the grievance," said Lynd. "You are guilty until proven innocent, not the other way around. And whatever the presumption, whether of guilt or innocence, who makes the decision?"[47] The answer, of course, is management. Lynd said that, in principle, a strike should be viewed "as a kind of court of last resort" in which workers walk off the job to show they believe an employer has acted unjustly and that a worker is innocent of some charge.[48] But, Lynd noted, most union contracts outlaw wildcat strikes. In grievance procedures, the matter is handled by a union staff man, with the final decision made by arbitrators, not a jury of one's peers.[49] At present, Lynd points out, there are few restrictions on an employer's right to fire. Employers, he says, "still function as judges without juries in administering organizational death. When all is said and done, we can't fire them but they can fire us."[50] And, he asks, "Why, in a society that insists on electing its political leaders, do Americans still take orders at work from people they did not choose?"[51]

Union workers, though, still possess a greater measure of job security than nonunion employees and even most white-collar professionals who are considered part of management. This lack of security for professionals causes them to be afraid to speak out, to say something controversial, to be a "whistle blower" on the company in the interests of the public. This means, said Ralph Nader, that

responsible scientists, lawyers, engineers and other professionals in the same company can be shown the door at 5:00 P.M. without any due process and without any grievance procedures. This obviously has a great inhibiting effect because there is an extremely effective grapevine among companies and governmental agencies that labels "trouble makers" very quickly, thus reducing the prospects of their employment to near zero. In short, the scientist has a skill right, and when that skill right is subjected to that kind of expulsion or administrative laceration, there is not much that the scientist can do because this skill right is not really considered as property by the courts. The field is littered with the bones of scientists who spoke out bravely about controversial issues and were forced to be at the mercy of a totally unresponsive and uncharitable society.[52]

Sounding a theme similar to Lynd's, Nader said that the Bill of Rights must be extended "to individuals as employees of private corporations or government agencies."[53] Theodore J. Jacobs, former executive director of Nader's Center for the Study of Responsive Law, made the point that we cannot depend on corporate good will to bring about the changes necessary to provide due process to employees. Because "men of good will" inside corporations have no right to due process themselves, they "aren't going to be in the vanguard of reforming their corporations,"Jacobs said, adding that "under present conditions, they can only go so far and remain in the corporations at all, let alone in positions of influence."[54] In addition to it being just that corporate employees have a right to due process, Jacobs also sees it as a means by which the role of the professions as countervailing institutions can be strengthened. "It will provide an internal limitation on corporate power if those who make the decisions know that there are some things that professionals cannot be ordered to do, and that they cannot be discarded for that refusal," Jacobs said.[55]

It detracts not at all from the achievements of unions to say that they are not the instruments through which significantly greater democracy in the workplace is likely to be accomplished. Democracy within unions is itself often a feeble thing. *Engineering News Record* reported in 1972 that less than 10 percent of the 3 million construction union members regularly attend union meetings.[56] Former labor organizer and teacher Stanley Aronowitz, in his 1973 book, *False Promises: The Shaping of American Working Class Consciousness*, made the point that most workers have given up on the notion of making their true grievances felt through union leadership.[57] This does not mean that workers have grown smug and that they see no need for greater protection from management, or do not desire a greater voice in how the company in which they work is run. Rather than being submissive and satisfied, Aronowitz said, workers today appear to be more militant about better working conditions than at any time in recent history. Since 1967, Aronowitz wrote, "the number of strikes as a whole, as well as rank-and-file rejections of proposed union settlements with employers, and wildcat actions has exceeded that in any similar period in the modern era."[58]

Aronowitz wrote that the union leaders often lag far behind the members. The leaders attempt to thwart membership initiative, support member-backed strikes publicly while sabotaging them behind the scenes, and emphasize grievances on wages and benefits while leaving the huge backlogs of grievances on working condition issues unresolved.[59] "Rank and file militancy has occurred precisely because of the refusal of the unions to address themselves to the issues of speedup, health and safety, plant removal, increased workloads, technological change, and arbitrary discharge of union militants," said Aronowitz.[60] Given this bad situation, workers stick with the trade unions, nonetheless, because no alternative to them exists.[61]

Writing from a radical perspective, Aronowitz noted that "the last thirty-five years of industrial unionism have failed to effect any substantive change in the distribution of income." With only partial (25 percent) unionization of the working force, he said, trade unionism "can do no more than redistribute income *within* the working class." Thus, workers in heavily organized industries—auto, rubber and steel—have relatively high wages compared to workers in consumer goods industries, retail and wholesale workers, and compared to most government and agricultural workers.[62] Aronowitz went on to say:

The tendency for employers in heavy industry to give in to union wage demands presupposes their ability to raise prices and productivity . . . Since advanced capitalism requires consumerism both as ideology and as practice to preserve commodity production, its payment of high wages to large segments of the working class—and minimum income to those excluded from the labor markets—is not objectively in the workers' interest. It is a means to take care of the market or demand side of production.[63]

From a probusiness standpoint, the *Engineering News Record* echoes some of Aronowitz's comments:

Intelligent and dedicated union members have become largely resigned to the futility of trying to effect changes within their organizations . . . , and often stay away from meetings.[64]

In the construction industry, the magazine said, low productivity wastes from 15 to 40 percent of every construction dollar—which in 1972 meant that "Americans this year are spending from $12 billion to $16 billion for something they aren't getting." Thus, with construction the nation's largest industry and a pacesetter for wages, "the economy of the entire nation and its 80 million workers may be adversely affected by 150,000 to 300,000 construction union members."[65]

Big unions attempt to tell their members how to vote without even consulting the rank-and-file members. In 1968, when the Democratic presidential nomination was still up for grabs among then-Vice-President Hubert H. Humphrey, then-Senator Eugene McCarthy (D–Minn.) and then–Senator Robert F. Kennedy (D–N.Y.), rank-and-file AFL–CIO members received duplicated letters signed by George Meany himself telling them that the federation supported Humphrey. The members were never consulted in advance on this, needless to say.

In 1972, leaders of The Newspaper Guild announced that the Guild supported Senator George S. McGovern (D–S.Dak.) over President Richard Nixon in the presidential race. Again, needless to say, Guild rank-and-file members were not consulted about this decision. This was especially questionable because members of the Guild who are reporters and editors are expected to handle political campaigns and other news without bias or partisanship.

Union leaders, again without any mandate from their rank-and-file members, also have immersed themselves in foreign policy. As one of the worst examples, the AFL–CIO under George Meany was a leading drum-beater for the disastrous Vietnam war. Edward Sadlowski, an insurgent who was elected director of the United Steelworkers Union District 31, which covers Chicago and Gary, is one of a new breed of labor leaders who sees Meany's jingoistic support of the Vietnam war as being not in the best interests of the nation or of labor. The position labor leaders took on Southeast Asia "was a tragedy," Sadlowski said. "It was a dastardly thing." He continued:

Who's the guy that was going? It was the kid—my son that works in the steel mill. It's not the banker's boy. Ain't too many steel worker guys bought their kids deferments and stuff. The kid that was in the goddamn trenches in Vietnam, or in that jungle over there, that was a working-class kid. If 50,000 kids laid dead in Southeast Asia, it was 50,000 sons of George Meany. That's the tragedy of the thing.[66]

Sadlowski went on to say that Meany and other labor leaders like him "get so plugged in with the goddamn Pentagon and the White House and everything else that they start believing generals. They start really believing that if there's no war they're going to shut down an armor-plate factory or something and put 500 men out of work. You've got to start instilling in them that instead of making armor plate, you start making books in that factory. It's just as easy. I don't know why you can't do that. And God knows you need books."[67]

Long before the Vietnam war, big labor was working with the CIA to keep foreign union movements out of the hands of leftists. Especially active in this was the AFL–CIO's international affairs department, which until 1974 was headed by Jay Lovestone, who had earned a reputation as a man who did the CIA's bidding in foreign affairs. Although Meany has said that the AFL–CIO, in its international programs, does "not even try to influence the structure of the labor movement in other nations," the facts are otherwise.[68] Columnist Tom Braden, who headed the CIA's program of anti-Communist fronts from 1950 to 1954, wrote that "in 1947 the Communist CGT led a strike in Paris which came near to paralyzing the French economy. A take-over of the government was feared. Into this crisis stepped Lovestone and his assistant Irving Brown. With funds from International Ladies' Garment Workers Union president David Dubinsky, they organized Force Ouvrière, a non-Communist union. When they ran out of money, they appealed to the CIA. Thus began the secret subsidy of free trade unions . . . Without that subsidy postwar history might have gone very differently."[69] Brown, according to Braden, received $2 million a year for the purpose of influencing overseas union movements. That amount undoubtedly grew as AFL–CIO agents were sent to other European nations, to the Far East and Latin America.[70]

Sidney Lens, an author and Chicago-based labor leader and radical activist, strongly makes the point that the mandate for all this foreign intrigue by union leaders has come not from the rank-and-file but from the leaders themselves:

Who gave the leadership of the AFL (and later of the AFL–CIO) a mandate to form this alliance with the U.S. government and its intelligence apparatus? In the last thirty years, the 13 million members of the AFL–CIO have never had the opportunity to vote on any issue of foreign policy, have never been consulted as to their wishes. Contrary to the popular image, the AFL–CIO is not a union as such, to which workers belong directly (except for a tiny number who are members of 'federal locals'). The AFL–CIO is a federation of unions; it does not have members but 'affiliates'—116 of them. The men with power at its biennial conventions are (again, with a few exceptions) the self-designated top leaders of the national unions (the 'affiliates'). Neither local union leaders nor rank-and-filers have any say.

The 116 affiliates and their hierarchs could have curbed Meany . . . Lovestone, and Brown, but they did not and do not because they are pragmatic men (no women were involved) who benefit substantially from the federation's alliance with the Government in international affairs. Among the benefits are representation on various Government boards, assurances to the seafarers' union that its members will haul a major portion of the Russian wheat deal, relaxation of pressures on certain building trades unions to integrate, winking at labor's illegal campaign contributions . . .[71]

But despite the many benefits to labor leaders from labor's collaboration with the CIA, the cost to free trade unions overseas has been substantial. Lens wrote that the AFL–CIO operation "split many labor movements abroad; it has served such nefarious purposes as financing a group of thugs . . . to break a strike of port workers in Marseilles who refused to unload ships with American arms; . . ."[72]

Under President Kennedy, the Lovestone-Brown operation began to get open government money in addition to CIA funds. Kennedy said this was needed so "the talents and experience of the U.S. labor movement could be brought to bear on the danger that Castro . . . might undermine the Latin American labor movement." The source of these new funds was the Agency for International Development.

When *Ramparts* magazine in 1967 disclosed secret CIA funding to the National Student Association, other publications followed with disclosures that labor unions and other organizations also were receiving covert CIA funds. The Newspaper Guild was among the labor organizations that received covert funding from the CIA through conduit front "foundations" for international-affairs programs.[73] Guild leaders never explained, satisfactorily if at all, precisely who had made a decision so dangerous to the reputations for independence and integrity of the members whose dues paid their salaries. They never explained why their curiosity had not been stirred by as improbable an act as foundations giving $1 million to a labor union, why they had failed to notice news stories naming the particular foundations as CIA funnels, why they had never looked at public records on their benefactors, and why they had not celebrated the gifts with large headlines in the *Guild Reporter.* Thanks to protests mainly by the Washington-Baltimore and Detroit locals, the International Executive Board in March 1967 terminated its relations with the foundations. Still, the Newspaper Guild gratuitously had damaged the credibility of reporters, particularly those in overseas assignments.[74]

While big union leaders have found time to dabble in national politics, foreign policy and clandestine dealings with the CIA, they, in concert with management, have evinced little interest in the democratization of the workplace or improving the quality of life for workers on the job. "Who the hell wants to go in a steel mill?" asked Ed Sadlowski, the steel-union leader.[75]

British economist E. F. Schumacher, author of *Small Is Beautiful: Economics As If People Mattered,* has said, "It is only necessary to assert that something would reduce the 'standard of living,' and every debate is instantly closed. That soul-destroying, meaningless, mechanical, monotonous, moronic work is an insult to human nature which must necessarily and inevitably produce either escapism or aggression, and that no amount of 'bread and circuses' can compensate for the damage done—these are facts which are neither denied nor acknowledged but are met with an unbreakable conspiracy of silence—because to deny them would be too obviously absurd and to acknowledge them would condemn the central preoccupation of modern society as a crime against humanity."[76]

What does technology do for the "standard of living?" "It obviously greatly reduces some kinds of work, while it increases other kinds," Schumacher says.

The type of work which modern technology is most successful in reducing or even eliminating is skillful, productive work of human hands, in touch with real materials of one kind or another. In an advanced society, such work has become exceedingly rare . . . A great part of the modern neurosis may be due to this very fact; for the human being with brains and hands, enjoys nothing more than to be creatively, usefully, productively engaged with both his hands and his brains.[77]

In a democratic workplace employees have decision-making power over matters of importance in their jobs. Nowhere is this concept more advanced than Sweden. Indeed, the Swedish government and the Confederation of Trade Unions proposed in 1975 a set of reforms under which workers will share control over virtually any decision traditionally reserved for employers. These include, Bernard Weinraub reported in the *New York Times*,

the appointment of directors as well as foremen, important management decisions such as expansion, pricing policies and mergers, and the right of unions to demand full information about a company's affairs.

"We are trying to come to grips with the problems of an industrial society," said Premier Olaf Palme in an interview. "We're at the beginning of major developments toward the rights of employees to influence decisions at work."

Allan Larsson, undersecretary of state in the Labor Ministry and an architect of the reforms, told Weinraub, "Workers should have more say over who gets dismissed, over how to lead and organize work, how a job should be done, what a company's policy should be. Workers should have more say in fields where employers had the options."[78]

Needless to say, business generally shrinks from the prospect of greater worker control. Most American labor unions have been generally uninterested, if aware at all, that such industrial democracy exists not only in many parts of Europe, but also in a small but growing number of businesses in the United States. Nat Goldfinger, research director for the AFL–CIO, has said that industrial democracy is not needed here. Other labor officials, notably some in the United Auto Workers, perceive a growing desire on the part of workers for democracy in the workplace.[79] For example, Irving Bluestone, head of the UAW's General Motors department, said in a speech in early 1972 that workers "question traditional authoritarian managerial prerogatives" and want "direct participation in the decision-making process." This desire "will evidence itself initially in the area of 'managing the workers' job';

then . . . it will spread to aspects of 'managing the enterprise,' " Bluestone predicted.[80]

Democratization of the workplace would mark "a radical change from the traditional rigid, pyramidal, authoritarian management structures that are virtually universally accepted," David Jenkins said in his book *Job Power: Blue and White Collar Democracy.*

At the very least, democracy means a firm check on the issuance of dictatorial management ukases from the airy reaches of the pyramidal peaks. It means an end to the assumption that "managers" and "employees" are somehow fundamentally different, the former endowed with vastly superior thinking powers, the latter totally incapable of formulating decisions on their own, able only to follow instructions, and at that only under threat of punishment. It means that the intelligence and knowledge of employees—assets often underutilized or nonutilized—can be put into action to the benefit of both employees and organization.[81]

Adam Smith, the champion of capitalism, foresaw the risks of the modern-day automobile assembly line two hundred years ago when he said: "The man whose life is spent in performing a few simple operations . . . has no occasion to exert his understanding or to exercise his invention in finding out expedients for removing difficulties which never occur . . . and generally becomes as stupid and ignorant as it is possible for a human creature to become."[82] When such work is performed by many people, Smith added, "all the nobler parts of the human character may be, in a great measure, obliterated and extinguished in the great body of the people."

Smith recommended that workers be paid high wages which would make them more productive. This is the "money instrumental" attitude toward work in which the worker is only an instrument purchased by the employer to perform a certain task.[83] In the late nineteenth century, the concept of scientific management—the idea that there was "one best way" of performing every job, and that this way could be scientifically established—was introduced by Frederick W. Taylor. Every worker could best do his job by following a preestablished, rigid pattern, he said. Among other things, Taylor invented time-and-motion studies. Taylor viewed man as incurably stupid, incapable of even understanding his work. This concept, which spread throughout American business, was the seedbed for much of the alienation that has grown up among many workers today. In his book *Alienation and Freedom*, Robert Blauner listed four ingredients of alienation: powerlessness (regarding ownership of the business, control over the work process); meaninglessness (with regard to the product or the production process); isolation (regarding the social aspect of work); self-estrangement (boredom, which can lead to "absence of personal growth").[84]

Nowhere is alienation more keenly felt than on the assembly line—especially the automobile assembly line. It features the most degrading aspects of work. Few of the jobs require much intelligence. The typical worker has no leeway to make the smallest decision on his own. He is completely subject to the machine, and generally sees only a small part of the overall production process.[85] Some defenders of the system say that it's a middle-class supposition that workers on the line are unhappy, and that in reality they are content with their lot because of their comparatively high wages. Reputable studies, however, indicate otherwise.

And it's not just on the job that workers are affected by boring, tedious, repetitive tasks; they also are affected in their home and leisure lives. Off the job, many psychologists and social research experts point out, alienation of workers also harms many companies. The most successful managers, they say, are generally those who in some manner share management with employees.

Although the sharing of management with the workers may strike some people, especially managers, as an undesirable radical change, it actually is very much in the capitalist mold of management self-interest. Many people may be surprised to learn that it's not just obscure little companies in remote nooks and crannies of the country that have adopted successful job democratization or forms of worker participation in management decisions. Take Texas Instruments. After rapid growth in the 1950s, this electronics giant's sales stagnated in the 1960–1962 period, and profits dropped by nearly half. It was during this period that personnel director Scott Myers tested workers and found all—from machine operators to scientists—had the same predominant motivating factor: achievement. Discovering a wide gap between managers and workers, he attempted to wipe it out by involving workers in the entire process—to make "every person a manager" so that he regards his work as something other than an ordeal. Myers cited an episode in which Texas Instruments had won a contract for some radar equipment, but had erroneously bid under its actual manufacturing cost and was losing money heavily. A foreman then laid out the the situation in detail to ten women assemblers and asked them for suggestions on how the company could stop losing money on the contract. After studying the assembly-line operation step-by-step, they made forty suggestions.

Under the prevailing work schedule, it was taking 138 man-hours to manufacture each unit. For the contract to be profitable, this figure would have to decline to under 100 hours. The women said that, by implementing their suggestions, the work could be done in 86 hours. Actually, they got the time down to 75 hours. They then asked for another meeting, made more suggestions and reduced the time to 57 hours and, eventually, to 32.

To break down the usual hierarchical structure, Texas Instruments has operators help to train supervisors. There are no executive dining rooms, no executive parking places, no hierarchy of office furnishings, no status symbols. Such innovations reveal, Myers says, "the wastefulness of bureaucracy and the advantages of democracy . . . It is necessary that we recognize people as individuals and realize that if they do not achieve their personal goals, they won't achieve company goals."[86]

Another big-name company, Corning Glass, started a successful participative program at a new electronics plant in New England. Under Michael Beer, manager of personnel research, the plant undertook programs in which workers got maximum responsibility; and decision making, rather than coming from the top, was pushed as far as possible down into the ranks. The first test came in a department where each woman on a traditional assembly line was doing only a small part of the job of producing hot plates for laboratories and hospitals. The assembly line was abolished, and each worker began to assemble entire products. The results were remarkable. After six months, absenteeism dropped from 8 percent to 1 percent. Productivity rose by 47 percent.

In another department, an assembly line turning out complex electronic instruments, some consisting of as many as 250 parts and selling for $4,000, was also abolished, and the operators began assembling entire products. Again, astounding results. Absenteeism fell from 8.5 percent to 3.4 percent and productivity increased by $1,500 per year per worker. Rejects dropped from 25 percent to 13 percent—this sharp drop in rejects came in spite of the fact that during the period in question, four new instrument models were introduced, including one which had been pushed so rapidly that no drawings were available and the women had to figure out how to assemble it on the basis of a prototype model.[87]

Even the systems set up by Corning Glass and Texas Instruments fall short of "open systems" or "total systems" two other industrial giants, General Foods and Procter & Gamble, have tried.

General Foods instituted a democratic work milieu at a pet-food factory in Topeka, Kansas. Management selected a planning group which determined that the plant's operation must mesh with the needs of the workers for self-esteem, sense of accomplishment, autonomy, and increasing knowledge of their performance. The planners omitted as many specialized functions as possible, abolished time clocks, held supervision to a minimum (team leaders replaced foremen), decentralized decision making, and minimized status symbols. For each of the three shifts, the planners set up an eight-member processing team and a sixteen-member packaging-warehousing team. There were no job categories. Instead, every worker learned all the jobs—cleaners, helpers, process operators, mechanics, boiler operators, quality control technicians, fork truck drivers, grain unloaders—which were needed by the teams. This system eliminates the difficulty of filling the most unpleasant and undesirable jobs—all workers share in the most desirable and most undesirable jobs. In addition, the employees are also involved in hiring and firing. Workers' responses to the set-up are overwhelmingly enthusiastic.

The democratization at Procter & Gamble takes on special significance because of the size of the company—the twenty-first largest in the United States—and the far-reaching nature and scope of the changes that it has initiated. P&G put its program of democratization into operation in the late 1960s at its plant in Lima, Ohio. About 125 people worked there, in three shifts, and produced two consumer products. According to Charles Krone, head of organizational development for P&G, "the plant was designed from the ground up to be democratic," with the basic principle being that all workers have growth potential. The plant has no jobs in the ordinary sense. Plants of this type set up along traditional lines would have between sixteen and twenty job classifications; at Lima there are none. Although each worker can improve his skills in a specialized field, all still must share responsibility for day-to-day operations, and must perform a variety of tasks. There are no time clocks. Everyone is on straight salary. The workers, then, have virtually total control of the plant. "The manager has very little decision-making power," Krone said. "Usually, instead of being seen as a resource, he is seen as an invader, fulfilling a directive and controlling role—there is much less of that here."

The workers devise their own budgets and pay scales; their salaries are known to everyone. At the same time, the company gives them financial figures on the plant's operation. Hypothetically, Krone said, this could have put management in a situation where the workers "could hold us up and say you're not paying us enough." But this hasn't happened. And, Krone said, "by now you could almost say these employees have less interest in their pay than management people do, who think Lima people are not being paid enough." Although pay levels are higher than is customary for this type of plant, the overall costs are only 50 percent of those at a conventional plant of this type. Much of the cost-saving is attributed to advanced technology, but such technology could not function so effectively were it not for plant democratization. The system also pays off in high-quality products. "It has the most outstanding quality record of any plant we have—it is virtually perfect quality," Krone said. Author David Jenkins said:

The outstanding characteristic of the P&G approach is its insistence on a truly "open" attitude. In line with the notion that the employee is a "growthful potential human being," no borders are erected to limit employee influence on company affairs. That these principles have been applied in a major U.S. company over a period of some years and widely scattered locations—with excellent results—is strong evidence of the benefits of giving power and freedom to employees . . .[88]

The industrial-democracy movement got its start in Norway in the early 1960s. At the time, surveys of the general population revealed a widespread feeling that a democratic nation must apply democratic principles to business organizations. Since then, Norway and other Scandinavian countries have developed substantial evidence that industrial democracy works in practice, as well as in theory.

In the United States, economic policy is often callously implemented. To combat inflation, economic thinkers here promote unemployment. Mass layoffs are carried out swiftly. Even high-level employees suffer from job insecurity. Compared to advanced European nations, we have a low level of public assistance to persons suddenly thrown out of a job. Until now, the emphasis here has been heavy on material gains, and light on psychic fulfillment. This is evident in the management techniques already discussed and in the attitudes of unions. Government policy-makers and political leaders have not promoted plans to give workers greater control in the workplace.

The contrast with Scandinavia is sharp. There, economic policy is more benevolent; full employment is a matter of firm government policy; and antiinflationary policies get lower priority. Compared with the United States, there is virtually no job insecurity.

In the case of some smaller American companies that were going bankrupt, the employees have bought the plant—and have shown themselves to be more efficient managers than the owners they replaced. In Lowell, Vermont, the workers in early 1975 bought a $5 million asbestos plant a year after the conglomerate GAF Corporation announced that it was going to close the plant rather than spend $1 million to meet federal air-pollution standards. All 280 employees, from plant manager to janitor, are stockholders in the company, Vermont Asbestos Group, Inc. Seven members of the union local, including two officers, sit on the board. While negotiations for the worker takeover were under way, production in the mine peaked and costs declined rapidly. The takeover was facilitated by a loan of $400,000 in working capital that was guaranteed by the Small Business Administration and by a $1.5 million loan guaranteed by Vermont's Agency for Development and Community Affairs. Among the costs that declined dramatically was equipment repair. "They realize that we all own this equipment now," said John J. Lupien, the plant's maintenance supervisor and board chairman. "It's amazing how careful people can be."[89]

441

. . .

Swedish Premier Palme has said that his government's "principal preoccupation" is with democracy on the job. "The reforms we have achieved have meant great progress, but without touching people's daily working lives," he has said. "We must introduce democracy into enterprises . . . In the 1970s and 1980s we are going to rebuild social life through democracy in work."[90] Numerous other countries, including England, Israel, and Yugoslavia, also have developed approaches to worker democracy. Here, barring a miracle of universal enlightenment in business and labor leaders, the path to democratization of the workplace will be long and hard.

The Declaration of Independence, once again, says that "life, liberty, and the pursuit of happiness" are inalienable rights. But a political process that does not secure these rights in the workplace is, for the men and women who spend most of their lives there, defectively accountable.

The burden of taxation and the ease of wealth continue to be unfairly and unwisely distributed. Reversing the ethic of Sherwood Forest, the system takes too much from those who haven't enough in order to bestow more on those who already have too much. Generation after generation, it has perpetuated gross inequities that are not only unjustifiable, but also irrational. Today, the system of taxation is no less unaccountable to most people than was the "taxation without representation" that helped to kindle the American Revolution; and it frustrates the prime purpose of government as perceived by the Founding Fathers: to assure the safety and happiness of the people.

Although exact measures of the impact of the primary mechanism of inequity, loopholes and subsidies, are unavailable, government and private studies indicate that they have proliferated to the point that they favor various special interests by more than $100 billion annually. With sums of such magnitude at stake, the relative few who share in them are powerfully motivated to try to assure the continuation and even enlargement of their favored situation. At the same time, of course, the many who are disadvantaged collectively have even more compelling reason to try to alter the status quo. But the minority, armed with great wealth and sustained high income, has what the majority lacks: the wherewithal and clout to get what it wants. To be sure, the rank and file have the sheer numbers to out-vote the minority, but at least insofar as the tax system is concerned are hopelessly fragmented. No wonder that when they go to the polling place—*if* they go— they find that in this area the political process has given them a choice of candidates who are Tweedledum and Tweedledee.

Beverly C. Moore, Jr., is a lawyer who, after working as an aide to Ralph Nader, set up an enterprise called the Center for the Study of Capitalist Institutions. He has emphasized "that the marginal utility of wealth and income declines"—that is, people need only so much money to live comfortably. He offers an extreme illustration: a billionaire will feel the loss of a dollar less than a beggar to whom the dollar is transferred will feel the gain. "More generally," Moore says, "the collective happiness derived by individuals from the use and ownership of economic resources is maximized by an equal distribution thereof." Most people would agree that $100,000 is a comfortable annual income. To a person in that income bracket, an additional $3,000 a year likely would provide only optional or luxury items. An additional

$3,000 a year for, say, a family of four with a $7,000 income, surely would provide necessities, such as more nutritious and better-quality food and more adequate housing.

Moore also points out that inequalities of income and wealth produce inequalities in other aspects of life. Persons with insufficient incomes generally have shorter life expectancies, suffer more physical and mental afflictions, are more alienated by their work, tend to spend fewer years in school and to get inferior educations, have less social mobility, and make little impact on the political system. According to Moore, then, a much more equitable distribution of wealth not only would increase the collective happiness but also would produce "a 'public good' that benefits society as a whole."[1]

Nobel Prize-winning economist Kenneth Arrow of Harvard argues that a fairer distribution of income is essential to the maintenance of liberty for all. As he sees it, "a commitment to democratic values strongly implies an ideal of redistribution of income and wealth." Arrow continued:

Many among both the intellectual and general publics regard redistribution as a deprivation of liberty, in that property is taken away by coercion. I disagree with this viewpoint most strongly. . . .

Income and property are certainly the instruments of an individual's freedom. Clearly the domain of choice is enhanced by increases in those dimensions. It is true not merely in the sense of expanded consumer choice but also in broader contexts of career and opportunity to pursue one's own aims and to develop one's own potential. *Unequal distribution of property and of income is inherently an unequal distribution of freedom. Thus a redistribution of income, to the extent that it reduces the freedom of the rich, equally increases that of the poor. Their control of their lives is increased.* (Emphasis supplied.)[2]

A more equitable distribution of the nation's wealth, in addition to creating a more just society, also could give the economy a substantial boost. Whereas the person of wealth, given an extra $3,000, would tend to use the money to produce more income, the poorer person would pump much of that money back into the economy for necessities that have been deferred because of the lack of money. Thus, income and wealth redistribution can also be said to be "good for business."

Arrow cited another important reason why wealth redistribution is essential: ". . . unequal economic power is bound to be translated into political power. The mechanisms that this transformation takes are no secret . . . Campaign contributions, the many rewards that can be conveyed by contributions of wealth to complaisant political leaders, the ability to control communication, the greater leisure and ability to be informed, all of them skew the distribution of political power. The aim of achieving an equal distribution of political power requires a restriction on the inequities of wealth and income."[3]

To illustrate the extent of the unequal sharing of income in the United States, Beverly Moore has devised a series of tables which show that in 1968 the wealthiest 5 percent of the citizenry received 22 percent of the nation's actual income before taxes (after-tax percentages were slightly lower). The wealthiest top 20 percent earned almost half—48 percent. This contrasts with the bottom 5 percent who received a minuscule 0.4 percent of the nation's income; the bottom 20 percent received only 3 percent.

The unequal distribution of wealth is glaringly evident in a category Moore calls business ownership claims. It covers, among other things, stocks, bonds, pensions, life insurance, and real estate. In this category, the nation's wealthiest 5 percent owned 61 percent of the claims. This, of course, leaves extremely little for the rest of the population. Thus, the bottom 5 percent owned none of these claims; the bottom 20 percent owned 0.5 percent.

A study released in late 1974 by three professors of finance at the Wharton School of the University of Pennsylvania showed that stock ownership continued to be an almost exclusive preserve of the rich. As of mid-1971, the study reported, the richest 0.2 percent of Americans owned 30 percent of all the stock. The richest 1 percent owned just over half of it.

In perhaps the most significant of the categories listed by Moore, the top 5 percent of the population are shown to have controlled, as of 1962, 53 percent of the nation's wealth. For the top 20 percent, the share was 77 percent. The bottom 40 percent controlled a trivial 2 percent.[4]

In 1944, Treasury Department figures show, individual income tax payments (including the full Social Security tax which, many economists say, in truth is borne entirely by the employee through lower wages and lower fringe benefits) amounted to 48.5 percent of all federal revenue receipts. By 1954, individuals were paying 52.7 percent; by 1964, 62.7 percent; by 1974, an estimated whopping 73.9 percent. Contrast this with corporate tax payments, which declined from 33.6 percent of total federal receipts in 1944 to 30.3 percent in 1954, to 20.9 percent in 1964, and to an estimated 14.6 percent in 1974. Thus, the gap between individual and corporate payments widened from 14.9 percent in 1944 to 59.3 percent in 1974. In 1944, individuals were paying into the treasury one and a half times as much as corporations; by 1974, individuals were paying five times as much. Curiously enough, this decline in the corporate tax burden came during a period when the supposed corporate tax rate as specified in the tax code had increased overall, rising from 31 percent in 1944 to 52 percent in 1954, then falling back to 50 percent in 1964 and 48 percent ten years later. In addition to dropping the corporate tax rate by four percentage points since 1974, the government has given corporations such a myriad of loopholes that their actual tax burden has declined much more than that.[5]

In 1974, eight large corporations, including Ford Motor Company and Lockheed Aircraft Corporation, had aggregate adjusted net income of $843,974,000 before federal income tax. But federal income tax was precisely what none of them paid, according to a study by the staff of the Joint Committee on Internal Revenue Taxation. Eighteen other corporations, including Chase Manhattan Corporation, Bankers Trust New York Corporation, Bank America Corporation, Continental Illinois Corporation, Texaco, Inc., and McDonnell Douglas Corporation, paid federal income taxes at rates of less than 1 percent to 10 percent.[6]

The loopholes go by a variety of exotic names—depletion allowances, intangible drilling expenses, investment tax credits, asset depreciation range. Taken together, they constitute a multibillion-dollar annual corporate dole that, as Ralph Nader has said, makes "middle-and-lower-income taxpayers pay more than they should, so that corporations and wealthy investors (who benefit from corporate tax loopholes) pay less than they should. So the many who have little subsidize the few who have much." Yet, as Nader notes, what little information is available indicates that the tax "windfalls are producing neither the additional investment nor the robust economic expansion and productivity which the law makers were told to expect."[7] For example, economists Edward Erickson and Stephen Millsaps examined the tax incentives for petroleum exploration to see if they actually achieved the intended result—a significant increase in domestic petroleum reserves. They determined that tax incentives which in 1968 cost the taxpayers $1.4 billion (and $3 billion or more a year after that) have not been shown to generate in excess of $150 million a year worth of additional petroleum reserves. The economists sensibly concluded that "the consensus of professional economic opinion is relatively certain that the special tax provisions [for petroleum] result in an inefficient allocation of resources, a smaller national income, and questionable distribution effects."[8]

The Erickson/Millsaps study was a rarity: a congressionally sponsored effort to determine whether a particular tax break was producing the result predicted by its advocates. On the overall issue, however, Congress and the Treasury Department have been strikingly slow to act on the common sense need to produce hard information on each loophole and subsidy. Commenting in late 1974 on the failure of tax bonanzas for the wealthy and private corporations to produce benefits for society as a whole, Nader said:

Given this unrequited subsidy, which directly burdens the small taxpayer, why is there not an annual evaluation by the Congress or the Treasury of such special corporate tax privileges? The small taxpayers should be informed about what they are not receiving in return for their subsidizing of these companies through the tax system. In recent days, corporate executives are once again telling the White House that they need even more "tax incentives," as they call them, or "welfare payments," as they should be described. Such incentives are needed, these industrial leaders say, to increase investment in plants and equipment. This corporate cry is becoming a routine Washington refrain—more tax subsidies for companies who vaguely promise more investment. But when they get their special tax reductions, the public is not shown what they receive in return.[9]

Nader, of course, has touched on something that the newspapers, magazines, and radio and television networks seldom make truly clear to the broad public: tax "subsidies," "incentives," and tax breaks for corporations are giveaways and handouts on a lavish scale. Notably, putatively conservative politicians and news organizations are routinely indignant about "welfare chiselers" and "ripoffs" in programs for lower-income persons, such as aid to dependent children and food stamps, but invoke a benign, soothing terminology in discussing the whopping amounts the government gives to the giants of industry and the wealthy elite. Just as the unaccountable language of the war in Southeast Asia translated invasions into "incursions" and concentration camps into "strategic hamlets," thus also have handouts to the rich and powerful been translated into "tax incentives" and "subsidies," while payments to the poor and politically impotent have become "welfare" and "handouts." Philip M. Stern, author of *The Great Treasury Raid*[10] and *The Rape of the Taxpayer,*[11] made this point in a satirical news story that was incorporated in his testimony to a congressional committee in early 1972. Here is that "story," in part:

WASHINGTON, D.C. (AP/UPI): Congress today completed action on the final part of a revolutionary welfare program that reverses the usual pattern and gives huge welfare payments to the super-rich but only pennies per week to the very poor. Under the program, welfare payments averaging some $720,000 a year will go to the nation's wealthiest families (those with annual incomes of more than a million dollars). For the poorest families (those earning $3,000 a year or less), the welfare allowance will average $16 a year, or roughly 30 cents a week.

The program—enacted by Congress in a series of laws over a period of years—has come to be called the Rich Welfare Program, after its principal sponsor, Senator Homer A. Rich, who, in a triumphant news conference, told newsmen that the $720,000 annual welfare allowances would give America's most affluent families "added weekly 'take-home pay' of about $14,000. Or to put it another way," the Senator added, "it will provide these families about $2,000 more spending money every day." Total cost of the program—the most expensive welfare program ever noted—comes to $77.3 billion a year.

Political observers have been surprised by the manner in which this huge sum has been allocated. Experts have calculated that only about $92 million—about one-tenth of one percent of the total—will go to the six million poorest families in the country (the under $3,000 income group). By contrast, experts said, Congress has voted about twenty-four times that amount—more than $2.2 billion—for families with incomes greater than one million dollars a year. (Informed government sources said there are roughly 3,000 such families in the United States.)

Moreover, Congress has allocated nearly 15 percent of the total—more than $11 billion annually—in welfare payments to families with annual incomes of $100,000 or more. Revelation of this fact brought angry protests from consumer groups here in Washington, who pointed out that this $11 billion outlay for the rich is four times the expenditures to provide food stamps for hungry poor families and one thousand times the Federal outlay for health programs for migrant farm workers.

Of greater consequence, political analysts here believe, is the potential discontent among the middle-classes (those in the $10,000–$15,000 income group) for whom the welfare payments under the Rich scheme will amount to $650 a year—or about $12.50 a week. While this is considerably more than the 30 cents a week allocated to the very poor, political pundits here feel that Congressmen who supported the Rich Plan might have trouble explaining to middle-class constituents why the very-rich should receive welfare payments of $60,000 per month, in contrast to the $55 per month allocated to middle-income families . . .

The kicker to this "story," is, Stern added, that it "is essentially true. The facts and figures in it are real. Such a system is, in fact, part of the law of the land. Only the law isn't called a welfare law. It goes by the name of 'The Internal Revenue Code of 1954, as amended.' It is the basic income tax law of the United States."

The Sixteenth Amendment, adopted in 1913, empowered Congress to tax incomes "from whatever source derived." But, Stern noted, "over the years, Congress has chosen to depart from that standard and to put into the law a special exception for this kind of income or a special deduction for that kind, or an exclusion or a waiver or an exemption or a special low rate or some other kind of escape hatch. And every time it did that it excused someone from paying what could and would have been collected if Congress had stuck to the Sixteenth Amendment and taxed 'incomes from whatever source derived'."[12]

Jean Paul Getty, reputedly one of the world's richest men, was said to be worth between a billion and a billion and a half dollars, and to enjoy a *daily* income of $300,000. He was hardly a person, one would think, who would need welfare payments; but the fact is that Getty got an annual government handout estimated at $70 million. But if Getty had been taxed as envisioned by the Sixteenth Amendment, he would have written a check to the Treasury Department for approximately $70 million each April, Stern said. Being an oil man, however, Getty enjoyed a number of tax loopholes. According to

Stern, President Kennedy in the early 1960s told two senators that Getty's annual taxes "amounted to no more than a few thousand dollars." The net effect of Getty's using the tax loopholes was the same as if Getty had been given a direct welfare payment of $70 million.[13]

Capital gains are the profits derived from the sale, after ownership of at least six months, of capital assets, such as stocks, bonds, land, buildings, factories, and machines. The tax rate on capital gains is no more than half that on an equivalent amount of wages. This is the biggest boondoggle for the wealthy and for corporations, amounting, according to Joseph A. Pechman and Benjamin A. Okner, of the Brookings Institution, to about $14 billion each year. Yet the benefit goes only to the one taxpayer in twelve fortunate enough to have any capital gains.

On the first $50,000 of a person's capital gains, according to Stern, the maximum tax is just 25 percent—compared to the 70 percent top rate applicable to earned income. But there is a loophole within the loophole. On capital gains held until death, the tax is not even 25 percent—but zero. Thus, according to Stern, "No one—neither the original owner of the assets nor his heirs—*ever* pays a tax on the rise in value that took place prior to his death. An estimated $10.4 billion passes tax-free in that manner every year."[14] This loophole, of course, helps those with great fortunes to preserve them through successive generations. As calculated from the Pechman/Okner figures, the capital-gains loopholes provide average "welfare" benefits of $640,667 annually for a person earning over $1 million; $22,630 annually for one in the $100,000–$500,000 bracket; $55 for one earning $15,000–$20,000; $1 for one earning $3,000–$5,000, and virtually nothing for one under $3,000. Under this kind of "tax redistribution" only the rich get richer.[15]

Another giveaway derives from the tax-free status of income from state and local bonds that, as Stern notes, "are overwhelmingly in the hands of financial institutions and wealthy individuals." The Pechman/Okner study shows that the annual average "welfare" benefits conferred by these bonds amounts to $36,333 for a person earning more than $1 million; $3,630 for one in the $100,000–$500,000 bracket; $1 for one in the $15,000–$20,000 category, and a dollar or less for one earning under that amount. The tax-free bond interest, plus the capital-gains tax breaks, account for about $15 billion of the $77.3 billion worth of tax preferences cited in the Pechman/Okner study. If all of these preferences were to be eliminated, Stern estimates, the result would be an across-the-board cut in the tax rate of 43 percent.[16]

More familiar to the average taxpayer are tax breaks such as the deductions that he is entitled to claim for medical expenses. Here again, as with the more exotic tax loopholes, it's the well-to-do who reap disproportionate benefits. In fiscal 1974, for example, persons earning up to $10,000 made up almost half (46.9 percent) of all taxpayers, but received just under 20 percent ($418 million) of the total deductions for medical expenses. For the large $10,000 to $20,000 income category, which includes 38.5 percent of all taxpayers, the medical-expense deductions amounted to just over 40 percent ($857 million) of the total; for the 13.4 percent of taxpayers in the $20,000–$50,000 bracket, 29.8 percent ($634 million), and for the 1.2 percent who earn $50,000 or more, 10.2 percent ($216 million). Thus, deductions for medical expenses, while averaging 99 cents for a taxpayer with income of under $3,000, and $30.15 for a typical taxpayer in the $10,000–$15,000 bracket, average $221.37 for the persons earning $50,000 to $100,000, and $443.75 for the person earning more than $100,000.

Deductions of mortgage interest and property taxes paid for owner-occupied homes also are widely assumed by middle-class taxpayers to give them a significant advantage. Again, however, the wealthy are disproportionately favored. In the case of mortgage interest, no deduction at all was enjoyed by the average person earning less than $3,000, only $1.72 by a person with income of $3,000 to $5,000, and only $55.54 by a person with $10,000 to $15,000. But the typical deduction for the $20,000–$50,000 range was $230.74, for $50,000–$100,000, $531.30, and for $100,000 and over, $593.75. The rewards of property-tax deductions were comparably phased: under $3,000, 25 cents; $3,000–$5,000, $3.17; $10,000–$15,000, $36.55; $20,000–$50,000, $196.98; $50,000–$100,000, $621.37, and $100,000 and over, $1,331.25.[17]

In addition to favoring the wealthy, these and other tax breaks for housing clearly discriminate against tenants, who while paying taxes and interest as a part of their rent, receive no deduction or direct tax benefit at all. Tax breaks for owner-occupied residences were, of course, ostensibly designed to encourage and facilitate home ownership, and to help the home-building industry. But the figures show that wealthier families—who are most likely to own their own homes with or without tax breaks—reap the largest benefits from the tax breaks. For them, therefore, the tax incentives are significantly a windfall for doing that which they would have done in any case. Moreover, the system in recent years significantly has failed to assist the building industry. New housing starts, numbering more than two million annually in 1971, 1972 and 1973, had declined to about one million in 1975. Surely direct subsidies to home-buyers would seem to be a fairer way to apportion housing benefits across the income spectrum—one that would spur the lagging housing market.[18] Indeed, everywhere in the tax structure one turns, one finds additional programs that had been ballyhooed as boons for lower-income persons, but that proved to hit those very persons hardest.

. . .

Social Security is by far the most regressive federal taxation. It now levies a flat 5.85 percent annually on the first $13,200 of a person's income. Thus, a person earning under $3,000 is taxed at the same rate as the person earning $13,200. Beyond that figure, the more he earns the smaller the share of income he pays for Social Security.

More than half the nation's taxpayers now are paying more Social Security tax than federal income tax. Also, the Social Security rates will have to keep increasing to keep pace with the benefits paid out to retired persons—which means the Social Security tax probably will become even more regressive. In addition, many economists say, Social Security taxes also result in lower wages because employers adjust wages to compensate for the requirement that they pay a sum equal to that paid by each employee.

In the past, there had been no way to get a handle on the extent of tax loopholes. But under the budget reform law enacted in 1974, the federal budget for fiscal 1975 disclosed for the first time that the cost of loopholes, called "tax expenditures" in the budget, was $91 billion. This, of course, was money that would have been collected had no special provisions been written into the law. Until 1975, figures on tax expenditures generally were kept from the public, although it is known that they totaled $36.6 billion in fiscal 1967. The figure had doubled seven years later, and in fiscal 1976 were two and a half times the 1967 level.

Even though the veil of secrecy has been lifted from the costs of loopholes, information remains scarce about which of them—if any—benefit the nation. Consider the tax code's export-subsidy provisions for Domestic International Sales Corporations (DISCs). The provisions permit companies doing business abroad to set up special sub-corporations—DISCs—and to postpone paying taxes on half of all the profits channeled through DISCs. The Treasury Department in 1971, when the secretary was John B. Connally, insisted that Congress approve the DISC provisions. His claim was that DISCs would provide an essential stimulus to exports. Congress went along. In 1971 alone DISCs cost the Treasury Department $200 million, which of course was made up by the taxpayers. By 1976, the cost had skyrocketed to $1.3 billion—and surely will go up much higher as more and more companies take advantage of the DISC provisions. Even by February 1974, more than five thousand DISCs were in existence, compared with only one thousand two years earlier.

The question is, How well have DISCs served their stated purpose of stimulating exports? In their first year, exports by companies using them actually declined 2.4 percent. In addition, a Treasury Department report showed that in 1972 a mere eight large firms had earned 22 percent of all untaxed DISC export income, and that 90 percent of all DISC receipts went to parent corporations that rank among the top one percent in assets. As Harvard Law Professor Stanley S. Surrey has said: "DISC is thus a windfall handed over to our largest corporations. Our largest corporations are our largest exporters and DISC simply reduces the current tax on export activity . . . Congress was . . . told that the tax on the DISC untaxed income would only be deferred, so that some day it would be paid. But Congress was not told that the deferral could be lengthy and that the present value of such deferral often would be worth about as much as the current exemption. DISC is thus built on paper and myths . . . do we as a nation gain anything? The answer is *no* . . ."[19]

Secrecy pervades administration of the tax code, mostly to the detriment of smaller taxpayers. For example, the Internal Revenue Service provides advance tax rulings for corporations and individuals. Many of these rulings have saved corporations and the rich millions of dollars. But not until 1975 did the IRS, under the pressure of a federal court ruling, propose new regulations under which it would make such rulings public and would name the person or firm who had sought the ruling. In the past, advance rulings had created a body of private law that was known only "to knowledgeable tax practitioners and those able to afford their services," Judge Aubrey E. Robinson, Jr., of the United States District Court in Washington, said in 1973. To deny the public access to these rulings was "an abomination," Robinson declared.

Numerous subsidies to business, in the words of Senator William Proxmire (D–Wis.), have been "hidden from public scrutiny." In chairing a Joint Economic subcommittee at the opening in early 1972 of the first congressional hearings ever held on these subsidies, which include loopholes, Proxmire said they totaled $63 billion. By late 1974, the figure had risen to $95 billion, a 50 percent increase attributed to larger subsidies and to underestimation in 1972. The $95 billion breaks down to more than $1,800 for every family in the nation. For the purposes of the 1972 hearings, the subcommittee staff, defined as subsidies government financial assistance that is designed to alter particular private market prices and incentives. Such subsidies include tax breaks, cash subsidies, credit subsidies and benefit-in-kind subsidies. In 1972, tax subsidies made up about 60 percent of the total; cash subsidies, 20 percent; credit subsidies, 6 percent, and benefit-in-kind subsidies, 14 percent. Harvard's Stanley Surrey, testifying in 1972 about subsidies, told Proxmire:

Less critical analysis is paid to these tax subsidies than almost any direct program that the Congress considers. These tax subsidies simply tumbled into the law without any supporting studies; they are propelled by cliches, debating points and scraps of data that are passed off as serious evidence. A tax system that is so vulnerable to this injection of extraneous, costly and ill-considered expenditure programs is simply in a very precarious state from the standpoint of the basic goals of tax fairness."[20]

Perhaps in no other area have subsidies had such a devastating effect on society as in agriculture. The huge subsidies of the past, the free research done for farmers, the federal government bailout programs when farmers overproduce—all of of these, perhaps, could be defended if they had gone chiefly to promote the family farm as part of the American way of life. But these programs undermined the family farm because the subsidy went mainly to agribusiness, the giants of the farming industry. As Jim Hightower, director of the Agribusiness Accountability Project, wrote in 1972, "Not only is agribusiness the largest American industry, but it also is the most heavily subsidized. The depth and range of these subsidies is far more than meets the public eye . . . It is unforgiveable naivete to think that it is the small farmer who receives this welfare . . ."[21]

At the time Hightower wrote that, farm subsidies were running at about $5 billion a year. Chief among them were price supports paid to growers on condition they not plant specified amounts of certain commodities; land-retirement payments for removing acreage entirely from production, and conservation payments to growers to improve their land. Charles Schultze, former director of the Bureau of the Budget, has noted that in 1969, large farms—the 7.1 percent then having more than $20,000 in sales—received almost two-thirds of the total commodity payments, while small farmers, who comprised more than half the total, received only 8.9 percent. In 1969, J. G. Boswell Company, a massive California agribusiness, alone received a $4.4 million subsidy—twice as much as the Department of Agriculture had available in grants to build housing for farm laborers. In 1970, Congress enacted a $55,000 limit on the subsidy any one grower could receive. Agribusinesses quickly found ways to get around this. The *Los Angeles Times* reported, for example, that California's big cotton growers were keeping enough land unplanted to receive the $55,000 subsidy, and were renting the balance "for 6 to 7 cents a pound of cotton, making most of the money they were expecting to lose in subsidies." The renters, of course, also could receive a subsidy of up to $55,000 by leaving some of the leased land unplanted.[22]

Enrichment of the well-to-do is also accomplished through tax deductions to charitable organizations. To illustrate, glowing publicity attended Nelson

A. Rockefeller's contribution of more than $1.6 million to charitable institutions in 1973. But it wasn't widely understood that more than two-thirds of this money—$1.16 million in uncollected taxes—was, in effect, federal funds directed to charities of Rockefeller's choice. A Boston College law professor, Paul R. McDaniel, in late 1975, suggested that a way to understand how charitable deductions work is to

imagine that the federal government made grants to match private contributions to charity, instead of simply allowing tax deductions. If the terms of that grant were identical to the present deduction system, this would be the formula: —If a donor's taxable income exceeds $200,000, the federal government will match each $1 contributed with $2.33 of federal funds.

—If a donor's taxable income is approximately $50,000, the federal government reduces its share and will match each $1 contributed with $1 of federal funds.

—If the donor's taxable income is only $10,000, then for each $1 of charitable contributions, the federal government reduces its share still further and provides only a 33 cent matching grant.

—Only those donors who itemize personal deductions on their tax returns—for mortgage interest, taxes, medical expenses and the like—are eligible for matching federal grants.

—The federal government provides no matching funds for the 65 per cent of individuals who either claim the standard deduction or do not have enough income to be required to file an income tax return. . . .

Were the secretary of the Department of Health, Education, and Welfare to propose such a plan, Congress, of course, would vote it down without serious debate, McDaniel said. "Yet this bizarre arrangement is the law of the land," he pointed out. "The system survives not because Congress is in fact convinced that the wealthy ought to control private charities, or that the federal government should help them to do so. It survives because very few people understand the way the present system works, and because no major group has tried to make it a political issue."[23]

Foundations are another device for the preservation of large fortunes with minimal accountability to the public. Consider the Government Affairs Foundation, Inc., of Albany, New York, which, between 1961 and 1964 received from its founder, then-Governor Nelson Rockefeller, gifts of $310,469—and paid out absolutely nothing to charity. Of Rockefeller's "contribution," $120,000 in salary and $40,000 in expenses went to New York's former Lieutenant Governor Frank C. Moore. The total of $160,000 paid out to Moore amounted to 57 percent of the foundation's total expenses of $284,193 for the period. The rest of the expenses were administrative costs. The result, according to the late Congressman Wright Patman (D–Tex.), former chairman of the House Banking and Currency Committee and a long-time critic of foundations, was a politician's dream come true. Rockefeller, Patman said, had found a "method by which he could hire a full-time liaison man, and be able to deduct that expense as a charitable item."

Upon resigning as governor in 1974, Rockefeller set up another tax-exempt arrangement with a potential to use the charitable donation provision of the tax code to his own advantage—possibly to improve his prospects for becoming President someday. One part of the arrangement was the National Commission on Critical Choices which, according to Rockefeller, would study the nation's problems into the next century. Its cost, estimated at $20 million, would be borne by the Third Century Corporation, which is a tax-exempt umbrella for the commission, and which is funded by grants from a half-dozen foundations and several governmental agencies.[24]

Henry Ford and his only son, Edsel, had owned 96.5 percent of all of the stock in the Ford Motor Company. Edsel died in 1943; Henry in 1947. Ovid Demaris wrote in his book *Dirty Business:*

The elder Ford's death came at a most inopportune time. The New Dealers had jacked up the inheritance tax to 91 per cent in the top bracket, and today's loopholes for marital deduction and estate splitting were not yet on the books . . . As matters stood at that crucial juncture, the government waited anxiously in the wings for its whopping 90 per cent chunk of the estate—unless, of course, the experts should conjure up an 11th-hour loophole. Thus was born the Ford Foundation . . .[25]

Actually, the Ford Foundation already had been in existence, having been incorporated by Edsel in 1936 with a $25,000 grant, but it had been kept small and had given mostly small gifts around Detroit that were beneficial to the Ford Motor Company. Henry Ford had often spoken out against public charity, but ironically it was the foundation established by Edsel that, according to Demaris, "provided the means for the family to retain absolute control of the company, saving it from outside factions seeking control. Even more importantly . . . it kept the money from the grasping hands of the hated New Dealers in Washington . . ." The foundation received 88 percent of Ford Motor assets in the form of a new issue of convertible, nonvoting stock, with the family retaining the voting stock. By this device, the family maintained control of both the foundation and the company. On property other than Ford stock, Demaris said, Henry and Edsel together paid inheritance taxes

of approximately $30 million on total assets with a market value of more than $3 billion—a flat rate of 1 per cent. Bear in mind that no capital gains tax was even paid on the appreciation of the Ford stock that grew from zilch to its staggering capital assets under the aegis of Henry . . .[26]

In the early 1950s, the late Howard Hughes, the recluse billionaire, transferred to the Howard Hughes Medical Institute, which he alone controlled, all of the stock of Hughes Aircraft Company. The institute then applied for a tax exemption. The IRS denied the application on the ground that the "whole setup was merely a device for siphoning off otherwise taxable income to an exempt organization, and accumulating that income." After the institute had filed a protest, and while the protest was pending, Richard Nixon, then the Vice-President-elect, requested and got a loan of $205,000 for his brother, Donald, from Hughes Tool Company (now Summa Corporation), of which Hughes Aircraft was a division, and which Howard Hughes owned. Collateral for the loan was a lot in Whittier, California, which was assessed for tax purposes at only $13,000. In March 1957, four months after the loan was made, the IRS, without explanation, reversed itself and ruled the institute tax-exempt. No connection between the loan and the agency reversal has been demonstrated.

Over the years, the institute annually paid out about $1 million—a relative trifle—for medical research. Its income from Hughes Aircraft, for contributions and for administrative expenses, was about $2.5 million, but it returned about $1 million to the company in the form of interest on a note. To end precisely such self-dealing and related abuses, Congress wrote the first significant controls on foundations into the Tax Reform Act of 1969. One of the controls requires an organization classified as a foundation to distribute to charity either its annual adjusted net income, or 6 percent of the fair-market value of its assets—whichever is greater. If classified as a foundation, the institute would have been required to pay out between $36 million and $60 million a year, on the basis of the market value of the institute's stockholdings in Hughes Aircraft as estimated by the staff of the House Banking Domestic Finance Subcommittee. But Hughes interests, represented mainly by former Senator George Smathers (D–Fla.), successfully lobbied Congress for an exclusion from the foundation classification of medical research foundations—meaning, for practical purposes, the institute.[27]

In an effort to circumvent the Smathers exclusion, the IRS proposed regulations to require medical research foundations to distribute to charity 4 percent of the fair market value of their assets. While this obviously was more lenient than the provision for nonmedical foundations, it still would have required the institute to pay out a hefty $24 million to $40 million annually. Not until five years later, did the IRS and its parent Treasury Department end what they call "study" and make the regulations final in February 1976, although with the required payout inexplicably reduced from 4 percent to 3½. Whether the regulations will apply to the institute was not immediately officially decided. During those five years, meanwhile, the institute, if it is a medical foundation, had been able to escape distributing $120 million to $200 million to research.

Incredibly, the institute—meaning Howard Hughes—had been secretly manuvering to be officially ruled a charity, such as a church or a hospital, so that it not only could wriggle free of restrictions on self-dealing and other abuses, but also could pay out for medical research as little as it cared to. The first inkling of all this came in testimony by a Hughes lawyer at a subcommittee hearing in April 1973. Congressman Patman, the subcommittee chairman, repeatedly pressed Treasury to end the "study" that was enriching the Hughes empire at a minimum rate of $24 million a year, but to no avail. The secret manuevering began in 1970; in 1969 and in 1970, Howard Hughes had made two contributions of $50,000 each to President Nixon or to his reelection campaign. In 1972, while the proposed regulations for a 4 percent payout were languishing in Treasury, Hughes openly gave $150,000 to the Finance Committee to Re-elect the President through Washington public relations man Robert F. Bennett. He, in turn, sent a private letter in July 1971 to John W. Dean III, then the White House counsel, asking help in getting charity status for the institute—the same outfit that the IRS once had found to be a mere siphon for otherwise taxable income. As of May 1976 there had been no final resolution of the institute's status.[28]

Although the 1974 elections deluged Capitol Hill with supposedly enlightened, progressive new members, the new Congress by late 1975 was showing that it was no hapless bumbler at continuing to soak the poor and middle class while sustaining the flow of welfare to the wealthy. In early November 1975, the House Ways and Means Committee adopted an obscure, seemingly routine amendment to a major tax bill that had been drafted by former IRS Commissioner Sheldon S. Cohen. The amendment, offered by Congressman Phil M. Landrum (D–Ga.), could have benefited Cohen's client, Texas millionaire H. Ross Perot, to the tune of an estimated $15 million, and a few other wealthy taxpayers $150 million. The amendment would have permitted individuals who had capital losses over $30,000 to carry them back for three years to offset taxes paid on capital gains in those years. Normally, such a tax break for special interests would have zipped through. In this case, however, Albert R. Hunt of the *Wall Street Journal* discovered and reported that Perot had contributed $1,000 to Landrum's election campaign in 1974, and a total of $27,400 to twelve of the thirty-eight Ways and Means Committee members. As the *Journal* noted, "Curiously, all the contributions except the one to Mr. Landrum were made after the November 1974 election." Ten of the twelve recipients of Perot's contributions voted for the amendment, but Landrum and the other nine disclaimed any knowledge that the amendment was to provide what the *Journal* said "may be the most gigantic tax break in history for one person." One may believe such a disclaimer if one cares to. Perot later denied he had inspired the amendment.

If it were to become law (it didn't), he would not use it to get a tax break, he said.

The amendment was just part of the committee's action in gutting the committee's own putative tax-reform bill. What had begun as a bill designed to bring an additional $2.6 billion into the treasury in 1976 ended up providing for only a $750 million gain when the committee was through with it.[29] On the House floor, the gain was enlarged to more than $1 billion.

At the state and local levels the record is also filled with examples of giveaways. For example, underassessments of West Virginia's coal companies and other giant land-owners are estimated to cost that state between $100 million and $200 million in tax revenues annually.[30] Byron Dorgan, North Dakota's state tax commissioner, estimated in late 1974 that avoidance of state tax liabilities by America's largest corporations runs into the "hundreds of millions and perhaps billions of dollars." Dorgan says that the corporations not only use legal loopholes in state laws, but also evade taxes illegally—and sometimes do so, he said, with impunity because most states lack enforcement machinery.[31]

And so it goes. Blame for the state of affairs must rest not only on the vested interests and the politicians and others who represent them, but also on the press, which with some notable exceptions, seldom has provided comprehensive, sustained coverage of the vast inequities in the tax system. To be sure, the press zeroed in on the obvious outrage of President Nixon paying only $792.81 in income taxes in 1969, and $878.03 in 1970 on a salary of $200,000 annually, and it regularly duly reports that certain millionaires— unidentified by the Treasury Department—pay no taxes at all. Congressman Henry S. Reuss (D–Wis.) was struck by the awe shown by the press in dealing in 1971 with Treasury Secretary John Connally, whom Reuss calls "Mr. Loophole." In response to questions by Reuss, Connally told the Joint Economic Committee that he favored retention of all of the ten or twelve leading tax loopholes. "Rather than reacting with outrage against the Treasury Secretary," Reuss has said, "about all the press wrote, as I recall, was that the Secretary of the Treasury knew so much about the tax laws. Well, that isn't being very energetic."[32]

Reuss pinpointed other reasons why the tax system continues increasingly to benefit the monied class. The contributors to the campaigns of Presidents Johnson and Nixon, he said, looked "very much like a roster of those who benefit by these loopholes." And, he added, "the Congress, the tax-writing committees, as is well known, are heavily peopled with worthy gentlemen who believe in these loopholes, and aren't about to do anything about them . . . And, finally, the Congress, the Senate and House itself, and here I criticize myself as much as anybody else, tends to follow its tax-writing committees like a troop of lemmings, with the result that we have the tax system we have."[33]

The federal tax system is accountable to the rich and powerful who are a minority, not to the ordinary citizens who are a great majority, and state and local taxation is similarly warped. Drastic structural reform is required. For starters, we should begin to think of evolving a system of taxation that is designed purely to raise revenues rather than to implement economic policies. It may well be that we will want to grant subsidies. If so, let us do it openly, not with tax breaks that obscure their effects and that are not subject to periodic and public congressional review.

In short, let us start to make the tax system accountable to the taxpayers. The goal of the Sixteenth Amendment—"to lay and collect taxes on incomes, from whatever source derived"—would start to be transformed from rhetoric into reality. "Life, liberty, and the pursuit of happiness" no longer would disappear through tax loopholes.

38

Hanging Judges

Over against the Nazi Storm Trooper you have got to set that typically
English figure, the hanging judge, some gouty old bully with his mind
rooted in the nineteenth century, handing out savage sentences.

George Orwell
A Collection of Essays by George Orwell

Sentences in England are always much shorter . . . far lighter than here.

James V. Bennett, former director,
United States Bureau of Prisons
Washington Post

Here I am, an old man in a long black nightgown making muffled noises
at people who may be no worse than I.

Judge Learned Hand
Criminal Sentences: Law Without Order

Winston Churchill once said that "the mood and temper of the public with
regard to the treatment of crime and criminals is one of the most unfailing
tests of the civilization of any country."[1] By that test, our society fails badly.
The question is not merely one of discriminatory application of police powers, or of terrible conditions in our jails and prisons. The problem runs deeper
—to the core of our criminal justice system, to the application of justice, or
injustice, itself.

Two distinct processes are involved in criminal trials: the determination
of guilt or innocence, and, if the verdict is guilty, the pronouncement of
sentence. Over the years, we have established elaborate procedural safeguards around the first process. Despite some obvious flaws, such as the
inability of the poor often to obtain counsel from anyone but overburdened
and underfunded public defenders, this process—rooted in the notions of
adversary proceedings and trial before one's peers—works tolerably well. It
is with the second process, sentencing, that the system breaks down.

With few institutional restraints, with no need to explain their reasons or motives, judges can and do impose widely disparate sentences on similar defendants convicted of the same crime. The late Robert F. Kennedy listed some stark specifics in a speech in October 1961:

Not long ago, a former Army officer, a first offender, was convicted here in the Midwest of charges involving several bad checks. He was sentenced to 18 years. About the same time, a young man with a sex record was convicted in the Southern District of California of robbing a bank of $5,000. He was sentenced to 98 days.

These are not isolated examples. The average sentences for auto theft vary from 11 months in the Western District of New York to 46 months in Wyoming and the Southern District of Iowa. Terms for forgery range from nine months in Maine and the Southern District of New York to 63 months in Oklahoma and 58 months in Western Arkansas . . .

In fact, the overall average of time spent in Federal prison varies nearly as greatly. Prisoners sentenced in Northern New York average 11 months. In my home State of Massachusetts the figure is 25 months. In Southern Iowa, it is 52 months.[2]

The late Simon E. Sobeloff, while a judge of the United States Court of Appeals for the Fourth Circuit (Maryland and Virginia), cited a classic case involving two men in Fort Worth, Texas. In 1960, one was convicted of fraudulently cashing a check for $58.40. "He was out of work at the time, his wife was ill, and he needed the money for rent, food, and doctors' bills, so he yielded to temptation," Sobeloff said. This man, he noted, had no prior record.

"At about the same time," the judge continued, "another defendant also fraudulently cashed a check, also for a small amount, $35.20. He, too, was out of work and in desperate financial condition under precisely similar circumstances. His only criminal record consisted of a drunk charge and a nonsupport charge.

"Now, what happened to these two men in these two cases that are as alike as two peas in a pod? One judge gave the first man 15 years in prison; in the second, another judge imposed a penalty of 30 days."[3]

In late 1975, the United States Court of Appeals for the Fourth Circuit overturned an eighteen-month sentence that had been imposed on one of the Baltimore businessmen who had cooperated with federal prosecutors in the investigation of former Vice-President Spiro T. Agnew. The appeals court returned the case to the district court for a new sentencing proceeding on the basis of a few remarks that one of the prosecutors had made to the defendant's attorney. The remarks had "misled" the defendant into believing he would not be imprisoned if he pleaded guilty to a tax charge as part of his cooperation, the court of appeals ruled. The court did not even touch on the propriety of imposing a prison term on the businessman after the main target of the investigation, Agnew, had used his high public office to escape with a fine and unsupervised probation as his only punishment.[4]

The treatment accorded the former Vice-President is all too typical of the disposition of white-collar and corporate crimes. For example, after four major oil companies had pleaded guilty to one count each of criminal pollution in connection with the 1969 oil well blowout in the Santa Barbara Channel, in California, a judge dismissed 342 other counts and fined each company $500. The companies had "suffered sufficiently" because of the many civil damage judgments in the case, the judge held.[5] In another case, an Oklahoma business operator who headed the Four Seasons Nursing Centers of America pleaded guilty to conspiracy in a stock fraud scheme in which he made $10 million and which cost investors $200 million. The judge sentenced him to a one-year prison term and imposed no fine at all.[6]

Contrast this with the five Ohio men who were confined to a state hospital for the criminally insane for a total of approximately 150 years. One had been sent to the hospital 41 years earlier for observation after being charged with attempted rape; another had been admitted 31 years earlier for observation after he admitted stealing three gallons of gasoline. The other three men also had been sent to the hospital for observation—one for 22 years for passing a bad check, another for 24 years after being charged with assault to commit rape, and the last for 32 years after he killed his wife. None of the men was ever convicted of a crime. They were released in 1972 after psychiatrists found them sane.[7]

For some judges, unaccountability in sentencing is a perquisite of office. A distinguished United States district judge, Marvin E. Frankel, of New York, recalls a cocktail party at which "Judge X"

told of a defendant for whom the judge, after reading the presentence report, had decided tentatively upon a sentence of four years' imprisonment. At the sentencing hearing in the courtroom, after hearing counsel, Judge X invited the defendant to exercise his right to address the court in his own behalf. The defendant took a sheaf of papers from his pocket and proceeded to read from them, excoriating the judge, the "kangaroo court" in which he'd been tried, and the legal establishment in general. Completing the story, Judge X said, "I listened without interrupting. Finally, when he said he was through, I simply gave the son of a bitch five years instead of the four."[8]

To be sure, the defendant acted disrespectfully and foolishly, and the judge's anger was understandable. But the important thing is that Judge X had it within his discretion to increase or decrease the sentence by a year or more. Initially he had decided on four years, but just as easily he could have chosen three years, or two, or probation without imprisonment. The choice was *his alone;* no mechanisms were in place to question his judgment. Having then been annoyed by the defendant, he unilaterally upped the sentence by a year. Again, the decision was wholly his—and final. No one, least of all the defendant, could know that the courtroom outburst had cost him up to a full year's freedom; consequently, no one could question the fairness or wisdom of the added deprivation of freedom. Sentences sometimes are purported to serve as warnings and deterrents to others, but the extra year could not be so categorized because, it will be remembered, Judge X had sat silently through the outburst and then "simply gave the son of a bitch five years instead of four." In short, the judge was unaccountable.

Judge X was not unique. James V. Bennett, former director of the United States Bureau of Prisons, and a crusader for appellate-review legislation, told a Senate Judiciary subcommittee in 1964:

That some judges are arbitrary and even sadistic in their sentencing practices is notoriously a matter of record. By reason of senility or a virtually pathological emotional complex, some judges summarily impose the maximum on defendants convicted of certain types of crimes or all types of crimes . . . There is one judge who, as a matter of routine, always gives the maximum sentence . . . I know of one judge who continued to sit on the bench and sentence defendants to prison while he was undergoing shock treatment.[9]

In most cases, the laws that define criminal conduct are reasonably intelligible, so that a person can know in advance whether his conduct will exceed the limits set by society. But once found guilty of exceeding those limits, the criminal defendant is more often than not at the mercy of vague and ill-defined punishment statutes. Judge Frankel, in his trenchant book *Criminal Sentences: Law Without Order,* citing "the unfettered discretion of miscellaneous judges" to impose a sentence that "may range from zero up to thirty or more years," said:

Everyone with the least training in law would be prompt to denounce a statute that merely said the penalty for crimes "shall be any term the judge sees fit to impose." A regime of such arbitrary fiat would be intolerable in a supposedly free society, to say nothing of being invalid under our due process clause. But the fact is that we have accepted unthinkingly a criminal code creating in effect precisely that degree of unbridled power.[10]

Our laws characteristically leave to a sentencing judge "a range of choice that should be unthinkable in a 'government of laws, not of men,' " Frankel said. ". . . the almost wholly unchecked and sweeping powers we give to judges in the fashioning of sentences are terrifying and intolerable . . ."[11]

The granting and use of this unchecked power riddles the judicial system from beginning to end. There is, to begin with, little if any apparent consideration of the sentencing power when judges are chosen. Even in the best of circumstances, where a judge may be chosen for his temperament, experience, and legal scholarship, there are no guarantees that he will be prepared to deal with the broad range of sentencing power suddenly given him, or that he always will wield that power judiciously.

All of these powers are exercised by judges who are—short of being found guilty of crimes themselves—essentially safe in their jobs until retirement or death. Federal judges may be removed through impeachment, a lengthy and cumbersome process. A number of states have procedures for investigating complaints against judges, but even in California, considered a leader in this field, no judge has ever been removed because of his courtroom conduct.[12]

Once on the bench, the judge is confronted with convicted defendants on whom he is expected to impose fair and reasonable penalties. Here the law gives him little guidance. Leaving aside the ludicrous examples of contradictory statutes—cases, for example, where the penalty for stealing a car is less than the penalty for stealing something from the car—the fact remains that the penalty sections of federal and some state criminal laws are written in terms of maximums, with imposition of anything less than the maximum left to the judge's discretion. When the maximum involves up to ten, twenty, or thirty years of a defendant's life, the discretionary power given to a judge in sentencing becomes truly awesome.

In deciding a civil suit, a judge may take weeks or months pouring over details of the dispute and researching the law. Not so in imposing a criminal sentence. To be sure, there are procedures to develop presentence reports, and judges presumably read these and think about them. But it is also true that a judge, after listening to the final oral arguments of attorneys and perhaps a few words from the defendant himself, often imposes sentence immediately.

We also tend to accept that as the end of the matter, because judges are not required to, nor do they usually, explain why they imposed a sentence of one duration rather than another. "But the absence, or refusal, of reasons is a hallmark of injustice," Frankel emphasized:

So it requires no learning in law or political philosophy to apprehend that the swift ukase, without explanation, is the tyrant's way. The despot is not bound by rules. He need not justify or account for what he does.

Criminal sentences, as our judges commonly pronounce them, are in these vital respects tyrannical.[13]

Because judges "usually say little or nothing to explain their sentences, the possibility that they were moved by absurd or vicious considerations is not usually open to inquiry," Frankel pointed out.

And the circle proceeds to be closed. The judges, if they are merely human rather than depraved, do not enjoy being caught in error. They know that an unexplained decision does not flaunt its possible fallacies. When they are not required to explain, many at least find this conclusive grounds for not explaining. There is no way of knowing, then, how many sentences, for how many thousands of years, have rested upon hidden premises that could not have survived scrutiny.[14]

Judges are free to assert such capricious and terrifying power over tens of thousands of persons a year because they have an astonishing degree of raw unaccountability even aside from the difficulty of removing them from the bench no matter how outrageous may be their conduct, whether in sentencing or some other area. With the exception of the United States, every Western nation gives all convicted persons the right to appeal a sentence on the ground that it is excessive. This tends inevitably to make for judicial accountability. In our country a federal prisoner also had such a right until 1891, when legislation creating the courts of appeal was assumed—erroneously, some scholars contend—to have wiped it out. Today, the right exists only in about seventeen states. To put it another way, judges in some thirty-three states and on the federal bench throughout the country have a free hand to impose excessive or discriminatory sentences because there is no provision for appellate court review and voiding of sentences solely on the ground that they are excessive.

Legislation to empower the United States Courts of Appeal to review sentences claimed by a convicted person to be out of line with sentences meted out to others for similar crimes has been sought for years by, among others, James Bennett, Judge Sobeloff, Senator Roman L. Hruska (R–Neb.) and former Senator Joseph D. Tydings (D–Md.). In 1958, the Judicial Conference of the United States, the organization of the federal judiciary, considered but rejected such legislation. In 1964, the conference backed down from this indefensible stance and approved such legislation. In 1967, the Senate passed an appellate-review bill, only to see it die in the House. As of May 1976, the proposal was part of S. 1, an omnibus bill to overhaul the United States Criminal Code. Regrettably, the bill also contains some extremely objectionable provisions unrelated to sentencing.

We would be remiss were we to leave the impression that ending judicial unaccountability for disparate sentencing alone would be sufficient. Sentences may be equal but still be either unfair to the convicted or irrelevant to the need to protect society. Again, incarceration may be equitably imposed but still be a wholly inappropriate way to deal with offenders who should be punished but who if not locked up not only may be no threat to the public, but may be converted into a positive asset.

. . . .

"One need not be a revolutionist or an enemy of the judiciary to predict that untrained, untested, unsupervised men armed with great power will perpetrate abuses," Judge Frankel has said.[15] Some of these abuses violate the "equal protection of the laws" guaranteed by the Constitution. Judges swear an oath to uphold the Constitution but daily, through bizarre disparities in sentencing, deny equal protection. Federal and state legislators also swear an oath to uphold the Constitution, but do not pass the laws that would make judges accountable for disparate sentencing. For such unaccountability, legislators and judges alike have offered no acceptable excuse.

In 1954, the Food and Drug Administration made an obscure decision which ultimately would unleash powerful forces of unaccountability, ranging from government lawlessness to misapplied technology. The consequent hazard, affecting most of the population, continued for more than twenty years.

The FDA decision was to grant cattle and sheep growers permission to use feed medicated with DES (diethylstilbestrol), a synthetic estrogen. Animals ingesting the chemical, it was believed, would get heavier faster with less feed than normal, although doubts persist that the presumed economy and efficiency actually are achieved.[1] Even at the time, DES was recognized to be a proved, potent carcinogen in several species of animals; necessarily, scientists suspected that DES might also be carcinogenic in humans. Within twenty years, DES in fact would be a proved carcinogen in at least some humans.

To this day, specialists in the causation of human cancer say unanimously that they are unable to determine a safety threshold for DES. They are unable to isolate a particle so minute that it might not in some persons cause cancer; even a single molecule of DES, so far as they know, might be carcinogenic. Nonetheless, the FDA confidently asserted the addition of DES to animal feed to be safe. Under its directives, livestock raisers were told not to exceed approved doses. They also were told to stop using medicated feed altogether at least forty-eight hours before slaughter. With these precautions, the agency assumed, cattle and sheep would excrete all traces of DES, and none would show up in edible tissue, principally liver, a major component of some prepared baby foods.

The theory correlated poorly with reality. For one thing, promotional materials for medicated feed actually encouraged cattlemen to exceed the FDA's legal limits on dose so as to achieve "faster gains and greater feed savings."[2] For another, DES pellets implanted in chickens and turkeys began in the late 1950s to be detected in poultry skin and tissue; and in 1959 the agency ruled the chemical "unsafe" as a poultry implant and banned it. Most important, the FDA overlooked a requirement—in a law prohibiting carcinogens in feed if residues show up in edible tissue—that manufacturers supply, and the agency approve and prescribe, a "practicable" method to test for residues. Consequently, the FDA, conveniently, did not know whether its dosage and withdrawal rules—even if scientifically sound—were being heeded. More ominously, the agency did not know whether DES residues in fact were present in the livestock fattened on medicated feed, which in the case of beef cattle was about 80 to 85 percent of the total. And similarly contrived or accepted ignorance prevailed for approximately eighty additional carcinogens, antibiotics, and other chemicals administered to feed animals. The obvious dangers to workers handling DES got almost no attention at all.

Strikingly, as early as 1959, other countries began to ban DES and other animal-fattening or growth-promoting chemicals. These countries, which within a few years numbered twenty-one, included Argentina and Australia, which are principal beef-producers, and Greece and Italy, which are not countries known to be at the cutting edge of sophisticated regulation. Indeed, Italy joined Sweden in going further: both banned importation of American beef from cattle that had been fed DES-treated feed.

In 1967, a teen-age girl, complaining of bleeding between her menstrual periods, entered Massachussets General Hospital in Boston. She turned out to have vaginal cancer (adenocarcinoma of the vagina) which had been virtually unheard-of in women under thirty. By 1969, six other women, none older than twenty-two, also had come to Mass General with the same disease, for which removal of the vagina is standard procedure, and which is sometimes fatal. Dr. Arthur L. Herbst, assistant surgeon at the hospital, and assistant clinical professor in obstetrics and gynecology at Harvard, began an investigation with two colleagues, Drs. Howard Ulfelder and C. C. Poskanzer. They used rigid controls to eliminate possible bias or distortion. Finally, in the *New England Journal of Medicine* for April 22, 1971, they reported their stunning finding: each victim was the daughter of a woman who while carrying her some twenty years earlier had taken DES prescribed by a physician to try to head off an apparent threat of miscarriage in the first trimester. A cause-effect relation was not merely suspected, but statistically demonstrated to be clear-cut. Notably, doctors in the 1940s and 1950s, particularly in the Boston area, were prescribing DES to prevent threatened abortion even though they had no substantial evidence that the hormone was effective in that usage—and a significant number of doctors write several thousand prescriptions for it annually even now, despite wide publicity given to the nonevidence of effectiveness, to Herbst's investigation, and to the plight of individual victims.[3]

On March 14, 1971—more than five weeks before publication of his report—Herbst sent his results to the FDA, but got no response for six months. In contrast, the New York State Department of Health, which maintains a unique Cancer Control Bureau, at once began a survey which uncovered seven additional cases of vaginal cancer in women whose mothers had taken DES while pregnant. In June 1971, Dr. Hollis S. Ingraham, New York State commissioner of health, alerted 37,500 physicians in New York State to the hazard and started a program of surveillance and monitoring to try to detect further cases as early as possible (detection is generally possible only after the onset of menstruation). In a letter to FDA Commissioner Charles C. Edwards, not only did Dr. Ingraham urge the agency to undertake similar steps nationally, but also recommended "most urgently" that the FDA "initiate immediate measures to ban the use of synthetic estrogens during pregnancy." Not until almost two months later, on August 10, did the FDA acknowledge Ingraham's letter; it then requested him to forward case histories and supporting data.

On October 27, the *Washington Post* published a page-one story which began, "The Food and Drug Administration has been sitting for four and one-half months on an appeal aimed at protecting tens of thousands of young women from a risk of vaginal cancer apparently caused by a drug their mothers took to prevent miscarriage, . . ."[4] By this time, the FDA knew of 62 cases of adenocarcinoma of the vagina or cervix in women no older than twenty-four. By 1976, the number listed in a registry, which Dr. Herbst had begun, was about 250. Of these, an association with vaginal cancer had been documented in about 120 (among the others were some foreign cases, some that were in a limbo of inconclusiveness, and some that involved mothers who had *not* taken DES or similar but less-often-prescribed estrogens). The number of American women estimated to have been prescribed DES to prevent abortion was in the broad range of one half million to two million, although one calculation was at least one million.[5] How many of their daughters ultimately would develop cancer is highly speculative. Dr. Peter Greenwald, director of the Cancer Control Bureau in Albany, said in 1975 that perhaps 90 percent of the "DES daughters" have an "apparently benign but perhaps precancerous lesion" known as vaginal adenosis.

For several months in 1971, the House Intergovernmental Relations Subcommittee, headed by Congressman L. H. Fountain (D–N.C.), had been investigating controls on drugs used in food-producing animals, including DES, and, a month before the appearance of Herbst's report, had held five days of oversight hearings. On November 10, on the eve of a further oversight hearing called by Fountain to find out why the FDA had not acted, the agency finally announced that it was advising doctors not to prescribe DES for pregnant women because "[a] statistically significant association has been reported between maternal ingestion of DES during pregnancy and the occurrence of vaginal carcinoma in the offspring."

At the hearing and, indeed, for nearly a year afterward, Commissioner Edwards—who in some other areas did a courageous and outstanding job—

continued to insist that the addition of DES to feed was safe. His arguments were rejected, or even ridiculed, by every one of the dozen or so experts on causation who spoke out, including Dr. Roy Hertz, former scientific director of the National Cancer Institute, and Dr. Umberto Saffiotti, the institute's associate director for carcinogenesis. Internal FDA papers showed that the agency's own experts—Edwards is a surgeon—were appalled. One of them, Dr. M. Adrian Gross, termed the FDA's position scientifically "absurd and indefensible." Striking back, Edwards at one point made a speech in which, in the context of the DES controversy, he attacked "the 'special interests,' the zealots, and the extremists." He interpolated the names of Ralph Nader and Morton Mintz, the *Washington Post* reporter covering the DES story.

The Department of Agriculture is responsible for monitoring the meat supply for the presence of DES residues, but did little or no checking for more than ten years after the chemical was first added to feed. By the mid-1960s, the Agriculture Department had in hand a method to detect DES residues down to ten parts per billion. That may seem a small concentration—ridiculously so, in Edwards' view—but DES already had been found, in 1964, to cause cancer in animals at 6.5 ppb.; and just *one* ppb. in liver translates into 340 trillion molecules in a single five-ounce serving. Using the relatively gross method, the Agriculture Department began a limited survey. Between 1968 and 1970, technicians detected DES residues in about 0.5 percent of the meat samples (mainly beef and lamb livers) analyzed. Agriculture reported this to the FDA, which told no one; the findings did not become public until the summer of 1970, when Senator William Proxmire (D–Wis.) got a tip and disclosed it. Despite the detection of residues, the FDA in 1970 proceeded to *double* the maximum permissible dose of DES in feed.

During the first half of 1971, Agriculture, making monthly reports to Capitol Hill at its request, claimed to be detecting no DES residues. But during the same period, David Hawkins, attorney for the Natural Resources Defense Council, a public-interest environmental group, was hearing from informants that Agriculture Department scientists not only had been detecting DES residues, but in fact had been detecting them in much higher concentrations than formerly. In October 1971, Hawkins publicly accused the Agriculture Department of misleading Congress and the public. Four days later, the department admitted an "inexcusable error," which was blamed on a communications lapse within the bureaucracy.

The FDA adopted rules requiring livestock men, on pain of possible criminal prosecution, to stop administering DES-treated feed not 48 hours but seven full days before slaughter. On December 13, 1972, Dr. Edwards, who by then was under considerable pressure, appeared before the Fountain subcommittee. "The fact of the matter is," Edwards testified, "if we find that our new program is not working, there is just one recourse for us and that is to ban its use totally." Thus did Edwards express his confidence that after the seven-day rule took effect in early January 1972, residues of DES would vanish from beef and lamb. The hope was a forlorn one, as Dr. Hertz, in testimony before the subcommittee in November, had predicted it would be. A matter of weeks after the new rules took effect, the Agriculture Department reported that DES residues continued to occur. After the new rules had been in effect for six months, Agriculture had detected residues at an average rate of 2.25 percent per week, or five times the old rate. The pressure on Edwards to redeem his December pledge of course mounted.

Under the so-called Delaney Amendment, the FDA is empowered, without holding a hearing, to ban any animal feed medicated with a drug that happens to cause cancer in either animals or men—provided that detectable residues are found in the meat, and that the agency first certifies the accuracy and reliability of the method used to establish the presence of carcinogens in the meat. In the case of DES, the FDA in fact had prescribed and published an official method to detect DES residues. Although cumbersome for the day-to-day work of Agriculture Department inspectors, the method was perfectly adapted for checking the results agriculture was obtaining with the unapproved method. Yet neither the FDA nor the department ever used the official method to check the unofficial results. Congressman Fountain expressed concern about this at the December hearing, but was unable to get either Commissioner Edwards or Peter Barton Hutt, the FDA's general counsel, to explain this peculiar nonfeasance. As a result, Edward was inhibited—or had inhibited himself—from invoking the Delaney Amendment and thereby cleanly resolving the matter, and protecting the public from exposure to a potent carcinogen in millions of beef cattle and sheep.

In the alternative, Edwards could have halted the use of DES-treated feed by ruling it an "imminent" hazard—but he himself not only had scorned the evidence that DES feed was hazardous, but had acclaimed it as a positive benefit to the public. Why? Because it purportedly was saving beef consumers an average of $3.85 each, or $800 million all told, per year. Edwards' assigned mission was to protect the public health, not to save each of us $3.85, or to decide for us that we should run a risk of contracting cancer by saving $3.85 each per year.[6]

Finally, Edwards could have withdrawn the approval the FDA had given manufacturers, principally the pharmaceutical firm of Eli Lilly & Company, to sell feed "premixes" medicated with DES. Such an action could have taken effect thirty days after interested parties had been given a chance to comment. Almost certainly, the FDA would have had to hold a hearing and then face a court challenge, during which proceedings sales of DES feed could continue.

But the commissioner opted for an even weaker course. Saying he remained "convinced" that DES was "safe when used as directed," Edwards on June 16, 1972, announced that the FDA would propose formally to withdraw permission to market DES—but only as a device with which to accumulate additional information at a public hearing. This action was denounced by Fountain and Senator Proxmire, who said it "evades the issue and disregards the law."

The heat on Edwards then rose intolerably with the disclosure of Agriculture's weekly reports for June on the occurrence of DES residues in beef and lamb livers. The rates soared to staggering levels—5.10 percent in the week ending June 10, 5.43 percent in the week ending June 17, and 10 percent —twenty times 1971's—in the week ending June 17. In addition, in an interview that reportedly infuriated Edwards, Dr. Frank J. Rauscher, Jr., director of the National Cancer Institute, publicly contradicted him by telling Mintz that banning DES feed would be the "prudent" course. DES is "a bona-fide example" of a carcinogen, he said. "Anything that increases the carcinogenic burden to man ought to be eliminated from the environment if it is at all possible—and in this case it is possible."

Rauscher's view reflected the concern of specialists in carcinogenesis that environmental factors, cigarette smoking being a major one, figure, in ways not always fully understood, in most human cancers—90 percent, according to an estimate by the World Health Organization. To put it another way, the great majority of human cancers are not inevitable because they are of environmental origin and therefore subject to control. The lesson is one the country has been slow to learn, having put minor emphasis on prevention and major emphasis on cures.

Rauscher, in the interview, went on to challenge the practicability of the FDA's seven-day withdrawal rules, saying that to implement them the agency might have to post an inspector, "in nearly every packing plant." Asked whether the estimated saving of $3.85 a year accruing to the average beef consumer warranted continued use of DES feed, Rauscher avoided a direct reply, but gave a telling indirect one. "My job is to protect people from cancer," he said.[7]

To make matters still more awkward, Senator Edward M. Kennedy (D–Mass.), chairman of the Senate Health Subcommittee, who had been highly critical of the FDA's performance in the matter, scheduled a hearing on the order. Testifying in July 1972, Edwards insisted that faulty compliance with administrative procedures was to blame for the rising incidence of DES residues.

Two weeks later, however, Edwards acknowledged new scientific evidence showing that DES residues occurred in meat even when cattle and sheep raisers had fastidiously observed the seven-day withdrawal requirement. Compelled to act, Edwards, on August 4, took another peculiar step, one which, it was widely noted, would eliminate any possibility that he would trigger an increase in beef prices before the November election. Such an increase presumably would be unwelcome by President Nixon, at whose pleasure Edwards served. The step Edwards took was in the form of an order immediately banning further *production* of DES-treated feed, but allowing manufacturers to continue to distribute and sell existing stocks for five more months, until January 1, 1973. In issuing the order, Edwards relied on the Delaney Amendment to ban the feed without a hearing, although the FDA still lacked a legal basis for asserting the Agriculture Department's detection of residues to be accurate and reliable. Moreover, Edwards gave the manufacturers the five-month bonus despite a requirement in the law that an order of the type he had issued take effect "forthwith." First the Fountain subcommittee and then the comptroller general said that the five-month delay was illegal. The manufacturers challenged the order in the United States Court of Appeals for the District of Columbia. There, figuratively, the FDA's chickens came home to roost.

In 1959, as was noted, the agency had banned DES in poultry production because residues were deposited in edible tissue. Manufacturers filed a challenge in the Court of Appeals for the Seventh Circuit in Cincinnati, but, in 1966, that court upheld the ban. At the Fountain subcommittee hearing in December 1971, the congressman explored the question whether the 1966 decision on poultry would apply to the DES residues in beef and lamb livers. In claiming that the rule was not applicable, Edwards used the same scientifically unacceptable arguments that the manufacturers had used— unsuccessfully—five years earlier in Cincinnati—that the residues were too inconsequential to be hazardous, and were insignificant alongside the estrogens naturally present in a number of common foods and produced naturally in the human body. FDA counsel Hutt, in addition, categorically denied to Fountain that the 1966 decision (*Bell* v. *Goddard*, 336 F. 2d. 177) had set a precedent obliging the agency to ban DES from livestock feed. But ten months later in the court of appeals, the FDA was so boxed in by its own flip-flops, and by its reluctance to keep carcinogens out of the food supply, that it was reduced to holding out *Bell* as the controlling precedent for its order against DES-treated feed. The pending case, the FDA contended, without visible contrition, "is essentially identical to *Bell.*"

The agency's case was fatally undermined by anomalies. First, the FDA was forced to ask the appellate court to uphold its invocation of the Delaney clause even though, as was noted, the agency still had not certified Agriculture's findings of residues as accurate and reliable. Second, after allowing manufacturers to go on distributing and selling DES-treated feed for five months in violation of the laws, the FDA could not be persuasive in contending that this same feed was a cancer threat. Third, after spurning the Delaney clause and then, in the August order, using it more or less at the gunpoint of congressional and public pressure, the agency was—justly— forced in court to fall back on the argument that DES-treated feed was— legally—hazardous. But if the hazard was not "imminent"—and the FDA had claimed all along that it was not—how could it defend its denial of a hearing to the manufacturers? Answer: it couldn't. The court of appeals, as it had to do, ultimately—in January 1974—ruled for the companies. Naturally, they continued to sell DES feed. Naturally, too, residues of the carcinogen continued to show up, with great frequency, in meat.

Dr. Rauscher, the Cancer Institute director, at a hearing held by Senator Kennedy in February 1975, advised women in the first trimester of pregnancy to shun beef liver because it may contain DES. Fetuses are extremely sensitive to cancer-causing chemicals. Most scientists doubt that the amounts of DES at issue are large enough to cause cancer, but the trouble is, Rauscher testified, that "we don't know." He urged an immediate ban on DES in feed. Later in the year, new studies indicated that some *sons* of DES mothers may be sterile.

The Senate in 1972 had passed a bill, sponsored mainly by Kennedy and Proxmire, to prohibit the use of DES in cattle feed, but it died in the House. Congressman Fountain, for one, questioned the wisdom and the precedent of passing a law to accomplish what existing laws already required the FDA to do. In 1975, Kennedy introduced a new bill not only to ban DES in feed, but, among other things, to require the President to submit nominations for FDA commissioner, deputy commissioner, and general counsel to the Senate for its advice and consent. The Senate passed the bill in September 1975, but in May 1976 it was reposing in a House Commerce subcommittee. Commissioner Edwards' successor, Dr. Alexander M. Schmidt, did not oppose it and, in fact in December 1975, instituted a bona-fide administrative effort to ban DES from feed.

To recapitulate some of the things that at last began to put the brakes on the FDA: a superb piece of medical detective work in Boston; an alert and responsive state health commissioner in Albany; a dedicated and expert

House oversight operation—one with a professional staff for FDA (and other) matters of only one person full-time and another part-time; Senate-level involvement; an activist public-interest environmental group; a top government cancer expert willing to challenge an FDA commissioner; a concerned press. Despite all of this, DES continued to be added to feed for twenty-one years—through mid-1976, at least.

Some agencies, such as the Civil Aeronautics Board, the Interstate Commerce Commission, and the Federal Maritime Commission, do little but obstruct competition and therefore are prime candidates for abolition. The FDA is not in this category, not only because it is a regulatory operation within the Department of Health, Education, and Welfare, but more importantly because the public safety absolutely requires some such mechanism. Yet the public safety, as the DES case demonstrates, will not be reliably served by the FDA unless it is made to shape up. An independent consumer protection agency could make it do so. Such an instrument would be as independent as possible from the Executive and would have no regulatory powers of its own. Instead, it would be empowered to intervene—solely as an advocate for consumers of goods and services—in decision-making by the Executive branch as well as by independent agencies. Thus, it could provide a vital offset across-the-board to powerful special interests. In an exchange of letters in 1974 with Senator Warren G. Magnuson (D–Wash.), a leading proponent of the agency, Professor Frederick C. Mosher, a University of Virginia political scientist who directed a study for the Senate Watergate committee on how to prevent future Watergates, said he had subscribed to the orthodox belief that a strong Presidency, because it "represented all the people," afforded the public its best protection. But, he said, events of the last few years had made it clear to him "that different Presidents feel different degrees of concern about their responsibilities toward the whole people."[8]

Ralph Nader, whose efforts to bring the agency into being constituted one of the supreme struggles of his career, said in 1975 that, during the previous six years, "a small corps of public interest advocates have often won surprising victories . . . But their occasional forays and successes should not obscure the need for a well-funded and on-going corporate counterweight in the federal agencies."[9] Later in 1975, the supposedly freshened and liberalized House passed a bill to create the consumer agency by a slim nine-vote margin, although the "old" House in 1974 had done so overwhelmingly—with three yes votes for each no vote. With President Ford determined to veto the bill, the effort to create the agency was stymied, at least temporarily. But as the DES episode shows, some such mechanism is vital.

*No right is more firmly established than the right of the patient to
informed consent to a prescription whether surgical or medical.
Knowledge sufficient for informed consent is a moral, medical, and legal
right to which malpractice suits testify. The classic statement of this right
is found in Plato's laws . . . where Plato distinguishes between the
physician who takes care of slaves, and the one who takes care of
freemen. Whereas the slave-doctor prescribed "As if he had exact
knowledge" and gave orders "like a tyrant," the doctor of freemen went
"into the nature of the disorder," entered "into discourse with the patient
and his friends," and would not "prescribe for him until he has first
convinced him."*

Herbert Ratner
Child and Family

Scientists constantly develop new medicines, new surgical techniques, and
new medical devices. Thus, they fuel an insatiable demand for more information. Some of it can be obtained only from testing in humans who are,
practically if not literally, helpless.

In the twelfth century, Moses Maimonides, a rabbi and physician, expressed succinctly and elegantly a view of the doctor-patient relationship in
which accountability is implicit: "May I never see in the patient anything
but a fellow creature in pain." It is not altogether too cynical to suggest that
some modern medical researchers might rewrite Maimonides' dictum this
way: "May I never see in the patient anything but a subject for experimentation." This, of course, is an expression of unaccountability.

The very phrase "human medical experimentation" is subject to many
definitions. Perhaps the best working definition was given in 1951 by a
professor of experimental medicine in an address to the Royal Society of
Medicine in Britain: "We should, I think, for present purposes, regard
anything done to the patient which is not generally accepted as being for
his direct therapeutic benefit or as contributing to the diagnosis of his

disease, as constituting an experiment, and falling therefore within the scope of the term experimental medicine."[1] Anything, therefore, that is done to the patient that is not directly intended to benefit him falls under the definition of human medical experimentation. Human experimentation poses a severe dilemma that Jay Katz, adjunct professor of law and psychiatry at Yale Law School, has summed up this way: "The controversy over the use of human beings in medical experimentation demonstrates the difficulty of reconciling two values basic to Western society: the desire to benefit from the advances in medical knowledge, and the commitment to individual dignity and autonomy."[2] Clearly, human experimentation of some kind is needed to assess in some way the benefits and risks of various drugs and medical procedures before they are used on vast numbers of people. But reliable safeguards for the human beings who run risks for the rest of us are essential.

In 1972, Jean Heller, then of the Associated Press, revealed in a series of articles that the United States Public Health Service had for forty years withheld all treatment from 399 syphilitic men in an experiment in Tuskegee, Alabama. The stated purpose of the experiment, begun in 1932, and carried out by the Public Health Service (PHS) in cooperation with local agencies, was to find whether the incidence of death and debilitation was higher in untreated syphilis than in a control group of 201 men who did not have syphilis. Another objective of the study was to compare the untreated syphilitics to an additional group of men with syphilis who were being treated with drugs which, at that time, contained heavy metals. Because these drugs were available but were withheld from the 399 syphilitics, and because treatment was not denied for the purpose of diagnosis, the Tuskegee study falls well within the definition of human medical experimentation. It should be noted as well that syphilis is a highly contagious infection spread by sexual contact, and that, if untreated, it can lead to blindness; deafness; deterioration of the bones, teeth, and the central nervous system; heart disease; insanity; and even death.

Some salient facts about the Tuskegee experiment are worth pointing out. First, all the men involved in the experiment were black. Second, although the director of the study says the participants were told of the nature of the experiment, a black Tuskegee physician who attended some of the men says the participants were *not* informed that they were joining in a medical experiment. And third, when penicillin became available in 1946, and when later it became the drug-of-choice in treating syphilis, the syphilitic men still did not receive the antibiotic. This is troubling because a goal of the experiment was to compare men with untreated syphilis with men who had undergone treatment with the now-obsolete earlier drugs. That is to say, the

477

advent of penicillin obviated the need for such a comparison, and in fact eliminated the rationale for the study. Consequently, the denial of the antibiotic was at best negligent.

Senator Abraham A. Ribicoff (D–Conn.) called the Tuskegee experiment a "frightening instance of bureaucratic arrogance and insensitivity."[3] Dr. John R. Heller, a PHS doctor who played a key role in the experiment, said in an AP interview following the disclosure of the experiment in 1972 that there were "absolutely no racial overtones to the study."[4] Were the men informed as to the nature of the experiment they were participating in? "We told them what they had," he said. When he was asked if any attempt was made to get penicillin for them, he said: "No. And it never occurred to us to ask because the demand was so great for other people who needed it much more than they did—the armed forces and people in civilian life."[5] Heller got to the heart of his explanation when he remarked, "Also, we were not responsible for getting it to them so we made no effort to get it. This was a community responsibility in Tuskegee . . . *it was not our ball of wax.*" (Emphasis supplied.) Since when is it not a physician's "ball of wax" to minister to the health of people with the best means at his disposal? Nor does Dr. Heller's explanation answer the question why penicillin and other antibiotics, when they became widely available later, were not offered to the subjects of the Tuskegee study.

In 1969, a follow-up study by the Center for Disease Control, in Atlanta, of 276 treated and untreated syphilitics involved in the Tuskegee study showed that 7 had died as a direct result of syphilis, and another 154 had died of heart disease. It was too late to determine if the heart-disease deaths were related to syphilis.

A final chapter in this experiment was written when a lawsuit brought by seventy survivors—both syphilitic and nonsyphilitic—resulted in an award by a Montgomery, Alabama, court of $37,500 to each individual. The experiment having lasted forty years, this came to $2.50 a day per man.[6]

Some physicians characterized the Tuskegee experiment as one of the worst violations of medical ethics in modern times. Yet, similar experiments —often with official government sanction—are carried out daily. Commonly, the subjects' backgrounds are similar to those of the men in the Tuskegee study—poor, sometimes retarded, sometimes prisoners. Almost always the subjects are persons less able to protect themselves and therefore less likely to hold accountable those who performed the experiments. "Possibly 80 per cent of all human experimentation that has occurred in this country involved the poor,"[7] Dr. Henry W. Foster of Meharry Medical College told a National Academy of Sciences forum in February 1975. At that same meeting, Dr. Franz J. Inglefinger, editor of the *New England*

Journal of Medicine, remarked that the poor are more "administratively eligible" for medical experimentation because of their reliance on government-funded medical care.[8] A plausible inference was that because the poor are much dependent on government, the government is freer to rely on their bodies for experimentation.

Prisons have long supplied men and women for medical experimentation, despite the obvious ethical problem of using as experimental medical subjects persons who have few free choices available to them. After World War II, the Nazis' use of concentration-camp prisoners as subjects for medical experiments became an issue at the Nuremberg war-crimes trials. In her book, *Kind and Usual Punishment,* Jessica Mitford said, "The Nuremberg tribunal established standards for medical experimentation on humans which, if observed, would end the practice of using prisoners as subjects. Yet in the twenty-six years since the Nuremberg judgment there has been a huge expansion of medical 'research programs' in many prisons in the U.S., sanctioned by federal health agencies and state prison administrations who do not choose to recognize these standards as applying to the captives in their custody."[9]

At a Senate hearing held by Senator Edward M. Kennedy (D–Mass.) in July 1975, a few prisoners testified about their experience as human subjects in medical experiments. One was James Downey, who had been a state prisoner in Oklahoma. He told of having participated in a planned thirty-day program to test a potent new drug intended to cure liver ailments. Downey said he was told it was a new "wonder" drug, and was assured it would have no adverse effects. Downey also said that he and others became subjects because they would be paid. The opportunity to earn money in prison—to purchase cigarettes and other items—is very limited and while the money reward in being a human subject is small, it was more than could be earned in other ways.

After eleven days on the drug, Downey said he began to feel quite ill. Because this happened on a weekend, he was unable to get adequate medical help for a couple of days. When he finally got to see the researcher conducting the drug experiment, he said, he was assured that his illness was *not* related to the drug. He was weak. Later, spots broke out on his body. The researcher told him he had measles. Finally Downey was so weakened that he was unable to work, and he stopped taking the drug. Later, his illness was diagnosed as hepatitis—drug-induced hepatitis. He testified that of the fifteen prisoners in that drug experiment, eight got sick. He testified also that he remains under a physician's care for his drug-induced liver problems.

In 1963, *Time* magazine reported that doctors in Oklahoma—where

Downey was incarcerated—were grossing some $300,000 a year from drug companies to test new drugs on prisoners. In Michigan, two drug companies, Upjohn and Parke-Davis, have acquired exclusive rights at Jackson State Prison to make drug-toxicity studies on prisoners.

A spokesman for the American Civil Liberties Union has estimated that about 20,000 prisoners—or approximately 10 percent of the total United States prison population—are participants in medical and drug-industry experiments.[10] Some states have banned such experimentation on prisoners—but more than twenty states allow it. Great Britain has banned it for a very simple reason: because a prisoner has limited choices, his consent to such experimentation cannot be obtained without at least the appearance of coercion. In her book, Ms. Mitford recalled one physician's remark that prisoners are ideal for medical experiments because they are "cheaper than chimpanzees" to experiment with. They are also selected for another reason, as Ms. Mitford reported: "Since the studies are carried out in the privacy of prison, if a 'volunteer' becomes seriously ill, or dies, as a result of the procedures to which he is subjected, it is unlikely this will ever come to anybody's attention."[11] What Ms. Mitford was saying, and what is the case, was that prisoners are selected for the explicit purpose of diminishing the possibility of accountability for the researchers for any injuries to the subjects. Notably, a prisoner signs a waiver which has dubious legal validity, but which has other benefits for the researcher. "The psychological effect of signing the waiver, coupled with the general helplessness of prisoners, makes lawsuits a rarity," Ms Mitford wrote.[12] And indeed she is correct.

The signing of a waiver by a prisoner—or by anybody who consents to become a human subject in a medical experiment—raises the question of informed consent, perhaps the most nettlesome legal question revolving around human medical experiments. Jay Katz addressed himself to this point: To safeguard their dignity, "subjects of research are now expected to be told of the proposed research procedures, of discomforts and risks, and of their right to ask questions and to withdraw at any time."[13] As Dr. Katz and others have repeatedly pointed out, such disclosure of all risks by the researchers to the human subjects is not always forthcoming. In fact, it is safe to say that in most cases, the human subject is *not* apprised of all the possibilities that might arise from his becoming a part of the experiment. The reason is simple. If subjects were to be told of the risks, and if they were able to comprehend the consequences, in many cases they probably would not volunteer. As Edmond Cahn noted in an article in the *New York Law Review:* "One of the major malpractices of our era consists in the 'engineering of consent.' "[14] Sir Austin Bradford Hill has pointed out, "If the patient cannot really grasp the whole situation, or without upsetting his faith in your judgment cannot be made to grasp it, then in my opinion the ethical decision still lies with the doctor, whether or not it is proper to exhibit, or withhold, a treatment. *He cannot divest himself of it simply by means of an illusory or uncomprehending consent.* "[15] (Emphasis supplied.) One way to obtain an uncomprehending consent is not to inform the subject that the procedure is experimental, and that its consequences are unknown. Another way was documented in the book, *Experimentation with Human Subjects,* edited by Paul Freund, the distinguished Harvard legal scholar:

A twenty-eight-year-old man of subnormal intelligence was treated in a hospital because of varicose veins. Informed consent was considered to have been obtained, but his subnormal intelligence made this impossible—particularly since he readily misconstrued as part of his treatment of varicose veins an incision in his groin permitting the passage of a catheter to the femoral artery and then to the heart. In passing the catheter into the heart, a coronary artery was blocked, causing collapse and an acute coronary attack—myocardial infarction—in an otherwise normal heart. A board of inquiry consisting of several directors of the hospital, several surgeons, and the hospital's Medical Director decided that the procedure was warranted in order to increase the skill of the surgeons and to bring therapeutic benefit to subsequent patients. The patient's subnormal intelligence *prevented informed consent;* nor were the family or other responsible persons informed of the procedure's purpose, which was of no possible benefit to the subject.[16] (Emphasis supplied.)

This documented case exposes not only the gaping loophole in the informed-consent provisions, but demonstrates as well a complete failure of accountability. The doctors were accountable to their peers at the hospital. The peers exonerated them with the claim that the experiment with an uncomprehending patient furthered medical science—a slender rationale, to be sure, but many medical experiments have none at all. Effectively, the doctors were accountable only to themselves—which, effectively, meant to no one.

In one prison experiment, several prisoners were exposed to scurvy. The disease was allowed to take its course for many, many weeks. Several of the prisoners, who were observed by the researchers, suffered excruciating complications, some of which were permanent. When the researcher wrote up the findings, he noted that the experiment *confirmed* findings which already had been well established. In other words, the prisoners could not break new medical ground by suffering the tortures of scurvy. Furthermore, they repeated a study which had no real relevance because treatments of the disease were then available.

In the early 1950s, the Army and the CIA both engaged in extremely questionable secret experiments with hallucinogenic drugs that, we believe, were a logical outgrowth of unaccountability in civilian experiments with humans. The stated purpose was to determine what effect the hallucinogens might have on human subjects. The stated rationale was "national security" —and the possibility that such drugs might be used to induce individuals to divulge secrets, or the possibility that the drugs might be used to disable this country's defenses so that a takeover by a foreign power could occur without the firing of a shot.

In the very first series of Army experiments in 1953, a mescaline derivative was administered to a man named Harold Blauer. He died as a result. Blauer had not been in the Army—he had been a civilian, a tennis professional from Long Island who had been at the New York Psychiatric Institute for treatment of depression. The Psychiatric Institute was under contract to the Army to perform these drug experiments. The circumstances under which Blauer got the drug are unclear. His daughter, on learning of the cause of her father's death more than twenty years after it happened, said emphatically that he had not volunteered to be a part of the experiment, and had not consented to the drug injection.

A short while after Blauer's death, during a CIA test of LSD, another death occurred. Frank R. Olson, a government biochemist, plunged to his death from a Manhattan hotel window after he had taken LSD. This time there was no confusion over informed consent. Olson had had no knowledge whatever that he was being given this powerful hallucinogen. Without his knowledge, it had been slipped into a cocktail. Those responsible never were reprimanded, the Senate Intelligence Committee said in April 1976.

While one might have expected the Army and the CIA to halt the experiments and reconsider their consequences, the only discernable reaction was to cover up what happened, something they managed to do for more than twenty years, until mid-1975. The Army in September 1975 made a similarly belated disclosure of the deaths of three of its civilian employees during experiments with anthrax, a rare disease.

Under great public pressure, the Army admitted that a total of 6,940 servicemen had been involved in drug and chemical testing over a period of twenty years.[17] Testing of LSD ended in 1967, but testing of other hallucinogenic drugs continued until it was suspended in mid-1975, following public disclosures of the testing. In these tests, the great majority of human subjects were military men, but about nine hundred civilians also were tested. Like the New York Psychiatric Institute arrangement, these experiments were carried out at university and research institutes under government contracts. There is very little to indicate what was told to the civilians prior to their becoming part of the experiment because the records are sketchy and incomplete. Research was contracted at institutions including the University of Maryland, the University of Wisconsin, and the University of Washington medical schools. Tulane University's Department of Neurology and Psychiatry was another test lab. The Air Force also financed at least five research projects on LSD. *Washington Post* reporter Bill Richards said in July 1975 that some of the LSD experiments were conducted with disturbed children and adult mental patients. The Air Force research was carried out at the University of Minnesota, New York University, Duke University, and the University of Missouri.

The military found "volunteers" within its ranks all over the country. The lure was simple and effective. The Army said those who "volunteered" for the testing—at Edgewood Arsenal in Maryland—would be given three-day passes and a $45 pay bonus, and could view movies showing girls on beaches. The Army later admitted that some commanders apparently had coerced their men into becoming "volunteers." The soldiers were told there would be "no hazards at all" in the experiment.

The release form the soldiers signed before the tests were administered said in part: "I recognize that in the pursuit of certain experiments transitory discomfiture may occur and when such reactions seem especially likely to occur, I will be so advised."[18] The signing of this consent form consigned the soldier "volunteer" to the discretion of the researchers conducting the experiment. No agency outside the military exercised any control over the experiment's procedures or its safeguards. Although the Food and Drug Administration has the legal power to exercise close supervision of drug testing, it had waived that right in a memorandum to the Defense Department and had reaffirmed the waiver in 1974. In essence, the FDA conceded the military full responsibility for the drug experiments and for the safeguarding of human life. This left the military accountable only to itself.

In addition to the deaths of some of those who knowingly and unknowingly participated in the experiments, many others suffered serious after effects. William Jordan, a former Army colonel who in 1960 had been one of the young officers given LSD during an experiment at Fort Benning, Georgia, said in an interview with the *Washington Post's* Richards that neither he nor any of the others in his test group had been apprised of the possible after effects of taking LSD. In the months following the experiment, Jordan said, he had experienced the first of a series of epileptic seizures and other "flashback" episodes. He believes some of this stemmed from LSD. "I was never sure that the epilepsy had anything to do with the LSD tests," he said, "but they never even told us there would be any after effects and no one bothered to check."[19]

An Air Force sergeant, also interviewed by Richards, told of having been in an LSD experiment in 1957. For two years following the experiment, he recalled, he had experienced deep depressions, sometimes had broken down in tears in front of his family, and had become moody. He said he once had contemplated suicide. Before the experiment, he said, he had considered himself happy-go-lucky. Because he was not told of potential after effects, he had not understood the cause of his behaviorial changes. "No one ever told us anything about those tests except that they said right before we drank the LSD that we'd get a little high like you do when you drink," he said. Some of the immediate reactions to the chemical included dizziness and vomiting. Some subjects were incapacitated for four days.

One reason for the long-standing secrecy about these experiments was the restrictions imposed by the Army on participating servicemen. They were told not to divulge the experiments and their part in them. No acknowledgement that they had participated was noted in their service record. The Army also failed to provide any follow-up examinations. In light of the potential harm, this confirmed the darkest suspicions about much human experimentation—that the care of the patient becomes a very minor consideration in the "advancement" of science. The Army was empowered to proceed with such human experiments; there was no law against it.

More significant than the laws and ethics of these experiments is the mentality of those who created them and allowed them to continue despite the obvious risks and hazards to the participants. A glimpse of that mentality was revealed by *New York Times* reporter Joseph Treaster when he quoted one of the few informed military officers willing to discuss the issue. "You have to look at these experiments like a combat operation," the officer said. "You start taking casualties in combat, and you don't stop. You press on. You take the objective. That is the way it was in these experiments. They were very important to national security, and we pressed on. It's unfortunate that somebody died. But we had to know what these drugs could do to people and how we could use them."[20] What was learned was that these drugs produced different reactions in different individuals; there was no single predictable reaction. Why it took twenty years and an incalcuable human cost to determine that remains unclear.

The attitude of the officer who spoke to the issue reflects other problems and incongruities. He did not differentiate between combat, in which the risks are known, and medical testing, in which the risks are not known, or not fully known, particularly to the individual who is taking them. He also did not distinguish between military men in battle and civilians in hospitals who were given these drugs under questionable circumstances and with sometimes fatal results.

Perhaps the most serious flaw in the man's thinking, and in the thinking of those who profess to see few ethical problems with human medical experimentation, is the fact that the "objective" outweighs the concern for human life. Supreme Court Justice Benjamin Cardozo once wrote that "every human being of adult years and sound mind has a right to determine what shall be done with his body." It is clear that many of the people involved in these drug experiments—as well as in the other experiments discussed—could not make such a determination for the simple reason that no one had offered them the opportunity to do so. Many were tested in ignorance that they were being tested, and others were given only the slightest hint of the possible consequences to their minds and bodies. It is neither unreasonable nor unfair to compare some of what was done in the name of "national security" by the military and the CIA with some of what was done in the human experiments revealed at the Nuremberg trials. In both cases, consent was coerced, even if with more abuse and cruelty in Germany; the possible consequences to the individuals were uncertain and not fully thought out; and the concern for the dignity of human life was minimal.

Preliminary legislation to assure protection of persons participating in government-sponsored biomedical and behavioral research was obtained in 1974 by Senator Kennedy, joined by Senator Jacob K. Javits (R–N.Y.). The bill provided for a temporary eleven-member commission under the Secretary of Health, Education, and Welfare to incorporate basic ethical principles into guidelines for research conducted with HEW funding. In late 1975, Kennedy, Javits, and Senator Richard S. Schweiker (R–Pa.) introduced a more ambitious bill. It would establish a permanent commission under the President, and would extend protection to those involved in all research conducted in government or private facilities receiving funds from any federal agency. The Senate passed the bill in May 1976.

Inhumane experimentation has gone on for a number of years and it expands as science and technology expands. In a sense, human experimentation is an ultimate step of technological evolution, because it erases one's control over one's own mind and body. The late and distinguished Sir Robert Hutchinson, addressed the growing number of human experiments when he wrote in 1953: "From inability to let well alone, from too much zeal for the new, and contempt for what is old; from putting knowledge before wisdom, science before art, cleverness before common sense; from treating patients as cases, and from making 'the cure' of the disease more grievous than the endurance of the same, Good Lord deliver us."[21]

It will take a major awakening, a major reappraisal of our attitudes and thinking, to slow down the momentum of human experimentation to place limits on what it can and cannot do to people, and to make it accountable.

The momentum to proceed with it has been growing, pushed by the sometimes mindless search for information and by the technology that guides it. It becomes finally one of the most fundamental human issues facing our technological age. It has proceeded for so long and so far because there has been meager accountability for what researchers want to discover by using human subjects, and for the methods they use to achieve it. They were accountable to themselves—cloaked in secrecy and anonymity, and able to proceed even when their research resulted in the death and disability of the humans they were experimenting with. Clearly, this kind of research thrives on the obscuring of accountability, accountability to the individuals and to the society. Addressing himself to this issue, Dr. Katz wrote: "Fidelity to the rights of research subjects may impede experimentation or indeed may make some research impossible to conduct. However, if we wish to authorize an invasion of individual dignity and autonomy under certain circumstances we must ask: Should society, on behalf of the affected subjects, give its 'informed consent' to the tolerable limits scientists can go in the use of human beings? It is imperative that answers to this and many other questions be sought by members of many disciplines in cooperative inquiry."[22]

Health is too serious a matter to be left to doctors.
Gough Whitlam, former Prime Minister of Australia
New York Times

To an extreme degree, society has delegated accountability for the practice of medicine to its practitioners. The rationale was the usual one: they have the expertise that laymen lack, and, being professionals, must be trusted to police their peers to prevent abuse of the public. The American Medical Association acknowledges its responsibility for "peer review" in its "Principles of Medical Ethics." The medical profession "should safeguard the public and itself against physicians deficient in . . . professional competence," Section 4 of the Code says.[1]

Organized medicine has created an imposing array of commissions, boards, committees, and panels that are charged with seeing to it that acceptable standards of care, if not achieved, at least are strenuously pursued. The titles of such bodies sound impressive. The membership is distinguished. The whole edifice appears to be reassuring.

The reality is something else. On the evidence of several studies carried out in recent years, these groups are passive, timid, and essentially powerless. In the words of Royce P. Noland, executive director of the American Physical Therapy Association, "Peer review has existed for some time, but it has been more of an exercise than a practical, meaningful force . . . peer review is treated like the country cousin, superficially recognized but generally ignored."

The sapper at work here is the "club" dynamic that makes one member hesitate to point a finger at another, particularly when the other member has been or may be helpful in a financial or professional way. Moreover, the profession has shown itself to be intensely protective of the prevailing non-system of medical care in which services are exchanged for fees in a one-to-one relationship. Anything that threatens to disrupt or alter that relationship traditionally has been regarded as a threat.

The great bulk of medical care is provided by individual physicians dealing with individual patients in the privacy of an office. How qualified a physician is to treat the specific disease, how abreast he is of recent advances, how thorough are his examinations—these are largely matters between the two individuals. Professor Avedis Donabedian, of the School of Public Health at the University of Michigan, has said, "The private office practice of medicine essentially remains *terra incognito,* outside the scope of effective professional or administrative observation or control."[2]

To begin with, the profession guards access to its ranks most zealously and efficiently. Applicants typically have to graduate from an accredited school and pass a stiff examination conducted by a state medical board (itself composed of physicians appointed by the governor) in consultation with the state medical society. But once admitted to practice, the new physician finds that the club takes over. His license permits him to practice in *any* field of medicine, no matter what his personal qualifications. Unlike his driver's permit, which he must renew periodically, his license to practice medicine is valid for a lifetime in all but a handful of states. The consequences have been spelled out in a report to Ralph Nader's Center for Study of Responsive Law entitled *One Life—One Physician: An Inquiry Into the Medical Profession's Performance in Self-Regulation.* "The effect of a single life-time license on the quality of medical care is obvious," the author, Dr. Robert S. McCleery, said:

If a physician does not update his medical knowledge, then he cannot practice high quality medicine. Conscientious physicians realize the necessity of guarding against educational obsolescence. But far too many physicians, because license maintenance is not conditioned by it, do not continue their medical education. Most of the medical practice acts require annual or biennial license renewal that is nothing more than payment of a fee. The physician need not indicate whether he has done anything to keep abreast of medical advances. Even if he received his license in 1930 and has learned nothing since, he is free to practice almost totally unimpeded by the law.[3]

State medical boards, in addition to their licensing functions, are responsible for monitoring physicians' activities. In this function, which McCleery said the boards regard as "secondary," they have "drastically failed. The failure is due partly to the gross inadequacy of the statutes, partly to the perceptions and attitudes of the state boards, and partly to the intrinsic value structure of the profession itself."[4] The operating assumption is that a state board depends on the county and state medical societies to monitor the quality of practice. To be sure, these societies have established "grievance" committees to handle complaints. But as many authorities have noted, these committees are generally passive. They don't move on an issue until a patient, or a representative of the patient, asks them to—in other words, they move at the behest of someone outside the medical profession, and after the purported damage already has been done. Furthermore, medical societies "do little or nothing to publicize" the existence of grievance committees, McCleery noted.

One executive secretary felt that the society did not have the facilities to handle all the complaints that would result from publicizing the existence of the committee. He went on to admit that this was a failure on the part of the society. Another felt that the public was aware of the existence of the committee. This was said in conjunction with the fact that in 1969 the grievance committee had handled less than 15 complaints.[5]

Under existing law the most extreme sanctions that a local medical society can apply in the event of "gross malpractice" is to expel an offender and to recommend to the state medical board that it revoke his license. Expulsion does not stop the offender from practicing or from maintaining his affiliation with a hospital. Should the ultimate—revocation of license—occur, the offender may simply move to another state, there to inflict surgical butchery or other malpractice on another population of unsuspecting victims.

But revocation of license is extraordinarily difficult to achieve, to begin with. "To prove incompetence," says Dr. Robert C. Derbyshire, an expert in this area who is an official of the New Mexico Board of Medical Examiners, "you have to prove a definite pattern—and waiting for the pattern to emerge is rather hard on patients." Of the some 380,000 doctors in the United States, state licensing boards took disciplinary action against fewer than two thousand between 1964 and 1974. The *Journal of the American Medical Association*, which publishes annual statistics on disciplinary actions taken by state boards and state societies, reported that in 1969 thirteen state boards listed no actions at all; as for state medical societies, thirty-two listed no actions.[6] In articles on unfit doctors in the *New York Times* on January 25 and 26, 1976, Boyce Rensberger cited authorities who estimate that sixteen thousand licensed physicians are unfit to practice medicine; that only about sixty-six of them lose their licenses each year; that they treat an estimated total of 7.5 million persons annually; and that one reason why the situation persists is the frequent inability of patients to discern that they have been incorrectly treated. Emphasizing the reluctance on the part of doctors, hospitals, and state licensing board to put the health and lives of patients over the reputation and livelihoods of professional colleagues, Rensberger told of the case of a New Mexico surgeon cited to him by Dr. Derbyshire. The surgeon had performed a gall bladder operation and tied off the wrong duct. The patient died and although the error was discovered at autopsy, the doctor was neither disciplined nor taught to avoid making the same mistake.

A few months later, the same surgeon performed the same operation and made the same mistake. Thus a second patient died and again the surgeon was neither punished nor taught which duct was which. Months later the same surgeon performed the operation a third time and again tied off the wrong duct.

Only after the doctor had lost a patient for the third time, within six months of the first death, Dr. Derbyshire recalled, did authorities act and, after weeks of investigation and days of hearings, take away the man's license.

The impotency of the peer review system extends into other areas. No questions seem to be raised, for example, about conflict of interest. In West Virginia, Dr. Rowland Burns, who was often a paid witness for coal companies in compensation cases, appeared before a state legislative committee considering legislation to deal with the problem of coal-miners' "black lung" disease. Burns acknowledged that he was a paid witness for the West Virginia Coal Association. How much was he being paid? he was asked. Burns said he could not recall the exact amount, but added, "I have not been paid near enough."[7]

The extent to which the medical profession protects its own was dramatically pointed up in 1975 at an AMA-sponsored conference on what the AMA terms "disabled physicians"—doctors afflicted by drug addiction, emotional problems, or alcoholism. Dr. Herbert C. Modlin, a Kansas psychiatrist and chairman of the AMA's Council on Mental Health, estimated that ten thousand doctors throughout the country might be rated "disabled"—but that most of them were professionally active. Dr. Aaron Ament, a Maryland psychiatrist, told the meeting of one respected physician who slowly deteriorated into a psychotic. Despite his repeated threatening phone calls to other physicians they refused to acknowledge that he was going out of his mind. Finally, after the man had called Ament and talked of mass murders, he was committed to a mental hospital. Even after the commitment, Ament disclosed, it was difficult to persuade other physicians that the man had been "disabled." "Doctors have a tendency to deny illness within their own profession," Modlin said.[8] Dr. Ernest Livingstone, a Portland, Oregon, internist who heads the AMA's committee on legislation, said, "other doctors are reluctant to intrude . . . One of the definitions of our profession is autonomy. Doctors have never been educated to expect that their colleagues should look into their practice."[9]

The AMA has proposed that states pass a disabled physicians' act which would require medical boards to investigate reports of doctors with mental or physical problems and, if the situation warrants, revoke their licenses. But the psychotic doctor or the fatally incompetent surgeon represents an extreme. What about the care provided to the average patient by a sane, presumably well-trained and well-intentioned physician in his office? Because this is where most medical care occurs, it should be a matter of intense scrutiny by the profession as society's surrogate. The reality is, however, that the principle of peer review collapses at the doorstep of the doctor's office. Dr. Kerr L. White, of the Johns Hopkins School of Hygiene and Public Health, said in 1968:

When it comes to disease and problems seen by doctors in their offices or in clinics, emergency rooms, or outpatient department, an even greater mystery is encountered. Virtually nothing is known about what doctors and nurses do for ambulatory patients. This is not a matter of invading the privacy and confidentiality of the patient-physician relations but of developing information about the content of medical practice, the accomplishment of end-results and the organization of responsible health services arrangements to meet the needs of the people . . . there is virtually no information available about complaints, symptoms, problems, or diseases brought to doctors in their offices and clinics.[10]

Such information as is available about the quality of care in private offices is not encouraging. Possibly the most comprehensive study was carried out in the mid-1950s under the direction of Dr. Osler Peterson of Harvard Medical School. Eighty-eight general practitioners in North Carolina were observed by an internist for periods averaging 3.5 days. The physicians were rated by several criteria, such as the thoroughness of the physical examination, the completeness of the clinical history and of subsequent record-keeping, and the therapy employed. The observers reported that 45 percent of the physicians permitted the patients to remain fully or almost fully clothed during the physical examination. Eighty-six percent failed to carry out a routine breast examination. Only 9 percent took reasonably thorough clinical histories. Sixty-one percent limited their questions to the patient's chief complaint or to the organ involved. Similar shortcomings turned up in the area of record-keeping. Thirty-six percent of the physicians noted medications, fees, and isolated data; 47 percent recorded minimal information on medications and positive findings. Only 17 percent recorded all positive findings in the clinical history and the physical examination, laboratory tests, and admissions to hospitals.

When it came to therapy, still more deficiencies were found. For example, 85 percent of the physicians treated cases of anemia with what was described as "shotgun preparations," as against the 15 percent who used appropriate treatment. In dealing with obese patients, 67 percent failed to recognize the condition as a problem and give adequate dietary advice. The results in dealing with hypertension were only slightly better, with some 57 percent making what was adjudged a poor assessment, using inappropriate drug therapy, and failing to suggest losing weight, low-salt diets and rest. Dr. McCleery commented in *One Life—One Physician:*

It is apparent from the data presented that the majority of these doctors do not measure up to even minimal standards of acceptable routine medical care. The general practitioner (GP) probably faces even more difficulties than do many other physicians in attempting to achieve and maintain excellence in the practice of medicine. By the very nature of his field, the GP does not tend to be associated with a teaching institution and thus can not easily avail himself of the opportunities in continuing education afforded physicians by the teaching hospital. In his office practice, the GP often represents the traditional "solo" ideal of the American physician—self-sufficient in practice, his work reviewed by no other members of his profession, and his standards of care set by no one but himself. The general practitioner, then, may well represent the practice of American medicine in its most unregulated form.[11]

Harvard's Dr. Peterson, in 1974, said that he believes the situation has improved since the study was carried out, largely because the new generation of general practitioners is better trained. "But there's still a fair amount of evidence that practice today isn't very good," he said.[12]

A major cause of inadequate or improper care is the failure of physicians to keep up with the newest discoveries in medicine. The present licensing system puts no pressure on them to do so. Dr. Thomas C. Chalmers, president of New York's Mount Sinai Medical Center, has pointed out that many doctors continued to prescribe diethylstilbestrol, a known carcinogen in some humans, to prevent miscarriages despite six well-documented studies that showed it to be ineffective and dangerous. Similarly, he said, a bland diet for ulcer patients and bed rest for patients with infectious hepatitis are still being prescribed widely despite evidence that the measures have little effect.[13]

Consumer groups have made tentative efforts to shed some light on how medicine is practiced, only to run into indignant resistance from local medical societies. These efforts have taken the form of directories of physicians in specific areas. The Health Research Group, which is financed by Ralph Nader's Public Citizen, Inc., undertook a pioneering effort in Maryland's Prince George's County near Washington, D.C. Traditionally, the only information available to the prospective patient was a Yellow Pages' listing of his name and possibly his specialty. Everything else was on a word-of-mouth basis. The Health Research Group's and other directories provided information on each listed doctor's training, hospital affiliation, specialty, fees, availability for house calls, and tests that he is equipped to administer. Some directories listed doctors who failed to respond as "uncooperative." In Prince George's County and in Sangamon County, Illinois, where a similar directory was prepared, the local medical societies cautioned their members that the listings might violate state laws against advertising by physicians. Subsequently, however, the American Medical Association's Judicial Council ruled that the directories do not violate medical ethics, provided that they are open to all physicians in the area and do not include "any self-aggrandizing statement or qualitative judgment" about his competency.[14]

The principal agency for overseeing the standards of hospitals is the Joint Commission on Accreditation of Hospitals, which was organized in 1952. The commission's sponsors are the American Medical Association and the American Hospital Association, each of which apoints seven commissioners, and the American College of Physicians and the American College of Surgeons, each of which names three commissioners. The mixed sponsorship builds in conflicts. This was indicated by Dr. John Porterfield, the commission director. "The extent to which the commissioners act as representatives of their organizations, rather than as individuals, varies both with the question on the table and with the man," he said. He added that "where an organization's house of delegates has taken a firm stand on a question, its commissioners feel obliged to vote that position regardless of their opinions. Often the commissioners from the AMA and the AHA are polarized, leaving the specialists either to arrange a compromise or to cast the swing votes."[15]

Membership in the commission is voluntary. Hospitals join mainly for prestige. As of 1969, 4,906 of the 7,137 hospitals in the United States had requested and received accreditation. The sole aim of accreditation, Dr. Porterfield has said, is to foster "the optimum environment for the practice of high-quality medicine." This "environment" is not necessarily synonymous with reliable accountability to patients. "Dealing only with the environment has made some people mad at us, yet how can we approach medical care quality directly?" he asked. "We wouldn't be caught dead—or we'd be dead if caught—saying, 'You made the wrong decision, Doctor.' "[16]

By general agreement, the most substantive element of commission monitoring is the provision for periodic review of the care provided by a hospital in specialized fields. A question exists, however, about the stringency of the provision and the lengths to which the commission will go in requiring compliance. Dr. Charles L. Hudson, a past president of the AMA, has indicated that the commission is not particularly tough. "Many physicians do not understand that the Joint Commission looks at the structure of the plant and of its organization but does not dictate to or evaluate the activities of professionals within the walls," he told a meeting of the American Association of Medical Clinics in 1968. "At the moment it is satisfied to see that a hospital has its procedures pre-planned and available in writing and that its physical plant is adequate to provision of good care."[17] When Dr. McCleery and his associates looked into the question of hospital staff review they found that

the fact that a hospital has an internal audit committee outlined in its bylaws offers no assurance that the committee meets. For example, one Commission surveyor found that the minutes of committee meetings seemed just too good to be true. When he questioned the secretary who had typed them, he found that she had made them up—that the meetings had never been held.[18]

"Many doctors resent the time that committee meetings take," McCleery said. "Many are reluctant to criticize a colleague since they often depend on one another for referrals. A physician may be hesitant to criticize for fear of losing referrals or the friendship and "respect" of his colleagues."[19]

McCleery also found that to determine whether a hospital is in compliance with the commission code, a physician-surveyor visits it periodically. He concentrates on those areas where the hospital staff indicates it is having problems. Occasionally the surveyor is able to double-check situations where the staff says it is in compliance, but commission spokesmen "admit that they do not have the time or personnel to check on all the questions." Joseph Stone, assistant director of the commission, said that the chief qualification for a surveyor was "availability." McCleery commented:

There are no set standards that applicants must meet. Most of the surveyors are retired or about to be retired physicians. Stone noted that it is hard to find qualified people who are willing to go out on the road for ten and a half months each year and that the per diem travel allowance and salaries they receive are not lavish.[20]

In two of the most comprehensive studies of the quality of institutional medical care, the Columbia School of Public Health and Administrative Medicine found that hospitals providing the best care were those affiliated with medical schools. ". . . a doctor at a teaching hospital, working under the critical eye of colleagues and the inquisitive prodding of students and residents, has an incentive to keep up with what's new."[21]

Among the most common abuses in hospital care are unnecessary operations and improper drug therapy. One study of several thousand pelvic operations in New England found that in about half, surgeons had removed a normal uterus.[22] An unprecedented review of the quality of American surgery was made on the basis of 1,493 operations performed in ninety-five hospitals. The study showed that one-third of the eighty-five deaths and 1,696 "untoward incidents" or complications that resulted were "preventable," Victor Cohn reported in the *Washington Post* on January 22, 1976. As for drugs, adverse reactions merely in hospital patients kill an estimated thirty thousand persons a year, according to Dr. Herschel Jick, director of the Boston Collaborative Drug Surveillance Program. "We ought to wonder if this is all justified," Jick said.[23]

The Commission on Professional and Hospital Activities analyzed tonsilectomies performed at one thousand hospitals and found that an elementary precaution, taking the patient's blood pressure before surgery, had not been taken in 43 percent of the cases. In addition, 30 percent of the patients showed signs of infection that should have precluded surgery.

Possibly the most significant factor in bringing into question the system of peer review in health care has been the development of the massive federally funded programs such as Medicaid and Medicare. Regional directors of these programs who were concerned about the quality of medical care have taken the initiative for more stringent auditing of procedures in both hospitals and private offices. As a consequence, Congress has passed legislation to try to insure control of quality and costs in government-supported programs. Under the law, doctors will be asked to establish regional Professional Review Standards Organizations (PRSO's) that will lay down norms for the treatment of various diseases, including the length of stay in the hospital, and the proper medical and surgical care. Physicians failing to meet the standards may be denied federal payments and conceivably fined as much as $5,000. Some see the new law as an acid test of peer review. Dr. Henry E. Simmons, while a top medical official of the Department of Health, Education, and Welfare, said in 1974, "PSRO's may be our last, best chance as an independent profession to do the job."[24]

Supervision of the dental profession by dentists generally ranks with supervision of the medical profession by physicians, except for one important and troubling difference: dentistry is even more of a "cottage industry," with each practitioner going his own, largely unsupervised way. By and large, no requirements for continuing education exist. Recognized standards of performance are even fewer than for doctors.

Herbert Denenberg, while insurance commissioner of Pennsylvania, said in his "A Shopper's Guide to Dentistry":

There is evidence that much dental care is substandard. A clinical evaluation of 1,300 Medicaid patients in New York State found 9 per cent of the work done was inexcusably poor quality dental care and another 9 percent involved fraud. The sample is not perfectly representative as 6,000 participants were asked to be checked and only 1,300 came in. A representative figure also from the New York Medicaid program indicates that 25 per cent of all amounts billed were for unnecessary dental treatment. A later evaluation of 11,000 Medicaid patients found that only 81.2 per cent of the patients received satisfactory dental care, although this again was not a representative sample.[25]

When a tooth decays, it is often possible to save it by removing the pulp and filling the empty space. The traditional procedure—done by a great many dental general practitioners as well as by a relative handful of specialists called endodontists—is called root-canal therapy. Performed properly, it is arduous, safe, and usually successful—but expensive. After World War II, dentists—especially some general practitioners—began to use a heavily promoted, "simplified" technique devised by Dr. Angelo Sargenti, a Swiss dentist, that is quick and relatively inexpensive, although profitable for dentists who otherwise might do no root-canal therapy.

At a hearing held by the House Intergovernmental Relations Subcommittee in October 1975, Chairman L. H. Fountain (D–N.C.) inquired of Dr. Ramon Werts, an advocate of the Sargenti method, how long it takes a dentist to learn the method. A single day, said Werts. Indeed, he added, the course is taught between 9 A.M. and 5 P.M., "with a break for lunch." Werts testified as executive director of the American Endodontic Society, which was formed in 1969 to spread the Sargenti gospel. Under questioning by Congressman Fountain, Werts acknowledged that "anyone" can join the society, which has "no requirements for membership." The annual dues are a modest $24.

Dentists using the Sargenti method fill the root canal with a paste-like drug of erratic composition—it has been formulated at least twenty-five different ways, and goes under names such as N-2 and RC-2B. While the filler used by endodonists is, to the maximum possible extent, inert and harmless, the Sargenti paste contains antiinflammatory agents that prevent wounds from healing, lead, and embalming fluid. Three endodontists testified that, because the bottom end of the root canal may be open, the toxic mixture can leach finally into the liver, other vital organs, and the bone marrow. The specialists—Drs. Howard Martin, of Georgetown University; Stephen Cohen of the University of the Pacific, and Dudley H. Glick of the University of Southern California—cited patients who had become "dental cripples" with numbness of the jaw and other serious injuries.

Drawing on the literature of the proponents, they cited an incredible claim that poisonous lead is "beneficial" in "proper concentrations," showed that the advocates had touted favorable results from a study with one dog while dismissing unfavorable results from studies with multiple animals, and proclaimed man to be "the highest experimental animal."

Finally, the critics disclosed that the Air Force and Army have not authorized their dentists to use the Sargenti method; that the method is not taught by dental schools in Sargenti's own Switzerland; that California forbids the manufacture, distribution, or use of the paste; that the State of Nebraska has warned dentists about the method, and that Australia, Norway, and Sweden have banned it. In addition, Fountain said that the Food and Drug Administration had banned importation of the paste in 1961. In December 1975 the FDA banned its shipment in interstate commerce and warned state health departments so that they might act against intrastate sales.

What may make you want to request a shot of novocaine was the disclosure at the hearing, apparently accepted everyone concerned, that an estimated thirty thousand American dentists—about one-quarter of the total —were using the Sargenti method.[26]

In *Dentistry and Its Victims,* written by a dentist using the nom de plume "Paul Revere," the author loosed these thunderbolts in what he termed "a deliberate, angry expose of bad dentistry and bad dentists":

"It is shocking but true that a considerable number of dentists actually choose to do poor work. All bad dentists know how to practice good dentistry; all of them know how to make more money from bad dentistry than they ever could by doing good work; and all of them choose a high income in preference to their patients' health."[27]

"For every dentist-hero in a white coat there may be one or more white-coated Poorworks [Revere invented a single, typical dentist to represent the bad dentists and named him Dr. Poorwork] leaning over victims in the dental chair. I say 'there may be' because organized dentistry will not publish, and actually suppresses, all studies on the quality of dentistry as it is practiced . . . it has been the policy of the American Dental Association to support the fiction that all dentists maintain high standards of care . . .[28]

"My own personal observations after fifteen years of practice are as follows:

1. Of patients coming for initial examination, the great majority had dental restorations that were below state licensing board standards.

2. A high proportion of this poor work fell so far short of minimum standards as to be disgraceful. Patients with this type of care can usually look forward to frequent dental pain and, over the years, progressive loss of teeth. . . .

To say anything that might be construed as criticism of another dentist's work is unethical, but intentionally to destroy a patient's tooth for increased profit is absolutely ethical. . . .[29]

The Code's message to the dentist is clear: The dentist himself is the sole judge and final authority on ethical behavior toward his patient. Such is the prescribed Code of Ethics of dentistry.[30]

A true profession must seek constantly to devise and enforce high professional ethics and standards. For this there is no satisfactory substitute. But the point must be reiterated that if war is too important to be left to generals, medicine and dentistry—and other professions and callings as well—cannot be abdicated solely to their practitioners, lest accountability run too much to them and too little to the public.

X
Unaccountable Technology: The End of the World?

Nuclear Power:
The "Faustian Bargain" **42**

We are still in a period of grace. In that time, let us hope, we can learn that the proper use of science is not to conquer the world, but to live in it.

Barry Commoner
*The Careless Technology: Ecology in
International Development*

During the eons in which man has been on earth he has looked upon nature as inexhaustible. With reason. "Nature always, so to speak, knows where and when to stop," E. F. Schumacher says in *Small Is Beautiful: Economics as if People Mattered.*[1] "Greater even than the mystery of natural growth is the mystery of the natural cessation of growth. There is measure in all natural things—in their size, speed, or violence. As a result, the system of nature, of which man is a part, tends to be self-balancing, self-adjusting, self-cleansing."[2] In the seventeenth century there began to evolve the enlightenment; and from this age, characterized by faith in the power of human reason, there evolved modern science, technology, and finally, in Schumacher's phrase, "man dominated by technology and specialisation." And, he emphasizes, technology "recognizes no self-limiting principle—in terms, for instance, of size, speed, or violence. It therefore does not possess the virtues of being self-balancing, self-adjusting, and self-cleansing."[3]

In our time nature, in the elemental form of fossil fuels for energy, at last got the message across that it is indeed exhaustible (although *when* is genuinely disputed by experts). Technological man was standing by with a substitute that would be inexhaustible. It was of course nuclear power. It would not pollute the air with smoke. It would spare us the need to adopt a program of far-reaching conservation. It would come to be regarded as indispensable to the quest for "self-sufficiency" in energy. It promised—overoptimistically —to be cheap. But could it be, in a phrase from another era, "a reckless shooting craps with destiny" for which the crapshooters cannot conceivably be held accountable?[4]

One of the great unsolved problems is nuclear wastes. These are radioactive, are the antithesis of any "self-limiting principle" of nature, and cause cancer and mutations. Cesium-137 and strontium-90 have a relatively brief half-life of thirty years—but go on emitting radiation for six hundred years, when finally they decay into harmlessness. Plutonium-239, one of the most poisonous elements man ever has handled in quantity, has a half-life of 24,400 years, or 244 centuries; but it remains dangerous for at least 2,000 centuries. One-millionth of a gram of it has been shown to be capable of causing cancer in laboratory animals.

Dr. Donald P. Geesaman, an authority on plutonium who for thirteen years did biomedical research for the Atomic Energy Commission (AEC), says that plutonium-239, "under a number of probable conditions," can powder into particles. These are insoluble, invisible, and incredibly tiny— about one-millionth of a meter in length. If for any reason—an explosion, an accident, sabotage—ten thousand particles of the metal were to escape into the air, Geesaman estimates, one human cancer would result. A mere pound of plutonium-239, according to Dr. John W. Gofman, a former associate director of the Lawrence Radiation Laboratory, "represents the potential for some nine *billion* human lung cancer doses."[5] In 1975 alone, thousands of pounds of plutonium-239 were being produced by the country's fifty-three commercial nuclear reactors, as a waste product of the enriched uranium "burned" as fuel.

President Ford has set a goal of having two hundred nuclear plants in operation by 1985. By the year 2000, the target, set by the AEC in 1972, was five hundred plants, although the government since has raised its sights to one thousand. A point ought to be made about this that usually is submerged. These plants will not last forever; indeed, they may become unserviceable after thirty, twenty-five, or even twenty years. "No one discusses the humanly vital point that they cannot be dismantled and cannot be shifted but have to be left standing where they are, probably for centuries, perhaps for thousands of years, an active menace to all life, silently leaking radioactivity into air, water and soil," E. F. Schumacher points out. "No one has considered the number and location of these satanic mills which will relentlessly accumulate. Earthquakes, of course, are not supposed to happen, nor wars, nor civil disturbances, nor riots like those that infested American cities. Disused nuclear power stations will stand as unsightly monuments to unquiet man's assumption that nothing but tranquillity, from now on, stretches before him, or else—that the future counts as nothing compared with the slightest economic gain now."[6]

Suppose that only five hundred plants are built by the year 2000. The annual production of plutonium-239 then would be two hundred thousand pounds. Will the nuclear industry contain 99.99 percent of its plutonium-

239 and other radioactive wastes? Constantly? For centuries? That is an extremely high degree of containment; and yet, in the year 2000, the putative five hundred plants—dispersing a mere 0.01 percent of their poisonous waste inventory—would be releasing in that year alone one-fifth of the radiation doses released by the combined atmospheric weapons testing conducted by the United States, the Soviet Union, and the United Kingdom over a decade. But is even 99.99 percent efficiency—if it could be achieved and maintained—good enough, especially for plutonium-239, with its 24,400-year half-life? Taking into account that it would be produced at the rate of some two hundred thousand pounds annually, and that a single pound has the potential for billions of human lung-cancer doses, Gofman thinks not. Indeed, he contends that containment exceeding 99.999 percent—allowing a loss of less than 0.001 percent—"is hardly good enough to avert disaster."

The plutonium created by the "burning" of uranium is contained in the fuel rods, which after being removed from a reactor are cooled for months at the site. Then the rods are transported—in huge self-cooling casks—to reprocessing plants for dissolution and separation of unusable wastes from reusable uranium and plutonium. These wastes, mostly in liquid form, are stored at the reprocessing plants in steel and cement tanks and eventually are reduced to cake form. Through 1974, about six hundred thousand gallons of wastes from commercial reactors have been processed (the weapons program has accumulated about 90 million gallons and is expanding that total at the rate of 7.5 million gallons a year).[7]

The problem of theft would enlarge were plutonium to be recycled in quantities sufficient to permit it to be "burned" as a supplement to nuclear fuel. Recycling would yield some economies—amounting to a saving of probably less than one-half of one percent on the nation's total energy bill.[8] But there would have to be created a large commercial plutonium industry to reprocess the metal for recycling. Facilities would have to be set up to haul plutonium to and from reprocessing and storage facilities. This would create opportunities which do not now exist for theft and for the consequent establishment of an illicit market in which terrorists might buy the small amounts of plutonium needed to build nuclear weapons. To protect against such a contingency, the government would have to set up a huge new security apparatus; after all, according to an AEC study, small groups committed more than four hundred acts of international terrorism in only six years.[9]

The AEC acknowledges that it has solved neither the problem of nuclear theft nor the problem of plutonium toxicity. Yet in August 1974, it proposed to allow the nuclear power industry to use plutonium as reactor fuel. This would result in "a dramatic escalation in the risks posed by nuclear power," said three members of the staff of the Natural Resources Defense Council. The staff members—biophysicist Arthur R. Tamplin, nuclear physicist Thomas B. Cochran, and attorney J. Gustave Speth—went on to warn, "We believe that the commercialization of plutonium will place an intolerable strain on our society. . . . our technology has again outstripped our institutions, which are not prepared or suited to deal with plutonium."[10] But the AEC staff was reversed by the Nuclear Regulatory Commission (NRC), which Congress established to take over the regulatory functions of the AEC. In May 1975, in its first major decision, the NRC put off a final decision on plutonium recycling until at least mid-1978, so that a number of safety studies could be completed, and so that the public would have time to prepare and file comments.

Compounding the problem, the government for several years has given its highest priority in energy to development of the Liquid Metal Fast Breeder Reactor. The overriding reason for this is the calculation that its production of plutonium fuel would exceed its consumption of uranium fuel, although the first breeders would be unable to do this for twenty-five years.[11] Critics say the breeder reactor would enlarge the ordinary hazards of conventional reactors; for example, the coolant would not be water, but radioactive molten sodium which reacts with violence on exposure to air or water. By the year 2020, by government estimate, nuclear reactors may have produced 60 million pounds of plutonium—a figure built on the assumption that breeder reactors would be the principal source.

The unimaginable hazards of this much plutonium aside, the Defense Council has cited revisions in the AEC's original cost-benefit analysis which show that "by the AEC's own reckoning, the present breeder program can no longer be justified economically."[12] Through fiscal 1975, the program had cost about $2 billion, with another $490 million allocated for fiscal 1976. The total cost had been estimated in 1973 to be less than $5 billion, but by 1975 even proponents were figuring $10 billion. The main test facility, in Hanford, Washington, was to have cost $87 million, but the estimate in 1975 was $933 million. The demonstration breeder plant, in Tennessee, was to cost $700 million; but in 1975 the estimates were running from $1.7 billion to $2.1 billion. The evil is not merely the enormous costs; it is that commitments on such a scale—and the accompanying neglect of alternative power sources—will generate irresistible pressures to use the breeder reactors and thus to multiply what the Defense Council staff justly regards as "the intolerable risks of utilizing plutonium."[13]

In pushing for the fast breeder and plutonium recycling, the government is reflecting a confidence—or arrogance—derived from having managed plutonium without harm to public health ever since the Manhattan Project of World War II, despite a major fire at one facility and other accidents. "For thirty years," the AEC said in a draft statement on plutonium recycling, "plutonium has been produced in reactors, recovered from reactor fuel, purified, made into many chemical and physical forms, fabricated, handled, transported and stored in large quantities involving many tons of materials." It detracts nothing from this accomplishment to examine whether it is a sufficient basis for accepting an enormous expansion of the hazards of plutonium-239 for a thousand generations to come.

To start with, the government has been pushing us into even greater reliance on nuclear power in the face of its failure, which goes back almost thirty years, to provide an ultimate solution to the problem of storing reactor wastes that will remain dangerous sources of radioactivity not merely for their half-lives, but for hundreds of thousands of years. "[T] here is no way of destroying radioactivity," an officially appointed British Working Party told the secretary of state for the environment. "So there is no alternative to permanent storage. . . . In effect, we are consciously and deliberately accumulating a toxic substance on the off-chance that it may be possible to get rid of it at a later date. We are committing future generations to tackle a problem which we do not know how to handle."[14] This has the profoundest moral implications. Indeed, as was noted in the Introduction, the Dutch philosopher Fred L. Polak has said "that responsibility for the *future* (especially for the far-away, but also for the near-future) forms the central core, is the crystallized essence of *all* responsibility of any kind, always and everywhere."[15]

In 1972, James R. Schlesinger, then chairman of the AEC, announced that the AEC would ask the help of the National Aeronautics and Space Administration in devising rocketry that would unload fission garbage on the sun.[16] This notion drew scorn from those advocates of nuclear power who did not suffer sunstroke from the Schlesingerian vision of a 93-million-mile haul to the solar trash dump. Yet the government treated it with a straight face for four years, until discarding it more or less officially in May 1976.

The genuine best hope for safe burial was and is salt caverns, which are deep geologic strata believed to have been stable for 250 million years. Initially, the AEC chose as a burial ground an unused salt mine near Lyons, Kansas. There, the AEC hoped to keep, in the spent-fuel casks, all of the radioactive wastes to be produced by commercial reactors until the year 2000. The plan generated strong resistance from environmentalists, the governor, and most of the state's congressional delegation. Then it turned out that nearby drilling for oil and natural gas had left countless holes through which 175,000 gallons of water entered from a working salt mine.

Water could combine with the salt and corrode the canisters. The AEC gave up in 1973, turning to a proposal—for above-ground double-walled concrete and steel tanks—which, it hoped, would get us by until a permanent solution became available. In 1975, however, the proposal was shelved by the Nuclear Regulatory Commission (NRC), Congress having dissolved the AEC and divided its functions between the NRC and the Energy Research and Development Administration. The NRC is making studies of a virginal salt bed which is presumably insulated from problems such as arose at the Kansas mine because it is mostly on federal and state property. The salt bed is in New Mexico between Hobbs and Carlsbad. There, it is hoped, nuclear wastes might be safely entombed for a million years.

There is not and cannot be total certainty that the plan will provide, say, 99.99 percent containment for thousands of years, let alone a million. Earthquakes and leaks, for example, are at least conceivable. And many other countries with increasing numbers of nuclear reactors are without deep salt caverns for their long-lived wastes. Meanwhile the reliance on nuclear power grows apace, just as if the storage problem had been forever solved, just as if the essential fact had to be rediscovered, by the General Accounting Office, in December 1974: "Technology for ultimate disposal is still in the research stages and offers no viable answers at the present time."[17]

Inexorably, the possibility of a catastrophic meltdown grows, too. In such an accident, the core of a reactor would melt down through the reactor vessel and into the earth. The toll would depend on the quantity of radioactive material released, winds, the presence of a temperature inversion that would hold a nuclear cloud near the ground, and the size of the population at risk.

In 1964, the AEC's Brookhaven National Laboratory, in an update of an earlier study that allowed for the increase that meanwhile had occurred in reactor size, calculated that a major meltdown might kill forty-five thousand persons, contaminate an area the size of Pennsylvania (which occupies 45,333 square miles), and cause property damage of $17 billion to $280 billion. Obviously, disclosure of the Brookhaven study, termed the Wash-740 revision, could chill the public's ardor for nuclear power. This was recognized in the AEC by an official, Stanley A. Szawlewicz, who said in a memo on November 27, 1964, "The impact of publishing the revised Wash-740 report should be weighed before publication." Moreover, C. K. Beck, then the commission's second-ranking regulatory official, worried about how to put the study "in 'proper perspective.' " In a memo to the AEC in March 1965, when it was headed by Dr. Glenn T. Seaborg, Beck went on to report that a special committee of the Atomic Industrial Forum, the industry's trade association and lobby, "strongly urge" that the Brookhaven report "not be published in any form at the present time." Instead, the forum proposed that the commission send to the public's putative watchdog, on Capitol Hill, the Joint Committee on Atomic Energy, "a very brief letter" saying very close to nothing—"if major accidents are assumed to occur without regard to the improbability of such events, very large damages, of course, would be calculated to happen . . ." Seaborg sent just such a letter on June 13, 1965, with the result that the Brookhaven study was not made public for precisely eight years—until after David Dinsmore Comey, director of environmental research of Businessmen for the Public Interest, had threatened to bring a suit under the Freedom of Information Act. In an account of all of this in the *New York Times*, David Burnham brought out, however, that the AEC found ways to try to justify its long burial of the report. In a release in June 1973, the commission said the study "was never completed" and insisted that the maximum estimated death toll of forty-five thousand persons was based on "grossly unrealistic assumptions."[18]

In 1957, a study made by the University of Michigan's Engineering Research Institute predicted that a far higher death toll, 133,000, would occur were radioactivity to be released in a meltdown at the experimental Fermi I breeder reactor near Detroit. In 1966, a partial meltdown did occur —without release of activity. The plant then was shut down.

The AEC has been consistently reassuring. At one point, for example, it said it had "concluded that for a thousand operating nuclear plants . . . the chances of a catastrophic accident is [sic] about one in 100 billion each year." Later, in a draft report released in August 1974, a group of experts put the chances at one in a billion per reactor per year. The experts, headed by Dr. Norman C. Rasmussen, a professor of nuclear engineering at the Massachusetts Institute of Technology and a consultant to five commercial firms in the nuclear field, had made the study for the AEC. The report compared the chances of one thousand deaths in a reactor accident to those of a meteor striking the earth and killing a similar number. If one hundred reactors were to be operating, the report said, an accident in one of them that would kill one hundred persons would be likely only once in ten thousand years, and an accident that would cause ten or so deaths would be likely once in twenty-five hundred years.[19]

These calculations, the product of two years of work for which the AEC paid $3 million, came under severe attack from the Union of Concerned Scientists, which is headed by Dr. Henry W. Kendall, a professor of physics at MIT, and from the Sierra Club, one of the oldest and largest conservation groups. In an analysis in November 1974, the critics charged that the hazards had been drastically underestimated. To compute the probability of an accident, the analysis said, the Rasmussen team had used a method which the National Aeronautics and Space Administration (NASA) had tried, found faulty, and abandoned. Specifically, NASA had used the method to predict that a particular rocket engine would fail once in every ten thousand starts—but in tests the engine failed four times in every one hundred.[20]

In concluding that casualties would be reassuringly low, the Rasmussen group assumed that at each of sixty-six sites studied, 90 percent of all citizens put at risk by an accident could be evacuated twenty miles from the menaced area—and within two hours, at that. Focusing on just one of these dubious assumptions, the Kendall analysis said, "No nuclear plant we are aware of has adequate plans or means to evacuate out to a distance of 20 miles. Moreover, one can hardly support the contention that evacuation only to 20 miles is adequate when lethal consequences can be induced at 15 miles."

Just north of New York City, at Indian Point, are three reactors. Within a radius of 5 miles are 66,000 people; of 20 miles, 900,000; and of 40 miles, 16 million. "Plans or no plans, one could not expect to be able to evacuate such a population as is around this site," the Kendall analysis said. "Moreover, no plans to our knowledge have been subject to test or drill of the type so familiar to school children, on a far smaller scale, to prepare for fire." The analysis further contended that the Rasmussen report made inconsistent assumptions about evacuation and shielding: specifically, it assumed people to be traveling away from the accident-damaged reactor *and* to be receiving the benefits of shielding from radiation by being, for example, in the basements of their homes.

A final major criticism of the Rasmussen study was that it failed to consider the implications of plutonium despite plans to use it as a fuel, and to give full allowance to the health hazards of radiation. On the basis of all of these flaws together, the Kendall analysis estimated that in a major nuclear reactor accident the toll of killed and injured would be 126,800, or sixteen times the Rasmussen study's estimate of 7,900.[21]

While the charges and counter-charges were being exchanged, twelve members of the American Physical Society led by Dr. Harold W. Lewis, of the University of California at Santa Barbara, were quietly winding up a year-long study funded by the AEC and the National Science Foundation. The study concentrated on light-water reactors, the type which powers most of the nuclear power plants now in operation, and which is intended to power most of the plants under construction or being planned. The scientists' report, released on April 28, 1975, severely faulted the Rasmussen report and thus implicitly vindicated the critique by the Union of Concerned Scientists. This was especially striking because, as was noted, the AEC had joined in funding the study.

At the center of the problem of assessing the likelihood of what is known as a "maximum credible accident"—a break in one of the huge pipes that carries cooling water into the hot nuclear core—is the question of how the emergency core-cooling system (ECCS) will perform. With a break in the pipe and the resultant loss of pressure on water in the core (called a "blow-down"), the core instantly would begin to overheat, and the coolant would be converted to steam. The ECCS must within a minute or so flood the core and hold down its temperature lest there be a meltdown of the core and a consequent release of radioactivity into the environment. "The uncontrolled release of even 5 to 10 percent of this inventory [of radioactivity] could bring death to persons from 60 to 100 miles from the reactor," Dr. Kendall has said. "Persons hundreds of miles distant could suffer radiation sickness, genetic damage, and increased incidence of many diseases including cancer."[22] Some engineers underscore his concern because they fear that the water with which the ECCS would flood the reactor core "also would be blown out as steam just as water bubbles away when dropped on a red-hot stove," David Brand reported in the *Wall Street Journal.*[23]

But how does one determine whether an ECCS will work as intended? The American Physical Society (APS) report said that the complexity of the phenomena involved and "inadequacies in the present data base and calculational curves" do not permit any "comprehensive, thoroughly quantitative" evaluation. Instead, the AEC has evaluated reactor safety principally with complex computer codes that simulate accidents. But the data available for use in such codes are, as noted, inadequate; and, in addition, the APS said, there is a danger that "the mere existence of extremely complicated computer codes, which few people understand, will lead to an overconfidence in reactor safety."[24] With that, the APS report expressed doubt that the computer simulations could measure the "effectiveness" of the ECCS— meaning, as Brand put it, "that there isn't any certainty that the critical safety systems on most of the nation's nuclear power plants will prevent a major accident and the release of radioactivity."

But it was the calculation of cancer deaths and genetic effects that led to the Rasmussen group's biggest comeuppance. The radioactivity released by a major reactor accident would lead over the long term to three hundred cancer deaths, the Rasmussen report estimated. The APS calculation was ten thousand to twenty thousand—thirty-three to sixty-six times as many; and for genetic effects, as much as sixty times as many as figured in the Rasmussen report. The Rasmussen group, it will be recalled, had calculated that with one hundred nuclear plants operating, an accident that would cause ten or more deaths would occur once in twenty-five hundred years. The APS scientists said bluntly that they don't "have confidence" in the way those numbers were arrived at.[25]

.   .   .

Five months after the Kendall analysis became public, and five weeks before the APS report was released, an accident of a kind that is not supposed to happen happened. The site was the Tennessee Valley Authority's power generation facility at Browns Ferry, Alabama, where the TVA had operated one giant nuclear reactor since August 1974, and a second for only three weeks. On March 22, 1975, an electrician was testing for an air leak in an area under the control room for the reactors. When he held a lighted candle near some plastic insulation, a fire resulted. Within seven hours the reactors —which together compromise the world's largest generating system—were turned off. The fire had destroyed sixteen hundred control cables, many of which had been used to operate the ECCS; consequently, the ECCS was unavailable in the event the regular cooling system should fail.

David Comey, of Business for the Public Interest, who had helped to prepare the Kendall analysis, said the avoidance of a meltdown was "largely the result of good luck." Daniel F. Ford, a Harvard economist who is director of the Union of Concerned Scientists, said, "One electrician with a candle may have refuted in an instant the industry's fundamental and long-standing claim about the reliability of reactor systems." The Nuclear Regulatory Commission, in a bulletin to utilities, said that the fire had "made several safety systems inoperable."

The seriousness of the affair was confirmed five months later by the Nuclear Energy Liability and Property Insurance Association, a pool of one hundred carriers that insured the plant. In a report in August 1975, the association termed the density of control cables in the area where the fire started "inexcusable," warned that unless the density was eased and unless an automatic fire-fighting system was installed "a loss beyond imaginatioin should be anticipated," and charged that "[m]inimal consideration was given to the obvious burning characteristics of the cables . . ." Seeking to benefit from the lessons learned, the report disclosed that the association has asked engineers in charge of other nuclear plants to provide reports of existing vulnerability.[26]

The following month, Senator Joseph M. Montoya (D–N.Mex.), acting chairman of the Joint Committee on Atomic Energy, added to the gloom. He said that the committee had information that "raises serious questions concerning the quality of the regulatory review and inspection system." He cited a law under which the Nuclear Regulatory Commission (or the AEC, its predecessor) should have, but did not, formally find that the facility had been built in conformity with the law and administrative regulations. And, he said, despite requirements in the law to the contrary:

• The government had approved the design of the reactor although it apparently had not met requirements in the regulations.

• Inspection procedures had failed to reveal the deficiencies.

• Regulatory review procedures apparently did not require either the persons running the reactors or state and local officials in coordination with those persons to develop effective emergency procedures.

Indeed, Dr. Stephen H. Hanauer, a regulatory commission official appointed to look into the long-term implications of the fire, testified that it had uncovered "serious inadequacies."[27]

The repairs at Browns Ferry were expected to cost about $5 million. In addition, TVA had to spend about $10 million a month for nine months to buy coal to generate steam for its turbines. Even if the total cost of the fire had been $50 million, as the insurance pool had estimated, it would have been, Ralph Nader said, "the most expensive . . . in history." Of the twenty-three reactors insured by the pool, said its general manager, Burt C. Proom, eighteen were in "substantial compliance" with recommended fire-protection standards. Bringing the other five—which were not identified—into compliance could cost hundreds of millions of dollars, mainly because of the need for them to burn coal while repairs were being made.[28]

In dealing with the safety issue, the government and the nuclear industry like to say, Look at the record. In 1972, for example, an industry spokesman said that "in the twenty years of experience in the operation of nuclear power plants there has been not one single injury due to radiation or radioactive materials, either inside or outside the plants." Again, it detracts nothing from such an achievement to question whether it is a sufficient basis for accepting a vast expansion of risks to very large numbers of people for a very long time to come. Even if something more than luck had controlled the TVA accident, it raised questions about the safety and reliability of nuclear reactors which will not go away. So does a series of other disturbing incidents.

At Hanford, Washington, to take a case in point, the government stores about three-fourths of its nuclear wastes from weapons production. Over a period of fifty-one days, before it was noticed, 115,000 gallons leaked out of corroded tanks. "Officials claim that none . . . penetrated the local water table, but environmentalists say the long-lived wastes have plenty of time to contaminate the ground water and even enter man's food chain," *Business Week* reported.[29] The General Accounting Office (GAO) made a review during which thirty storage tanks were newly "identified," and of which three had not been monitored for leaks since 1949, the GAO said in a report in December 1974.

The unreliability of nuclear power plants "is becoming one of their most dependable features," the *Wall Street Journal* said in 1973. "The incredibly complex facilities are plagued by breakdowns that experts blame on faulty engineering, defective equipment and operating errors. Failures range from hour-long annoyances to months-long closedowns."[30] In January 1975, Commonwealth Edison Company in Chicago said that it had found five cracks in two ten-inch-diameter pipes in the emergency core cooling system of one of its nuclear plants at Morris, Illinois. The Nuclear Regulatory Commission then ordered twenty-three other nuclear plants to shut down so that a check for possible cracks in their emergency cooling system pipes could be made.[31]

All nuclear power plants are designed to withstand earthquakes, which, of course, have the potential to release lethal radioactivity. No nuclear power plant having been subjected to an earthquake, however, the design is unproved. Meanwhile, the most elementary precaution is not to build over a geologic fault. That, it happens, is precisely what the Virginia Electric Power Company (Vepco) did. The sequence was this:

Consultants to Vepco investigated a site for a four-reactor plant at North Anna, in Louisa County, Virginia, in 1968 and 1969. They reported finding no fault. In February 1970, the late Dr. John Funkhouser, a professor of geology at John Tyler Community College in Chester, Virginia, did discover the fault. In a deposition to the Nuclear Regulatory Commission, Funkhouser said he had reported the discovery to Herbert Engelman, Jr., the Vepco engineer on the site. Engelman, at a hearing, testified he could not remember being told, and Vepco officials said he never had reported Funkhouser's finding to the company. Vepco's own consultants confirmed the existence of the fault in May 1973, and the company reported it to the NRC at that time. A citizens' group, the North Anna Environmental Coalition, brought the existence of the fault to public attention in August 1973, and then pushed hard for action against Vepco.

The real issue did not appear to be genuinely one of safety, because most geologists involved in the case agreed that the earth at North Anna has been stable for millions of years; NRC criteria require evidence that a site has been stable for at least thirty-five thousand years. Rather, the issue was whether the government will demand the candor and integrity from the operators of nuclear facilities without which maximum protection from terrible hazards cannot possibly be attained. In this case, a regulatory unit called the Atomic Safety and Licensing Board (ASLB) was dealing with a company which already had received three of the nine civil penalties meted out against utilities in the history of the use of nuclear energy, and which, it concluded, had made twelve "material false statements" to the NRC in reference to the geologic fault. "In essence, they were that Vepco said there were no faults at the North Anna site and none were suspected," Hal Willard reported in the *Washington Post*.[32] On September 11, 1975, the ASLB fined Vepco $60,000, the maximum allowed by law, and laid down strict conditions for

Vepco to meet if it is to keep its license for the plant. Vepco claimed it never had "any intent to mislead or deceive anyone." It wanted to make its customers for electricity compensate it for the $60,000 fine, but was ordered by the Virginia Corporation Commission to pay it out of profits.[33]

Financial accountability counts. It makes one put one's money where one's mouth is. Government and industry advocates of nuclear power tell us that a catastrophic reactor accident is wildly improbable. They logically should not, then, seek to limit their financial accountability. If they do, they should expect their assurances to be taken for what they are: words.

In 1954, when the government decided to encourage electric utilities to venture into nuclear power, the companies at first were enthusiastic; but after studying the consequences of a possible major nuclear accident, they and such equipment manufacturers as General Electric and Westinghouse backed off. They feared damage claims that could bankrupt them. Insurers refused then and refuse now to provide full coverage. And so the utilities told Congress they would build nuclear plants only if they first were to be immunized from full liability. Congress responded with the Price-Anderson Act of 1957. Because of this law—a law that legalized financial unaccountability—nuclear power technology exists and is growing today, although this fact "has been artfully concealed from public view so that consideration of the . . . legislation would not trigger public debate as to whether nuclear power was needed and whether its risks were acceptable," Professor Harold P. Green, an expert on the subject at the National Law Center of George Washington University, has said.[34]

The Price-Anderson Act limits liability in a single nuclear accident to $560 million, although a major accident, as shown by the AEC's own studies, could inflict merely on property damages several times as large. "In the end the figure . . . was chosen because it was small enough 'not to frighten this country to death' but probably large enough to protect industry," a Columbia University study said. The decision to limit liability, the study added, "represents a determination that a major share of the costs of an accident should be borne by its victims."[35] In 1965, when it recommended that the Price-Anderson Act be renewed, the Congressional Joint Committee on Atomic Energy "reported that one of the Act's objectives had been achieved —the deterrent to industrial participation in the atomic energy program had been removed by eliminating the threat of large liability claims," Dr. Dixy Lee Ray said while chairman of the AEC.[36]

Under Price-Anderson, the liability of $560 million is shared, with the current maximum exposure of the government being $435 million and of private industry—utility insurers, for the most part—being $135 million. If damages exceed $560 million, the claimants are entitled only to pro-rata shares of what's left of that sum after utilities have deducted their legal fees and losses, if any, at facilities other than the reactor. No further relief is permitted. Nor is there any refuge in homeowners' and other private insurance policies: these bar claims for nuclear accidents. Before payments can be made, the government must certify that the accident was an "extraordinary nuclear occurrence." A victim must accept the judgment of the government and the insurers as to the size of his payment; if he doesn't, his only recourse is to sue and await a court judgment. Up to twenty years may elapse between exposure to radiation and a manifestation of cancer or genetic injury that is detectable; but claims relating to the accident will not be paid if filed more than ten years after it happened. "The government and the insurance companies will surely contest any claims involving cancer that develops after an accident," P. C. Gardette said in a fact sheet that was the primary source for the foregoing summary. Gardette, who prepared the paper for Senator Mike Gravel (D–Alaska), went on to say:

The case of Edward Gleason, a truck dock worker is instructive. In 1963, Gleason handled an unmarked, leaking case of plutonium that was being shipped to a nuclear facility. Four years later, he developed a rare cancer; his hand and then his arm and shoulder were amputated. He sued, but even though plutonium is among the deadliest of radioactive poisons, company insurers contended that Gleason's cancer could not be proven to have resulted from his contamination. Gleason's suit was dismissed in 1970 on statute of limitations grounds, although a settlement was later made. He died of cancer in 1973 at the age of 39.[37]

Referring to 1972, when the maximum liability of the insurers was $95 million, Herbert S. Denenberg, then insurance commissioner of Pennsylvania, has said, "The insurance industry says it's not a safe technology. They will go on the line for $95 million worth, whereas if two planes collide in midair, they may be on the line for half a billion dollars. If it's so safe, why do they insist on limiting their liabilities to $95 million?"[38] The Price-Anderson Act was scheduled to expire in 1977. The utility industry was unwilling to let it do so. Congress in 1974 voted to extend it, but the legislation took a form unacceptable to President Ford who, surprisingly, vetoed it. In December 1975, however, Congress voted to extend the law for ten more years—a victory for well-financed power- and nuclear-industry lobbyists, and a defeat for public-interest forces centered in Critical Mass, a Washington-based citizens' movement to stop nuclear power which is affiliated with Ralph Nader's Public Citizen, Inc.

During floor debate, Senator John O. Pastore (D–R.I.), chairman of the Joint Committee on Atomic Energy, and a foremost proponent of Price-

Anderson, admitted that a single accident at one plant causing damages in excess of $560 million might force a shutdown of *all* nuclear plants. "Do you know what would happen?" he asked. "We would close down the whole caboodle." In the House, Congressman Wayne L. Hays (D–Ohio) summed up the issue in simple terms that ought to be remembered: "I do not know whether it is a safe technology or not, but if it is so safe as these power companies have us believe, then they ought to stand behind it and be willing to pay if lives are lost, and property is destroyed and if human lives are trespassed against."[39]

The great dilemmas created by the radioactive rubbish for which there is no good riddance, by the specter of accidental catastrophe, and by congressionally decreed financial unaccountability for disaster are not the end—and are perhaps only the beginning—of nuclear crapshooting. There remain additional horrendous problems. Dr. Hannes Alfven, the Nobel laureate in physics, has summarized them:

Fission energy is safe only if a number of critical devices work as they should, if a number of people in key positions follow all their instructions, if there is no sabotage, no hijacking of the transports, if no reactor fuel processing plant or repository anywhere in the world is situated in a region of riots or guerrilla activity, and no revolution or war—even a "conventional one"—takes place in these regions. The enormous quantities of extremely dangerous material must not get into the hands of ignorant people or desperados. No acts of God can be permitted.[40]

Plutonium-239, in addition to being at the heart of the nuclear power industry, is at the heart of nuclear weapons; the other essentials for bomb making are available from normal commercial sources. Dr. Theodore B. Taylor, a nuclear physicist who for seven years was a designer of such weapons at Los Alamos, has said that ten pounds of the metal would be enough to destroy the New York financial district. A single breeder reactor, as contemplated for the year 2000, would be producing plutonium-239 at the rate of 350,000 pounds annually.

Taylor has been warning since 1966 that a person without extensive background in nuclear science, working only with publicly available documents and texts, could design a nuclear explosive device. He also has warned that security precautions are inadequate. There is, he says, a consequent continuing danger of nuclear blackmail and destruction. The point was dramatically underscored by "The Plutonium Connection," which John Angier produced in 1975 for the Educational Television Network's "NOVA" science series. As a test, the program challenged a twenty-year-old chemistry student to design a plutonium-based atomic bomb. He was to use only publicly available documents and texts. He was given five weeks. He succeeded, saying, "I was pretty surprised about how easy it is . . . I kept thinking there's got to be more to it than this, but actually there isn't much to it." NOVA flew the report to Stockholm for assessment by Jan Prawitz, a scientist in the Swedish Ministry of Defense. "It's a shocking report even if there is a fair chance that this bomb will not go off," Prawitz said. "On the other hand there is also a fair chance that it will go off but then the yield, the explosion yield would probably be rather low, less than a kiloton and probably less than point one kilotons." An accidental chemical explosion in that range of force destroyed Texas City, Texas, in 1947. On the television program, Taylor said that the same force, if loosed in a crowded urban area, would be enough "to kill fifty or 100,000 people." Prawitz said, "I think that in the hands of a terrorist, and from the point of view of the authorities negotiating with the terrorist, the fact that the bomb might go off is the important thing."[41]

To be able to design an atomic, or fission, bomb that might go off is not necessarily to be able to build one, but there is little solace in this. Taylor explained why in testimony before the Senate Banking Subcommittee on International Finance in July 1974. One person with about ten kilograms of plutonium and a substantial amount of high explosive "could, within several weeks, design *and build* a crude fission bomb," he testified (emphasis supplied). Taylor returned to the point on the NOVA program, when he said "that it would be possible for a small group of people, possibly even one person working alone, to make what I would call a crude fission explosive."[42] Such a weapon would have a yield of approximately one hundred tons of high explosive and would be small enough to be carried in an automobile, the scientist told the subcommittee. The person making it, he said, would need a working knowledge of nuclear physics or engineering, and would have to be skilled with his hands and be willing to run a significant risk of killing himself while constructing the bomb. How many persons actually have the basic facts needed to assemble a nuclear weapon? Between one hundred thousand and 1 million, by estimate of Dr. Edward Teller, the scientist known as the father of the hydrogen bomb.[43]

How good are the security precautions? One disturbing indication that they are not always what they should be came on June 4, 1975, when two professional security men, at a press conference with Ralph Nader in Washington, released a statement charging that "lax security standards" existed at the Three Mile Island (TMI) nuclear power plant near Harrisburg, Pennsylvania. They had advised the management of the problem, only to be told to withdraw their complaints; on refusing to do so, they said, they were laid off. For security guards to "go public" and thereby to jeopardize their futures was extraordinary, but the press widely ignored the affair. The guards, John Darcy and Joseph Shapiro, gave eight examples of "lax security," including falsification of records, hiring of most any "warm body," "insufficient and improper training," faulty electronic-security systems, unauthorized distribution of keys to delivery men by guards "apparently . . . too lazy to unlock and lock the gate, as required, for each delivery," and an unguarded entry to the reactor vessel building.[44]

The stakes being what they are, and the warnings from such as Dr. Taylor and the two guards mounting as they are, pressures are building up for elaborate security arrangements to see to it that plutonium at no stage can come into the hands of a blackmailer, a saboteur, or a deranged person. Nader, who considers the construction of nuclear power plants a form of "technological suicide," and John Gofman, among others, have concluded that in the end this will mean a mini-garrison state. Personnel security checks and classifications will have to be so extensive as to be "reminiscent of the fifties in our country," Nader said on the NOVA program.

In the long run, even a garrison state would be an incomplete guarantor of our security, because for more than twenty years we increasingly have been entrusting it to others. "Only a social psychologist could hope to explain why the possessors of the most terrible weapons in history have sought to spread the necessary industry to produce them," Leonard Beaton has said.[45] Rhetorical overkill? The record makes one wonder. The United States, at the start of the atomic age, sought to limit membership in the nuclear "club." In 1953, President Eisenhower announced his "Atoms for Peace" plan through which we began to share our nuclear technology. In this way, the United States, ironically, opened the doors of "that fearsome club," Senator Stuart Symington (D–Mo.) said in a Senate speech in March 1975. "Atoms for Peace," he said, "has resulted in an expanding web of nuclear cooperation agreements . . . France, Canada, Sweden, the Federal Republic of Germany, Great Britain, and the Soviet Union have joined the United States as exporters of nuclear reactors; and . . . other countries may soon join this group."

The exports proceed with casual accountability that Symington compared to the controls on exports of wheat, soybeans, and carrots. Fred C. Iklé, director of the Arms Control and Disarmament Agency, shares Symington's apprehensions. The transfer of nuclear technology "provides not only the means but also the cover" for a spread of nuclear weaponry, he has said.[46] Canada provided nuclear technology, for peaceful purposes, to India; but on May 18, 1974, India exploded a nuclear device and—"blew open the door to membership in the nuclear club," as Symington put it. Five days later, India signed a pact for "nuclear cooperation" with Argentina, which has been reported to be one of the "several places" Iklé had in mind when he said that an "intent to make nuclear weapons exists . . . even though the capability is not yet there." If Argentina in fact develops a nuclear-weapons capability, Symington asked, "would not her rivals for pre-eminence in South America want the same?"

Only two and a half months after Symington raised that question, West Germany made a multibillion-dollar deal to sell Brazil a complete nuclear industry—including the technology that would enable it to produce nuclear weapons. United States officials "are concerned that the military dominated government has decided to opt for the bomb," Lewis H. Diuguid said in an early report in the *Washington Post*.[47] Then, in an interview with the *Frankfurter Allgemeine Zeitung*, Dr. Iklé said American concern did not stem from the eight huge power reactors, which comprise the bulk of the sales agreement, and which, at least in theory, can be subjected to international safeguards. Rather, he said, the problem "is with the reprocessing equipment which, in treating the spent fuel of reactors, can produce plutonium for weapons. We also have a problem with the uranium-enrichment equipment which can make weapons-grade uranium. American firms have not been permitted to sell this type of equipment abroad." For its civilian pursuits, Iklé said, Brazil has no need for this kind of equipment.[48]

India's explosion stilled the lullaby that less advanced countries could not manage the separation of fissionable material from reactor fuel waste. Now we know, Symington said,

that the production of nuclear material for bomb-making does not require an elaborate commercial re-processing plant; that a country intent upon nuclear weapons development could build its own plant, hire foreign scientists and within a year achieve the desired results. Some nations may already have built such facilities and begun to covertly produce and stockpile nuclear explosive devices. . . .

Only 10 to 20 pounds of plutonium is necessary for making an atomic bomb with the same destructive power as the one dropped on Hiroshima. Yet today, close to 90,000 pounds of plutonium have been produced by commercial nuclear power plants—not including amounts used for nuclear weapons programs of the Big Powers.

Five years from now some half-million pounds of plutonium may be commercially available throughout the world. As the amount of plutonium grows internationally so does the risk of its diversion from peaceful uses to weapons-development.

But India's crashing of the club seemed to exert no restraining influences. At the time, Symington said, plutonium or uranium suitable in quality and quantity to a nuclear weapons program was in the hands of approximately thirty countries exclusive of the now-six nuclear powers—the United States, the Soviet Union, Great Britain, China, France, and India. Of the thirty countries, more than half have refused to ratify the 1968 Treaty on the Non-Proliferation of Nuclear Weapons, the pact which the signatory super-powers drew up to give other nations an incentive, help with peaceful uses of atomic energy, not to develop nuclear weapons.

Despite this volatile situation, the United States proposed in June 1974 —less than a month after the Indian explosion—to sell reactors to two nations that were chronically either at or near war with each other, Egypt and Israel. Along with India, Argentina, and Brazil, Egypt and Israel are, moreover, among the countries that have refused to ratify (although Egypt has signed) the treaty. The proposal drew hostility from Congress and the public. The Ford Administration then insisted upon tougher "safeguard" and security measures; this led to stalemated negotiations. France, which is not a treaty signatory, then made a substitute offer to Egypt. The Union of South Africa is also not a signatory and is believed by disarmament experts to have the will and the technology to produce and test nuclear weapons. "All it needs is weapons-grade uranium," Congressman Les Aspin (D–Wis.) said in April 1975. And, he disclosed, the United States in the last year had provided enough of it—ninety-seven pounds—for seven atomic bombs, with twenty-eight additional pounds, sufficient for two more bombs, scheduled to be shipped. The South Africans bought the uranium for a research reactor with assurances that it would not be diverted.[49]

Even among the eighty-four countries that have signed the treaty there is little coordinated regulation. Purchasers shop around for the best deal, which may be the one with the least stringent safeguards. "Unhappily, shortsighted commercial interests sometimes militate against the application of effective controls," Fred Iklé, the disarmament chief, said. He was re-ported to have been referring especially to France but in some degree also to West Germany.[50] But after each of these countries had sold two reactors to Iran, a treaty signer which, because of its superabundance of oil, would seem to have no pressing need for them, the United States arranged to sell it six more. "This would give her a potential, if she had access to reprocessing facilities, to produce at least eight hundred or one thousand atomic weapons per year," Symington said. The presumption must be that Iran will build nuclear weapons, and that the United States Government itself so presumed, but that we cared more about dollars than about responsibility, no matter all of the pious talk.

Early in 1975, after the United States had imposed an arms embargo on Turkey, that country's defense minister said that it has "plans to manufac-ture atom bombs."[51] The president of Libya, Colonel Muammar al-Qadh-dhafi, has said, "Soon the atom will have no secrets for anybody. Some years ago we could hardly procure a fighter squadron. Tomorrow we will be able to buy an atom bomb and all its parts. The nuclear monopoly is about to be broken."[52] Turkey invaded Cyprus in 1974; Qadhdhafi has openly boasted of supplying weapons to the Irish Republican Army, and has been credited by President Anwar Sadat of Egypt with an unsuccessful plan to torpedo the *Queen Elizabeth 2* during a voyage to Israel in 1974. The Soviet Union agreed in mid-1975 to provide Libya with its first nuclear reactor, but it was too small, experts said, to produce plutonium in weapons quantities.[53]

In the unlikely event that Argentina, say, or South Africa, or maybe Turkey or Libya, should be unable to build or buy nuclear weapons, there is the serious possibility of acquiring ready-made bombs. The United States by 1975 had stockpiled some seven thousand "tactical" nuclear weapons in European countries, and thousands more in other nations and aboard her warships. In his Senate speech, Senator Symington took note of reports, such as those by Walter Pincus, then executive editor of the *New Republic*, that some of these weapons may not be adequately protected against potential nuclear thieves—"especially those who may have the armed capability and intelligence information necessary to overcome security systems protecting these weapons." Symington went on to say:

The mere presence of such large numbers of nuclear weapons around the globe provides an ever-present risk of seizure—not only by criminal groups but host governments themselves. A change in government, or government policy, in a country where U.S. nuclear weapons are stored could lead to a takeover of these weapons. It is no secret that during the Cyprus crisis, . . . the United States has been concerned with the security of its nuclear arsenals in Greece and Turkey.

Security of nuclear weapons is not only a problem for the United States, [but] also for France, Great Britain, the Soviet Union, the People's Republic of China—or any other country which has nuclear arms. Indeed all nations take the risk that the security and potential use of these weapons may be affected by the political stability of the countries that possess or store them.

Symington's concerns about a problem which, he would say later, "could be the most important . . . that the world faces today," were underlined six weeks later, when the Pentagon declassified portions of a report on a "highly secret" inspection and review of the arrangements in Europe for storing nuclear weapons. Two senators had made the inspection, in the spring of 1973, and had requested the declassification: John Pastore, chairman of the Joint Committee on Atomic Energy, and Howard H. Baker, Jr. (R–Tenn.), a committee member. The report "may shock some people," Pastore told the Senate on April 30, 1975. It shows "that nuclear weapons sites appeared to be vulnerable to terrorist attacks; that certain nuclear weapons sites appeared to be particularly vulnerable to surprise attack by Communist forces . . ." Some of the depositories were used during World War II, before there was an atomic capability, "and it just does not do," Pastore said. In order to guarantee security at these sites, some of which are outside of military bases,

what do we do? We have got these tremendous spotlights. Very frankly, we do not tell people what is there, but a man would have to be a fool not to know what is there. . . .

We were told that in many of these places even a small group could actually invade one of these compounds and cause us a lot of trouble. . . .

I say this: Unless we can protect these bombs—and there are about 7,000 nuclear weapons in Europe—we ought to take them out. . . .

Despite recurrent "[deleted]" in the report, it made clear why Pastore had reason to be so disturbed. At one site, nuclear weapons were stored in the basement of an administrative building then under repair. Not until the day of the Pastore-Baker visit was a guard posted, for the first time, at the entrance ramp to the basement facility. The equipment for emergency demolition was "about 25 miles (round trip) from the barracks." At two sites, "individuals have been fired on by guards . . . Inasmuch as in both cases the individuals did not stop after being fired on, it at least suggests the possibility of a hostile 'casing' . . ."

"We nuclear people have made a Faustian bargain with society," Dr. Alvin M. Weinberg, then director of the Oak Ridge National Laboratory, said in 1972. "On the one hand, we offer—in the catalytic burner—an inexhaustible source of energy. . . . But the price that we demand of society for this magical energy source is both a vigilance and a longevity of our social institutions that we are quite unaccustomed to." He went on to say:

We make two demands. The first, which I think is easier to manage, is that we exercise in nuclear technology the very best techniques and that we use people of high expertise and purpose. . . .

The second demand is less clear, and I hope it may prove unnecessary. This is a demand for longevity in human institutions. We have relatively little problem dealing with wastes if we can assume always that there will be intelligent people around to cope with eventualities we have not thought of. . . . Before agriculture, social institutions hardly required the long-lived stability that we now take so much for granted. And the commitment imposed by agriculture was in a sense forever. . . . In the same sense, though on a much more highly sophisticated plane, the knowledge and care that goes into the proper building and operation of nuclear power plants and their subsystems is something we are committed to forever, so long as we find no other practical source of infinite extent.[54]

This candid appraisal helps us to get to the bottom of the matter. Dr. Weinberg acknowledges that the indispensable "longevity of our social institutions" transcends human experience. "No government," he said, "has lasted continuously for 1000 years; only the Catholic Church has survived continuously for 2000 years or so."[55] He found it appropriate to name the "bargain" after Johann Faust, who in medieval legend was said to have sold his soul to Mephistopheles in exchange for money and power. Satan and Faust knew what they were agreeing upon, and why; otherwise the story would have been pointless. Whether the "nuclear people" knew what they were doing is argued even by some of them; whether "society" knew what it was doing is extremely doubtful. There was no referendum—approval was had instead from the Executive branch and Congress. The legitimacy with which Presidents and legislators acted in the name of "society" is not at issue; but it cannot be said that our elected leaders gave or tried to give the electorate any authentic choices in the matter. No President, no chairman of the Congressional Joint Committee on Atomic Energy, and no chairman of the AEC ever came before the American people to say that the bargain —before, during, or after its making—was a Faustian one and to urge, because of its gravity, a debate of all of its implications. Rather, they all have been promoters of nuclear power, tending to drown in happy advocacy rhetoric the issues Dr. Weinberg would define, in 1972, with clarity.

After military ascendancy over atomic energy was broken and civilian control established, and after the AEC began to promote peaceful uses of the atom, the agency continued to have responsibility for safety. These missions—promotion and regulation for safety—were incompatible. Yet the AEC retained both for approximately twenty years, until legislation to abolish the commission became law in 1974. By allowing this, Congress and a succession of Presidents demonstrated a gross indifference to a bureaucratic environment constructed to encourage unaccountability. The public had a right to expect that Congress, if it would not change this environment, at least would try to hold the AEC accountable within it. But Congress had delegated its responsibility to the Joint Committee on Atomic Energy which, most of the time, was the agency's chum rather than its overseer.

In choosing one presidential or legislative candidate over another, the electorate never gave any kind of specific nuclear mandate to any President or Congress. For such a mandate to have been given, the "Faustian bargain" first would have had to have been a consequential political issue. It never was. Neither "the politicians" nor the voters—Democrats or Republicans—ever made it one. It may be that a large bloc of voters would prefer the bliss of ignorance, but it is certain that they did not give truly informed consent. By and large, they lacked the information and the debate which would have made such consent possible; and for that the news media are significantly to blame.

There is a good deal more to it. Dr. Weinberg, as was noted, gave as one of the "demands" of the nuclear managers the need on their part to exercise "the very best techniques" and to use "people of high expertise and purpose." There remain grave questions about how well that demand is being fulfilled. Beyond that, "society" has a reasonable "demand" of its own to make of government administrators: to be always forthcoming, level, and open, so that the modest degree of accountability which is possible may attend them and—in this case—their arcane technology. Conceding recent improvements, the AEC, during most of its life, has not hesitated to serve its public relations interests by invoking indefensible secrecy and suppression in the most vital safety matters. Often, the AEC has yielded key papers only when forced to do so in litigation brought by sometimes impecunious public-interest groups.

Public hearings held by administrative agencies fulfill their proclaimed purpose when they serve to elicit information and views which then are taken fairly into account by officials whose minds were not made up beforehand. Commonly, however, public hearings are a fake—a ritual to be gone through in order to present a facade of accountability. For fifteen months, Dr. Steven Ebbin, a political scientist, and Dr. Raphael Kasper, a nuclear engineer, looked into the kind of public hearings held by the AEC. In a report on their study, which was financed by the National Science Foundation, they said:

to the extent that the AEC hearing process is designed to be an adequate and fair forum for the expeditious public consideration of an application to construct or operate a nuclear plant, it is a failure; to the extent that it is designed to resolve scientific or technological questions or issues, it is a failure; to the extent that it is expected to satisfy the legitimate needs of applicants, proponents or opponents by demonstrating the validity or lack of validity of their contentions, it is a failure. . . . the only consensus among all of the parties to the proceedings appeared to be a general evaluation that the whole process as it now stands is nothing more than a charade, the outcome of which is, for all intents and purposes, predetermined.[56]

Ebbin and Kasper, who took no pro or con stand on nuclear power, found nonetheless that "the licensing process is one which is geared to the promotion of nuclear power plants. . . . it is evident to us that the decision to build remains one that has already been made by the time citizens are afforded an opportunity to express their views on the matter." They had harsh words for certain citizen groups—not including the Union of Concerned Scientists, which was among the citizen organizations for which they expressed high regard—that had displayed "strong evidence . . . of know-nothingism, blind anti-technology and anti-government sentiments, pessimism and doom forecasting." But their indictment of unaccountability in those paid by all of us to serve all of us was much more disturbing: "We have found that despite lip service paid to citizen participation in governmental decision-making, agency arrogance, expert elitism, stacked-deck proceedings and the consigning of citizens to helplessness before the steamroller of big government is more the rule rather than the exception."[57]

The two "demands"—Alvin Weinberg's for "the very best techniques," the present authors' for openness—fused in 1972, when the AEC held an unprecedented public hearing on a matter in which the possibility of catastrophe was central, thus opening itself to an unprecedented accounting.

The hearing concerned the design of emergency core cooling systems (ECCS) for commercial reactors which, it will be recalled, are needed to prevent overheating, melting, and release of radiation from uranium fuel cores. The background was this: The AEC's criteria for an acceptable system were considered too stringent by manufacturers and by the agency's licensing division. The same criteria were considered too lenient by the Union of Concerned Scientists (UCS) and its allies (who would come to be designated intervenors) as well as by experts within the AEC itself. In addition, the safety of the emergency systems was being questioned in hearings at local sites chosen for reactors. Finally, the commission agreed to hold a single, consolidated national hearing, starting in January 1972. For the first time, the AEC agreed to make its own reactor safety experts available for questioning. But the agency refused to permit the intervenors either to subpoena agency personnel or documents, or to examine underlying data in the possession of the AEC or equipment manufacturers. And in written instructions for its technical witnesses that came into the hands of the intervenors by chance, the AEC said, "Never disagree with established policy."[58] Even so, the UCS's Henry Kendall and Daniel Ford would say later, the hearing provided "an unparalleled opportunity to see how this large agency . . . has dealt with a most critical public safety issue."[59] It did indeed. Limited though they may have been, the disclosures—in testimony, and in sixty internal papers which the AEC released in February 1972, to stave off a threatened Freedom of Information Act lawsuit—are profoundly troubling. Some of them, at least, merit a close look:

• The AEC had licensed nuclear power plants without first actually testing their emergency core cooling systems; rather, it will be recalled, the AEC relied on computerized mathematical models intended to evaluate the effects of a loss of coolant. In the fall of 1970, Aerojet Nuclear Company, the AEC's safety contractor, ran a series of tests with a small (nine-inch-diameter) reactor of the pressurized-water type. The emergency cooling systems failed; so did the mathematical models.

• Spurred by such signs of trouble, the AEC's regulatory staff formed a task force to review the state of the art. In turn, the task force, headed by Dr. Stephen Hanauer, director of the Office of Technical Advisor, retained Aerojet Nuclear as its chief consultant. In a two-volume report, the company found that in several critical areas the ability to predict what would happen during a loss-of-coolant accident was simply "beyond the present capability of engineering science."[60] Five months later, in September 1971, Hanauer told colleagues in a memo that publication of a paper summarizing the two volumes had been "temporarily forestalled" but not finally dealt with. "The present goal should be a paper that can be published without hurting the A.E.C. and without inciting a cause celebre for squelching a paper because of technical dissent," he said.[61] The Hanauer memo was among hundreds which were examined by David Burnham of the *New York Times*. He concluded that AEC officials seemed to be "more concerned about the possible public relations impact of safety studies than the actual safety of reactors," and that during the decade in which the memos were written, starting in 1964, "the commission has repeatedly sought to suppress studies by its own scientists that found nuclear reactors were more dangerous than officially acknowledged or that raised questions about reactor safety devices."[62]

• About a year after receiving the Aerojet Nuclear report, Hanauer was asked at the hearings if he had read it. "I leafed through it," he replied. "I did not read it." Had he "dismissed it as not helpful?" "It did not seem to me to help any," he said.[63]

• A later Aerojet general report divided the knowledge or capability needed for effective operation of emergency core cooling systems in pressurized-water reactors into twenty-nine subject areas. In seven areas, the report said, techniques to deal with problems that might arise did not exist. In the remaining twenty-two, in the summation of Kendall and Ford, the methodology was "incomplete, unverified, inadequate, imprecise, or preliminary."[64] Aerojet gave a rating of very high urgency to eight of the areas and of high urgency to fifteen.

The company gave the report to the AEC's Division of Reactor Development and Technology in August 1971. One might think that the division, headed by Milton Shaw, would have passed it along promptly to the AEC regulatory staff. But the staff saw the report for the first time seven months later, in March 1972, "when it was handed to them by the Intervenors, who had received an unsolicited copy," Kendall and Ford said.[65]

• The commission's National Reactor Testing Station in Idaho Falls,

Idaho, was submitting monthly reports to Shaw's division. Was he "censoring" the reports? he was asked at the hearing. "Censoring?" Shaw responded. "If you want to use that terminology in the sense I think you are using it, yes."[66] The next day, J. Curtis Haire, general manager of the Idaho safety program, was asked what the motive might be for "censoring." "Well," Haire replied, "I believe that R.D.T. [Shaw's division] is trying to avoid the problems or burden, if you will, of having to spend a lot of time answering public inquiries that are addressed to Congress and referred to them. . . . on general questions of nuclear safety." A few months later, Haire was relieved of his duties in the AEC's safety research program.[67]

• In a cover letter accompanying a report by his division in November 1971, Shaw termed a major loss-of-coolant accident "extremely unlikely." He also said that should such an accident occur, existing emergency core cooling systems "are expected to mitigate the consequences . . ." He went on to say, with emphasis supplied:

However, present experimental data and analysis techniques are not now sufficient to provide the degree of ECC [emergency core cooling] *assurance deemed necessary by the AEC.* It is for this reason that a major emphasis is on the performance of ECC systems. . . .

As reactor designs and their operating characteristics changed, the analysis methods were "patched up," rather than redeveloped, with the net result that overall, existing methods are inefficient, inflexible, and do not adequately represent the physical phenomena intended.[68]

• In June 1971, the AEC had formally published, in the *Federal Register*, so-called Interim Acceptance Criteria, which codified existing informal standards for emergency cooling systems. The *Register* notice did not acknowledge a division in the regulatory staff as to whether the criteria could provide sufficient assurance for a clear basis for licensing. They couldn't, according to a memo prepared by Dr. Morris Rosen, who from the start had been in charge of analyzing emergency cooling systems, and his deputy, Robert J. Colmar. The memo was dated June 1, 1971—four weeks before the *Federal Register* notice appeared.

• In December 1971—a few weeks before the year-long hearing began—William Cottrell, director of the Nuclear Safety Program at Oak Ridge National Laboratory, wrote a letter to L. Manning Muntzing, the AEC's director of regulation. "To summarize what follows herein," Cottrell said, "we are not certain that the Interim Criteria for ECCS adopted by the AEC will, as stated in the *Federal Register* 'provide reasonable assurance that such systems will be effective in the unlikely event of a loss-of-coolant accident.' " This was inconsistent with the written testimony the regulatory staff would file almost on the eve of the hearing, on December 28, in which the conclusion was that "the conservatism in today's criteria and today's evaluation models suffice to provide reasonable assurance of the safety of today's reactors." Muntzing was spared any immediate inconvenience when he got a phone call from a superior of Cottrell who claimed the letter was a "draft" and unrepresentative of the views of the laboratory's personnel and who asked that the "draft" be returned to Oak Ridge. At the hearing, Cottrell's testimony showed the letter to have been neither a "draft" nor unrepresentative of the views of his Oak Ridge colleagues.[69]

• Like the *Federal Register* notice six months earlier, the written testimony of the regulatory staff gave no indication of substantial and serious internal disagreement. Morris Rosen, called as a witness at the hearing, testified that the staff lacked "knowledge sufficiently adequate to make licensing decisions for the approximately 100 reactors now under construction," but was persisting despite this in basically disregarding the advice of many—or "more likely a majority"—of the knowledgeable persons available to it for consultation.[70]

• Under cross-examination, Stephen Hanauer, who headed the AEC task force to review the state of the art of emergency core cooling systems, said that the three most knowledgable members of the commission's "watchdog" Advisory Committee on Reactor Safety had "serious reservations about the effectiveness of ECCS."[71]

• Alvin Weinberg, the director of the Oak Ridge National Laboratory, which was not consulted by the AEC about the Interim Criteria, wrote AEC chairman James Schlesinger in February 1972 that he had a "basic distrust" of the mathematical models, or computer codes, that supposedly ensured the safe performance of the ECCS. Similar distrust was expressed in testimony by Rosen and by witnesses from Oak Ridge and Aerojet Nuclear.

• In a telegram to Schlesinger and Muntzing, the director of regulation, C. M. Rice, president of Acrojet, asked that witnesses from his firm be allowed to cross-examine manufacturers' witnesses about their testimony on the AEC's reactor safety research and development program. The appeal was turned down.

The foregoing evidence, a mere sampling of the whole, shows that the AEC constructed a facade of assurances of reactor safety, this being essential if dependence on nuclear power were to grow, but that behind the facade the AEC has engaged in suppression, manipulation, and other familiar techniques of cover-up. Its response to the disclosures included: cutbacks of numerous research programs into reactor safety, although its support of such programs was, at least in the view of such critics as Kendall and Ford, already inadequate; assurances from chairman Schlesinger that there "would be no threat whatever to public health or safety"; and an announcement by the AEC that it intended to license seventeen nuclear power plants to go to full-power operation by February 1973.[72]

In India in the third century B.C., according to an envoy from the Selucidian dynasty, Megasthenes, the powerful Brahman caste monopolized science. "Megasthenes also claimed that Indian scientists were exempt from forced labor and met annually in a great conclave to advise the state on impending droughts, public health, and other matters of import," Thomas W. Africa says in *Science and the State in Greece and Rome.*[73] But these scientists were held accountable, according to the Greek historian Diodorus Siculus. A sage, he said, was permitted three errors before he was banished to a "life of silence."[74]

The nuclear sages—scientific, political, industrial—made one transcendent error: attempting to claim for this generation what John Gofman termed "the arrogance of possibly compromising the earth as an habitable place for this and essentially all future generations."[75] Redemption lies not in silence for them but in an end to silence for the citizen. With that there would be hope that nuclear power ultimately would be phased out, for that is what accountability would require, and that more conservation and alternative power sources be phased in, for that is what accountability also would require.

The government is insufficiently disposed to do this, as shown by a close analysis by Congressman Charles A. Vanik (D–Ohio) of the budget of $3,747,308,000 proposed by the Ford administration for the Energy Research and Development Administration in fiscal 1976:

One. The largest item in the Agency's budget has nothing to do with energy research. Exactly 30 percent of the Agency's funds will be spent for national security.

Two. Direct research and development into nonnuclear energy forms—coal, solar, geothermal—account for a little over one-tenth of the Agency's total budget.

Three. Less than one percent of the budget will be devoted to finding ways to use energy more efficiently.

Four. Excluding administrative costs, over 78 percent of the ERDA budget is related directly to research and development of various applications of nuclear energy.

Five. Exploring the profound issues of nuclear safety will account for only a little over five percent . . .

Six. Solar energy research accounts for only a little over one percent of the total . . ."[76]

The allocation for solar power is only $57 million, although it is, the National Science Foundation (NSF) and the National Aeronautics and

Space Administration said in a report in 1972, "an inexhaustible source of enormous amounts of clean energy," one which poses "no technical barriers to wide application to meet U.S. needs." Vanik, in an article in *Environmental Action,* recalled a 1973 report by a panel of NSF experts who suggested two energy budgets, one "accelerated" and the other "minimal." The $57 million for solar power in the ERDA budget "does not even meet the 'minimum' suggested budget," the congressman said. "In fact, it falls over $10 million short."

The ERDA budget also provides only $28 million for research into geothermal power, which draws on the heat of the earth, and the steam it produces, to generate electricity. The Cornell Workshop on Environment and Energy said in 1972 that with the so-called hot rock technology—in which a fracturing of rock, at extreme depths, between two wells enables a water-steam cycle to proceed unassisted—"geothermal energy alone is capable of meeting all American power requirements for several centuries."[77]

There is also wind power, another frequently disregarded source, and one which, like solar energy, is not susceptible to monopolization by oil companies. In the Midwest, farm windmills have been making a comeback as power sources. In Maine, the Office of Energy Resources was planning development of a wood alcohol (methanol) industry that would convert some of the state's abundant timberlands—including bark, pine needles, leaves, and stumps—into this clean-burning fuel for automobiles and home heating. Methanol, which can be produced from any cellulose-based material, including garbage and manure, was used as fuel in Germany and Japan in World War II and in the United States in the last century.[78]

Monfort of Colorado, the world's largest feedlot operator, plans to convert manure into 4 million cubic feet of methane daily; the gas can be captured from other sources, including coal mines.[79] Paris for many years has burned its wastes for steam heating. The Congressional Research Service says that in the year 2020, bioconversion for the production of natural gas—through the cultivation of algae or floating plants on about 5 percent of the country's land area—could provide *all* of this fuel that we then would be needing.[80] Ocean tides and even ocean waves are potential power sources.

If we pass over or neglect such alternatives, if we fail seriously to practice conservation, if we do not start to dismantle the perpetual-danger machine built by the scientific-political-industrial-nuclear complex, we will be the most unaccountable generation in the history of mankind. Our legacy, enduring through eternity, will be radioactive poisons. This would be, says E. F. Schumacher, "a transgression against life itself, a transgression infinitely more serious than any crime ever perpetuated by man. The idea that a civilisation should sustain itself on the basis of such a transgression is an ethical, spiritual, and metaphysical monstrosity. It means conducting the economic affairs of man as if people really did not matter at all."[81] If rulers had to be accountable, people *would* matter.

"The seas we shan't replace," Noël Mostert warns in *Supership*. It is a measure not only of his reporting and eloquence, but also of a generalized ignorance of the consequences of advancing technology, that such a truism takes on a stirring power. "During the past two decades," Mostert tells us, "we have undone much of the structural gift of the eons; by the end of this very decade we might have destroyed it altogether; and so have brought to extinction the only truly eternal feature of this planet."[1]

The principal instrument of this depradation is of course the supertanker. The possibility that it may extinguish the seas was remote from the considerations of those who brought it into being. They were pursuing routine concerns. This is succinctly shown in a newspaper article that touched upon the evolution of the relatively small (54,000 deadweight tons) *Tina Onassis*:

The ship was built in Germany, mortgaged in the United States, insured in London, financially controlled from Monaco and manned by Greeks. It flew the flag of Liberia.[2]

Routine concerns regularly have been the midwives for other momentous technologies. Charles Frankel emphasized this in 1955, when he cited the impact of television. "It has affected education and home life, changed the patterns of congressional behavior and political discussion, and fundamentally altered, for better or worse, the operating conditions and purposes of traditional political institutions," he said. "But the decisions on how to use television, and how not to use it, have been made almost entirely by men whose area of responsibility is very narrow, and who have to think about only a very few, selected values."[3]

When supertankers inflict massive damage on the seas, the shores, marine life, and bird life, as they regularly do, there is minimal accountability. When they are built, mortgaged, controlled, manned, and chartered like the *Tina Onassis*, how could it be otherwise? Mostert taught this lesson stunningly, and subsequent events do not give us much of a chance to forget it. On August 9, 1974, for example, the *Metula*, a Shell Oil supertanker, ran aground in the easternmost Strait of Magellan close to the coast of Chile. An estimated fifty thousand tons of oil were spilled. Approximately forty miles of coastline were spoiled. Marine life in two tidal estuaries was destroyed. The fisheries of the Straits of Magellan were ruined for at least a year. As many as four thousand birds—mostly penguins—were killed. According to a scientist who led a study at the site soon after the spill, adverse effects will be felt "for another decade."[4] In a study published a year after the spill, the Chilean Patagonian Institute said that the slick was continuing to damage animal and plant marine life, and bird life on the northern coast of Tierra del Fuego island.[5] The *Metula*'s ranked as the second-largest oil spill in history until January 29, 1975, when the Danish supertanker *Jakob Maersk* struck a sandbar off the coast of Portugal, exploded, and burned, and leaked or spilled 28 million gallons of oil. At least twenty miles of coastline were despoiled.

The unaccountability of supertankers begins with their staggering dimensions, which, Mostert tells us, are "one of the technological audacities of the century." At the end of World War II, the largest tankers had a deadweight of 18,000 tons. By 1956, tankers of 45,000 tons, of which the *Tina Onassis* was one, were at sea; in the early 1960s, 100,000; in 1968, 326,000; in 1972, 372,000; and in 1973, 476,000. As of 1974, when *Supership* was published, there were plans for a 1-million-ton supertanker, large enough, Mostert says, to accommodate in one of her five major tanks "[a]lmost any of the great cathedrals of western Europe." Even a ship of between 200,000 and 400,000 tons, designated a VLCC (Very Large Crude Carrier), must be guided and steered from a bridge set nearly a quarter-mile from the bow and one hundred feet above the water. A man must walk one hundred and fifty feet from port to starboard to see what is happening on the other side.

"It takes at least three miles and twenty-one to twenty-two minutes to stop a 250,000 tonner doing sixteen knots," Mostert says. The international rules of the road "have served shipping well until now but for supertankers they have proven to be often impracticable or downright dangerous." The riding lights, intended to identify a ship and its course at night, "have caused confusion, which can be fatal. Many instances have been reported of smaller ships trying to steer *between* the forward and after lights of a supertanker, on the understandable assumption that the great distance between them indicated two different ships."[6] Mostert provides yet other measures of supertankers to enable us to grasp why oil spills are inevitable and why the consequences are so ominous:

The size of supertankers places such distance between their sailors and the sea that tanker crews may not even be aware that they have run down a smaller vessel. The inexplicable loss of trawlers and coasters has sometimes been attributed to these ships.[7]

. . . surveys are essential to detect hull or tank damage or faults. . . . A 25,000 ton tanker has about 400,000 square feet of plating in her tanks. A 350,000 tonner has around 3 million, and the tanks themselves may be 100 feet deep. F.N. Boylan, deputy chief surveyor of Lloyd's Register of Shipping, and F.H. Atkinson, senior principal ship surveyor, have described the survey task on a VLCC as being "roughly equivalent to climbing Mount Everest and still having another 6,000 feet to go."[8]

The technology that made such size possible, while audacious, proved to be often unsound. "The long hulls had shown a great deal less than their estimated strength," Mostert says. "They had a propensity to buckle and crack under certain pressures, sometimes even in dock or on the slipway while still under construction. . . . A number of tankers simply tore apart in heavy seas . . ."[9] All of this reflected haste in innovation, which was aggravated by haste in workmanship. Thus, the Japanese Ministry of Transport, whose inspectors examined Japanese-built superships whenever they returned to Japan for overhaul, "found a high rate of defective workmanship in vessels built between 1962 and 1969, which were the years of most intensive supertanker production. Some ships had been sailing with vital parts of their structure not welded at all, or imperfectly welded. A 58,000-ton tanker built in 1964 had four ribs without any welding whatsoever. A 60,000 tonner built in 1967 had hull cracks caused by faulty welding."[10]

The problems created by quantum leaps in size, hurried innovation, and sloppy workmanship were enlarged by dangerous shortcuts in both operation and design. The waters off the Cape of Good Hope, to take a case in point, are exceedingly dangerous—so much so that since 1967, when the closing of the Suez Canal caused oil ships to be rerouted between the Persian Gulf and Europe, "hundreds of tankers have been smashed, disabled, or lost," Mostert says. "Possibly the most astonishing aspect of all this is that, during the southern winter, every loaded tanker rounding the Cape is loaded deeper than was formerly thought safe for those waters. . . . If she is too heavily loaded for winter seas, the effort of countering them can strain a vessel's plates and frames and spring leaks, so that she can start sinking from the damage."[11] Actually, storms cause lesser fears among the crews of VLCCs than their overlarge oil tanks, "the seat of frightening and still incompletely understood forces when empty. Three 200,000 tonners were torn by tank explosions so severe that their long decks rolled back as though opened like cans of sardines. . . . Supertankers thus altered the maritime scale in disaster to the same outlandish degree that they have affected it in everything else."[12]

Gulf Oil–Ludwig 326,000 tonners can crash-stop and manuever as well as much smaller tankers, because they are equipped with twin rudders and twin screws. But they are rarities. Because of "penny-pinching," almost all VLCCs have been built with a single rudder and a single screw, Mostert says. This is "on the face of it ludicrous: relatively low drag allows supertankers to roll easily through the water, so the single-screw system is adequate for thrust, but it is wholly inadequate for emergencies, and hopeless as a means of braking the considerable momentum of the ship in a hurry."[13] Similarly, in most VLCCs, prudence dictated but penny-pinching denied a second boiler and an emergency source of power capable of running both engines and electrical plant if steam was lost.[14]

Mostert's conclusion, meticulously documented, persuasive, and frightening, is that "the world's seas cannot be expected to survive the oil ships if they continue to be built to and operated and sailed by the sort of standards that now largely prevail. At any rate, what is left of the seas by the time they have done with them might not be worth the having. As this basis of management is transferred to chemical ships, the outlook becomes even bleaker."[15]

If some system of responsibility is to be established in time to be useful, it somehow must shatter the international legal milieu in which technological unaccountability flourishes. A large proportion of the world's tankers are registered in countries which are attractive for this purpose because their quintessential appeal is, go and sin some more. These countries, including Liberia, Panama, Costa Rica, Honduras, Lebanon, and Cyprus, offer so-called flags of convenience. The master of a ship flying such a flag who dumps oil at sea and continues into international waters is subject to the penalties only of the nonseafaring nation in which the ship is registered and which it is unlikely ever to visit. Putting it gently, Mostert says the master "would not feel unduly perturbed about the punitive consequences at his home port, whose conscience and standards on these matters might be questionable..."[16]

After examining Liberia's recent record, Mostert said, "it often seems to make little difference aboard a Liberian ship whether it has the newest equipment or the oldest; too often those in charge of an ultramodern bridge don't know how to use what's there, or don't know how to repair anything that breaks down, or, worse, don't even bother to report a fault when they get to port."[17] It is, then, not to be wondered that Liberian ships have been involved in most of the major oil spillage calamities, including the *Ocean Eagle*, which after a wreck fouled the beaches of San Juan, Puerto Rico, in 1967, and the *Juliana*, which in 1971 hit a breakwater, broke in two, and gave Japan its worst oil spill. In October 1970, Mostert recalls,

two fully laden supertankers, the 77,648-ton *Pacific Glory*, Chinese owned, and the 95,445-ton *Allegro*, Greek owned, both flying the Liberian flag, and between them carrying 170,000 tons of crude oil, ran into each other off the Isle of Wight. The *Pacific Glory* suffered a violent explosion and was burned out; fourteen of her crew died. Most of the oil in their tanks fortunately remained intact. The third officers of both ships were on watch at the time; the *Allegro's* third officer had no certificate whatsoever. Two of her engineers, Greek as well, had no certificates either. Two of *Pacific Glory's* engineers also had no certificates.[18]

It was a Liberian tanker, the 120,000-ton *Torrey Canyon*, that first dramatized for most of us, in 1967, the environmental threat of supertankers. Fully laden, it ran onto the rocks of the Scilly Isles, with devastating impact on the adjacent coasts of the English Channel. The ship's master had an outstanding reputation and record as a seaman, but Mostert points out, had been aboard for 366 days.

As the British and French governments discovered when they tried to hold someone responsible for the accident, the task of trying to pin down a flag of convenience ship within any accessible range of legal jurisdiction is well-nigh impossible. The *Torrey Canyon* was owned by the Barracuda Tanker Corporation, a financial offshoot of the Union Oil Company of California, which leased the ship and had, in turn, subleased it to British Petroleum Trading Limited, which was a subsidiary of the British Petroleum Company. The ship, built in the United States, and rebuilt in Japan, was registered in Liberia, insured in London, and crewed by Italians. For an international lawyer any suit involving such a vessel must, one assumes, be the sort of stuff of which dreams of eternal litigation are made.[19]

In this case, as it happened, the British and French "pretended they weren't looking and, when one of *Torrey Canyon's* sister ships, the *Lake Palourde*, ambled into the first port where the law was held to be firm, they pounced and had her arrested until her insurers, the only accessible body with responsibility, paid up $7,500,000 as a settlement for damage."[20]

The *Lake Palourde* aberration aside, the situation becomes more depressing when it is realized that the Soviet Union now has one of the largest of the merchant navies. It is the state itself that owns the ships. If a complaint is made that one of them has dumped oil in the sea during bilge and ballast operations, would the state, Mostert asks, "flagellate itself? The same might be asked of any of the many national fleets that have arisen in recent years and whose accountability is only to themselves."[21]

An American, British, or Scandanavian seaman whose errors result in a mishap knows that he must account for them to a formal board of inquiry and that he could face serious consequences. He also knows, Mostert says, that the inquiry "will be impartial, and incorruptible." Admittedly, the highest standards do not guarantee against accidents, but, as the author points out, "they create a better climate of vigilance and responsibility, and responsibility itself is ensured by accountability." But the flags of convenience

have advanced by their casual standards on even the most modern of ships a disrespect and indifference to a ship and the ways of the sea whose influence has become widespread, mainly by creating a body of seamen which is well on its way to being the largest in the world and whose view of the sea and ships is entirely that of the vessels in which they have trained and served. They have brought the credentials of the sea into disrepute by making them easily available through minimum standards or modest purchase, or even not necessary at all. By removing themselves from accountability, they have virtually suspended law upon the sea, and diminished the oldest collaboration and responsibility in the world.[22]

The flags-of-convenience fleets continue to grow. How much accountability there is to be, if any, remains a national concern. There is no visible way to compel the flags-of-convenience nations to cede their sovereignty in this matter to anyone. "It is quite impossible to visualize any sort of international authority with real teeth which in the immediate or even foreseeable future would have the means and administration and executive power to control the seas," Mostert says. This conclusion is the more disheartening because the seas are bearing not only unaccountable supertankers, but ships of growing size which carry poisonous chemicals and liquefied natural gas. Mostert says:

Chemical tankers used to be small ships, usually in the 500 to 1,000 ton range, gross, but they already are up to 24,000 tons. The products they carry vary in danger from being highly inflammable to being highly toxic to touch and inhale. Defoliants for Vietnam were carried in such vessels. In February 1971, an American chemical carrier, the 21,000-ton *V.A. Fogg* vanished, presumably from an explosion; only small pieces of wreckage were found. The ignorance about the full effects of crude oil dumped in the sea must be small change against our ignorance of what such chemicals can do if deposited in the mainstream flow of a major current such as the Gulf Stream—indeed, if deposited *anywhere*. At a maritime symposium . . . it was admitted that there were no laws to stop chemical tankers from dumping their slops into the sea, as doubtless they do when they clean their tanks.[23]

In 1970 two tankers collided in San Francisco Bay. Had one of them been a liquefied natural gas (LNG) tanker, "the impact might have released a cloud of combustible gas vapor and engulfed several square miles of San Francisco in flames," Timothy M. Ingram, a contributing editor of the *Washington Monthly*, has said.[24] There were in 1974 fewer than thirty LNG tankers on the seas, but by 1985 between two hundred and two hundred and fifty are expected to be in service. Each carries 75,000 cubic meters of LNG, which is the energy equivalent of the oil carried by a 250,000- to 300,000-ton supertanker, and which is one-sixth-hundredth the volume taken up by the gas in its normal state. The gas is converted into LNG by refrigerating plants and then put into ship's tanks where it is preserved at minus 160 degrees centigrade. At this extremely low temperature, LNG, were it to escape in large amounts, "would make the hull of the ship so brittle that any damage already suffered might be swiftly enlarged by cold-induced cracks and fractures, perhaps leading to the cracking and breaking of other tanks," which is "an entirely new factor" in collisions and shipwrecks, Noël Mostert says.[25] Still more awful to contemplate is a collision or accident in which large amounts of LNG would spill onto the sea and, after freezing it, would evaporate into a lethal cloud close to the surface. "The gas is lighter than air, and most experiments so far suggest that it would quickly disperse," Mostert says. "Tests carried out in the United States indicated that a spillage of one large tank from one of these ships occurring off Staten Island could result in a gas cloud extending from seven to twelve miles from the point of collision. It would, it was said, swiftly disperse. On a subzero windless day? Vagueness, however, is an endemic factor in explanations of these matters."[26]

Ingram said the cloud "could drift into cities, ships, or whatever else was in the vicinity. . . . Then, with the slightest spark, the cloud could create a holocaust equivalent to the burning of 100 *Hindenburgs.*" He recalled what happened in Cleveland on October 20, 1944, when, after three successful years of operation, one of the four storage tanks in the country's first successful LNG plant

suddenly ruptured, spewing forth 1.2 million gallons of LNG (equivalent to about 100 million cubic feet of gas). It was ignited, possibly by a cigarette, and burning LNG poured into the streets and sewers. Once in the confined space of the sewer pipes, the quickly vaporizing, burning liquid gas exploded with tremendous force. . . . When it was all over, 133 people were dead, 300 injured; 10 industrial plants, 80 houses, and 200 automobiles were seriously damaged, and the city sewer system over an area of more than 30 acres was destroyed.

Ingram went to Boston harbor, which was the first to become experienced in handling LNG shipments, to see firsthand how it's done. Lieutenant David Blomberg of the Coast Guard, which checks the safety equipment of the ships, told him, "The last two LPG ships in here were shitboxes. . . . One didn't even have the gas detector system turned on. It was disconnected. It hadn't been properly set, and they were getting a continuous alarm on it, and had just shut it off entirely. They didn't have a repair manual for it, didn't know how to fix it, and couldn't have cared less." Ingram learned that crew members of the French tanker *Descartes* had concealed cracks in her tank membranes in a manner intended to deceive Coast Guard inspectors. He found that no one really is certain how to fight an LNG fire. While the nuclear establishment hurried to build power plants with untested emergency core cooling systems and without knowing how to deal with long-lived radioactive poisons, the LNG establishment was investing some $1 million to study the hazards—but only, Ingram said, "after the LNG boom is already under way." In the end, he said, "the hardest question to answer is who should be responsible for heading off the holocaust. All along the line, officials shuffle their feet when asked this question and point at the man down the hall."[27]

Like the oil supertankers, the LNG supertankers and the chemical ships fly flags of convenience and are being sailed, Mostert says, "by unskilled or uncaring men whose minimal terms of employment are part of the basis of a profit for the shipowners and operators gross beyond any previous calculation of avarice." In sum, what we have is a picture of almost unrelieved grimness, of accountability for the preservation of the infinitely precious oceans being captured and drowned by an undertow of cosmically reckless technology. While Mostert confines himself to the threat to the seas, his advice has broad implications for our approaches to other great dilemmas of unleashed technology:

If a battle is to be fought . . . it must be fought with tankers; if anything is achieved, the benefits will transfer as a matter of course to the other vessels. For the moment, therefore, it is the tankers that must engage our fullest interest . . . it is they that principally distribute pollution and destruction out upon the deep sea; and there is no law on earth at present that can be effective against them there. All that we can do is to hedge them with accountability: that is, ensure that those men who profit from them should be held accountable for making these ships as fail-safe as possible; that they should also be held accountable for the health and standards and efficiency of their crews; and that they should be held accountable for every drop of oil that goes on board. If we hold them to account for these things, we will still have no guarantee of absolutely clean seas, because ordinary merchantmen will still be dumping their bilges where they wish, but the main offenders will be under a program of chastisement, and the difference will bring us closer to survival of the oceans than to the possibility of their dying.[28]

Mostert would not permit any more supertankers to be built without twin screws, a stronger rudder system, and a major auxiliary boiler capable of handling the ship's entire electrical and automatic system as well as its engines. "If airline pilots are compelled to undergo health examinations, why not the masters of supertankers?" Mostert asks. "The state of health of [the captain] of the *Torrey Canyon* alone would seem to have made that an indisputable requirement. Nor should any master take command of a super-ship without intensive simulator training of the airline sort, which is now provided at Delft; and, in model ships, in France."[29]

Just as we cannot wait for some international authority to make multinational corporations accountable, we also cannot wait for some such authority to save the sea and the environment. "Only ruthless arbitrary unilateral action can do that," Mostert says. "Nothing else can possibly be effective." That means that a relatively few nations—the United States, Canada, Japan, and the countries of Europe—have but to require tankers entering their waters to observe rigorous safety and operational standards, and to penalize or even bar those that may not.[30]

"In no other age have men lived with so dizzying a sense of change, or seen their basic material and social environment being made over, and made over again, so steadily," the philosopher Charles Frankel said in 1955. He viewed technological change as "the fundamental dynamic element in modern society," as one of those "tidal movements such as wars, the business cycle, and international disorganization." He also viewed it as profoundly unaccountable. "The decision as to when, where, and how to introduce a technological change is a *social* decision, affecting an extraordinary variety of values," he said. And yet the engineers and industrialists who make such decisions, who assert enormous power over the quality and conditions of our lives, do so "in something very close to a social vacuum." Professor Frankel pointed out that

the traditional liberal mechanisms of public consultation and consent, on which the authority for such basic decisions has been supposed to rest, have next to no influence here. From the point of view of most of us these decisions just seem to happen; and it is one reason why so many ordinary men and women have come to feel that they are being manipulated by invisible persons whom they do not know and cannot control.[1]

Some years later, Mrs. T. A. Conger of Athens, Georgia, wrote a letter to *Life* magazine to tell how an unseen person in a military aircraft had suddenly and roughly manipulated her: "Last spring as I was riding in the upper reaches of Yosemite Valley, I was nearly thrown from my mount because of a sonic boom. The horse jumped, the birds stopped singing and I was sick at heart. If this is progress, then progress be damned." Mrs. Conger was not, apparently, using the primary dictionary definition of "progress," which is simply the action of moving forward or onward. One can move forward into the path of a car and onward to the morgue. Instead, as do most of us, she implicitly was imparting to "progress" a subordinate definition, that of a gradual betterment. On that basis, she was protesting the notion that "progress" possibly could embrace a machine that, flying at supersonic speeds, would send down a boom heard and felt at every point on its flight path.

The distinction between the primary and subordinate definitions deserves attention, because it has been the widespread, persistent, and generally uncritical acceptance of the latter which helps to explain the ease with which technological change of drastic kinds has escaped accountability—has moved forward and onward in "something very close to a social vacuum," as Professor Frankel said. That is to say, we—virtually everyone—bought the notion that technological change equates with improvement. Sometimes it may; but often, and in matters of the utmost importance, such as the sanctity of the earth's atmosphere and the seas, it assuredly does not. The ancient Hippocrates elegantly distinguished between the progress that is change and the progress that is betterment when he was moved to wonder by those "who praise what seems outlandish before they know whether it is good, rather than the customary which they already know to be good; the bizarre rather than the obvious."[2]

In our time, British economist E. F. Schumacher, in *Small Is Beautiful*, has done the same. "The whole point is to determine what constitutes progress," he says.[3] "Scientific or technological 'solutions' which poison the environment or degrade the social structure and man himself are of no benefit, no matter how brilliantly conceived or how great their superficial attraction."[4] Lewis Mumford, who was born in 1895, and who has been architecture critic for the *New Yorker* since 1931, has been one of the most incisive assessors of the technological era that coincided with his lifespan. He has mocked the "doctrine of progress," but only, he said, "to attack the simpleminded notion that human improvements are guaranteed by purely scientific and technological advances—that they are the predictable outcome of today's panacea, 'research and development.' "[5]

It should not overstrain the implications of Mrs. Conger's letter to suggest that she would empathize with these men. Taking a Hippocratean view, she did not object to a customary aircraft which she knew to be good, but only to an outlandish one which, for the sake of marginal and questionably useful increases in speed, hurled down a boom that startled her horse and silenced the birds. With Lewis Mumford, she might "[b]ehold the ultimate religion of our seemingly rational age—the Myth of the Machine! Bigger and bigger, more and more, farther and farther, faster and faster became ends in themselves, . . . The going was the goal—a defensible doctrine for colliding atoms or falling bodies but not for men."[6]

As so often happens with unbridled technologies, the first problem to be discovered turns out to be not the only one and not necessarily the worst one. This is not to minimize the boom in the case of supersonic aircraft: the environmental panel of an SST Ad Hoc Review Committee warned in 1969 that the sonic boom would be "considered intolerable by a very high percentage of the people affected," and that it was "essential" to prohibit supersonic flights over land.[7]

"Thank God, men cannot as yet fly, and lay waste the sky as well as the earth," Henry David Thoreau once said.[8] He died innocent of the knowledge that the supersonic transport would come along a century later to threaten to lay waste the ozone layer, which is concentrated eight to thirty miles above the earth, in the stratosphere, and which shields the earth against excessive exposure to the sun's ultraviolet rays. By so doing, the ozone shield controls the incidence of human skin cancer, and affects weather patterns, the production of food crops, and, ultimately, the habitability of the planet.

Mankind's first major assault on the ozone layer occurred between 1952 and late 1962, the period during which the United States and the Soviet Union conducted test explosions of heavy nuclear weapons at high altitudes. Dr. Harold S. Johnston, a professor of chemistry at the University of California at Santa Barbara, has said that the explosions released large quantities of nitrogen oxides. These drifted slowly upward into the ozone layer, which as a result began to diminish, in 1971, through a catalytic process in which the oxides break down the molecules of ozone, each into a molecule of stable oxygen and a free atom of oxygen. Normally, the free atoms are available to replenish the ozone that is constantly being lost in natural processes; but the nitrogen oxides would combine with these atoms. Consequently, Johnston said, the process would continue the destruction of ozone "indefinitely."[9] Dr. Fred C. Iklé, director of the Arms Control and Disarmament Agency, has warned that thermonuclear warfare, in addition to its familiar terrors, would destroy a large part of the ozone layer.[10]

It was Dr. Johnston who, in 1971, sounded the alarm about SSTs. His calculations, he told fellow scientists, showed that SSTs in large numbers, flying in the lower stratosphere, would endanger the ozone shield, because their exhausts contain oxides of nitrogen that would move up into it.[11]

A year earlier, with a rare combination of luck and foresight, Congress had manifested a concern that SSTs might induce a variety of environmental changes. It asked the Department of Transportation to undertake the Climatic Impact Assessment Program, a $20 million effort. In a report to Congress on January 21, 1975, the department validated Johnston's calculations. The report found no reason for worry in a small number of SSTs, such as the thirty French-British Concordes and Soviet TU-144s then scheduled to go into operation; these would have effects too inconsequential to be detected. A moderate-sized fleet of 120 similar SSTs, the report estimated, would deplete the ozone supply by 0.5 percent. Such a depletion would be expected to increase the ultraviolet radiation reaching the earth by 1 percent. The result would be a 1 percent increase in the less severe of the two forms of skin cancer, or approximately 6,000 additional cases annually in the United States (the principal victims of this form of skin cancer are fair-skinned; in this country the incidence is normally about 250 per 100,000 per year, although this is an average reflecting substantial regional variations). Because the hazard lies in prolonged dosage, the reduction in ozone would not register its full impact on the skin-cancer rate for several decades; but by the same token, according to Drs. Frederick Urbach and Ronald E. Davies of Temple University's Skin and Cancer Hospital in Philadelphia, a restoration of the previous ozone level would not be followed by an immediate return to the normal skin-cancer rate; instead, that would take sixty years.[12]

Substantial confirmation came two months later, on March 31, 1975, with the release of another report, this one based on a two-year study by an expert panel of the National Research Council, operating arm of the National Academy of Sciences. The NRC panel said that fewer SSTs, 100 rather than 120 of the Concorde or TU-144 class, might destroy more ozone, 0.7 rather than 0.5 percent, but also said that the reduction, because of uncertainties, might range between one-third and three times 0.7 percent.[13]

What the Department of Commerce report termed "serious consequences" would result, with existing engines and fuel, "if *either* supersonic or subsonic fleets are expanded to large numbers without imposing strict limitations on engine emissions" (emphasis supplied). Essentially concurring, the NAS panel said it might cost $100 million and take ten years to develop engines with acceptably low emissions of nitrogen oxides.

Until Congress killed the plan in 1971, the government in fact was bent on having built in the United States a large fleet of SSTs—three to four hundred of them. Most would have flown where the risk to people is greatest, over the Northern Hemisphere. There, the NRC experts estimated, the SSTs would decrease the ozone layer by 10 percent while increasing the occurrence of skin cancer by 20 percent. A threat of this order of magnitude remains, however, because the sponsors of the Concorde and the TU–144 have been said to be contemplating having perhaps three hundred of these SSTs in the skies by the end of the century.

Some seventeen hundred subsonic jets operate in the lower stratosphere. Their exhausts also tend to deplete the ozone shield, although the "jumbo" jets, because of the huge volume of their emissions, account for a disproportionate share of the problem. To reduce the risk, the engines of the subsonics should also be modified, the NRC panel said.

In sum, to achieve a dubious sort of progress, toward large numbers of superbig and superfast aircraft flying at superaltitudes, tens of thousands of persons, each year for many decades, could be put at risk; and nature's screen against the sun could be thinned, with unassessed implications for weather and crops. If mistakes should be made now accountability would not be possible later. "The engineers, we say with pride, are the true revolution-aries," Charles Frankel said. "We forget to add that if they came dressed as social planners many of us would regard them as tyrants."[14]

Astounding though it may seem, the potential threat to the ozone shield from even a large fleet of SSTs may pale alongside the threat apparently already created by the gases used to propel various substances out of aerosol spray cans. This could be a much more deeply troubling example of what another philosopher, Professor H. S. Thayer, perceives as "our stubborn predilection against thinking carefully and seriously about what we are do-ing," a predilection which "is due no doubt to already imbalanced forces within ourselves and our culture."[15] Indeed, Paul Brodeur reported in the *New Yorker,* two scientists who investigated the problems created by the gases, chlorofluorocarbons, set out upon the trail on October 1, 1973, "never suspecting that before the end of the year it would lead them to contemplate the possibility of an end to life on earth."[16]

In the early 1950s, chemists at E. I. du Pont de Nemours & Company found that a mixture of two of the gases, trade-named Freon, was an ideal propellant that could be confined in aluminum or tin-plate cans. Also in the early 1950s, Robert H. Abplanalp invented a valve that could be mass-produced from plastic and metal and that, at a touch, could dispense the contents of a can. "By 1970," Brodeur wrote, "practically every product that was conceivably sprayable either had been packaged or was being considered for packaging in aerosol form. As a result, more than three hundred different uses have been devised for aerosols, which dispense everything from baby powder, slip preventive for bathtubs, breath sweeteners, and cheese spreads, to cooking-pan coatings, nasal sprays, oven cleaners, rug shampoo, shoe polish, telephone disinfectant, waxes, weed killers, and whipped-cream sub-stitutes. . . . Today, with personal products such as deodorants, hair sprays, and shaving lathers accounting for fifty per cent of the take, aerosols are a three-billion-dollar-a-year industry in the United States." Notably, few items on that list are not available in nonaerosol form—and more economically. In 1974, more than 3 billion aerosols were produced and sold in the United States. In more than half, because of its superior efficiency, Freon was the propellant, especially in fine-mist cosmetic items such as body (but not room) deodorants and hair sprays. Other propellants were used for foam—espe-cially oven cleaners, shaving cream, and whipped cream substitutes—and for insecticides and paint.

The first hint of possible environmental peril came in 1970 from a British chemist, Dr. James E. Lovelock of the University of Reading. In the ambient air over western Ireland he detected one of the gases, trichloromonofluoro-

ОЗE LAYER

methane. He assumed that the second gas, dichlorodifluoromethane, which has been used as a refrigerator and air-conditioner coolant since its discovery by General Motors researchers in 1928, must also be present, and later he was shown to have been correct. In 1971, in air samples taken in the North and South Atlantic, Lovelock found that trichloromonofluoromethane had pervaded the troposphere, which is six to ten miles high and which lies under the stratosphere. At the time, he and other investigators were not alarmed because both gases were known to be nontoxic and chemically inert. "In fact, it was their chemical inertness, that, together with a high volatility, had made them ideal as an aerosol propellant, which must vaporize at room temperature and not react with any of the ingredients it is designed to propel," Brodeur said.

At the University of California in Irvine, Professor F. Sherwood Rowland, a specialist in the chemistry of radioactive isotopes, wondered for more than a year about where the gases were going and what eventually would become of them. In mid-1973, he requested and got permission from the Atomic Energy Commission to investigate. Dr. Mario J. Molina, a Mexico City photochemist, joined his research group. On October 1, 1973, they began the investigation; before the year ended they were contemplating "the possibility of an end to life on earth." Summarizing Brodeur's account:

Because the troposphere has no known mechanisms to break down the gases; and because they are relatively insoluble in water, so that rainfall and the oceans cannot absorb them, the two men presumed that the gases— several million tons of them—would survive long enough to rise into the stratosphere. The process would be slow; Rowland and Molina calculated it would take between forty and a hundred and fifty years for an average molecule to encounter ultraviolet light and be decomposed. During that period, they estimated, sustained production of the gases for propellants and coolants worldwide at the 1972 rate, almost a million tons annually, could enlarge the load in the troposphere from several million tons to nearly a hundred million tons; and the decomposition of chlorofluorocarbons would increase correspondingly.

The scientists had known that decomposition would release chlorine atoms. In November 1973, they discovered that this could have awesome significance. Each chlorine atom, they determined, would, within one or two seconds, seek out and react with a molecule of ozone. There would then be initiated an extensive and complex chain reaction resembling that which occurs with nitrogen oxides in jet exhausts; and over a year or so, as many as a hundred thousand ozone molecules could be converted into oxygen molecules and eliminated from the atmosphere.

"Uneasy at finding that a single atom of chlorine was capable of such

545

destruction, Rowland and Molina returned to their earlier calculation that nearly a hundred million tons of chlorofluorocarbons could be expected to build up in the troposphere within the next century or so, and estimated that enough chlorofluorcarbon molecules would thereafter be decomposed annually in the stratosphere to unleash five hundred thousand tons of chlorine atoms," Brodeur said. "Chlorine in this amount, they concluded, was roughly sufficient to roughly double the depletion of ozone known to occur naturally each year, . . . The chlorine would thus bring about a situation in which ozone would be destroyed much faster than under normal conditions." It was shortly before Christmas when the scientists reached this conclusion. They then made a rough calculation that a loss of 20 to 40 percent of the ozone shield was within the realm of possibility. They came "to the further chilling conclusion that if chlorofluorocarbon propellants and refrigerants continued to be used at present rates, chlorine might one day take over chemical control of the stratosphere, with consequences that could conceivably disrupt, if not destroy, the biological systems of the earth," Brodeur said. He continued:

Moreover, they realized that even if the use of the two gases were to cease at once, destruction of part of the ozone layer—though the effect would not be felt for a decade or two—was foreordained by the fact that the chlorofluorocarbons already in the troposphere were inexorably seeping up into the stratosphere. In effect, they had discovered a planetary time bomb.

Not being specialists in atmospheric chemistry, Rowland and Molina initially were disbelieving; but a review of their calculations turned up no errors. They then went for advice to Dr. Harold Johnston, the University of California chemist who in 1971 had alerted the scientific community to the threat from SST exhausts. Johnston not only confirmed their conclusion, but said that atmospheric scientists in the Climatic Impact Assessment Program had worked out similar theories on the potential role of chlorine in the stratosphere. In addition,he said, recent work in England has indicated that the chain reaction initiated by free chlorine atoms is six times more efficient at destroying ozone than the chain reaction begun by nitrogen oxides.

Over the next several months, Brodeur said, Rowland and Molina calculated and then, on September 11, 1974, told a meeting of the American Chemical Society in Atlantic City,

that if chlorofluorocarbon production continued to increase at the present rate of ten per cent a year until 1990 and remained constant thereafter, between five and seven per cent of the ozone layer would be destroyed by 1995, and between thirty and fifty per cent of it would disappear by the year 2050. To underscore the gravity of even a five-per-cent depletion, they cited studies indicating that the resulting increase in ultraviolet radiation would, after 2050, cause forty thousand additional cases of skin cancer each year in the United States alone. They went on to warn that greater losses of ozone could cause other serious biological damage, such as genetic mutation and crop damage, and might even shift stratospheric temperatures sufficiently to create changes in the world's weather patterns. To point out the irreversible aspect of the problem, they predicted that if nothing was done over the next decade to prevent further release of chlorofluorocarbons, the vast reservoir of the gases that would have built up in the meantime would provide enough chlorine atoms to insure continuing destruction of the ozone layer for most of the twenty-first century.

Within two weeks, confirmation of this grim assessment came in the form of announcements of similar findings by Dr. Paul Crutzen, a government meteorologist, and by Drs. Ralph J. Cicerone and Michael B. McElroy, each the chairman of a unit of the Climatic Impact Assessment Program. The unit chairmen's calculations, Brodeur said, "indicated that the chlorofluorocarbons would, if anything, destroy ozone even faster than Rowland and Molina had estimated." And in November 1974, in a petition to ban Freon aerosol sprays, the Natural Resources Defense Council told the Consumer Product Safety Commission that, using high-altitude aircraft, Philip W. Krey, an Atomic Energy Commission scientist, had detected chlorofluorocarbon molecules in the lower stratosphere, twelve miles above the earth.

In Atlantic City in September, when their findings first got attention in news media, Rowland and Molina also had recommended a ban on the sprays; and they were supported in this about six weeks later by Dr. Donald M. Hunten, an atmospheric physicist who in mid-September had been named chairman of a five-member panel set up by the National Academy of Sciences to assess the situation. Initially, the du Pont Company emphasized that Rowland and Molina had offered not conclusive proof, but a hypothesis developed under laboratory conditions. Other questions rested on the natural occurrence of significant quantities of chlorine in the atmosphere. In addition, du Pont's Freon Products Division announced that scientists at several universities would undertake studies to measure fluorocarbons in the troposphere, and to observe their chemical reactions under simulated high-altitude conditions. The studies are to require three years for completion; be coordinated by the Manufacturing Chemists Association, a trade group, and be financed by nineteen producers of the gases, including the six American manufacturers—du Pont, Allied Chemical Corporation, Union Carbide Corporation, Pennwalt Corporation, Kaiser Aluminum & Chemical Corporation, and Racon, Inc. The resulting long delay of any decisive action—three years at the very least—would be particularly welcomed by the industry because the public was continuing to buy aerosol sprays in large numbers. Thus, for a time at least, there appeared to be support for the concern of H. S. Thayer, the philosopher, with a generalized "refusal to be disturbed about how we are disrupting nature's delicately balanced and compensatory mechanisms . . ."[17]

Under the sponsorship of the White House Council on Environmental Quality and the Federal Council for Science and Technology, fifteen agencies began a study which resulted, in June 1975, in a finding that the two fluorocarbons pose "a legitimate cause for concern" that the ozone layer is being destroyed, but not a cause so urgent as to warrant an immediate ban. Instead, the task force recommended that the fluorocarbons be banned as a propellant of aerosol sprays by January 1, 1978, provided that the National Academy of Sciences, in a report due in 1976, upholds its finding.[18] Meanwhile, fortunately, many manufacturers were substituting pump mechanisms for aerosol sprays. With the task force advising against an immediate ban, there seemed to be no chance of Congress or regulatory agencies instituting one. In effect, industry's request for a delay in regulatory action was granted, and everyone concerned was spared the necessity of making a decision that, particularly in a sagging economy, would be, Brodeur said, "politically unpalatable."

The use of chlorofluorocarbons to propel antiperspirants out of a can into an armpit may represent an ultimate idiocy, but, as Dr. Russell W. Peterson, chairman of the Council on Environmental Quality, put it, "It is difficult to perceive that when you are spraying an anti-perspirant in your bathroom, you are endangering the health of everyone in the world."[19] In addition to the threat to the skies, there is a threat to the user and to those—his children, say—who may come too soon into the vicinity. If inhaled in high concentrations the gases can cause fatal cardiac arrest; if in smaller concentrations, an altering of normal heart rhythms in humans and a weakening of heart muscle and a lowering of blood pressure in laboratory animals. To avoid such risks, one need but use antiperspirant or deodorant creams, lotions, or roll-ons. These achieve "levels of perspiration control quite comparable to those achieved" by aerosols, the Antiperspirant Panel, a group of expert advisers to the Food and Drug Administration, has said.

The story of the aerosol sprays illuminates a key point: Despite laws that supposedly protect the public interest, we seem to suffer from catatonic inertia when it comes to applying and enforcing effective, reliable, and timely accountability to technology that is radical, perilous, and unnecessary—but that has important financial stakes.

Perplexed and anguished because reports of the threat to the ozone shield were received with indifference, Professor H. S. Thayer has asked, "Why is it so difficult to recognize and acknowledge this danger to the continuance of life?" The same question could be asked about other drastic impacts of technology. "[W]e must inquire how it is that the very rational methods through which modern technology has prospered have taken so little account of the dangers of nonrational technology," Thayer said. "We need to study why man is his own worst enemy, and why he stubbornly refuses to clarify his ethical responsibility to himself and his future."[1]

Thayer's questions cannot be fully and satisfactorily answered, involving as they do so many obscure areas of human nature, societal arrangements, the preoccupations of any given moment, the economy, the performance of political leaders and the press, and so forth. Yet it is useful to identify some of the factors that contribute or relate to our seeming paralysis of will in making technology accountable. For example:

• The discovery, development, and application of new technologies traditionally has been perceived by most of us as an almost unalloyed good—an engine of progress that provides jobs, profits, and solutions to our problems. The forces behind technology are organized, diligent, and purposeful. They are powerful, often combining business, labor, and government into an almost irresistible lobbying force. In contrast, even the realization that some technologies are not worth the candle and indeed may threaten life on earth has come, in any general sense, relatively recently. Mechanisms for timely assessment and action were slow in coming. The National Environmental Policy Act, which requires a study of environmental impact by federal agencies undertaking major actions, and which created the Council on Environmental Quality, became law—thanks mainly to Senator Henry M. Jackson (D–Wash.)—in January 1970; not until December 1970 was the Environmental Protection Agency established, by an Executive reorganization order of President Nixon. Valuable as they are, the law and the agencies are insufficient and lack an adequate and demonstrably durable constituency. Public-interest environmental groups are indispensable supplements, with staffs skilled and sometimes dedicated to the point of self-sacrifice, but are severely handicapped by small budgets.

• Our social bookkeeping is a nonsystem that does not provide a realistic balance sheet on the price of technological change and thus obscures the need for the requisite accountability. Take Southern agriculture. The old sharecropping system started to die when cultivators and tractors began to replace men. By 1949, Daniel Fusfeld has written, the need for hand labor had gone from everything but summer weeding and fall harvesting. This forced many black sharecroppers off their homesteads into Southern towns and cities, where they were available for seasonal and harvest labor. They were poor—they subsisted—but they stayed.

Then disaster struck. Machine harvesting of cotton and corn was introduced on a large scale in 1950 and substantial expansion of soybean acreage (which uses little labor) resulted in a huge decline in use of labor. For example, in the space of only three years from 1949 to 1952 the use of unskilled agricultural labor in twenty Mississippi delta counties fell by 72 percent, and five years later was down to only 10 percent of the 1949 level.[2]

For the employers in the twenty counties the drastic reductions in employment brought sharply lowered production costs and thereby contributed to Progress. This was counted a plus. Many of the families progressed ("forward and onward") onto the welfare rolls of Chicago, New York, and St. Louis. This kind of cost to the taxpayers was not always reckoned a minus.

The ancient Pharaohs came closer to keeping an honest count. When one built a pyramid, Edmond Cahn, a philosopher and law professor once said, "it is possible that his more methodical overseers might have reported that the cost of construction had included some thousands or hundreds of thousands of human lives. Proper accounting would have computed these lives as part of the over-all expense to the Egyptian throne." Writing in the context of human experimentation in the development of new drugs, some of which turned out to be catastrophes, Cahn said, "As we in our day can smile condescendingly at the primitives and ancients who practiced human sacrifice for what they considered to be the general good of the tribe or nation, future generations may ask how we could make human sacrifice more acceptable in our day by calling it 'social cost.' At least the ancients were honest; they called a spade a spade even when it was used to bury a human statistic of 'social cost.' "[3] Much later, in the first century A.D., the genial Roman emperor Vespasian displayed a similar candor, but as an act of compassion. Rejecting a new machine that would lower the cost of hauling pillars, he asked, according to the historian Suetonius, " 'Who will take care of my poor'? Nevertheless, the emperor paid the inventor a handsome fee."[4]

• Technological developments have enhanced feelings of futility and isolation in large segments of the population.

• There is a pervasive blind faith—one of sanity's defenses against despair —that the government, or *somebody*, must be keeping technology under control and guiding it in our interests.

Rather than extend the list, let us look more closely at aspects that may help to bring fundamental issues of unaccountable technology into sharper focus. These are: the problem of the burden of proof, which arises whenever technological change leads to a confrontation between economic interests and protection of human beings or the environment against actual or potential harm; the role played by "the doctrine of Progress" in bringing us to our present condition; and a central religious concept that may help to clarify what Thayer termed man's "ethical responsibility to himself and his future."

The problem of the burden of proof is essentially this: Is it safety or "unsafety" that should be demonstrated? For the most part, the burden has fallen overwhelmingly on those who would claim "unsafety" if they had the information and resources to do so, which often they haven't. Freed of the burden to prove safety, sponsors of technological change have had a clear field through most of the industrial era; and once they have established a change so as to make it part of the economy, and once it has as a result acquired a dependent business-and-jobs constituency, it can be hard to dislodge, should hazards be discovered. "The religion of economics promotes an idolatry of rapid change, unaffected by the elementary truism that a change which is not an unquestionable improvement is a doubtful blessing," Ralph and Mildred Buchsbaum said in 1957. "The burden of proof is placed on those who take the 'ecological viewpoint' . . . Common sense, on the contrary, would suggest that the burden of proof should lie on the man who wants to introduce a change. . . . But this would take too much time, and would therefore be uneconomic."[5]

The burden of proving lack of safety can be staggering. One need but consider certain chemicals that may contaminate man's food, drink, or medicine, his workplace, or the ambient atmosphere. Suppose research is undertaken which establishes that such chemicals cause cancer in laboratory animals. Leading specialists in carcinogenesis agree unanimously not only that the presumption then must be that the chemicals probably cause cancer in man, but also that no one has found a particle of a carcinogen so small that it may not cause cancer. Furthermore, the latent period during which a carcinogen may be causing human cancer, and during which it is not detected, may be twenty or even thirty years. "Evidence based upon human subjects is virtually impossible to obtain," Russell E. Train, administrator of the Environmental Protection Agency (EPA), has said. "The general human population is continually exposed to a variety of chemicals. A significant 'control group' is thus impossible to establish. . . . to await the 20 to 30 years of exposure necessary to determine the ultimate effect is only to wait until the damage to an entire generation of humans is complete."[6] That is to say, when laboratory testing shows a chemical to be cancer-causing, the burden must not be on those who ultimately could prove their case only with a "body count"; rather, those who would introduce or retain the chemical in man's environment must show it to be safe, or at least to have a highly favorable ratio of benefits to risks. (It should be noted that Milton Friedman, the famed economist and *Newsweek* columnist, has cited serious flaws in federal regulation of food and drugs as a basis for arguing—repeatedly—that it should be abolished and replaced by "consumer sovereignty." The surpassing foolishness of this advice is illustrated by the safety problems of chemical carcinogens.[7])

Train took his position in August 1974, when he proposed to halt, as an "imminent hazard to public health," sales of two popular Shell Chemical Company pesticides which had been used mainly in corn fields since 1955. One of the pesticides was Dieldrin, to which the other, Aldrin, converts on application. Dieldrin causes cancer in mice. Thus was posed the burden-of-proof issue. Residues of the pesticides pervade the food supply and threaten to cause cancer in "thousands of people" annually, Dr. M. Adrian Gross, a Food and Drug Administration pathologist and statistician, testified at a hearing on Train's proposal. A Shell research scientist, Don E. Stevenson, however, could not "equate mice and men. . . . To me, the mouse is a warning flag, not a crash barrier."

After a fifteen-day hearing, Herbert L. Perlman, an administrative law judge for the EPA, upheld Train. He found it easy to strike down the mice-are-not-men argument because the record was "overwhelmed" by evidence that "an agent causing cancer in rodents or other experimental animals poses a high risk of causing cancer in man." A conclusion that this is so "represents established, traditional and 'conventional wisdom,'" he said. Citing other evidence showing that Dieldrin "is a persistent chemical which pervades our diet at significant residue levels," and to which man is exposed "via the air and other routes," Perlman said the pesticide "has probably accumulated in the tissue of every individual." As a result, he said, to insist on advance knowledge of the actual mechanisms by which the pesticide may cause cancer, or to wait twenty or thirty years for proof that it is carcinogenic, would be "irresponsible in the extreme."[8] Train followed up by banning Aldrin and Dieldrin, which were producing sales of about $10 million annually for Shell. The company litigated in the U.S. Court of Appeals for the District of Columbia, lost, and finally, in April 1975, gave up, saying it would stop producing the pesticides.

It might seem that here was an idea whose time had come: accountability delayed for body counts is accountability defeated. Perhaps so. But it was rejected in 1974 and 1975—pretty late in the game—by three-judge panels that decided crucial cases in two United States courts of appeals.

The first case involved the Reserve Mining Company, a subsidiary of ARMCO and Republic Steel Corporations. In 1956, Reserve's plant in Silver Bay, Minnesota, a town on Lake Superior about fifty miles upstream from Duluth, began to use a new technology for extracting iron from deposits of taconite ore. Pulverized waste tailings were dumped in the lake at a rate that reached 67,000 tons per day by the mid-1960s; simultaneously, large amounts of mineral dust were wafted through smokestacks into the air. In mid-1973, the Environmental Protection Agency announced that Duluth's public water system, supplied by Lake Superior, was laden with a material that turned out to be amphiboles. These are silicate minerals containing varieties of asbestos that, when inhaled, are known to have caused an irreversible and often fatal lung scarring called asbestosis, lung cancer, certain benign tumors, and cancer of the gastrointestinal tract.

During the trial resulting from litigation brought by the EPA, the states of Minnesota, Wisconsin, and Michigan, and environmental groups to stop the dumping, Dr. William J. Nicholson, of the Environmental Sciences Laboratory of the Mount Sinai School of Medicine, testified that he had analyzed Duluth water and had found that a quart could contain between 20 million and 100 million amphibole fibers, and that a cubic meter of air contained as many as 11 million. Dr. Harold L. Stewart, chief of pathology at the National Cancer Institute for fifteen years until his retirement in 1969, judged the fibers in the water supply a carcinogen. "You give it to the infants," he said. "You give it to young children. This is a captive population. They not only ingest the water, it's virtually a food additive. . . . All the sheets and the pillowcases are laundered in the asbestos water. It must be in the atmosphere. It must be floating around. The dryer that dries the clothes in the cellar must blow this out somewhere." Toward the end of his direct testimony, Paul Brodeur wrote in *Expendable Americans,* "Dr. Stewart said that anybody who permits such a situation 'must realize that he's condemning people to exposure to a carcinogen that may take their lives and probably will.' "[9]

Dr. Irving J. Selikoff, a pioneer in asbestos epidemiology and director of the Environmental Sciences Laboratory, testified that the airborne concentration of asbestos in Silver Bay was the highest he had ever seen. He joined his colleague, Nicholson, in saying that persons drinking or using the contaminated water—mostly the one hundred thousand in Duluth—were exposed to a distinct health hazard. Selikoff compared it to "a form of Russian Roulette, and I don't know where the bullet is located." Nicholson said, "If we waited until we saw the bodies in the street, we would then be certain that there would be another thirty or forty years of mortality experience before us."

Reserve Mining contended that its dumping of taconite wastes and asbestos-type materials—hundreds of millions of tons, in all—into Lake Superior did not account for the fibers in the water Duluth drew from the lake. In reply to repeated questions by the plaintiffs and U.S. District Judge Miles W. Lord, Reserve witnesses denied that the company had prepared alternative plans to discharge the refuse on land. But on March 1, 1974, it was revealed that Reserve in fact had prepared four or five such plans, the first of them in 1970. A month later, Reserve president Edward M. Furness admitted to Judge Lord that he was "familiar" with the plan prepared in 1970 and had authorized a key Reserve witness to testify that such plans did not exist. Subsequently, C. William Verity, head of ARMCO and chairman of Reserve, asked Lord to rule that there was no health menace—a request that the judge said was tantamount to asking him "to violate the oath of his office."

Finally, on April 20, 1974, the chief executive officers of ARMCO and Republic testified that they were unwilling to abate the discharge. The same day, Lord enjoined Reserve from dumping into Lake Superior and from discharging amphibole fibers into the air, effective at 12:01 A.M. April 21. Three judges of the Court of Appeals for the Eighth Circuit convened hastily in a motel in Springfield, Missouri, and granted Reserve a temporary reprieve. In May, during oral arguments on Reserve's appeal, John P. Hills, a Justice Department lawyer, told the three-judge panel:

I concede that the burden was on the Government in this to show that it's in the water. At that point I seriously wonder if the burden doesn't shift. When you put a carcinogenic agent in drinking water and you show that some company is putting it there . . . I think it should be seriously considered that that burden shifts at that point.

You poison a man's well, do you have to show dead bodies and so forth, or do you just say that you poisoned his well, it should be stopped.

On June 4, 1974, the panel said that the original decision to permit the discharge of tailings into Lake Superior was "a monumental environmental mistake" that ought to stop as quickly as possible. But it ruled that the dumping could continue. Judge Lord "apparently took the position that all uncertainties should be resolved in favor of health safety," the panel said. This represented "a legislative policy judgment, not a judicial one. . . . The discharges may or may not result in detrimental health effects, but, for the present, that is simply unknown." The failure of the plaintiffs "to prove that a demonstrable hazard exists," the judges said, "is not reflective of any weakness which it is within their power to cure but rather, given the current state of medical and scientific knowledge, plaintiffs' case is based only on medical hypothesis and is simply beyond proof . . ."[10]

As translated by Russell W. Peterson, chairman of the White House's Council on Environmental Quality, the panel was saying that "counting dead bodies through an after-the-fact epidemiology study then becomes virtually the only way the government could 'prove' its case." The decision prompted Senator Philip A. Hart (D–Mich.), chairman of the Subcommittee on the Environment of the Senate Commerce Committee, to propose legislation intended to make it easier to hold polluters such as Reserve Mining accountable. The proposal was that where proof—by which Hart said he meant "dead bodies"—of a demonstrable health hazard cannot be produced, the courts "shall consider the likelihood and magnitude of risk of harm . . ." The proposal, attached as an amendment to an unrelated bill, passed the Senate but died in a conference in the House. In 1975 Senators Gaylord Nelson (D–Wis.) and Charles H. Percy (R–Ill.) joined Hart in sponsoring a tougher bill to shift the burden of proof firmly onto polluters.

Meanwhile, in a decision the Supreme Court declined to review, the full Court of Appeals for the Eighth Circuit—including the three judges on the panel—sharply tempered the panel's ruling. Most important, the court held that a district judge can act on a health hazard without waiting for "dead bodies in the streets," as Judge Myron H. Bright put it during final arguments. Taking a middle ground in an opinion written by Bright, the court refused to sustain Judge Lord's order closing the Reserve plant but termed it "a potential threat to the public health" which requires immediate steps to clean up the air pollution and steps in an undefined "reasonable" time to clean up the water pollution. The economic hardships resulting from closing the plant, as well as the inland taconite mine that supplies it, "may be more certain than the harm from drinking Lake Superior water or breathing Silver Bay air," the court said. It found the air pollution to be a "more significant" threat. Saying that an assessment of the risk in the water "was made impossible by the absence of medical knowledge," the court returned the case to Lord for a new hearing. Later, in violation of a court order, he involved himself in negotiations between the State of Minnesota and Reserve Mining over a possible site on land where the water pollutants could be deposited. Acting on an appeal by the company, the court in January 1976 removed Lord from the case, reprimanding him for showing "great bias" and "substantial disregard for the mandate of this court." Lord, conceding "irregular" conduct, said that "sometimes the stakes are so high you have to take risks." Judge Edward J. Devitt, who replaced Lord, gave the environmentalist cause a clear victory in May 1976, when he fined Reserve Mining $837,500 for violating state water discharge permits during the eleven-month period from May 20, 1973, when contamination of Duluth's water system was reported, and April 20, 1974, when Lord enjoined Reserve from further dumping. Devitt fined Reserve an additional $200,000 for having "violated court rules and orders as to discovery," and directed the company to reimburse the city of Duluth for the $22,920 it had spent to acquire "interim clean water facilities and supplies" for its residents.

The second court of appeals case involved lead which, when ingested, poisons the blood, kidneys, and brain, among other things. Lead poisoning in 1972 alone, it is estimated, killed 200 children, injured 150 more so severely that they had to be sent to institutions for lifetime care, and caused neurological handicaps, including mental retardation, in 6,000; in addition, 80,000 children suffered asymptomatic lead poisoning, and 600,000 more had dangerously high blood levels. The victims are mainly the poor, many of whom eat chips of lead-containing paint. But it is the addition of lead to gasoline (to retard engine knocking) which makes it something like a universal hazard, because it is blown out the tailpipe in tiny particles that become part of the air we breathe and, along city streets and busy freeways, part of the dust and dirt ingested primarily but not entirely by poor children.

The case arose from regulations promulgated by the Environmental Protection Agency to require half of the nation's filling stations to offer unleaded gasoline by July 1, 1974 (so as to protect catalytic mufflers on 1975 cars), and to reduce the lead content of gasoline year by year, in order that the total supply in 1979 would contain only 35 percent as much as in 1975. Manufacturers of lead compounds, including the Ethyl Corporation and E. I. du Pont de Nemours & Company, sued the EPA, contending that a danger to public health from leaded gasoline had not been proved and that the proposed 65 percent reduction in lead content consequently was unwarranted. A coalition of environmental and poverty groups also sued EPA. Their contention was that the EPA hadn't gone far enough, because its own medical scientists in 1972 had said a 65 percent lead reduction "must be considered inadequate to protect the public health," because the reduction will be especially insufficient to protect children living along heavily traveled arteries, and because *all* lead could be phased out of gasoline in five years at an annual cost to the average motorist of $15—half of which he would get back in the form of a reduced need for maintenance, according to Louis V. Lombardo, president of the Public Interest Campaign.[11]

Just as in the Reserve Mining case, a three-judge panel—this one in the Court of Appeals for the District of Columbia—put a burden on the EPA that it could not bear. In a 2-to-1 decision written by Judge Malcolm R. Wilkey and concurred in by Judge Edward E. Tamm, the panel held in January 1975 that the agency did not "conclusively prove" that emissions from leaded gasoline had an adverse cause-effect relationship with public health; that the EPA had not proved beyond doubt that the amount of lead a person absorbs is determined by the amount to which he is exposed and the proximity of the exposure (although an EPA study in Newark, New Jersey, revealed a correlation between the distance children lived from throughways and the amount of lead in their bodies), and even that EPA Administrator Russell Train, by promulgating regulations to reduce the lead content of gasoline, had exceeded his authority. Wilkey was distressed by the "anguish" Train had caused the lead industry—which, it happens, he had been part of. "From 1963 until 1970, when he was appointed to the Court of Appeals by former President Nixon, Wilkey served as general counsel to Kennecott Copper Corp., one of the nation's major lead producers," Judith Miller reported in the *Progressive*. "Wilkey has refused to comment on whether he, or any member of his family, now owns stock or bonds in Kennecott, oil refineries [some oil companies were co-plaintiffs with the lead producers], or lead-producing corporations."[12]

The dissenter, Judge J. Skelly Wright, argued that his colleagues—"stabbing blindly through a curtain of ignorance"—would have the EPA administrator "sit idly by as the storm approaches, consigned to wait until its damage is felt before taking then largely superfluous preventive action." He also said that Wilkey and Tamm, while "without scientific background or access to expertise," had ignored much of the evidentiary record of ten thousand pages. "And with due deference to the 'anguish' the Administrator has inflicted on the suppliers of lead for the petroleum industry, it is the anguish of children and urban adults who must continue to breathe our lead-polluted air that moves me," Wright concluded.[13]

Now and then, virtue triumphs; and it did so, barely, on March 19, 1976, when the full court of appeals, in a 5-to-4 decision, reversed the three-judge panel and held that the EPA has wide-ranging authority to control dangers to the public health. After World War I, the equating of technological change with human improvement was an idea whose time had not only come, but was going to continue to come for many decades; and while it was coming most people would not entertain—and might consider benighted or even perverse—the idea that "Progress" ought to be accountable. The evidence of this was everywhere at hand. To take a case in point:

In 1896, Elihu Root found that X-rays could injure body tissue. In 1922, an estimated one hundred radiologists died in the practice of their profession. In 1923 there sprang up a business in which beauticians used X-rays to remove unwanted hair. In 1927, Hermann J. Muller, the geneticist ultimately awarded a Nobel Prize, reported that X-rays caused genetic mutations. In 1929, after X-ray hair removal—an enterprise in folly dependent upon blind faith that a marvel of science would do no harm—had flourished for six years, the American Medical Association issued the first public condemnation. There had been no action by a government agency, federal, state, or local, although thousands of the trusting suffered burns, cancer, and even fatal injury.[14]

It was only after Hiroshima, in 1945, that Muller won a serious hearing for his case that physicians and dentists were so casually using X-ray as to give far more radiation than necessary. Not that they then began always to use it wisely. Among other things, Ralph Nader told the Senate Commerce Committee in 1968, standard radiation exposures were set higher for blacks than for whites. Inquiries established that *X-Ray Technology,* a textbook widely used by technicians, had in its 1960 and 1964 (but not 1968) editions recommended an exposure to radiation 40 percent to 60 percent higher for patients whose "physical condition" is "Negroid." One of the coauthors acknowledged to a reporter that the recommendation was "absolutely ridiculous."[15] A few days later, on May 22, 1968, a New York State Health Department official disclosed that "a significant proportion" of the state's X-ray technicians apparently have routinely exposed blacks to higher doses of radiation than whites.[16]

Some years afterward, Dr. Priscilla Laws, associate professor of physics at Dickinson College, asked her dentist if a particular X-ray was necessary. He wouldn't answer the question. She then wrote a *Consumer's Guide to Unnecessary Surgery,* aided by the Health Research Group, which is supported by Nader's Public Citizen, Inc. Some principal findings: Of the total dosage of X-rays given Americans, more than half is unnecessary, because too many are given, and dosages are sometimes excessive; better than nine out of ten X-rays are done without protective shielding of patients; one out of five X-ray machines were found by state inspectors in 1972 not to comply with laws intended to minimize unneeded radiation, and 30 percent of all X-rays are done not because they are medically justified, but to protect doctors from malpractice suits. Dr. Sidney Wolfe, director of the Research Group, said the result of all of this excess may be as many as one thousand deaths a year from cancer and genetic injury.[17]

The X-ray episode is instructive in diverse ways, but its pertinent lesson would seem to be this: For almost eighty years it has been known that the benefits of a marvelous new technology were offset by serious risks. It is also true that the wherewithal was always at hand to hold the risks to a perfectly acceptable minimum, or, to put it another way, to make it an accountable technology. And yet, lethal misuse of X-rays—by trained and supposedly expert persons—never has been eradicated and persists to this day. If this is the case with X-rays, how could one sensibly expect to find accountability mechanisms for a plethora of technological changes that had—or seemed to have—no or minor disadvantages?

Must we go on permitting technology to be unaccountable? Permitting the fate of the planet to be determined by Faustian bargains, flags of convenience, and aerosol sprays for the armpit market? By dead souls putting the burden of proof on dead bodies?

"The earth is the Lord's, and the fullness thereof; the world and they that dwell therein," begins Psalm 24. This is a beautiful expression of a point repeatedly made in the Old Testament: simply that man is the custodian or guardian—not the owner—of the earth, and is responsible to God for his fidelity to that trust. The Book of Genesis says that God put Adam in a paradise, the Garden of Eden, and directed him "to work it and to guard it," or, in the King James version, "to dress it and to keep it." In a commentary on Genesis, Benno Jacob said,

Adam's relation to the Owner of the garden in the terminology of the Halakah, Jewish law, is that of a guardian. To guard may simply mean careful treatment and protection against damage. Primarily, however, this term is meant to characterize the garden as someone else's property. It is a garden that belongs to God, not man.[18]

When Adam and Eve violated God's command not to eat "of the tree of knowledge of good and evil," He "called unto Adam and said unto him, Where art thou?" Here was the origin in our culture of personal accountability. Adam and Eve had been given everything they needed, but, God told them, it was not theirs to do with as they pleased; and when they disobeyed His command to forgo the one fruit which was forbidden, and which they did not need, God took steps, persuasive ones, to establish that man is answerable.

God put Abraham to a terrible test: "Take now thy son, thine only son Isaac, whom thou lovest, and get thee into the land of Moriah; and offer him for a burnt offering . . ." Biblical scholars puzzle over and dispute the justification for God's command. Rabbi Joshua O. Haberman, of Washington Hebrew Congregation, perceives yet another reenforcement of the concept of trusteeship. God's purpose, Dr. Haberman reasons, was to show that even a beloved only son does not belong totally to his father, and to compel Abraham to prove his belief in this.[19]

It is with no thought of seeking religious conversions that we cite the strikingly timeless emphasis in the Bible on conservation. It is an emphasis which "seems to speak directly to contemporary man, for whom the environment is high on the scale of priorities," Eric G. Freudenstein has said. He cited the specific prohibition in Deuteronomy (20:19–20) on the despoilation of trees, even in time of war: "When you besiege a city many days to bring it into your power by making war against it, you shall not destroy the trees thereof by swinging an axe against them; for from them you may eat but not destroy them, for the tree of the field is man's life."[20]

If accountability were to be accorded its just importance, trees possibly would not have an Almighty as their advocate, but they would have a mighty army to protect them.

"Even now, perhaps a majority of our countrymen still believe that science and technics can solve all human problems," Lewis Mumford says. "They have no suspicion that our runaway science and technics themselves today constitute the main problem the human race has to overcome."[1] How could they be restrained? The first step toward an answer is a more precise definition of the problem. The problem, says the philosopher Charles Frankel, is the

drift of decision-making authority into key positions that are anonymous, the development of an institutional structure that denies the individual genuine options, and the increasing inadequacy of our inherited mechanisms of public discussion and consent to control this situation. It is a problem to which none of the old models apply. . . .

Frankel concludes that it is essential to restore responsibility—that is to say, accountability—to the decision-making process. He provides this key definition of responsibility/accountability:

A decision is responsible when the man or group that makes it has to answer for it to those who are directly or indirectly affected by it. To introduce this kind of responsibility, those who are affected by social decisions have to be in a position to ask the relevant questions; they have to know whom to ask; they have to have enough power to force their questions to be taken seriously; and, in the end, they have to have some power of free choice.[2] (Emphasis supplied.)

Writing presciently in 1955, Frankel said, "To create such a structure of responsibility in a mass society is the overarching problem."[3] He fashioned "no single strategy," but he made two key observations from which his most important approach naturally evolved. The first observation was that major social decisions—"decisions affecting a broad spectrum of values—are made by specialized agencies whose business it is to be concerned with only one or two of those values." The second observation was that "[t]he pattern of competition is the basic pattern which liberal societies have traditionally employed to make the decision-making process responsible." Consequently, he reasoned, "The essential point is to introduce a competition of powers into the decision-making process that does not now exist."[4]

Starting with Ralph Nader in the mid-1960s, and continuing with environmental and public-interest groups, there has been introduced "a competition of powers." It in no way derogates their impressive accomplishments to say that they have been wholly insufficient. The explanation is in part that radical technology has proliferated rather than standing still during the twenty years since Frankel's analysis was published. Moreover, resistance to "a competition of powers" remains essentially as great as ever, not only among businessmen seeking a profit, but also among bureaucracies and among those scientists who, if they do not see themselves as an elite, have yet to develop, in the polite phrasing of Harold P. Green, of the National Law Center of George Washington University, "the capability of functioning within the institutional framework in a manner consonant with the basic principles of our form of democratic society."[5] These are among the reasons why radical technology continues to retain the initiative, and why those who would slow it down, who would tame it, who would take care to make it accountable, continue to face great obstacles. Two examples, each concerning an audacious new technology of great potential impact, and raising questions of utmost gravity, will make the point.

Even as it was about to be phased out, the Atomic Energy Commission, in a bureaucratic death rattle in January 1975, took a bizarre initiative in behalf of wide-scale use of heart pacemakers powered by plutonium-238. This metal is 280 times more toxic than plutonium-239, which, the director of the National Cancer Institute said in 1971, "is one of the most potent respiratory carcinogens known."[6] Depending on the model and manufacturer, the plutonium content of a single pacemaker would be between 0.15 and 0.5 grams. If optimally dispersed, this would be sufficient to contaminate to the maximum levels permitted under official guidelines 10,000 cubic kilometers of air or 1,000 square kilometers of ground; and it would be enough, says Dean E. Abrahamson, a physician and professor at the School of Public Affairs of the University of Minnesota, to achieve "maximum permissible lung burdens to 16 billion people."[7] The obvious question is also the right one: Who needs it?

As of mid-1975, an estimated one hundred twenty-five thousand Americans were using pacemakers to correct problems in the electrical conduction system that triggers heartbeats. These units, powered by chemical batteries, were, on the whole, a technological triumph—and one which, importantly, created no environmental problems. Some units were faulty; indeed, by May 1975, the Food and Drug Administration had recalled twenty-three thousand of them, and they had been associated with twenty-eight deaths. In addition, Senator Abraham A. Ribicoff (D–Conn.) disclosed serious deficiencies in the manner in which the FDA exercised, or neglected to exercise, its regulatory authority to protect those persons in whom the proper functioning of a pacemaker was literally a matter of life or death.[8] This raises a question: If inadequate regulation occurred in the case of battery-powered pacemakers, what reason is there to believe it would not occur in the case of the plutonium pacemaker, which meanwhile had been invented and tested, on a limited scale?

The Atomic Energy Commission, no doubt, tried hard to make the use of plutonium fail-safe against release; but the difficulty of such an enterprise may be suggested by the fact that in the shooting gallery which is the United States, it is conceivable that a person fitted with a plutonium pacemaker might be shot through the heart. Indeed, one of six patients in a control group in a study of nuclear pacemakers happened to be shot to death in a filling station robbery in which he was an innocent bystander.[9]

Undeterred, the AEC in January 1975 issued a draft environmental impact statement on its proposal to authorize large-scale use of nuclear pacemakers. The statement was supposed to conform to guidelines prepared for all federal agencies by the Council on Environmental Quality. One of these guidelines directs an agency to seek out organizations with an interest in the matter at issue. To comply, clearly, is to enhance Charles Frankel's "competition of powers" and thereby to help assure bureaucratic accountability. It surprised no one familiar with the AEC's record of arrogance, secrecy, and suppression that insofar as Dr. Abrahamson could determine, it made no effort to alert public-interest, environmental, and medical groups to the existence of the paper. "In particular, the medical community appears to have been totally, and one must assume deliberately, excluded from any notice," he has said.[10] Nonetheless, the draft did come to the attention of, among others, Abrahamson and a physicist colleague at the School of Public Affairs, Associate Professor Donald P. Geesaman. They were among those who, in March, filed comments with the Nuclear Regulatory Commission, which meanwhile had taken over the AEC's regulatory functions. Their analyses of the AEC's draft statement are forceful and at times astonishing reminders of the lengths to which boosters of radical new technologies will go.

The *only* benefit claimed by the AEC for the nuclear pacemaker is that it will decrease surgical mortality among persons who, if fitted with battery units, would have to undergo replacement operations. The AEC computed the benefit at 59 lives per 100,000 wearers per year. Abrahamson devastated the AEC computation. He pointed out, most importantly, that the AEC had assumed the surgical mortality rate to be 1 percent, although it is in fact zero; that the AEC had assumed the operational life of the nuclear pacemaker to be ten years, although that is "simply the design objective of the promoters" and has "no evidence" behind it; that in contrast, clinical use has demonstrated the lifetime of conventional pacemakers to be at least six years; and that chemical power sources, including the commercially available lithium-iodide battery, have a much longer life than six years.

The AEC draft was at least as depressing because of its omissions. Nowhere did it discuss the toxic nature of plutonium and its implications, making its evaluation of hazards "meaningless," Abrahamson pointed out. The statement said that "[a] regulatory framework will be needed" because of the plutonium—but did not make at all clear that this would mean, Abrahamson said, "stringent requirements for licensing, record keeping, [and] monitoring," involving "patients, hospitals, physicians, morticians, operators of crematoria, medical examiners, individuals and organizations (e.g., police, firemen, ambulance crews) . . ." Neither did the AEC statement discuss the ability of the plutonium capsule to withstand the impact of a bullet fired from a handgun or a rifle.

Elsewhere in his forty-two pages of comments, Abrahamson said that to make plutonium pacemakers widely available would be to increase the opportunities for accidental exposure of the public and workers in enterprises that would produce the devices, and also for theft and terrorist activities. In fact, Dr. L. D. DeNike, and Watson Morris, of ECOS, Inc., in Chapel Hill, North Carolina, wrote a paper entitled, "How to Convert a Plutonium-Powered Heart Pacemaker into a Terrorism Weapon Capable of Making Up to Two Square Miles of Any City Uninhabitable." They said that no radiation detector or knowledge of chemistry would be needed; that the materials, with the possible exception of three common chemicals, "can be obtained very easily without arousing any suspicion," and that the operation could be carried out in a motel room or other temporary location which a terrorist could swiftly abandon. Associate Professor Chester E. Gleit, of the Department of Chemistry of North Carolina State University in Raleigh, said in a critique of the paper that the procedure could be "simplified to: Dump the capsule [containing the plutonium] in acid mixture on hot plate in a room near the target area, open the window, and leave area. Truly a frightening possibility."[11]

Donald Geesaman, in his separate paper, said the AEC had not established an absolute need for an extra-long-lived pacemaker, had not established the superiority of nuclear power in any event, and had not established that a nuclear power source will "result in reduced mortality, morbidity, anxiety or expense for the patient." Thus, the draft statement had left the residual impression of being "simply a technology in search of a need," he said.

If nuclear pacemakers by the tens of thousands should come into use, and if this should occur without proof of significant benefits that outweigh the enlargement of grave risks, it again will be made resoundingly clear that technology which is potentially nihilistic as well as unaccountable remains ascendant—and with the power of government coalescing rather than competing with the power of industry.

The second example of audacious technology involves genetic manipulation. In quite pure form it raises the question, as Senator Edward M. Kennedy (D–Mass.) put it, whether scientists alone should "determine the scope and nature of their own work, especially when that work poses considerable risks for society as a whole"; and it also raises the question "whether the principles that the interests of science and those of society usually coincide, and that the pursuit of knowledge, any knowledge, is, in of itself, a noble and positive endeavor, are valid."[12] These are profound questions, questions that reach to the heart of unaccountable technology.

Genetic manipulation or "engineering" is a revolutionary development which holds out the possibility that scientists in their laboratories can create new forms of life. They have discovered enzymes which chemically cleave strands of DNA, the genetic material, at specific places, and leave them with "sticky ends" which can be "spliced" to a special kind of genetic material and transplanted into fast-growing bacteria. To put it another way, methods now have been discovered which overcome the natural barriers to the union of hereditary characteristics from organisms that are widely dissimilar. Using these methods, scientists have transplanted hereditary material from bacteria, viruses, and even frogs; thus they have created forms of life that in nature do not exist.

In testimony before Kennedy's Health Subcommittee in April 1975, Dr. Stanley N. Cohen, a Stanford University microbiologist and associate professor of medicine who has pioneered in this work, said that "it is now potentially possible to construct bacteria capable of producing a wide variety of biological substances such as hormones, antibiotics, and other drugs, vaccines, food nutrients, and enzymes—all of which are currently obtainable only from their original plant or animal sources." The possibility also emerges, Dr. Halsted Holman, a colleague of Dr. Cohen's at Stanford, told the hearing, "of modification of specific genes of an individual or group which will immediately alter the functions of the individuals and possibly their offspring."

The new technology held out a promise of the richest kind of rewards, including inexpensive new medicines and relief of shortages of food and energy and of environmental pollution. But it also held out the possibility that it might create new strains of germs resistant to treatment and increase the risks of cancer. Researchers were in addition concerned that safety guidelines had not been established for experiments in microbial gene manipulation. As a result, participants at an experimental research conference at which the new experimental methodology was described asked the National Academy of Sciences to establish a committee to consider "the possibility that potentially biohazardous consequences might result from widespread or injudicious use" of genetic manipulation. In the interim, on an informal basis, researchers deferred two specific types of gene manipulation experiments. The committee in the spring of 1974 formally recommended deferral of the same experiments until, Dr. Cohen testified, "it was determined whether there are ways in which the scientific work could be undertaken safely, and until adequate safety precautions could be made available." And so, Senator Kennedy said, "in a move unprecedented in the history of science, molecular scientists from around the world ceased doing a particular kind of research."

In February 1975, at a meeting in Asilomar, California, the issues were exhaustively discussed for three and a half days. It was all out in the open: indeed, Cohen said, one of every eight persons attending was from the press. The scientists reached a general consensus that genetic manipulation offers hope for solving a wide variety of problems that beset society and science and medicine as well; that there are hazards for which safeguards must be erected so that, Cohen testified, "most experiments" can proceed "with minimal risk to laboratory workers, to the public at large, and to the animal and plant species sharing our ecosystems, and that, finally, "there are certain experiments in which the potential risks are of such a serious nature that they ought not to be done with the presently available containment facilities." It ought to be said, with gratitude, that this was not a replay of the Faustian bargain that "we nuclear people" made with "society" to provide an inexhaustible source of power in exchange for stable institutions through eternity.[13] At the same time, Kennedy said in opening the hearing, scientists alone largely made the decisions voluntarily to adopt a moratorium on genetic manipulation research and then to lift it. "They weighed the risks and benefits," he said. "They defined them. They decided. And the work will go on." The Senator queried, "Was it proper for *scientists alone* to decide to stop and then resume the research?"

Cohen said that "it is appropriate for the public to be assured that experiments using this basic knowledge are carried out safely," but took the position that "it would be contrary to the public interest if the initiative of the scientific community in raising issues of experimental safety should lead to a decision by the public to direct the scientific course of such investigations." Dr. Donald D. Brown, of the Department of Embryology at the Carnegie Institution of Washington, who like Cohen has been working in the field of genetic manipulation, was more explicit in urging that the public's role be subordinate. "When a new line of research is under investigation, only the scientists actively engaged in the work will be in a position to see a potential safety problem," he testified. Brown went on to say:

experience has shown that neither nonscientists nor scientists can measure the future benefits of a line of research with sufficient vision to direct the overall priorities of research. There is a very simple solution to this apparent dilemma. We should permit scientists to choose their own projects and require that their research be of highest quality. Quality is something that can be measured. The decision of what science is good and the responsibility to reduce the risks of this science to levels acceptable to society *must be borne by scientists themselves.* (Emphasis supplied.)

This could lead to irresponsible decision-making as Charles Frankel—we believe correctly—had defined it. In contrast, Dr. Holman, an investigative immunologist testifying "primarily as a physician and as a citizen," saw the issue correctly: as "a struggle to achieve a healthy relationship between science and citizens who support and are affected by it. Science as a human endeavor, like medicine, can develop appropriately only with the consent and support of those whom it affects. Scientists, like physicians, should be partners of the public."

Holman built his case on the rules developed to regulate experimentation on humans and the use of dangerous medical practices. "Central to every code are three principles," he said. "1. the purpose of the experiment or treatment must have high importance unattainable in other ways. 2. probable gain must clearly outweigh probable risk for the subject, and 3. *the subject must be fully informed of the nature of the experiment or treatment, assent to it freely, and be able to terminate it at will.*" (Emphasis supplied.) The experiences acquired "in devising social policies to govern human experimentation and to secure informed consent to treatment" are applicable to genetic engineering, Holman testified. "We need an informed consent of society which is analogous to informed consent of an individual."

Holman proceeded to apply the three principles to experiments in genetic manipulation and found that they "do not clearly meet the test":

Because of the newness and power of genetic manipulation the risks are not known; the benefits must therefore be very great to justify the experiments. However, for example, genetic manipulation is clearly not essential for the achievement of increased agricultural production. Output could be greatly increased through many conventional methods. Similarly, the production of materials such as hormones can continue to be achieved by other means. For another example, most major human illnesses appear to result from actions of many genes. Useful genetic manipulation in these instances would probably be unattainable. For single gene illnesses, there are alternate approaches. . . . Thus, while genetic manipulation would theoretically be useful in these circumstances, it is not the only path to a possible solution.

If the foregoing arguments are valid, increasing general human knowledge remains as the predominant reason for conducting the experiments. This is a problematic justification. Because the purpose is not specific, *it is virtually impossible to balance benefits and risks. It is particularly difficult for those who might be affected to be fully informed or to assent freely.* Additionally, if for instance dangerous bacteria escaped from the laboratory to the general environment, it would be impossible to terminate the experiment easily. (Emphasis supplied.)

Dr. Brown urged that the consciences of researchers should delineate the limits of what should and should not be done in the pursuit of more information. While requiring that research be of "highest quality," he testified, "[w]e should permit scientists to choose their own projects." Holman disagreed:

Without impugning the investigators, I consider this a dangerous position. It raises questions of conflicts of interest. More important, it raises questions of uses and misuses of knowledge. . . . The social responsibility of those who have knowledge is to make it understandable and available to all. *It follows that decisions concerning the development and uses of knowledge are a public concern, and a joint responsibility of the public and those with the knowledge.* (Emphasis supplied.)

Dr. Willard Gaylin, a psychoanalyst at the Institute for Bioethics and the Life Sciences, expressed a similar view. "It is the very success of modern technology that has redefined its private pursuits as the public concern," he testified. "The mass success of the scientific enterprise and its technologies have made it an indispensable part of our common culture. Because we can no longer do without it, like water and air and other essentials of life it must enter into the public governance and the public domain."

Holman explored what happens when knowledge is "treated as a private possession, to be deployed and exploited for private purpose":

the needed social relationship is disrupted. Experts become semi-autonomous. Their individual or group interests prevail.

Dr. Brown seemed to imply by his emphasis on research of high quality ("Quality is something that can be measured") that its attainment protects us. In the case of genetic manipulation, Holman agreed that "[t]he goals are laudable," but emphasized that the precise outcome of experiments in this field "cannot be predicted." No matter the quality, researchers cannot predict what harmful but unintended consequences might arise. "Organisms such as bacteria or viruses containing human or other foreign genes could affect in quite unexpected ways the plants or animals they subsequently encounter," Holman testified. "Persons exposed to the experiments could suffer an infection unsusceptible to present therapy. Genetic alterations induced in domestic animals or in man might have overt or subtle consequences unanticipated by the experimenters."

. . .

All these things having been said, two fundamental, related questions remain. The first is, in an issue as complicated as genetic manipulation, Can the public learn enough to make an informed judgment? "This question is unanswerable with certainty," Dr. Holman acknowledged to Senator Kennedy. But, he said, his experience in medicine teaches him that "the public can learn. Physicians can attest to the willingness and capability of citizens to learn about, and deal effectively with, complex issues relating to their health when given the opportunity."

The second question is, Can the public intelligently supervise science? The important thing here is to understand the distinction between scientific decisions and moral and political decisions. Dr. Gaylin testified:

There is probably not a member of Congress to this day who completely understands the physics behind the creation of the atom bomb, and it is not necessary that they do so. The decisions on whether to build bombs, how many they should build and how and when, if ever, they should be used require a minimal knowledge of that technology. It would be appalling if it were deemed a problem in physics. *The decisions are political and must rest with the people and their representatives. . . .*

Indeed, the question might be asked, does the scientist in this day of early specialization have the training and expertise to intelligently supervise his own establishment? The very nature of the problems to be resolved and the values to be balanced are usually beyond the expertise of the scientific experts who so value expertise.

Ralph Nader in 1974, drawing on vast experience with environmental, nuclear, safety, and other technologies, had made a related point. "It is an unfortunate attribute of many specialized roles such as those of scientists to be accompanied by a commensurate narrowing of their range of accountability and their perceived duty," he said. "This is particularly the case when these roles are performed within bureaucratic structures of power, governmental or corporate, which command the resources and priorities for their use."[14]

Dr. Gaylin went on to caution:

In defense of a free science, a scientist often protests the intrusion of the public who is not trained to understand his methodologies in an area in which he himself is untrained to understand the moral and political implications of his work. (Emphasis supplied.)

How could the public intelligently supervise science? The mechanism that first springs to mind, legislation, is sometimes appropriate and sometimes inappropriate; Gaylin thinks it would be "unwanted and unwise" in the case of genetic manipulation. Nonetheless, the public's right to decide through the legislature cannot be questioned without at the same time questioning its sovereignty; and it has the right to make a mistake. But there are other mechanisms, including the funding to be provided through taxes, an insistence that Congress monitor what the scientific community is doing, and greater public support of public-interest groups that most consistently and with greatest dedication contribute to the infusion of "a competition of powers into the decision-making process."

The technologies discussed in this book, along with a great many others we haven't touched upon, challenge the public and its elected leaders to decide, while there may still be time, who is minding the store. "We nuclear people"? Supertanker owners? Aerosol merchants? Genetic manipulators?

Or is the public in charge? Them or us?

One prediction may be ventured: If the American polity deliberately or by default leaves it to scientists alone to control their radical undertakings it will be poorly positioned to deny like latitude to industry and the government bureaucracy. The outlook for making technology accountable, for making it the dutiful servant rather than the arrogant master of the public sovereignty, then will be bleak. And the prospects for the planet will be dimmed.

XI
What to Do

In the deliberations on the Constitution there was a pervasive and indeed dominant theme, here distilled by historian Jackson Turner Main: "In order to guard against the tyranny of power and preserve popular rule, the men entrusted with power had to be kept responsive to public opinion. If they were allowed to act independently, history proved that the results were evil. . . ." Main pointed out that "[t]he corruption of power, the oppression of strong government, had been vital, immediate dangers to those who waged the Revolution because of them." Consequently, he said, the crucial question for the Founding Fathers was, "How could responsibility [i.e., accountability] be maintained?"[1]

Relentlessly distrusting power, which in our immediate context we define to mean the ability to influence substantially the lives of a significant number of people, or to dictate how they live, the Framers separated and divided governmental powers, these being the powers which preoccupied them. In addition, the Founders made the centers of governmental power—the Executive, the Congress, and the Judiciary—accountable each to the other. They reserved certain powers for the states. Finally, they reposed sovereignty in the people, so that all governmental power ultimately would be accountable to the citizenry it is supposed to serve.

But in its role as a guarantor of accountability, which is the foundation of a true democratic process, the Constitution over the past two centuries has been sapped. Unaccountability—both perceived and unperceived—has come to infest every facet of a complex and swollen government establishment. Furthermore, we now find ourselves confronting a paradox, particularly insofar as the Executive branch is concerned: great reservoirs of power are essential if the nation is to cope with a proliferation of immediate as well as long-range problems of transcendent importance.

Moreover, the question considered by the Framers to be crucial—How could accountability be maintained?—requires new answers, not only as to public government, but equally as to private governments. The Constitution, designed as it was to deal only with public government, is not a ladder with which to scale strongholds of unaccountable nongovernment power.

In our book *America, Inc.: Who Owns and Operates the United States,* published in 1971, the two final sentences captured the essence of our message: "Concentrated economic power lies at the core of much of the unrest, injustice, and unresponsive government that besets us. Until it is

removed we can fiddle with this and that, but true progress will elude us."
Our sober purpose now is not to say we told you so; instead it is to say that
the message, while correct as far as it goes, does not go nearly far enough.
Specifically, we continue to believe that the diffusion of power is and must
remain a foremost goal—but our eyes are open to the existence of unaccountable power centers too numerous and too entrenched to permit us to believe
that legislation, or other conventional tools, ever will bring them satisfactorily and durably under control.

If significant or concentrated power cannot be adequately and reliably
diffused, broken up, checked and balanced, or restrained by a putatively
sovereign electorate, what can be done? Is there a way to make such power
accountable, by which we mean, as we have said, to make it answerable in
another place—a place effectively equipped for that purpose?

Ever since the Watergate scandal and the Vietnam debacle began to put
such questions before a wide public, a profusion of articles, speeches, reports,
and books has, late in the game, recognized and grappled with the need for
accountability.[2] Various remedies have been suggested, some of which are
excellent. For example, an ombudsman mechanism of one kind or another
frequently has been urged for the Executive branch, Congress, and administrative agencies.[3] Congress has been urged to exercise oversight powers after
nearly allowing them to atrophy from disuse in several critical areas.[4] In
behalf of consumers, Congress came close to passing legislation to give them
an independent advocate in government departments and agencies, but set
it aside because it faced a certain veto by President Ford, which, at least in
early 1976, would not be overridden. Additional legislation has been proposed to attach personal accountability to government employees who fail
to enforce the laws, or who neglect or improperly or incompetently perform
their public duties; possibly of greater significance, the bill would protect the
rights of those federal employees who expose administrative failures, incompetence, dishonesty, and corruption. As matters stand, government
workers who make such exposures invite martyrdom.

In another effort to make government accountable, Congress has gone far
toward moving operations and decision-making of government agencies, and
of its own committees, out into the open—"government in the sunshine,"
in a phrase much used by the principal advocate, Senator Lawton Chiles
(D–Fla.). Similarly, Senator Lee Metcalf (D–Mont.) continues to try to open
up government advisory committees to full public scrutiny. The Freedom of
Information Act also makes an important contribution to openness.

It does not derogate such advances, however, to point out that they
incorporate no mechanisms with which to enforce accountability. And there

is a common denominator under each item of legislation described in the preceding paragraph as well as under each of the "sunshine" steps: one source of unaccountable power (Congress, say) takes on the task of making another source of unaccountable power (the President, say) accountable. The problem, delineated by long experience, is that sources of unaccountable power tend to work out accommodations with each other. In the long run, the watchdog often ends up most in need of being watched. Who was watching the congressional watchdogs who were nonwatching the Presidents who took us, by stealth, into the Bay of Pigs, Vietnam, and Watergate, who accumulated totalitarian "emergency" powers, and who had the services of an unmonitored CIA, FBI, IRS, and NSA?

An imaginative exception to the approaches we have described has been advanced by Gerry Spann and Alan B. Morrison, who are associates of Ralph Nader. To deal with illegal actions by government, they would, through legislation, confer the right to sue, or legal standing, on citizens, organizations, and governmental units affected directly or indirectly by those actions. Uniquely, it would give the citizen a clear-cut and effective opportunity to challenge governmental actions in an open forum, the federal courts, in which effective remedies are available. The proposal does have an inherent serious limitation, applying as it would only to federal government violations of the Constitution or federal laws. Additionally, the "cases and controversies" section of Article III of the Constitution, as interpreted by the courts, would severely limit the number of persons who could initiate the actions.

A unique proposal for making the President accountable has been made by Joseph A. Califano, Jr., who was a White House aide in the Johnson Administration. In his book *A Presidential Nation*, published in 1975, Califano suggested enactment of a law to require the President (and Congress) to publish an advance analysis of the impact on the power of the Presidency that would be had by any major new legislative program. In addition, the presidential term would be extended from four years to six.[5] As devices to achieve accountability, these would clamp toothless gums on a sinewy problem.

A proposal to make Congress more accountable emerged at a Conference on Constitutional Principles held by the Center for Democratic Institutions: either through legislation or amendment of the Constitution, the people would elect a certain number of representatives and senators at large. Such legislators would have a national constituency, as only the President has had up to now.[6] On balance this must be counted another dubious approach. A national constituency certainly has not made the Presidency accountable; what reason is there to believe that a number of at-large legislators would make Congress significantly if at all more accountable than it is now? Indeed, a good argument can be made that the larger a legislator's constituency, the more difficult it is to make him accountable. No one seriously contends that a senator is more accountable to his state-wide constituency than is a congressman to his district-wide constituency. Congress is providing a better answer to the problems of its own overall unaccountability simply by making more and more of its decisions in open rather than closed committee and House-Senate conference sessions.

Another proposal for congressional accountability has been put forth by Marcus Raskin, of the Institute for Policy Studies in Washington. He would establish local "congressional grand juries" primarily "to develop the ideas and programs of the citizens," and apparently to advise Congress and to assure that legislators listen to their constituents.[7] We doubt that congressmen need congressional grand juries to help them relate to the problems of their constituents. In any event, the grand juries, however much they might improve the flow of information between districts and legislators, either would not reach the heart of the matter, which is accountability, or would tend to do something highly questionable, which would be to substitute a concept of accountability to grand juries for traditional accountability to full constituencies. The grand juries would become watchdogs of congressmen, renewing the question we raised earlier: Who would watch the watchdogs?

A parliamentary system, such as England's, never loses its appeal to some Americans. But England's system has not worked all that marvelously, even conceding certain obvious advantages. Most importantly, we simply have strong doubts that a parliamentary system, which in other countries has evolved logically and naturally from their own particular backgrounds, possibly could be adapted to our wholly different historical, political, and social context. Besides, a parliamentary system tends to coalesce more power in the Executive than already exists under our system. We are indebted to Professor Philip B. Kurland, the University of Chicago constitutional lawyer, for this salient observation: "The proposed [parliamentary] system could work in this country only if there were a real two-party system in this nation. Today there is not. The so-called national parties are faction-ridden. And in a parliamentary system with a multiplicity of parties, the instability overweighs any possible gain from responsibility."[8]

Some urge a return to smaller units of government. For certain functions and purposes this assuredly is clearly desirable, but for others it is impractical nostalgia. In any case, our history reminds us that power in small units of government can be quite unaccountable, or quite prepared, say, to deny the rights of minorities, as blacks, Spanish-speaking and Indian citizens are not likely to soon forget. In sum, Robert Maynard Hutchins has said the giving of power to a smaller community often merely substitutes a small barony for a larger one.[9]

. . .

Numerous remedies or palliatives also have been proposed to tame large corporations, particularly the multinationals. These include two that we believe are especially meritorious.

The first proposal would put public directors on the boards of large corporations, so as to compel them to pay more attention to the environment, minorities, and other social responsibilities; this is essentially an ombudsman approach. It would ameliorate, but cannot solve, problems of corporate accountability.

The second proposal, which was the centerpiece of our recommendations in *America, Inc.*, was for federal chartering of corporations. We remain completely convinced of the desirability, rationality, and urgency of this approach; it is preposterous to go on letting the unaccountable government of little New Jersey, say, charter Exxon, the world's largest industrial corporation. In a six-hundred-page report prepared over a five-year period, Ralph Nader's Corporate Accountability Research Group urged legislation to require federal chartering of any industrial, retailing, or transportation corporation with annual domestic sales of at least $250 million, or with at least ten thousand employees. The purpose is to recognize such corporations for what they are, private governments, and to try to make them accountable by, for example, forcing them to make full disclosure of financial data.[10]

Committed though we are to federal chartering, we must note that it and other proposals for corporate restructuring would entrust one major center of unaccountable power, in this case the federal government, to control another center of unaccountable power, in this case the megacorporation. Moreover, these proposals, as well as those for making government accountable, can be implemented only by legislation. After a prolonged gearing up, legislation may or may not be enacted, and if enacted could be weakened or even repealed by later legislation. Great economic interests with much at stake would work resolutely to do just that. A final point: without effective, sustained congressional oversight of federal laws, the good intentions with which they may have been enacted tend to fade away. That is what the record shows. And if there is anything to be learned from the record of oversight, it is that Congress usually cannot or will not sustain it over any long period of time. Similar caveats attach to other legislative proposals which we nevertheless have strongly endorsed during the course of this book.

Two additional points of critical importance remain to be made about the proposed remedies we have listed. The first is that none of them, or, for that matter, others of which we are aware deals with nongovernmental centers of unaccountable power such as the medical, dental, legal, accounting, and other professions, although, as we have pointed out, they greatly influence our daily lives. The second point is that, whatever the merits of any of the listed proposals, none is addressed to the structural defects in the Constitution that have allowed unaccountability to impress itself on so much of our society.

"In the perspective of American history," *Saturday Review/World* said in an editorial, "the most important lesson of Watergate is that the ultimate power of this society must be consolidated in the hands of the American people. How this can be done in the modern world, with all its complexities and tensions, many of which call for prompt response, is the largest and finest test yet to confront the American intelligence."[11] This was a call for a return to the basic principle of sovereignty of the people on which the Framers built the Constitution (although they restricted the direct vote to the election of members of the House of Representatives). Clearly, the editorial acknowledges that the Constitution has failed to consolidate ultimate power in the hands of the people. This failure, we believe, may be closely related to some of the feelings of inability to control events, of inadequacy, and even of insignificance that many Americans feel.

In explaining man's destructiveness, the psychoanalyst Erich Fromm, in his book *The Anatomy of Human Destructiveness,* has said that help in any broad sense can be achieved only through radical changes in the social and political structure that restore man to his supreme role in society.[12] If such a restoration is to occur, each person must be given some effective means to exercise his fraction of the sovereignty that is the whole people's; he must have, and feel he has, the power to react constructively to events that affect him.

"Democracies do not survive unless elected officials do what they are supposed to do and citizens maintain vigilance to see that they do," the Office of the Watergate Special Prosecutor said in its final report.

The public unfolding of Watergate abuses resulted from citizen, press and official actions. Nothing can replace that kind of vigilance; and recommendations for new laws or new institutions are insignificant when compared to the stubborn, plodding daily work of Americans and their elected representatives in watching over and channeling the power of their national Government, the power of concentrated wealth, the power of officially spoken and written words, and the power of secret bureaucracies.[13]

But *how* can Americans effectively watch over and, more importantly, deal with rampant unaccountability?

Our answer is an accountability amendment to the Constitution. Only such an amendment can equip the people with the tools with which to make the public government—including Congress—and nongovernmental power centers properly accountable. Only such an amendment can make whole the concept of sovereignty which, so long as it can be implemented only by occasional trips to the polling place, never will adequately restrain unaccountable public and private power. Only such an amendment can harness the sovereignty of the people to fulfill the sole legitimate justification for government as seen by the Founding Fathers: the safety and happiness of the citizenry.

DRAFT CONSTITUTIONAL AMENDMENT

Any citizen eligible to vote in a Federal election[1] shall have standing to bring a claim in a Federal court of appropriate jurisdiction challenging any act or conduct of a person which act or conduct threatens to cause or is causing substantial harm[2] to the safety or happiness of a consequential[3] number of people.

The court may grant such relief as it deems appropriate and may award reasonable costs of litigation, including attorney's fees.[4]

"Person" includes any individual, governmental entity (including any department or agency), or nongovernmental entity (including any unincorporated association, corporation, or partnership).

"Happiness" means the rights of citizens to fundamental justice, fundamental liberties, fundamental fairness, and the perpetuation and protection of environmental quality.

"Fundamental justice" includes, but is not limited to, the principles of "distributive justice"[5] to the extent that any governmental entity, by legislation or otherwise, establishes barriers or lessens the opportunities of citizens to share in the entitlements, wealth, and resources of the United States on an equitable basis.

This amendment which we propose simply would give every citizen standing —the right to sue—so that he could go into a United States District Court and challenge conduct, whether governmental or nongovernmental, which substantially threatens the safety or happiness of a not insignificant number

---

[1]Inasmuch as the purpose of this amendment is to furnish a better alternative to the vote for asserting sovereignty, standing under this amendment is limited to citizens elegible to vote.

[2]The amendment is limited to "substantial" harm because its purpose is to deal with those problems causing more than minimal damage to a consequential number of people rather than attempting to provide a remedy for specific harm done to specific persons. It is not intended to apply to those acts which are quantifiably *de minimus* insofar as their effects on any part of society are concerned.

[3]The same reasoning as in "2" above applies to the requirement that a "consequential" number of citizens be involved, the amendment being intended as a means of dealing with problems generally rather than with specific harm to an individual. Although "consequential" is a purposely vague standard, it is intended, for example, that acts affecting the physical health or safety of citizens would require a fewer number of citizens to be affected than would acts affecting "happiness."

[4]The purpose of allowing the court to award attorney's fees is to encourage members of the bar to represent potential litigants who otherwise might find it difficult to obtain legal representation.

[5]"Distributive justice" as used here applies to the rights and opportunity of citizens to share in the entitlements, wealth, and resources of the United States on an equitable basis. This portion of the amendment, therefore, would make unconstitutional legislation, rules, regulations, or any acts of a governmental entity which interferes with, lessens, or results in the establishment of inequitable barriers to the opportunity of citizens to share in such entitlements, wealth, and resources.

of citizens. Power that is now unaccountable, of the kind described in this book, would be made answerable to the individual citizen, as intended by the Framers.

"Safety" is relatively easy to define, because it can be laid against an objective standard, our physical and mental health.

As for "happiness," which is at the heart of the amendment, it is not, we hasten to say, a synonym for pleasure. Rather, the Founding Fathers (and we) define it to embrace values so basic as to be preconditions to the well-being of society.

The Constitution is the prime instrument through which society declares its values. Our proposed amendment would empower the individual citizen to move to protect society against those who would erode or destroy those values.

In our judgment, any definition of happiness in a constitutional context begins with the presumption that power must not be used in ways that either diminish fundamental justice and liberty, or that unreasonably deny fundamental fairness. This accords with the Preamble. There, "We the people" stated why they "do ordain and establish this Constitution":"in order to form a more perfect union, *establish justice,* insure domestic tranquility, provide for the common defense, and *secure the blessings of liberty to ourselves and our posterity . . ."*

The rationales of immediate concern are those we have italicized. They are obviously generalities, but down through the years, the Supreme Court, notably in cases involving the first nine amendments of the Bill of Rights, and the concept of "liberty" in the Fourteenth Amendment, has particularized them.

William O. Douglas, the former associate justice, did this sweepingly in a concurring opinion in 1973 in which he discussed the Ninth Amendment. He said that it

obviously does not create federally enforceable rights. It merely says, "The enumeration in the Constitution, of certain rights, shall not be construed to deny or disparage others retained by the people." But a catalogue of these rights includes customary, traditional, and time-honored rights, amenities, privileges, and immunities that come within the sweep of "The Blessings of Liberty" mentioned in the Preamble to the Constitution. Many of them, in my opinion, come within the meaning of the term "liberty" as used in the Fourteenth Amendment.

First is the autonomous control over the development and expression of one's intellect, interests, tastes, and personality. . . .

Second is freedom of choice in the basic decisions of one's life respecting marriage, divorce, procreation, contraception, and the upbringing of children. . . .

Third is the freedom to care for one's health and person, freedom from bodily restraint or compulsion, freedom to walk, stroll, or loaf. . . .[14]

An iron logic requires that the protections afforded a citizen from governmental interference under the Constitution as it now stands must be extended to comparable interference by all forms of private power. In addition, a person should have standing not merely to sue when he himself is injured by government, as at present, but when the liberty or freedom of a substantial number of citizens is injured or threatened, by either public or private power, even if he is not one of them. Our proposed amendment would accomplish these extensions of standing for the citizen. Necessarily, judges would have to assess the impact of abuses brought before them. This properly would come to be regarded, openly, as one of their principal duties, reversing the present trend of judges' resistance to being considered interpreters of fundamental principles.

Our definition of happiness (still in a constitutional sense) has an additional dimension: protection of the environment. In a seminal essay, Christopher D. Stone proposed that legal rights be accorded to natural objects "in the environment—and to the natural environment as a whole."[15] Such rights having been granted to the corporation, a wholly synthetic creation, why should they be denied a lake, a river, a mountain, or a tree?

In a minority opinion in a key Supreme Court decision affecting the environment, Justice Douglas, citing Stone, pressed the argument to its ultimate:

The ordinary corporation is a "person" for purposes of the adjudicatory processes, whether it represents proprietary, spiritual, aesthetic, or charitable causes.

So it should be as respects valleys, alpine meadows, rivers, lakes, estuaries, beaches, ridges, groves of trees, swampland, or even air that feels the destructive pressures of modern technology and modern life. The river, for example, is the living symbol of all the life it sustains or nourishes—fish, aquatic insects, water ouzels, otter, fisher, deer, elk, bear, and all other animals, including man, who are dependent on it or who enjoy it for its sight, its sound, or its life. The river as plaintiff speaks for the ecological unit of life that is part of it. Those people who have a meaningful relation to that body of water—whether it be a fisherman, a canoeist, a zoologist, or a logger—must be able to speak for the values which the river represents and which are threatened with destruction.

The problem of course is they do not and cannot. Justice Douglas continued:

Those who have that intimate relationship with the inanimate object about to be injured, polluted, or otherwise despoiled are its legitimate spokesmen.[16]

Justice Douglas' designs are not the law. Our proposed amendment, however, would give each citizen credentials to protect the environment. In Douglas' words, "before these priceless bits of Americana (such as a valley, an alpine meadow, a river, or a lake) are forever lost or are so transformed as to be reduced to the eventual rubble of our urban environment, the voice of the existing beneficiaries of these environmental wonders [would] be heard."[17]

To recapitulate for a moment: for purposes of our constitutional amendment, we have defined happiness to be inconsistent with acts of public or private governments that either decrease fundamental justice or liberty, or deny fundamental fairness, and to include protection of the environment. The definition must be further expanded, however, to take into account an additional element: what is commonly known as distributive justice, i.e., an allocation of society's wealth and resources among its citizens in ways that need not (and actually should not) be equal, but that must not be grossly inequitable.

The Founding Fathers felt strongly that the right to share in the property of the nation was essential to the happiness of free men. This was attributable in part to the strong influence had on them by John Locke's philosophy of natural rights and natural law. Samuel Adams provides a case in point. In his essay "The Rights of Colonists," he said that among the natural rights of the colonists are: "first, a right to life; secondly, to liberty; thirdly, to property, together with the right to support and defend them in the best manner they can. . . ."[18]

"Whenever there are in any county uncultivated lands and unemployed poor," Thomas Jefferson said, "it is clear that the laws of property have been so far extended as to violate natural rights. The earth is given as a common stock for man to labor and live on. If for the encouragement of industry we allow it to be appropriated, we must take care that other employment be provided to those excluded from the appropriation. If we do not, the fundamental right to labor the earth returns to the unemployed."[19]

The First Continental Congress, which met in the autumn of 1774 to petition the British for a redress of grievances, reflected this approach. In its Declaration and Resolves, the First Right was "life, liberty and property."[20] Similarly, the Massachusetts Bill of Rights listed as an inalienable right ". . . that of acquiring, possessing and protecting property. . . ."[21]

A draft constitution for Virginia, which Jefferson is believed to have written in 1776, said that "Every person of full age neither owning nor having owned [50] acres of land, shall be entitled to an appropriation of [50] acres or to so much as would make up what he owns or has owned [50] acres in full and absolute dominion, and no other person shall be capable of taking an appropriation."[22]

In the original draft of the Declaration of Independence the rights proclaimed to be inalienable were, "life, liberty, and property," not, as in the final version, ". . . and the pursuit of happiness." Jefferson made the change. Certainly it is reasonable to presume that he intended "the pursuit of happiness" to include "property."

Finally, "Cato," the pseudonym of an articulate opponent of the Constitution, took a strongly equalitarian stance, writing in 1780: ". . . government [to express the popular will] required a relatively equal division of property. Since dominion follows Property . . . an equality of estate will give equality of power; and an Equality of Power is a Commonwealth or Democracy; whereas Very great Riches in Private Men . . . destroy amongst the Commons, that Balance of Property and Power, which is necessary to a Democracy."[23]

Over the last two centuries the concept of property has changed drastically. Once it was land, farm animals, the tools of a trade. Today it is also, and often more importantly for most of us, something determined by one's status in an organization, such as job security, medical insurance, or a pension.

The United Nations in 1948 adopted the Universal Declaration of Human Rights. None of the nations that signed it having observed it, so far as we know, it is an artifact of interest only for its adventurous expansion of the definition of property to far frontiers, so as to include a citizen's right to work, to a free choice of employment, to just and wholesome working conditions, to protection against unemployment, to just compensation for his work, and to a standard of living adequate for the health and well-being of himself and his family—meaning sufficient food, clothing, housing, medical care and social services, and the right to security in the event of becoming unemployed, sick, disabled, widowed, old, or otherwise rendered, by circumstances beyond his control, incapable of earning a livelihood.[24]

In the United States, as was noted in our chapter on taxes, the distribution of wealth and income is highly inequitable. For example, the top 20 percent of the population, as of 1962, controlled 77 percent of the wealth, and, as of 1968, received 43.5 percent of the actual income before taxes; in the same years, the bottom 20 percent of the population controlled less than 2 percent of the wealth, and received only 6.9 percent of the income.

Surely such imbalances in some degree can be righted. One obvious move is to eliminate personal tax deductions and exemptions—provided that this is done in lockstep with moves to assure equity for middle- and low-income taxpayers and the poor, such as downward adjustments in their basic tax rates. The appeal of any single, grand, convulsive scheme for a massive redistribution of wealth may be strong, but we seriously question its practicality or workability.

This is not to counsel despair. Rather, it is to propose—more modestly and, we hope, more realistically—the need to block the enlargement of existing inequalities while trying to erode them. We would do this through our proposed amendment, which simply would rule out, as unconstitutional, any new federal, state, or local legislation that unreasonably interferes with the just entitlements of the least-advantaged. This would bar, for example, legislation that would enlarge the share of the wealth already in the hands of the much-advantaged; and it would require the assessment—by the courts, if not by the legislatures—of the impact of legislation on the have-nots. Thus, the trend toward concentration of wealth would be halted while— with luck—successful efforts to cut it back would be made. These efforts would be primarily in the form of new laws. Our concern, however, is with providing a constitutional back-up and control, so that all new laws henceforth could point us in only one direction: away from inequality.

In his profound book *A Theory of Justice,* Harvard professor John Rawls argues against any governmental policy that, in the long run, will not benefit the least-advantaged.[25] In contrast, Professor Robert Nozick, his colleague at Harvard, contends in a later book, *Anarchy, State, and Utopia,* that it is unwise and unfair for the state to use its power to redistribute wealth.[26] Our own position is that the happiness of society (again in the constitutional context) is incompatible with extreme inequalities of wealth, and that our proposed amendment deals with this dilemma in a way congenial to the spirit of the Founders.

Now we turn to objections to the amendment that we believe may be made.

The first objection might be that if citizens were to have standing to challenge important public or private assertions of unaccountable power, the courts would be deluged with cases. This point has been made against most every piece of major legislation to come before Congress in the past decade. But the courts have proved that they can adapt to the need; they have, for example, devised procedures to cope with complex class-action litigation sometimes involving hundreds of thousands of persons, and they also have devised procedures to consolidate similar or related lawsuits originally filed in several districts. Furthermore, the courts have developed methods for early resolution of matters which they find on their face to be without merit. In matters not susceptible to such methods, careful use of discovery techniques determines at an early stage of a proceeding whether a litigant has a substantial possibility of eventually prevailing; if not, judges cut matters short by granting motions for dismissal or for summary judgment. In the end the court system may have to be enlarged. So be it.

A second objection is that the courts themselves exercise unaccountable power. This is correct—but less impressive than it may seem at first blush. The reason is that suits brought in the federal courts, under our proposed amendment, would be distributed among literally hundreds of judges, each of whom is significantly independent from the others. Admittedly, each has a degree of unaccountability, but it is not of the kind that coalesces into concentrated, pervasive power.

Moreover, it is entirely consistent with democratic principles for courts to play an active role in checking bureaucratic and corporate abuse, Simon Lazarus pointed out in his book *The Genteel Populists*. ". . . And from a pragmatic standpoint courts should be relatively effective in this role," he said. He related their effectiveness to their independence, saying that this characteristic "is the first resource the federal courts can use to aid public and majority interests systematically neglected by the elective branches."[27]

Finally, there is a measure of deliberate, routine accountability in the right of parties to litigation to appeal a lower-court decision to a court of appeals, and a decision of that body to the Supreme Court. To be sure, the High Court regularly declines to hear cases without stating its reasons for doing so; and for this and other reasons admittedly wields unaccountable power. Historically, however, the Supreme Court has shown itself reluctant to overreach. The Court knows itself to be in some ways a fragile institution that needs substantial public acceptance of its rulings if it is to withstand attack. This serves as a strong external restraint on the Court's power, although it is of course a restraint nowhere to be found in the words of the Constitution.

One of the authors has had considerable experience with the federal courts in cities across the country. Insofar as the motivations, diligence, fairness, and wisdom of judges are concerned, the experience has left him, on the whole, not disillusioned, but without illusions. It also has prepared him to accept and to urge this non-Utopian, practicable proposition: On balance, the courts are the only institution capable of achieving, over time, the solid, stable, workable accountability of public and private power that the safety and happiness of the country require. Conceding their many failures and weaknesses, it should not be forgotten that ultimately it was the courts which weakened or struck down Executive privilege, impoundment of funds appropriated by Congress, and other unconstitutional usurpations of power by the White House, and which significantly exposed and dealt with the Watergate horrors.

Lawyers are expensive, sometimes almost prohibitively so for persons of moderate income, and so is litigation. Consequently, the opportunity to initiate litigation has been unduly restricted to persons of means and to corporations and organizations, leaving aside a relative handful of public-interest and poverty-law groups. And so there is no evading the question whether only the affluent could sue under our proposed amendment. The answer, not as satisfactory as we would wish, is that public-interest, environmental, and other groups, individuals, and law firms dedicating a portion of their resources to *pro bono publico* work would litigate at least some of the most important cases, particularly those in which standing cannot be contested and there is a good prospect of winning. But the amendment would take an affirmative approach by guaranteeing payment of costs and attorney's fees to successful litigants.

Yet another argument against the proposed amendment might be that it would become a tool of persons who would use it to endanger national security (whatever that is), or to pry legitimate trade secrets out of corporations. This argument is owed little weight, because the courts have an arsenal of devices, such as *in camera* inspection of devices and protective orders, to keep matters in hand. Indeed, the record suggests that a more serious problem, one of an opposite kind, may be that the courts will be too much inclined to credit dubious arguments for national security or trade secrets, or to keep their dockets clear by peremptorily dismissing meritorious suits at early stages.

In this regard, it should be borne in mind that a degree of conservatism is built into the very selection of judges. The selection process is a political one in which the President makes the formal nomination. But influential politicians are in *de facto* control from start to finish, and the opposition of the senior senator from a nominee's or possible nominee's state is almost always absolutely decisive. In addition, the establishment-oriented American Bar Association exercises a degree of oversight which tends further to assure that the judiciary as a whole would take a cautious approach to lawsuits challenging the constitutionality of governmental or nongovernmental acts.

Under the amendment, would federal judges be philosopher-kings? Actually, they have been playing that role since 1803, when the Supreme Court decided *Marbury* v. *Madison*. The difference would be that we would stop pretending that they don't. The great Judge Learned Hand did not so pretend. "I venture to believe," he wrote almost a half-century ago,

that it is as important to a judge called upon to pass on a question of constitutional law, to have at least a bowing acquaintance with Acton and Maitland, with Thucydides, Gibbon and Carlyle, with Homer, Dante, Shakespeare and Milton, with Machiavelli, Montaigne, and Rabelais, with Plato, Bacon, Hume, and Kant, as with the books which have been specifically written on the subject. For in such matters everything turns upon the spirit in which he approaches the questions before him. The words he must construe are empty vessels into which he can pour nearly anything he will. . . . [Judges] must be aware that there are before them more than verbal problems; more than final solutions cast in generalizations of universal applicability. They must be aware of the changing social tensions in every society which make it an organism; which demand new schemata of adaptation; which will disrupt it, if rigidly confined.[28]

A candid recognition of the crucial role of the federal bench would, we hope, have the effect of inducing citizens, civic organizations, and the press to pay more serious attention than in the past to the selection of judges. The presumption should be that only the best should even be considered. But that will not happen unless the traditional cozy political arrangements—particularly that in which each of the fifty senior senators, for all practical purposes, chooses the judges for his state—are replaced by mechanisms that put the premium on quality.

"Every four years we elect a President through democratic processes," Richard L. Strout, writing as "TRB," has said. "Between elections, however, he reigns out of reach of any sanctions—as long as he avoids getting caught committing an indictable felony. Absent such a mistake, no matter how outrageously he defaults in the exercise of presidential powers, nor what the consequences are to the country, he remains in office. . . . This is a situation that Americans tolerate in few other institutions."[29] Admittedly, our amendment would not meet this problem head-on. But it would enlarge the opportunity, through the courts, to hold to account any President and the Executive branch.

The amendment would not provide the opportunity to deal satisfactorily with all of the agonizing problems of unaccountable power, even with the array bared by Watergate. We emphatically do not hold out the amendment as a perfect solution, if such a solution can be imagined. Most of the Founding Fathers certainly did not think in terms of perfection; they accepted the postulate that justice depends on the virtue of rulers. We do not expect rulers in the future to be more virtuous than those in the past, and we cannot conceive of a process that would give us virtuous rulers all of the time. No, we think we are in the real world. There we derive comfort from a definition of a virtuous Bostonian: a man who is afraid of the police. Taking it from there, we seek in rulers, through the amendment, the virtue, or the added virtue, that comes from making them effectively, openly, and strictly accountable for their uses of power.

Acknowledging that the amendment is imperfect, perhaps even in ways that have not even occurred to us, we say nonetheless that it is the most promising, the most supple, and, in the light of our American heritage, the most philosophically and pragmatically right instrument available. It would put sovereignty over power into the hands of the people. That is where the Founders intended it to be. That is where it should be.

The prescient reader at this point will be wondering if we have painted ourselves into a corner. Have we not argued as forcefully as we could that an amendment along the lines we have proposed is essential? But have we not also asserted the unaccountability of Congress, the very body empowered by the Constitution to propose an amendment, and of the legislatures of the states, three-fourths of which would be needed for ratification?

Have we painted ourselves into a corner? Yes. But accountability is an idea whose time has come. The paint will dry.

Postscript

The end of the institution, maintenance and administration of government is to secure the existence of the body politic; to protect it, and to furnish the individuals who compose it with the power of enjoying, in safety and tranquillity, their natural rights and the blessings of life; and whenever these great objects are not obtained, the people have a right to alter the governement and to take measures necessary for their safety, happiness and prosperity.

John Adams, preamble to a
draft constitution for the
Commonwealth of Massachusetts, 1778

Notes

Introduction

[1]"Accountability and the Federal Contractor," *Journal of Public Law* 20 (1971): 473.

[2]National Consumers League, *Consumers Almanac and Calendar* (Washington, 1975), p. 1.

[3]Ibid.

[4]Arthur Jay Silverstein, "Consumer Protection in Talmudic Law," *Reform Judaism*, November 1974.

[5]*London Review*, 1835; reprinted in Mills *Dissertations and Discussions: Political, Philosophical, and Historical*, 1 (New York: Haskell House, 1975), p. 475.

[6]*History of Greece* (London, 1849), 5:475.

[7]*Science and the State in Greece and Rome* (New York: Wiley, 1968), p. 38.

[8]*Thomas Jefferson on Democracy*, ed. Saul K. Padover (New York: Pelican, 1946), pp. 21–23.

[9]Richard McKeon, "The Development and the Significance of the Concept of Responsibility," *Revue Internationale de Philosophe* 11 (Brussels, 1957): 5.

[10]Ibid.

[11]Ibid., pp. 6–7.

[12]Ibid., p. 8.

[13]Ibid., p. 23.

[14]Ibid., p. 9.

[15]Ibid.

[16]Op. cit. (above, n. 8), p. 22.

[17]"Public Accountability and Audit: A Reconnaissance," *The Dilemma of Accountability in Modern Government*, ed. Bruce Smith and D. C. Hayne (New York: Macmillan, 1971), p. 312.

[18]"Responsibility Towards Oneself and Others," *Revue Internationale de Philosophe* 11 (Brussels, 1957): 51.

[19]*Resignation in Protest* (New York: Grossman, 1975), p. 86.

[20]Radio address from London to America, 11 October 1931.

[21]*The Case for Modern Man* (New York: Harper, 1955), p. 203.

[22]"New Migrant Housing Rules Assailed," *Washington Post*, 23 January, 1975.

[23]*The Dilemma of Accountability in Modern Government*, p. 358.

[24]"The Greatest Judge," *Washington Post*, 12 January, 1975.

[25]"Responsibility for the Future and the Far-Away," *Revue Internationale de Philosophe* 11 (Brussels, 1957): 100.

[26]Ibid.

[27]Op. cit. (above, n. 8), p. 138.

[28]"The Defeat of America," *New York Review of Books*, 5 October 1972.

[29]"Watergate Panel Cure: Constitutional Band-Aids," *Washington Post*, 21 July 1974. Professor Miller expanded his views in "Implications of Watergate: Some Proposals for

Cutting the Presidency Down to Size," *Hastings Constitutional Law Quarterly* 2 (1975): pp. 33–74.

[30]Ibid.

[31] *Washington Journal. The Events of 1973–1974* (New York: Random House, 1975), p. 181.

Chapter 1. The Framers' Grand Design: Why It Failed

[1]a)James Madison, *Notes of Debates in the Federal Convention of 1787* (New York: Norton, 1969).

b)Alexis de Toqueville, *Democracy in America,* the Henry Reeve text as revised by Francis Bowen, now further corrected and edited with a historical essay, editorial notes, and bibliographies by Phillips Bradley (New York: Knopf, 1945), 1:118.

c)Probably as accurate and objective an evaluation as any has been written by the historian Irving Brant, in his classic work *James Madison: Father of the Constitution 1787–1800* (Indianapolis: Bobbs Merrill, 1950), p. 159:

The longer a believer in democracy studies the work of the framers of the Constitution, the higher his estimate of them is bound to become. That is due in part to the cumulative evidence of their integrity and ability, in part to the fact that, property-minded though they were, they accepted the people as the final custodians of public power. The convention opened on the note of the fury and follies of democracy. Safeguards against democratic excesses were planted in the Constitution, and local interests and selfishness crowded their way in. But the convention ended on a note of trust in the people. No greater error can be made than to say that the Constitution was written either in a spirit of blind self-interest or of hostility to democracy.

Contrast this with Madison's own appraisal, as cited by Brant (pp. 59–60) and taken from James Madison, "Preface," *Writings,* 2:411:

But whatever may be the judgment pronounced on the competency of the architects of the Constitution, or whatever may be the destiny of the edifice prepared by them, I feel it a duty to express my profound and solemn conviction, derived from my intimate opportunity of observing and appreciating the views of the convention, collectively and individually, that there never was an assembly of men, charged with a great and arduous trust, who were more pure in their motives, or more exclusively or anxiously devoted to the object committed to them.

[2] *Works of the Honorable James Wilson* (Philadelphia: Lorenzo Press, 1804), 3 Vols.

[3]Op. cit. (above, no. 1a), p. 52.

[4]Ibid., p. 76.

[5]Ibid., p. 135.

[6]Ibid., p. 77.

[7]Alexander Hamilton, James Madison, and John Jay, *The Federalist* (New York: Mentor, 1961), no. 51, p. 324.

[8]Ibid., p. 371.

[9] *Documents of American History,* ed. Henry S. Commager, 9th ed. (Englewood Cliffs, N.J.: Prentice-Hall, 1973), p. 107.

[10]Op. cit. (above, n. 7), no. 47, p. 301.

[11]"Implications of Watergate: Some Proposals for Cutting the Presidency Down to Size," *Hastings Constitutional Law Quarterly* 2, no. 1 (Winter, 1975), p. 47.

[12]Ibid., p. 46.

[13]Op. cit. (above, n. 7), no. 51, p. 322.

[14]Ibid., p. 323.

15 *Thomas Jefferson on Democracy*, ed. Saul K. Padover (New York: Penguin, 1946), p. 171.

16 *The Defeat of America* (New York: Simon and Schuster, 1974), p. 112.

17 *The Writings of Samuel Adams* (New York: G. P. Putnam's, 1908), 4 Vols.

18Op. cit. (above, n. 15), p. 67.

19Op. cit. (above, n. 16), pp. 42–43.

20"The Challenge Beyond Nihilism," *New York Times*, 27 September 1975.

Chapter 2. Separation and Division: The Presidency

1"Tying the Imperial Purse Strings," *Washington Monthly*, September 1975.

2Edward Weisband and Thomas M. Franck, *Resignation in Protest: Political and Ethical Choices between Loyalty to Team and Loyalty to Conscience in American Public Life* (New York: Grossman, 1975), pp. 123–24.

3 *The Imperial Presidency* (Boston: Houghton Mifflin, 1973), p. 219.

4"The Nature of the Presidency," radio speech, 19 September, 1968.

5"Ends: Watergate Reflections," *New York Times Magazine.* 19 May 1974.

6 *The President: Office and Powers* (New York: New York University Press, 1974), p. 18.

7Ibid., p. 28, taken from Woodrow Wilson, *Constitutional Government in the United States* (Columbia, 1908), 67–73 passim.

8 *The Defeat of America* (New York: Simon and Schuster, 1974), p. 61.

9Cited in Commager book (above, n. 8), p. 63, from *Works of James Madison*, Hunt, ed. 6:174.

10Op. cit. (above, n. 8) p. 63.

11The Final Report of the Committee on the Judiciary, House of Representatives, Ninety-third Congress, Second Session, *Impeachment of Richard M. Nixon, President of the United States* (New York: Bantam, 1975), p. 422.

12Special Senate Committee on National Emergencies and Delegated Emergency Powers in Support of a Recommended National Emergencies Act, "Interim Report," reprinted in *Congressional Record*, 22 August 1974, pp. S15789–15791.

13 *Congressional Record*, 22 August 1974, p. S15784.

14"The Principal Unlearned Lesson of Watergate: The Need for a Responsible Presidency" (Talk given at the Annual Meeting of the Delaware Bar Association, Wilmington, Delaware, 4 June 1975).

15"The New Constitutional Crisis," *Progressive*, March 1973.

16Op. cit. (above, n. 1).

17Ibid.

18Op. cit. (above, n. 8), p. 121.

Chapter 3. Separation and Division: Congress

1Marjorie Hunter, "Congress Takes Slowly to the Age of Computers," *New York Times*, 2 October 1975.

2Mark J. Green, with Bruce Rosenthal and Lynn Darling, *Who Runs Congress?* rev. ed. (New York: Bantam, 1975), p. x.

3Thomas W. Africa, *Science and the State in Greece and Rome* (New York: Wiley, 1968), p. 30.

4David Burnham, "Quality of Appointments to 9 U.S. Agencies Scored," *New York Times*, 7 November 1975.

[5]James Reston, "Revolt in the House," *New York Times,* 17 January 1975.

[6]Op. cit. (above, n. 2), p. 327.

[7]*Let Them Eat Promises: The Politics of Hunger in America* (Englewood Cliffs, N.J.: Prentice–Hall, 1969). Excerpts are from the chapter "The Subcommittee Chairman," reprinted in *American Politics and Public Policy,* ed. Michael P. Smith (New York: Random House, 1973), pp. 141–151.

[8]*Inside the House* (Chicago: Follett, 1975).

[9]David R. Mayhew, *Congress: The Electoral Connection* (New Haven: Yale University Press, 1974), p. 6.

[10]Ibid., p. 109.

[11]Op. cit. (above, n. 2) p. xi.

[12]Ibid., p. xii.

[13]"Rules Committee Rulers," *Washington Post,* 24 December 1974.

[14]"For the Record," *Washington Post,* 14 January 1975.

[15]"News Television Can't Cover," *Congressional Record,* 7 June 1975.

[16]Robert A. Caro, *The Power Broker: Robert Moses and the Fall of New York* (New York: Knopf, 1974), p. 196.

[17]"Congress' Pace on Economy, Energy Attacked and Defended," *Washington Post,* 13 September 1975.

[18]James Madison, *Notes of Debates in the Federal Convention of 1787* (New York: Norton, 1969), pp. 59–60.

[19]Edward Weisband and Thomas M. Franck, *Resignation in Protest: Political and Ethical Choices between Loyalty to Team and Loyalty to Conscience in American Public Life* (New York: Grossman, 1975), p. 125.

[20]"The Presidency: Ventures in Reappraisal," *The Presidency Reappraised,* ed. Rexford G. Tugwell and Thomas E. Cronin (New York: Praeger, 1974), p. 5.

Chapter 4. Separation and Division: The Courts/the States

[1]George E. Reedy, "On the Isolation of Presidents," *The Presidency Reappraised,* ed. Rexford G. Tugwell and Thomas E. Cronin (New York: Praeger, 1974), p. 122.

[2]"PresiGovernoMayor," *New York Times,* 2 October, 1975.

[3]John J. Flynn, "The Crisis of Federalism: Who is Responsible?" *American Bar Association Journal* 51, (March 1965).

[4]"The Constitution and the Presidency," *Congressional Record,* 19 December 1974, p. H12457.

Chapter 5. Private Governments

[1]*Thomas Jefferson on Democracy,* ed. Saul K. Padover (New York: Penguin, 1946), letter to James Madison, p. 47.

[2]"Profits of Doom," *Washington Post,* 19 January 1975.

[3]"The Menace of 'The Company,'" *Progressive,* September 1975.

[4]Arthur S. Miller, "Legal Foundations of the Corporate State," *Journal of Economic Issues* vol. 6 (Spring 1972).

[5]"An Inquiry into the Relevance of the Intention of the Founding Fathers with Special Emphasis upon the Doctrine of Separation of Powers," reprinted from the *Arkansas Law Review,* vol. 27 (Winter 1973).

[6]Op. cit. (above, n. 1), letter to Dr. J. Curie, 1786, p. 98.

[7]Ralph Nader, "Obligation of Scientists to Respond to Society's Needs," *Scientists in the Legal System: Tolerated Meddlers or Essential Contributors?*, ed. William A. Thomas (Ann Arbor, Mich.: Ann Arbor Science Publishers, 1974), p. 46.

Chapter 6. The Fourth Branch: Bureaucracies

[1]The case against the CAB, ICC and FMC is persuasively made in, among other places, *The Monopoly Makers*, ed. Mark J. Green (New York: Grossman, 1973), pp. 103–189.

[2]Bob Woodward, "IRS Chief Blocks Audit of Montoya's Taxes," and Morton Mintz, "FPC Laxity Blamed in Gas Crisis," *Washington Post*, 19 October 1975.

[3]"Justice Without Politics," *Progressive*, April 1974.

[4]*Air Safety: Selected Review of FAA Performance*, December 1974, p. 6.

[5]Ibid., p. 8.

[6]Kenneth Bredemeier, "Bureaucratic Rigidity Contributes to Air Safety Lapses," *Washington Post*, 23 February 1975.

[7]Op. cit. (above, n. 4), p. 2.

[8]Op. cit. (above, n. 3).

[9]Ibid.

[10]"FBI Veiled Illegal Break-Ins," *Washington Post*, 26 September 1975.

[11]*Olmstead* v. *United States*, 1928.

[12]*How the Government Breaks the Law* (New York: Stein & Day, 1972).

[13]Colman McCarthy, "Ravaging the Land and the Law," *Washington Post*, 23 March 1974. His other columns were published 29 January 1974 and 15 February 1974.

Chapter 7. The End of Government by and for the People

[1]Alexander Hamilton, James Madison, and John Jay, *The Federalist* (New York: Mentor, 1961), no. 51, p. 322.

[2]"The Principal Unlearned Lesson of Watergate: The Need for a Responsible Presidency" (Talk given at the Annual Meeting of the Delaware Bar Association, Wilmington, Delaware, 4 June 1975).

[3]"The Case for Not Voting," *New York Times*, 7 September 1974.

[4]*Sin and Society: An Analysis of Latter-Day Iniquity* (1907, reprint ed., Gloucester, Mass.: Peter Smith, 1965), p. 156.

[5]*Washington Post*, 27 January 1975.

[6]William Chapman, "Voter Turnout Lower, Particularly in North," *Washington Post*, 17 November 1974.

[7]Merrill Moss, Letter to the Editor, *New York Times*, 30 November 1975.

[8]Page Smith, *John Adams* 1735–1784 (Garden City: Doubleday, 1962), 1:440.

[9]Op. cit. (above, n. 1), no. 84, p. 513.

[10]Alan M. Dershowitz, "The First Ten in Jeopardy," *New York Times*, 25 June 1972.

[11]*Criminal Sentences: Law Without Order* (New York: Hill and Wang, 1973), p. 103.

[12]Ibid., p. 104.

[13]*Justice Denied: The Case for Reform of the Courts* (New York: Praeger, 1971), pp. 3, 4.

[14]Ibid., pp. 13, 14.

[15]"A Plea to Prevent Rikers Island Jail Conditions from Exploding into Bloodshed and Death," *New York Times*, 15 August 1975.

[16]Op. cit. (above, n. 13), p. 14.

[17]William M. Kunstler, "The Vanishing Jury," *New York Times,* 27 September 1975.

[18]Edward S. Corwin, *The Constitution and What it Means Today,* rev. Harold W. Chase and Craig R. Ducat (Princeton: Princeton University Press, 1974), p. 243.

[19]Op. cit. (above, n. 10).

Chapter 8. The Executive

[1]"Watergate and Beyond: The Issue is Secrecy," *Progressive,* December 1973, pp. 15–19.

[2]U. S. Congress, Senate, hearings before the Subcommittee on Reorganization, Research, and International Organizations of the Committee on Government Operations, *Government in the Sunshine,* 93d Cong., 2d Sess., 21 and 22 May and 15 October 1974, p. 51.

[3]"Accepting the Consequences for Secret Policies," *Washington Post,* 3 May 1975.

[4]*Washington Cover-Up,* (Garden City: Doubleday, 1962).

[5]Ibid., p. 9.

[6]The Final Report of the Committee on the Judiciary, House of Representatives, 93d Cong., 2d Sess., *Impeachment of Richard M. Nixon, President of the United States* (New York: Bantam, 1975), dissenting views pp. 443–44.

[7]*The Politics of Lying: Government Deception, Secrecy, and Power* (New York: Vintage, 1973), p. x.

[8]*New York Times,* 24 June 1975, p. 33.

[9]Op. cit. (above, n. 2), p. 1.

[10]"Lessons of Watergate," *New York Times,* 19 February 1975.

[11]*The Defeat of America* (New York: Simon and Schuster, 1974), p. 87.

[12]Op. cit. (above, n. 2), p. 3.

[13]Op. cit. (above, n. 7), p. 89.

[14]Ibid., p. 160.

[15]"A Madness for Secrecy," *Washington Post,* 12 December 1971.

[16]Op. cit. (above, n. 7), pp. 162–63.

[17]Morton Mintz, "Secrets of the Bureaucracies," *Washington Post,* 25 June 1971.

[18]Op. cit. (above, n. 7), p. 510.

[19]Op. cit. (above, n. 4), pp. 45–46.

[20]Ibid., p. 53.

[21]Op. cit. (above, n. 1).

[22]Ibid.

[23]Ibid.

[24]"Text of Supreme Court Ruling Ordering Nixon to Turn Over Data," *New York Times,* 25 July 1974.

[25]Op. cit. (above, n. 1).

[26]Op. cit. (above, n. 7), p. 50.

[27]*Anything but the Truth: The Credibility Gap—How the News is Managed in Washington* (New York: Putnam, 1968), p. 7.

[28]Op. cit. (above, n. 7), p. 21.

[29]"The Defeat of America," *New York Review of Books,* 5 October 1972.

[30]*Public Philosophy* (New York: New American Library, 1955), p. 99.

Chapter 9: Congress/Advisory Committees/Lobbying

[1]Prudence Crewdson, "Hill Cuts Secret Meetings," *Washington Post,* 14 February 1974.

[2]"Open Committee Trend in House and Senate," *Congressional Quarterly,* 11 January 1975.

[3]"Reform Penetrates Conference Committees," *Congressional Quarterly,* 8 February 1975.

[4]Ibid.

[5]Ibid.

[6]"House Feels Clout of New Rules," *Washington Post,* 2 March 1975.

[7]Morton Mintz, "CAB Unit Closes Sessions to Public" and "CAB Dropping Disputed Unit," *Washington Post,* 26 April 1971 and 30 May 1971.

[8]Senator Lee Metcalf (D–Mont.), "LEAA Advisory Committee Schooled in How to Thwart the Law," *Congressional Record,* 20 June 1975.

[9]Morton Mintz, *By Prescription Only* (Boston: Houghton Mifflin, Beacon, 1967), p. 143.

[10]Ibid., pp. 230–247d. See also Sanford J. Ungar, "Get Away With What You Can," *In the Name of Profit* (Garden City: Doubleday, 1972) pp. 106–128.

[11]Op. cit. (above, n. 9), p. 144.

[12]"Freedom of Information," *Washington Post,* 13 June 1975.

[13]Martin Arnold, "The New Rules On Freedom of Information," *New York Times,* 16 February 1975.

[14]Op. cit. (above, n. 12).

[15]Ibid.

[16]Robert Blanchard, "Knowing and *Knowing,"* *New York Times,* 8 March 1975.

[17]John P. MacKenzie, "Court Upholds Secrecy if Specific Law Allows It," *Washington Post,* 25 June 1975.

[18]U. S. Congress, Senate, testimony of John W. Gardner, chairman of Common Cause, before the Government Operations Committee 22 April 1975.

[19]"Revisions Seen in Lobbying Law," *New York Times,* 20 April 1975.

[20]Ibid.

Chapter 10. The Supreme Court

[1]Arthur S. Miller, "Watergate and Beyond: The Issue is Secrecy," *Progressive,* December 1973.

[2]*Thomas Jefferson on Democracy,* ed. Saul K. Padover (New York: Penguin, 1946), p. 65.

[3]"Secrecy and the Supreme Court: On the Need for Piercing the Red Velour Curtain," *Buffalo Law Review* 22 (1973).

[4]Ibid., p. 799.

[5]"Behind the Marble, Beneath the Robes," *New York Times Magazine,* 16 March 1975.

[6]"High Court and Disqualification," *New York Times,* 3 March 1975.

[7]*Lord Acton and His Circle,* ed. A. Gasquet (1906), p. 799.

Chapter 11. Secrecy and the Press/Agencies/States/Cities

[1]"S.1: A Bill to Make the Press a Whimpering Lackey," *Guild Reporter,* 30 May 1975.

[2]Ibid.

[3]"The Role and Rights of the Press," *Washington Post,* 11 November 1974.

[4]Victor Marchetti and John D. Marks, *The CIA and the Cult of Intelligence* (New York: Dell, 1975), p. 22.

[5]Ibid.

[6]"Gagging the Press in the Courtroom," *Washington Post*, 17 November 1974.

[7]"Press Group Fights Secret Jury Concept," *Washington Post*, 26 May 1975.

[8]"U.S. Hit by News Suppression Wave," *Washington Post*, 26 June 1975.

[9]"Keeping Secrets," *New Republic*, 7 May 1975.

[10]U.S. Congress, Senate, testimony before the Subcommittee on Reorganization, Research, and International Organizations of the Committee on Government Operations, 22 May 1974.

[11]*The Power Broker: Robert Moses and the Fall of New York* (New York: Knopf, 1974), pp. 716–17.

Chapter 12. The Federal Reserve System

[1]*Congressional Record*, 5 March 1975, p. H1395.

[2]Congressman Wright Patman (D–Tex.), *Congressional Record*, 19 June 1975, pp. H5792–5795.

[3]Frank Aukofer, "Reuss (D–Wis.), A Demanding Man," *New York Times*, 2 March 1975, sec. 3.

[4]In 1974, the Fed's revenues actually reached $6.3 billion. *Congressional Record*, 10 March 1975, p. H1494.

[5]*Congressional Record*, 4 March 1975, p. H2185.

[6]U.S. Congress, House Subcommittee print published by the Subcommittee on Domestic Finance, Committee on Banking and Currency, 88th Cong., 2d Sess., *The Federal Reserve System After Fifty Years*, 25 August 1964.

[7]Congressman Wright Patman (D–Tex.), "What's Wrong with the Federal Reserve and What to do About It," *American Bar Association Journal*, February 1975, reprinted in *Congressional Record*, 14 March 1975, pp. H1775–1778.

[8]Ibid.

[9]Ibid., also, *Congressional Record*, 29 May 1974, pp. H4532–4534.

[10]Op. cit. (above, n. 2).

[11]Ibid.

[12]Op. cit. (above, n. 7), *Congressional Record*, 14 March 1975, p. H1774.

[13]*Congressional Record*, 14 March 1975, p. 1775.

[14]Ibid.

[15]Op. cit. (above, n. 6), p. 21.

Chapter 13. Who Owns the Corporations

[1]Ralph Nader, Introduction, Morton Mintz and Jerry S. Cohen, *America Inc.: Who Owns and Operates the United States* (New York: Dial, 1971), p. xi.

[2]U.S. Congress, Senate, Hearings before the Subcommittee on Monopoly of the Select Committee on Small Business, *The Role of Giant Corporations in the American and World Economies, Corporate Secrecy: Overviews*, 92d Cong., 1st sess., 9 and 12 November 1971, pt. 2:1089.

[3]*The History of the Standard Oil Company* (1904, reprint, ed., Gloucester, Mass.: Peter Smith, 1963), 2:127.

4Ibid., p. 129.

5Ibid., pp. 129, 130.

6Op. cit. (above, n. 2), p. 1097.

7Op. cit. (above, n. 1), p. 1.

8"The Corporation," CBS News documentary telecast 6 December 1973.

9Op. cit. (above, n. 1), p. 1.

10Op. cit. (above, n. 2), p. 1110.

11Ibid., Senator Gaylord Nelson (D–Wis.), p. 1041.

12Ibid., pp. 1112, 1113.

13Corporate Power in America, ed. Ralph Nader and Mark J. Green (New York: Grossman, 1971), p. 74.

14Theodore Roosevelt, First Annual Message to Congress, December 1901.

15Op. cit. (above, n. 13), p. 75.

16Op. cit. (above, n. 14).

17Global Reach: The Power of the Multinational Corporations (New York: Simon and Schuster, 1974), p. 370.

18U.S. Congress, Senate, Subcommittee on Intergovernmental Relations, and Budgeting, Management, and Expenditures of the Committee on Government Operations, "Conclusions and Recommendations," Disclosure of Corporate Ownership, 27 December 1973, pp. 10–11.

19Op. cit. (above, n. 2), p. 1095.

20Ibid., p. 1151.

21Op. cit. (above, n. 2), p. 1044.

22Jaime Friedman, "Firms Fight FTC Data Bar," Washington Post, 16 June 1974.

23Ibid.

24Ibid.

25U.S. Congress, House, Testimony before the Renegotiation and Oversight Subcommittee of the House Banking and Currency Committee, 12 June 1975.

26Op. cit. (above, n. 2), p. 1129.

27Morton Mintz, "Secrecy Shrouded Oil Accord," Washington Post, 17 February 1974.

Chapter 14. Ignorance Is Pain

1Morton Mintz and Jerry S. Cohen, America Inc.: Who Owns and Operates the United States (New York: Dial, 1971), pp. 257–264.

2U.S. Congress, Senate, Hearings before the Subcommittee on Monopoly of the Select Committee on Small Business, The Role of Giant Corporations in the American and World Economies, Corporate Secrecy: Overviews, 92d Cong., 1st Sess., 9 and 12 November 1971, pt. 2:1084.

3Op. cit. (above, note 1), p. 268.

4U.S. Congress, Senate, Testimony at Joint Hearings of the Subcommittee on Health of the Committee on Labor and Public Welfare and the Subcommittee on Administrative Practice and Procedure of the Committee on the Judiciary, 10 July 1975.

5Morton Mintz, "FDA Seeks Role of Drug Co.," Washington Post, 8 April 1976.

6The Food and Drug Administration in October 1975 rejected a petition by the Health Research Group intended to prevent overprescribing of Flagyl.

7Morton Mintz, The Pill: An Alarming Report (Boston: Beacon, 1970), pp. 26–28.

8Op. cit. (above, n. 2), p. 1066.

⁹Morton Mintz, *Washington Post,* 20 May 1974.

¹⁰Op. cit. (above, n. 2), p. 1066.

¹¹"Abbott Pleads No Contest In Adulterated Drug Case," *New York Times,* 5 June 1974.

¹²Op. cit. (above, n. 2), p. 1065.

¹³Ibid., p. 1067.

¹⁴"Tactical A-Weapons Called 'Option,' " *Washington Post,* 8 July 1975.

¹⁵Vernon Guidry, "Cost Clause Slowed Oil Bug," *Washington Star-News,* 31 January 1975, and letter from Senator William Proxmire (D–Wis.) to James R. Schlesinger, Secretary of Defense, 17 January 1975.

¹⁶U.S. Congress, House, Testimony of Admiral H. G. Rickover, Renegotiation and Oversight Subcommittee of the House Banking and Currency Committee, 12 June 1975.

¹⁷Ibid.

¹⁸Morton Mintz, "Oil Expert Says IRS Section Favors Industry," *Washington Post,* 11 January 1972.

¹⁹Op. cit. (above, n. 1), p. 6.

Chapter 15. Buying Elections

¹George Thayer, *Who Shakes the Money Tree?* (New York: Simon. and Schuster, 1973), p. 25.

²Ibid., p. 30.

³Ibid., pp. 51 and 53.

⁴Archibald Cox, Special Watergate Prosecutor, Louis D. Brandeis Memorial Lecture, Brandeis University, adapted in *New York Times Magazine,* 19 May 1974.

⁵Lawrence Meyer, "Watergate Probe told of Pressure for Funds," *Washington Post,* 15 November 1973.

⁶"Why They Did What They Did," *New York Times,* 9 March 1975, sec. 3.

⁷Morton Mintz and Nick Kotz, "Auto Firm Rejected Nixon Fund Bid," *Washington Post,* 17 November 1972.

⁸"Two Kinds of Justice," *Washington Post,* 22 March 1975.

⁹"The Steinbrenner Case—Realities of Sentencing," *Los Angeles Times,* 28 September 1974.

Chapter 16. More Election Buyers

¹Morton Mintz, "1 of Every 7 on Hill Got Dairy Gifts," *Washington Post,* 16 June 1974.

²George Lardner, Jr., "Anatomy of a Scandal: The Milk Fund," *Reader's Digest,* November 1974.

³Common Cause, in July 1975, cited the total in correspondence with the Department of Justice and the Securities and Exchange Commission. The thirty-one contributors together had given $1,745,000, the citizens' lobby said.

⁴Morton Mintz, "Millionaire Got Refund, but not Ambassadorship," *Washington Post,* 10 November 1973.

⁵Morton Mintz and Stephen Isaacs, "CPA May Have Passed Nixon Gift," *Washington Post,* 25 November 1973.

⁶James R. Polk, 9 August 1974.

⁷*Howard: The Amazing Mr. Hughes* (New York: Fawcett, 1972), p. 241.

⁸Ibid., pp. 242–43.

[9]Morton Mintz, "Hughes Payout to Politicians Is Surfacing," *Washington Post*, 7 October 1973.

[10]Ibid.

[11]Ibid.

[12]Ibid.

[13]George Thayer, *Who Shakes the Money Tree?* (New York: Simon and Schuster, 1973), p. 233.

[14]"The Shakedown Cruise," *Washington Monthly*, October 1969.

[15]*Wall Street Journal*, 11 July 1969.

[16]"U.S. Starts Enforcing Laws Banning Political Gifts by Firms, Unions," *Wall Street Journal*, 21 November 1969.

[17]Morton Mintz and Jerry S. Cohen, *America, Inc.: Who Owns and Operates the United States* (New York: Dial, 1971), p. 166.

[18]Howard Saxner, "On Traveled Waters," *The Monopoly Makers*, ed. Mark J. Green, (New York, 1971), p. 118.

[19]Ibid.

[20]Robert Trumbull, "Union Gifts Stir Storm in Canada," *New York Times*, 15 December 1974.

[21]Morton Mintz, "Maritime Funds Spread in Hill Races," *Washington Post*, 2 November 1974.

[22]David Burnham, "The Maritime Industry Floats on Tax Dollars," *New York Times*, 14 September 1975, sec. 4.

[23]"Bribery and Contributions," *New Republic*, 21 December 1974.

[24]Op. cit. (above, n. 13), p. 300.

Chapter 17. Corporate Bribery

[1]"Not Just Your Corner Drugstore," *New York Times*, 19 June 1975.

[2]The Simon testimony, and the Lockheed episode generally, were extensively reported in the press, e.g., by Jack Egan and William H. Jones of the *Washington Post* and Robert M. Smith of the *New York Times*.

[3]Robert M. Smith, "Lockheed Documents Disclose a $106-million Saudi Payment," *New York Times*, 13 September 1975.

[4]On 7 January 1975, the *Washington Post* and the *New York Times* reported that the CIA had begun a greatly stepped-up program of providing covert financing to non-Communist political parties in Italy, including $6-million in direct support principally for the Christian Democratic Party.

[5]Robert M. Smith, "Exxon Canada Gifts $234,000 Each Year," *New York Times*, 16 July 1975.

[6]Spencer Rich, *Washington Post*, 4 December 1975.

[7]*Inside the House* (Chicago: Follett, 1975), p. 203.

[8]In addition to Gruenstein's article ("Auditors Question Payment of $5.5 million to Northrop"), the Northrop case, like others in this chapter, was extensively reported by, among others, William H. Jones, Jack Egan, and Jim Hoagland of the *Washington Post*, and Robert M. Smith, Henry Weinstein, and Michael C. Jensen of the *New York Times*.

[9]Michael C. Jensen, "Watergate Donors Still Riding High," *New York Times*, 24 August 1975, sec. 3.

[10]William H. Jones, "Need for New Business Ethic Cited," *Washington Post*, 23 July 1975.

[11]*Sin and Society: An Analysis of Latter-Day Iniquity* (1907, reprint ed. Gloucester, Mass., Peter Smith, 1965), p. 109.

[12]Ibid., pp. 122–23.

[13]Ibid., p. 125.

[14]Ibid., pp. 126–29.

Chapter 18. The Executive/Congress/Courts/Agencies

[1]Congressman John D. Dingell (D–Mich.), *Congressional Record*, 19 December 1974, p. H12444.

[2]*U.S.* v. *Mississippi Valley Generating Co.*, 364 U.S. 520, 549 (1961).

[3]"Tax Questions Surround Rocky," *People and Taxes*, November 1974, Tax Reform Research Group, Washington, D.C.

[4]"Rockefeller Family Holdings Touch Every Economic Sphere," *Washington Post*, 22 September 1974.

[5]U.S. Congress, Senate, Committee on the Judiciary together with Supplemental, Dissenting, and Separate Views, *Confirmation of Nelson A. Rockefeller as Vice President of the United States*, 93d Cong., 2d sess., 17 December 1974, p. 41.

[6]Congressman Wright Patman (D–Tex.) put Nader's letter into the *Congressional Record*, 20 December 1974, pp. 12646–12649.

[7]*Congressional Record*, 10 December 1974, p. S20979.

[8]Mark Barbash, "Energy in Bondage," *Progressive*, April 1975; William E. Clayton, "Justice Department Calls Simon 'Foolish' for Appointing FEO Aide," *Washington Post*, 15 December, 1974.

[9]"G.A.O. Study Queries Holdings By Officials of Geological Survey," *New York Times*, 5 March 1975.

[10]Morton Mintz, *By Prescription Only* (Boston: Houghton Mifflin, Beacon, 1967), pp. 52e–52m.

[11]Ibid., pp. 175–184, 184q.

[12]*Congressional Record*, 26 March 1975, p. S5058; Henry Weinstein, "Abuse is Charged in Defense Hiring," *New York Times*, 19 August 1975; Jensen's article, "Retired Generals Employed by Northrop in Varied Tasks," appeared 26 June 1975.

[13]Philip M. Stern, "Sikes Linked to Sellers of G.I. Insurance," *Washington Post*, 20 October 1974.

[14]"Sikes Linked to Many Banks," *Washington Post*, 1 July 1975, and "Retired Admirals Rebuked for Role in Banks," *Washington Post*, 16 October 1975.

[15]"Northrop Flew Senators Gratis," *Washington Post*, 14 June 1975.

[16]*Congressional Record*, 26 March 1975, p. S5065.

[17]*The Appearance of Justice* (New York: Scribners, 1974), p. 228.

[18]Ibid., p. 101.

[19]Ibid., p. 108.

[20]Ibid., p. 190.

[21]Morton Mintz, "FPC Hit on Gas Pricing," *Washington Post*, 14 September 1974.

[22]"G.A.O. Study Queries Holdings by Officials of Geological Survey," *New York Times*, 5 March 1975.

[23]Phone Interview of Mrs. Nassikas by Morton Mintz, September 1974.

[24]Op. cit. (above, n. 5), p. H12427.

Chapter 19. Physician, Heel Thyself

[1]Herbert Ratner, M.D., put this in the context of the Hippocratic Oath in "The Oath —IV. Why?," *Child and Family* (Oak Park, Illinois, 1971), no. 3, 16:196.

[2]Ibid.

[3]Morton Mintz, *By Prescription Only* (Boston: Houghton Mifflin, Beacon, 1967), p. 325d.

[4]Ibid., pp. 311–325d.

[5]Lloyd Shearer, "Unnecessary Surgery," *Parade*, 7 September 1975.

[6]Ibid.

[7]"The Surgeon's Dilemma," *Harper's*, May 1975.

[8]"The Professions in the Society of Today," *New England Journal of Medicine*, 8 September 1949.

[9]Letter from Johnny H. Killian, Legislative Attorney, American Law Division, 6 December 1968, to Benjamin Gordon, Staff Economist, Senate Select Committee on Small Business.

[10]Op. cit. (above, n. 3), pp. 71–92.

[11]Op. cit. (above, n. 8).

[12]Op. cit. (above, n. 10).

[13]Op. cit. (above, n. 3), pp. xii, xviii, 28, 32, 34–36, 62–64, 94, 149–152, 248–264.

[14]Op. cit. (above, n. 3), pp. 92a–92n; Morton Mintz, "Drugs: Deceptive Advertising," *New Republic*, 6 July 1968; Morton Mintz, "The AMA's Overdose of Drug Advertising," *Progressive*, October 1965.

[15]Op. cit. (above, n. 3), pp. 92b–92e.

[16]Op. cit. (above, n. 14).

[17]"AMA Invests Millions in Drug Firms," *Washington Post*, 25 June 1973, and "AMA Free to Buy Drug Firm Stocks," *Washington Post*, 27 June 1973.

[18]Morton Mintz, "AMA 'Captive' of Drug Firms, Top Aides Say," *Washington Post*, 7 February 1973.

[19]U.S. Congress, Senate, Hearings before the Subcommittee on Monopoly of the Select Committee on Small Business, *Competitive Problems in the Drug Industry*, 91st Cong. 7 May 1969, pp. 5029–30.

[20]Ibid., 6 May 1969, p. 5000. Morton Mintz, "AMA Refusal to Print Drug Attack Cited," *Washington Post*, 8 May 1969; Morton Mintz, "3 Score Advertising of Condemned Drugs," *Washington Post*, 7 May 1969; Morton Mintz, "AMA Denies Refusing to Print Attack on Combination Drugs," *Washington Post*, 12 May 1969.

[21]Op. cit. (above, n. 19), 6 May 1969, p. 5000.

[22]Stuart Auerbach, " 'Sore Throat' Gives AMA High Fever," *Washington Post, (Outlook)*, 13 July 1975.

[23]Ibid.

[24]Op. cit. (above, n. 22).

[25]Ibid.

[26]"A.M.A. Aided Drive on Drug Cost Cut," *New York Times*, 20 July 1975.

[27]Stuart Auerbach, "Drug Firms Gave AMA $851,000," *Washington Post*, 1 July 1975.

[28]David Burnham, "A.M.A. Aide Let Upjohn Use Letter to Sell Drug," *New York Times*, 8 July 1975; Stuart Auerbach, "AMA Official Let Company Use Name," *Washington Post*, 9 July 1975.

[29]Thomas W. Africa, *Science and the State in Greece and Rome* (New York: Wiley, 1968), pp. 11–12.

Chapter 20. Unaccountable Accountants

[1]"Accounting: A Crisis Over Fuller Disclosure," *Business Week,* 22 April 1972.

[2]Ibid.

[3]*A Search for Fairness in Financial Reporting to the Public* (Chicago: Arthur Andersen, 1969), 1:2.

[4]Richard J. Barnet and Ronald E. Muller, *Global Reach: The Power of the Multinational Corporations* (New York: Simon and Schuster, 1974), p. 263.

[5]"Market Place: Accounting Rule on Research Changes," *New York Times,* 24 January 1975.

[6]Op. cit. (above, n. 4).

[7]Op. cit. (above, n. 1).

[8]Norman Medvin, *The American Oil Industry: A Failure of Anti-Trust Policy* (Washington, D.C., 1973), pp. 114–15.

[9]Ibid., p. 116.

[10]Op. cit. (above, n. 1).

[11]Op. cit. (above, n. 3), from a 1960 speech, p. 151.

[12]Op. cit. (above, n. 1).

[13]"Guidelines and Standards to avoid Potential Conflicts Between Accountants and Clients" (Address to the SEC Reporter Group Conference, Washington D.C., 17 March 1975).

[14]"Integrity in the Business Landscape," *New York Times,* 12 December 1975.

Chapter 21. Blue Cross and Other Conduits of Private Power

[1]Sylvia A. Law, principal author, *Blue Cross: What Went Wrong?,* prepared by the Health Law Project, University of Pennsylvania (New Haven: Yale, 1974), p. 1.

[2]Ibid.

[3]Ibid., p. 26.

[4]William Stockton, "Public Role Scant in Health Plans," Associated Press, *New York Times,* 6 August 1975.

[5]Ibid.

[6]Morton Mintz, "Virginia Blue Cross Costs Cited," *Washington Post,* 22 January 1971; op. cit. (above, n. 1), pp. 21–23 and 174–75.

[7]Ibid.

[8]Ibid.

[9]Ibid.

[10]Ibid.

[11]Ibid.

[12]Ibid.

[13]Ibid.

[14]Ibid.

[15]Op. cit. (above, n. 1), p. 39.

[16]Ibid., p. 89.

[17]Ibid., p. 92.

[18]"Pathologist Paid a Percentage of the Profit in Department," *Washington Post,* 1 November 1972.

[19]Op. cit. (above, n. 1), p. 96.

[20]*The Brain Bank of America: An Inquiry into the Politics of Science* (New York: McGraw Hill, 1975), p. 6.

[21]*Science,* 14 April 1967.

[22]Morton Mintz, "U.S. Debates 'Acceptable' Level of Cancer Risk," *Washington Post,* 21 December 1971; Jacqueline Verrett, Ph.D., and Jean Carper, *Eating May be Hazardous to Your Health: The Case Against Food Additives* (New York: Simon and Schuster, 1974), pp. 84–86; *op. cit.* (above, n. 20), pp. 167–72.

[23]Op. cit. (above, n. 20), p. 167.

[24]Ibid., pp. 167–68.

[25]Ibid., p. 165.

[26]Ibid., p. 168.

[27]Ibid., pp. 168–70.

[28]Op. cit. (above, n. 22).

[29]Op. cit. (above, n. 20), p. 163.

[30]Ibid., p. 203.

[31]Ibid., p. 200.

[32]Ibid., p. 253.

[33]*The Cholesterol Controversy* (Los Angeles: Sherbourne, 1973).

[34]Ibid., pp. 140–41; Morton Mintz, "Eat, Drink and Be Merry," *Washington Post (Book World),* 18 March 1973.

[35]"Conflict Charged on Mining Panel," *New York Times,* 30 December 1974.

[36]Stephen D. Isaacs, "The Oil Lobby Abroad," *Washington Post,* 9 January 1975.

[37]U.S. Congress, Senate Hearings before the Committee on Interior and Insular Affairs, *Market Performance and Competition in the Petroleum Industry,* 93d Cong., 1st Sess., 5 and 6 December 1973, pt. 2:470–76.

Chapter 22. Banks/Unions/Hospitals

[1]Memorandum Opinion and Order, Willie Roy Blankenship, et al., Plaintiffs, v. W. A. (Tony) Boyle, et al., Defendants, Civil Action no. 2186–69, in the United States District Court for the District of Columbia, Judge Gerhard H. Gesell, 28 April 1971.

[2]Ibid.

[3]Ibid.

[4]Congressman Wright Patman (D-Tex.), *Congressional Record,* 26 March 1975, p. H2410.

[5]"U.S. Banks $3.9 Billion, Gets No Interest," *Washington Post,* 17 November 1974.

[6]*Who Shakes the Money Tree? American Campaign Financing Practices from 1789 to the Present* (New York, 1973), p. 45.

[7]Wayne Slater, "W. Va. Bank Scandal Latest in a Line," *Washington Post,* 31 May 1975.

[8]*The Fall and Rise of Jimmy Hoffa* (New York: Saturday Review Press, 1972), p. 522.

[9]Ibid., pp. 531–32.

[10]"Pension Fund of Teamsters Scanned for Clues on Hoffa," *New York Times,* 12 August 1975.

[11]Jonathan Kwitny, *Wall Street Journal,* series began 22 July 1975.

[12]Morton Mintz, "Health Insurors Scored on Investment Policies," *Washington Post,* 22 May 1970.

[13]"Banks With Officers on Blue Cross and Blue Shield Boards Use Their Funds," *New York Times,* 5 August 1975.

[14]"Conflict of Interest Marks Hospital Center Management," *Washington Post,* 30 October 1972.

[15]"Trustees' Banks Use Hospital Money," *Washington Post*, 4 February 1973.

[16]Ibid.

[17]The suit was filed by Alan S. Novins of Lobel, Novins and Lamont, a Washington, D.C., law firm.

[18]Memorandum Opinion and Order, David M. Stern, et al., Plaintiffs, v. Lucy Well Hayes National Training School for Deaconesses and Missionaries, et al., Defendants, Civil Action no. 267–73, United States District Court for the District of Columbia.

[19]Op. cit. (above, n. 15).

[20]Victor Cohn, "GAO Bids Hospitals Disclose Overlaps," *Washington Post*, 3 May 1975.

Chapter 23. The Press

[1]George Seldes, "Recollections of George Seldes: When the American Press Sold Itself Out—Lock, Stock and Barrel—to the Advertisers," *Media and Consumer*, September 1974.

[2]Ibid.

[3]David P. Garino, "Louisville Newspapers Cherish Independence, Guard It Jealously," *Wall Street Journal*, 11 July 1974.

[4]Bob Schulman, "Will the New York Times Ever 'Tell It Like It Is' about Itself?" *Louisville Times*, 26 September 1974.

[5]"On the Profession of Journalism," Speech to International Press Institute, London, 27 May 1965, reprinted in *Congressional Record*, 15 June 1965.

[6]Stephen E. Nordlinger, "We've Got a Secret" [*More*], December 1974.

[7]Charles B. Seib, "Columnists and Conflicts," *Washington Post*, 2 January 1975.

[8]Ibid.

Chapter 24. Eroding Competition

[1]U.S. Congress, Senate, hearings before the Subcommittee on Antitrust and Monopoly of the Committee on the Judiciary, *The Industrial Reorganization Act*, Ground Transportation Industries, 93d Cong., 2d Sess., 26, 27, 28 February; and 1 March 1974, pt. 3:1776–1777.

[2]Ibid., pp. 1839–1926; pt. 4A—appendix to pt. 4; and Morton Mintz, "GM Said to Ruin City Rail Systems," *Washington Post*, 25 February 1974. GM on April 10 submitted "The Truth about 'American Ground Transport'—a Reply by General Motors," and, at its request the Subcommittee printed it in full as a hearing volume.

[3]Op. cit. (above, n. 1), pt. 4A:A–31, A–32.

[4]Ibid., pp. 1840–1841.

[5]Ibid., pp. 1985–2045; and Morton Mintz, "U.S. Auto Antitrust Inaction Disclosed," *Washington Post*, 1 March 1974.

[6]Letter from Mark Green to Robert Liedquist, Acting Director of the Bureau of Competition of the Federal Trade Commission, cited in *New York Times (Business)*, 4 August 1975.

[7]Testimony before the House Judiciary Committee, 25 February 1914; and "Interlocking Directorates," *The Brandeis Guide to the Modern World*, ed. Alfred Lief (Boston: Little, Brown, 1941).

[8]*Commercial Banks and their Trust Activities: Emerging Influence on the American Economy*, vol. 2, 90th Cong., 8 July 1968, esp. "Summary and Conclusions," pp. 1–5.

[9]U.S. Congress, Senate, Subcommittee on Intergovernmental Relations, and Budgeting, Management, and Expenditures of the Committee on Government Operations, *Disclosure of Corporate Ownership*, 27 December 1973; and Morton Mintz, "8 Institutions Control Most Top Firms," *Washington Post*, 6 January 1974.

[10]Morton Mintz, "Refinery Divestiture Urged," *Washington Post*, 24 February 1974.

[11]Norman Medvin, *The American Oil Industry: A Failure of Antitrust Policy* (Washington, D.C.: Stanley H. Ruttenberg and Associates, 1973), p. 61.

[12]U.S. Congress, Senate, Testimony before Subcommittee on Antitrust and Monopoly, Committee on the Judiciary, 27 June 1973.

[13]Ida M. Tarbell, *The History of the Standard Oil Company* (1904, reprint ed., Gloucester, Mass.: Peter Smith, 1950), 2:283.

[14]Op. cit. (above, n. 12).

Chapter 25. Words, Words, Words

[1]Christopher Lehmann-Haupt, "The Days of George S. Patton," review of *The Patton Papers, 1940–1945*, by Martin Blumenson, *New York Times*, 27 October 1974.

[2]Edward Weisband and Thomas M. Franck, *Resignation in Protest* (New York: Grossman, 1975), p. 79.

[3]Ibid.

[4]*Progressive*, February 1975, p. 42.

[5]*Congressional Record*, 20 March 1975, p. S54604.

[6]"Perfectibility: False Premise, False Promise," *New York Times* (Sec. 4), 30 March 1975, p, 16.

[7]"Careless, Careless," *New York Times Magazine*, 6 April 1975.

[8]From *America Now*, ed. John G. Kirk, copyright © 1968, Metromedia, Inc.; and *The Defeat of America: Presidential Power and the National Character* (New York: Simon and Schuster, 1974), pp. 46–47.

[9]"Politics and the English Language," 1946, reprinted in *A Collection of Essays on George Orwell* (New York: Doubleday, Anchor, 1954), pp. 172–73.

[10]*The Politics of Lying: Government Deception, Secrecy, and Power* (New York: Vintage, 1973), p. 42.

[11]John T. Watts, of the crew of USS E.F. Larson (DD 830), a U.S. destroyer, in a letter on 22 April 1971, to Senator John V. Tunney (D–Calif.), published in *Defeated: Inside America's Military Machine*, by Stuart H. Loory (New York: Random House, 1973).

[12]*Ibid*.

[13]Israel Shenker, "Obfuscation Fighters Anoint Ziegler and Envoy," *New York Times*, 27 November 1974.

[14]Ibid.

[15]Richard Gambino, "Through the Glass Darkly," *New York Times*, 29 July 1974.

[16]*The American Food Scandal: Why You Can't Eat Well on What You Earn* (New York: Morrow, 1974), pp. 2–4.

[17]Ibid.

[18]Morton Mintz, "The Pill and the Public's Right to Know," *Progressive*, May 1970.

[19]Morton Mintz, "FDA Watered Down Pill Warning," *Washington Post*, 5 August 1973.

[20]Morton Mintz, "FDA and the Dangers of 'The Pill,' " *Washington Post*, 20 November 1975.

[21]Tom Wicker, "This Is an Arms Limitation?," *New York Times*, 10 December 1974.

[22]*Uncle Sam: The Last of the Bigtime Spenders* (New York: Simon and Schuster, 1972), p. 104.

[23]Attorneys for Daniel Ellsberg and Anthony Russo, defendants in the Pentagon Papers case, made the transcript of Hunt's testimony public on 3 May 1973.

[24]David Hapgood, *The Screwing of the Average Man* (Garden City: Doubleday, 1974), p. 26.

25Russell Baker, *New York Times*, 31 August 1974.

26Morton Mintz, and Jerry S. Cohen, *America, Inc.: Who Owns and Operates the United States* (New York: Dial, 1971), p. xv.

27*Strictly Speaking: Will America Be the Death of English* (Indianapolis: Bobbs-Merrill, 1974), p. 5.

28Interview with Arthur Cooper, *Newsweek*, 18 November 1974.

29Morton Mintz, "Squibb Doctor Faced Built-In Conflict," *Washington Post*, 8 June 1969.

30"Small Type Upsets an Insurance Policy," *New York Times*, 16 March 1975.

31U.S. Congress, Senate, Hearings before the Subcommittee on Antitrust and Monopoly of the Committee on the Judiciary, *The Life Insurance Industry*, 93d Cong., 1st Sess., 23 February 1973, pt. 3:1518. In March 1975, the New York State Insurance Department for the first time approved an "easy-to-understand" policy issued by Sentry Insurance (Leonard Sloane, "Prepared Finance: Readable Policies," *New York Times*, 31 March 1975). At about the same time Nationwide Mutual Insurance Company produced a clear-language automobile policy.

32Charles M. Wiltse, *The Jeffersonian Tradition in American Democracy* (New York: Hill and Wang, 1935, 1960), p. 111.

33Fred Rodell, *Woe Unto You, Lawyers!* (New York: Reynal and Hitchcock, 1959), p. 7.

34Ibid., p. 12.

35*The Power Broker: Robert Moses and the Fall of New York* (New York: Knopf, 1974), p. 625.

36U.S. Congress, Senate, Hearings before the Subcommittee on Antitrust and Monopoly of the Committee of the Judiciary, *Controls on Competition*, 92d Cong., 2d sess., sec. 4, 18, 19, 20, and 21 January 1972, pp. 266–68.

37Murray Edelman, "On Policies that Fail," *Progressive*, May 1975.

38*The Working-Class Majority* (New York: Coward, McCann & Geoghegan), p. 25.

39Morton Mintz and Bob Kuttner, "Renegotiation Panel Chief on the Way Out," *Washington Post*, 2 October 1974; and Morton Mintz, "Negotiation Board Criticized," *Washington Post*, 3 October 1974.

40U.S. Congress, Senate, Hearings before the Subcommittee on Monopoly of the Select Committee on Small Business, *Role of Giant Corporations, Corporate Secrecy: Overviews*, 93d Cong., 1st. sess., 9 and 12 November, 1971, pt. 2:1088–1089.

41*Consumer Reports*, June 1975.

Chapter 26. Conservatives, Liberals, Criminals

1Morton Mintz and Jerry S. Cohen, *America, Inc.: Who Owns and Operates the United States* (New York: Dial, 1971), p. xvi.

2In sworn Senate testimony, Kleindienst had falsely claimed never to have been contacted by the White House in regard to an appeal of an International Telephone and Telegraph antitrust case to the Supreme Court. Actually, President Nixon and White House Aide John D. Ehrlichman had phoned on April 19, 1971, to order him not to appeal. Kleindienst pleaded guilty to a reduced charge of refusing to testify accurately—a misdemeanor—and, on June 7, 1974, came before United States District Judge George L. Hart, Jr., in Washington to be sentenced. The maximum possible penalty was a year in jail and $1000 fine. Calling the violation "technical" and one that "reflects a heart that is too large and considerate of the feelings of others," Hart put the former attorney general on one year's unsupervised probation and fined him $100.

[3]"The Defeat of America," *New York Review of Books*, 5 November 1972; reprinted in slightly different form, *The Defeat of America* (New York: Simon and Schuster, 1974), p. 98. In the article Commager says the government "audaciously," in the book "contemptuously."

[4]Jonathan Schell, "Reflections—The Nixon Years—1," *New Yorker*, 2 June 1975.

[5]Nicholas von Hoffman, "How Conservatives Cause Centralized Government," *Washington Post*, 19 February 1975.

[6]"House Voting a Reflection of Liberal Trend in South," *New York Times*, 25 February 1975.

[7]Eileen Shanahan, "House Panel Hears Explanation of How Tax Shelters Help Rich," *New York Times*, 4 September 1975.

[8]Ibid.

[9]"Putting Yourself on the Line," *Washington Monthly*, October 1974.

[10]*The Case for Modern Man* (New York: Harper, 1955), p. 28.

[11]Marvin E. Frankel, *Criminal Sentences: Law Without Order* (New York: Hill and Wang, 1973), pp. 8–9.

[12]"The Other Crime Wave," *Washington Post*, 17 September 1974.

[13]Address before the Associated Industries of New York, Lake Placid, N.Y., 4 October 1974; see also Bob Kuttner, "Saxbe Asks Jail for Antitrust Tax Violators," *Washington Post*, 5 October 1974.

[14]"Headin' for Stir," *New York Times*, 30 May 1975.

[15]Philip Elman, Letter to the Editor, *Washington Post*, 16 June 1975.

[16]*Muscle and Blood: The Massive, Hidden Agony of Industrial Slaughter in America* (New York: Dutton, 1974), p. 293.

[17]Op. cit. (above, n. 12).

[18]*Sin and Society: An Analysis of Latter-Day Iniquity* (1907, reprint, ed. Gloucester, Mass., Peter Smith, 1965), pp. vii–viii.

[19]Op. cit. (above, n. 18), pp. 29–30.

[20]Ibid., "The Criminaloid," pp. 45–71.

Chapter 27. Wedge-Driving

[1]Congressman Benjamin S. Rosenthal (D–N.Y.), "The Impact of Federal Consumer and Environmental Regulation," a study released 13 March 1974; DeLorean's data were in a paper prepared for Allstate Insurance Company.

[2]*The Power Broker: Robert A. Moses and the Fall of New York* (New York: Knopf, 1974), pp. 476–77.

[3]Douglas Watson, "U.S. Reports $57 Billion in Overruns," *Washington Post*, 26 February 1975.

[4]"Trouble in Mass Transit: Why Can't the People Who Put a Man on the Moon Get You Downtown," *Consumer Reports*, March 1975; Jack Eisen, " 'Personal Transit' System is Rescued," *Washington Post*, 22 May 1975.

[5]Ibid.

[6]*Defeated: Inside America's Military Machine* (New York: Random House, 1973), p. 342.

[7]Ibid.

[8]Ibid., p. 344.

[9]Michael Getler, "Second Report Scores U.S. Radar Plane Plan," *Washington Post*, 23 February 1975; and Peter J. Ognibene, "AWACS: The Plane that Would Not Die," and "Congress and the Pentagon," *New Republic*, 5 and 12 July 1975.

[10]Seymour Melman, "Getting the Biggest Bang for the Buck," *New York Times*, 4 December 1974.

[11]"The Air Force's Secret War on Unemployment," *Washington Monthly*, July–August 1975.

[12]Ibid.

[13]The GAO report, "Status of Selected Major Weapon Systems," was said by Senator William Proxmire (D–Wis.) to show that "what we have in the weapon economy is double digit and triple digit inflation," press release, 6 February 1975.

[14]"Navy Estimates on F-18 Found $1.6 Billion Short," *New York Times*, 17 July 1975.

[15]*The High Priests of Waste* (New York: Norton, 1972), p. ix.

[16]Op. cit. (above, n. 6), p. 10.

[17]Ibid., p. 374.

[18]Op. cit. (above, n. 15), p. 159.

[19]Ibid., p. 312.

[20]Walter Pincus, "$1 Billion Wings Eyed for C-5 Jet," *Washington Post*, 17 September 1975.

"The Lockheed Loan Revisited," *New York Times*, 29 August 1972.

[22]"Staff Study of the C-5A," General Accounting Office, March 1972.

[23]"Troublesome Cargo Plane," *Parade*, 25 May 1975.

[24]Op. cit. (above, n. 21).

[25]Op. cit. (above, n. 15), p. ix.

[26]Ibid.; and Bernard Nossiter, *Washington Post*, 21 November 1969.

[27]Winston Groom, "Final Payoff for the Man Who Blew the Whistle on the Pentagon," *Washington Star*, 31 December 1975.

[28]Morton Mintz, "FDA Harassment Alleged," and "Official Hit on Blocked Drug Data," *Washington Post*, 16 August 1974, and January 30, 1975.

[29]Lockheed located three new subassembly plants for the C-5A in the districts of influential House committee chairmen, in addition to choosing Russell's "home ground" for the main assembly plant, the *Washington Post* said in a page-one story on 14 November 1968. Three days later, in an editorial, the *Post* identified another beneficiary: Congressman Harley O. Staggers (D–W. Va.), then chairman of the House Interstate and Foreign Commerce Committee.

[30]Morton Mintz, "$1 Billion C-5A Overpayment Charged," "Lockheed Critics Sees GAO 'Whitewash'," and "Sen. Proxmire Tells of New Threats," *Washington Post*, 28 March and 19 and 20 December 1972; see also Erwin Knoll, "The Further Education of Henry Durham," *Progressive*, June 1974.

Chapter 28. The Donkey's Tail

[1]Morton Mintz, "Drug Firm on Trial In Birth Defects Suit," *Washington Post*, 9 March 1969.

[2]Morton Mintz, *The Theraputic Nightmare* (Boston: Houghton Mifflin, 1965), p. 477.

[3]Ibid., pp. 56–65, 479–86.

[4]*The CIA and the Cult of Intelligence* (New York: Dell, 1974), p. 225.

[5]William McGaffin and Erwin Knoll, *Anything But the Truth* (New York: Putnam, 1968), pp. 128–29.

[6]Ibid.

[7]Morton Mintz and Nick Kotz, "Pesticides Firms Aided Whitten Book," *Washington Post*, 14 March 1971.

[8]Morton Mintz, "Firm Pledges to Aid Magazine Writers," *Washington Post*, 25 May 1972.

[9]*Columbia Journalism Review*, July/August 1975, p. 5.

[10]Op. cit. (above, n. 4), pp. 334–35.

[11]"CIA News Service Reported," *Washington Post*, 3 July 1975.

[12]Morton Mintz, "AMA Promotion of Eldercare Examined," 1 April 1965.

[13]Morton Mintz, "SEC Lawyers Oppose Giant Power Merger," *Washington Post*, 26 August 1972.

[14]Morton Mintz, "Running Over No-Fault," *Washington Post (Outlook)*, 27 August 1972.

[15]Stuart Auerbach, "Drug Firms Gave AMA $851,000," *Washington Post*, 1 July 1975.

[16]Morton Mintz, "FDA and Panalba: A Conflict of Commercial, Therapeutic Goals?" *Science*, 29 August 1969.

[17]U.S. Congress, Senate hearings before the Subcommittee on Monopoly of the Select Committee on Small Business, *Competitive Problems in the Drug Industry*, 94th Cong., 1st Sess., 19 March 1975, pt. 20: 11650–11651.

Chapter 29. Potpourri

[1]Morton Mintz, "Golden Days of Retirement," and "Policy Value for Elderly Questioned," *Washington Post*, 18 February 1972, and 29 July 1974.

[2]P. B. Medawar, *Induction and Intuition in Scientific Thought* (London: Methuen, 1969), cited by Paul D. Stolley, "Assuring the Safety and Efficacy of Therapies," *International Journal of Health Services*, vol. 4, no. 1, 1974.

[3]Ibid.

[4]David H. Spodick, Letters to the Editor, *American Journal of Cardiology*, 1 July 1974, and *New England Journal of Medicine*, 17 May 1973, and 29 August 1974.

[5]*The Genteel Populists* (New York: Holt, Rinehart & Winston, 1974), pp. 130–131.

[6]"On TV, Government and 'Betrayed' Children," letter to the editor, *New York Times*, 6 December 1974.

[7]Morton Mintz, " '50s Suit Linked Ash to False Affidavits," *Washington Post*, 2 January 1973.

[8]*The Power Broker: Robert Moses and the Fall of New York* (New York: Knopf, 1974), pp. 318–319.

[9]Ibid., p. 558.

[10]Ibid., p. 491.

[11]Ibid., p. 510.

[12]"H.E.W. Held Weak in Investigations," UPI, *New York Times*, 4 May 1975; and "H.E.W. Forms Unit To Look for Fraud in Use of Its Funds," AP, *New York Times*, 6 December 1975.

[13]*The CIA and the Cult of Intelligence* (New York: Dell, 1974), pp. 110–111.

[14]Morton Mintz, "Commodity-Shortage Policy Hit," *Washington Post*, 30 April 1974. TRB, "Planning Ahead," *New Republic*, 29 March 1975.

[15]A. Ernest Fitzgerald, *The High Priests of Waste* (New York: Norton, 1972), p. 362.

[16]Morton Mintz, "Foundations' Vagaries Muddle Health Plans," *Washington Post (Outlook)*, 22 October 1967.

[17]William Raspberry, "The Merit Trap" and "Conducting a Job Lottery," *Washington Post*, 19 March 1975, and 26 March 1975.

[18]Morton Mintz, "Dingell Hits U.S. Oil Leasing Policy," *Washington Post*, 27 March 1974.

[19]Morton Mintz, "Oil Shale Tract Vastly Undervalued, House Probe Says" and "Oil Tract Let For Less Than Worth," *Washington Post*, 3 March 1974, and 2 September 1974.

[20]"Keeping Experts on 'Tap'Not on 'Top,' " *Congressional Record*, 19 December 1974, p. S 22401.

[21]Ibid.

[22]Saul Friedman, *New York Times Book Review*, 4 May 1975, review of *The Experts: 100 Years of Blunder in Indo-China*, by Clyde Edwin Petty (Seacausus, N.J.: Lyle Stuart, 1975).

[23]The phrase may always evoke bitter memories of the catastrophic American involvement in Vietnam thanks to David Halberstam, author of *The Best and the Brightest* (New York: Random House, 1972).

[24]Op. cit. (above, n. 20), pp. S22399–22491.

[25]Lee Metcalf, "The Vested Oracles: How Industry Regulates Government," *Washington Monthly*, July 1971; Carole Shifrin, "Sen. Metcalf Files Suit in Petroleum Council," *Washington Post*, 22 March 1975; U.S. Congress, Senate, hearings before the Committee on Interior and Insular Affairs, *Market Performance and Competition in the Petroleum Industry*, 93d Cong., 5 and 6 December 1973, pt. 2: 470–474.

[26]Ibid., *Washington Monthly*.

[27]U.S. Congress, House, hearings before a Subcommittee of the Committee on Government Operations, *Use of Advisory Committees By the Food and Drug Administration*, 93d Cong. 6, 7, 8, 12 and 13 March; 30 April, and 21 May 1974, pt. 1: 1–2.

[28]Ibid., p. 2.

[29]Ibid.

[30]U.S. Congress, House, report by the Committee on Government Operations, *Use of Advisory Committees by the Food and Drug Administration*, 94th Cong. 1st sess. 26 January 1976, pp. 18–26, 56.

[31]"Final Report," *National Commission on Product Safety*, June 1970, p. 55.

[32]Ibid.

[33]Morton Mintz, *Washington Post (Book World)*, 26 November, 1972 review of *The Great American Auto Repair Robbery: A Report on a Ten-Million Dollar National Swindle and What You Can Do About It*, by Donald A. Randall and Arthur P. Glickman (New York: Charterhouse, 1972).

[34]William Robbins, *The American Food Scandal: Why You Can't Eat Well on What You Earn* (New York: Morrow, 1974), p. 77.

[35]Ibid., pp. 78–79.

[36]Ibid., p. 80.

[37]James McCartney, "The Vested Interests of the Reporter," *Nieman Reports*, December 1963.

Chapter 30. Setbacks and Hopes

[1]Morton Mintz, *By Prescription Only* (Boston: Houghton Mifflin, Beacon, 1967), p. 44.

[2]Ibid., pp. 48–49.

[3]U.S. Congress, Senate, Dr. Charles C. Edwards, Commissioner of the Food and Drug Administration, Statement to the Subcommittee on Monopoly of the Select Committee on Small Business, 18 January 1971.

[4]"Ex-Convicts Win Brutality Suit," *New York Times*, 27 November 1974.

[5]*Kind and Unusual Punishment: The Prison Business* (New York: Knopf, 1973), p. 82.

[6]Leroy Aarons, "U.S. Penal System 'Truths' Questioned," *Washington Post*, 17 August 1975.

[7]The Mudge Rose firm's fee may exceed $1 million: Ovid Demaris, *Dirty Business: The Corporate-Political Money-Power Game* (New York: Harper's Magazine Press, 1973), p. 365; and *Time*, 10 April 1972.

[8]Address at National Press Club, Washington, D.C., 29 July 1974, reprinted in *Congressional Record*, 29 July 1974, pp. H7297–7301.

[9]Mike Causey, "End to Mail Monopoly Foreseen," *Washington Post*, 15 December 1974.

[10]Simon Lazarus, *The Genteel Populists* (New York: Holt, Rinehart & Winston, 1974), p. 271.

[11]Ibid.

[12]Ibid.

[13]*The Buffalo Creek Disaster* (New York: Random House, 1976).

[14]"From Chaos to Responsibility" (Paper presented at Annual Meeting of the American Psychiatric Association, Anaheim, California, 5 May 1975).

[15]Don Stillman, "Pittston Admits Buffalo Creek Guilt; 625 Survivors Win $13.5 Million," *United Mine Workers Journal*, 16–31 July 1974.

[16]Op. cit. (above, n. 15).

[17]Ibid.

[18]"Innocent Bystanders," *Newsweek*, 2 September 1974.

[19]Op. cit. (above, n. 14).

[20]Gerald M. Stern, interview with Morton Mintz, 13 September 1975.

Chapter 31. Setting the Agenda

[1]This material, without substantial change, was taken from "Professionalism in the Newsroom," the Consumers Union Lecture given by Morton Mintz on May 18, 1972, at the Consumer Journalism Conference, Graduate School of Journalism, Columbia University. In slightly modified form, *Nieman Reports* published the lecture, under the same title, in the December 1972/March 1973 issue. Excerpts were published by *Columbia Journalism Review* ("Auditing the Media: A Modest Proposal"), November/December 1972, and *Progressive* ("The Test is Truth"), December 1972.

[2]One of the earliest comprehensive examinations by a newspaper (Morton Mintz, *Washington Post*) appeared as a five-article series 13–17 December 1959—but even this was quite late.

[3]Op. cit. (above. n. 1).

[4]Morton Mintz, "Cancer Death Rate Up," *Washington Post*, 7 November 1975.

[5]In *Don't Blame the People: How the News Media Use Bias, Distortions and Censorship to Manipulate Public Opinion* (Los Angeles: Diversity Press, 1971), Robert Cirino presents detailed information on noncoverage of such major issues as pollution, overpopulation, hunger, auto safety and smoking.

[6]*New Republic*, 20 February 1961, p. 7.

[7]Paul Brodeur, "Annals of Chemistry: Inert," *New Yorker*, 7 April 1975.

[8]From *Public Opinion* (New York: Penguin, 1922); reprinted in *The Essential Lippmann* (New York: Vintage, 1965), p. 401.

[9]*Congress: The Electoral Connection* (New Haven: Yale, 1974), p. 177.

[10]*Guild Reporter*, 13 June 1975, and 4 July 1975; and "Television's Profits," AP, *Washington Post (Style)*, 8 September 1975.

[11]Donnie Radcliffe, "A Message for the Medium," *Washington Post (Style)*, 8 April 1975.

¹²Strikingly, the treaty was disclosed not in a news story, but in a letter to the editor of the *New York Times.*

¹³David McAteer, "You Can't Buy Safety at the Company Store," *Washington Monthly,* November 1972.

¹⁴U.S. Congress, Senate, hearings before the Subcommittee on Antitrust and Monopoly of the Committee on the Judiciary, *The Industrial Reorganization Act,* Ground Transportation Industries, 93d Cong., 2d sess., 4, 9, 10, and 11 April 1974, pt.4A: 68A–69A, and 102An.

¹⁵In the judgment of Dan Morgan, of the *Washington Post,* formerly a correspondent in Eastern Europe.

¹⁶In much of the United States, title firms and lawyers have charged helpless home-buyers high, fixed fees for minimal performance and service; only recently, thanks to litigation, has this structure begun to crack.

¹⁷U.S. Congress, Senate, Hearings before the Subcommittee on Antitrust and Monopoly of the Committee on the Judiciary, *International Aspects of Antitrust,* 93d Cong., 2d sess., 30 April 1974, pp. 633–699, 710–750, and 997–1024.

¹⁸Peter Barnes, "Socialist Experiment in Canada," *New Republic,* 13 October 1973.

¹⁹Ibid.

²⁰Ibid.

²¹David Jenkins, *Job Power: Blue and White Collar Democracy* (New York: Doubleday, 1973).

²²Bingham wrote Miller on March 6, 1975.

²³Bob Schulman, "Can Journalistic Eavesdropping Be Justified?" *Louisville Times,* 9 May 1974; and David P. Garino, "Louisville Newspapers Cherish Independence, Guard It Jealously," *Wall Street Journal,* 11 July 1974.

²⁴These decisions are elaborated in Sanford J. Ungar, *The Papers and the Papers* (New York: Dutton, 1972) and in Bob Woodward and Carl Bernstein's *All the President's Men* (New York: Simon and Schuster, 1974).

²⁵"Should a TV License Be Immune From Any and All Challenges?" *New York Times,* 30 June 1974.

²⁶Op. cit, (above, n. 11).

²⁷Letter to [*More*], July 1975.

²⁸Op. cit. (above, n. 22).

²⁹Bob Schulman, "Shortcomings of the Press Endanger Its Freedom," *Louisville Times,* 15 April 1974.

³⁰"Still New Under the Sun: Truth," *New York Times,* 7 November 1975.

³¹With few exceptions, the items on the list derived from Mintz's own experience as a reporter in Washington since 1958. Assuredly the list easily could be extended for several pages.

³²Alfred Balk, "Britain's Great Thalidomide Cover-Up," *Columbia Journalism Review,* May/June 1975; other sources include Harold Evans, *The Listener* (London), 1 February 1973; and Bernard D. Nossiter, "A Courtroom Conflict Over the Thalidomide Tragedy," *Washington Post,* 11 February 1972.

Chapter 32. Overseeing the Overseer of the Overseer

¹*The Liberal Hour* (New York: New American Library, 1964), p. 96.

²"Room at the Top," *New York Times,* 5 December 1974.

³Morton Mintz, Second Annual Consumers Union Lecture, "Professionalism in the News-room," Graduate School of Journalism, Columbia University, 18 May 1972; printed in slightly altered form in *Nieman Reports,* December 1972/March 1973.

⁴"Checking Up," *The New Republic,* 14 December 1974.

⁵Ibid.

⁶"Wilbur Mills: The Ways and Means of Conning the Press," *Washington Monthly,* December 1974.

⁷Ibid.

⁸Ibid.

⁹Ibid.

¹⁰Ibid.

¹¹Ibid.

¹²*Time,* 31 December 1973.

¹³"Congress and the Media: Partners in Propaganda," *Columbia Journalism Review,* January/February 1974.

¹⁴"On the Profession of Journalism," address to the International Press Institute, London, 27 May 1965; published in *Congressional Record,* 15 June 1965, pp. A3116–3117.

¹⁵Speech at the annual convention of the American Political Science Association, New York, 1966.

¹⁶Quoted by Tom Bethell, an editor of the *Washington Monthly,* in a letter of 24 March 1975, seeking funds for *The Mountain Eagle* from its admirers.

Chapter 33. Flacking

¹William McGaffin and Erwin Knoll, *Anything But the Truth* (New York: Putnam, 1968), pp. 22–23.

²Ibid., p. 72.

³Ben H. Bagdikian, "The Fruits of Agnewism," *Columbia Journalism Review,* January/-February 1973.

⁴Ibid.

⁵Ibid.

⁶*[More],* December 1972.

⁷Barry Sussman details this episode in *The Great Coverup: Nixon and the Scandal of Watergate* (New York: New American Library, 1974), pp. 122–30.

⁸Op. cit. (above, n. 1), p. 205.

⁹Principal sources for this account of the Glomar episode were: Jack Anderson, "Press Forgets Prime Responsibility," *Washington Post,* 25 March 1975; Elizabeth Peer and others, "Salvaging the Substory," *Newsweek,* 31 March 1975; Charles B. Seib, "The Confusing Coverage of the Submarine Story," *Washington Post,* 27 March 1975; Martin Arnold, "C.I.A. Tried to Get Press to Hold Up Salvage Story," *New York Times,* 20 March 1975; Stephen Isaacs, "Withholding of Story Defended," *Washington Post,* 20 March 1975; and Arthur S. Miller, "The Servile Press," *Progressive,* May 1975.

¹⁰Letter to the Editor, *New York Times,* 19 June 1975.

¹¹"All the President's Friends," *New York Times,* 1 July 1975; adapted from *The Promise and the Performance: The Leadership of John F. Kennedy* (New York: Crown, 1975).

¹²"Rocky in Medialand," *[More],* January 1975.

¹³Morton Mintz and Jerry S. Cohen, *America, Inc.: Who Owns and Operates the United States* (New York: Dial, 1971), p. 9.

[14]*APME News*, publication of the Associated Press Managing Editors Association, July 1971.

[15]David Wise, *The Politics of Lying: Government Deception, Secrecy, and Power* (New York: Vintage, 1973), pp. 499–500.

[16]Morton Mintz, "Anti-Profiteer Agency Called Hacks' Haven," *Washington Post*, 13 June 1975.

[17]Ibid.

[18]"Curbing the Tappers," *New York Times*, 27 June 1975.

Chapter 34 The CIA, FBI, NSA, and IRS

[1]U.S. Congress, Senate Final Report of the Select Committee to Study Governmental Operations With Respect to Intelligence Activities, *Intelligence Activities and the Rights of Americans*, Book 2, April 1976.

[2]Ibid.

[3]"Intelligence 'Oversight' Is Done With A Blindfold," *New York Times*, 29 December 1974.

[4]Laurence Stern, "Church Says Kissinger Imposed Covert Angola Role," *Washington Post*, 15 January 1976.

[5]Nicholas M. Horrock, "President Bars House Unit From Seeing Secret Data," *New York Times*, 13 September 1975.

[6]Donald P. Baker, "Allen Dulles Testified CIA, FBI Would Lie," *Washington Post*, 22 November 1974.

[7]Tom Braden, "CIA: Power and Arrogance," *Washington Post* (Outlook), 27 April 1975 (reprinted from Saturday Review).

[8]John M. Goshko, "Kelley Says FBI Is 'Truly Sorry' For Past Abuses," *Washington Post*, 9 May, 1976.

[9]Op. cit. (above, n. 1).

[10]Laurence Stern, "Relentless Growth," *Washington Post*, 29 April 1976.

[11]David Kahn, "Big Ear or Big Brother," *New York Times Magazine*, 16 May 1976.

[12]Ibid.

[13]Ibid.

[14]Ibid.

[15]Francis Biddle, *In Brief Authority*, (Garden City, N.Y.: Doubleday, 1962), p. 166.

[16]Op. cit. (above, n. 1).

[17]Op. cit. (above, n. 15).

[18]"The Kennedy Vendetta: How the CIA Waged a Silent War Against Cuba," *Harper's*, July 1975.

[19]" 'Only Congress Itself,' " *New York Times*, 18 September 1975.

[20]Speech at Denison College, Granville, Ohio, October 3, 1975.

[21]Op. cit. (above, n. 19).

[22]Victor Marchetti and John D. Marks, *The CIA and the Cult of Intelligence* (New York: Dell, 1974), p. 281.

[23]Ibid.

[24]John M. Crewdson, "House Committee Finds Intelligence Agencies Generally Go Unchecked," *New York Times*, 26 January 1976.

[25]"The Menace of 'The Company,' " a review of Philip Agee's *Inside the Company: CIA Diary*, in *Progressive*, September 1975.

Chapter 35. World, Inc.

[1] *Hale* v. *Henkle,* 201 US 74 (1906).

[2] U.S. Congress, Senate, hearings before the Subcommittee on Antitrust and Monopoly of the Committee on the Judiciary, *The Industrial Reorganization Act, Ground Transportation Industries,* 93d Cong., 2d sess., 26, 27, 28 February; and 1 March 1974, pt. 4A: 17.

[3] Ibid., p. 17.

[4] Morton Mintz; "GM, Ford Units Criticized on WW II Role," *Washington Post,* 27 February 1974.

[5] Op. cit. (above, n. 2), p. 22.

[6] Thurman Arnold, *Fair Fights and Foul: A Dissenting Lawyer's Life* (New York: Harcourt, Brace & World, 1965), pp. 115, 145; interviews of Joseph Borkin, who was a top aide to Arnold, by Morton Mintz; contemporary new accounts, particularly by Thomas Stokes of United Press and in the newspapaer *PM;* Anthony Sampson, *The Seven Sisters: The Great Oil Companies and the World They Shaped* (New York: Viking, 1975), pp. 79–80 (Sampson omits that the proceeding against Exxon was a *criminal* one).

[7] *The Sovereign State of ITT* (New York: Stein and Day, 1973), pp. 27, 28.

[8] Ibid., p. 40.

[9] Ibid., p. 43.

[10] Ibid., p. 47.

[11] Ibid., pp. 27, 28.

[12] Mark J. Green, *The Other Government: The Unseen Power of Washington Lawyers* (New York: Grossman, 1975), pp. 94–95.

[13] Ibid, p. 95.

[14] Op. cit. (above, n. 7), p. 47.

[15] U.S. Congress, Senate, hearings before the Subcommittee on Multinational Corporations of the Committee on Foreign Relations, *Multinational Corporations and United States Foreign Policy,* 93d Cong., 2d sess., 20 and 21 February; 27 and 28 March 1974 (Executive sessions held on 28 January and 20 June 1974), pt. 7:47.

[16] U.S. Congress, Senate, Committee print, prepared for the use of the Subcommittee on Multinational Corporations of the Committee on Foreign Relations, *The Internationl Petroleum Cartel, the Iranian Consortium and U.S. National Security,* 21 February 1974, p. 7.

[17] Ibid., p. 14.

[18] U.S. Congress, Senate, Report to the Committee on Foreign Relations by the Subcommittee on Multinational Corporations, *Multinational Oil Corporations and U.S. Foreign Policy,* 2 January 1975, pp. 37–38.

[19] Eric Pace, *New York Times,* 18 March 1976.

[20] U.S. Congress, Senate, Committee print prepared for the use of the Subcommittee on Multinational Corporations of the Committee on Foreign Relations, *A Documentary History of the Petroleum Reserves Corporation 1943-1944,* 8 May 1974, p. 63.

[21] Op. cit. (above, n. 16), pp. 12–13.

[22] Op. cit. (above, n. 15), p. 65.

[23] U.S. Congress, Senate, Staff Report to the Federal Trade Commission, submitted to the Subcommittee on Monopoly of the Select Committee on Small Business, *The International Petroleum Cartel,* 22 August, 1952, p. 104.

[24] Op. cit. (above, n. 15), pt. 8: 116–117.

[25] Op. cit. (above, n. 18), pp. 49–50.

[26] Ibid., p. 81.

27Ibid., p. 84.

28Ibid., p. 85.

29Op. cit. (above, n. 24), p. 160.

30Op. cit. (above, n. 18), p. 92.

31Op. cit. (above, n. 18), p. 92.

31Ibid.

32Morton Mintz, "Oil Expert Says IRS Favors Industry," *Washington Post*, 11 January 1972.

33Op. cit. (above, n. 18), p. 93.

34Press conference held by Stephen J. Spingarn, acting Chairman of the Federal Trade Commission, at the FTC, December 17, 1952.

35*The Seven Sisters: The Great Oil Companies and the World They Made* (New York: Viking, 1975), p. 123.

36Op. cit. (above, n. 16), p. 43.

37Op. cit. (above, n. 34).

38Op. cit. (above, n. 16), p. 6.

39Ibid., p. 15.

40Op. cit. (above, n. 34).

41Statement by Federal Trade Commissioner Stephen J. Spingarn, January 15, 1953, in an FTC press release the same day.

42Ibid.

43Op. cit. (above, n. 34).

44Ibid.

45Op. cit. (above, n. 15), p. 32.

46*Op. cit.* (above, n. 15), pt. 8: 3–5.

47Ibid., p. 5.

48Ibid., p. 7.

49Ibid., p. 11.

50Ibid., pp. 10–12.

51Ibid., p. 12.

52Ibid.

53Ibid.

54Ibid., pp. 12–13.

55Op. cit. (above, n. 7), pp. 102–103.

56Morton Mintz, "Oil Tax Break in 1950 Laid to Security," *Washington Post*, 24 February 1974.

57CBS Reports: "The Hot and Cold Wars of Allen Dulles," 26 April 1962.

58David Wise and Thomas B. Ross, *The Invisible Government* (New York: Random House, 1964), p. 113.

59Op. cit. (above, n. 15), p. 74.

60Op. cit. (above, n. 16), p. 52.

61Op. cit. (above, n. 15), p. 110.

62Op. cit. (above, n. 18), p. 67.

63Ibid., p. 68.

64Op. cit. (above, n. 16), p. 76.

65Op. cit. (above, n. 35), p. 131.

66Op. cit. (above, n. 16), p. 92.

67Op. cit. (above, n. 15), pt. 5: 251.

[68]Op. cit. (above, n. 16), p. 91.

[69]Op. cit. (above, n. 15), p. 32.

[70]Ibid., p. 33.

[71]Op. cit. (above, n. 16), p. viii.

[72]Statement of Senator Frank Church upon release of the Senate Subcommittee on Multinational Corporations Report *Multinational Oil Corporations and U.S. Foreign Policy*, 12 January 1975.

[73]Ibid.

[74]Morton Mintz, "Hart Says Oil-Price Increases Cost More Than Vietnam War," *Washington Post*, 29 April 1974.

[75]Op. cit. (above, n. 72).

[76]Op. cit. (above, n. 15), p. 504.

[77]Op. cit. (above, n. 18), p. 142.

[78]Op. cit. (above, n. 15), p. 547.

[79]Ibid.

[80]Ibid.

[81]No evidence to support the warning about "Japanese, European, and perhaps Russian interests" was offered by McCloy, and so he is owed a presumption that he had none. Almost a year later, at an executive session of the Senate Subcommittee on Multinational Corporations on June 20, 1974, Senator J. William Fulbright (D–Ark.) was questioning George M. Keller, vice-chairman of Socal and a director of Aramco, about Saudi Arabia, which is almost fanatically anti-Communist:

Q. How about the British or Italians or Japanese, you don't think they would step in if they were invited?
A. The problem, as I say, is a practical one. In the first place, I think this is a very fair statement: the Saudis don't really trust any of the others but the United States.
Q. They prefer you?
A. They can deal with us. So there would be a several year period during which, I will make a guess, Aramco production might drop in half and then recover over 3 years. . . .

[82]Op. cit. (above, n. 15), p. 517.

[83]Ibid., p. 516.

[84]Ibid., p. 418.

[85]Ibid., p. 515.

[86]Ibid., p. 421.

[87]Ibid., p. 419. (For a fuller exploration of this issue, see U.S. Congress, Senate, Hearings before the Permanent Subcommittee on Investigations, of the Committee on Government Operations, *Cutoff of Petroleum Products to U.S. Military Forces*, 93d Cong., 2d sess., 22 April 1974.)

[88]Ibid., p. 430.

[89]Op. cit. (above, n. 18), p. 148.

[90]Ibid., p. 161.

[91]Op. cit. (above, n. 16), p. viii.

[92]At the opening of a six-day hearing on the Overseas Private Investment Corporation on July 18, 1973, Stanford G. Ross, a former Treasury Department tax expert, told the Senate Subcommitee on Multinational Corporations that an American-based multinational may pay negligible taxes at home on income from a foreign operation so long as it prospers. But if the operation should be expropriated, the United States Treasury will compensate the company with a reduction in income taxes of up to 48 percent of its loss.

An exchange between Ross and Subcommittee Chairman Frank Church also brought out this anomaly: if a multinational builds a new plant in one of the fifty states, it will pay taxes, at a low rate, to that state; if it builds abroad it will pay income taxes to a foreign country at a much higher rate. Yet it will have an incentive to build abroad; the payment to a state would be deductible only as a business expense; the foreign taxes would be subtracted directly from American income taxes.

The professed objective of the United States Government in taxing foreign income is "neutrality," that is, to provide neither an incentive nor a disincentive to foreign investment. Do our tax laws achieve that neutrality? Church asked. "No," said Ross. "They are tipped in favor of foreign investment."

As for OPIC, its professed purpose is to protect the public interest mainly by insuring American corporations against expropriation of their operations in developing countries. The investigation established that OPIC was serving the interests of big business at public expense.

Chapter 36. The Workplace

[1] Morton Mintz, "Stars in Our Eyes, Dust in Our Lungs," *Washington Post (Book World)*, 20 October 1974.

[2] *Safety in the Mines: A Look at the World's Most Hazardous Occupation*, a comparative study of mine health and safety in Europe and the United States; done in 1971 for Ralph Nader's Center for Study of Responsive Law in Washington, D.C., p. 7.

[3] Ibid.

[4] Ibid.

[5] Ibid.

[6] Ibid.

[7] Ibid., p. 56.

[8] Ibid., pp. 56–57.

[9] Ibid., p. 57.

[10] Ibid.

[11] Ibid., p. 11.

[12] Ibid., p. 2.

[13] Thomas O'Hanlon, "Anarchy Threatens the Kingdom of Coal," *Fortune*, January 1971.

[14] Jeremy Brecher, *Strike* (Greenwich, Conn.: Fawcett, 1974), p. 337.

[15] Ibid.

[16] *Death and the Mines: Rebellion and Death in the United Mine Workers* (New York: Grossman, 1971).

[17] Ibid., p. 55.

[18] Ibid., p. 65.

[19] Ibid.

[20] Ibid., p. 75. In a House floor speech on October 27, 1969, Hechler asked a question with which all of us—public officials, the press, citizenry—ought to be confronted relentlessly: "When are we going to start placing the priority where it belongs—on the value of human life?"

In an additional contribution to debate on the then-pending coal-mine safety bill, Hechler said that in the year since the seventy-eight deaths at Farmington, twice as many men had been killed in mine accidents; that in West Virginia one out of every three hundred men who went down into the mines had perished, and that one out of ten miners had suffered a lost-time injury in the mines.

"Did you hear that figure?" Hechler asked a hushed House. "One out of ten injured." Morton Mintz and Thomas O'Toole, "Industrial Hazards Exact a Rising Toll," *Washington Post,* 28 December 1969.

[21]Congressman David R. Obey (D–Wis.), "Death on the Job," *Progressive,* September 1975.

[22]Ibid.

[23]Stuart Auerbach, "Cancer: A Work Hazard Industry Is Forced To Face," *Washington Post,* 30 March 1975.

[24]Ibid.

[25]Ibid.

[26]Ibid.

[27]Ibid.

[28]Stuart Auerbach, "Job-Caused Cancers Are Found Spreading To Workers' Families," *Washington Post,* 25 March 1975.

[29]Ibid.

[30]Ibid.

[31]Ibid.

[32]Op. cit. (above, n. 1); for a full account, see Paul Brodeur, *Expendable Americans* (New York: Viking, 1974), p. 163.

[33]Ibid.

[34]Op. cit. (above, n. 1).

[35]*Op. cit.* (above, n. 28).

[36]Ibid.

[37]Ibid.

[38]Ibid.

[39]Hobart Rowen, "A Loss of Hands: Rule on Machines Controversial," *Washington Post,* 8 June 1975.

[40]Ibid.

[41]Ibid.

[42]Ibid.

[43]Ibid.

[44]Ibid.

[45]*Muscle and Blood: The Massive, Hidden Agony of Industrial Slaughter in America* (New York: Dutton, 1974), p. 239.

[46]"No Supervision Without Representation," *Working Papers,* Summer 1974.

[47]Ibid.

[48]Ibid.

[49]Ibid.

[50]Ibid.

[51]Ibid.

[52]"Obligation of Scientists to Respond to Society's Needs," in *Scientists in the Legal System: Tolerated Meddlers or Essential Contributors?,* ed. William A. Thomas (Ann Arbor, Mich.: Ann Arbor Science Publishers, 1974), p. 53.

[53]Ibid.

[54]"New Paths to Corporate Accountability" (Paper presented at a conference on "The Corporation and the Quality of Life," Center for the Study of Democratic Institutions, September 27–October 1, 1971).

[55]Ibid.

[56]"Low Productivity: The Real Sin of High Wages," 24 February 1972.

[57] *False Promises: The Shaping of American Working Class Consciousness* (New York: McGraw-Hill, 1973), pp. 214–215.

[58] Ibid., p. 214.

[59] Ibid., p. 214–215.

[60] Ibid., p. 215.

[61] Ibid.

[62] Ibid., pp 254–255.

[63] Ibid., p. 255.

[64] Op. cit. (above, n. 56).

[65] Ibid.

[66] Barbara Newman, "They Didn't Know Who They Were Jazzing With," interview of Edward Sadlowski for National Public Radio as excerpted in the *Washington Post (Outlook)*, 23 March 1975.

[67] Ibid.

[68] Sidney Lens, "Partners: Labor and the CIA," *Progressive*, February, 1975.

[69] Ibid.

[70] Ibid.

[71] Ibid.

[72] Ibid.

[73] Guild leaders said they had solicited the money. "ANG Probes Foundations Supplying Overseas Funds," *Guild Reporter*, 24 February 1967.

[74] On August 31, 1964, at a hearing of a House Select Small Business Subcommittee headed by Congressman Wright Patman (D–Tex.), the Andrew Hamilton Fund was among several "foundations" identified as fronts for the CIA. This was widely reported by, among others, the *Washington Post* (Morton Mintz, "Hearing Looks Into CIA Role in Tax Probe of Charity Fund,"1 September 1964), and United Press International (the *New York Times* for September 1 began the UPI account on page one).

Not until February 1967, however, did Guild members learn that the Hamilton Fund was a CIA conduit to the American Newspaper Guild, as the international union was then named. On February 18, 1967, the *Post* and *Times* each published acknowledgements by Charles A. Perlik, Jr., then secretary–treasurer (and later president of the ANG, and Richard P. Davis, then international affairs director of the union, that the ANG had received money through CIA front "foundations," while claiming not to have known of the CIA connection.

In the resulting flaps, the ANG ended its ties with the "foundations," ("IEB Cuts Foundation Ties," *Guild Reporter*, 24 March 1967), and, a few months later, Guild members at their annual convention adopted a resolution barring the ANG from accepting government funds, for any purpose, covertly or overtly.

[75] Op. cit. (above, n. 66).

[76] *Small Is Beautiful: Economics As If People Mattered* (New York: Harper & Row, 1973), p. 35.

[77] Ibid., pp. 140–141.

[78] Bernard Weinraub, "Swedes Propose Reform to Widen Worker Role," *New York Times*, 22 October 1975.

[79] David Jenkins, *Job Power: Blue and White Collar Democracy* (Garden City: Doubleday, 1973) pp. 315, 319.

[80] Ibid., p. 319.

[81] Ibid., p. 1–2.

[82] Ibid., p. 23.

[83] Ibid.

[84]Ibid., pp. 38–39.

[85]Ibid., p. 39.

[86]Ibid., pp. 194–196.

[87]Ibid., pp. 196–197.

[88]Ibid., p. 235.

[89]William Claiborne, "When Workers Are Owners," *Washington Post*, 22 April 1975.

[90]Op. cit. (above, n. 79), p. 281.

Chapter 37. Taxes

[1]*A Modest Proposal for the Reform of the Capitalist System: Politically Impossible Solutions to Our Economic Ills* (Washington, D.C., Center for the Study of Capitalist Institutions, 4914 Belt Rd., N.W., 1974), p. 3. Moore also says, it should be noted, that "some degree of economic inequality is necessary to maintain work incentives and economic growth."

[2]"Taxation and Democratic Values," *New Republic*, 2 November 1974.

[3]Ibid.

[4]Op. cit. (above, n. 1), p. 1.

[5]Ralph Nader, "Corporate Taxes—⅓ of Legal Rate," *People & Taxes* (Public Citizen Tax Reform Group, P.O. Box 14198, Ben Franklin Station, Washington, D.C.), June 1975.

[6]Data were compiled—entirely from public sources—by the Joint Committee on Internal Revenue Taxation, with the aid of the General Accounting Office, and were published by Congressman Charles A. Vanik (D–Ohio) in the *Congressional Record*, 18 December 1974.

[7]"Taxes, Goods, and Efficiency: Petroleum and Defense," published in *The Economics of Federal Subsidy Programs*, pt. 3, *Tax Subsidies*, a compendium of papers submitted to the Joint Economic Committee, 15 July 1972.

[8]Ibid.

[9]Op. cit. (above, n. 5).

[10]New York: Random House, 1964.

[11]New York: Random House, 1973.

[12]U.S. Congress, Senate and House, Hearings before the Subcommittee on Priorities and Economy in Government of the Joint Economic Committee, *The Economics of Federal Subsidy Programs*, 92d Cong., 1st Sess., 13, 14, and 17 January 1972, pp. 77–79.

[13]Ibid.

[14]Ibid., p. 80.

[15]Ibid., p. 81.

[16]Ibid. In fiscal 1976, Thomas J. Reese, legislative director of Taxation with Representation, a public-interest taxpayers' lobby based in Washington, D.C., told the House Ways and Means Committee on January 21, 1976, the tax exemption for interest on state and local bonds will save state and local governments about $3.6 billion but cost the Treasury about $4.8 billion. "The remaining $1.2 billion stayed in the pockets of banks and high income individuals who own tax exempt bonds," he said.

[17]"How Much Do Loopholes Leave You?," *People & Taxes*, June 1975.

[18]Samantha Senger, "Taxes: Our Biggest Housing Problem," *People & Taxes*, July 1975.

[19]DISC Repeal Called Needed Tax Reform," *Washington Post (Business and Finance)*, 16 June 1974.

[20]Op. cit. (above, n. 12), p. 43.

[21]"Agribusiness and Agrigovernment: Power, Profits, and Poverty," *The Politics of Exploitation*, ed. Gene L. Mason and Fred Vetter (New York: Random House), p. 181.

[22]Ibid.

[23]"Governmental Charity: A Proposal for Direct Grants," *Working Papers,* Winter 1975.

[24]Ovid Demaris, *Dirty Business: The Corporate-Political Money-Power Game* (New York: Harper's Magazine Press, 1974), p. 284.

[25]Ibid., p. 253.

[26]Ibid., pp. 253–254.

[27]Morton Mintz, "Hughes Medical Institute Seeks $36 Million Tax Break," and "White House Had Role in Hughes Case," *Washington Post,* 27 October 1973, and 7 November 1973.

[28]Ibid.

[29]"Perot Would Gain $15 Million Benefit In Tax Panel's Bill," *Wall Street Journal,* 7 November 1975, and Peter Milius, "Tax Reform Gutted by House Panel," *Washington Post,* 6 November 1975. With "an enlarged, younger, more liberal membership," and with Congressman Al Ullman (D–Ore.) displacing Wilbur Mills as chairman, House Ways and Means supposedly was a "new" committee, Milius wrote. But, he said, it "has turned out to be not much different from the old. The Committee . . . gutted its own tax bill."

[30]"Schools Hurt By Operators' Low Taxes," *United Mine Workers Journal,* 16–31 March 1975. The article said: "Six months of research by Tom D. Miller, a reporter for the Huntington (W. Va.) *Herald Dispatch,* established that absentee landlords own or control at least two-thirds of the privately held land in the state. He found that 24 out-of-state corporations and land companies—many of them coal companies—own a third of the state's private acreage.

First among them is Continental Oil, which through Consolidation Coal Co. owns over a half million acres. Eastern Gas & Fuel owns more than a quarter million acres, and Bethlehem Steel and Pittston Co. each own another 125,000.

Miller calculated that W. Va. schools lose at least $100 million and possibly as much as $200 million each year because of the underassessment of coal owners and other giant landowners.

See also, Reginald Stuart, "Higher Appalachia Coal Taxes Asked," *New York Times,* 22 June 1974.

[31]James Rosapepe, "Corporations and State Taxes: The Big Ones Get Away," *Washington Monthly,* January 1975.

[32]Op. cit. (above, n. 2), pp. 92–93.

[33]Ibid., p. 93.

Chapter 38. Hanging Judges

[1]Marvin E. Frankel, *Criminal Sentences: Law Without Order* (New York: Hill and Wang, 1973), p. 9.

[2]Morton Mintz, "A Quest for Criminal Justice," *Washington Post,* 29 November 1968.

[3]Ibid.

[4]Edward J. Walsh, "Agnew Witness's Jail Term Upset," *Washington Post,* 31 October 1975.

[5]"4 Oil Companies Fined $500 in Santa Barbara Oil Spill," AP, *New York Times,* 13 January 1972.

[6]" 'Appropriate' Sentence?," editorial, *New York Times,* 1 October 1973.

[7]"Ohio Hospital Frees Sane Prisoners," *Washington Post,* 24 April 1971. The judge who ordered the release of the inmates was David O. Steiner of Allen County (Lima), Ohio. A hospital official said at the time that none of the five men was "ever diagnosed as being

psychotic and thus had no business in being committed to the hospital." He estimated that up to 150 more such men may be in the institution.

[8]Op. cit. (above, n. 1), p. 18

[9]Op. cit. (above, n. 2).

[10]Op. cit. (above, n. 1), p. 8.

[11]Ibid., p. 5.

[12]Tom Goldstein, "How To Measure A Judge's Conduct?," *New York Times* (Sec. 4), 17 August 1975.

[13]Op. cit. (above, n. 1), p. 39.

[14]Ibid., p. 42.

[15]Op. cit. (above, n. 1), p. 17.

Chapter 39. Cattle Feed and Human Fodder

[1]In a letter to Secretary of Agriculture Earl Butz on November 21, 1973, Congressman L. H. Fountain (D–N.C.), chairman of the House Intergovernmental Relations Subcommittee, cast doubt on claims—made mainly by pharmaceutical firms—that medication of feeds with DES reduce the need for them by 10 to 15 percent, and antibiotics by an additional 10 percent.

He cited statistics, gathered by the Department of Agriculture's own Economic Research Service, showing that the efficiency of feed in producing beef cattle appeared to be at the lowest level in fifty years. According to the ERS, for example, the number of "feed units" consumed to produce 100 pounds of calves and cattle was 904 in 1955–56, when use of DES was relatively light, and 1,086—182 more—in 1970–71, when use of DES was massive.

[2]Jacqueline Verrett and Jean Carper, *Eating May Be Hazardous to Your Health* (New York: Simon and Schuster, 1974), p. 160.

[3]In 1975, on the basis of marketing data, Dr. Sidney M. Wolfe, director of the Health Research Group, a Washington, D.C., organization supported by Ralph Nader's Public Citizen, Inc., estimated that physicians wrote eleven thousand prescriptions for DES as an abortifacient.

[4]Morton Mintz, "Drug Linked to Cancer In Daughters," *Washington Post*, 27 October 1971.

[5]Dr. Wolfe, identified in op. cit. (above, n. 3).

[6]This was the per capita savings estimated by the Department of Agriculture at House Intergovernmental Relations Subcommittee hearings, but see op. cit. (above, n. 1).

[7]Morton Mintz, "Cancer Institute Head Urges FDA Ban DES," *Washington Post*, 10 July 1972.

[8]Morton Mintz, "Consumer Bill Scored by Ervin," *Washington Post*, 22 July 1974.

[9]"The State of the Consumer," Address to the Consumer Federation of America, Washington, D.C., 31 January 1975.

Chapter 40. Human Guinea Pigs

[1]Robert Alexander Mc Cance, Professor of Experimental Medicine, University of Cambridge, Presidential Address to the Royal Society, 1951, cited in M. H. Pappworth, *Human Guinea Pigs: Experimentation on Man* (Boston: Beacon, 1968), p. 10.

[2]"Experiments on Humans," *New York Times*, 20 February 1975.

[3] *Congressional Record*, 1 August 1972, p. S12430; Jean Heller's articles are reprinted on pp. S 12432–12435.

[4] Frank Carey, reprinted in *Congressional Record*, 1 August 1972, pp. S 12431–12432.

[5] Ibid.

[6] Victor Cohn, "Experiment Settlement Is Faulted," *Washington Post*, 18 December 1974.

[7] "Human Experiments and Civil Liberties," *Washington Post (Style)*, 30 March 1975.

[8] Ibid.

[9] *Kind and Usual Punishment: The Prison Business* (New York: Knopf, 1973), p. 139.

[10] Op. cit. (above, n. 7).

[11] Op. cit. (above, n. 9), p. 143.

[12] Ibid., p. 144.

[13] Op. cit., (above, n. 2).

[14] Op. cit. (above, n. 1, Pappworth), p. 192.

[15] "Medical Ethics and Controlled Trials," *British Medical Journal*, 20 April 1963.

[16] Herrman L. Blumgart, "The Medical Framework," *Experimentation On Human Subjects*, ed. Paul A. Freund (New York: Braziller, 1970), pp. 51–52.

[17] Bill Richards, "6,940 Took Drugs; Army Still Testing," *Washington Post*, 23 July 1975.

[18] Bill Richards, "Drug Tests Stir Debate on Ethics," *Washington Post*, 10 August 1975.

[19] Op. cit., (above, n. 7).

[20] Joseph B. Treaster, "The LSD Connection: To National Security," *New York Times* (Sec. 4), 21 September 1975.

[21] *British Medical Journal* 1 (1953): 671; cited by Pappworth, op. cit. (above, n. 2), p. 219.

[22] Op. cit. (above, n. 2).

Chapter 41. Doctors and Dentists

[1] American Medical Association, *Opinions and Reports of the Judicial Council* (Chicago, 1969), p. vi.

[2] "Promoting Quality Through Evaluating the Process of Patient Care," *Medical Care*, May–June 1968.

[3] *One Life—One Physician: An Inquiry Into the Medical Profession's Performance in Self-Regulation*, Report to the Center for Study of Responsive Law (Washington, D.C.: Public Affairs Press, 1971), pp. 129–130.

[4] Ibid, p. 67.

[5] Ibid, pp. 86–87.

[6] Op. cit. (above, note 3), p. 87.

[7] Brit Hume, *Death and the Mines: Rebellion and Death in the United Mine Workers* (New York: Grossman, 1971), p. 129.

[8] "Physicians Focus on Own Ailments," *New York Times*, 14 April 1975.

[9] Ibid.

[10] "Research in Medical Care and Health Services Systems," *Medical Care*, March–April 1968.

[11] Op. cit. (above, n. 3), p. 30.

[12] Op. cit. (above, n. 6).

[13] Ibid.

[14] "The Doctors Guide," *Newsweek*, 18 November 1974.

[15] "The New JCAH Standards," *Journal of the American Hospital Association*, 16 October 1969.

16"Self-Evaluation by Professionals," *Group Practice*, November 1968.
17Op. cit. (above, n. 3), pp. 103–104.
18Ibid.
19Ibid., p. 102.
20Op. cit. (above, n. 6).
21Ibid.
22Ibid.
23Ibid.
24Ibid.
25Howard S. Shapiro, *How to Keep Them Honest* (Emmaus, Pa.: Rodale Press, 1974), p. 211.
26Morton Mintz, "FDA Assailed on Use of Toxic Dental Drug," *Washington Post*, 1 November 1975, and "FDA Acts on Dental Drug Use," *Washington Post*, 19 December 1975.
27*Dentistry and Its Victims* (New York: St. Martin's Press, 1970) p. 3.
28Ibid., pp. 3, 5.
29Ibid., p. 6.
30Ibid., p. 25.

Chapter 42. Nuclear Power: The "Faustian Bargain"

1*Small Is Beautiful: Economics As If People Mattered* (New York: Harper & Row, 1973), p. 138.
2Ibid.
3Ibid., pp. 138–139.
4General Hugh Johnson, once the most powerful administrator in the New Deal, said after World War II broke out in September 1939, that the United States, by engaging in warlike acts while "utterly, tragically unprepared for war," was engaging in a "reckless shooting craps with destiny for the sake of democracy."
5"Time for a Moratorium," an article in *The Case for a Nuclear Moratorium* (Environmental Action Foundation, Washington, D.C., 20036).
6Op. cit. (above, n. 1), pp. 129–130.
7Interview with Daniel F. Ford of the Union for Concerned Scientists. See also, "Can Nuclear Waste Be Stored?," *Newsweek*, 18 November 1974, and "The Deadly Dilemma of Nuclear Wastes," *Business Week*, 3 March 1975.
8J. Gustave Speth, Arthur R. Tamplin, and Thomas B. Cochran, "Plutonium Recycle: The Fateful Step," *Bulletin of the Atomic Scientists*, November 1974.
9W. C. Bartels and S. C. T. McDowell, cited in *Nuclear News*, August 1974.
10Op. cit. (above, n. 8).
11J. Gustave Speth, Arthur R. Tamplin, and Thomas Cochran, "Plutonium: An Invitation to Disaster," *Environmental Action*, 23 November 1974.
12Ibid.
13J. Gustave Speth, Arthur Tamplin, and Thomas Cochran, "Bypassing the Breeder," *Environmental Action*, 12 April 1975.
14Op. cit. (above, note 1), p. 136.
15"Responsibility for the Future and the Far-away," *Revue Internationale de Philosophie* 11 (Brussels, 1957): 100.
16Op. cit. (above, n. 5).

[17]Cited by Senator Mike Gravel (D–Alaska), a leading critic of nuclear power, in a "factsheet" prepared by an aide, P. C. Gardette, and dated 15 April 1975.

[18]"A.E.C. Files Show Effort to Conceal Safety Perils," *New York Times*, 10 November 1974.

[19]The AEC released the study in August 1974.

[20]David Burnham, "Panel Disputes Estimate of Toll in Reactor Mishap," *New York Times*, 24 November 1974.

[21]Ibid.; the Kendall analysis (Union of Concerned Scientists, 1208 Massachusetts Ave., Cambridge, Mass. 02138).

[22]Ibid.

[23]"Safety Systems at Nuclear Power Plants Might Not Prevent Accidents, Study Says," *Wall Street Journal*, 29 April 1975.

[24]Walter Sullivan, "Physicists Voice Long-Term Worry on Reactor Peril," *New York Times*, 29 April 1975. See also *Wall Street Journal* story of same day.

[25]Ibid.

[26]Key news stories on the Browns Ferry fire were: David Burnham, "Fire Raises Issue of Safe Reactors," *New York Times*, 26 March 1975; Barry Kramer, "Fire Knocks Out Nuclear Facility, Reigniting Clash Over Safety of Plants," *Wall Street Journal*, 25 March 1975, and Cynthia Gorney, "25 A-Plant Safety Reports Sought After $50 Million Fire," *Washington Post*, 14 August 1975.

[27]David Burnham, "Fire Raises Doubts on Atom Plants' Safety," *New York Times*, 22 September 1975.

[28]Ibid.

[29]"The Deadly Dilemma of Nuclear Wastes," 3 March 1975.

[30]Thomas Ehrich, "Breakdowns and Errors In Operation Plague Nuclear Power Plants," *Wall Street Journal*, 3 May 1973.

[31]"Cracks in Reactor Force 23 N-Plants To Close for Probe," *Boston Globe*, 30 January 1975.

[32]Ibid.

[33]"Vepco Fined $60,000 for A-Plant Fault," *Washington Post*, 2 September 1975.

[34]"Nuclear Power: Risk, Liability, and Indemnity," *Michigan Law Review*, January 1973.

[35]"Issues of Financial Protection in Nuclear Activities," quoted in *Hearings before the Joint Committee on Atomic Energy*, "Possible Modification or Extension of the Price-Anderson Insurance and Indemnity Act," 1974, p. 256.

[36]Testimony before the Joint Committee on Atomic Energy, 31 January 1974.

[37]The paper was dated February 22, 1975.

[38]Howard S. Shapiro, *How To Keep Them Honest* (Emmaus, Pa.: Rodale Press, 1974), p. 117.

[39]"Nuclear Industry Wins Price-Anderson Vote," *Critical Mass*, January 1976; this is the publication of The Citizens' Movement to Stop Nuclear Power (P.O. Box 1538, Washington, D.C. 20013).

[40]"Energy and Environment," *Bulletin of the Atomic Scientists*, May 1972.

[41]A transcript appears in *Congressional Record*, 11 March 1975, pp. 53617–53622.

[42]Ibid.

[43]Senator Stuart Symington, "Controlling the Cancer of Nuclear Proliferation," *Congressional Record*, 13 March 1975, pp. S3843–3844.

[44]Despite the importance of the subject, and despite the rarity of a press conference by security guards, the event was found unworthy of notice in major news media including the *New York Times* and *Washington Post*.

45Op. cit. (above, n. 1), p. 133.

46Leslie H. Gelb, "Arms Expert Warns on Nuclear Spread," *New York Times.*

47"Brazil Nuclear Deal Raises U.S. Concern," 1 June 1975.

48Cited in "Bonn's Atomic Sale," editorial, *New York Times* 29 June 1975.

49Thomas O'Toole, "S. Africa Gets A-Bomb Type U.S. Uranium," *Washington Post,* 14 April 1975.

50Op. cit. (above, n. 46).

51Ibid.

52Ibid.

53Richard L. Homan, "Libya to Get Soviet-Built Nuclear Plant," *Washington Post,* 3 June 1975.

54"Social Institutions and Nuclear Energy," *Science,* 7 July 1972.

55Ibid.

56Op. cit. (above, n. 38), pp. 114–115.

57Ibid.

58Op. cit. (above, n. 17).

59Daniel F. Ford and Henry W. Kendall, "Nuclear Safety," *Environment,* September 1972.

60Ibid.

61David Burnham, "A.E.C. Files Show Effort to Conceal Safety Perils," *New York Times,* 10 November 1974.

62Ibid.

63Ibid.

64Op. cit. (above, n. 59).

65Ibid.

66Op. cit. (above, n. 61).

67Ibid.

68Op. cit. (above, n. 59).

69Ibid.

70Ibid.

71Ibid.

72Ibid.

73*Science and the State in Greece and Rome* (New York: Wiley, 1968), p. 6.

74Ibid., pp. 6, 30; author Africa is dubious of Siculus's reliability.

75Op. cit. (above, n. 5).

76*Environmental Action,* 24 May 1975.

77Op. cit. (above, n. 17).

78Myron W. Levin, "An Energy Alternative," *Progressive,* May 1975.

79Op. cit. (above, n. 17).

80Ibid.

81Op. cit. (above, n. 1), p. 137.

Chapter 43. Supertankers

1*Supership* (New York: Knopf, 1974), p. 331.

2Albin Krebs, "Shrewd and Adventurous" (an obituary of Aristotle Onassis), *New York Times,* 16 March 1975.

3*The Case For Modern Man* (New York: Harper & Row, 1955), p. 198.

4Thomas O'Toole, "Vast Damage In Oil Spill Off Chile Seen," *Washington Post,* 14 February 1975.

[5]"Oil Spill Off Chile in 1974 Said to Still Cause Damage," UPI, *New York Times*, 13 August 1975.

[6]Op. cit. (above, n. 1), pp. 30–32.

[7]Ibid., p. 32.

[8]Ibid., p. 40.

[9]Ibid., p. 76.

[10]Ibid., p. 77.

[11]Ibid., p. 83.

[12]Ibid., p. 84.

[13]Ibid., p. 159.

[14]Ibid., pp. 159, 161, 162.

[15]Ibid., p. 326.

[16]Ibid., p. 55.

[17]Ibid., p. 60.

[18]Ibid., p. 61.

[19]Ibid., p. 60.

[20]Ibid.

[21]Ibid., p. 191.

[22]Ibid., p. 321.

[23]Ibid., p. 323.

[24]"Peril of the Month: Gas Supertankers," *Washington Monthly*, February 1973.

[25]Op. cit. (above, n. 1).

[26]Ibid., p. 324.

[27]Op. cit. (above, n. 24).

[28]Op. cit. (above, n. 1), p. 326.

[29]Ibid., p. 329.

[30]Ibid., p. 330.

Chapter 44. The Ozone Layer

[1]*The Case For Modern Man* (New York: Harper & Row, 1955), pp. 198–199.

[2]Hippocrates, *On Wounds of the Head* 1.

[3]*Small Is Beautiful: Economics As If People Mattered* (New York: Harper & Row, 1973), p. 149.

[4]Ibid., p. 31.

[5]"Reflections: Prologue to Our Time," *The New Yorker*, 10 March 1975.

[6]Ibid.

[7]Philip Boffey, *The Brain Bank of America: An Inquiry into the Politics of Science* (New York: McGraw-Hill, 1975), pp. 140–142. Although the warning was sounded in March 1969, the public did not hear it until October 31, 1969, when Congressman Sidney R. Yates (D–Ill.) obtained and released a copy.

[8]Thoreau (1817–1862) was cited in *Harper's*, March 1975, p. 8.

[9]Walter Sullivan, "Concern Over the Ozone Layer," *New York Times*, 31 March 1975.

[10]In a speech in Chicago, September 5, 1974.

[11]Paul Brodeur, "Annals of Chemistry: Inert," *New Yorker*, 7 April 1975.

[12]Walter Sullivan, "Data Link Drop in Ozone to Skin Cancer," *New York Times*, 7 February 1975.

[13]Harold M. Schmeck, Jr., "Jet Study Warns of Skin Cancer Risk," *New York Times*, 1 April 1975.

[14]Op. cit. (above, n. 1), p. 198.

[15]"The Good Is Oft Interred," *New York Times*, 27 October 1974.

[16]Op. cit. (above, n. 11).

[17]Op. cit. (above, n. 15).

[18]Stuart Auerbach, "Banning of Aerosol Sprays as Hazardous to Ozone Proposed," *Washington Post*, 13 June 1975.

[19]Ibid.

Chapter 45. Burdens of Proof

[1]"The Good Is Oft Interred," *New York Times*, 27 October 1974.

[2]"The Basic Economics of the Urban and Racial Crises," *Review of Black Political Economy* 1, no. 1, (Summer/Spring, 1970): 63; cited in "Black Land Loss: The Plight of Black Ownership," *Southern Exposure*, Fall 1974.

[3]"Drug Experiments and the Public Conscience," *Drugs in Our Society*, ed. Paul Talalay (Baltimore: Johns Hopkins, 1964), pp. 260–261.

[4]Thomas W. Africa, *Science and the State in Greece and Rome* (New York: Wiley, 1968), p. 73.

[5]In *Basic Ecology* (Pittsburgh, 1957); cited by E. F. Schumacher, *Small Is Beautiful: Economics As If People Mattered* (New York: Harper & Row, 1973), p. 126.

[6]"Guns, Butter, and Phytoplankton: The New Economics of Ecology—and Vice-Versa" (Address to the Conference on the Prevention and Control of Oil Pollution, San Francisco, 25 March 1975).

[7]Friedman's peak exposure for his case was in his *Newsweek* column of January 8, 1973. For a detailed critical analysis, see Morton Mintz, "Should the FDA Be Dismantled?" and "FDA: Battling, Embattled," *Washington Post (Style)*, 4 and 5 February 1973. Senator Gaylord Nelson (D–Wis.), as chairman of the Senate Subcommittee on Monopoly, held hearings on proposals such as Friedman's in February 1973. He invited Friedman to testify, but the professor, perhaps exercising consumer sovereignty, chose not to accept.

[8]Morton Mintz, "Scientist Warns of Cancer Threat in Aldrin and Dieldrin," and "Plan to Ban 2 Pesticides Is Upheld; Cancer Risk Cited," *Washington Post*, 15 August 1974, and 22 September 1974.

[9]*Expendable Americans* (New York: Viking, 1974), p. 234.

[10]Ibid., pp. 273–274.

[11]"Get the Lead Out," *Progressive*, August 1974.

[12]"Putting the Lead Back," *Progressive*, April 1975.

[13]Ibid.

[14]Morton Mintz, *The Therapeutic Nightmare* (Boston: Houghton Mifflin, 1965), pp. xi–xii.

[15]Morton Mintz, "Textbook Erred on X-Ray for Negroes," *Washington Post*, 18 May 1968.

[16]Morton Mintz, "X-Ray Use for Negroes Altered," *Washington Post*, 23 May 1968.

[17]Victor Cohn, "X-Rays: Some Words of Caution," *Washington Post (Style)*, 19 December 1974.

[18]*Das Erste Buch der Tora*, Genesis (Schocken Verlag, 1934), p. 91; cited in *Judaism and Human Rights*, selected and edited by Milton Konvitz (New York: Norton and Viking, 1972), p. 271.

[19]Interview of Dr. Haberman by Morton Mintz, April 16, 1975.

[20]"Ecology and Jewish Tradition," in *Judaism and Human Rights*, (op. cit., above, n. 18).

Chapter 46. Nuclear Pacemakers/Genetic Engineering

[1]"Reflections: Prologue to Our Time," *New Yorker,* 10 March 1975.

[2]*The Case for Modern Man* (New York: Harper & Row, 1955), pp. 202–203.

[3]Ibid., p. 203.

[4]Ibid., p. 204.

[5]"The Risk-Benefit Calculus in Safety Determinations," *George Washington Law Review,* March 1974.

[6]Dean E. Abrahamson, "Comments on Draft Generic Environmental Statement on the Wide-Scale Use of Plutonium Powered Cardiac Pacemakers," 8 March 1975, p. 20. Abrahamson, a physician and Ph.D., is professor, School of Public Affairs, University of Minnesota. Assisting in the preparation of his "informal" staff paper were Mary Trigg, Steven Emmings, Donald Geesaman, and Dr. William Lindsay.

[7]Ibid. The original draft erroneously calculated 20 billion (rather than 16 billion) people.

[8]Stuart Auerbach, "More Heart Pacemakers Recalled, Bringing 3-Year total to 23,000," *Washington Post,* 22 May 1975, and Richard M. Cohen, "FDA Tied to Lax Pacemaker Rules," *Washington Post,* 13 March 1975.

[9]Op. cit. (above, n. 6), p. 29.

[10]Ibid., p. 39.

[11]Letter of March 26, 1975, to Watson Morris, ECOS, Inc. Box 1055, Chapel Hill, N.C. 27514.

[12]Opening Statement at Senate Health Subcommittee hearing on Genetic Engineering, 22 April 1975.

[13]Alvin M. Weinberg, "Social Institutions and Nuclear Energy," *Science,* 7 July 1972.

[14]"Obligations of Scientists to Respond to Society's Needs" (Talk before a symposium of the annual meeting of the American Academy for the Advancement of Science, Washington, D.C., December 1972); reprinted in *Scientists in the Legal System: Tolerated Meddlers or Essential Contributors,* William A. Thomas, ed. (Ann Arbor, Mich.: Ann Arbor Science, 1974), p. 46.

Chapter 47. Constitution Avenue

[1]*The Antifederalists: Critics of the Constitution* (New York: Norton Library, 1974) p. 11.

[2]See, for example: Philip B. Kurland, Professor, University of Chicago Law School (Speech delivered at Annual Meeting of the Delaware Bar Association, Wilmington, Delaware, June 4, 1975); Editorial, *SR/World,* 7 September 1974; "The Constitution Under Strain, A Conversation About Watergate," the *Center Magazine,* March/April 1974; Arthur Selwyn Miller, "Implications of Watergate: Some Proposals for Cutting the Presidency Down to Size," *Hastings Constitutional Law Quarterly* 2, no. 1, Winter 1975; Elizabeth Drew, "A Reporter in Washington, D.C.," *New Yorker,* 14 October 1974; *The Presidency Reappraised,* ed. Rexford G. Tugwell and Thomas E. Cronin (New York: Praeger, 1974); Theodore C. Sorensen, *Watchman in the Night: Presidential Accountability After Watergate* (Cambridge: MIT Press, 1975); Joseph A. Califano, Jr., *A Presidential Nation* (New York: Norton, 1975); Frederick C. Mosher et al., *Watergate: Implications for Responsible Government* (New York: Basic Books, 1974); Senator Walter F. Mondale, *The Accountability of Power: Toward a Responsible Presidency* (New York: McKay, 1975); Clark R. Mollenhoff, *Game Plan for Disaster: An Ombudsman's Report on the Nixon Years* (New York: Norton, 1975).

[3]Ibid., Kurland, *Center Magazine,* Miller, and Mosher.

[4]Op. cit. (above, n. 2), Sorensen.

[5]Ibid., Califano.

[6]Ibid., *Center Magazine.*

[7]Marcus Raskin, *Notes on the Old System: To Transform American Politics* (New York: McKay, 1974).

[8]Op. cit. (above, n. 2), Kurland.

[9]Ibid., *Center Magazine.*

[10]Ralph Nader, Mark Green and Joel Seligman, *Constitutionalizing the Corporation: The Case for the Federal Chartering of Giant Corporations* (Washington: Corporate Accountability Research Group, 1976).

[11]Editorial, *SR/World,* 7 September 1974.

[12]Erich Fromm, *The Anatomy of Human Destructiveness* (New York: Holt, Rinehart & Winston, 1973), p. 10.

[13]The Report, authored by Special Prosecutor Henry S. Ruth, was discussed in an editorial, "Wrapping Up Watergate," in *Washington Post,* 20 October 1975, from which this excerpt was taken.

[14]*Roe* v. *Wade,* 410 U.S. 113, 98 S. Ct. 705, 35 L. Ed. 2d 147, p. 186.

[15]Christopher D. Stone, *Should Trees Have Standing? Toward Legal Rights for Natural Objects* (Los Altos, Calif.: William Kaufman, 1974).

[16]*Sierra Club* v. *Rogers C. B. Morton,* 445 U.S. 727, 92 S.Ct. 1361, 31 L. Ed. 636, p. 649.

[17]Ibid., p. 651.

[18]Sam Adams, *The Rights of Colonists* (Boston, 1772), reprint ed. Saul K. Padover, *The World of the Founding Fathers* (New York: T. Yoseloff, 1960).

[19]*The Life and Selected Writings of Thomas Jefferson,* ed. Koch & Peden (New York: Modern Library, 1944), Letter to James Madison, p. 390.

[20]Henry Steele Commager, *Documents of American History,* 4th ed. (Englewood Cliffs, N.J.: Prentice Hall, 1973), 1: 83.

[21]Ibid., p. 107.

[22]*The Portable Thomas Jefferson,* ed. Merrill D. Peterson (New York: Viking, 1975), p. 248.

[23]Op. cit. (above, n. 1), p. 10. Main says of Cato: *"Cato's Letters,* the joint product of Thomas Gordon and John Trenchard, was written during 1720–23 and had passed through a number of English editions by the time of the Revolution. . . . Although it was never published in America, it was widely read in the colonies and became 'a favorite textbook of the patriots'. . . . The writers who adopted 'Cato' as their nom de plumes were probably thinking as often of the British authors as of the Roman original."

[24]*Human Rights: A Compilation of International Instruments of the United Nations* (New York: United Nations, 1973).

[25]John Rawls, *A Theory of Justice* (Cambridge: Harvard University Press, 1971).

[26]Robert Nozick, *Anarchy, State, and Utopia* (New York: Basic Books, 1974).

[27]Simon Lazarus, *The Genteel Populists* (New York: Holt, Rinehart & Winston, 1974), pp. 244, 245.

[28]Judge Learned Hand, "Sources of Tolerance," *University of Pennsylvania Law Review* 79 (1930): 12.

[29]*New Republic,* 17 May 1975.

Index

653